David Gemmell's first novel, *Legend,* was published in 1984. He has written many bestsellers, including the Drenai saga, the Jon Shannow novels and the Stones of Power sequence. He is now widely acclaimed as Britain's king of heroic fantasy. David Gemmell lives in East Sussex.

Find out more about David Gemmell and other Orbit authors by registering for the free monthly newsletter at www.orbitbooks.co.uk

DRENAI TALES

VOLUME TWO

Quest for Lost Heroes
Waylander II
The First Chronicles of Druss the Legend

David A. Gemmell

www.orbitbooks.co.uk

An *Orbit* Book

First published in Great Britain by Orbit 2002

Copyright © 2002 by David A. Gemmell

Quest for Lost Heroes Copyright © 1990 by David A. Gemmell
Waylander II Copyright © 1992 by David A. Gemmell
The First Chronicles of Druss the Legend Copyright © 1994 by David A. Gemmell

The moral right of the author has been asserted.

A CIP catalogue record for this book
is available from the British Library.

ISBN 1 84149 130 6 (Hardback)
ISBN 1 84149 085 7 (C Format)

Typeset by Hewer Text Ltd, Edinburgh
Printed and bound in Great Britain
by Clays Ltd, St Ives plc

Orbit
An imprint of
Time Warner Books UK
Brettenham House
Lancaster Place
London WC2E 7EN

Contents

DRENAI TALES

VOLUME TWO

QUEST FOR LOST HEROES

Some men climb mountains, or found empires, others make fortunes or create classics. But *Quest for Lost Heroes* is dedicated with love to Bill Woodford, who took on the role of stepfather to a shy, introverted and illegitimate six-year-old boy, and never once let him down. Through his patient encouragement, his quiet strength and his endless affection he gave his son the pride and the confidence to fight his own battles – both in life and on the printed page. Thanks, Dad!

Acknowledgements:
Grateful thanks also to Liza Reeves, for the direction, Jean Maund for copy-editing, and Tom Taylor, Stella Graham, Edith Graham and Val Gemmell for the test reading.

Introduction

By 1989 I had been a full time writer for three years. Those early years were a struggle. *Legend*, *The King Beyond the Gate* and *Waylander* had been written while I was a journalist, working in a happy environment in Hastings, on the south coast of England.

In 1986, following the publication of *Waylander*, I was made redundant. As far too many people have discovered, redundancy is a harsh and scarring business. The hunter is told by his tribe that he is no longer needed. He walks out into the wilderness, suddenly confused and uncertain. Confidence begins to leech away.

Each subsequent job application and rejection further accelerated feelings of self-doubt.

The first three novels had been successful in a minor way, earning a little money, and just about remaining in print. To make enough money to support a growing family I began to write feverishly, increasing my output to two novels a year. The thinking was simple: the more I wrote, the more shelf space I would get in WH Smiths and other leading booksellers. *Wolf in Shadow*, *Ghost King*, *Last Sword of Power*, and *The Last Guardian* were literally powered out during the first two years of losing my job. Sales began to grow. 'Shelf talkers' – those little tags on bookshelves carrying the name of prominent authors – began to appear. Debts began to disappear and slowly the realisation dawned that I had become relatively safe again, financially at least.

Yet the scars did not seem to fade.

A friend of mine, a psychologist, suggested I used the experience in my writing. This would have a dual purpose: it would earn me money, and help exorcise the demons.

Around the same time a great number of quest novels were appearing, and with them an increasing flood of games-related stories with heavy quest overtones. A gallant band of heroes would come together and seek out a number of magical tokens or relics. When these were successfully gathered they were handed in like a lottery prize to defeat the great menace and restore a golden age to the world. The quests were always epic, and, in a genre where the readership was largely teenage, conducted by youthful heroes. Misunderstood scullery boys who were, in fact, the lost sons of great kings, wizards, or mighty heroes.

Most were highly entertaining. Some were mind-numbingly derivative.

I rarely have more than a skeletal plot when I begin a story. The beginning of *Quest for Lost Heroes* was no different. All I knew was that I would find a group of redundant, middle-aged heroes and set them on a quest they knew was small and, in terms of the world at large, meaningless.

The journey was an eye-opener for me.

Quest for Lost Heroes healed my scars, revitalised the sales of all the previous Drenai novels, and continues – twelve years later – to generate readers' letters demanding a direct sequel.

Prologue

Three men were down, the other four formed a half circle around the huge, ugly man in the bearskin jerkin.

'You want to know what it's like on the mountain?' he asked them, his voice slurred. He spat blood from his mouth, which stained his red and silver beard. His attackers hurled themselves forward and he met the first with a crashing blow to the chin which sent the victim sprawling to the sawdust-covered floor. Blows rained in on him. He ducked his bald head and charged at the remaining three, but his foot slipped and he fell, dragging a man with him. A booted foot lashed into his face but he swung his arm to knock the man from his feet. The ugly man staggered upright and leaned back against the wooden counter, his eyes narrowing as two of his attackers drew daggers from their belts. Dropping his right arm, he pulled a long skinning-knife from his boot. It was double-edged and wickedly sharp.

The innkeeper moved silently behind him and the blow to the back of the ugly man's neck was sudden. His eyes glazed. The knife dropped from his fingers and he fell face down to crash alongside his victims.

'I'll cut his puking heart out,' said one of his attackers, moving forward.

'That would not be wise,' the innkeeper told him. 'The man is a friend of mine. And I would be obliged to kill you.' The words were spoken softly, but with a confidence which cut through the atmosphere of anger and sudden violence.

The man slammed his dagger home in its sheath. 'Someone will kill him one day,' he said.

'Sadly that is true,' the innkeeper agreed, opening the flap on the counter and kneeling beside the unconscious man in the bearskin. 'Are your friends alive?'

Two of the men were groaning, and a third struggled to sit. 'Yes, they're alive. What was that nonsense about a mountain?'

'It's not important,' replied the innkeeper. 'There's a pitcher of ale by the barrel. You're welcome to it – and there'll be no charge for your drinks this evening.'

'That's good of you,' said the man. 'Here, let me give you a hand with him.' Between them they hauled the ugly man upright and carried him through to a room at the rear of the inn, where a lantern burned brightly and a bed was ready, the sheets drawn back. They laid the unconscious warrior on the bed and the innkeeper sat beside him. He looked up at his helper; all the man's anger had disappeared.

'Go and enjoy your ale,' said the innkeeper. 'My wife will bring it to you.'

After the man had gone the innkeeper checked his friend's pulse. It was beating strongly.

'You can stop pretending now,' he remarked. 'We are alone.'

The ugly man's eyes opened and he eased himself up on the thick pillows. 'I didn't want to have to kill anyone,' he said, smiling sheepishly and showing a broken tooth. 'Thanks for stopping it, Naza.'

'It was nothing,' Naza told him. 'But why do you not let it rest? The past is gone.'

'I was there, though. I was on the mountain. No one can take that from me.'

'No one would want to, my friend,' said Naza sadly.

The ugly man closed his eyes. 'It wasn't what I dreamed of,' he said.

'Nothing ever is,' replied Naza, standing and blowing out the lantern.

Later, after Naza and his wife Mael had cleared away the tankards, pitchers and plates, and locked the doors, they sat together by the dying fire. Mael reached over and touched her husband's arm; he smiled and patted her hand.

'Why do you put up with him?' asked Mael. 'That's the third fight this month. It's bad for business.'

'He's my friend.'

'If he was truly your friend, he would not cause you so much grief,' she pointed out.

He nodded. 'There's truth in that, Mael my love. But I feel his sadness; it hurts me.'

Moving from her seat, she leaned over to kiss his brow. 'You are too soft-hearted. But that is one of the reasons I love you. So I won't complain too much. I just hope he doesn't let you down.'

He pulled her into his lap. 'He will; he can't help it. He climbed the mountain, and now he has nowhere to go.'

'What mountain?'

'The worst kind, Mael. The kind that first you climb – and then you carry.'

'It is too late for riddles.'

'Yes,' he agreed, surging to his feet and holding her in his arms. 'Let me take you to bed.'

'Which bed? You put your drunken friend in ours!'

'The upper guest room is free.'

'And you think you're still young enough to carry me there?'

8

He chuckled and lowered her to the floor. 'I could – but I think I'll conserve what little strength I have for when we get there. You go up and light the lantern. I'll be with you in a little while.'

He wandered back to his own room and pulled the boots from the sleeping man. A second knife clattered to the floor. Covering his friend with a blanket, he crossed the room.

'Sleep well,' he whispered, pulling shut the door behind him.

1

Seventeen people watched the duel, and not a sound could be heard above the whispering of the blades and the discordant music of steel upon steel. The Earl rolled his wrist and sent a lancing stroke towards the face-mask of his opponent, but the man dropped his shoulder and swayed aside, flashing a riposte which the Earl barely parried. For some minutes the two duellists were locked in a strategic battle, then the Earl launched a blistering attack. His opponent – a tall, lean man wearing the grey habit of a monk beneath his mask and mail-shirt – defended desperately. With a last hissing clash the swords came together, the Earl's blade sliding free to touch the monk's chest.

The duellists bowed to one another, and a light ripple of applause came from the spectators. The Earl's wife and his three sons moved out on the floor of the hall.

'You were wonderful, Father,' said the youngest, a blond-headed boy of seven. The Earl of Talgithir ruffled the boy's hair.

'Did you enjoy the exhibition?' he asked.

'Yes, Father,' the boys chorused.

'And what was the move by which your father defeated me?' asked the monk, pulling off his mask.

'The *Classic Chare*,' replied the eldest.

The monk smiled. 'Indeed it was, Lord Patris. You are studying well.'

The Earl allowed his wife to lead his sons from the hall and waved away his retainers. With the hall empty he took the monk's arm and the two men strode to the south gallery where a pitcher of fruit juice and two goblets had been set aside.

The Earl filled the goblets. 'Are you really content here?' he asked.

The monk shrugged. 'As content as I would be anywhere, my lord. Why do you ask?'

The Earl gazed into the eyes of the man before him. The face he saw was strong, the nose long and aquiline, the mouth full below a trimmed moustache. 'There are many legends concerning you, Chareos,' he said. 'Some have you as a prince. Did you know that?'

'I have heard it,' Chareos admitted. 'It is unimportant.'

'What is important? You are the finest swordsman I ever saw. You were one of the heroes of Bel-azar. You could have been rich beyond the dreams of common men.'

11

'I am rich beyond the dreams of common men, my lord. And *that* is what is important. This life suits me. I am by nature a student. The libraries here in Gothir are among the best anywhere. Far south, they say, the libraries of Drenan contain more books, but here are the complete works of Tertullus. It will take me many years to study them all.'

'It doesn't seem right,' said the Earl. 'I remember my father putting me on his shoulder so that I could see the heroes of Bel-azar as they marched through the streets of New Gulgothir. I remember everything about that day. You were riding a white stallion of some seventeen hands, and wearing a silver mail-shirt and a helm with a white horsehair plume. Beltzer was behind you, carrying his axe. Then Maggrig and Finn. People in the crowd reached out to touch you, as if you were some lodestar. It was a wonderful day.'

'The sun shone,' agreed Chareos, 'but it was only a parade, my lord – and there are many parades.'

'What happened to the others?' asked the Earl. 'Did you remain friends? I have heard nothing of them for years.'

'Nor I,' Chareos answered. The dark-eyed monk looked away, seeing Beltzer as he had been on the last day – drunk, red-eyed and weeping, his axe auctioned to settle his debts. The farmer had become a hero, and it had destroyed him in a way the Nadir could not. Maggrig and Finn had been there; they had left Beltzer alone in the back room of the inn and walked with Chareos out into the sunshine.

'We are going back to the mountains,' said Finn.

'There's nothing there,' Chareos told him.

Finn had smiled. 'There's nothing anywhere, Blademaster.' Without another word the black-bearded archer had taken up his pack and moved off.

The youth Maggrig had smiled, offering Chareos his hand. 'We will meet again,' he said. 'He probably only needs a little time to himself, away from crowds.'

'How do you suffer his moods and depressions?' asked Chareos.

'I do not see them,' Maggrig answered. 'I see only the man.'

Now Chareos sipped his fruit juice and gazed out of the tall window. He was sitting too far back to see the courtyard and the gardens beyond. But from here he could look over the high wall of the monastery and off into the southern distance, where the forest lay like a green mist on the mountains. His gaze swept across to the east, and the ridges of hills which led to the Nadir Steppes. For a moment only, he felt the touch of icy fear.

'You think the Nadir will attack come summer?' asked the Earl, as if reading his thoughts. Chareos considered the question. The Nadir lived for war – a dour, nomadic tribal people, joyous only in battle. For centuries Gothir kings had held them in thrall, sure in the

12

knowledge that the tribes hated one another more than they detested the conquerors. Then had come Ulric, the first great warlord. He had united them, turning them into an invincible force, an army numbering hundreds of thousands of fierce-eyed warriors. The Gothir were crushed, the King slain and refugees fled here to the north-west to build new homes. Only the great Drenai citadel of Dros Delnoch, far to the south-east, had turned them back. But a century later another warlord arose, and he would not be thwarted. Tenaka Khan had crushed the Drenai and invaded the lands of Vagria, his armies sweeping to the sea at Mashrapur and along the coastline to Lentria. Chareos shivered. Would they attack in this coming summer? Only the Source knew. But one point was as certain as death – one day the Nadir would come. They would sweep across the hills, their battle cries deafening, the grass churned to muddy desolation under the hooves of their war ponies. Chareos swallowed, his eyes fixed to the hills, seeing the blood-hungry hordes flowing across the green Gothir lands like a dark tide.

'Well?' queried the Earl. 'Do you think they will attack?'

'I could not say, my lord. I do not listen to the reports as once I did. It is said that the Drenai are in rebellion again, led by yet another who claims to be the Earl of Bronze reborn. I think that makes it the fifth in the thirty years since Tenaka Khan stormed Dros Delnoch. But perhaps such an uprising will put off the Nadir plans.'

'He went the way of all the others,' said the Earl. 'He was caught and crucified; the rebellion was crushed. It is said the new Khan has ordered his troops north.'

'People have been saying that for years,' said Chareos. 'There is little here for them. The spoils they took from the conquests of Drenan, Vagria and Lentria made them rich. We have nothing to offer them – we are not even a gateway to richer kingdoms. Beyond New Gulgothir is the sea. Perhaps they will leave us alone.' Even as he spoke, Chareos felt the lie sitting cold in his throat. The Nadir did not live for plunder but for blood, and death, and conquest. It would matter nothing to them that the riches were few. No, they would be fired with thoughts of ancestral revenge on the Gothir people.

'You do not believe that, Blademaster. I see it in your eyes,' said the Earl, standing. 'No, the Nadir hate us for the past, and they are tormented by the memory of Bel-azar – the only defeat to stain the reputation of Tenaka Khan.'

Chareos rose and assisted the Earl into his caped coat. He looked into the younger man's face. 'Bel-azar was a miracle. I do not know how we did it – nor why Tenaka Khan *allowed* us to hold. But it was twenty years ago; I very rarely think of it now.'

'The old fortress is in ruins,' said the Earl. 'It's as good as Nadir territory now. Thank you for the lesson. I think I am getting closer to you.'

'Better than that, my lord. You beat me today.'

'Are you sure you did not let me win – just because my sons were watching?'

'You won fairly, my lord. But next week I will be better.'

'Next week, you come to the castle. Afterwards we will ride out into the Hunting Woods and see if we can flush out a boar or two.'

Chareos bowed as the Earl strode from the hall. There was still some juice in the pitcher, and he refilled his goblet and wandered to the window, watching as the Earl's retinue rode from the monastery.

It had been a long time since those names had been voiced: Beltzer, Maggrig and Finn. He could still see the red-bearded giant hammering his battle-axe into the Nadir as they swarmed over the gate-tower wall. And each evening the bowmen, Maggrig and Finn, would compare scores and write them in charcoal on the granite wall. *Maggrig killed eleven today, making his tally 31. Death to the Nadir!* Old Kalin would dispute their figures as he cooked the evening meal over the brazier. Such a way with food, that man, Chareos remembered – he could make sirloin steak taste like sheep's bowels. He had died on the last day.

The gate-tower section took the most casualties throughout. Of the original complement of forty-five only Beltzer, Maggrig, Finn and Chareos had survived. The Nadir had taken the fortress, but Beltzer had leapt from the gate-tower and singlehandedly retaken the Gothir standard, hacking and cutting his way back to the tower door. Once inside, the soldiers had barricaded themselves in and defied the encircling Nadir warriors. For most of the day the enemy had scaled the wall, only to be repulsed by the swords and axes of the defenders.

That night Tenaka Khan himself had walked, with his shaman, below the gate-tower.

'Surrender to me, and you may leave here alive,' he had called.

'That would be contrary to our orders,' Chareos had answered him.

'What is the most important to you, duty or freedom?' the Khan had asked.

'An interesting question, sir,' Chareos replied. 'Why not come up here and debate the point?'

'Throw down a rope,' the Khan had answered.

Chareos smiled at the memory now as he heard footsteps in the hall behind him and turned to see the Senior Brother approaching.

'Am I disturbing you?' asked the old man.

'Not at all, Parnio. Please join me.'

The white-robed Senior sat by the table and gazed up at the sky. 'The Heavens are incredible,' he whispered. 'Ever changing, yet constant in their beauty.'

'Indeed they are,' agreed Chareos, sitting opposite the old man.

'Have you touched the power of the Source yet, my son?'

'No, Father. I am still a doubter. Is this a concern to you?'

The Senior waved a slender hand. 'Not at all. Those who seek Him find Him . . . but in His own time. But you have been here two years now, and I wonder what holds you. You do not need to wear the robes in order to use the library.'

Chareos smiled. 'There is comfort in belonging, Father. There is a certain anonymity.'

'If it was anonymity you were seeking, you would not have kept your own name, and certainly you would not have acceded to the Earl's request to teach him the finer techniques of swordsmanship.'

'True. Perhaps the answer is, simply, that I do not know. Yet I have no desire to leave.'

'By my lights, my son, you are a young man. You should have a wife and children; there should be love in your life. Am I at fault in my thinking?'

Chareos stood and moved once more to the window. 'Not at fault, Senior Brother. I loved once . . . and in truth I could love again. But the pain of loss was too much for me. I would rather live alone than suffer it.'

'Then you are here to hide, Chareos, and that is not a good reason. The gift of life is too great to waste in such a fashion. Think on it. Why should the famed hero of Bel-azar fear such a wondrous joy as love?'

Chareos swung on the old man, his dark eyes hooded and angry. 'Bel-azar! I have heard that name twice today. It means nothing. I had a sword . . . I used it well. Men died. I see nothing heroic in that, Senior Brother. A long time ago I watched an old man, crippled in the joints, try to aid a woman who was being attacked. One blow from a fist killed that old man. But his action was heroic – for he had no chance. Do you understand what I am saying? The soldier always has a chance. There are men and women in the world who perform heroic acts daily, and no one sees them. But I – because of a good eye and a fast arm – I am one of the heroes of Bel-azar. My name is sung in the long halls and the taverns.'

'You are wrong, Chareos. *Men* sing of you. But the action of that old man was sung before God. There is a difference.'

'There would be – if I believed. But I do not.'

'Give it time – and beware of the Earl, my son. There is strength in him, but there is cruelty also. And when you go to teach him at his castle, do not wear the Grey. We are not warriors here; this is no Temple of the Thirty.'

'As you wish, Father.'

The old man rose. 'When I came upon you,' he said softly, 'you were lost in thought. Will you share your memories?'

15

'I was thinking of Bel-azar and Tenaka Khan. I was wondering about that last night when he climbed the wall alone and sat with us until the dawn. He talked of his life and his dreams and we spoke of ours. Beltzer wanted to hold him for a hostage, but I overruled him. At dawn he climbed down from the gate-tower and led his force away. We still had the Gothir standard, so – in theory, at least – the victory was ours.'

'You admired the man?'

'Yes. There was a nobility of spirit. But I do not know why he let us live.'

'Did he not tell you?'

'No. But he was not a man to act without a reason and it has haunted me for years. When he died I journeyed into Nadir lands and stood before the great tomb of Ulric, where Tenaka Khan was buried. I was drawn there. I rode into the camp of the Wolves and knelt before the shaman. I asked him why we were spared on that day. He shrugged. He told me we were the *Shio-kas-atra* – the ghosts-yet-to-be.'

'Did you understand him?'

'No. Do you?'

'I will pray on it, my son.'

Beltzer awoke to a roaring sea of pain within his skull. He groaned and hauled himself to a sitting position, his stomach heaving. He pulled on his boots and staggered upright, wandered around the bed to the window and opened it. Fresh air drifted in on a light breeze. He hawked and spat; his lip was split and a little blood could be seen in the phlegm. There was a mirror on the dresser and he sank down into the seat before it and stared at his reflection. One eye was swollen and dark; his forehead was grazed and there was a shallow cut on his right cheek; his red and silver beard was matted with dried blood. He felt sick. The door opened behind him, causing the curtains to billow. He turned to see Mael entering, bearing a tray on which was a platter of toasted bread and cheese and a jug – he prayed it contained ale.

'Thank you,' he said, as she set down the tray. She looked at him and shook her head.

'You are a disgrace,' she told him, planting her hands on her ample hips.

'No lectures, Mael. Have pity! My head . . .'

'Your pain is your own affair. And I have no pity for drunken louts. Look at the blood on these sheets! And the stink is enough to turn a decent man's stomach. How long since you bathed?'

'It was this year, I know that.'

'When you've finished your breakfast, you will go to the woodshed.

16

There you will work until you have settled your bill. Axe and saw will clear your head.'

'Where's Naza?' he asked, straining to focus on the flaxen-haired woman.

'He's gone into the city. It's market day. When he returns you will be gone – you understand that?'

'He . . . owes me.'

'He owes you nothing. You hear me? Nothing! You've been here two months. You've not paid a single Raq for food, lodging or ale, and in that time you've insulted our customers, picked fights and generally done your best to ruin the trade my husband lives on. You will chop wood and then you will go.'

His fist slammed down on the dresser and he surged to his feet. 'You dare to talk to me like that?' he stormed. 'You know who I am, woman?'

'I know,' she said, moving closer. 'You are Beltzer. Beltzer the drunkard. Beltzer the sloth. Beltzer the braggart. And you stink. You stink of sweat, sour ale and vomit. Of course I know who you are!'

He raised his hand as if to strike her, but she laughed at him. 'Go ahead, mighty hero of Bel-azar. Come on!'

Beltzer pushed past her and out into the empty room beyond, but she followed him, her anger lashing him with whips of fire. He stumbled out into the yard beyond the tavern, blinking in the harsh sunlight. The woodshed was to his right; open fields lay to his left.

He took the left path and headed off into the high country, but he had travelled only a half-mile when he sat down on a rock and gazed over the rugged countryside. Three miles ahead was his cabin. But there would be no one there: no food, no drink; merely the howling of the wolves and the emptiness only the lonely could know.

His heart full of shame, he turned back towards the woodshed.

Stopping at a stream he stripped himself of his bearskin jerkin and grey woollen tunic. Then placing his boots beside his clothes, he stepped into the water. With no soap to cleanse himself, he scrubbed at his body with mint leaves and washed the blood from his beard. When he returned to the bank and lifted his tunic the smell from it almost made him nauseous. 'You've fallen a long way,' he told himself. He washed the tunic, beating it against a rock to drive out the dirt, then wrung it clear of excess water and struggled into it. His bearskin jerkin he carried over his arm.

Mael watched him walk back into the yard and cursed softly under her breath. She waited until she heard the sound of the axe thudding into the tree rounds and then returned to the kitchen, preparing the pies and pasties the farm workers and labourers would require at noon.

In the woodshed Beltzer worked hard, enjoying the heft of the

17

single-bladed axe and the feel of the curved wood. His arm had lost none of its skill and each stroke was clean, splitting the rounds into chunks that would burn on the iron-rimmed braziers at each end of the tavern's main room.

Just before noon he stopped and began to cart the wood across the yard. Then he carried it into the tavern to stack beside the braziers. Mael did not speak to him, and he had no desire to feel the sharpness of her tongue. She handed him a plate of broth and some bread when the noon-time custom died down and he ate it in silence, longing to ask for a tankard of ale but fearing the inevitable refusal.

Naza returned at dusk and carried a pitcher of ale out to the woodshed.

'How are you feeling, my friend?' he asked, filling a tankard and passing it to the grateful Beltzer.

'Worse than death,' he replied, draining the tankard.

'You didn't have to do all this,' said Naza. 'You should have rested today. You took quite a beating last night.'

Beltzer shook his head. 'Your wife understands me better than you. This is what I need,' he said, lifting the tankard. 'You know, there's an insanity to it all, Naza. I was the most famous person in Gothir. I was the standard-bearer. I was wined and dined, money and presents poured into my hands. I was on top of the mountain. But there was nothing there. Nothing. Just clouds. And I found that you can't live on that mountain. But when it throws you off – oh, how you long for it! I would kill to climb it again. I would sell my soul. It is so stupid. With fame I thought I would *be* someone. But I wasn't. Oh yes, the nobles invited me to their castles for a while, but I couldn't talk to them in their own language, of poetry and politics. I was a farmer. I can't read or write. I stood with them and sat with them and I felt like the fool I am. There is only one skill I know – I can swing an axe. I killed a few Nadir. I took the standard. And now I can't even become a farmer again. The mountain won't let me.'

'Why don't you visit Maggrig and Finn? They still have that house in High Valley. They'd be glad to see you and you could talk of old times.'

'They were always loners and we were never close. No, I should have died at Bel-azar. Nothing has gone right since then.'

'Death comes soon enough to all men,' said Naza. 'Don't wish for it. Come inside and have a drink.'

'No, tonight I will sit out here and think. No drinking. No fighting. I will sit here.'

'I'll send a jug out to you – and a hot meal. I'll have some blankets brought out too.'

'You needn't do this for me, Naza.'

'I owe you, my friend.'

'No,' said Beltzer sadly, 'you owe me nothing. And from now on I work for my food.'

Forty wooden pegs two inches in diameter had been driven into the lawn; each was set some three feet apart in rows of eight. The eight young students stood before the pegs awaiting instructions from Chareos. The morning sun was bright and a light breeze caressed the elm trees which bordered the lawn.

'Now, gentlemen,' said Chareos, 'I want you to walk along the pegs, turn and come back as swiftly as you can.'

'Might I ask why?' enquired Patris, the Earl's eldest son. 'Are we not supposed to learn the use of the sword?'

'Indeed you are, my lord. But you hold a sword in the hand, and that is only one aspect of the bladesman's skill. Balance is everything. Now kindly take your positions.'

The youngsters stepped on to the pegs and made a wary start. Patris moved smoothly out, turned and ran back to where Chareos waited. The other youths followed more carefully. Three slipped and had to make the attempt a second time; these three Chareos took aside.

'You will continue on the pegs until I return,' he told them. One was the fat child, Akarin, son of the city's Elder Magistrate. He would never be a swordsman, but he was a game boy and Chareos liked him.

He took the other five youths to the Run. It had been finished the day before and Chareos was well pleased with it. A long plank was angled up to join a platform of logs some six feet above the ground. The logs were balanced on greased spheres of wood, allowing them to roll gently. At the end of the log run was tied a knotted rope. With this it was possible to swing the twenty feet to the second set of logs and down a greased plank to the ground. The youths looked at the structure, then gazed one to the other.

'Who wishes to be first?' asked Chareos. No one spoke. 'Then it will be you, young Lorin,' said the monk, pointing to the red-headed son of Salida, the Earl's Captain of Lance.

Gamely the boy ran up the plank and on to the logs. They rolled and twisted under his feet and he half fell, but righted himself and slowly made it to the rope. With a leap he sailed over to the second run, released the rope and missed his footing, tumbling to the soft earth. The other youths did not laugh; they knew their turn would come. One by one each of them failed the Run until, at last, only Patris was left. He nimbly ran up the plank and on to the logs. Moving carefully, he reached the rope and then swung. Just before landing he angled his body sideways and, bending his knees, dropped into a crouch. Although the log rolled, his balance was perfect. But the

19

greased plank at the end of the Run foxed him, and he slipped and fell sideways to the mud.

Chareos called them to him. Their fine tunics of embroidered silk were covered in mud and grime.

'Gentlemen, you are in sorry condition. But war will render you yet more sorry. The soldier will fight in rain and mud, snow and ice, drought and flood. It is rare that a warrior ever gets to fight in comfort. Now make the attempt twice more – in the same order, if you please. Patris, walk with me a moment.' He led the Earl's son some way from the others. 'You did well,' he said, 'but it was not innovative thought. You watched and you learned from the errors of your friends. The greased plank fooled you because you did not consider the problem.'

'I know now how to descend it, master Chareos,' said the boy.

'I don't doubt it. But in real war an officer may have only one chance to succeed. Consider each problem.'

'I will.'

Chareos wandered back to the three youths on the pegs. Each was coping more ably with the course, save Akarin. 'Let me look at you,' said the monk and the boy stood red-faced before the Swordmaster as Chareos gripped the flesh above the youth's hips. 'You know, of course, that you are carrying too much weight. Your legs are strong, but your body is out of balance. If you truly wish to become a swordsman, then limit your diet to one meal a day. Make it a broth, with meat and vegetables. No honey-cakes. No sweetmeats. You are a fine boy, but your mother spoils you.'

The other two boys were allowed to attempt the Run, but they fared badly. Akarin pleaded with Chareos to be allowed to try.

'They will make fun of me,' he pleaded. 'Please let me attempt it.'

Chareos nodded and the fat youngster ran at the plank, made it to the logs and wobbled towards the rope. Under his great weight the logs did not roll as badly as with the other youths. He swung on the rope, but lost his grip and dropped into a mud pool. A huge splash went up, followed by a roar of laughter from the other boys.

Akarin hauled himself clear of the pool and stood blinking back his tears.

There was always one, Chareos knew, who had to endure the taunting. It was the nature of the pack.

He led them to a nearby pasture and opened the chest containing swords, masks and mail-shirts. Then he paired off the youngsters, partnering Patris with Akarin. The Earl's son stalked across to the monk. 'Why must I have the Piglet?' he demanded.

'Because you are the best,' answered Chareos.

'I do not understand.'

'Teach him.'

20

'And who teaches me?'

'As an officer, my lord, you will have many men under your command and not all will be gifted. You must learn to use each man to his best advantage. Akarin will gain more from partnering you than he would with any other boy . . . and I will teach you.'

'So from now on he is my problem?'

'I believe that will be in his best interests – and yours.'

'We will see,' said Patris.

When the afternoon session ended, Akarin had learned a great deal from Patris, but his arms and legs were bruised from the countless blows the older boy landed with their wooden practice blades.

'I will see you tomorrow, gentlemen,' said Chareos, watching as they trudged wearily back to their homes. 'Wear something more in keeping tomorrow,' he called after them.

The following afternoon the youths assembled by the pegs and Chareos came out to them. Akarin was not present; instead, a slim boy stood beside Patris.

'And who is this?' enquired Chareos.

'My cousin, Aleyn,' answered Patris.

'Where is Akarin?'

'He has decided not to continue his lessons.'

'And you arranged this, my lord?' asked Chareos softly.

'I did. You were wrong, master Chareos. When I am an officer I will have no one in my force who is not excellent in every department. I shall certainly have no pigs.'

'Neither will I, my lord. I suggest that you and your cousin remove yourselves immediately. The rest of you gentlemen can begin on the pegs.'

'No one move!' ordered Patris and the youths froze. 'You dare to insult me?' the boy demanded of Chareos.

'You have brought discredit on yourself, my lord,' Chareos answered him icily, 'and I will no longer be at your service. Since these youngsters are your friends, and in some way dependent on your good graces, I shall not ask them to remain and incur your displeasure. There will be no more lessons. Good day to you.'

Chareos bowed to the group and walked away.

'You'll pay for this!' Patris shouted.

The monk ignored him and returned to his rooms, his fury hard to control. He was not angry with Patris, but with himself; he should have seen it coming. The Earl's son was a fine athlete, but his personality was flawed. There was in him an arrogance which could not be curbed, and a cruelty which would never be held in check.

After a while he calmed his emotions and walked to the library. Here in the cold, stone quiet of the reading hall he sat and studied the writings of the philosopher Neucean.

Lost in his studies, he did not feel the hours flow by. A hand touched his shoulder.

'The Earl is waiting for you in the Long Hall,' said the Senior Brother.

Chareos left the library and walked through the arched gardens towards the steps to the Long Hall. He had expected some reaction to his dismissal of Patris – but a visit from the Earl? And so swiftly? It made him feel uneasy. In Gothir the old feudal laws had been much revised, but the Earl was still the ultimate power in the Southlands and, on a whim, he could have a man flogged or imprisoned or both.

Chareos gathered his thoughts and climbed the stairs to the Hall. The Earl was standing alone by the south window, his fingers tapping rhythmically at the sill.

'Welcome, my lord,' said Chareos and the slim young man turned to him, forcing a smile. His face was fine-featured, his hair long and blond, heat-curled in the manner of the Lord Regent's Court.

'What are we to do about this business, Chareos?' asked the Earl, beckoning the monk to a seat by the window. Chareos sat but the Earl remained standing.

'You are speaking of the lessons?'

'Why else would I be here? You have caused quite a stir. My wife wants you flogged; the Captain of the Guard wishes to challenge you; my son wants you hanged – though I pointed out that withdrawing from lessons is hardly a crime. So, what can we do?'

'Is the subject so important, my lord? There are many sword-masters.'

'That is not the point and you know it, Chareos. You have insulted the heir to the earldom and, in doing so, it could be argued that you have insulted me.'

'The question of right and wrong must be considered,' said the monk.

'The fat boy? Yes. But I want this business resolved. I suggest you invite the child – what's his name? Akarin? – to return to the classes. You can then pair him with someone else, and the lessons can continue.'

Chareos considered the question and shook his head. 'I am indeed sorry that you feel the need to be involved in this . . . petty matter. What with thoughts of the Nadir, the Slave raids and the many duties you face, this is an unnecessary irritant. However, I do not see that the resumption of lessons is what is called for here. Your son is highly gifted, but arrogant. Resumption of lessons will, for him, be a victory. It will be the better for the boy if he is placed with another master.'

'You speak of arrogance?' snapped the Earl. 'He has every right to be arrogant. He is my son – and we of the House of Arngir are used to victory. The lessons will resume.'

Chareos rose and met the Earl's icy stare. 'I should point out, my lord, that I receive no pay. I chose – as a free man – to administer the lessons. I choose as a free man to cease them. I am contracted to no one, and therefore am not under the law.'

'Then you are telling me that the insult to my family stands? Be careful, Chareos. Think of what that means.'

The monk took a deep, slow breath. 'My lord,' he said at last, 'I hold you in the highest regard. If you feel that my actions have brought discredit to you, then accept my sincerest apologies. But at the beginning it was made clear to the students that, in the matter of my lessons, they had no rank. There would be no privilege. Patris not only dismissed one of my pupils, but stopped the others from obeying a command. By all the rules that he – and you – agreed, he had to go. I cannot reverse that decision.'

'Cannot? Say it honestly, man. You *will* not.'

'I will not.' A cold silence grew between the men, but the Earl seemed unwilling to end the meeting and paced by the window for several minutes.

'Very well,' he said finally. 'It will be as you say. Logar will take over the duties of Swordmaster. I will see you, as agreed, at the castle hall on Petition Morning.'

'You still wish me to practise with you, my lord?'

'I do. Or are you withdrawing from that duty also?'

'Not at all, sir. I will look forward to it.'

The Earl smiled. 'Until then,' he said, turning on his heel and striding from the hall. Chareos sat down, his hands trembling and his heart beating wildly.

It did not make sense for the Earl to retain him, and he had an uneasy feeling that the next practice would not be a pleasant experience. Was he to be publicly humiliated?

He wandered to the window. Now would be a good time to leave. He could travel north to the capital, or south-east into Vagria. Or even south through the lands of the Nadir and on to Drenan and the Great Library.

He thought of the twelve gold coins he still had hidden in his room. He could buy two horses and supplies for a journey. His gaze flickered around the Hall; he had been almost content here.

His mind journeyed back to the last night on the gate-tower, as they sat with Tenaka Khan, the violet-eyed Lord of the Nadir.

'Why did you let us live?' whispered Chareos.

The two-hour service was drawing to a close. Chareos enjoyed the singing of hymns, the chanting of the ritual prayers and the feeling of belonging that accompanied the morning worship. It did not matter to him that his faith was less than that of his brothers. He felt at one with the Grey Order, and that in itself was enough for the former soldier.

He rose from his knees and filed out with the others, head bowed, face shadowed by the deep hood. The morning sunshine was welcome after the cold of the Nave as Chareos stepped out into the Long Garden and down the terraces towards the southern gate. Once beyond it, the peace of the monastery was lost within the noise of the crowds heading for the market meetings. Chareos allowed himself to be swept along until he reached the main square, where he pushed clear of the crowd and moved down a narrow alleyway to the Live-stock Market. Daily auctions were watched here by discerning farmers and noblemen, the pedigrees of bulls and horses discussed at length in the stalls surrounding the circular arena. Chareos eased himself on to the front bench by the rail, and sat in silence while the bulls were led into the circle. The bidding was brisk, especially for the Drenai bulls – powerful beasts, short-horned but weighed down with flesh. After an hour the horses were led in. Chareos bid for a bay gelding, but lost out to a young nobleman sitting three rows back. He bid again for a dun mare, but this time was beaten by a bid from the back of the arena. Most of the other horses were swaybacks, or past their prime, and he began to lose interest. Then the grey was brought in. Chareos had no wish to bid for a grey; out in the Wildlands they stood out too much, unlike the bay or the chestnut. But this animal had the look of eagles about him. His neck was long and arched, his ears flat to his skull, his eyes fierce and proud. The man leading him had a nervous look, as if fearing that at any moment the beast would rear and smash his skull. Bidding was slow, and Chareos was surprised to find himself raising an arm, and even more surprised when he won the auction with a price less than half the sum he had bid for the gelding.

The man beside him leaned in close. 'Beware, brother, that is the mount that killed Trondian – threw him, then trampled him to death.'

'Thank you for your concern,' said Chareos, rising and moving to the rear of the arena. The stallion had been stabled there and the monk moved in alongside him, stroking his gleaming flank. 'I understand you are a killer, White One. But I daresay there is another side to your story.' Carefully he checked the stallion's legs. 'You are a fine beast.' Edging back, he made his way to the auction table.

'I will ride him this afternoon,' he said, 'but I wish him stabled with you until Petition Day.'

'As you wish,' replied the auction clerk. 'That will be twelve silvers for the horse, and six coppers for the week. Will you require a saddle? We have several that would suit.'

Chareos chose a Vagrian saddle with high pommel and a good harness, settled his account and left the market. After a short walk he entered Wool Street. Here he purchased riding clothes – soft leather boots, dark woollen troos, two thick white shirts and a leather topcoat, double-shouldered and vented at the ribs to allow for ease of movement. He also bought a cloak of shining black leather lined with fur.

'A fine choice, sir,' the merchant told him. 'The leather is Ventrian and will stay soft through the fiercest winter. It is deeply oiled and will repel rain.'

'Thank you. Tell me, who is the finest swordsmith here?'

'Well, that is a matter of debate, of course. But, my brother . . .'

'Does your brother supply the Earl?'

'No, but . . .'

'Who does supply the Earl?'

The man sighed. 'It is not far from here. You are seeking Mathlin, he has a forge by the Eastern Gate. Follow Wool Street until you reach the Grey Owl tavern, turn right and continue to the Temple. Then it is the second on the left.'

Mathlin – a dark-bearded, powerfully built Drenai – took the monk through his workshop to a building behind the forge. Here on the walls hung swords of every kind – broad-bladed glaves, short stabbing swords, sabres and the rapiers carried by the Gothir noblemen. There were even tulwars and double-headed axes on display.

'What blade were you seeking, sir monk?'

'A cavalry sabre.'

'Might I suggest that you try Benin's establishment? His weapons are cheaper than mine, and would probably suit you just as well.'

Chareos smiled. 'What suits me, swordsmith, is the best. Show me a sabre.'

Wandering to the far wall, Mathlin lifted clear a shining weapon. The blade was only slightly curved, the hilt topped with a crossguard of iron. He tossed it to Chareos, who caught it expertly, then hefted the blade, slashed the air twice, rolled his wrist and executed a lunge. 'The weight is wrong,' he said. 'The lack of balance makes it unwieldy. Perhaps you should direct me to Benin.'

Mathlin smiled. 'That was made by my apprentice and he has much to learn. Very well, sir monk. Perhaps you would follow me.' He led the way through to a second room. The swords here were beautifully fashioned, but without adornment – no gold leaf, no filigree silver. Mathlin took down a sabre and passed it to Chareos. The blade was no wider than two fingers and sharp as a razor. The hilt-guard extended around the fist, protecting the sword hand.

'Forged of the finest Ventrian steel, and tempered with the blood of the smith,' said Mathlin. 'If there is a finer sabre, then I have not seen it. But can you afford it?'

'What are you asking?'

25

'Three gold pieces.'

'I could buy five horses for that sum.'

'That is the price. There is no haggling to be done here, sir monk.'

'Throw in a hunting-knife and a good scabbard and we will strike the bargain,' said Chareos.

Mathlin shrugged. 'So be it. But the knife will be one made by my apprentice. Nothing I make comes cheap.'

2

That afternoon, in his new clothes, Chareos prepared to ride the grey for the first time. He checked the saddle's underblanket for rucks or folds which would rub at the beast's back, then examined the bridle and bit. The latter was heavy and ridged.

'Take it out,' Chareos told the hostler.

'This is a trouble beast, sir. You may need that bit.'

'I want a sound horse. That . . . monstrosity . . . will tear his mouth to pieces.'

'Maybe so. But it will keep him in check.'

Chareos shook his head. 'Look at his mouth – there are scars there already . . . old scars. And on his flanks. His masters have been hard men.'

He took an apple from the barrel by the door and cut it into quarters with his new hunting-knife. Then he offered a quarter to the grey, who turned his head away. Standing to one side of the horse, Chareos ate the first quarter himself; then he offered another. This time the grey accepted the gift, but his eyes were still wary.

'I reckon he'll be fast,' said the hostler. 'He's built for it. And with that colour he'll need to be. You using him for afternoon rides, sir?'

'Perhaps. I may take him on a journey or two.'

The hostler chuckled. 'Don't try the Wildlands. They'll see a horse of this colour from a mile away and you'll have robbers around you thicker than flies on dog droppings.'

'I'll bear that in mind,' said Chareos irritably. Stepping into the saddle, he steered the stallion out into the back street behind the auction yard.

Twenty minutes later he was in the foothills to the south of the city, with the wind in his hair and the stallion galloping at full stretch. He let the beast have his head for a full quarter mile and then drew him back, pulling left to climb a gentle rise. At the top he allowed the horse to walk for a while, watching the beast's breathing. He need not have been concerned; within a few minutes the stallion was no longer snorting, and there was little evidence of sweat on his flanks.

'You are strong,' said Chareos, stroking the long sleek neck, 'and fast. But when will you let me know why you are such a troubled beast?'

The stallion plodded on, but when Chareos urged him into a canter over the hills the horse responded instantly. At the end of an hour's riding the city was far behind, though Chareos could still see its turrets in the misty distance. He made up his mind to turn back, for dusk was fast approaching and the great stallion was finally tired. Angling the beast down a short slope, he spotted billowing clouds of smoke from the south, beyond the hills. He rode on, entering a circle of trees. In a clearing he came on a group of soldiers sitting around several small fires. He recognised the officer – who was sitting apart from his men – as Logar, the Earl's champion.

'There is a large fire south of you beyond the hill,' Chareos told him. 'Have you not noticed the smoke?'

'What business is it of yours?' asked Logar, rising smoothly. A tall, lean young man with cold eyes and a dark trident beard, he moved forward to stand close to the stallion. The horse did not like the proximity of the soldier and backed away; Chareos calmed him.

'It is not my business,' he said. 'Good day to you.' He rode from the clearing, topped the rise and gazed down on a scene of devastation. There were twelve homes burning, and several bodies lay sprawled on the ground. Elsewhere people were trying to bring the blaze under control at a large communal barn. Chareos cursed and returned to the soldiers' camp.

Logar was dicing with a junior officer and both men looked up as Chareos rode in. 'There is a village close by,' said Chareos, 'which has been under attack. You will take your men and help with the fire-fighting. And know this – I shall report you to the Earl for dereliction of duty.'

All colour fled from Logar's face as he rose and grasped the hilt of his sabre. 'Step down, you whoreson! I'll not be insulted by the likes of you.'

'You have been,' said Chareos. 'Now do as I told you.' Swinging the stallion he rode to the village, tethering the horse upwind of the smoke before running to help the villagers. The fire at the barn was out of control. As a man ran by him bearing a bucket of water, Chareos dragged him to a halt. 'You must get out what you can. The barn is beyond saving,' he told him. The man nodded, and ran on to the others as the soldiers arrived and hurled themselves into the work. Three of the homes were saved, but the barn fire raged on. Several axemen hammered an entrance at the rear of the building, allowing

27

others to enter and drag clear what grain sacks could be saved. The battle went on long into the evening, but finally the fires died down.

Chareos walked to a nearby stream and washed his face and hands of grime. He looked down at his new clothes. The jerkin was singed, as were the troos; the shirt was blackened by smoke, the boots scuffed.

He sat down. His lungs felt hot, and his mouth tasted of woodsmoke. A young man approached him.

'They took eleven of our women, sir. When will you ride after them?'

Chareos stood. 'I am not a soldier, I was merely passing by. You need to see the officer with the troop; his name is Logar.'

'A thousand curses on him!' spat the young man. Chareos said nothing, but looked more closely at the villager. He was tall and slender, with long dark hair and keen blue eyes under thick brows. The face was handsome, despite the blackening of the smoke and charcoal.

'Be careful what you say, youngster,' warned Chareos. 'Logar is the Earl's champion.'

'I don't care. Old Paccus warned us of the raid and we sent to the Earl for aid three days ago. Where were the soldiers when we needed them?'

'How did he know of the raid?'

'He's a seer: he told us the day and the hour. We tried to fight them, but we've no weapons.'

'Who were they?'

'Nadren. Outlaws who trade with the Nadir. For slaves! We must get them back. We must!'

'Then see the officer. And if that does not satisfy you, go to the Earl. It will soon be Petition Day.'

'Do you think he will care about what happens to a few poor farmers?'

'I do not know,' said Chareos. 'Where is Paccus?'

The young man pointed across the ruined village to where an old man was sitting on the ground, wrapped in a blanket. Chareos made his way over to him.

'Good day, sir.'

The old man looked up, his eyes bright in the moonlight. 'So, it begins,' he said softly. 'Welcome, Chareos. How can I help you?'

'You recognise me? Have we met?'

'No. How can I help you?'

'There is a young man who claims you knew of the raid. He is angry – understandably so. How did you know?'

'I saw it in a dream. I see many things in dreams. I saw you in the clearing beyond the hill asking the vile Logar about the smoke. He and his men have been camped there all day but he did not want to be involved in a battle. Who can blame him?'

28

'I can. There is no place for cowardice in an army.'

'You think it cowardice, Chareos? We are talking of a man who has killed sixteen men in duels. No, he was paid by the Slavers. Since slavery was outlawed in Gothir lands the price per head has quadrupled. Our eleven women will fetch perhaps fifteen gold pieces each; Ravenna will fetch more.'

'That is a great deal of money,' Chareos agreed.

'The Nadir can afford it. Their treasuries are bulging with gold and jewels from Drenan, Lentria, Vagria and Mashrapur.'

'How do you know that Logar accepted a bribe?'

'How do I know that you are planning to leave the city on Petition Day? How do I know that you will not travel alone? How do I know that an old friend awaits you in the mountains? How? Because I am a seer. And today I wish I had never been born with the Talent.'

The old man turned his head away, gazing down at the cinder-strewn ground. Chareos rose, and as he walked back towards his stallion a tall figure stepped into his path.

'What do you want, Logar?' he asked.

'You insulted me. Now you will pay the price!'

'You wish to duel with me?'

'I do not know you, therefore the Laws of the Duel do not apply. We will merely fight.'

'But you do know me, Logar. Look closely, and picture this face above the robes of a grey monk.'

'Chareos? Damn you! Will you hide behind the rules of the Order? Or will you meet me like a man?'

'Firstly, I will see the Earl and discuss your . . . curious behaviour today. Then I will consider your challenge. Good night to you.' He moved on, then turned. 'Oh, by the by . . . when you spend the gold you made today, think of the bodies that lie here. I noticed two children among the corpses. Perhaps you should help to bury them.'

The stallion stood quietly as Chareos stepped into the saddle. The rider looked back once at the smouldering remains of the village and then rode warily for the distant city.

'I am deeply sorry that you have decided to leave us,' said the Senior Brother, rising from his chair and leaning across the desk with one hand extended. Chareos accepted the handshake.

'I also am full of regrets, Father. But it is time.'

'Time, my son? What is time but the breath between birth and death? I had thought you were coming to understand the purpose of Being, to establish the Will of the Source in all things. It saddens me greatly to see you armed in this way,' he said, pointing to the sabre and the hunting-knife.

'Where I am travelling I may have need of them, Father.'

'I learned long ago that the sword is no protection, Chareos.'

'I have no wish to argue, Father. Yet it must be said that the monks exist here in peace and security only because of the swords of the defenders. I do not belittle your views – I wish all men shared them. But they do not. I came to you as a broken man and you made me whole. But if all men lived as you and I, there would be no children and no humanity. Where then would be the Will of the Source?'

The Brother smiled. 'Oh, Chareos, how narrow is your thinking! Do you believe that *this* is all there is? You were an acolyte, my son. In five or ten years you would have been ready to study the true Mysteries, and you would have seen the magic of the universe. Give me your hand once more.'

Chareos reached out and the monk took his fingers and turned his palm upwards. The Senior Brother closed his eyes and sat statue-still, seeming not even to breathe. Slowly the minutes passed and Chareos found his shoulder stiffening as he sat with arm stretched. Easing his hand from the Brother's grip, he waited in silence. At last the monk opened his eyes, shook his head and reached for a goblet of water.

'Your journey will be long, my friend, and perilous. May the Lord of All Harmony travel with you.'

'What did you see, Father?'

'Some sorrows are not for sharing before their time, my son. But there is no evil in you. Go now, for I must rest.'

Chareos took a last stroll around the monastery grounds before walking on towards the Keep at the centre of the city. Several centuries ago the Keep had been built to guard the northern toll road, but when the Nadir hordes of Ulric first gathered they destroyed the great southern city of Gulgothir, the capital of the Gothir kingdom, and the land was torn in two. Refugees streamed north, over the mountains and far from Nadir tyranny. A new capital was built on the western edge of the ocean, and the Keep at Talgithir became the southernmost point of Gothir lands. It had grown in size since those early days, and now the Keep was but a small island at the centre of a bustling metropolis.

The Great Gates of Oak and Iron were shut, but Chareos joined the queue at the side gate which slowly filed through to the outer courtyard. There were the petitioners, men and women with grievances only the Earl could settle. There were more than two hundred people already present, and each carried a flat disc of clay stamped with a number. When that number was called, the petitioner would walk inside the main hall and present his case to the Earl. Of the hundreds waiting, only about a dozen would be dealt with, the rest returning next Petition Day.

Chareos walked up the wide stone steps towards the two guards at the top; their spears were crossed, but they lifted them to allow him to pass through into the inner chambers. Three times already he had tried to contact the Earl, to inform him of the deeds of his soldiers. But on each occasion he had been turned away and told that the Earl was too busy to be interrupted.

A servant led Chareos through to the Dining Hall. The long tables had been removed and now the Earl and his retainers sat facing the doors. The first petitioner was already before them, talking of a broken promise in the matter of the sale of three bulls; he had received half the payment on delivery, but the remainder had been denied him. The accused was a nobleman, a distant relative of the Earl. The case was found to be proved and the Earl ordered the money to be paid, plus five silver pieces to be given to the plaintiff to offset the waste of time the case had incurred. He also fined the nobleman twenty gold pieces.

The plaintiff bowed low and backed from the chamber. The next person to be called was a widow, who claimed that her inheritance had been stolen by a man who claimed to love her. The man was dragged into the hall, weighted down with chains. His face was bruised and bloody and he admitted the charge against him. The Earl ordered him hanged.

One by one the petitioners came forward until, at noon, the Earl rose. 'Enough for one day, by the gods,' he said.

A young man pushed through the main doors, the guards running after him. 'My lord, hear me!' he called. The two guards seized the man's arms and began to drag him away.

'Wait!' called the Earl. 'Let him speak.'

Chareos recognised the tall young villager and eased himself forward to hear him.

'My village was attacked by raiders. Eleven of our women were taken to be sold to the Nadir. We must get them back, my lord.'

'Ah yes, the village. A sad affair,' said the Earl. 'But there is little we can do. We followed their tracks to the mountains, but they escaped into Nadir lands and I have no jurisdiction there.'

'Then you will do nothing?' the man shouted.

'Do not raise your voice to me, peasant!' roared the Earl.

'We pay taxes to you, and we look to you for protection. But when we asked for it, your men stayed hidden in a wood while our people were slaughtered. Do cowards now rule the Gothir?'

'Take him!' shouted the Earl and the guards leapt on the villager, pinning his arms. 'I want him flogged. Get him out of here.'

'Is that your answer?' yelled the youth. 'Is this justice?'

The Earl ignored him and the youth was hauled away, the doors closing behind him. 'Ah, Chareos,' said the Earl. 'Welcome. Are you ready for the exhibition?'

31

'I am indeed, my lord,' replied Chareos, stepping forward. 'But may I first say a word about the young man's claims?'

'You may not!' snapped the Earl. 'Logar!' The champion rose from his seat and walked out to stand with the two men. 'I hurt my shoulder during last week's exhibition,' said the Earl, 'and it is troubling me still. But rather than disappoint our guests, would you take my place against the hero of Bel-azar?'

'It would be a pleasure, my lord,' replied Logar. 'Might I suggest that it would imbue the spectacle with greater tension were we to exhibit our skills without masks and mail-shirts?'

'Is that not dangerous?' the Earl queried. 'I would not like to see a tragic accident.'

'There is danger, my lord, but it might add spice to the exhibition.'

'Very well,' agreed the Earl, ignoring Chareos. 'Let it be as you say.'

A page came forward bearing two rapiers. Chareos chose the left-hand blade and moved away to loosen his muscles. He laid his sabre and knife on a ledge, his mind racing. He had no doubt that Logar would try to kill him, yet if he killed Logar the Earl would have him arrested. Mechanically he went through his exercises, stretching the muscles of his arms, shoulders and groin. He glanced at the two rows of spectators, his eye catching the young Lord Patris. The boy was grinning wolfishly. Chareos turned away and approached Logar.

The two men lifted their blades high, saluting each other, then touched swords.

'Begin!' called the Earl.

Logar launched a sudden attack, rolling his wrist in the *Classic Chare*, but Chareos parried the blow, moving smoothly to his right. Logar's eyes narrowed. Three times the soldier hurled himself forward, and on each occasion was parried. Chareos was growing angry. Logar was making no attempt to defend himself, sure in the knowledge that Chareos could not – in an exhibition – deliver a killing thrust. Twice his blade flashed by Chareos' throat, and the monk knew it was only a matter of time before the Earl's champion found a way through his defences. Chareos blocked a thrust and leapt back, wrong-footing Logar. As the champion cursed and moved forward, Chareos took a deep breath and prepared to meet the attack, knowing now that Logar intended to kill him. But was it the Earl's plan, or merely the result of Logar's wounded pride? Logar's sword-blade lanced for his eye but he sidestepped, spun on his heel and jumped back. Logar swung and grinned broadly. Back and forth across the hall the two swordsmen battled. The spectators could not hold themselves in silence and began wildly cheering every attack made by Logar. Several minutes passed, and still there was no resolution to the encounter. Logar lunged. Chareos only partly blocked, and felt his opponent's sword blade slice into the skin of his cheek.

At the sight of blood a hush fell on the spectators, who looked to the Earl to end the exhibition. But he made no move. So it was the Earl's plan, thought Chareos and anger flared within him, but he held it trapped. He could not kill Logar, for then the Earl would have him arrested and on trial for murder. Coldly furious, Chareos circled, then moved swiftly to his right. Logar lunged forward. Chareos parried three thrusts, then slashed his own blade high over Logar's sword. The point of Chareos' rapier split the skin above Logar's right eye and sliced on across his brow. Blood billowed into the swordsman's eyes and he fell back.

Chareos turned to the Earl. 'Is the exhibition over, my lord?'

'That was foul work,' said the Earl. 'You could have killed him.'

'Indeed I could, for he is not very skilful. But for good luck this blow,' said Chareos, pointing to the cut on his own cheek, 'would have pierced me to the brain. Happily there is little harm done; his cut is not serious. And now, with your permission . . .' A sound from behind made him spin on his heel. Logar had wiped most of the blood from his face and was running at him with sword extended. Chareos sidestepped and rammed his hilt guard behind Logar's left ear and the champion fell unconscious to the marble floor. 'As I was saying,' said Chareos coldly, 'with your permission I will leave.'

'You are not welcome here,' hissed the Earl, 'nor anywhere within my jurisdiction.'

Bowing, Chareos backed three steps and took up his sabre and knife. He marched from the hall with head held high, feeling the hostility following him.

Out in the courtyard most of the petitioners had remained to watch the flogging. Chareos descended the steps, his eyes locked to the writhing form of the villager as the lash snaked across his skin.

Approaching the Captain of the Guard, he asked, 'How many strokes has he suffered?'

'Eighteen. We'll stop at fifty.'

'You'll stop at twenty,' Chareos told him. 'That is the penalty for insubordinate behaviour.'

'The Earl did not specify the number,' the officer snapped.

'Perhaps he thought you would know the law,' remarked Chareos as the lash sounded once more.

'That's enough,' said the Captain. 'Cut him down.' They dragged the villager out through the postern gate and left him lying beside the path.

Chareos helped him to his feet. 'Thank you,' the man whispered.

'You'll not get home in that state,' Chareos told him. 'You'd best come with me. I'll book a room at the Grey Owl tavern and we'll see to your back.'

The Grey Owl tavern was a rambling building, built around an ancient inn which sat on the mountain road leading to Gulgothir. At its centre was an L-shaped hall, where drinkers and diners were waited upon by serving-maids. Two new buildings had been constructed on the east and west sides, and a stableyard added to the rear.

As Chareos eased his way through the milling taverners, his jutting scabbard cracked against a man's leg.

'Watch what you're doing, you whoreson!' hissed the drinker. Chareos ignored him, but as he walked on he gripped the hilt of his sabre, holding the scabbard close to his leg. It was a long, long time since he had worn a sword-belt and it felt clumsy, out of place.

He passed through a doorway and mounted the circular stair to the first-floor corridor. At the far end he entered the double room he had paid for that afternoon. The villager still slept, his breathing deep and slow; the draught of *lirium* administered by the apothecary would keep him unconscious until dawn. Chareos had cleaned the whip wounds and covered them with goose-grease, pressing a large square of linen to the villager's back. The lash cuts were not deep but the skin around them had peeled back, burnt by the leather of the whip.

Chareos banked up the fire in the hearth on the south wall. Autumn was approaching, and a chill wind hissed through the warped window-frames. He removed his sword-belt and sat in a wide, deep leather chair by the fire. Tired now, yet his mind would not relax. The sanctuary of the monastery seemed distant, and depression hit him like a physical blow. Today the Earl had tried to have him killed – and for what? All because of the actions of an arrogant child. He glanced at the sleeping villager. The boy had seen his village razed, his loved ones taken, and had now been whipped to add to his agony. Justice was for the rich . . . it always had been. Chareos leaned forward and threw a chunk of wood on the fire. One of the three lanterns on the wall guttered and died and he checked the others. They were low and he pulled the bell-rope by the west wall.

After some minutes a serving-maid tapped at the door. He asked for oil and ordered a meal and some wine. She was gone for half an hour, in which time a second lantern failed.

The villager groaned in his sleep, whispering a name. Chareos moved over to him, but the youth faded back into slumber.

The maid returned with a jug of oil. 'I'm sorry for the delay, sir, but we're full tonight and two of the girls have not come in.' She refilled the lanterns and lit them with a long taper. 'Your food will be up soon. There is no beef, but the lamb is good.'

'It will suffice.'

She stopped in the doorway and glanced back. 'Is he the villager who was scourged today?' she whispered.

'He is.'

'And you would be Chareos the monk?'

He nodded and she stepped back into the room. She was short and plump, with corn-coloured hair and a round, pretty face. 'Perhaps I shouldn't speak out of turn, sir, but there are men looking for you – men with swords. One of them has a bandage upon his brow.'

'Do they know I am here?'

'Yes, sir. There are three men in the stable and two others are now sitting in the main hall. I think there may be more.'

'Thank you kindly,' he said, pressing a half silver piece into her hand.

After she had gone he bolted the door, returned to the fire and dozed until there was another tap at the door. He slid his sabre from the scabbard. 'Who is it?' he called.

'It's me, sir. I have your food and wine.'

He pulled back the bolts and opened the door. She came in and laid the wooden tray on the narrow table by the chair. 'They are still there, sir. And the man with the bandage is talking to Finbale – the owner.'

'Thank you.'

'You could leave through the servants' quarters,' she offered.

'My horses are in the stable. Do not fear for me.'

She smiled. 'It was good what you did for him,' she said and then she left, pulling the door shut behind her. Chareos pushed home the bolt and settled down to his meal. The meat was tender, the vegetables soft and overcooked and the wine barely passable; even so, the meal filled his belly and he settled down to sleep in the chair. His dreams were troubled, but when he awoke they vanished like smoke in the breeze. Pre-dawn light had shaded the sky to a dark grey. The fire was almost dead, the room chill; Chareos added tinder to the glowing embers, blowing the flames to life, then piled on larger chunks. He was stiff and cold, and his neck ached. With the fire blazing once more, he moved to the villager. The youth's breathing was more shallow now. Chareos touched his arm and the villager groaned and opened his eyes.

He tried to sit up but pain hit him and he sank back.

'Your wounds are clean,' said Chareos, 'and though they must be painful I suggest you rise and dress. I have bought a horse for you. And we leave the city this morning.'

'Thank you . . . for your help. My name is Kiall.' The youth sat up, his face twisted by the pain clawing at his back.

'The wounds will heal well,' Chareos told him. 'They are clean and not deep. The pain is from the whip-burns, but that will pass in three or four days.'

'I do not know your name,' said Kiall.

'Chareos. Now get dressed. There are men waiting who will make our departure troublesome.'

'Chareos? The hero of Bel-azar?'

'Yes,' snapped Chareos, 'the wondrous giant of song and tale. Did you hear me, boy? We are in danger. Now get dressed.'

Kiall pushed himself to his feet and struggled into his troos and boots, but could not raise his arms to pull on his shirt. Chareos helped him. The lash marks extended all the way to Kiall's hip and he could not fasten his belt. 'Why are we in danger?' he asked.

Chareos shrugged. 'I doubt it is to do with you. I had a duel with a man named Logar and I would imagine he is feeling somewhat humiliated. Now I want you to go down to the stable. My horses are there. Mine is the grey and the saddle is by the stall. You know how to saddle a horse?'

'I was once a stable-boy.'

'Good. Make sure the cinch is tight enough. Two stalls down, there is a swaybacked black gelding; it was the best I could find for you. He's old and near worn out, but he will get you back to your village.'

'I will not return to the village,' said Kiall softly. 'I will hunt down the raiders who took Ravenna and the others.'

'A sound and sensible idea,' said Chareos irritably, 'but for now be so good as to saddle my horse.'

Kiall reddened. 'I may owe you my life, but do not mock me,' he said. 'I have loved Ravenna for years and I will not rest until she is free, or I am dead.'

'The latter is what you will be. But it is your life. My horse, if you please?'

Kiall opened his mouth, but said nothing. Shaking his head, he left the room. Chareos waited for several minutes and then walked down the stairs to the kitchen where two scullery servants were preparing the dough for the day's bread. He summoned the first and asked her to pack some provisions for him – salt beef, a ham, corn biscuits and a small sack of oats. With his order filled, he paid her and wandered through the now deserted main hall. The innkeeper, Finbale, was hanging freshly washed tankards on hooks above the bar. He nodded and smiled as Chareos moved towards the door and Chareos stopped and approached the man.

'Good morning,' said Finbale, a wide grin showing the gaps in his teeth.

'And to you,' responded Chareos. 'Will you have my horse brought to the door?'

'The stable is only across the yard, sir. And my boy is not here yet.'

'Then do it yourself,' said Chareos coldly.

'I'm very busy, sir,' Finbale answered, the smile vanishing and he turned back to his chores.

So, thought Chareos, they are still here. Holding his provisions in his left hand, he stepped out into the yard. All was quiet, and the dawn was breaking to the east. The morning was chill and fresh, and the smell of frying bacon hung in the air. Glancing around the yard, Chareos saw a wagon close by and a short wall leading to the chicken-run. To the left the stable door was open, but there was no sign of Kiall. As Chareos moved out into the open, a man ran towards him from the side of the building; he dropped his provisions and drew his sabre. Two more men came into view from behind the wagon and then Logar appeared from the stable. His forehead was bandaged, but blood was seeping through the linen.

'You are very good with a rapier,' said Logar. 'But how do you fare with the sabre?'

'I am better with a sabre,' Chareos answered.

'In that case we will take no chances,' hissed Logar. 'Kill him!'

As two swordsmen leapt forward Chareos blocked a wild slash, spun on his heel to avoid a second thrust and backhanded his blade across the first man's throat. Blood welled from the cut and the attacker fell, dropping his sword and thrusting his fingers at the wound in a vain attempt to stem the flow of his life. The second attacker sent a cut at Chareos' head but he ducked under it and thrust his own blade through the man's chest. A third swordsman fell back, his eyes widening.

'Well?' said Chareos, glaring at Logar, and the Earl's champion screamed and launched an attack. Chareos blocked the first slash, leapt back from a sweeping slice which would have disembowelled him, then swept a flashing riposte that plunged into Logar's groin, severing the huge artery at the top of the inner thigh. Logar dropped his sabre and stared in disbelief at the blood drenching his leggings; then his legs gave way and he fell to his knees before Chareos. He looked up at his killer and blinked before toppling sideways to the ground. Chareos moved to the body, pulling free the sword-belt and sliding the dead man's sabre back into the scabbard. When Kiall rode into the yard, leading Chareos' grey, the former monk tossed Logar's sabre to the villager, gathered his provisions and swung into the saddle. The last swordsman stood by, saying nothing. Chareos ignored him and steered his mount towards the southern gate.

The yard had been roped off and guards stood by the entrances. Behind them a crowd had gathered, straining to see the stiffening corpses. The Earl stood over the body of Logar, staring down at the grey, bloodless face.

'The facts speak for themselves,' he said, pointing at the body. 'See, he has no sword. He was murdered and I want the killer brought to justice. Who would have thought that a hero of Bel-azar would stoop to such a base deed?' The retainers grouped around him said nothing, and the surviving swordsman turned his eyes from the Earl.

'Take twenty men,' the Earl ordered Salida, his Captain of Lancers, 'and bring Chareos back here.'

Salida cleared his throat. 'My lord, it was not like Logar to walk unarmed – and these other two men had swords drawn. Chareos is a master bladesman. I cannot believe . . .'

'Enough!' snapped the Earl and swung to the survivor. 'You . . . what is your name again?'

'Kypha, my lord,' replied the man, keeping his eyes fixed on the ground.

'Was Logar armed when Chareos slew him?'

'No, my lord.'

'There you have it then,' said the Earl. 'And you have the evidence of your eyes. Do you see a sword?'

'No, my lord,' said Salida. 'I will fetch him. What of the villager?'

'He was an accessory to murder; he will hang alongside Chareos.'

The twenty-two captive women sat close together in four open wagons. On either side, warriors rode, grim men and fierce-eyed. Ravenna was in the second wagon, separated from her friends. Around her were women and girls taken in two other raids. All were frightened, and there was little conversation.

Two days before a girl had tried to escape; she had leapt from a wagon at dusk and run for the trees, but they had ridden her down in seconds and dragged her back. The captives had been assembled in a circle to watch the girl being whipped, and her whimpering screams still sounded in Ravenna's ears.

After that, several of the men had dragged her away from the camp and raped her. Then her arms were tied and she was flung down near the other prisoners.

'There is a lesson to be learnt here,' said a man with a scarred face. 'You are slaves and you will begin to think like slaves. That way, you will survive. Any slave who attempts to run will be treated more harshly than this one. Remember these words.'

Ravenna would remember . . .

The time to escape would not be while the Nadren held them. No, it was necessary to be more cunning. She would wait until she was bought by some lecherous Nadir. She would be pliant and helpful, loving and grateful . . . and when he had grown confident of her emotions – then she would run.

'Where are you from?' whispered the woman beside her. Ravenna told her.

'I visited your village once. For the Summer Solstice Fair.' Ravenna looked at the bony figure, scanning the lean, angular face and the shining black hair. She could not remember her.

'Are you wed?' she asked.

'Yes,' said the woman, shrugging. 'But that does not matter any more.'

'No,' Ravenna agreed.

'And you?'

'I was due to marry. Eighteen – no, seventeen – days from now.'

'Are you a virgin?' asked the woman, her voice dropping lower.

'No.'

'You are from now on. They will ask. Virgins fetch higher prices. And it will mean these . . . pigs . . . will not touch you. You understand?'

'Yes. But surely the man who buys me . . .'

'What do they know? Men! Find yourself a sharp pin, and on the first night cut yourself.'

Ravenna nodded. 'Thank you. I will remember that.'

They lapsed into silence as the wagons moved on. The raiders rode warily and Ravenna could not stop herself scanning the horizon.

'Do not expect help,' the woman told her.

'One should always hope.'

The woman smiled. 'Then hope for a handsome savage with kindly ways.'

The mountains towered before them like a fighting line of white-bearded giants and an icy wind drifted over the peaks into the faces of the riders. As Chareos pulled his fur-lined cloak about him and belted it, he glanced at the villager. Kiall's face was grey and he swayed in the saddle, but offered no complaint. Chareos gazed back towards the city. It was far behind them now, and only the tallest turrets could be seen beyond the hills.

'How are you faring?' he asked Kiall. The villager gave a weak smile. The *lirium* was wearing off and pain was eating into his back like hot coals. The old swayback gelding was a serene beast and normally the ride would have been comfortable, but now every movement pulled at Kiall's tortured flesh. 'We will stop in a while,' said Chareos, 'once we are in the trees. There are lakes there, with crystal-clear water. We will rest and I will see to your injuries.' Kiall nodded and gripped the pommel of his saddle. He felt sick, and sweat had formed a sheen on his face. Cursing inwardly, Chareos moved alongside the swayback. Suddenly the white stallion arched its neck and flashed a bite at the older animal. Chareos dragged on the reins and the gelding reared. Kiall all but toppled from the saddle. The stallion bucked and dipped its head, but Chareos clung on grimly, his thighs locked tight to the barrel of the animal's body. For several seconds the horse tried to unseat him, then settled down as if nothing had happened and stood calmly. Chareos stepped down from the saddle, stroking the stallion's long neck. Moving to stand before the horse's head, he rubbed at its nose, then blew a long slow breath into each of its nostrils. 'Know me,' whispered Chareos, over and over again. 'I will not harm you. I am not your master. I am a friend.'

At last he remounted and continued the journey south. Chareos had never travelled these hills, but travellers spoke of a settlement built around a tavern. He hoped the village was close – and that they had a healer. Kiall's fever was climbing, and for all Chareos knew the wounds could be festering. As a soldier, he had seen many men die from what appeared to be small wounds. The skin would swell and discolour; fever would deepen and flesh melt away. He recalled a young warrior at Bel-azar who cut his hand on a thorn. The hand had swelled to three times its size, then turned blue, and finally black. The surgeon had cut it from him. But the boy died . . . And he died screaming. Chareos glanced at Kiall and forced a smile, but the youth did not respond.

By late afternoon Kiall could ride no more. He was feverish and moaning, and two of the long wounds in his back had opened. Chareos had lashed the young man's wrists to the pommel and was now leading the gelding as he guided the horses along the shores of a wide lake; it was smooth as a mirror and the mountains were reflected on its surface. Dismounting, he hobbled the horses and helped Kiall to the ground. The villager sagged, his knees giving way. Chareos let him lie and built a fire. As a soldier he had seen many men flogged. Often the shock of the beating was what laid a man low, the humiliation more than the agony. With the fire blazing, he turned Kiall to his stomach and sniffed at the wounds. There was no smell of corruption. Chareos covered him with a blanket. The young man was strong and proud. He had not complained about his pain and Chareos admired that.

He sat by the fire, staring out over the mountains and the stands of pine which grew green through the snow. There was a time when such a view had made him think of freedom, the wide beauty, the towering grandeur of the peaks. Now, he realised, they spoke only of the futility of Man. Wars, plagues, kings and conquerors were as nothing to these peaks.

'What do you care for my dreams?' asked Chareos, his mind drifting back to Tura as it so often did when the reflective mood came upon him. Beautiful, black-haired Tura. She had made him feel more of a man than he could have wished for. With her he was complete. But what she seemed to give so freely, she had cruelly stolen back. Chareos' face reddened with the memory. How many lovers had she taken before Chareos discovered her infidelity? Ten? Twenty? How many of his friends had accepted the gift of her body? The hero of Bel-azar! If only they knew. Chareos the Bladesman had not gone there to fight; he had gone there to die.

There was little heroism in that. But the bards did not care for realism. They sang of silver blades and dashing deeds – the cuckold's shame had no place in the saga of Bel-azar.

He stood and wandered to the lakeside, kneeling to drink, closing his eyes against his reflection. Returning to the fire he saw that Kiall was sleeping peacefully. The sun drifted low in the west and the air grew cooler. Chareos loosened the saddle cinches on the horses and stretched out his blanket close to the fire.

Lying back, he stared at the stars. He had wanted to forgive Tura, to take her far from the fort and start a new life, but she had laughed at him. She liked it where she was – where there were men to hand, strong men, lusty men, men who would give her presents. In his mind's eye he could see himself striking her and smashing her beauty beneath his fists. But he never had. He had backed from the room, forced by the strength of her laughter – the love he had allowed into his heart torn away by the talons of treachery. He had never loved again, never taken a woman to his heart or his bed.

A wolf howled in the distance, a lonely mournful sound. Chareos banked the fire and slept.

Bird-song drifted through his dreams and he awoke. He did not feel refreshed for his sleep, and knew that he had dreamt of Tura. As always he could remember little, save her name echoing in his mind. He sat up and shivered. The fire was near gone and he knelt before it, blowing the embers to life and adding twigs to the tiny flames. Then he rose and wandered from the camp-site, gathering dead wood.

With the fire blazing once more he moved to the stallion, stroking its neck. He took some cold meat from his sack of provisions and returned to the warmth of the blaze. Kiall woke and carefully sat up. His colour had returned, and he smiled at Chareos.

The former monk sliced the ham with his hunting-knife and passed it to the villager.

'Where are we?' asked Kiall.

'About ten miles from the old toll road. You look better.'

'I am sorry to be a burden to you. And even more sorry that you had to kill for me.'

'It wasn't for you, Kiall. They were hunting me. A haughty child is disciplined and now three men are dead. Insane.'

'You were amazing in the fight. I have never seen anything like it. You were so cool.'

'You know why they died?' Chareos asked.

'They were not as good as you?' ventured Kiall.

41

'No, they weren't, but that's not the whole reason. They died because they had something to live for. Finish your breakfast.'

For three days they moved higher into the range, crossing streams and rivers. Above them the snow-geese flew, heading for their distant breeding grounds. In the waters the beaver battled against the floods, building their dams. Kiall's wounds were healing fast in the clean mountain air, and now he wore Logar's sabre at his side.

The companions had spoken little during the climb and at night, at the camp-fire, Chareos would sit facing north, lost in thought.

'Where are we going?' asked Kiall as they saddled their horses on the fifth morning.

Chareos was silent for a moment. '*We* are heading into a settlement called Tavern Town. There *we* will purchase supplies. But after that *I* will be riding south across the Steppes. And I will be riding alone, Kiall.'

'You will not help me rescue Ravenna?' It was the first time since the tavern that the villager had spoken of the raid. Chareos tightened the saddle cinch on the stallion before turning to face the young man.

'You do not know which direction the raiders took. You do not know the name of their leader. By now the women will be sold. It is a hopeless cause, Kiall. Give it up.'

'I cannot,' said the young man. 'I love her, Chareos. I have loved her since a child. Have you ever been in love?'

'Love is for fools. It is a surging of blood in the loins . . . there is no mystery, and no magic. Find someone else, boy. By now she has been raped a dozen times and she may even have found she likes it.'

Kiall's face went white and Logar's sabre flashed into the air. Chareos leapt back. 'What in the devil's name are you doing?'

'Apologise! Now!' ordered Kiall, advancing with sabre pointing at Chareos' throat.

'For what? For pointing out the obvious?' The sabre lanced forward but Chareos swayed aside from the point and drew his own sword. 'Don't be a fool, boy. You are in no condition to fight me. And even if you were, I could cut you to pieces.'

'Apologise,' repeated Kiall.

'No,' said Chareos softly. The villager attacked wildly, but Chareos parried with ease and, off balance, Kiall tumbled to the ground, dropping the sabre. He reached for it, but Chareos' boot trapped the blade. Kiall twisted and dived, his head ramming into Chareos' belly, and both men fell. Kiall's fist cracked against Chareos' chin. The former monk blocked a second blow, but a third stunned him and he lost his grip on his sabre. Kiall swept up the blade and lurched upright. Chareos tried to rise, but the point of his own sabre touched the skin of his throat.

42

'You are a surprising lad,' remarked Chareos.

'And you are a whoreson,' hissed Kiall, dropping the sabre to the snow and turning away. His wounds had opened and fresh blood was seeping in jagged lines through the back of his tunic.

Chareos rose and slid the sabre back in its scabbard.

'I am sorry,' he said and Kiall stopped, his shoulders sagging. Chareos moved to him. 'I mean it. I am not a man who likes women very much, but I do know what it is to be in love. Were you married long?'

'We were not wed,' Kiall told him.

'Betrothed?'

'No.'

'What then?' asked Chareos, mystified.

'She was going to marry another man. His father owns the whole of the east pasture land and it was a good match.'

'But she loved you?'

'No,' admitted Kiall. 'No, she never did.' The young man hauled himself into the saddle.

'I don't understand,' said Chareos. 'You are setting off on a quest to rescue a woman who doesn't love you?'

'Tell me again what a fool I am,' Kiall said.

'No, no, forgive me for that. I am older than you, and cynical, Kiall. But I should not mock. I have no right. But what of her betrothed? Is he dead?'

'No. He has made an arrangement with Ravenna's father and now he will marry her younger sister, Karyn – she was not taken.'

'He did not grieve for long then,' Chareos observed.

'He never loved her; he just wanted her because she is beautiful and her father is rich – he breeds pigs, cattle and horses. He is the ugliest man I ever saw, but his daughters have been touched by Heaven.'

Chareos picked up the boy's sabre and handed it to him, hilt first.

Kiall gazed down at the blade. 'There's little point in my carrying this sword. I have no skill with such things.'

'You are wrong,' said Chareos, smiling. 'You've a good hand, a fast eye and a proud heart. All you lack is tuition. I'll supply that – as we search for Ravenna.'

'You'll come with me? Why?'

'Never count the teeth of a gift horse,' answered Chareos, moving to the grey and stepping into the saddle. The horse trembled.

'Oh no,' whispered Chareos. The stallion bucked violently, then reared and twisted in the air and Chareos flew over his head to land in the snow with a bone-jarring thud. The stallion walked forward to stand over him. He pushed himself upright and remounted.

'A strange beast,' observed Kiall. 'I don't think he likes you.'

'Of course he does, boy. The last man he didn't like he trampled to death.'

Chareos touched his heels to the stallion and led the way south.

He stayed some lengths ahead of Kiall as they rode through the morning, aware that he had no answers which the boy would understand. He could have told him of a child thirty years ago who had no hope, save that a warrior named Attalis had rescued him and become a father to him. He could tell him of a mother also named Ravenna, a proud, courageous woman who had refused to leave the husband she adored, even for the son she loved. But to do so would mean sharing a secret that Chareos carried with shame – a duty unfulfilled, a promise broken. He felt the fresh breeze whispering against his skin, and could smell the trees and the promise of snow. He glanced at the sky.

There was nothing he could say to Kiall. The boy was happy. The legendary Blademaster had agreed to accompany him and in Kiall's mind success was assured.

Chareos' thoughts turned to the farm-girl and the man who loved her – just as he had loved Tura, a hopeless one-sided emotion. Yet even now, after the bitterness and the pain, Chareos would walk through a lake of fire if Tura needed him. But she did not need him . . . she never had.

No, the one in need was a pig-breeder's daughter. He twisted in the saddle and looked back at Kiall, who smiled and waved.

Returning his gaze to the mountains ahead, Chareos remembered the day Tura had left him. He was sitting alone in the small courtyard behind the house. The sun was sinking behind the clouds, which seemed to burn like red fire. Finn had found him there.

The bowman sat alongside him on the stone seat. 'She didn't love you, man,' said Finn, and Chareos had wept like a child. For some time Finn sat in silence, then he placed his hand on Chareos' shoulder and spoke softly. 'Men dream of many things, Blademaster. We dream of fame we can never know, or riches we can never win. But the most foolish of all is the dream of love, of the great abiding love. Let it go.'

'I can't,' answered Chareos.

'Then mask it, for the troops are waiting and it is a long ride to Belazar.'

3

The stag dipped its head to the stream, its long tongue lapping at the clear water. Something struck it a wicked blow in the side; its head came up and an arrow sliced through one eye, deep into the brain. Its forelegs buckled and it dropped to the earth, blood seeping from its mouth.

The two hunters rose from the bushes and splashed across the stream to the carcass. Both were wearing buckskins, fringed and beaded, and they carried curved hunting-bows of Vagrian horn. The younger of the men – slight, blond-haired, with wide eyes of startling blue – knelt by the stag and opened the great artery of the beast's throat. The other man, taller and heavily bearded, stood watching the undergrowth.

'There's no one about, Finn,' said the blond hunter. 'You are getting old, and starting to imagine things.'

The bearded man swore softly. 'I can smell the bastards – they're hereabouts. Can't see why. No raiding for them. No women. But they're here, right enough. Puking Nadren!'

The smaller man disembowelled the stag and began to skin the carcass with a double-edged hunting-knife. Finn notched an arrow to his bow and stood glaring at the undergrowth opposite.

'You are making me nervous,' the younger man told him.

'We been together twenty years, Maggrig, and you still read sign like a blind man reads script.'

'Truly? Who was it last year said the Tattooed Men were hunting? Stayed guard for four days and not a sight of the head-hunters?'

'They were there. They just didn't want to kill us right then,' said Finn. 'How long you going to be quartering that beast?'

Just then four men rose from the bushes on the other side of the stream. They were all armed with bows and swords, but no arrows were notched and the blades were scabbarded.

'You want to share some of that?' called a lean, bearded man.

'We need it for the winter store. Deer are mighty scarce these days,' Finn told him. Maggrig, kneeling beside the carcass, sheathed his hunting-knife and took up his bow, sliding an arrow from his quiver.

'There's two more on this side,' he whispered.

'I know,' said the older man, cursing inwardly. With two Nadren hidden in the undergrowth behind them, they were trapped.

'You are not being very friendly,' said the Nadren warrior as he and the others began to wade towards the hunters.

'You can stop there,' Finn told him, drawing back the bow-string. 'We are in no need of company.' Maggrig, confident that Finn could contain the men at the stream, notched an arrow to his bow, his blue eyes scanning the undergrowth to the rear. A bowman rose from the bushes with his arrow aimed at Finn's back. Maggrig drew and loosed instantly, his shaft flashing through the man's throat, and the raider's arrow sailed over Finn and splashed down into the water before the four men.

'I didn't order him to do that,' said the lean man across the water,

45

waving his arm at the men alongside him. They began to back away but Finn said nothing, his eyes fixed on them.

'The other one is ready to chance a shaft,' whispered Maggrig. 'Do you have to stand there inviting it?'

'Hell's Gates, I'm tired of standing around in the cold,' said Finn. 'Make the whoreson show himself.' Maggrig drew back on the bow-string and sent an arrow slicing into the bushes. There was a yelp of surprise and a bowman reared up with a shaft through his upper arm. Finn spun on his heel and sent a second arrow into the man's chest and he fell face down into the undergrowth. Finn swung back, but the men across the stream had vanished into the bushes.

'Getting old, am I?' snapped Finn. 'Your boots have more brains than you.' Maggrig grabbed Finn's jerkin, hauling him from his feet as three arrows slashed the air where he had been standing. Maggrig loosed a shaft back across the stream, but he knew he had struck nothing.

'Time to be going home, old man,' said Maggrig. An arrow hit the ground before him, striking a stone and ricocheting into the carcass. Hastily the two men dragged the butchered deer back out of range, stacked the choicest cuts of meat inside the skin and faded into the woods. They moved warily for several miles, but there was no sign of pursuit.

Finally they angled across the slopes of the mountain to the partially hidden cabin set against the north face. Once there Finn built up the fire and tugged off his wet boots, hurling them against the stone of the hearth. The cabin was two-roomed. A large bed was placed against the wall opposite the fire, and a single window was fashioned beside the door. Bearskin rugs covered the floor. Maggrig opened the door to the workshop beyond, where they crafted their bows and arrows and beat the iron for the heads. He heard Finn swear.

'Damn Nadren! When I was your age, Maggrig, we had mounted patrols that scoured the mountains for scum like that. It's a bad day when they feel they can come in, bold as a brass mirror, to steal an innocent man's supper. Damn them!'

'Why so annoyed?' asked Maggrig. 'We killed two of them, *and* kept our supper. They haven't caused us a problem, save for three lost arrows.'

'They will. Murderous savages, the lot of them. They'll be hunting us.'

'Ah yes, but we have the Great Hunter Finn, the smeller of trouble! Not a bird can break wind in the mountains without Finn picking up the scent.'

'You're as funny as a broken leg. I've got a bad feeling, boy; there's death in the air smelling worse than winter.' He shivered and stretched out his large, bony hands to the fire.

46

Maggrig said nothing. He could feel it too.

Carrying the quartered stag through to the back of the workshop, Maggrig hung it on iron hooks by the far wall. Then he spread the skin and began the long job of scraping the fat from it. He'd need a new shirt for the winter, and he liked the russet colour of the hide. Finn wandered in and sat at the work-bench, idly picking up an arrow shaft and judging the line. He put it down. Normally he would cut feather flights, but now he merely sat staring at the bench-top.

Maggrig glanced up at him. 'Your back troubling you again?'

'Always does when winter's close. Damn! I hate going down to the Tavern Town, but needs must. Have to pass the word about the raiders.'

'We could look in and see Beltzer.'

Finn shook his head. 'He'll be drunk as usual. And one more insult from that pig and I swear I'll gut him.'

Maggrig stood and stretched his back. 'You don't mean that. Neither does he. He's just lonely, Finn.'

'Feel sorry for him, do you? Not me. He was cantankerous when he was married. He was vile at Bel-azar. There's a streak of mean in the man – I can't stand him.'

'Then why did you buy his axe when they auctioned it?' demanded the blond hunter. 'Two years of trapping to pay for that! And what have you done with it? Wrapped it in oilskin and left it at the bottom of the chest.'

Finn spread his hands. 'No accounting for myself sometimes. Didn't like the thought of some northern nobleman hanging it on his wall, I guess. Wish I hadn't now; we could do with some ready coin. Buy some salt. Damn, but I miss salt. I suppose we could trade some bows. You know, we should have stopped long enough to take the weapons from those Nadren. Could have got some salt for them, right enough.'

A wolf howl rent the night.

'Puking sons of bitches!' said Finn, standing and striding back into the main room.

Maggrig followed him. 'Got it in for wolves now, have you?'

'Wolf call makes no echo, boy. Don't you remember nothing at all?'

'I was raised to be a priest, Finn. My father didn't think I'd have much need for wolf calls and echoes.'

Finn chuckled. 'If they find the cabin, you can go out and preach to them.'

'How many do you think there are?'

'Hard to say,' Finn told him. 'Usually they keep to bands of around thirty, but there may be less.'

'Or more?' suggested Maggrig, softly.

Finn nodded. The wolf call sounded once more.

And this time it was closer . . .

Chareos drew rein on a hill-top and glanced back down towards the valley. 'What is it?' asked Kiall. 'That's the fourth time you've checked the back trail.'

'I thought I saw riders, sunlight gleamed from helms or lances. It could be a patrol.'

'They would not be looking for us, would they? I mean, we have broken no laws.'

Chareos looked into Kiall's face and read the fear there. 'I have no idea. The Earl is a vengeful man and he feels I have insulted him. But even he could find no way to accuse me on this matter. Let's move. We should be in Tavern Town by mid-morning, and I would sell my soul for a hot meal and a warm bed.'

The clouds above them were heavy with the promise of snow, and the temperature had dropped sharply during the past two days. Kiall wore only a woollen shirt and leggings, and just looking at him made Chareos more cold. 'I should have bought gloves,' he said, blowing at his hands.

'It is not too cold yet,' said Kiall cheerfully.

'It is when you are my age,' Chareos snapped.

Kiall chuckled. 'You don't look much past fifty.'

Chareos bit back an angry retort and urged the stallion on down the slope. All life is a circle, he reminded himself, remembering the days when he had chided old Kalin for being near senile. Old Kalin? The man had been forty-two – nearly three years younger than Chareos was now.

The stallion slithered on the slope. Chareos pulled his head up and leaned back in the saddle. The grey recovered his balance and reached the foot of the hill without incident. The trail widened into a mountain road, flattened by the wide leather-rimmed wheels of the wagons that carried timber to Talgithir. The trees gave shelter from the wind and Chareos felt more comfortable. Kiall rode alongside, but the grey nipped at the gelding, which reared. The villager clung on grimly.

'You should sell that beast,' said Kiall. 'There is a devil in him.'

It was good advice, but Chareos knew he would keep the grey. 'He is bad-tempered and a loner. But I like him. He reminds me of me.'

They emerged from the woods above a cluster of buildings, at the centre of which was a tavern. Grey smoke rose from its two stone chimneys, and men could be seen gathering outside the main doorway.

'Bad timing,' muttered Chareos. 'The timber workers and labourers are waiting for their midday meal.'

The two men rode down into the settlement. The stables were at the rear of the tavern, and there Chareos unsaddled the grey and led him

48

into a stall. He forked hay into the feeding-box and brushed the animal's back. Then he and Kiall walked through into the tavern. It was near full and there was no room close to the fires, so the two men sat at a bench table.

A plump woman approached them. 'Good morning, sirs. We have pies, and good roast beef and a rich honey-cake served hot.'

'Do you have rooms available?' asked Chareos.

'Yes, sir. The upper guest room. I will have a fire lit; it will be ready shortly.'

'We will take our food there,' he told her. 'But for now, two goblets of mulled wine, if you please.'

She curtseyed and moved back into the throng. The crowd made Chareos uncomfortable; the air was close and reeked of wood-smoke, sweat and broiling meat. After a while the woman returned and led them through to the stairs and on to the upper guest room. It was large and cold, despite the newly-lit fire, but there were two soft beds, a table and four deep leather chairs.

'It will warm up soon enough,' said the woman. 'Then you'll need to open the window. The left shutter is a little stiff, but a good push will move it; the wood has warped. I will bring your food presently.'

Chareos removed his cloak and dragged a chair to the fire. Kiall sat down opposite him, leaning forward; his back was healing fast, but still the wounds were sore.

'Where do we go from here?' he asked.

'South-west into Nadir lands. There we'll hear of the Nadren who raided your village. With luck Ravenna will have been sold and we should be able to steal her back.'

'What of the others?'

'For pity's sake, boy! They'll be spread all over the Nadir lands. Some of them will be sold twice over and we'd never find them all. Use your brain. Have you ever been to the Steppes?'

'No,' admitted Kiall.

'It's a big land. Huge. Endless prairies, hidden valleys, deserts. The stars seem close, and a man could walk for a year without seeing a single tent village. The Nadir are a nomadic people. They could buy a slave in . . . Talgithir, say . . . and three months later be in Drenan. They go where they will – unless they are summoned to war by the Khan. It will be task enough merely to find Ravenna. Believe me!'

'I keep thinking of her,' said Kiall, turning to stare at the fire. 'How frightened she must be. It makes me feel guilty to be sitting in comfort by a fire.'

'Nothing worth while was ever done in haste, Kiall. She is a beautiful woman, you say. Therefore they will not harm her. Is she virgin still?'

'Of course!' hissed Kiall, face reddening.

'Good. Then they will not rape her either. They will set a high price, and that might mean they keep her for a month or two. Relax, boy.'

'With respect, Chareos, would you mind not calling me boy? I last heard that more than five years ago. I am nineteen.'

'And I am forty-four – that makes you a boy to me. But I am sorry if it offends you . . . Kiall.'

The villager smiled. 'It does not offend me. I think I am too sensitive. It is just that, in your company, I feel . . . young and useless. I am an apothecary's assistant; I know herbs and medicines, but nothing of swordplay. I wouldn't know where to begin to look for Ravenna. Calling me "boy" just highlights my . . . lack of worth in this quest.'

Chareos leaned forward and added a chunk of wood to the blaze. Then he looked up into the earnest grey eyes of the young man. 'Do not speak of lack of worth,' he said. 'You proved your worth when you spoke out before the Earl . . . and more. Not one man in a hundred would set out on a quest such as this. You will learn, Kiall. Every day. And this is your first lesson: a warrior has only one true friend. Only one man he can rely on. Himself. So he feeds his body well; he trains it; works on it. Where he lacks skill, he practises. Where he lacks knowledge, he studies. But above all he must believe. He must believe in his strength of will, of purpose, of heart and soul. Do not speak badly of yourself, for the warrior that is inside you hears your words and is lessened by them. You are strong and you are brave. There is a nobility of spirit within you. Let it grow – you will do well enough. Now where is that damned food?'

Outside two hunters were loping into the settlement. The taller man glanced back and cursed.

From the woods came forty riders, swords in their hands.

Finn ran up the tavern steps, hurled open the door and all but recoiled from the mass of humanity wedged inside. 'Raiders!' he bellowed, then turned and sprinted across to the barn, where Maggrig was scaling a rope to the hayloft. The rolling thunder of hooves grew louder. Finn did not look back, but leapt for the rope and hauled himself up to kneel alongside his slender companion. Maggrig notched an arrow to his bow. 'We should have stayed in the woods,' he said. 'I don't believe it will be safer here.'

Finn said nothing. The riders galloped in to the settlement, screaming war-cries and slashing the air with their curved blades. Some among them were Nadir warriors in lacquered breastplates, others were renegade Gothir outlaws bearing axes and knives. All carried small round bucklers strapped to their left forearms. As they leapt from the horses and ran for the buildings, Finn sent an arrow which skewered a man's neck. Maggrig loosed a shaft, but it struck a horned

50

helm and glanced away to tear at the flesh of another warrior's arm. Seven of the raiders charged towards the barn and Finn cursed. A second shaft sang from his bow, but thudded against a raised buckler. Maggrig's next arrow hammered into a man's groin and he stumbled and fell. The six remaining raiders ran into the barn below.

Finn stood and scanned the hay-loft, seeing a ladder by a trapdoor some ten paces back. He moved to it and began to haul it up, but before he could lift it out of reach a tall raider leapt and dragged it back. Pulled forward, Finn almost toppled into the trap.

'I remember you, you puking bastard,' yelled the Nadren warrior at the foot of the ladder, staring up at Finn. 'You are dead meat. I'll rip your guts out through your bowels.'

Holding his buckler ahead of him, he began to climb. Finn swore and ran back to Maggrig.

'Good place you chose,' whispered Finn. Maggrig drew back on his bowstring and sent an arrow slicing into the back of a man running towards the tavern.

'You think we should leave?' he asked.

'No, I think we should stay and plant flowers,' muttered Finn. Behind them the Nadren warrior had reached the hay-loft. Finn sent a shaft at him, but the man blocked it with his buckler and began to haul himself through the opening. Dropping his bow, Finn launched himself at the warrior feet first, his right foot cracking home against the man's chin. Half stunned, he slumped back, but he still had a grip on his sword which he swung wildly. Finn rolled away from the cut. Maggrig ran back to aid him, but Finn waved him away. Rolling to his feet, the black-bearded hunter scooped up his bow and quiver, and looped them over his shoulder. 'Let's go!' he shouted at Maggrig. 'Now!' Dropping to his belly, he grabbed the rope and slithered over the hay-loft opening. Half-way down he released his hold and dropped to the ground. Maggrig joined him.

Deep in the barn, behind the winter wood-store, Beltzer awoke. His head was pounding and he sat up and groaned. He blinked and saw the Nadren warriors around the ladder. Worse, one of them swung round and saw him. Staggering upright as the man raised his sword and charged, Beltzer curled his right hand around the haft of a hatchet whose head was half-buried in a round of wood. He dragged it clear and leapt to meet the swordsman. The thin sabre slashed for his head, but Beltzer ducked and sent the hatchet blade cleaving through the man's ribs. The wooden haft snapped under the impact. Four more warriors came at him and, with a bellow of rage, Beltzer dropped his head and dived at them. Three of the Nadren were hurled from their feet but the fourth moved in with sword raised. An arrow punched through his temple and he staggered before dropping to his knees. Beltzer's huge fists clubbed at the men around him – in the close confines of the brawl they could not use their swords. He scrambled to his feet, kicked a man in the head and ran back towards the wood-store. The Nadren surged after him.

At the back of the barn the long-handled tree-axe rested against the wall. Beltzer swept it into his hands and swung on the attackers. Two men died in the first seconds of the combat, the survivor first backing away and then turning to sprint for the safety of the outer yard. An arrow from Finn stopped him in his tracks and he pitched face first to the floor.

'What in the Seven Hells is going on?' bellowed Beltzer – but Maggrig and Finn were gone and he sat down on a tree round and stared at the bodies. A movement from the ladder caught his eye and a Nadren warrior clambered down from the hay-loft. The man took one look at the giant with the axe and made off at speed.

Outside, Finn had dropped his bow and now held two bloodstained hunting-knives. Beside him lay two Nadren warriors and the body of Maggrig. Eight raiders circled him. 'Come on, my boys,' he snarled. 'Come in and die!'

Beltzer strolled out into the open with his axe on his shoulder and saw Finn surrounded. 'Bel-azar!' he screamed. The circle around Finn broke as the giant charged, and the slashing axe scattered the attack-ers. A warrior carrying a short stabbing spear rushed at Finn, but he sidestepped and rammed his hunting-knife into the man's belly.

Inside the tavern all was chaos. The raiders had forced their way in and hacked and slashed at the defenceless workers. Several were dead, others wounded. The survivors cowered on the floor, eyes averted from the warriors who stood guard over them. One Nadren warrior had climbed over the counter and was holding Naza's wife, Mael, by the throat. A knife-blade hovered over her right eye. Naza lay in a pool of blood by the man's feet.

'Where is it, you fat cow?' hissed the warrior, but suddenly a movement at the back of the room caused him to twist, his eyes narrowing. A door had opened and a tall man stepped into view carrying a shining sabre. Behind him came a second man, younger but also armed. The Nadren's eyes flickered back to the first man; he was no youngster, but he moved well. 'Don't just stand there,' the Nadren told the warriors. 'Take them!'

The farm workers scrambled back to form a pathway and several of the Nadren ran at the newcomers. Swords flashed and the clash of steel was punctuated by the screams of the dying. The Nadren holding Mael watched as his men were butchered by the tall swordsman. Hurling Mael aside, he vaulted the counter and ran to the door, shouting for aid.

But he stopped in the doorway – and cursed, for galloping from the woods to the north were twenty lancers. He leapt down and stepped into the saddle of the nearest horse, dragging the reins clear of the post round which they had been loosely tied.

'To horse! To horse!' he shouted. Then the lancers were upon them. The raiders, most of them on foot, scattered before the charge, but the lancers wheeled their mounts and bore down on the fleeing Nadren. A dozen of the raiders, mounted now, counter-attacked, trying to cut a path to the south.

Inside the tavern Chareos stumbled. A sword flashed for his head and he hurled himself to his right, landing on the massed forms of the labourers. The last Nadren loomed over him with sword raised, but Kiall slashed his sabre across the man's throat. Chareos regained his feet and moved to the doorway. On the open ground beyond he saw Salida and his lancers battling desperately against the raiders. The Nadren, realising now that they outnumbered the soldiers, were attacking with renewed frenzy. Chareos sheathed his sabre and drew his hunting-knife. He ran among the milling horsemen and dragged a Nadren from the saddle, plunging his knife between the rider's ribs. Vaulting to the horse's back, he drew his sabre and battled his way towards Salida.

Inside the tavern, Kiall glared at the workmen. 'Is this what you will brag about to your children?' he shouted. 'How you cringed in the face of danger? Get up! Arm yourselves!'

Seven of the men pushed themselves to their feet, but most of them remained where they were. The seven took weapons from the dead Nadren and followed Kiall out into the open. 'At them!' yelled the young villager, running forward and plunging his sabre deep into the back of a horseman.

By the barn Beltzer knelt by Finn, who sat with Maggrig's head in his lap. The blond hunter was bleeding from a wound to the scalp.

Beltzer reached for Maggrig's wrist. 'He's not dead,' he said, but Finn ignored him. Beltzer cursed and stood, pushing Finn aside and grabbing Maggrig by his shirt. He dragged the unconscious hunter back into the barn, away from the slashing, stamping hooves of the milling horses.

Finn blinked and followed him. 'Not dead?' he whispered.

'Stay with him,' said Beltzer, hefting his axe.

'Where are you going?' asked Finn.

'I'm going to kill a few Nadren. Then I am going to have a drink – many drinks.'

The giant vanished back into the fray. Finn sat back and looked down at Maggrig. He felt for the younger man's pulse; it was strong and even.

'You are nothing but trouble for me,' said Finn.

Slowly the battle turned. The lancers, fighting with sabres now, were more disciplined than the raiders and Chareos had linked with Salida at the centre. The two swordsmen seemed invincible.

Several of the Nadren turned from the fight and kicked their horses into a gallop. Others followed them. In all, seventeen Nadren escaped.

The others were killed where they stood . . .

Eleven lancers were dead, four more seriously wounded, and the open ground before the tavern was blood-drenched. Six horses had been killed and two others crippled and put down. Everywhere lay the corpses of dead warriors. In the sudden calm Salida lifted one leg and slid from the saddle. He wiped his sabre clean on the shirt of a dead man, and returned it to his scabbard. Chareos dismounted alongside him.

'A timely arrival, Captain,' said the former monk.

'Indeed, Chareos. My thanks. You fought well.'

'Needs must when demons rise,' quoted Chareos.

'We need to talk,' said Salida, leading his horse away from the slaughter field. Chareos followed him to a well at the rear of the tavern where both men drank, then Salida sat down on the well wall. 'The Earl has ordered your arrest. He means to see you hanged.'

'For what?' said Chareos. 'Even an earl must have a reason.'

'The murder of Logar.'

'How can a man be accused of murder when he is attacked by three swordsmen?'

'Logar was unarmed.'

'Un . . . Wait a moment.' Chareos moved back to the battle-ground and called Kiall to him. 'Give me your sword for a second.' He took the sabre to Salida. 'You recognise this?'

The Captain examined the blade and looked up. 'Yes, it is Logar's sabre. But that means nothing, Chareos. There is a witness against you and the Earl wishes you dead.'

'Do you believe me?'

The Captain smiled wearily. 'I believed in you even before I saw the sword. Logar was a snake. But that is not the point at issue and you leave me with a problem. My orders are to take you back – if I do, you will hang for certain; if I don't, I will be stripped of my command. Why in Bar's name did you cancel those cursed lessons?' Without waiting for an answer, Salida stood and returned to the tavern. He summoned an under-officer and gave instructions for the clearing away of the bodies.

Chareos sat by the well with Kiall beside him. 'What will you do?' asked the villager. Chareos shrugged. 'You can't go back,' said Kiall.

'No,' Chareos agreed, 'I can't go back.' A shadow fell across them and Chareos was suddenly lifted from his feet and held in a crushing bear-hug. Beltzer spun him round several times, then kissed him on both cheeks.

'I couldn't believe my eyes,' said the giant. 'Blademaster? What are you doing here? Did you come to see me? Have you a task for me? Dear Gods of Heaven, what a day!'

'Put me down, you ape!' thundered Chareos. Beltzer dropped him and stepped back, hands on hips.

'Gods, but you look older. Maggrig and Finn are here. We're all here! It's wonderful. I've been waiting for something to happen. Anything! But to have you here . . . well, say something, Blademaster.'

'You look dreadful,' said Chareos, 'and your breath would make rotting fish smell like perfume. Moreover I think you've broken one of my ribs.'

'Who is the boy?' asked Beltzer, jerking a thumb at Kiall.

'His name is Kiall. We are travelling together.'

'Good to meet you,' said Beltzer, thumping Kiall on the back. The villager groaned and staggered. 'What's the matter with him?'

'He suffered a whipping,' snapped Chareos, rubbing at his ribs, 'which I think you just reminded him of. Do you live here now?'

'After a fashion. I've been helping Naza – the tavern owner. Come, you must be dying of thirst. Let's have a drink or two . . . or three. Gods, what a lucky day! I'll fetch us some ale.' Beltzer ambled away towards the tavern.

'What *was* that?' Kiall asked.

'*That* was Beltzer. Once seen, never to be forgotten.'

'Beltzer?' whispered Kiall. 'The golden-haired hero of Bel-azar?'

'You will find, Kiall, that song and fable are not reliable. There could once have been a blind sow who would have considered Beltzer handsome – but I doubt it. I've seen whores turn him away while his pockets were bulging with gold coin.'

'It's incredible,' whispered Kiall. 'He's ugly and fat – and he smells.'

'Those are his good points,' said Chareos. 'Wait until you get to know him.' He stood and walked towards the barn, where Finn was helping Maggrig to stand.

'Still drawn to trouble like moths to candles,' remarked Chareos, smiling.

'It would seem so, Blademaster,' answered Finn. 'The boy here got a crack to the skull.'

'Bring him to my room.'

'I don't want to stay here too long,' said Finn. 'I hate crowded places – you know that.'

'I remember. But spare me an hour, if you will. Kiall will show you the way.'

Chareos walked over to where Salida sat on the raised walkway around the tavern.

'I have met some old friends, Captain. I will be in my room if you wish to talk to me.'

55

Salida nodded. 'Get your friend another sabre. I will take Logar's back to the Earl.'

'And what of me, my friend? And what of you?'

'You go where you will, Chareos. And may the Source guide you. As for me . . . who knows? I wasn't always a Captain of Lance – there may be other roles I will enjoy. But I think the Earl will send others after you. He is no longer rational where you are concerned.'

'Be careful, Salida.'

'Yes, this is a world for careful men,' he replied, waving a hand at the battlefield.

Inside the tavern the bodies had been dragged away, leaving trails of blood on the wooden boards. The eastern end of the dining room was now a hospital area, where soldiers were stitching wounds and applying bandages. Chareos saw the innkeeper's wife sitting beside her husband. With a deep wound in his shoulder and a lump on his temple, Naza was white-faced and deeply in shock.

Chareos joined them and the woman looked up and smiled wearily. 'Thank you for your aid, sir,' she said. 'I thought they would kill me.'

'What did they want?' asked Chareos.

'The timber workers are paid tomorrow. We keep the silver coin hidden here. There are four hundred men, and they are paid each quarter year; it is a sizeable sum.'

'I see. Would you mind if I took some food from the kitchen? My companion and I still have not eaten.'

'I will prepare you something presently,' she offered, her face flushing.

'Not at all,' said Chareos swiftly. 'Stay with your husband. It is no trouble to me, I assure you.'

'You are kind, sir,' said Mael.

Chareos walked through to the kitchen. Several tables had been overturned and there were broken pots and crockery on the floor, but a large pot of stew still simmered on the huge iron stove. A serving-maid entered from the rear of the building. Short and slender, with dark, curled hair, she curtseyed. 'May I help you, sir?' she enquired.

'Bring some food, stew, meat, bread . . . whatever, to the upper guest room. We will also need some wine – five goblets. Oh yes, and some linen for bandages. Will you do it now?' he asked, handing her a half silver piece. She pocketed the coin and curtseyed once more.

Chareos returned to his room where Finn was sitting on one wide bed, dabbing with a cloth at the wound on Maggrig's head; it was a shallow cut, and his temple was bruised and swollen. Beltzer was sitting by the fire with a pitcher of ale in his hands; Kiall was standing by the window, looking down at the former battleground. He had surprised himself today, leading the farm workers into the fight – the excitement had been great, and his fears had vanished in the chaos of the skirmish. Now he felt like a warrior. He glanced up at the sky. How blue it was, how fresh and clean the air. He turned and smiled at Chareos, then switched his gaze to Beltzer. Ugly the man was, but he had swung his axe like a giant of legend. He had not seen Maggrig and Finn in action, but merely to be in the same room as the heroes of Belazar filled him with pride.

A serving-maid brought food, but Kiall was no longer hungry. Beltzer took his share, while Chareos sat quietly opposite the giant, gazing into the fire. Finn had applied a linen bandage to Maggrig's head and the younger man lay back on the bed and fell asleep. There was no conversation and Kiall pulled up a chair and sat in silence. His hands began to shake, and his stomach heaved. Chareos saw this and passed across a chunk of black bread.

'Eat it,' he said. Kiall nodded and chewed at the crust and the nausea passed.

'What now?' said Beltzer, laying the empty pitcher beside the chair. 'Back to chopping wood and punching timber men?'

'What do you want?' asked Chareos softly.

'I want it to be the way it was,' the giant answered him.

'Nothing is the way it was. And I'll tell you something, Beltzer, old friend – it never was the way it was.'

'I'm supposed to understand that, am I? You always were so clever with words. But they don't mean pig-wind. I'm not old, I can hold my own with any man. I can drink a mountain of ale and still lift a barrel of sand over my head. And there's no man alive can stand against me in battle.'

'That's probably true,' Chareos agreed, 'but you are not young either. What are you, Beltzer? Fifty?'

'Forty-eight. And that's *not* old.'

'It's older than Kalin was at Bel-azar. And didn't you advise him to go home and leave the fighting to the younger men?'

'It was a jest,' snapped Beltzer. 'And I didn't know then what I know now. Gods, Blademaster, there must be something for me!'

Chareos eased himself back in his chair and stretched his legs to the fire. 'I am on a quest,' he said softly.

Beltzer leaned forward, his eyes shining. 'Tell me,' he invited.

'I am helping young Kiall to rescue a woman stolen by the Nadren.'

'A noblewoman? A princess?'

'No, a village girl – the daughter of a pig-breeder.'

'What? Why? Where is the glory in that? The Nadren have been stealing women for centuries. Who'll sing a song about the rescue of a pig-breeder's daughter?'

'No one,' admitted Chareos, 'but if you'd rather stay here and chop wood . . .'

'I didn't say that – don't put words in my mouth. Which group took her?'

'No one knows.'

'Which Nadir camp did they head for?'

Chareos shrugged. 'We don't know.'

'If you are mocking me I'll break your head,' said Beltzer. 'What DO we know?'

'We know she was taken. Now all we have to do is find her – and steal her back.'

'You'd need the Tattooed Man for that – and he's gone. Probably dead by now.'

'My thoughts exactly,' agreed Chareos, 'but I shall ride into the Valley and seek him. Unless you have a better plan?'

'Anything's better than that,' said Beltzer. 'They'll take your head and shrink it down to wear on a belt. You don't even speak the language.'

'You do.'

'I need some more ale,' said Beltzer, lurching to his feet and striding from the room.

'Who is the Tattooed Man?' asked Kiall. 'And where is the Valley?'

'The Gateway is not of this world,' answered Finn, moving to join them. 'And only a moonstruck fool would venture there. What game are you playing, Chareos? No one goes into the Valley.'

'It is no game, Finn,' Chareos told him. 'The quest, as it stands, is impossible . . . unless we can find a man who can follow spirit-trails. Do you know of any as skilled as Okas?'

'None,' admitted Finn. 'But the Valley? I wouldn't go there if my soul depended on it. Neither will Beltzer. They don't like visitors.'

'I'll go there with you,' said Kiall. 'I'll go anywhere if it means a chance to find Ravenna.'

'I can remember when we sounded like that,' mused Finn. 'It's a wonder we've survived so long, Blademaster. If you want to die, why not leap from a cliff, or open your veins with a sharp blade? The Tattooed People will kill you slowly. But then you know that.'

Chareos turned to Finn and smiled. 'I know the perils, Finn, and I won't go without Beltzer. For some reason, Okas seemed to like him.'

'Perhaps it was the smell,' offered Finn. 'He was the only man I ever met who stank worse than the big man. Even so, it is not a journey I would undertake.'

'What is so terrible there?' Kiall asked.

Finn scratched at his beard. 'According to Okas the land is hot, and there are beasts there who feed on human flesh. Also, the Tattooed People collect heads and shrink them down by magic. About twenty years ago a nobleman named Carsis led a small force into the Valley; their shrunken heads were left on spears at the entrance. For ten years, whenever a traveller passed by, the heads would shriek warnings. I saw them once – aye, and heard them. They spoke of the terrors of Hell.'

'They are not there now, then?' said Kiall.

'No. The Lord Regent sent a section of lancers into the hills – they built a great fire and burned the heads.'

'Do the Tattooed People venture into our lands?'

'Sometimes, boy. And that's when a man locks his doors and sits up at night with sword and bow close to hand. You still want to go there?'

Kiall swallowed hard. 'I will go wherever I have to.'

'Spoken like a hero,' said Finn sourly.

The door opened and Beltzer entered, carrying two pitchers of ale. 'I'll come with you,' he told Chareos.

'Spoken like an idiot,' whispered Finn.

The soldiers dug a shallow trench a half-mile from the settlement. The bodies of the Nadren, stripped of their armour and weapons, were unceremoniously flung into it. The corpses of the soldiers, eleven in all, were wrapped in their blankets and reverently placed on the back of a wagon, ready for burial with honours in Talgithir.

Salida ordered the Nadren grave to be filled with rocks, to prevent wolves and foxes from digging for food. It was almost dusk, and he was bone-weary. Seven of the dead had been new recruits, unused to war, but four were seasoned veterans. One of these had been his valet, a bright, amusing man named Caphes; he had a wife and five sons in Talgithir and Salida did not relish the visit he would have to make to the family home. The sound of a horse's hooves made him turn, and he saw Chareos riding towards him on a huge white stallion.

The former monk dismounted and approached.

'I wanted to make sure,' said Chareos, 'that you had no second thoughts on the matter of my arrest.'

Salida gazed into the man's dark eyes, unable to read the thoughts of the tall swordsman before him. 'No, I have not,' he said and Chareos nodded.

'You are a good man, Salida. Here, I have brought Logar's sabre.' He handed the scabbarded weapon to the officer. Dipping his hand into the sack hung behind his saddle, he produced a wineskin and two leather-covered brass cups. 'Join me?' he enquired.

'Why not? But let's move away from the stench of death – I've had my fill of it.'

'You look tired,' Chareos told him. 'And not just because of the battle, I think?'

They strolled to a group of boulders and sat down; Salida un-buckled his iron breastplate and laid it beside him. 'No, it is not. I am a family man now, Chareos. There was a time when I believed that soldiers could make a difference.' He accepted a goblet of red wine and sipped it. 'But now? I have three sons and a beautiful wife. The Nadir are gathering again, and one day soon they will cross the mountains and destroy the Gothir. What then of my sons and their dreams?'

'Maybe they will not come,' said Chareos. 'The Gothir have little; this is not a rich land.'

'They don't care about riches, they live for war. And what do we have to oppose them? The army has been cut to two thousand men. We couldn't even hold Bel-azar now.' He drained his wine and held out the cup for more. Chareos filled it and sat silently.

'I was born out of my time,' continued Salida, forcing a smile. 'I should have been an officer in the great days when the Gothir swept across Nadir lands all the way to the Delnoch mountains.'

'It is all a circle,' Chareos told him. 'The Gothir had their day, as did the Drenai and the Vagrians. Now we live in Nadir days. Their time will come, and then an officer just like you will sit at the last outpost of the Nadir empire bewailing his fate, and wondering about the dreams of his sons.'

Salida nodded. 'May that day come soon,' he said, grinning. 'Is it true that you were once a Drenai prince?'

Chareos smiled and refilled his own cup. 'So the singers would have us believe.'

'Have you never thought to return to your homeland?'

'This is my homeland. But yes, I have considered crossing the Delnoch mountains . . . one day, perhaps.'

'I once visited Castle Tenaka,' said Salida. 'It is an incredible place: six great walls and a keep with walls three feet thick.'

'I knew it as Dros Delnoch,' Chareos told him. 'It was said that it could never be taken. I was raised on stories of Druss the Legend, and Rek, the Earl of Bronze. Strange that it should have been conquered by one of Rek's descendants. Castle Tenaka? I don't like the sound of the name.'

'You met him once, did you not? The Great Khan?'

'Yes. A very long time ago. Another lifetime.' Chareos rose. 'If you do not object, I would like to find my companion another sabre. I doubt the Nadren had anything of similar workmanship, but then he is no swordsman.'

'There's no point in going through the Nadren weapons – poor iron, badly fashioned. I gave a sword to my valet. It is a good blade, and he will have no further use for it. Take it with my blessing.' Salida walked across to the wagon and lifted clear a cavalry sabre in a wooden, leather-covered scabbard. 'The balance is good, the edge keen.'

'Thank you, my friend,' said Chareos, offering his hand. Salida gripped it.

'At least I can tell my sons I fought alongside a hero of Bel-azar.'

'May the Source go with you, Salida.'

The Captain watched as Chareos swung into the saddle. The stallion reared and came down at a run. Salida stood for several minutes as the rider grew ever smaller, then he returned to the tasks at hand – ordering the wagon hitched, and the riderless horses tied to the rear.

It would be a sad ride back to Talgithir.

4

An eerie silence covered the high forest like an invisible cloak as the dawn light bathed the tavern. Kiall gazed around the seemingly deserted settlement. There were few signs now of the battle, save for the dried bloodstains on the snow. Beltzer hoisted his pack to his shoulders and stamped his feet. 'I hate the cold,' he declared.

'We haven't started yet,' said Finn, 'and already you're complaining.'

Kiall struggled to get his arms through the pack ropes and Maggrig assisted him, lifting the loops over the thick goatskin jerkin Kiall now wore.

'It's too big for me,' said Kiall.

'There's gratitude,' snapped Beltzer, 'after all the trouble I took to get it for you.'

'You stripped it from a dead Nadren,' Chareos pointed out.

'Had to kill him first,' retorted Beltzer, aggrieved.

Chareos ignored him, and shrugged into his pack. Finn had loaned him a fur-lined cloak with a deep hood, which he lifted into place and tied under his chin. Moving away from the others, he drew his sabre. After several practice lunges and parries, he scabbarded the sword and adjusted the loops of the pack. He dropped his arms and the pack fell away . . . the sabre flashed into the air. Twice more Chareos repeated the manoeuvre. At last, satisfied, he rejoined the others. The pack was less comfortable now, the ropes biting into his shoulders, the weight too low on his back. But it could be swiftly jettisoned if the need arose, and that was worth a little discomfort.

The group set off on the ice-covered trail. Chareos had never enjoyed walking but on Finn's advice had left the horses in the settlement, paying Naza a retainer to feed and groom the mounts while they were gone.

Both the bowmen had declined the opportunity to join the three questors, but Finn had at least agreed to guide them to the Shrieking

Gate. As he walked behind Finn, Chareos considered all aspects of the way ahead. The Nadren were still in the forest, but these were not a great fear. Five well-armed men should prove deterrent enough, especially after the mauling the raiders had received. No, the biggest problem was what awaited them beyond the Gate.

The Tattooed People were a mystery. Some said they had once been of this world, forced back by the migration of nations ten centuries before when the war-like Drenai, the Gothir and the ferocious Nadir tribes came sweeping from north, south and east. One legend claimed the Tattooed People used sorcery to open a doorway between worlds, allowing the tribe to escape to a hidden land of riches and plenty. Another maintained that the Gateway had been there from the days before the Ice Fall, a last remnant of a once proud civilisation and that beyond it lay mountains of gold.

But whatever the truth the Gateway did exist and, on rare occasions, one or more of the Tattooed People passed through it. Such had been the case when Okas had wandered into the army camp six months before the battle at Bel-azar. He had squatted down at Chareos' camp-fire and waited in silence until Beltzer offered him a plate of meat and bread. He was a small man, no more than five feet tall, pot-bellied and wearing only a loin-cloth decorated with pale stones. His entire body was covered in blue tattooes – some in the shape of leaves, others in runic symbols around what appeared to be camp-fire scenes. His face also was tattooed with curving lines and his beardless chin was completely blue, shaped like a beard with a waxed moustache above it. Amazingly he spoke a little of the Common Language and, more amazing still, in the four months Okas was with them the uncouth Beltzer mastered the tribesman's tongue. Okas proved invaluable during that time. In the skills of tracking he had no peers – at least not among the Gothir. And he was a great 'finder'. Chareos' senior officer, Jochell, lost a valuable golden ring and had the quarters of all enlisted men searched. Through Beltzer, Okas told the officer that he would find the missing item.

Jochell was dubious, yet he had seen Okas' skills in action during the hunt for Nadir raiders. Much to the amusement of the men Okas took the officer's hand and held it in silence for a while, eyes closed. Then he released his grip and trotted from the camp. Jochell saddled his horse and rode after him; Chareos and Finn followed, anxious to see the outcome. Two hours later they were at the scene of the previous day's battle with Nadir outriders. There was a small stream to the west of the battlefield. Okas moved to it and knelt by the water-line. Then he grunted and pointed. Jochell joined him. There, just below the surface, nestling among the pebbles was the gold ring, its pale central opal glistening blue.

Jochell was delighted and gave Okas two gold pieces. The tribesman stared at them for a while, then tossed them to Chareos. That night Okas left them, but not before he had sat with Beltzer for more than an hour. He said farewell to no one else, merely gathered up his blanket and walked from the camp.

In the morning Chareos had asked Beltzer, 'What did he say to you?'

'He told me to stay close to you, Maggrig and Finn during the coming days. He also told me that Jochell's ring would grace a Nadir hand before the winter moon.'

'I wish I hadn't asked,' Chareos said.

'He's only been gone a few hours – and already I miss him,' said Beltzer. 'You think we'll see him again?'

Now, as he walked through the early morning frost, Chareos remembered that conversation and the many which had followed it. Beltzer told him of the land beyond the Gateway. It was hot and humid, with towering trees and vast open veldts and lakes. There were huge animals there, higher than houses, and hunting cats with fangs like long knives. It was a world of sudden storms and sudden deaths.

'Are you thinking of going there?' Chareos had asked. Beltzer looked away, his face reddening.

'I would have liked to, but Okas said the Tattooed People kill any interlopers. Their history is full of massacres and the murder of their people by our races – they are terrified it will happen again.'

The sky darkened and thunder jolted Chareos' mind back to the present. Finn called a halt and turned to face Chareos. 'It will be dusk soon and there's going to be a heavy snowfall,' he said. 'I suggest we look for somewhere to camp and sit it out. We will build two shelters and gather wood for fires.' The group walked on into a thick stand of pine; Finn and Maggrig scouted the area, locating two good sites. Kiall watched as the hunters tied twine to the tops of four sapling trees. These were then pulled together and fastened. Finn sent Beltzer and Chareos out to cut branches from the surrounding pine, and these were threaded through the tied saplings to form a spherical shelter some ten feet across. The bowmen left Kiall, Chareos and Beltzer to complete the walls, then walked some thirty feet away to build their own shelter.

Snow began to fall – gently at first, then thick and fast. The wind strengthened, gusting the snow into the faces of the workers, ice forming on brows and beards. Chareos continued to pack the walls of the shelter while Beltzer and Kiall gathered dead wood for a fire. The temperature plummeted as the sun dipped below the peaks.

Chareos had left a rough doorway on the south side of the structure and Kiall and Beltzer crawled inside. A tiny fire surrounded by stones was burning at the centre of the circle, but there was not heat enough to warm a man's hands, let alone keep death from his body, thought

Kiall miserably. The snow fell harder, covering the shelters, blocking the gaps in the walls and cutting out the icy draughts.

The temperature began to rise. 'Take off your cloaks and jerkins,' ordered Chareos.

'I'm cold enough already,' Kiall argued.

'As you please,' said Chareos, removing his fur-lined cloak and heavy woollen overshirt. Adding fuel to the fire he lay down, his head resting on his pack. Beltzer did likewise, having discarded his bearskin jerkin. Kiall sat shivering for some minutes. Neither of the others spoke for a while, then Kiall unclipped the brooch which held his Nadren cloak in place. Immediately he struggled out of the goatskin jerkin, the warmth from the fire enveloped him.

'I don't understand,' he said. Chareos raised himself on one elbow and smiled.

'Wool and fur are made not just to keep cold out, but to keep warmth in. Therefore it will work in reverse. If your body is cold and there is heat outside, the furs will stop it getting through to you.'

'Why did you not just tell me?'

'I find some men learn best by suffering,' said Chareos.

Kiall ignored the rebuke. 'Why did Finn and Maggrig choose to have their own shelter?' he asked. 'Surely there is enough room in here with us?'

'They prefer their own company,' answered Beltzer. 'They always did. But I am sorry they will not be coming with us beyond the Gate. I never knew a better shot than Maggrig, nor a cooler fighting man than Finn.'

'Why won't they come with us?' Kiall asked.

'They have more sense,' Chareos told him.

Ravenna's dreams were strange and fragmented. She was a child in the arms of her mother – safe, warm and comforted. She was a doe running through the forest, pursued by wolves with long yellow fangs, sharp as swords. She was a bird, trapped in a gilded cage and unable to spread her wings.

She awoke. All around her the other women lay sleeping. The air was close and there were no windows. Ravenna closed her eyes. Tomorrow she would stand naked on the auction block. Her heart began to beat wildly; she calmed her breathing and tried to relax.

The dreams flowed once more. Now she saw a knight in shining armour riding through the gates, the Nadren scattering before him. Leaning from his saddle, he plucked her from the auction platform and rode out across the steppes. Safe in the trees he helped her down and dismounted beside her. He lifted his visor . . . the face inside was rotted and long dead, the flesh hanging in leather strips from the grinning skull.

64

She screamed . . .

And woke. The other women were still sleeping – the scream then had been part of the nightmare. Ravenna was glad of that. Wrapping the thin blanket round her shoulders, she sat up. Her dress of yellow-dyed wool was filthy, and she could smell stale sweat upon it.

'I will survive this,' she told herself. 'I will not give in to despair.'

The thought strengthened her for a moment only, but the weight of her captivity bore down on her, crushing her resolve.

She wept silently. The woman from the wagon rose from her blankets and walked over to her, putting a slender arm about her shoulders.

'Tomorrow,' she said, 'when you stand on the platform, do not try to entice a buyer. The Nadir put no stock in women. They view them like cattle. They fear proud women. You understand me? Keep your head down, and obey the commands of the auctioneer. Do not think of nakedness. Be meek and submissive.'

'If they fear proud women, perhaps no one would buy me.'

'Do not be a fool!' snapped the older woman. 'If you look defiant, the auctioneer will have you whipped into submission – or you'll be bought by a man who enjoys inflicting pain on women. What you need is a master who will treat you casually. There is no such animal as a gentle Nadir, but better to be bedded swiftly by an indifferent savage than to be beaten like a dog.'

'How is it you know so much?' asked Ravenna.

'I have been sold before,' said the woman. 'I spent three years as a whore in New Gulgothir. Before that I was sold to a Nadir chieftain.'

'But you escaped?'

'Yes. And I will escape again.'

'How is it you are so strong?'

'I was once wed to a weak man. Sleep now. And if you cannot sleep, rest. You will not want dark rings under those pretty eyes.'

'What is your name?'

'What does it matter?' the woman answered.

Salida strode into the main hall, his armour dust-stained and dull, his eyes bloodshot and weary. Yet still he kept his back straight, his chin high. There were more than forty noblemen present. He bowed before the Earl and their eyes met.

'Do you bring me Chareos?' asked the Earl softly.

'No, my lord. But I bring you Logar's sabre.' He held the scabbarded blade high and placed it on the dais before the Earl. 'Also I bring you the owner of the Grey Owl tavern, who witnessed the fight; he is outside. He says that Logar and two others attacked the monk, and that Chareos defended himself nobly. The man Kypha was lying.'

'You took this investigation on yourself?' said the Earl, rising from his ebony chair, his eyes cold.

'I know, my lord, how highly you value justice. I must also tell you that Chareos and the villager, Kiall, fought alongside myself and the men from Talgithir against a large band of Nadren. Chareos slew at least six of them in a pitched battle. Without him, and Beltzer, Maggrig and Finn, we might well have lost the encounter. I judged – perhaps wrongly – that you would not appreciate the waste of time involved in bringing Chareos back.'

The Earl stood in silence for several seconds, then he smiled. 'I like my officers to show initiative, Salida, and this you have done. You also destroyed a band of raiders and showed, I understand, great personal courage. You are to be commended – both for your action in battle and your discretion. Go now. Rest. You have earned it.'

Salida bowed and backed two paces before turning and striding from the hall. Aware that all eyes were on him, the Earl turned back to his guests. For an hour he moved among them, his mood light, his humour good. Just before dusk he left the hall and walked swiftly through the stone corridors of the Keep until he reached the stairway to his private rooms.

He entered the study and pushed shut the door. A tall man was standing at the window. Lean and hawk-faced, with pale eyes separated by a curved beak of a nose, a scar ran from his brow to his chin in an angry white line. He wore a black leather cloak that shimmered in the lantern light, and three knives hung from a baldric on his chest.

'Well, Harokas?' said the Earl.

'The man, Kypha, is dead. Somehow he contrived to drown in his bath,' answered Harokas. 'I hear the other business is finished.'

The Earl shook his head. 'Nothing is finished. The man insulted me, through my son, then disgraced me publicly. Find him – and kill him.'

'I am skilful with a blade, my lord – but not that skilful.'

'I did not say fight him, Harokas. I said *kill* him.'

'It is not for me to criticise . . .'

'No, it is not!' stormed the Earl.

Harokas' green eyes narrowed, but he said nothing.

'I want him to know why he is dying,' the Earl continued.

'What should I tell him, my lord?' asked Harokas. 'That a hero of Bel-azar is doomed because he disciplined an arrogant boy?'

'Beware, Harokas,' the Earl hissed. 'My patience is not limitless – even with those who have served me well and faithfully.'

'It will be as you order,' said Harokas. He bowed and left the study.

Kiall's dreams were troubled. Again and again he saw the Nadren sweep down on the village, heard their wild battle cries and saw the sunlight gleaming on their swords and helms. He had been high in the woods, supposedly gathering herbs for the apothecary – but in reality he had been wandering, dreaming, imagining himself as a knight, or a bard singer, or a nobleman on a quest. In his fantasy he was a man of iron courage and lethal skills. But when the Nadren war cries sounded he had stood frozen to the spot, watching the carnage, the looting, raping and burning. He had seen Ravenna and the others hauled across the saddles of the conquering raiders and taken away to the south. And he had done nothing.

He knew then, as he knew now, why Ravenna had rejected him, and suffered again the pain of their meeting in the high meadow by the silver stream.

'You are a dreamer, Kiall,' she had said, 'and I like you. Truly I do. But I need more than dreams. I want a man who will build, who will grow. I need a strong man.'

'I can do all these things,' he had assured her.

'Only in your head. Now you must leave me. If Jarel sees you talking to me, he will be jealous. And it would not be wise for you to make Jarel angry.'

'I am not afraid of Jarel. But I *love* you, Ravenna. I cannot believe that means nothing to you.'

'Poor Kiall,' she whispered, stroking his cheek. 'Still the dreamer. Love? What is love?' She had laughed at him then and walked away.

Kiall awoke. His body was warm under the blanket, but his face was cold. Raising himself on one elbow, he saw that the fire was dying. He added wood and sat up. Beltzer was snoring and Chareos remained in a deep sleep. The flames licked the fuel and rose. Kiall warmed his hands and wrapped his blanket around his shoulders.

He sniffed. The air inside the shelter was close and full of smoke, but still he could smell the rank odour emanating from Beltzer. This was no dream. Here he sat with the heroes of Bel-azar, on a quest to rescue a beautiful maiden from the clutches of evil. Yet in no way did the reality match the fantasies. A bad-tempered Swordmaster, a vile-smelling warrior, and two hunters who spoke barely a civil word to anyone but each other.

Beltzer snorted and turned over, his mouth open. Kiall saw that he had lost several teeth and that others were discoloured and bad. How could this fat old man *ever* have been the golden-haired hero of legend?

I should have stayed in the village, he told himself, and learned the apothecary's skills. At least then I would have been able to afford to take a wife, and build a home. But no, the dreamer had to have his way.

He heard the crunching of boots on the snow outside, and fear rose in him as he pictured the Nadren creeping up on them as they slept. He scrambled to his feet and dressed swiftly. Then he heard Maggrig's voice. Pulling on his boots, he dropped to his knees and eased himself out into the snow-covered clearing. The sky was a rich velvet blue, and the sun was just rising above the mountains to the east. Maggrig and Finn were skinning four white rabbits, the nearby snow spattered with blood.

'Good morning,' said Kiall. The younger man smiled and waved, but Finn ignored the villager. Kiall moved alongside them. 'You're out early,' he remarked.

'Early for some,' grunted Finn. 'Make yourself useful.' He tossed a rabbit to Kiall, who skinned it clumsily. Finn gathered up the entrails and threw them out into the bushes, then he scraped the fat from the furs and pushed them deep into his pack.

Kiall wiped his blood-covered hands on the snow and sat back on a rock. Finn's bow was resting against it and Kiall reached for it.

'Don't touch it!' snapped Finn.

Kiall's anger rose. 'You think I would steal it?'

'I don't much care – but don't touch it.'

Maggrig moved alongside Kiall. 'Don't take it to heart,' he said softly. 'No bowyer likes another man to touch his bow. It is . . . a superstition, I suppose. You see, each bow is made for one archer. It is designed for him alone. Finn makes his own bows. Even I am not allowed to use them.'

'No need to make excuses for me,' said Finn sourly.

Maggrig ignored him. 'When we get to the cabin,' he told Kiall, 'you will see many bows. Finn will probably give you one – a weapon to suit your length of arm and your pulling strength.'

'It would be no use,' said Kiall. 'I have no eye for archery.'

'Neither had I when I first met Finn. But it is amazing what a man can learn when he is paired with a master. Finn won every prize worth the taking. He even took the Lord Regent's talisman against the best archers of six lands: Drenai, Vagrians, Nadir, Ventrians, and even bowmen from Mashrapur. None could compete with Finn.'

'Not then or now,' muttered Finn, but his expression softened and he smiled. 'Don't mind me, boy,' he told Kiall. 'I don't like people much. But I don't wish you harm – and I hope you find your lady.'

'I am sorry you will not be travelling with us,' said Kiall.

'I'm not. I have no wish to have my head shrunk on a pole, or my skin flayed outside a Nadir tent. My battle days are long gone. Quests and the like are for young men like you.'

'But Beltzer is coming,' Kiall reminded him.

Finn grunted. 'He never grew up, that one. But he's a good man in a scrap, right enough.'

'Chareos too,' said Maggrig softly.

'Yes,' agreed Finn. 'A strange man, Chareos. But you watch him, boy, and learn. His kind don't come around so often, if you catch my meaning.'

'I'm not sure that I do.'

'He's a man with iron principles. He knows the world is shades of grey, but he lives like it's black and white. There's a nobility in him – a gallantry, if you like. You'll see what I mean, come the finish. Now that's enough of talking. Wake your companions. If they want to break their fast, they'd better be up. I'll not wait for them.'

The snow held off for several days, but even so the travellers made slow progress across the peaks. On the fifth day Maggrig, leading the group, came too close to the lair of a snow leopard and her cubs. The leopard seemed to explode from the undergrowth, spitting and snarling. Maggrig was hurled from his feet, a jagged tear across one arm of his tunic. Beltzer and the others ran forward, shouting at the tops of their voices – but the animal crouched before them, ears flat to her skull and fangs bared. Finn dragged Maggrig clear and the travellers gave the beast a wide berth. Maggrig's arm was slashed, but not deeply, and the wound was stitched and bound by Finn.

On the following morning they reached the valley where the hunters' cabin was hidden. A blizzard blew up around them and they forced their way, heads bowed against the wind, to the frozen doorway. Snow had banked against it, blocking the door and filling the window-frame alongside. Beltzer cleared it, shovelling it aside with his huge hands. Inside was icy, but Finn got a fire going; it was more than an hour before the heat warmed the cabin.

'That was good luck,' said Beltzer, finally stripping his bearskin jerkin and squatting on the rug beside the fire. 'That blizzard could have hit us days ago, and we'd have been trapped out in the mountains for weeks.'

'It may be lucky for you, dung-brain,' said Finn, 'but I do not relish my home being filled with sweating bodies for days on end.'

Beltzer grinned at the black-bearded hunter. 'You're the least welcoming man I've ever known. Where do you keep the drink?'

'In the well outside. Where else?'

'I mean the ale, or the wine, or even the malt spirit?'

'We have none here.'

'None?' asked Beltzer, eyes widening. 'None at all?'

'Not a drop,' answered Maggrig, smiling. 'Now how lucky do you feel?' His face was white and sweat dripped into his eyes. He tried to stand, but sank back in his chair.

'What's the matter with you?' said Finn, rising and moving to the younger man.

Maggrig shrugged. 'I don't . . . feel . . .' He sagged sideways from

69

the chair. Finn caught him and carried him to the bed, where Chareos joined him.

'He has a fever,' said Chareos, laying his hand on the hunter's brow. Maggrig's eyes opened.

'Room's going round . . . thirsty . . .' Finn brought him a goblet of water and lifted his head while he drank.

Kiall cleared his throat. 'If you boil some water, I'll make a potion for him.'

Finn swung on him. 'What are you . . . a magician?'

'I was an apothecary's assistant, and I bought some herbs and powders back in Tavern Town.'

'Well, come and look at him, boy. Don't just stand there!' stormed Finn. Kiall moved to the bedside. First he examined the wound on Maggrig's temple; it had closed and healed well, but his master had always told him that blows to the head often shocked the system. Perhaps the second injury, caused by the leopard's attack, had caught the hunter in a weakened state. Trying to remember what Ulthen had told him of such wounds, he removed the bandage from Maggrig's arm; the cut was jagged and angry, but there was no pus or obvious sign of infection.

Kiall filled a small copper pot with water and hung it over the fire. Within a few minutes the contents were boiling. Then he opened his pack and took out a thick package, wrapped in oiled paper. Inside were a dozen smaller packages, each decorated with a hand-drawn leaf or flower. Kiall selected two of the packets and opened them. Bruising the leaves, he dropped them into the water and stirred the brew with a spoon. Then lifting the pot from the fire, he laid it in the hearth to cool.

'Smells fine,' said Beltzer.

'How would you know?' hissed Finn. 'What have you made there, boy?'

'It's a potion from willow leaves and comfrey. Both are good for fighting fevers, but the comfrey helps to clean the blood and give strength to a sick man.'

'What else is it good for?' asked Beltzer.

'It helps to heal bones and reduce swellings, and stops diarrhoea. It has also – so my master told me – been used to prevent gangrene in wounds. Oh yes . . . it is good for rheumatic pain too.'

'Then while you have the ingredients there, my boy,' said Beltzer, 'better make another pot. I have the rheumatism in my knee. Hurts like Hades.'

When the mixture had cooled, Kiall carried it to Maggrig's bedside and Finn held the hunter's head while he drank. At first he choked, but he swallowed half of the contents and sank back. Kiall covered him with a blanket and Finn sat at the bedhead, mopping the sweat from Maggrig's brow. Beltzer strolled over and finished the brew, belching loudly.

For an hour or more there was no change in Maggrig's condition, but at last he drifted off into sleep. 'His colour is a little better,' said Finn, looking to Kiall for confirmation. The youngster nodded, though he could see little change. 'Will he be all right now?' Finn asked.

'We'll see tomorrow,' answered Kiall cagily. He stood and stretched his back. Looking around, he saw that Beltzer had fallen asleep by the fire and Chareos was nowhere in sight. The back-room door was open and Kiall wandered through. It was colder here, but not uncomfortable. Chareos was sitting at the work-bench examining sections of wood shaped for a long-bow.

'May I join you?' asked the villager.

Chareos looked up and nodded. 'How is Maggrig?'

'I don't really know,' whispered Kiall. 'I have only been working with Ulthen for a few months. But the potion will reduce the fever. I'm not sure, though, about the arm wound. Perhaps the cat had something trapped beneath its claws – dung, rotting meat . . .'

'Well, he has two choices – live or die,' said Chareos. 'Keep an eye on him. Do what you can.'

'There's nothing much I can do at the moment. That's a thin bow, isn't it?' he went on, looking at the slender length of wood in Chareos' hand.

'It is just a section: one of three. Finn will bond them together for more flexibility. You know what wood this is?'

'No.'

'It is yew. A curious wood. When you slice it there are two shades – light and dark. The light is flexible, the dark compactable.' He lifted the piece and showed it to Kiall. 'You see? The light wood is used for the outer curve, where maximum flexibility is needed; the dark for the inner, where it compacts. It is beautiful wood. It will be a splendid weapon.'

'I didn't know you were an archer?'

'Nor am I, Kiall, but I was a soldier and it pays a soldier to understand the workings of all weapons of death. I'm getting cold in here – and hungry.' Chareos replaced the wood and strolled out into the main room where Finn was asleep beside Maggrig, while Beltzer lay unmoving on the floor. Chareos stepped over the giant and added wood to the fire, then he took dried meat and fruit from his pack and shared it with Kiall.

'Thank you for agreeing to help me,' said Kiall softly. 'It means much to me. Finn told me you were gallant.'

Chareos smiled and leaned back in his chair. 'I am not gallant, Kiall. I am selfish, like most men. I do what I want, go where I want. I am answerable to no one. And do not thank me until we have freed her.'

'Why *did* you come with me?'

'Why must there always be answers?' countered Chareos. 'Perhaps I was bored. Perhaps it was because my mother's name was Ravenna. Perhaps it is because I am secretly a noble prince who lives to quest for the impossible.' He closed his eyes and was silent for a moment. 'And perhaps I do not know myself,' he whispered.

By mid-morning Maggrig's fever had broken and he was awake and hungry. Finn showed no relief, gathered his bow and quiver and, with Chareos and Beltzer, set off into the snow to scout the trail to the Valley of the Gateway. Kiall remained with the younger hunter; he prepared a breakfast of oats and honey and built up the fire. Then he dragged a chair to Maggrig's bedside and the two men sat and talked for much of the morning.

Maggrig would not speak of the battle at Bel-azar, but told Kiall how he had been a student at a monastery. He had run away on his sixteenth birthday and joined a company of bowmen from Talgithir. He had spent two months with them before being sent to the fortress; there he had met Finn and the others.

'He is not the friendliest man I have known,' said Kiall.

Maggrig smiled. 'You learn to look beneath the harsh words and judge the deeds. Had I not met him, I would not have survived Bel-azar. He's canny and a born fighter. There's more give in a rock than Finn. But he's never liked company much. Having you all here must be driving him insane.'

Kiall glanced around the cabin. 'How do you stand it? Living here, I mean? You are days from civilisation and the mountains are savage and unwelcoming.'

'Finn finds cities savage and unwelcoming,' said Maggrig. 'This is a good life. Deer are plentiful, and mountain sheep. There are pigeons and rabbits, and many roots and tubers to spice a broth. And you should see the mountains in spring, ablaze with colour under a sky so blue it would bring tears to your eyes. What more could a man need?'

Kiall looked at the blond hunter – at the clear blue eyes and the handsome, almost perfect features. He said nothing. Maggrig met his gaze and nodded, and an understanding passed between them.

'Tell me of Ravenna,' invited Maggrig. 'Is she beautiful?'

'Yes. Her hair is dark and long, her eyes brown. She is long-legged and her hips sway when she walks. Her laughter is like sunlight after a storm. I will find her, Maggrig . . . one day.'

'I hope that you do,' said the hunter, reaching out and patting Kiall's arm, 'and I also hope that you will not be disappointed. She may be less than you remember. Or more.'

'I know. She may be wed to a Nadir warrior and have babes at her heels. It does not concern me.'

'You will raise them like your own?' enquired Maggrig. His expression was hard to read and Kiall reddened.

'I had not thought of it. But . . . yes, if that is what she wished.'

'And if she wishes you to leave her be?'

'What does that mean?'

'I am sorry, my friend – it is not my place to criticise. But, as I understand it, the lady turned you down once. Perhaps she will do so again. When a woman has children she changes; they become her life. And if their father loves them – and the Nadir are fond of their children – then she may wish to remain with him. Have you considered that possibility?'

'No,' answered Kiall honestly, 'but how much must I consider? She could be dead, or sold as a whore. She could be diseased. She could be wed. But whatever the situation, short of death, she will know that someone cared enough to come after her. That is important, I think.'

Maggrig nodded. 'You are correct in that, my friend. You have a wise head on those young shoulders. But answer me this, if you can: does the lady have any virtues other than beauty?'

'Virtues?'

'Is she kind, loving, understanding, compassionate?'

'I . . . I don't know,' admitted Kiall. 'I never thought of it.'

'A man should not risk his life for beauty alone, Kiall, for that fades. You might as well risk it for a rose. Think on it.'

Finn walked around the deserted camp-site. The snow was packed tight by heavy boots, and there were three abandoned shelters.

'How many men?' asked Chareos.

'I'd say around seven, maybe eight.'

'How long ago?' questioned Beltzer.

'Last night. They moved off to the east. If they come across our tracks, they will be led straight back to the cabin.'

'Can you be sure they are Nadren?' Chareos asked.

'There is no one else up here,' said Finn. 'We should be heading back. Maggrig is in no condition to fight, and your villager is no match for them.'

Kiall stood in the doorway, feeling the warm sun on his face. The long icicles hanging from the roof were dripping steadily. He turned back inside.

'How bizarre,' he said to Maggrig, who was slicing venison into a large iron pot. 'The sun is as warm as summer and the ice is melting.'

'It is only autumn,' Maggrig told him. 'The blizzard was a foretaste of winter. We often get them. The temperature plummets for several days, and then it is like spring. The snow will clear within a day or two.'

Kiall pulled on his boots and took up the sabre Chareos had given him.

'Where are you going?' asked Maggrig.

Kiall grinned. 'Before they get back, I'd like to practise a little with this blade. I am not much of a swordsman, you know.'

'Nor I. I could never master it.' Maggrig turned back to the broth, adding vegetables and a little salt. Having hung the pot over the fire, he sank back into a chair. He felt weak and dizzy and his head was spinning.

Kiall stepped out into the sunshine and slashed the air with the sabre, left to right. It was a fine blade, keen-edged, with a leather-covered hilt and an iron fist-guard. Many was the time during his youth when he had walked alone in the woods holding a long stick, pretending to be a warrior knight – his enemies falling back from the demon blade he carried, dismayed by his awesome skills. He hefted the sabre, cutting and lunging at imaginary opponents: three, four, five men died beneath the glittering steel. Sweat dripped from his back, and his arm was growing tired. Two more opponents died. He spun on his heel to block a thrust from behind . . . his blade clanged against an arrow-head, shattering the shaft. Kiall blinked and gazed down at the ruined missile on the snow.

Then he looked up and saw the Nadren at the edge of the under-growth. One man held a bow, his mouth open in surprise. There were seven men in all – four of them with bandaged wounds to head or arms. All were standing silently, gazing at the swordsman.

Kiall stood frozen in terror, his mind racing.

'That was a pretty trick,' said one of the newcomers – a short, stocky man, with a black and silver beard. 'I have never seen an arrow cut in flight, nor believed any man could move so swiftly.'

Kiall glanced once more at the arrow and took a deep breath. 'I was wondering when you would show yourselves,' he said, surprised that his voice was smooth and even.

'I did not tell him to shoot,' said the Nadren leader.

'It does not concern me,' replied Kiall loftily. 'What do you want here?'

'Food. That's all.' He saw the man's eyes flicker to his right and glanced back. Maggrig now stood in the door of the cabin with his bow in his hands, an arrow notched to the string. An uneasy silence developed. The Nadren were tense, hands on their weapons.

One warrior eased himself alongside the leader and whispered something Kiall could not hear. The leader nodded; he looked at Kiall.

'You were one of the swordsmen back in the town. You were with the tall one – the ice warrior.'

'Yes,' admitted Kiall. 'It was quite a battle, was it not?'

'He cut us to pieces. I have never seen the like.'

'He is quite skilled,' said Kiall, 'but a hard taskmaster for a student like myself.'

'He is your Swordmaster?'

'Yes. It would be hard to find a better.'

'I can see now why you find it so easy to cut an arrow from the air.' The Nadren spread his hands. 'However, since we must fight or starve, I think it is time we put your skills to the test.' He drew his short sword from the leather scabbard at his hip.

'Is this wise?' asked Kiall. 'There are four of you wounded. It does not seem much of a contest – and warriors should fight over something more valuable than a pot of broth.'

The man said nothing for a moment, then he smiled at Kiall. 'You would allow us inside?' he asked softly.

'Of course,' Kiall told him. 'But naturally, as a token of good manners you would leave your weapons here.'

'Ha! And what then would stop you from butchering us?'

'What stops me now?' countered Kiall.

'You are a cocky young snipe,' snapped the leader. 'But then I've seen you in action, and I guess you've reason to be.' He slammed his sword back in its scabbard, loosened the buckle on his belt and dropped the weapon to the ground. The other Nadren followed his lead. 'Now where is the broth?' Kiall sheathed his blade and gestured towards the cabin. Maggrig stepped back inside. Kiall took a deep, slow breath, calming himself, then followed them.

At first the atmosphere within the cabin was tense. Maggrig sat back on the bed, honing a hunting-knife with long, rasping sweeps against a whetstone while Kiall ladled out the broth. It was under-cooked, but the Nadren wolfed it down. One of the men seemed weaker than the others. He had a wound to the shoulder; it was heavily bandaged, yet still blood seeped from it steadily. Kiall moved to him. 'Let me see that,' he said. The Nadren did not complain as Kiall gently unravelled the bandage. The flesh was sliced back, the cut angry and swollen. Kiall replaced the bandage and took herbs from his pack. Selecting the leaves he needed, he walked back to the man.

'What is that?' grunted the warrior. 'It looks like a weed.'

'It has many names,' Kiall told him. 'Mostly it is called Fat Hen. It is used to feed chickens.'

'Well, I'm no chicken!'

'It also heals festering wounds. But it is your choice.'

'You are a surgeon, too?' asked the leader.

'A warrior needs to know of wounds, and ways of healing them,' replied Kiall.

'Let him do it,' said the leader and the warrior settled back, but his dark, slanted eyes fixed to Kiall's face and the young man felt the hatred in his stare. He pushed the flap of skin in place and stitched the wound, then he laid the leaves on top of it. Maggrig brought a section of linen for a new bandage, and this Kiall applied.

The warrior said nothing. He moved to the wall and curled up to sleep on the floor. The Nadren leader approached Kiall. 'My name is Chellin,' he said. 'You have done well by us. I thank you for it.'

'I am Kiall.'

'I could use a man like you. If ever you travel south past the Middle Peaks, ask for me.'

'I'll remember that,' Kiall said.

The tension in the room eased and the Nadren settled back. Kiall built up the fire, and helped himself to a little broth. He offered food to Maggrig, who shook his head and smiled.

As the afternoon sun began its slow descent towards the western mountains, Chellin roused his men and walked with Kiall out into the sunlight. Just as they gathered their weapons Chareos, Finn and Beltzer appeared. Chareos had his sabre in his hand.

Kiall waved to them casually, then turned to Chellin. 'Good luck on your journey,' he said.

'And you. I am glad the ice warrior was not here when we arrived.'

Kiall chuckled. 'So am I.'

The warrior whose arm Kiall had treated approached him. 'The pain has mostly gone,' he said, his face expressionless. He held out his hand and gave Kiall a golden Raq.

'That is not necessary,' Kiall told him.

'It is,' retorted the man. 'I am no longer in your debt. Next time I see you I will kill you – as you killed my brother during the raid.'

When the Nadren had gone Kiall wandered back to the cabin. Chareos' laughter came to him as he mounted the three steps to the doorway. Inside Maggrig was regaling them with the tale of Kiall the Arrow-slayer. Kiall flushed. Chareos rose and walked to him, clapping a hand to his shoulder.

'You did well,' he said. 'You thought fast and took control. But how did you deflect the arrow?'

'It was an accident – I didn't even know they were there. I was practising with the sabre and I spun round. The arrow hit the sword-blade.'

Chareos smiled broadly. 'Even better. A warrior needs luck, Kiall, and those Nadren will carry the tale of your skill. It could hold you in good stead. But it was an enormous risk. Maggrig told me how you threatened to kill them all single-handed. Let's walk awhile.'

Together the Swordmaster and the young villager walked out into the fading sunshine. 'I am pleased with you,' said Chareos, 'but I think it is time I gave you a little instruction. Then perhaps the next time you face armed men, you will not need to bluff.'

For an hour Chareos worked with the villager, showing him how to grip the sabre, how to roll his wrist, to lunge and parry. Kiall was a swift learner and his reflexes were good. During a break from the exercise, Chareos and his student sat on a fallen log.

'To be skilful requires hard work, Kiall, but to be deadly requires a little more. There is a magic in sword-play that few men master. Forget the blades, or the footwork – the battle is won in the mind. I once fought a man who was more skilful than I, faster and stronger. But he lost to a smile. He thrust, I parried and, as our blades locked, I grinned at him. He lost his temper, perhaps feeling that I mocked him. He came at me with great frenzy and I killed him . . . just like that. Never let anger, or outrage, or fear affect you. That is easy advice to give, but hard to follow. Men will bait you, they will laugh at you, they will jeer. But it is just noise, Kiall. They will hurt the people you love. They will do anything to make you angry or emotional. But the only way you can make them suffer is to win. And to do that you must remain cool. Now let us eat – if the Nadren left us any broth.'

Chareos sat beneath the stars, his cloak wrapped loosely around his shoulders, the night breeze cool upon his face. Inside the cabin all was silent, save for Beltzer's rhythmic snoring. A white owl soared and dived. Chareos could not see its prey, nor whether the owl made a kill. A fox eased itself from the undergrowth and loped across the snow, ignoring the man.

Memories crowded into Chareos' mind, days of youth and ambition, times of wonder and glory, nights of despair and dark melancholy. What have you achieved, he asked himself? Indeed, what was there to achieve? He remembered the parting from his parents and the long, cold journey that followed it; that had been hard on a young boy. The memories were jagged, and he pushed them away. His adolescence in New Gulgothir had been lonely – despite the friendship and guidance of Attalis, his Swordmaster and guardian. Chareos was never at ease among the boys of his own age but, worse than this, he could not adapt to the curious lifestyle of the Gothir nobility. It was on a journey north that he began to understand them. He had passed a village that nestled against a mountain. Above the settlement was a monstrous overhang of rocks and boulders.

'That looks perilous,' Chareos observed to Attalis and the old man nodded.

'It will fall one day,' he said. 'Few will survive it.'

'Then why do people live there?'

'They always have, lad. And after a while they don't notice it any more. You can only live with fear so long, then you absorb it and it loses its power.'

The Gothir were like that, living always with the threat of a Nadir invasion they could not prevent. The nobility organised endless feasts, banquets, dances and diverse entertainments: keeping only a token army to man the ramparts of Bel-azar. Chareos had come to manhood in those days of apathy and instant gratification. An expert swords-man, thanks to the tutelage of Attalis, he won a commission to the Sabres – the elite force formed by the Lord Regent. He recalled now with embarrassment his pride when the white cloak and silver sabre had first been presented to him. He had stood with two hundred other young men before the gallery, his back straight, his eyes fixed on the Lord Regent on his ebony throne. He felt like a man, and destiny was smiling upon him.

Two weeks later his world lay in ashes. Attalis, always a proud man, became involved in a minor dispute with Targon, the Lord Regent's champion. The dispute festered into a blood feud and Targon chal-lenged the old man publicly. The duel was fought in the Royal Courtyard. It did not last long. Chareos, on patrol with the Sabres, heard of it two days later. Attalis had been crippled by a piercing thrust to the shoulder and had fallen to his knees, his sword clattering to the stone. Targon had then stepped forward and sliced open the old man's throat.

Chareos asked for compassionate leave to attend the funeral and this was granted. He used his meagre savings – and a pledge against next year's pay – to purchase a plot of ground, a marble sarcophagus and a statue above the grave. This done, he sought out Targon. The man was taller by a head than Chareos, and whip-lean; he was fast, and confident of his talents. Once more, the duel took place in the Royal Courtyard.

Targon had flashed a mocking grin at the young officer. 'I hope you'll offer more sport than the old man,' he said. Chareos did not reply. His dark eyes fixed on Targon's swarthy features as he drew his borrowed rapier. 'Frightened, boy?' asked Targon. 'You should be.'

The Lord Regent lifted his arm and both men presented their swords. The duel began in a blistering series of thrusts, parries and ripostes. Chareos knew within seconds that he was outclassed but he remained calm – sure in the knowledge that, no matter what, his blade would find its home in the flesh of the man he faced. Back and forth across the courtyard the two warriors fought, their blades shimmering in the early morning sunlight. Three times Chareos felt his opponent's sword nick his skin – twice on the upper arm, once on the cheek. A thin trickle of blood dripped to his chin. But Targon could find no opening for the killing thrust. Beginning to lose patience, he attacked with greater fury, but his young opponent blocked him at every turn.

The two men stepped back from one another, sweat on their faces. 'You take a long time to die, boy,' remarked Targon.

Chareos smiled. 'You have the sword skill of a Nadir tent-wife,' he said. Targon flushed red and launched another attack. Chareos blocked the blade, rolled his wrist and lanced his rapier deep into Targon's right shoulder, slicing the muscles and tearing through ligament and sinew. Targon's rapier fell from his hand and for the first time fear showed in his pale eyes. For several seconds Chareos stood watching his opponent, then his blade cut the air with a hissing slash to rip across Targon's throat.

The Lord Regent's champion staggered back, clutching the wound. Blood bubbled through his fingers as he fell to his knees. Chareos walked forward and placed his boot against the dying man's chest. With one contemptuous push, he hurled Targon to his back. There was silence among the spectators and then the Lord Regent called Chareos forward, while pages ran to Targon, seeking to stem the bleeding.

'You took not only his life, but his dignity,' said the Lord Regent.

'If I could, my lord, I would follow him into Hell and destroy his soul as well,' Chareos told him.

That afternoon Chareos had stood alone by Attalis' tomb. 'You are avenged, my friend,' he said. 'He died as you died. I don't know if that is important to you. But I remembered your teaching and I did not allow my hatred to control me. You would have been proud of that, I think.' He was silent for a moment, and his eyes filled with tears. 'You were a father to me, Attalis. I never told you how much you meant to me, nor ever thanked you for your friendship and your company. But I do so now. Rest easy, my friend.'

A quarter of a century later, outside Finn's cabin, Chareos the Blademaster wept again for the old man, for the ruin of his hopes and the failure of his dreams.

It had always been Attalis' wish that one day they would return home and restore all that had been lost. Without the old man Chareos had viewed that dream with cold logic – and ruthlessly pushed it aside.

Now he dried his eyes with the edge of his cloak. 'What would you think of this quest, Attalis?' he whispered. 'The hunt for the pig-breeder's daughter? Yes, I can almost hear your laughter.'

He stood and entered the cabin where the fire was low, the room warm and cosy. Kiall and Beltzer were asleep before the hearth, Maggrig deep in dreams in the bed by the far wall. Lantern light was streaming from the back room and Chareos walked quietly across the cabin floor and looked in. Finn was sitting with his feet on the work-bench, idly cutting flights for new arrows.

'I couldn't sleep,' said Chareos, moving in to sit opposite the black-bearded hunter.

Finn swung his legs to the floor and rubbed his eyes. 'Nor me. What happened to us, eh?'

Chareos shrugged. In the lantern light Finn looked older, his face seemingly carved from teak. Deep shadows showed at his eyes and neck, and silver hairs glistened within his matted beard. 'You seem to have found peace, my friend,' said Chareos. 'Up here in the mountains you have freedom and more land than some kings.'

'Not much of a life for the boy – though he doesn't complain.'

'The *boy* must be thirty-six years old. If he doesn't like the life he is old enough – and man enough – to say so.'

'Maybe,' said Finn, unconvinced. 'And then again, maybe it is time to move on.'

'You'll find nowhere more beautiful, Finn.'

'I know that,' snapped the hunter, 'but there's more to it. I'm no youngster, Chareos, I feel old. My bones ache in winter, and my eyes are not what they were. One day I'll die. I don't want to leave the . . . Maggrig . . . up here alone. I don't like people much – nasty minds, foul manners, always looking to steal, or lie or slander. But maybe that's just me. Maggrig, he gets on with folks, likes company. It's time he learned how to live with people again.'

'Think about it some more, Finn,' advised Chareos. 'You are happy here.'

'I *was*. But nothing lasts forever, Blademaster. Not life, not love, not dreams. I reckon I've had more than my share of all three. I'm pretty much content.'

'What will you do?'

Finn looked up and met Chareos' gaze. 'I never had many friends. Never needed them, I reckon. But you – and that fat pig – are the closest I got to family. So we'll come with you – if you want us, that is.'

'You don't need to ask, Finn.'

'Good,' said Finn, rising. 'That's a burden off my heart. Maybe we'll even find the girl. Who knows?'

Tsudai watched the auction with little interest. He had no taste for these pale-skinned Gothir women with their cold blue eyes and their huge cow-like breasts. He swung away from the window and looked at the dark-haired woman seated on the satin-covered divan. Now here was a *real* Nadir beauty.

The first time he had seen her was when Tenaka Khan brought her to Ulrickham. She had been fourteen years old, her skin golden, her eyes proud. Tsudai had always believed proud women were the devil's curse and he had longed to take a whip to her, to see her kneeling at his feet. Even now the memory brought a surge of arousal.

80

He moved to sit beside her. As she smiled thinly and edged back from him, his face reddened, but he forced himself to remain calm.

'Your brother, Jungir, sends greetings. He hopes that you are in good health,' said Tsudai. 'I will tell him that you are, for I have never seen you look more beautiful, Tanaki.'

'Why should I not be in good health?' she asked him. 'Did Jungir not send me to this desolate land in order that I might enjoy the freshness of the air?'

'It was for your own safety, Princess. There were rumours of plots and fears for your life.'

She laughed then, the musical sound doing little to ease Tsudai's physical discomfort. Her eyes met his, and for the first time it seemed to him that she smiled with genuine warmth.

'Why do we play such foolish games, Tsudai? There is no one else here, and we both know why my brother sent me here. He killed his own brothers and, possibly, his own father. Why should he baulk at slaying his sister? I'll tell you why. Because I am the only hope the Nadir have for providing a male heir. For all his skill with horses and weapons, Jungir is sterile.'

Tsudai blanched. 'You must not say that! If I was to repeat that to the Khan . . .'

'Not even you would dare to voice that, even at second hand. Now why are you really here, Tsudai?'

He swallowed his anger, feeling uncomfortable sitting here dressed in the full armour of his rank. He reached for the buckle of his black and silver breastplate.

'Do not undress,' she chided him. 'That would not be seemly.'

'Seemly? What would you know of seemly? You take a succession of barbarian lovers, discarding them daily. That is no way for a person of your blood-line to behave.'

Tanaki stood and stretched her arms over her head. Her figure was slim and lithe and the short, silken tunic rode up to show smooth golden thighs.

'You do this to fire my blood,' snapped Tsudai, rising to his feet aware of arousal coursing through him.

'A volcano could not fire you,' she said. 'Now, for the last time, tell me why you are here.'

He looked hard into her violet eyes and suppressed the desire to strike her, to hammer her to her knees before him.

'Your brother merely wishes to know of your well-being,' Tsudai said. 'Is that so hard to understand?'

She laughed, the sound rippling across his emotions like bee-stings. 'My well-being? How sweet of him! I saw your aide looking over the new slaves. The great warrior, Tsudai, now reduced to finding concubines. Have you seen any that please you, Tsudai?'

'I do not find any of them attractive, though there are one or two that may suit. But you wrong me, Tanaki. I came here in order that I might speak with you. You know how perilous is your position. You know that at any time your death could become expedient. Four years ago you had the opportunity to become my wife. Now I offer that gift to you once more. Agree and you will be safe.'

She moved closer, her perfume washing over him. Lifting her hands, she rested them on his shoulders and looked deeply into his dark, slanted eyes.

'Safe? With you? I remember when you sought my hand. I considered it with due seriousness. I sent spies into your palace, Tsudai. Not one of your women lacks scars from the whip. I know what you want,' she whispered huskily, 'and you will never have it!' Then she laughed again and stepped back. His hand lashed out. She swayed out of his reach, then stepped inside. Tsudai froze as the dagger-point touched his neck. 'I could kill you now,' she told him.

It was his turn to laugh as he pushed her hand away. 'You still want to live, though, do you not? And an attack on me would bring you down. I offered you my hand, Tanaki. But now I will wait. And when the day comes for you to suffer, it will be Tsudai who rides to you. It will be Tsudai to whom you will beg. And I tell you now that no pleas will be heard. When next we meet, you will not be so haughty.'

The warrior spun on his heel and stalked from the room. Tanaki returned the small dagger to its sheath and poured herself a goblet of wine.

It had been foolish to anger Tsudai. As Jungir Khan's most trusted adviser, his was a friendship it would have been wise to court. But there was something about the man, a coldness within the soul, a meanness of spirit that she could not tolerate. Her father, Tenaka, had distrusted him. 'I have nothing against a man who disciplines his household,' Tenaka told his daughter, 'but any man who needs a whip to deal with a woman has no place in my service.'

Tanaki swallowed hard as she pictured her father, his violet eyes full of warmth, his smile like the dawn light – welcoming, reassuring. Her stomach knotted and tears welled in her eyes. How could he be dead? How could the greatest man in the world be dead?

Blinking away her tears, she wandered to the window and watched the auction, wondering which of the women Tsudai would purchase. Rarely did she feel sorry for any of the slaves. But today . . .

She saw a dark-haired young woman pulled to the block, her yellow dress stripped from her. She had a good figure and her breasts were not over-large. Tanaki's eyes flickered to Tsudai's bidder and she saw his hand rise.

There were several other bidders, but the woman was sold to the Nadir general.

'Tread warily, girl,' whispered Tanaki. 'Your life depends on it.'

5

Maggrig's fever-induced weakness lasted a further five days, during which time Chareos continued to teach Kiall the elementary moves of swordplay. Beltzer, his mood foul, took to walking alone in the mountain woods. Finn spent much of the time in his workshop, completing a new long-bow.

The snow all but disappeared from around the cabin, and the sun shone with summer warmth over the mountains.

On the morning of the sixth day, as the questors prepared to set off for the Valley of the Shrieking Gateway, Finn called Beltzer to his workshop. The others gathered round as the hunter pulled clear a brass-bound oak chest from its hiding place beneath a bench seat. Finn opened the chest and lifted out a long object, wrapped in oiled skins. He placed it on the bench-top and cut the thong bindings with his hunting-knife. He gestured to Beltzer. 'It's yours. Take it.'

The giant unwrapped the skins and there lay a gleaming, double-headed axe. The haft and handle were as long as a man's arm – oiled oak and reinforced with silver wire. The heads were curved and sharp, acid-etched and decorated with silver runes. Beltzer's hand curled around the haft, lifting the weapon.

'Nice to have it back,' he said and, without another word, stalked from the workshop.

'Ignorant, ungrateful pig,' stormed Maggrig. 'He didn't even say thank you.'

Finn shrugged, and gave a rare smile. 'It is enough that he has it,' he said.

'But it cost you a fortune. We had no salt for two years, and precious little else.'

'Forget it. It is past.'

Chareos moved forward and placed his hand on Finn's shoulder. 'That was nobly done. He wasn't the same man without that axe. He sold it while drunk in Talgithir and never knew what became of it.'

'I know. Let's be on our way.'

The journey to the Valley took three days. They saw no sign of any Nadren, and only once caught sight of a single rider far to the south.

The air was thin here and the questors talked little. At night they sat beside campfires, but slept early and rose with the dawn.

Kiall found it a curious time. It was an adventure, full of promise – yet these men, these comrades of war, hardly spoke at all. When they did it was to discuss the weather, or the preparation of food. Not once did they mention the Gateway, or the Nadir, or the quest. And when Kiall tried to introduce such topics to the conversation they were brushed aside with shrugs.

The Valley proved an anti-climax to Kiall. It was just like several others they had journeyed through, its pine-cloaked flanks dropping away into a deep cleft between the mountains. There were meadows at the base, and a stream ran along its length. Deer moved across the gentle hills, and there were sheep and goats grazing close by.

Finn and Maggrig chose a camp-site, removed their packs, took up their bows and moved off to hunt for supper. Chareos climbed a nearby hill and scanned the surrounding countryside while Beltzer prepared a fire and sat, watching the flames flicker and dance.

Kiall seated himself opposite the bald giant. 'It is a beautiful axe,' he said.

'The best,' grunted Beltzer. 'It is said that Druss the Legend had an axe from the Elder Days that never showed rust, and never lost its edge. But I don't believe it was better than this one.'

'You carried that at Bel-azar?'

Beltzer glanced up, his small, round eyes fixing to Kiall. 'What is this fascination you have with that place? You weren't there – you don't know what it was like.'

'It was glorious. It is part of our history,' said Kiall. 'The few against the many. It was a time of heroes.'

'It was a time of survivors – like all wars. There were good men there who died on the first day, and cowards who lasted almost until the end. There were thieves there, and men who had raped or murdered. There was the stench of open bowels, and split entrails. There was screaming and begging, and whimpering. There was nothing good about Bel-azar. Nothing.'

'But you won,' persisted Kiall. 'You were honoured throughout the land.'

'Aye, that was good – the honour, I mean. The parades and the banquets, and the women. I never had so many women. Young ones, old ones, fat ones, thin ones: they couldn't wait to open their legs for a hero of Bel-azar. That was the real glory of it, boy – what came after. By the gods, I'd sell my soul for a drink!'

'Does Chareos feel as you do – about Bel-azar, I mean?'

Beltzer chuckled. 'He thinks I don't know . . . but I know. The Blademaster had a wife,' he said, twisting his head to check that Chareos was still high upon the hill. 'Gods, she was a beauty. Dark

84

hair that gleamed like it was oiled, and a body shaped by Heaven. Tura, that was her name. She was a merchant's daughter. Man, was he glad to be rid of her! Anyway, Chareos took her off his hands and built a house for her. Nice place. Good garden. They'd been married maybe four months when she took her first lover. He was a scout for the Sabres – just the first of many men who romped in the bed Chareos made for her. And him? The Blademaster, the deadliest swordsman I ever saw? He knew nothing. He bought her presents, constantly talked about her. And we all knew. Then he found out . . . I don't know how. That was just before Bel-azar. Man, did he try to die! He tried harder than anyone. But that's what makes life such a bitch, isn't it? No one could kill him. Short sword and dagger he carried, and his life was charmed. Mind you, he had me alongside him and I don't kill easy. When the Nadir rode away you've never seen a man so disappointed.'

Kiall said nothing but gazed into the fire, lost in thought.

'Shocked you, did I, boy?' said Beltzer. 'Well, life's full of shocks. It's all insane. There never was a better husband. Gods, he loved her. You know where she ended up?'

Kiall shook his head.

'She became a whore in New Gulgothir. The Blademaster doesn't know that but I saw her there, plying her trade by the docks. Two copper coins.' Beltzer laughed. 'Two of her front teeth were gone, and she wasn't so beautiful. I had her then. Two copper coins' worth. In an alley. She begged me to take her with me; she'd go anywhere, she said. Do anything for me. She said she had no friends, and nowhere to stay.'

'What happened to her?' whispered Kiall.

'She threw herself from the docks and died. They found her floating among the scum and the sewage.'

'Why did you hate her?' asked Kiall. 'She did nothing to you.'

'Hate her? I suppose I did. I'll tell you why. Because in all the time she was cuckolding Chareos, she never once offered it to me. She treated me like dirt.'

'Would you have accepted?'

'Sure I would. I told you, she was beautiful.'

Kiall looked into Beltzer's face and remembered the song of Bel-azar. Then he looked away and added fuel to the fire.

'Don't want to talk any more, young Kiall?' asked Beltzer.

'Some things it is better not to hear,' said the villager. 'I wish you hadn't told me.'

'Whores' lives don't make pretty stories.'

'No, I suppose they don't. But I wasn't thinking of her; I was thinking of you. Your story is as disgusting as hers.'

Kiall rose and walked away. The sun was fading, the shadows lengthening. He found Chareos sitting on a fallen tree, gazing at the sunset. The sky was aglow, red banners flowing over the mountains.

'It is beautiful,' said Kiall. 'I have always enjoyed the sunset.'

'You are a romantic,' stated Chareos.

'Is that bad?'

'No, it is the best way to live. I felt that way once – and I was never happier.' Chareos stood and stretched his back. 'Hold on to your dreams, Kiall. They are more important than you realise.'

'I shall. Tell me, do you like Beltzer?'

Chareos laughed aloud and the sound, rich and full of good humour, echoed in the valley. 'No one likes Beltzer,' he said. 'Least of all Beltzer.'

'Then why do you have him with you? Why did Finn buy his axe?'

'You are the dreamer, Kiall. You tell me.'

'I don't know. I can't imagine. He is so gross; his speech is vile, and he doesn't understand friendship or loyalty.'

Chareos shook his head. 'Don't judge him by his words, my friend. If I was standing alone down there in the valley, surrounded by a hundred Nadir warriors, and I called his name, he would come running. He would do the same for Finn, or Maggrig.'

'I find that hard to believe,' said Kiall.

'Let us hope you never see the proof of it.'

At dawn the next morning the questors moved north into the shadowed pine woods, following a deer trail that wound down to a shallow stream. This they waded across, climbing a short, steep slope to a clearing beyond. The wind gusted and an eerie, high-pitched scream echoed around them. Finn and Maggrig leapt from the trail, vanishing into the undergrowth. Beltzer lifted his axe from the sheath at his side, spat upon his hands, and waited. Chareos stood unmoving, hand on sword-hilt.

Kiall found his limbs trembling and suppressed the urge to turn and sprint from the clearing. The scream came again, an ululating howl that chilled the blood. Chareos walked on, Beltzer following. Sweat dripping into his eyes, Kiall could not bring himself to move. He sucked in a deep breath and forced himself forward.

At the centre of the clearing, some fifty paces away, stood a huge stone edifice and before it, on lances decorated with feathers and coloured stones, were two severed heads.

Kiall could not tear his eyes from the shrunken faces. The eye-sockets were empty, but the mouths trembled with each scream. Maggrig and Finn stepped back into view.

'Can we not stop that noise?' hissed Beltzer and Chareos nodded. He walked swiftly to the first lance and held his hand behind the severed head. The scream stopped instantly. Chareos lifted the head and placed it on the ground, then repeated the action with the second. All was silent now, save for the gusting wind. The other questors approached. Chareos squatted down and lifted the silent head, turning it in his hands. Taking his hunting-knife he plunged it deep through the scalp, peeling back the skin, which stretched impossibly before snapping clear of the wooden skull beneath. Chareos stood and lifted the wood to his lips – immediately the blood-curdling scream sounded. He tossed the object to Finn. 'It is merely a kind of flute,' said the former monk. 'The winds enter through the three holes in the base, and the reeds set in the mouth supply the sound. But it is beautifully crafted.' Stooping, he gathered the skin, lifting it by the hair. 'I do not know what this is,' he said, 'but it is not human flesh. See, the hair has been stitched in place.'

Kiall picked up the second head and looked closely at it. It was difficult to know now why it had inspired such fear. He turned it. The wind whistled through it and a low moan came out. Kiall jumped and dropped the head, cursing himself even as the others laughed.

Chareos moved on to the edifice. There were two stone pillars, twelve feet high and three feet square, covered with an engraved script he did not recognise. An enormous lintel sat above the pillars, creating the impression of a gateway. Chareos squatted before it, running his eyes over the script.

Kiall moved around to the rear. 'There are symbols here,' he said, 'and the stone seems a different colour. Whiter, somehow . . .' He stepped forward.

'Stop!' yelled Chareos. 'Do not attempt to pass through.'

'Why?' Kiall asked.

Chareos picked up a round pebble. 'Catch this,' he said, tossing it through the opening. Kiall opened his hands, but the stone vanished from sight. 'Throw one to me,' commanded the Blademaster. Kiall obeyed. Again the pebble disappeared.

'Well, do we go through?' asked Beltzer.

'Not yet,' Chareos told him. 'Tell me again all that Okas told you of the Gateway.'

'There was precious little. It leads to another world. That is all.'

'Did he not say it leads to many worlds?'

'Yes,' admitted Beltzer, 'but we do not know how the magic works.'

'Exactly,' said Chareos. 'Did Okas give an indication of when he would pass through the Gateway. Daytime, midnight, sunset?'

'Not as I recall. Is it important?'

'Did he say which side he entered, north or south?'

'No. Let's just go through and see what we find,' urged Beltzer.

Chareos stood. 'Take my hand, and hold to it tightly. Count to five, then draw me back.' He moved to the entrance and held out his arm. Beltzer gripped his wrist and Chareos leaned forward, his head slowly disappearing from view. Beltzer felt the body sag – he did not count, but dragged Chareos back. The Blademaster's face was white, and ice had formed on his moustache; his lips were blue with cold. Beltzer laid him down on the grass, while Finn began rubbing at the frozen skin. After a while Chareos' eyes opened; he stared angrily at Beltzer.

'I said count to five,' he said. 'Not five thousand.'

'You were in there for only a few heartbeats,' Finn told him. 'What did you see?'

'Heartbeats? It was an hour at least on the other side. I saw nothing, save snow and ice blizzards. Not a sign of life. And there were three moons in the sky.' He sat up.

'What can we do?' asked Beltzer.

'Build a fire. I'll think on it. But tell me everything you can remember about Okas and his tribe. *Everything*.'

Beltzer squatted down on the grass beside Chareos. 'It's not a great deal, Blademaster. I never had much of a memory for detail. They call themselves the People of the World's Dream, but I don't know what that means. Okas tried to explain it to me, but I lost hold of it – the words roared around my head like snowflakes. I think they see the world as a living thing, like an enormous god. But they worship a one-eyed goddess called the Huntress, and they see the moon as her blind eye. The sun is her good eye. That's all.'

Finn lit the fire and joined the two men. 'I have seen them,' he said. 'In the mountains. They move at night – hunting, I think.'

'Then we will wait for moonlight,' said Chareos. 'Then we shall try again.'

The hours passed slowly. Finn cooked a meal of venison, the last of the choice cuts he had taken from the deer killed the previous evening. Beltzer wrapped himself in his blankets and slept, his hand on his axe. Kiall wandered away from the fire, walking to the crest of a nearby hill. There he sat down alone and thought of Ravenna, picturing the surge of joy she would feel when he rode to her. He shivered, and depression struck him like a blow. Would he ever ride to her? And if he did would she just laugh, as she had laughed before? Would she point to her new husband and say, 'He is my man. He is strong, not a dreamer like you'?

A sound came from behind and Kiall turned to see Finn walking towards him. 'You wish to be alone?' asked Finn.

'No, not at all.'

Finn sat down and stared over the rugged countryside. 'This is a beautiful land,' he said, 'and it will remain so until people discover it and build their towns and cities. I could live here until my dying day – and never regret it.'

'Maggrig told me you hated city life,' said Kiall. The hunter nodded.

'I don't mind the endless stone and brick – it's the people. After Belazar we were dragged from city to city so that crowds could gawp at us. You would have thought we were gods at the very least. We all hated it – save Beltzer. He was in a kind of Heaven. Chareos was the first to say, "No more". One morning he just rode away.'

'He has had a sad life, I understand,' said Kiall.

'Sad? In what way?'

'His wife. Beltzer told me about it.'

'Beltzer has a big mouth, and a man's private business should remain so. I saw her in New Gulgothir three years ago. She is happy at last.'

'She is dead,' said Kiall. 'She became a street whore and killed herself.'

Finn shook his head. 'Yes, Beltzer told me that but it's not true. She was a whore, but she married a merchant – bore him three sons. As far as I know they are still together. She told me she had seen Beltzer – it was the lowest point of her life. That I can believe. Every time I see Beltzer I feel the same way. No, Beltzer heard of a whore who drowned and the rest was wishful thinking. She was happy when I saw her – for the first time in her life. I was pleased for her.'

'You did not hate her, then?'

'Why should I hate her?' asked Finn.

'She betrayed Chareos,' Kiall answered.

'She was sold to him by her father. She never loved him. She was fey and high-spirited – reminded me of a fawn I saw once. I was hunting and the creature saw me. It did not recognise a bow or a hunter, it had no fear. When I stood with bow bent, it trotted towards me. I dropped the arrow and the fawn nuzzled my hand. Then it went its way. Tura was like that. A fawn in search of a hunter.'

'You liked her, then?'

Finn said nothing but stood and walked back down the hill. The sun was setting, and a ghostly moon could be seen shimmering behind the clouds.

Chareos waited as the moon rose higher. Silver light bathed the clearing and the ancient stone Gateway shimmered and gleamed like cold iron. He stood and rolled his head, stretching the muscles of shoulder and neck, trying to ease the tension born of fear. Something deep within him flickered, a silent voice urging him to beware. He sensed himself on the verge of a journey that would take him where he did not want to go, on pathways dark and perilous. There were no words of warning, merely a feeling of cold dread.

'Are you ready then?' asked Beltzer. 'Or would you like me to try it?'

Chareos did not reply. He walked to the Gateway and held out his arm. Beltzer gripped his wrist as he leaned forward, half his body disappearing. Seconds later he drew back.

'I do not know if that is the place, but it fits the description. There is

89

jungle beyond. The sun is bright.' He swung towards Maggrig and Finn. 'I need only Beltzer with me. The rest of you should stay here and await our return.'

'I get bored just sitting,' said Finn. 'We'll come with you.'

Chareos nodded. 'Then let us go, before good sense can assert itself.'

He turned – and was gone from sight. Beltzer followed him, Maggrig and Finn stepped through together. Kiall found himself alone in the clearing. His heart was beating wildly and fear surged through him. For several heartbeats he stood rooted and then, with a wild cry, he leapt through the Gateway – cannoning into Beltzer's back and sprawling to the mud-covered trail. Beltzer swore, leaned down and hoisted Kiall to his feet. Kiall smiled apologetically and looked around. Huge trees festooned with vines surrounded them. Plants with leaves like spears, and heavy purple flowers, grew at their bases. The heat was oppressive and the questors began to sweat heavily in their winter clothes. But what impressed Kiall most was the smell – overpowering and cloying, decaying vegetation mixed with the musky scent of numberless flowers, plants and fungoid growths. A throaty roar sounded from some distance to their left, answered by a cacophony of chittering cries in the trees above them. Small, dark creatures with long tails leapt from branch to branch, or swung on vines.

'Are they demons?' whispered Beltzer.

No one answered him. Chareos looked back at the Gateway. On this side it shone like silver and the runic script was smaller, punctuated by symbols of the moon and stars. He gazed up at the sun.

'It is near noon here,' he said. 'At noon tomorrow we will make our way back. Now, I would suggest we follow this trail and see if we can locate a village. What do you think, Finn?'

'It is as good an idea as any. I will mark the trail, in case any should become lost.' Finn drew his hunting-knife and carved an arrow-head pointing at the gateway. Beside it he sliced the number 10. 'That represents paces. I will swing a wide circle around our trail, marking trunks in this manner. If we do become separated, seek out the signs.' Aware that Finn was directing his remarks to him, Kiall nodded.

The group set off warily, following a meandering trail for almost an hour. In that time Finn disappeared often, moving to the left and reappearing from the right. The small, dark creatures in the trees travelled with them, occasionally dropping to the lower branches, where they hung from their tails and screeched at the newcomers. Birds with glorious plumages of red and green and blue sat on tree-limbs preening their feathers with curved beaks.

At the end of the hour Chareos called a halt. The heat was

incredible and their clothes were soaked with perspiration. 'We are travelling roughly south-east,' Chareos told Kiall. 'Remember that.'

A movement came from the undergrowth to their right. The spear-like leaves parted . . . and a monstrous head came into sight. The face was semi-human and black as pitch, the eyes small and round. It had long sharp fangs and, as it reared to its full height of around six feet, its enormous arms and shoulders came into view. Beltzer dragged clear his axe and let out a bellowing battle-cry. The creature blinked and stared.

'Move on. Slowly,' said Chareos. Warily the group continued on the trail, Chareos leading and Finn, an arrow notched to his curved hunting bow, bringing up the rear.

'What an obscenity,' whispered Kiall, glancing back at the silent creature standing on the trail behind them.

'That's no way to talk about Beltzer's mother,' said Maggrig. 'Didn't you notice the way they recognised each other?' Finn and Chareos chuckled. Beltzer swore. The trail widened and dropped away towards a low bowlshaped depression, cleared of trees. There were round huts there, and cooking-fires still burned. But no one would use them. Bodies lay everywhere – some on the ground, some impaled, others nailed to trees at the edge of the village. Huge, bloated birds covered many of the corpses or sat in squat and ugly rows along the roofs.

'I think we've found the Tattooed People,' said Finn.

Kiall sat on the slope above the devastated village and watched his companions moving about the ruins. Finn and Maggrig skirted the round huts, reading sign, while Beltzer and Chareos walked from hut to hut looking for survivors. There were none. Kiall felt a sense of despair creeping over him. This was the third time in his young life that he had seen the results of a raid. In the first Ravenna had been taken, but other, older, women had been raped or abused. Men had been slain. In the second he had witnessed – and taken part in – a wild, frenzied slashing of swords and knives, his blood hot, fired by a need to kill. Now here was the third – and the worst of all. From his vantage point he could see the bodies of women and children, and even his unskilled eye could read the mindless savagery which had taken place here. This was no slave raid. The Tattooed People had been exterminated.

After a while Maggrig shouldered his bow and strode up to sit alongside Kiall.

'It is revolting down there,' said the hunter. 'It seems that nothing was taken in the raid. Some two hundred warriors surrounded the village earlier today, moved in and killed almost everyone. There are some tracks leading north and it looks as if small groups of the

91

Tattooed People fought clear and fled. Maybe a dozen. But they were followed.'

'Why would anyone do this, Maggrig? What is gained by it?'

The hunter spread his hands. 'There is no answer I can give you. I took part in a raid on a Nadir camp once. We had found several of our men tortured over camp-fires, their eyes burned out. We followed the raiders to their village and captured them. Our officer, a cultured man, ordered all the children to be brought out to stand before the captives. Then he slew them in front of their parents. After that the Nadir were hanged. He told us the Nadir did not fear death, so to kill them was no real punishment. But to butcher their children before their eyes – that was justice.' Maggrig fell silent.

Kiall looked back at the village. 'There is no justice in any of it,' he said. The others joined them and the group moved back from the slope to make camp. Finn was unable to light a fire because the wood was too damp, and the questors sat in a circle, saying little.

'Was Okas among the dead?' asked Kiall.

Chareos shrugged. 'Difficult to tell. Many of the corpses have been stripped almost clean, but I saw no tattooes I could remember.'

'Have we arrived in the midst of a war between them?'

'No,' answered Finn. 'The Tattooed People are small, and pigeon-toed. The tracks of the raiders show them to be tall. I found this,' he went on, pulling a broken gold wristband from the pocket of his deerskin jerkin. Beltzer gasped as he saw it.

'Sweet Heaven!' he exclaimed. 'How heavy is it?' Finn tossed it to him. 'It must be worth around a hundred Raq,' said the giant.

'The owner threw it away when it broke,' said Finn. 'Gold cannot be worth that much here.'

'It isn't,' agreed Chareos, producing a small, barbed arrow-head – it too was gold.

'I am beginning to like it here,' remarked Beltzer. 'We could go back to Gothir as rich men.'

'Let us be content to be going back as *live* men,' snapped Chareos.

'I am with you on that,' whispered Finn, holding out his hand to Beltzer, who reluctantly returned the wristband.

Chareos rose. 'It is coming on towards dusk,' he said, 'I think we should make our way back to the Gate and camp there.' He shouldered his pack and led the others towards the north-west. They moved warily, stopping often while Finn scouted the trail ahead, and Kiall grew increasingly nervous. There would be little chance of hearing the approach of a legion of enemy warriors, not above the chittering of the dark creatures in the trees, the distant roar of hunting cats and the rushing of unseen rivers and streams. He kept close to Chareos, Beltzer bringing up the rear with his huge axe in his hands.

Up ahead Finn dropped to his haunches, raising his arm and pumping his fist three times in the air. Then he rolled to the left and out of sight. Maggrig ducked into the undergrowth, followed swiftly by Chareos and Beltzer. Kiall stood for a moment alone on the trail. Three tall warriors came into sight, dragging a young woman; they saw Kiall and stopped, perplexed. They were tall men, bronze of skin with dark, straight hair. Gold glittered on their arms and ankles. Two of them carried weapons of dark wood, while the third had a long knife of burnished gold. They wore necklets of coloured stone, and their faces were streaked with many colours. The woman was small, her skin copper-coloured. On her brow was a blue tattoo. She wore only a loincloth of animal skin.

Slowly Kiall drew his sabre. One of the warriors screamed a war-cry and ran at him, his wooden club raised high. Kiall dropped into the sideways crouch Chareos had taught him, then sprang forward, the sabre lancing the man's chest. The bronze warrior staggered back as the sword slid clear. He looked down at the wound, saw the blood burst from it and slumped face first to the ground. The young woman tore herself free of her captors and ran down the trail towards Kiall who stepped aside to let her pass. The remaining warriors stood, uncertain. But from behind them came a score more of their comrades.

Kiall plunged left into the undergrowth as the hunters rushed forward. The ground dropped away and he lost his footing, slipping and sliding down a mud-covered slope to land in a sprawling heap at the bottom.

Half winded, he struggled to rise. Gathering his sabre he glanced up: the bronze warriors were coming down towards him. Spinning on his heel, he raced down a narrow trail. Broad, overhanging leaves lashed at his face, thorn-covered branches ripping at his clothes. Twice he slipped and fell, but the bloodcurdling cries of the pursuing hunters fed his panic, giving strength to his flight.

Where were his friends? Why were they not helping him?

He forced his way through a last section of dense undergrowth and emerged on the muddy bank of a great river, wider than the lakes of his homeland. His breathing was ragged, his ears filled with the drumming of his heart.

Where can I go?

He had lost all sense of direction and thick, lowering clouds obscured the sun. He heard shouts from his left and swinging to the right, he ran along the river-bank.

A huge dragon reared from the water, its elongated mouth rimmed with teeth. Kiall screamed, and leapt back from the river's edge. A spear sliced the air by his head and he turned in time to see a bronze warrior diving at him. The warrior crashed into Kiall, hurling them both back towards the river-bank. His sabre knocked from his hand, Kiall surged up and crashed his fist into the man's face, knocking him sideways. The warrior sprang upright but Kiall leapt feet-first, his boots thudding against the man's chest and propelling him back into the dark water. As the warrior struggled to the surface and began to wade ashore, the dragon's head reared behind him, the monstrous jaws clamping home on his leg. He let out an agonising scream and began to stab at the monster's scaled hide with a golden knife. Blood billowed to the river's surface and Kiall watched in horror as the warrior was dragged from sight.

Kiall tore his eyes from the scene and took up his sabre. He scanned the trees for sign of the enemy. A sudden movement behind made him spin round with sword raised. It was the young woman and she waved him towards where she was hidden in the undergrowth. He ran to her, dropped to his knees and crawled inside the spike-leaved bushes. Carefully she eased leaves back across the opening.

Within seconds more of the enemy arrived on the scene. They stood at the river-side, watching the struggle between the dying warrior and the dragon. When it was over the hunters squatted in a circle and spoke in low voices; one pointed up the trail, and it seemed to Kiall they were arguing about which direction to take. A large spider, hairless and bloated, crawled on to Kiall's hand. He stifled a scream. The girl swiftly leaned over him, plucking the insect from his skin and carefully placing it on a leaf.

The hunters rose and moved off into the jungle.

Kiall lay back and smiled at the young woman. She did not respond in kind, but touched her hand to her breast, then to her brow, then pressed her fingers to Kiall's mouth. Not knowing how to respond, Kiall lifted her hand and kissed it. She settled down beside him, closed her eyes and slept.

For some time he lay awake, too frightened to leave the sanctuary of the undergrowth. Then he too drifted off into a light doze – and awoke with the moon shining high above the trees. The woman sat up and crawled into the open. Kiall followed. She whispered something to him, but it was a language he had never heard.

'Okas?' he asked. Her head tilted. 'I am looking for Okas.'

She shrugged and trotted off along the river-bank. He followed her through the moonlit jungle, up over hills and rises, down through vine-choked archways and on to a wide cave where she stopped outside and held out her hand. He took it and was led inside. Torches flickered and he saw more than thirty of the Tattooed People sitting around fires built within circles of stone. Two young men approached them. After the woman had spoken to them for a few moments, he was led further into the cave.

An old man, near toothless, sat cross-legged on a high rock. His body was completely covered in tattooes and his lower face was stained blue, as if emulating a beard and an upturned moustache.

The woman spoke to the old man, whose face remained expressionless throughout. Finally she turned to Kiall and dropped to her knees. Taking his hand she kissed it twice, then rose and was gone.

'I am Okas,' said the old man.

'I am . . .' Kiall began.

'I know who you are. What do you want of me?'

'Your help.'

'Why should I seek to aid the soul of Tenaka Khan?'

'I do not know what you are talking about,' said Kiall. 'I am seeking to rescue a woman I love – that is all.'

'Where is fat Beltzer?'

'I lost them when we were attacked.'

'By the Azhtacs, this also I know! Give me your hand.' Kiall reached out and Okas took his hand and turned it palm upwards. 'You lost your woman – and yet not your woman. And now you are on a quest you do not understand, that will determine the fate of a people you do not know. Truly, Kiall, you are a part of the World's Dream.'

'But will you help me? Chareos says you can follow spirit trails; he says that without you we will never find Ravenna.'

The old man released his hand. 'My people are finished now, the day of the Azhtacs has dawned. But soon another day will dawn, and the Azhtacs will see the destruction of their homes, the torment of their people. Yet that gives me no pleasure. And I do not wish to be here when they come for my children. I had thought to die tonight, quietly, here on this stone. But now I will come with you and die on another stone. Then I will join the World's Dream.'

'I don't know how to thank you,' said Kiall.

'Come,' said the old man, dropping to the floor beside him, 'let us find the *ghosts-yet-to-be*.'

Chareos dragged his sword clear of the dying Azhtac and swung to see if any of his companions needed help. Beltzer was standing over a dead warrior with axe raised. Maggrig and Finn had sheathed their knives and notched arrows to their bows. Nine dead Azhtacs lay sprawled around them. Chareos glanced up at the sun; it was almost noon and the silver-grey Gateway beckoned him.

'Where in Bar's name is Kiall?' hissed Chareos.

Finn joined him. 'I marked as many trees as I could, Chareos. I think he must be dead.'

Beltzer dropped to his knees beside a corpse and began to tug at the gold circlet the man wore on his brow. At that moment Maggrig shouted a warning and a large group of Azhtacs raced from the trees.

'Back!' shouted Chareos. Beltzer cursed and rose. Maggrig and Finn ran through the Gateway. Beltzer raised his axe and bellowed a battle-cry and the Azhtacs slowed. Beltzer turned and sprinted through the Gate, followed by Chareos.

The moonlight was bright on the other side, and the cold was numbing after the heat of the jungle. A spear flashed through the Gateway, striking the ground and half burying itself in the snow. Beltzer moved to one side of the Gateway; when an arm and a head showed through, his axe smashed into the head, catapulting the man back through the opening. Then there was silence.

'All that gold,' said Beltzer, 'and I didn't get a single piece of it.'

'You have your life,' Finn told him.

Beltzer swung on him. 'And what is that worth?'

'Enough!' roared Chareos. 'We have a comrade on the other side. Now cease your arguing and let me think.'

Within a circle of boulders, within sight of the Gateway, Maggrig lit a fire and they all gathered around it. 'You want to go back, Blade-master?' asked Maggrig.

'I don't know, my friend. We were lucky to escape the first time. I should think they would place guards on the Gate – and that makes it doubly perilous.'

'I think we should go back,' said Beltzer. 'I'm willing to risk it.'

'For the boy or the gold?' asked Maggrig.

'For both, if you must know,' Beltzer snapped.

Chareos shook his head. 'No,' he said, 'that would be foolhardy. Kiall is alone there, but he is a resourceful lad. Finn marked the trees and if he still lives Kiall will follow the trail back to the Gate. We will wait for him here.'

'And what if you are right about guards, eh?' enquired Beltzer. 'How will he get past those?'

'My guess is that they will be watching the Gate to see who passes from this side. He may have an opportunity to run at it.'

'Aren't you forgetting something, Chareos?' asked Maggrig. 'If he chooses the wrong time, there is no knowing where the Gate will take him.'

'As I said, he is resourceful. We wait.'

For some time they sat in silence. The wind picked up, gusting the snow around them; the fire spluttered and little heat seemed to emanate from it. 'We could freeze to death waiting here,' grumbled Beltzer. 'At least it is warmer on the other side.'

'It is colder than it ought to be,' remarked Finn suddenly. 'When we left the thaw had set in. The weather should not have turned so swiftly.'

'It has not necessarily been swift,' said Chareos, drawing his cloak more tightly about his frame. 'When I first looked beyond the Gate I seemed to be there, frozen, unable to move, for an hour at least. You said it was but a few heartbeats. Well, we were beyond the gate for a day – that could be a week here, or a month.'

'It better not have been a month, Blademaster,' said Maggrig softly. 'If it is, we are trapped in this valley for the winter. And there is not enough game.'

'Rubbish!' snorted Beltzer. 'We would just pass through the Gate and wait for a few of their days, returning in spring. Isn't that right, Chareos?'

The Blademaster nodded.

'Well, what are we waiting for?' asked Beltzer. 'Let's go back and find the lad.'

Finn bit back an angry response as Beltzer pushed himself to his feet. Just then a spark lifted from the fire and hung in the air, swelling slowly into a glowing ball. Beltzer's mouth dropped open and he took up his axe. Chareos and the others stared at the floating sphere – watching, astonished, as it grew to the size of a man's head. The colour faded until the globe was almost transparent and they could see the Gate reflected there, and the snow gusting around it. Finn gasped as two tiny figures showed inside the sphere, stepping through the miniature Gateway.

'It is Okas,' said Beltzer, peering at the ball. 'And the lad with him.' He spun round, but the real Gateway was empty. The scene inside the floating sphere shimmered and changed; now they could see Finn's cabin, and a warm fire glowing in the hearth. Okas was seated cross-legged before the blaze, his eyes closed. Kiall sat at the table.

The sphere vanished.

'He found the old boy,' said Beltzer. 'He found Okas.'

'Yes, and arrived back before us,' continued Finn.

The four men stood. Chareos doused the fire and they set off through the snow.

In the cabin Okas opened his eyes. 'They come,' he said.

'I had begun to give up hope,' replied Kiall. 'Twelve days is a long time to be trapped in that jungle.'

Okas chuckled. 'They left before we did. But I know how to use the Gate.' He stood and stretched. A small man, no more than five feet tall, he was round-shouldered and pot-bellied. He could have been any age from sixty to a hundred, and looked as if a stiff breeze could snap his bones. Yet he had walked through the snow clad only in a loin-cloth and had appeared to suffer no discomfort, neither through cold nor exhaustion. And he left barely a print on the snow, as if his weight was no more than that of a bird. He looked up at Kiall. 'So tell me all you know about the Great Khan.'

'Why are you interested? I don't understand,' said Kiall.

'I was here when he led his armies into Drenai lands,' Okas told him. 'And again when they marched against Bel-azar. Strong man, the Khan. Great man, perhaps. But he is dead, yes?'

'I don't know much about him. He conquered the Drenai and the Vagrians. He died some years ago; he is buried in the tomb of Ulric.'

'No, he is not,' said Okas. 'He is buried in an unmarked grave. But I know where it is. How did he die?'

'I do not know. His heart gave out, I would suppose. That is how most people die – even kings. Are you sure Chareos is coming?'

Okas nodded. He poured himself a goblet of water. 'I sent them a message. They come. Fat Beltzer is disappointed. He wanted to go back through to the jungle to find you – and to be rich. Fat Beltzer always wanted to be rich.'

'He is your friend?'

'All men are my friends,' said Okas. 'We are all of the Dream. But, yes, I like very much fat Beltzer.'

'Why? What is there to like?' Kiall asked.

'Ask me again in half a year. I will sleep now. I am older than I look.'

Kiall thought that barely credible, but he said nothing. Okas sat down before the fire, crossed his arms and slept upright. Kiall blew out the lantern and lay back on the bed by the wall.

The others were coming. The search for Ravenna was under way.

He slept without dreams.

It was a further two days before the exhausted travellers reached the sanctuary of the cabin. Beltzer was the first inside. He hoisted Okas into a bear-hug and spun him round until the little man laughed delightedly. 'How come you still live, fat man?' he asked. 'How come no one kill you yet?'

'They do keep trying,' replied Beltzer. He put the old man down and stared closely at his wrinkled skin and rheumy eyes. 'By the Source, you look all but dead yourself.'

'Soon,' said Okas, smiling. 'The Dream calls. But I will stay a little while with my old friends.' He turned to Chareos, who had shed his ice-covered cloak and was stripping his wet clothes from him and standing before the fire shivering. 'You and I, we speak,' Okas said. 'Back room good place.'

'This minute?'

'Yes,' answered Okas, moving through to the workshop. Chareos pulled a fresh tunic from his pack and dressed, then he walked to where Okas waited. The old man reached out and took his hand, holding it firmly for several seconds. 'Sit down,' he ordered, 'and tell me of quest.'

Chareos explained about the raid on the village, and Kiall's love for Ravenna. 'The others are coming along for different reasons. Beltzer is a lost soul, down from the mountain. Finn fears his death will leave Maggrig alone.'

'And you?'

'Me? I have nothing better to do with my life.'

'Is that true, Chareos? Do you not carry a dream?'

'Another man's dream. It was never my own.'

Okas clambered up on the edge of the work-bench, and sat down, his short legs dangling less than half-way to the floor. He looked closely at Chareos. 'Not your dream, you say. So, you also do not understand nature of this quest, nor where it take you. Tell me of Tenaka Khan, and gate-tower night.'

Chareos smiled. 'Do you know everything, Okas?'

'No, that is why I ask.'

'He climbed up to sit with us and we talked of many things: love, life, power, conquest, duty. He was a knowledgeable man. He had a dream, but he said the stars stood in his way.'

'What did he mean by it?'

'I don't know. He was no youngster then. Perhaps he meant death.'

'How did he die?'

'As I understand it, he collapsed at a feast. He was drinking wine and his heart gave out.'

'What happened then? After feast?'

Chareos spread his hands. 'How would I know? They buried him in Ulric's tomb. It was a great ceremony and thousands witnessed it. Our own ambassadors – and others from Ventria and the east – attended. Then his eldest son, Jungir, became Khan. He killed all of his brothers and now rules the Nadir. What has this to do with our quest? Or are you merely curious?'

Okas lifted his hand, the index finger pointing up, and spun it in the air. Golden light streamed from the finger, forming a circle. Other circles sprang up, criss-crossing the first until a sphere hung there. He dropped his hand and traced a straight golden line. 'This line is how you see your quest; flat, straight, start, finish. But this,' he said, raising his eyes to the globe, 'is how it really is. Your line is touched by many others. I know your secret, Chareos. I know who you are. You are son of last Earl of Dros Delnoch. You are heir to Armour of Bronze. And that makes you blood relative of Tenaka Khan and descendant of both Ulric and Earl Regnak, the second Earl of Bronze.'

'That is a secret I hope you will share with no one else,' whispered Chareos. 'I have no desire to return to the Drenai, and I want no one seeking me out.'

'As you wish . . . but blood is strong and it calls across the centuries. You will find it so. Why did Tenaka Khan let you live?'

'I don't know. Truly I don't.'

'And the *ghosts-yet-to-be?*'

'Just another riddle,' answered Chareos. 'Are not all men the ghosts of the future?'

'Yes. But in the Nadir tongue the phrase could be translated as *Companions of the ghost*, or even *Followers of the ghost*. Is that not so?'

'I am not skilled in the nuances of the Nadir tongue. What difference does it make?'

Okas jumped down to the floor, landing lightly. 'I will take you to Nadren village where Ravenna and the others were held. Then we see.'

'Is she still there?'

'I cannot say. I will pick up the spirit-trail at her home.'

Okas returned to the main room, where Kiall had lifted a heavy bundle to the table-top. When he opened it golden objects fell across the wooden surface, glinting in the lantern light. There were arm-bands, necklets, brooches, rings, and even a belt with solid gold clasp.

'Oh, joy!' cried Beltzer, dipping his huge fingers into the treasure and lifting a dozen items clear. 'Chareos said you were resourceful, but he didn't do you justice.'

'With this we should be able to buy back Ravenna,' said Kiall.

'With this you could buy a hundred women,' countered Beltzer. 'When do we share it out?'

'We don't,' Kiall stated. 'As I said, this is for Ravenna.'

Beltzer reddened. 'I worked for this too,' he said, 'and you must have stripped it from the bodies of the men I slew at the Gateway. Part of it is mine. Mine!' He scooped up a handful of golden objects and began to cram them into his pockets. Kiall stepped back and drew his sword, but Beltzer saw the move and swept up his axe.

'Stop this foolishness!' roared Chareos, moving between them. 'Sheath the blade, Kiall. And you, Beltzer, put back the gold.'

'But Chareos . . .' began Beltzer.

'Do it now!'

Beltzer slammed the gold back to the table, and stalked off to sit by the fire. Chareos turned his angry eyes on Kiall. 'There is truth in what he said. Think on it!'

Kiall stood silently for a few moments, then he relaxed. 'You split it fairly, Chareos,' said the young man. 'I will use my share to buy Ravenna.'

Finn stepped to the table, lifted a single ring and slipped it on his finger. 'This will do for me,' he said. Maggrig chose a wristband. Chareos took nothing.

Beltzer stood and glared at the others. 'You will not shame me,' he hissed. 'I will take what is mine!' He shovelled a number of items into his deep pockets and returned to the fire.

'We leave at first light for Tavern Town,' said Chareos. 'We will buy extra horses there. Since you are now rich, Beltzer, you can buy your own – and all the food and supplies you will need.'

6

'You tell me I face great danger – and yet you do not know from whence it comes?' asked Jungir Khan, his manner easy, his voice cold. He lounged back on the ivory inlaid throne and stared down at the shaman kneeling before him.

Shotza kept his eyes on the rugs below him, considering his words with great care. He was the third shaman to serve Jungir Khan; the first had been impaled and the second strangled. He was determined there would be no fourth. 'Great Khan,' he said, 'there is a magic barrier at work which will take me time to pierce. I already know where the magic originates.'

'And where is that?' whispered Jungir.

'From Asta Khan, sire.' Shotza risked a glance to see the effect the name had on the man above him.

Jungir's face betrayed no emotion, but his dark eyes narrowed. 'Still alive? How can this be? He was an old man when my father became Khan. He left the city of tents to die more than twenty years ago.'

'But he did not die, lord. He lives still in the Mountains of the Moon. There are many caves there, and tunnels that go through to the centre of the world.'

Jungir rose to his feet. He was tall for a Nadir, as his father Tenaka had been. He had jet-black hair drawn back in a tight topknot, and a short, trimmed trident beard. His eyes were slanted and dark, betraying no evidence of his half-breed ancestry. 'Stand up,' he ordered the little shaman and Shotza rose. He was just over five feet tall, wiry and bald. Less than sixty years old, the skin of his face hung in wrinkled folds.

Jungir looked into the shaman's curiously pale eyes and smiled. 'Do you fear me?' he asked.

'As I fear the winds of death, lord.'

'Do you love me?'

'Love? You are my Khan. The future of the Nadir rests with you,' answered Shotza. 'Why would you need my love also?'

'I do not. But the answer is a good one. Now tell me of Asta.'

The Khan returned to his throne and sat with his head back, gazing up at the silken roof which gave the throne hall the appearance of a vast tent. The silks were gifts from the Eastern kingdom of Kiatze, dowry for the bride they had sent him.

'After Asta left the Wolves, he passed from the knowledge of men,' began Shotza. 'We all thought he had died. But at the last full moon, when I tried to trace the Silver Thread of your destiny, I found a great mist had settled over the sign of your house. I tried to pierce it, and at first had some success. Then it hardened into a wall. I flew high, but could not find the top. Using all the arcane powers my masters taught me, I finally breached the wall. But all too briefly. Yet I saw the face of Asta Khan. And I sensed the perils that await you in the coming year.'

Shotza licked his lips and once more considered his words. 'I saw gleaming Armour of Bronze, floating beneath a star, and a swordsman of great skill. But then Asta became aware of me – I was, thrown back, and the wall sealed itself once more.'

'And that is all you saw?' asked Jungir softly.

'All that I could see clearly,' Shotza answered, wary of offering a direct lie to his king.

The Khan nodded. 'Find Asta Khan – and kill him. Take a hundred of my Guards. Scour the mountains. Bring me his head.'

'With respect, Great Khan, you could send a thousand men and not find him. Asta was the greatest of shamen; he cannot be taken by men.'

'His magic is stronger than yours?'

Shotza closed his eyes. 'Yes, lord. There is not one man alive who could overcome him.'

'It is not my way, Shotza, to have inferior men serve me.'

'No, lord. But there is a way in which I could defeat him. I have six worthy acolytes. Together – and with certain necessary sacrifices – we could overcome Asta.'

'Necessary sacrifices?'

'Blood kin of Asta Khan, sacrificed on the night of Midwinter.'

'How many such sacrifices?'

'Twenty at least. Maybe thirty. Each one will weaken the old man.'

'And you, of course, know the whereabouts of Asta's family?'

'I do, lord.'

'Then I leave the preparations to you, Shotza. Now this peril from the Armour of Bronze – does it herald yet another Drenai uprising?'

'I do not think so, lord. I saw the image of the armour, and yet the star was in the north. There can be no Drenai threat from the lands of the Gothir. But once I have breached Asta's wall, I will know more. I will know it all.'

Shotza bowed deeply. Jungir waved him away and the shaman made his way to his chambers and sat down on a silk-covered divan. Free from the piercing eyes of Jungir Khan, he lay back and allowed his fear to show. His heart was palpitating and he found it difficult to breathe. Slowly he calmed himself, thanking the gods of the Steppes that Jungir had not pressed him about the other images.

He had seen a babe, wrapped in a cloak, lying on a cold stone floor.

And hovering over the child was the grim ghost of Tenaka Khan, Lord of the Wolves.

Jungir watched the little man leave, then sat in silence for several minutes. He could smell Shotza's fear and knew full well there was more the shaman could have said. None of these sorcerers ever gave the whole truth. It was against their natures. Secretive, deceitful and cunning, they were weaned on subtlety and guile. But they had their uses. Shotza was the best of them and it must have taken great courage to admit that Asta Khan was more powerful. Jungir rose and stretched. He walked to the hanging tent wall which masked the window and pulled it aside.

The new city of Ulrickham stretched out before his eyes, low single-storey dwellings of mud-dried brick and stone. Yet inside all of them were the tent hangings that meant home to the Nadir. Nomads for ten thousand years, they were ill-suited to cities of stone. Yet Tenaka had insisted on the building of the cities, with their schools and hospitals.

'It ill behoves the world's greatest nation to live like savages,' he had told Jungir. 'How can we grow? How can we fasten our grip on the events of the world if we do not learn civilised ways? It is not enough to be feared on the battlefield.'

Such talk had made him unpopular with the older Nadir warlords, but how could they turn on the man who did what the mighty Ulric could not? How could they betray the man who had conquered the round-eyed southerners?

Jungir stepped back from the window and wandered into the Hall of Heroes. Here, after the fashion of the conquered Drenai, were the status of Nadir warriors. Jungir paused before his father's likeness and stared into the cold, grey eyes. 'Just how I remember you, Father,' he whispered. 'Cold and aloof.' The statue was expertly carved, showing the lean power of the Khan, the fine jaw and the noble stance. In one hand he held a long-sword, in the other the helm of Ulric. 'I loved you,' said Jungir.

A cool breeze caused the torches to flicker and shadows danced on the stone face, seeming to bring it to life. Jungir could almost see the stone eyes gleaming violet, the mouth curving into that long-remembered cynical smile. He shivered. 'I did love you,' he repeated, 'but I knew of your plan. You trained me well, Father. I had my spies too. No man should think to live forever . . . not even Tenaka Khan. And had you succeeded, where would Jungir have found a place? The eternal heir to a living god? No. I too am of the blood of Ulric. I had a right to rule, to make my own life.'

The statue was silent. 'How strange, Father. There is no difference in talking to you now, from when you were alive. It was always like speaking to stone. Well, I wept when you died. And I almost stopped you drinking that poison. *Almost.* I reached out my hand to you. You looked into my eyes, and you said nothing. A single word from you and I would have stopped you. But you looked away. Did you know, I wonder, as the poison touched your soul? In those last moments, as you lay upon the floor with me kneeling by you, did you know that it was I who put the black powder in your wine? Did you?' He gazed once more into the cold eyes. 'Why did you never love me?' he asked.

But the statue was silent still.

The twelve days lost beyond the Gate cost the questors dear, for a savage blizzard kept them trapped within the cabin for eighteen days. Food ran short and Finn almost died after setting off to hunt for meat. After killing a deer, he was caught in a second blizzard and had to take refuge in a cave. An avalanche blocked the entrance and it was only through the magic of Okas that Chareos and the others found the hunter and dug a tunnel through to him.

The winter storms eased off on the nineteenth day, but even then it took another three weeks before the exhausted group topped the last rise before Tavern Town.

Beltzer led the way down to the inn, pounding on the door and calling for Naza. The little man shouted with delight when he saw the giant and embraced him.

'I feared you dead,' he said. 'Come in, come in! Mael has just lit the fire. It will soon be warm. Come in!'

'Where is everyone?' asked Kiall.

'They don't fell the timber at this time of year,' replied Naza. 'There will be no one here for another two months. Most of the passes are blocked. Sit down by the fire. I will fetch you some wine.' His smile faded as Okas entered the tavern. 'He's . . . he's . . .' stammered the innkeeper.

'Yes, he is,' said Chareos swiftly. 'He is also a friend who, like us, last ate three days ago.'

'Wine first,' grunted Beltzer, throwing his arm around Naza's shoulder and leading him back towards the cellar.

The flames took hold of the logs and began to rise, but even so it was cold inside the inn. Chareos pulled up a chair and sat. His eyes were dull, and purple rings showed under them. Even the hardy Finn was exhausted. Only Okas and Kiall seemed none the worse for the ordeal in the mountains. The old man had been untroubled by the cold, and the youngster had grown in strength as the days passed.

'We're too old for this,' said Finn, reading Chareos' thoughts. Chareos nodded, too tired to reply. Returning with wine, Beltzer thrust a poker deep into the fire and waited until the iron glowed red and bright. Then he plunged it into the wine pitcher. He poured five goblets and handed one to each of the questors. He downed his own swiftly and refilled the goblet. Naza brought them bread, smoked cheese and cold meat.

After the meal Chareos slowly climbed the stairs to the upper guest room, pulled off his boots and was asleep almost as soon as his head touched the bolster. Maggrig and Finn took a second room, while Okas lay down on the stone hearth and slept before the fire.

Beltzer and Kiall sat together, the giant calling out for a third pitcher of wine.

Mael brought it. 'I take it you still have no money?' she asked.

'Oh yes, he has,' said Kiall. 'Pay the bill, Beltzer.'

Beltzer muttered a curse and dipped into his pocket, producing a thick gold ring. Mael took it, judging the weight. 'That should settle about half of what you owe Naza,' she said, leaving her hand extended.

'You are a hard woman,' grumbled Beltzer. He fished around in his pocket, seeking a small token, but he had only larger items. Finally he produced a wristband. 'That's worth ten times what I owe,' he told her.

Mael laughed at him, as she took the band and examined it. 'I have never seen workmanship like it, nor gold as red as this. Naza will give you a fair price – and you are right. It is worth far more than you owe. I will see to it that you are reimbursed.'

'Don't bother,' said Beltzer, flushing. 'Keep it. I'll probably come back one day, with not a copper coin to my name.'

'There's truth in that,' she told him.

After she had gone Beltzer turned to Kiall. 'What are you staring at, boy? Never seen a man settle a debt before?'

Kiall had drunk too much wine and his head was light, his thoughts serene. 'I never thought to see *you* settle one.'

'What does that mean?'

'I took you for a selfish, greedy pig,' said Kiall, smilingly oblivious to Beltzer's growing anger.

'I pay my debts,' declared Beltzer.

'Truly? You didn't even thank Finn for buying back your axe – and that cost him dear.'

'That is between Finn and me. You don't count, boy. Now curb your tongue – before I cut it out!'

Kiall blinked and sobered swiftly. 'And you are a liar,' he said. 'You told me Tura was dead, drowned in a dock. All lies. And I don't fear you, you fat-bellied pig. Don't threaten me!'

Beltzer lurched to his feet and Kiall rose, scrabbling for his sabre, but not before Beltzer's fingers grabbed the front of his jerkin and hoisted him into the air. As Beltzer's fist rose Kiall's foot lashed up into his groin and the giant bellowed with pain, dropping the younger man and staggering back. Now Kiall drew his sabre. Beltzer grinned at him – and advanced.

'What are you going to do with that, boy? You going to stick old Beltzer? Are you?' Kiall backed away, aware that the situation had careered out of control. Beltzer lunged at him, slapping the sabre aside. Kiall hit him with a straight left that slammed into Beltzer's face. The giant ignored the blow and struck Kiall's jaw open-handed, cartwheeling the younger man across the floor. Half-stunned, Kiall came to his knees and dived head-first at Beltzer's belly. Beltzer's knee came up with sickening force, snapping Kiall's head back . . .

He awoke to find himself in the chair by the fire with Beltzer sitting opposite him.

'Want some wine?' Beltzer asked. Kiall shook his head. Hammers were beating inside his skull. 'You are a game fighter, boy, and one day you may even be a wolf. But wolves know better than to tackle a bear.'

'I'll remember that,' Kiall promised. 'And I'll have that wine now.'

Beltzer handed him a goblet. 'I love old Finn. And he knows how much it meant to me to have that axe back; he didn't need any words. Back at Bel-azar, Finn was dragged from the ramparts by the Nadir. Chareos, Maggrig and me, we jumped down to haul him clear. It was I who carried Finn on my back, and cut a path to the gate-tower. He didn't thank me then; he didn't need to. You understand?'

'I believe I do.'

'It's the drink. It makes me talk too much. You don't like me, do you?'

Kiall looked at the flat, ugly face under the shining bald head; he stared into the small round eyes. 'No, not much,' he admitted.

Beltzer nodded solemnly. 'Well, don't let it concern you. I don't like myself much, either. But I was on the mountain, boy. No one can take that away from me.'

'I was on the mountain too,' said Kiall.

'Not *my* mountain. But maybe you will, one day.'

'What is so special about it?'

'Nothing,' replied Beltzer.

'Then why should I wish to go there?'

Beltzer looked up from his wine. 'Because that's where your lady is, Kiall.'

Moonlight bathed the grey stone walls, and a hunting owl swooped low over the deserted ramparts. Chareos could hear the screams of the

106

wounded and the dying, yet there were no bodies sprawled on the stone, no blood pooling by the gate-tower steps. As he sat down on the edge of the crenellated battlement, staring out over the valley of Bel-azar, the screams faded into the echoes of memory. The land was now empty of life. Where Nadir camp-fires had lit the valley like fallen stars, now there was only the shimmering grass, the lonely boulders and a long-dead lightning-struck tree.

Chareos was alone. He could not remember travelling to Bel-azar, but that did not seem to matter. He felt, in some strange way, that he was home – safe among the ghosts of the past.

Safe? Dark shapes moved at the edge of his vision, vanishing into the shadows as he swung to confront them. He backed away to the rotted gate-tower door and climbed the spiral steps to the circular battlement. There he drew his sword and waited. He could hear the scratching of talons on the stairway, smell the fetid odours of the dwellers in the dark: slime on fur, the sweet, sickly stink from mouths that fed on corpses.

He slammed shut the top door. There was no bolt and he dropped his sword into the catch, wedging the door shut. Heavy bodies beat upon the wood.

'Beltzer!' called Chareos. 'Help me!'

But there was no answer. 'Maggrig, Finn!'

'It would seem you are alone, kinsman,' said a quiet voice and Chareos turned slowly, knowing whom he would see. The tall man sat on the battlement's edge, his black hair tied at the nape of the neck, his violet eyes seeming grey in the moonlight.

'Will *you* help me?' whispered Chareos.

'Blood always aids blood, my friend. Are you not my kinsman?'

'Yes. Yes, I am. Will you help me? Please?'

The door splintered and a taloned hand broke through, ripping at the wood.

'Begone!' shouted Tenaka Khan. The hissing cries beyond the doorway faded into silence and the hand slid back from view.

'Are they your creatures?' Chareos asked.

'No, but they know a voice of power. And they can smell fear like a lion smells blood. Why are you afraid, Chareos?'

'I don't know how I came here. I am alone.'

'That is not an answer. Fear brought you, but what caused the fear?'

Chareos laughed, but there was no humour in the sound. 'You can ask that? You who slew my father and mother and made me an outcast? I should hate you, Tenaka. Once I thought I did. But then you climbed alone to this tower, and you sat and talked with us.' Chareos stared at the man before him. He was dressed exactly as he had been on that night so many years ago, in black riding-boots and leather leggings, topped by a shirt of black silk embroidered with silver. 'You called me kinsman,' whispered Chareos. 'You know who I am?'

'I knew you when first I saw you on this tower,' answered Tenaka. 'Blood recognises blood.'

'I should have killed you!' hissed Chareos, 'for all the pain. I was twelve when they sent me from Dros Delnoch. The night when your hordes finally stormed the last wall, I was taken from the fortress and brought to the lands of the Gothir. My father's last words to me were, "Avenge me, my son. And remember the Drenai". My mother was already dead. And for what? So that a treacherous cur like you could take Nadir savages into the last bastion of civilisation. What caused my fear? You dare ask me that?'

'I still ask it,' replied the Khan smoothly. 'And all you tell me is a history I already know.'

'You were descended from the Earl of Bronze and raised by the Drenai. How could you destroy them?'

'How indeed?' replied the Khan. 'If you truly knew the story of my life, you would not ask such a question. As you know, I was raised by the Nadir until I was fourteen. You think you were the only child who ever suffered pain and rejection? I was hated for being part Drenai. Then I was sent, as part of my mother's marriage agreement, to live among the Drenai. Were they different from the Nadir? No. To them I was a savage from the Steppes – something they could bait and torture. Yet I learned to live among them. And I fought for them. I rode with the Dragon. I even made a few friends among them. But when the mad emperor Ceska brought terror to the land, I risked my life and my soul to aid the Drenai. I paid my debt to them. I brought the Nadir to crush the emperor's army, and I allowed Rayvan and your father to form a new republic. Why did I take Dros Delnoch years later? Because I was the Khan! Because the day of the Nadir had dawned. Yet if I can be accused of treachery, what of you? Why did you not obey your father's command? Why did you not return home?'

'For what purpose?' shouted Chareos. 'To die? Achieving what?'

'So that is your fear?' responded Tenaka Khan. 'You were afraid to try. Afraid to fail.'

'Don't you dare to judge me!' Chareos stormed. 'I will not be found wanting by a murderous traitor.'

Tenaka Khan spread his hands. 'And who did I betray, Chareos? I was the Khan of the Nadir. I had saved the Drenai once. I gave them good warning that I would return. But you – you betrayed your father and all your ancestors back to Regnak, second Earl of Bronze. He held Dros Delnoch against seemingly insurmountable odds. Generations of Drenai warriors have died to protect their homeland, but not you. No, you would be content to marry a whore and win a little battle here at Bel-azar.'

Chareos dragged his sword from the bolt latch of the door and swung on Tenaka.

'Is this how you repay me for saving your soul?' asked Tenaka, mildly. 'Only a few moments ago, you were asking for my help against the beasts of the night.'

Chareos lowered his sword. 'Am I a coward then?' he whispered.

'There are many forms of cowardice, Chareos. One man can face a score of enemies with a sword, but not a sickness which paralyses him. Another can face death with a smile, yet fear the years of hardship and toil which are living. Are you a coward?'

Chareos sat down on the battlements, staring at the sword in his hand. 'I have never feared an opponent. But yes, I am a coward. I did not have the strength to return to the Drenai . . . I still haven't.'

'You found the Tattooed Man?'

'Yes. Yes, we found him. And he will come with us on our . . . journey.'

'You feel this quest is below you?' asked the Khan.

'We are seeking to rescue a pig-breeder's daughter, taken by Nadren raiders. Will the sun fall from the sky if we fail?'

Tenaka stood and placed his hands on Chareos' shoulders. 'I returned to the lands of the Drenai to kill a madman. Instead I found a friend, and a love, and a home I never knew I had lost. From being the Prince of Shadows I became the Great Khan, and I took the Nadir to heights undreamed of. Do not judge your quest until you have completed it. You remember that other night on this very tower?'

'How could I forget? You let us live.'

'One day soon, you will know why.'

Chareos awoke. The fire had died, the room was cold; he shivered and pulled the blankets over his chilled frame. He could still picture the slanted violet eyes and feel the strength of the grip on his shoulders.

The door opened and Okas stepped in. He moved silently to the bed and sat upon it.

'The dawn is up,' said Okas. 'Your quest awaits.'

'I had a dream, Okas.'

'I too. I dreamt of a bed of rushes and a soft woman.'

'And I of Tenaka Khan.'

'Was he at Bel-azar?' enquired the Tattooed Man.

'Yes.' Chareos sat up. 'How do you know that?'

'I did not,' replied Okas, blinking. 'It was a question.'

'But why did you ask it?'

The old man was silent for a moment. 'There is a mystery here. Tenaka Khan was buried with his ancestor Ulric in the Great Tomb. It was sealed by his son, Jungir, and a thousand spells were cast upon it so that it should never be opened.'

'I know all this,' snapped Chareos.

'You do not know,' said Okas, 'or you would solve mystery. I understand magic that is hidden in the world; I can read hearts of men. Yet the Source of All Things has his own secrets, and I cannot read those. Tenaka Khan died and was buried – this we know. His son was anxious that no one should enter the tomb; this also we know. But here is the mystery, Chareos: why do Tenaka Khan's bones lie hidden at Bel-azar?'

'That is impossible. It would be sacrilege.'

'Indeed so.'

Chareos shook his head. 'Our quest has nothing to do with Tenaka Khan. We will be travelling nowhere near Bel-azar.'

'Are you sure?'

'I will stake my life on it.'

Okas said nothing.

7

Chien-tsu was not a man who liked to travel. He did not like the dust of the Steppes, nor the arid, inhospitable country; most especially he abhorred the squat dwellings, the stench of the towns and the barely concealed hostility of the Nadir. It was said, back in Hao-tzing, that the Nadir were closely related to the people of the Middle Kingdom. Chien-tsu doubted it – despite the similarity of skin colour and language, he could not believe that their origins were identical. He put forward the entirely reasonable view that the gods made the Nadir first and then, realising the ghastly flaws inherent in the species, created the perfect people and gave them the Middle Kingdom for their own. This hateful visit only confirmed his theory. The Nadir did not seem disposed towards bathing, and their clothes remained unwashed from season to season – in fact, probably from decade to decade, he thought.

And what a country! Though he travelled light, which did not befit an ambassador from the Supreme City, he still found it difficult to obtain lodgings for his forty-two servants, eleven concubines and sixty members of the Guard Royal. He had been reduced to purchasing sixteen wagons to carry necessities like tents, beds, tables, chairs, soft linen sheets, harps, flutes, two enamel baths and five full-sized mirrors. And he had brought a mere twenty-five chests of personal luggage containing his own – entirely inadequate – travelling wardrobe.

Chien-tsu found it curious that the Emperor should have allowed one of his daughters to wed a savage, but a wise man did not question the decisions of the Divine One. And Chien-tsu, as all civilised men knew, was wise far beyond his thirty-two years.

He reined in his horse before the city, and sighed. The buildings were in the main unlovely, and the palace which towered at the centre – despite having an arrogant, almost primal simplicity – lacked any sense of aesthetic beauty. There were six square towers and a crenellated battlement. No banners flew. Chien-tsu halted the wagons and ordered his tent pitched. Once this was done, he had his mirrors assembled and a bath prepared. His hand-maidens washed the dust from his body and massaged him with aromatic oils; his long dark hair was carefully greased and combed, drawn back from the brow and held in place by ivory combs. Then he dressed in leggings of gold-embroidered blue silk, and shoes with golden straps. His shirt was of the whitest silk, and over this he placed a lacquered breastplate of wood and leather decorated with a golden dragon. His long, curving sword hung between his shoulder-blades, and two knives in gleaming wooden scabbards were carefully placed within the satin sash tied around his waist. He ordered the presents for Jungir Khan to be carried forward: there were seventeen chests – matching the age of the new Queen of the Nadir. It would, Chien-tsu decided, be pleasant to see Mai-syn once more. The youngest of the Emperor's legitimate daughters, she was quite breathtakingly beautiful and could play the ninestringed harp with exquisite style.

He stepped into the saddle and led his entourage of five footmen and thirty-four bearers down towards the palace.

They were greeted by twenty soldiers, led by an officer wearing a silver chain who inclined his head in a perfunctory bow. Chien-tsu stiffened, for the bow was some six inches short of politeness. Raising his head, he looked the officer in the eye . . . the silence grew. It would not be good manners to speak first, but Chien-tsu found his irritation growing.

'Well?' snapped the officer at last. 'What do you want?' Chien-tsu was taken aback but controlled his rising temper. It would not be seemly to kill a man on his first day in the city.

'I am Chien-tsu, ambassador of the Supreme Emperor to the court of Jungir Khan. I have come with suitable gifts on the anniversary of the Queen's birthday. Kindly take me to the royal presence.'

As Chien-tsu expected, the man's expression changed; he bowed once more, this time exceeding the distance required. Then he barked out a command and the twenty soldiers turned. 'Follow me,' he told Chien.

There was no open courtyard within the great gates, merely a maze of tunnels. They emerged swiftly into a large shrub garden to the east of the gate. A line of stables stretched to the right and Chien-tsu

111

dismounted, allowing his horse to be led away. The party was passed on to a second officer – taller than the first, he wore a silver breastplate and helm. He bowed correctly to Chien and smiled.

'Welcome, ambassador. The Lord Khan was not expecting you so swiftly.'

'Is this not the day of the anniversary?'

The man seemed confused. 'Please follow me,' he said. Chien and his party moved on into another intricate system of tunnels and corridors that opened on to a wide hallway before huge double doors of oak, mounted with silver.

Four guards stood before the doors. They stepped aside as the officer approached and the doors swung open.

Inside, to Chien's surprise, the main hall resembled a giant tent with curtains and hangings of the finest silk. At the far end, on a raised dais, the Great Khan lounged on a satin-covered divan. Chien entered and bowed low, holding the pose for the obligatory ten heartbeats.

The Khan waved him forward. 'Welcome, ambassador, this is an unexpected pleasure.' The man's voice was deep and powerful. He rose, and stepped from the dais. 'We did not expect you until tomorrow.'

Chien lifted his hands and clapped them and the thirty-four bearers moved forward to place the chests in a line before the Khan. The men backed away with heads low, eyes averted. Chien bowed once more. 'Great Khan, I have come bearing gifts from the Divine Lord of the Golden Realm, to celebrate the year of your marriage and to enquire, on behalf of His Majesty, whether Mai-syn has continued to bring exquisite joy to your hearth.'

'Indeed she has,' answered Jungir. 'Now to the chests, if you please.'

This was not the response which Chien had been expecting, but he hid his consternation and opened the first of the silver-bound chests. Lifting clear a handsome coat of silver silk, decorated with pearls, he held it before the Khan.

'Pleasant,' commented the Khan. 'Are they all clothes?'

'No, Great Khan,' said Chien, forcing a smile. He opened the second chest, which was filled with emeralds, some the size of a man's fist.

'What is this worth in your land in, say, horses and men?' asked the Khan.

'A man could equip an army of ten thousand lances for a full summer,' Chien answered.

'Good. I like them. And the others?'

Some contained gold, others perfumes and spices or articles of clothing. The last chest produced the strongest response from the Nadir warlord. From it Chien lifted a sabre of dazzling brightness. The hilt-guard was of gold inset with gems, and the hilt was bound with gold thread. But the pommel-stone was milky-white and carved into the head of a wolf.

112

Jungir took the blade and slashed the air. 'It is perfect,' he said, his eyes shining. 'The balance is beyond belief and the edge is remarkable. Truly I am pleased. Relay my thanks to your king; tell him I had not realised his lands delivered such wealth. When will you be starting back – tomorrow?'

'As you wish, Great Khan.'

'Tomorrow would be good for you, for the winter will be closing in on the ports and I would not like your journey to be uncomfortable.'

'It is kind of you to concern yourself over my comforts; but His Majesty has required me to see his daughter, and to carry her a message of his love and devotion.'

'I will give her that message,' said Jungir loftily.

'And I do not doubt, Great Khan, that you would deliver it more skilfully than I. But my king ordered me to see her and, as I am sure you will agree, a subject must always obey the order of his liege lord.'

'Indeed,' said Jungir, 'but I fear that will not be possible. The . . . Queen is at my palace in the south. It is a two-month journey. I am sure your king will understand that you could not fulfil his wishes.'

'But I can, Great Khan. I will travel to the south, and then journey home. With your permission, of course?'

Jungir's face darkened, but his expression remained friendly. 'It would not be advisable, ambassador. The lands of the Steppes are . . . perilous for outsiders. Many tribes continue to harass . . . foreigners.'

'I understand, sire. Even within the Middle Kingdom there are bandits and rogues who disobey the Emperor's will. But I am sure my soldiers will be a match for them. And I much appreciate your concern over the safety of a humble ambassador.'

Jungir gave a tight smile and stepped back to the dais. 'Quarters will be allocated to you, ambassador, and my chamberlain will furnish you with the guides and supplies you will need for your journey. And now I have matters of state to occupy me.'

Chien bowed – but not low. He straightened. 'I cannot thank you sufficiently, sire, for the time you have allowed me.' He backed seven paces, instead of ten, and turned.

As the great doors swung shut Jungir turned to a broad-shouldered warrior at his side. 'You will guide them south for a week. Then there will be an attack on them. No one survives. You understand, Kubai?'

'I do, sire.'

'And see that they do not move around in the palace. I want no one to mention the yellow-faced bitch.'

'As you wish, Lord Khan.'

The chamberlain led Chien through the maze of tunnels to three large, square adjoining rooms. Windows in the west walls looked out over an exquisitely ugly garden of shrubs. In the first room was a bed, four chairs, a table and three lanterns. the second contained only a narrow bed and a single lantern, while the third boasted a metal bath, three barrels of water and several thin towels.

'It is almost too luxurious,' said Chien, without a hint of mockery. The chamberlain gave a thin-lipped smile and left. Chien turned to his manservant, Oshi, a wiry ex-slave who had served Chien's family for forty years. 'Find the spy-holes,' ordered Chien, using an obscure Kiatze dialect. Oshi bowed and moved around the room for several minutes.

'There are none, lord,' said Oshi finally.

'Is there no end to their insults?' snapped Chien. 'Do they feel I am not important enough to spy on?'

'They are savages, lord.'

'Go and find where they have put Sukai and the others. Send Sukai to me.'

'At once, lord. Or should I prepare your bath first?'

'I will bathe tomorrow. I would not put it past these Nadir to have urinated in the water-barrels.' Oshi chuckled and left the room. Chien pulled a linen handkerchief from his pocket and dusted one of the chairs. A dark shape scuttled across the room behind him and Chien swivelled, his hand snapping a small throwing-knife from his sleeve. The blade flashed across the room and the black rat died instantly, almost cut in half.

Minutes later, as Chien stood at the window staring down at the grey-green shrubs in what passed for a royal garden, there came a discreet tap at the door.

'Enter!' he commanded.

Sukai marched into the room and bowed as low as his lacquered leather breastplate would allow. The officer carried his iron helm against his chest. He was neither tall nor especially formidable in appearance, yet his skill with the long, curved *chantanai* blade was known throughout the Middle Kingdom. He had served Chien for eleven years – and not once in that time had Chien seen him without his hair combed, oiled and lacquered. Now it was hanging lank about his shoulders.

'Why do you come here looking like the basest peasant?' asked Chien, still using the Kiatze dialect.

'A thousand apologies, noble lord,' Sukai replied. 'I was preparing for my bath – I did not think you would wish to wait for me to dress properly.'

'You are correct in that, Sukai. But it was improper to prepare to bathe without first ascertaining whether I had need of you. However, in a city of barbarians it is difficult to retain hold of civilised behaviour. Have you checked your room?'

'I have, lord. There are no passageways hidden, and no secret hearing tubes.'

114

'Disgraceful!'

'They are an insulting people.'

Oshi entered silently, bowed twice – then saw the dead rat. He retrieved Chien's knife and removed the corpse by the tail. 'It has fleas,' he said, holding the body at arm's length.

'Throw it from the window,' ordered Chien. 'If we leave it here, we will probably find it served to us for supper.' Oshi hurled the rat to the gardens below and wandered off to the back room to clean the knife, while Chien turned back to the warrior. 'Tomorrow we will be leaving for the south.'

'Yes, lord.'

Chien hesitated and closed his eyes. His concentration hardened and he felt the floating presence of a spirit within the room. He smiled. So, he thought, they are not quite such savages. His fingers flickered against his belt; Sukai read the message, and smoothly moved from Kiatze to Nadir.

'Will the Lord Khan be supplying us with guides, sir?'

'But of course. He is a noble king, of a noble line. But I do not think we should all presume upon his hospitality. You will arrange for a guard of twenty men to take the women and all manservants bar Oshi back to Kiatze. I will send a message to the Divine Emperor, telling him of the success of our mission and the kind words of Jungir Khan. The journey south would be too hard on my girls.'

'Yes, lord.'

'We will take only one wagon – with gifts for the Queen. All my goods will go back to Kiatze.'

'With the exception of your tent, my lord?'

'No, that also. I will take my paints and brushes, that is all. There may be some interesting flowers along the way.' His fingers appeared to brush a speck of dust from his sleeve.

Sukai bowed. 'I have noticed many red blooms, sir.'

'You will see many more.'

Sukai's face hardened. 'May I be permitted to write to my family, lord?'

'Of course. Now leave me. I will see you at dawn.'

As the officer departed Oshi returned to the room with Chien's freshly cleaned knife in his hands. Chien returned the blade to the oiled sheath in his sleeve.

Oshi moved the cleaned chair to the window and Chien sat, seemingly lost in thought. He focused his mind on the intrusive spirit in the room and saw a thin, wrinkled old man with pale eyes and a weasel face. He was floating just below the high ceiling. Chien sat silently until the watcher's presence faded.

'Oshi!'

'Yes, lord?'

'Go to the kitchens and find some bread. They will have no fish, but choose me some dried meat that is not full of corruption.'

'At once!'

Chien folded his arms and thought of Mai-syn. To her this place must have seemed worse than squalid. He concentrated on the beauty of her face, trying to communicate with her spirit. But there was only a cosmic silence. Perhaps she is too far from here, he thought. Perhaps not, the darker side of his nature told him.

The chamberlain knocked at the door and told Chien that the Lord Jungir Khan had arranged a feast in his honour. It would be this evening at moonrise. It would be acceptable if the Lord Ambassador wished to bring the Chief of his Guards. Chien bowed and accepted.

What new humiliation will the savages plan for tonight, he wondered?

The great hall was packed with warriors, seated around a score of bench tables pushed together to make an enormous open square. Jungir Khan – in tight-fitting tunic of black leather embroidered with gold thread – sat at the southern end of the hall, the throne dais behind him. Chien was seated at his right hand and to his right sat Sukai, ill at ease and eating little. To Jungir's left was a wizened man whom the Khan introduced as Shotza, the court shaman. Chien inclined his head to the man. 'We have heard much of the skills of the Nadir shamen,' he said.

'As we have of the court magicians of the Kiatze,' responded Shotza. 'Is it true they make tiny golden machines that fly in the air, imitating birds?'

'The Divine King has three,' answered Chien-tsu.

Shotza nodded, but seemed unconvinced.

The feast involved eating an extraordinary amount of meats which, back in Kiatze, would have been refused by the court dogs. In the main, it was high beyond the point of rotting. To offset this, the guests covered the food with spices. Chien ate sparingly and drank less. The liquor being consumed by the Nadir was distilled, he was told, from rancid goats' milk. 'How clever,' he remarked. How apt, he thought.

Between the interminable courses there were performances by jugglers or acrobats. They were not especially skilled, though Chien applauded politely.

'We have heard much,' said Jungir Khan suddenly, 'of the martial skills of the Kiatze. Would your officer honour us with an exhibition?'

'Of what kind?' enquired Chien.

'Swordsmanship.'

'With respect, Lord Khan, that is not possible. The soul of a warrior partly resides in his blade. It is not to be drawn unless to take blood – and that, I fear, would not represent an exhibition of skills.'

116

'Then let him fight to the death,' said the Khan.

'I am afraid I do not understand you, sire. Is this a jest of some kind?'

'I never jest about war, ambassador. I merely ask that your man shows me the skills of the Kiatze. I would take it badly were you to refuse me.'

'I hope, my Lord Khan, that you will not interpret my words as a refusal. I merely ask you to reconsider. Is it not bad fortune for there to be a death at a feast?'

'That depends on who dies,' answered the Khan coldly.

'Very well, sire,' said Chien, turning to Sukai. 'The Khan wishes to see the battle skills of a Kiatze officer. Oblige him.'

'As you order,' answered Sukai. He rose and vaulted the table. He was not a tall man, nor did he have great width of shoulder. His face was broad and flat, his eyes dark; he was clean-shaven, but for a thin moustache which drooped to his chin. He drew his long curved double-handed sword and waited; his fingers brushed his chest. Chien read the signalled question and found it difficult to keep the pride from his eyes. 'Do you require me to die?' Sukai had asked. Chien lifted his hand to touch his carefully lacquered hair. Sukai understood – and bowed.

Jungir Khan pointed to a warrior at the far end of the hall. 'Show our guest how a Nadir fights,' he called, and the man leapt into the square.

'Excuse me, sire,' said Chien, his face expressionless.

'What is it?'

'It seems hardly fair to have only one man face Sukai. He will be mortally offended.'

The Khan's face darkened and he held up one hand. Silence fell. 'Our guest, the ambassador for the land of Kiatze, has said that one Nadir warrior is no match for his champion.' An angry murmur began. Again the Khan's hand cut the air and silence followed the move. 'Can this be true?'

'No!' came a roar from the feasters.

'But he also says that his champion will be insulted if he faces only one opponent. Should we insult so fine-looking a warrior?' There was no response and the Nadir waited for the lead from their Khan. 'No, we cannot insult our guests. Therefore you, Ulai, and you, Yet-zan, will join your comrade.' The two Nadir warriors clambered into the square. 'Let the battle commence,' Jungir ordered.

The Nadir warriors spread out in a circle around the still, motion-less figure of Sukai, his great sword resting lightly on his shoulder. Suddenly the first Nadir ran forward, the others following. Sukai spun on his heel, his sword slicing out and down to cleave through the collarbone and chest of the first attacker. He swivelled and blocked a thrust, cut the head from the sword wielder, dropped to one knee and rammed his blade through the belly of the third man.

Sukai returned the great sword to its scabbard on his back, and waited with hands on hips. At his feet lay three corpses, their blood staining the mosaic floor.

'He is a fine warrior,' said Jungir Khan, his voice cutting the silence.

'Not especially, my lord,' replied Chien, masking his delight. 'I thought the last thrust sloppily executed. A fourth man might well have killed him at that moment.'

Jungir Khan said nothing but waved his hand. Servants moved into the square and the tables were pulled back to allow the bodies to be dragged from the hall. Sawdust was spread on the blood.

The feast continued for another hour, but Jungir did not speak again to the ambassador from the land of Kiatze.

Towards midnight the feasters began to drift away. Chien stood and bowed to Jungir. 'With your leave, my lord?'

The Khan nodded. 'Good fortune follow you on your journey,' he said.

'I am sure that if you will it, then it will be so,' answered Chien. 'My thanks to you for the feast. May the Gods bring you all the blessings you deserve.'

With Sukai following, Chien-tsu marched from the hall.

Back in his rooms he turned to Sukai.

'I apologise,' he said, 'for the affront to your dignity. It was unseemly to have agreed to the Khan's request.'

Sukai bowed low, dipping his head three times. 'No apology is necessary, lord. I live to serve you.'

Chien entered his rooms to find that Oshi had stripped the Nadir linen from the bed and covered the mattress with sheets of fine silk and a coverlet filled with goose down. The servant himself was asleep at the foot of the bed.

Chien removed his clothes and carefully folded them, placing them on the chair by the window. Then he climbed into bed and lay back, wishing that he could enjoy a hot, scented bath.

Oshi rose from the foot of the bed. 'Is there anything you require, my lord?'

'Nothing, thank you.'

Oshi settled down on the floor once more, and Chien stared out of the window at the bright stars. In all probability Mai-syn was dead. He could sense no warmth from her spirit. No more would her laughter be heard under Heaven, no more would her sweet singing grace the night. But he could not be sure and therefore would have to begin, at least, his journey to the south. Yet if she was dead, then once away from the city Chien had no doubt the party would be attacked and slaughtered. Jungir Khan would have no wish for news of his daughter's death to reach the Emperor. No, Chien's murder would be put down to robbers or bandits, and thus the flow of costly presents would continue for at least one more year.

There had to be a way to thwart the Khan. Honour demanded it. For several hours he lay awake. At last a smile touched his face. And he slept.

Despite the closeness of the midwinter solstice the warmth of an early spring was in the air as the questors rode down the long hills into the valley of Kiall's settlement. The young man found his emotions torn as he gazed down on the wooden buildings and the new stockade. He was home – and yet he was not home. All his dreams of childhood were resting here, the ghosts of his youth still playing in the high woods. He knew every bend and turn of the trails, all the secret places, the fallen trees and the hidden caves. Yet the village was changed. The burned-out buildings were no longer in evidence, and twelve new houses stood on the outskirts. Tanai the baker had been killed in the raid, his house and bakery gutted. Now a new bakery stood on the site, and Kiall felt that someone had reached into his memories with a hot knife, cutting and hacking at images dear to him.

Chareos led the small group down into the settlement and on through the unfinished stockade wall to the main square. People stopped their work to watch the riders and a tall, fat man in a tunic of green wool – a wide leather belt straining to hold his bulging belly – marched out to stand before them with brawny arms folded across his chest.

'What do you want here?' he asked, his voice deep, his tone pompous.

Chareos stepped down from the saddle and approached him. 'We are looking for shelter for the night.'

'Well, there's no welcome here for strangers.'

Kiall could stand no more; he lifted his leg over the pommel of his saddle and jumped to the ground. 'I'm no stranger?' he stormed. 'But who, in Bar's name, are you? I don't know you.'

'Nor I you,' said the man. 'State your business – or suffer the consequences.'

'Consequences?' snorted Beltzer. 'What is he talking about?'

'He's talking about the bowmen hidden in the alleyways around us,' explained Finn.

'Oh,' said Beltzer.

Chareos glanced around and saw the archers. They seemed nervous and frightened, their fingers trembling on the drawn bowstrings. At any moment an accidental shot could turn the square into a battle-field, Chareos knew. 'We are not Nadren,' he said softly. 'I came here on the night of the raid and tried to aid the people. The young man here is Kiall, who is of this village.'

'Well, I don't know him and I don't believe I care to,' retorted the man sourly.

'My name is Chareos. It would at least be polite if you told me yours.'

'I don't need to be polite to the likes of you,' said the man. 'Be off with you!'

Chareos spread his hands and stepped closer. Suddenly he seized the man's tunic with his left hand, dragging him forward. His right hand flashed up holding his hunting-knife, the blade point resting against the man's throat.

'I have an abhorrence for bad manners,' he said quietly. 'Now order your men to lower their weapons, or I will cut your throat.'

The man swallowed hard, the action causing his flabby skin to press on the knife point. A thin trickle of blood traced a line to his tunic.

'Put . . . put down your weapons,' the leader whispered.

'Louder, fool!' hissed Chareos and the man did as he was told.

Reluctantly the archers obeyed, but they crowded in to surround the group. Still holding on to the fat man, Chareos turned to the crowd. 'Where is Paccus the Seer?' he called. No one answered him.

Kiall stepped forward. 'Does no one remember me?' he asked. 'What about you, Ricka? Or you, Anas? It's me – Kiall.'

'Kiall?' said a tall, thin man with a pockmarked face. He moved closer to peer at the young warrior. 'It *is* you,' he said, surprised. 'But you look so different. Why have you come back?'

'To find Ravenna, of course.'

'Why?' asked Anas. 'She'll be some Nadir's wife by now – or worse.'

Kiall reddened. 'I will find her anyway. What is going on here? Who is this man? And where is Paccus?'

Anas shrugged. 'After the raid a lot of families chose to move north, to settle nearer Talgithir. New families moved in. He is Norral; he's a good man, and our leader. The stockade was his idea – as were the bows. We are going to defend ourselves in future, Kiall. The Nadren will not find us an easy target the next time they ride into Gothir lands.'

'What about Paccus?'

'He died three days ago.'

In the background, Chareos sheathed his knife and pushed Norral away from him. Beltzer and the others dismounted.

Kiall looked at the rest of the crowd. 'We are not raiders,' he said. 'I am of this village, and we will be leaving come morning to seek the women stolen in the raid. We will bring them back. These warriors with me may not be known to you by sight, but you do know of them. This one is Chareos the Blademaster, and this is Beltzer of the Axe.

The man with the dark beard is the famed archer Finn, and beside him is his friend Maggrig. They are the heroes of Bel-azar, my friends. The other man is a mystic from the lands of the Tattooed People; he will follow the spirit trail that leads us to the saving of our people.'

Anas stared hard at Beltzer. '*He* is the famous axeman?'

'Yes I am, goat brain!' thundered Beltzer, drawing his axe and holding the shining blade under Anas' chin. 'Perhaps you'd like to see more proof?'

'Not at all,' said Anas, stepping back.

Norral stepped alongside Chareos. 'A thousand apologies,' he whispered. 'I didn't know, of course. Please make my home your own. I would be honoured if you would spend the night at my house.'

Chareos nodded. 'That is kind,' he said at last, forcing a smile. 'I also must apologise. You were quite right to be concerned at the appearance of six armed men, and your precautions were commendable.'

Norral bowed.

The food he supplied them was excellent, cooked by his two plump comely daughters, Bea and Kara. But the evening was dominated by Norral, who told them the story of his largely uninteresting life in great detail, punctuating it with anecdotes concerning famous Gothir statesmen, poets or nobles. Each story had the same ending: how the famous complimented Norral on his sagacity, wit, far-sightedness and intelligence.

Beltzer was the first to grab a jug of wine and wander out into the cool night air. Maggrig and Finn soon followed. Unconcerned by the stream of sound from Norral, Okas curled up on the floor to sleep.

Chareos and Kiall sat with the fat farmer until after midnight, but when he showed no sign of fatigue Chareos yawned theatrically. 'I must thank you,' he said, 'for a most entertaining evening. But we will be leaving soon after dawn and, if you will excuse me, I will leave you in Kiall's company. He is younger than the rest of us, and I am sure will learn much from you.'

Rigid with boredom, Kiall contained his anger and settled himself for more of Norral's history. But with the last of the heroes of Bel-azar gone, Norral had no wish to converse with a former villager. He excused himself and took to his bed.

Kiall stood and walked out into the night. Only Beltzer remained awake and Kiall sat down beside him.

'Did the old windbag run out of stories?' the giant asked.

'No. He ran out of listeners.'

'By the Gods, he doesn't need a stockade; he could just visit a Nadren village for an evening. The raiders would avoid this place like a plague pit.'

Kiall said nothing, but sat with his chin resting on his hands staring at the homes around him. Golden light showed in thin beams from the closed shutters of the windows.

'What ails you, boy?' asked Beltzer, draining the last of his wine.

'It is all changed,' replied Kiall. 'It's not my home any more.'

'Everything changes,' said Beltzer, 'except the mountains and the sky.'

'But it was only a few months ago. Now . . . it's as if Ravenna never existed.'

'They can't afford to stay in mourning, Kiall. Look around you. This is a working village; there are crops to be planted, cultivated, harvested; animals to be fed, watered, cared for. Ravenna was last year's crop. Gods, man, we're all of us last year's crop.'

'It shouldn't be that way,' argued Kiall.

'Wrong, boy. It is the only way it *can* be.' He picked up the empty jug and passed it to Kiall. 'What do you see?'

'What is there to see? You finished it all.'

'Exactly. The wine was good, but now it isn't here any more. Worse, I'll piss it against a tree tomorrow – then no one could tell if it was wine or water.'

'We're not talking about wine – we're talking about people. About Ravenna.'

'There's no difference. They mourned . . . now they're living again.'

Soon after dawn Okas vanished into the hills to seek the spirit trails. Kiall wandered in search of Ravenna's sister and found her at the house of Jarel. She smiled and invited him inside where Jarel was sitting by the window, staring out over the mountains. Karyn poured Kiall a goblet of watered wine.

'It is good to see you again,' she said, smiling. She looked so like Ravenna that his heart lurched – the same wide eyes, the same dark hair gleaming as if oiled.

'And you,' he replied. 'How are you faring?'

'I'm going to have Jarel's child in the autumn,' she told him.

'I congratulate you both,' he said.

Jarel swung from the window. He was a strongly built young man with black, tightly curled hair and deep-set blue eyes.

'Why must you pursue this business?' he asked. 'Why chase after the dead?'

'Because she is not dead,' answered Kiall.

'As good as,' snapped Jarel. 'She is tainted . . . finished among civilised people.'

'Not for me.'

'Always the dreamer. She used to talk of you, Kiall; she used to laugh at you for your silly ideas. Well, don't bring her back here, she won't be welcome.'

Kiall put the goblet down on the table-top and rose, his hands

122

shaking. 'I will say this once to you, Jarel. When I bring her back, if there is one evil word from you I will kill you.'

'You?' snorted Jarel. 'Dream on, Kiall.'

Kiall walked forward to where Jarel stood with hands on hips, grinning. He was a head taller than Kiall and far the heavier. Kiall's fist slammed into the bigger man's face, rocking him back on his heels. Blood spurted from his smashed lips and his jaw dropped, then anger blazed in his eyes and he sprang forward – only to jerk to a stop as he saw the long hunting-knife in Kiall's hand. Fear touched him then.

Kiall saw it and smiled. 'Remember my warning, Jarel. Remember it well.'

'I'll remember,' said the farmer, 'but you remember this: no one here wants the women back. So what will you do? Build a new place for them? Two of the men whose wives were taken have remarried. Twenty other families have gone, and no one knows where. What do the captives have to come back to? No one cares any more.'

'I care,' said Kiall. 'I care very much.' He turned to Karyn. 'Thank you for your hospitality.' She said nothing as he sheathed his knife and walked out into the sunlight.

8

Okas sat cross-legged beneath a spreading elm and concentrated on the village below. His vision swam and the buildings blurred and faded like mist under sunlight. He had no control now, and time ceased to have meaning. He saw mountains of ice swelling on the land, filling the hollows, rearing from the peaks. Slowly, reluctantly through the centuries, the ice gave way and the long grass grew. Huge lumbering creatures moved across the face of the valley, their massive limbs brushing against new trees and snapping the stems. Aeons passed and the grass grew. The sharp hills were smoothed by the winds of time. The first oak tree took root on the southern hill, binding the soil. Birds flocked to its branches. Seeds in their droppings caused other trees to grow and soon Okas saw a young forest stretching across the hills.

The first group of men appeared from the west, clad in skins and furs and carrying weapons of bone and stone. They camped by the stream, hunted the great elk and moved on.

Others followed them, and on one bright day a young man walked the hills with a woman by his side. He pointed at the land, his arm sweeping to encompass the mountains. He built a home with a long

123

sloping roof. There was no chimney; two holes were left at the points of the roof's triangle and Okas saw the smoke drifting from them as the snows fell. Other travellers settled close by over the years and the young man, now a leader, grew old.

A savage tribe entered the valley, slaying all who lived there. For some time they took over the homes but then, like all nomads, they moved on. The houses rotted and fell to feed the earth; grass grew over the footings.

Okas watched as the centuries slid by, waiting with limitless patience, judging the passage of time by the movement of the stars. At last he saw the familiar buildings of the near present and moved his spirit close to the village. Focusing on Kiall, he found himself drawn to a small house on the western side. There he watched the birth of a boy, saw the proud smile on the face of the weary mother, saw the happiness in the eyes of Kiall's father as he tenderly lifted his son.

Okas relaxed and let the vision flow. He saw Kiall's mother die of a fever when the boy was first walking, saw the father injured in a fall and losing his life to gangrene from the poisoned wound. He watched the boy – raised by strangers – grow tall. Then he saw the dark-haired girl, Ravenna.

At last he came to the raid, the Nadren thundering into the village with bright swords and gleaming lances.

Okas pulled his gaze from the slaughter and waited until the raiders had taken their captives back into the hills, where wagons stood loaded with chains and manacles.

He followed them for a hundred miles to a stockaded town, but there the vision faded.

He opened his eyes and stretched his back, suppressing a groan as the ligaments above his hip creaked and cracked. The wind was cold on his skin and he was mortally tired.

Yet still there was another flight to be made. The call was still strong and he allowed himself to link to it, his spirit lifting from his body to be drawn swiftly across the Steppes. The mountains were beautiful from this height, cloaked in snow and crowned with clouds. His spirit fell towards the tallest peak, passing through it deep into the dark. At last he entered a cavern where torches flickered on the walls and an old man sat before a small fire. Okas looked at him closely. He wore a necklace of lion's teeth around his scrawny throat, and his thin white beard had no more substance than woodsmoke. When the man's dark eyes opened and fixed on Okas there was pain in them, and a sorrow so deep that Okas was almost moved to tears.

'Welcome, brother,' said Asta Khan. The Nadir shaman winced and cried out.

'How can I help you?' asked Okas. 'What are they doing to you?'

'They are killing my children. There is nothing you can do. Soon they will send their forces against me and that is when I shall require your aid. The demons will fly, and my strength will not be enough to send them fleeing back to the pit. But with you I have a chance.'

'Then I shall be here, brother . . . and I will bring help.'

Asta Khan nodded. 'The *ghosts-yet-to-be*.'

'Yes.'

'Will they come if you ask it?'

'I think that they will.'

'They will face nightmares beyond description. The demons will sense their fears – and make them real.'

'They will come.'

'Why do you do this for me?' asked Asta. 'You know what I desire. You know everything.'

'Not everything,' said Okas. 'No man knows it all.'

Asta screamed and rolled to the floor. Okas sat quietly and waited until the old shaman pushed himself upright, wiping the tears from his eyes. 'Now they are killing the little ones; I cannot block out their anguish.'

'Nor would you wish to,' said Okas. 'Come forth and take my hand.'

The spirit of Asta Khan rose from the frail body. In this form he seemed younger, stronger. Okas took the outstretched hand and allowed his own strength to flow into the shaman.

'Why?' asked Asta once more. 'Why do you do this for me?'

'Perhaps it is not for you.'

'Who then? Tenaka? He was not your lord.'

'It is enough that I do it. I must return to my flesh. When you have need, I will be here.'

Kiall's anger was short-lived. As the questors waited on the edge of the woods for Okas, the young man sat beside Chareos and vented his rage.

Chareos cut across his words. 'Follow me,' he said sharply. The Blademaster stood and walked away into the trees, out of earshot of the others. Once there he turned on Kiall, his dark eyes angry, his face set.

'Do not waste your self-righteous wrath on me, boy. I'll not have it. When the raiders came, you – and all these villagers – did nothing. Of course they *think* they don't want the captives back. And why? Because it would be like looking in a mirror and seeing their own cowardice. They would have to live every day with that mirror. Every time they passed a former prisoner, they would see their own short-comings. Now stop whining about it.'

'Why are you so angry?' Kiall asked. 'You could have just explained it to me.'

'Explained . . .?' Chareos threw back his head and stared at the sky. He said nothing for several seconds and Kiall realised he was fighting for control of his temper. Finally he sat down and indicated that Kiall should join him. The young man did so. 'I don't have time to explain everything, Kiall,' said the older man patiently, 'and I do not have the inclination. I have always believed that a man should think for himself. If he relies on others for his thoughts and his motives, then his brain becomes an empty, useless thing. Why am I angry? Let us examine that for a moment. How do you think the Nadren know which villages to hit, where attractive young women live?'

'I don't know.'

'Then think, damn you!'

'They send out riders to scout?' ventured Kiall.

'Of course. How else?'

'They listen to traders, merchants, tinkers who pass through such villages?'

'Good. And what do you think they are listening for?'

'Information,' Kiall answered. 'I do not understand where this is taking us.'

'Then give me time. How does one village know what is going on at another village?'

'Traders, travellers, poets – all carry news,' said Kiall. 'My father said it was one way in which they encouraged trade. People would gather round their wagons to hear the latest gossip.'

'Exactly. And what *gossip* will the next trader carry?'

Kiall reddened and swallowed hard. 'He will tell the tale of the heroes of Bel-azar who are hunting Ravenna,' he whispered.

'And who will hear of this band of heroes?' asked Chareos – his eyes narrowing, his mouth a thin tight line.

'The Nadren,' admitted Kiall. 'I'm sorry. I didn't think.'

'No, you did not!' stormed Chareos. 'I heard of your dispute with the farmer and your threat with the knife. Bear this in mind, Kiall, that what we do is easy. Understand that. Easy! What the villagers do is hard. Hoping and praying for just enough rain to make the seeds grow and just enough sun to ripen the harvest; never knowing when drought, famine or raiders will destroy your life and take away your loved ones. Do not ever ask me for explanations. Use your mind.'

Finn pushed through the undergrowth. 'Okas is back. He says we have a hundred miles to travel. And it's rough country, for the most part. I've sent Maggrig back to purchase supplies. Is that all right, Blademaster?'

'Yes. Thank you, Finn. We'll set off once he's back and camp away from here. I couldn't stand another night with that sanctimonious bore.'

'Just think, Blademaster. Tonight he'll be entertaining the villagers with how you complimented him. You'll be remembered in future times as Chareos, the friend of the great Norral.'

'There's probably truth in that,' agreed Chareos, chuckling.

He strode through the undergrowth to where Okas was sitting quietly with Beltzer. The old man looked dreadfully weary.

'Would you like to rest for a while?' Chareos asked him.

'No rest. It is a long journey ahead. I will sleep tonight. There is a good camping place some four hours' ride to the south.'

'Is the girl alive?' asked Chareos. Kiall moved in behind him.

'She was when they took her to the fort town,' said Okas. 'I could not see beyond that; the distance is too great for me. And I have no hold on her – but for the love of Kiall. It is not enough. Had I known her, I would be able to find her anywhere.'

'How long for the journey?'

'Maybe three weeks. Maybe a month. It is rough country. And we must move with care. Nadir tribesmen, outlaws, Wolfsheads, Nadren. And . . . other perils.'

'What other perils?' asked Beltzer.

'Demons,' answered Okas. Beltzer made the Sign of the Protective Horn on his brow and chest, and Finn did likewise.

'Why demons?' Chareos asked. 'What has sorcery to do with this quest?'

Okas shrugged his shoulders and stared down at the ground. He began to trace circular patterns in the dust.

Chareos knelt beside him. 'Tell me, my friend, why demons?'

Okas looked up and met Chareos' dark eyes. 'You asked me here to help you,' he said. 'I help you. What if I ask you to help me?'

'You are a friend,' replied Chareos without hesitation.

'If you need me – or any of us – you have only to ask. Are the demons hunting you?'

'No. But there is old man – enemy of Jungir Khan. He lives alone in mountains far from here. He is the one I am pledged to help. But if I go alone, I will die. Yet I must go.'

'Then I shall go with you,' declared Chareos.

'And I,' echoed Beltzer, clapping his large hand on Okas' shoulder.

Okas nodded, then returned to tracing his patterns in the dust. He spoke no more and Chareos left him alone.

Kiall moved alongside Chareos. 'I need to speak with you,' he said, walking away from the others. Chareos followed him to a shaded spot beneath a spreading elm. 'How does this help us find Ravenna?' asked the young man.

'It doesn't, Kiall. We may die here.'

'Then why? Did we come so far for nothing?' Kiall stormed.

'Friendship is not *nothing*. That old man will die without us. What would you have me say? There are few virtues in this world, boy, but friendship is one that I prize. But if you want a reason which has naught to do with honour, then consider this: what chance do we have of finding Ravenna *without* Okas?' Chareos gripped Kiall's shoulder. 'I have no choice, my friend. None at all.'

Kiall nodded. 'I shall go too,' he said.

Maggrig returned with supplies of food – dried meats, oats, salt and a sweet tisane made from dried honey and turmeric root. The questors set off towards the south with Okas and Chareos riding at the front, Kiall, Beltzer and Maggrig following. Finn galloped off into the distance, scouting for sign of raiders or outlaws.

Kiall rode alongside Maggrig. 'The thought of fighting demons terrifies me,' he confided.

'And me,' owned Maggrig. 'I saw the stuffed corpse of a Joining once, when we were in New Gulgothir. A wolfman some ten feet high – he was killed by Ananais, the Drenai hero, during the Ceska wars decades ago. But no demons. Finn had a friend killed by them, so he told me. They were hunting him in his sleep and he would awake screaming. One night he screamed but did not wake. There was not a mark upon him.'

Kiall shivered.

Beltzer dropped back to ride alongside them. 'The Nadir shamen summon the creatures,' he said. 'I knew a man once who survived an encounter with them. He'd robbed a Nadir shrine. Then the dreams began; he was being hunted through a dark wood; he had no weapons, and the beasts came closer to him on each night.'

'What did he do?' Maggrig asked.

'He journeyed to a Temple of the Thirty near Mashrapur. They made him pass over the ornament he'd stolen – a goblet, I think it was. Then two of the warrior priests sat with him while he slept. He dreamt of the wood again – but this time the priests were with him, all dressed in silver armour and carrying swords which blazed brighter than lanterns. They fought off the demons and took the man's spirit to the Nadir shaman that sent them. They agreed to return the goblet and the dreams stopped.'

'He was a lucky man,' said Maggrig.

'Not really. He died soon after in a fight over a tavern whore.'

Beltzer spurred his mount forward and followed Chareos and Okas over a small rise.

Ahead of them was a long valley, and beyond that the seemingly arid, windswept landscape of the Nadir Steppes.

Tanaki rose from her bed, stretched and walked to the window, opening the shutters and staring out over the empty square.

Movement from behind made her turn and she smiled at the newcomer.

128

'It is considered polite to announce yourself, Harokas,' she told the hawk-faced assassin.

He shrugged. 'Not in my line of work,' he said, with a broad grin.

'I had not expected you for some weeks. Tell me you rode day and night to feast your eyes on my beauty.'

'Would that I could, Princess. But I did bring news that will interest you. There is a group of men riding here, intent on rescuing one of the slave women. It is likely your life will be in some danger from them.'

'How many?'

'Six.'

She chuckled. 'You think I should fear six men? I could probably tackle that many myself on a good day.'

'These men are special, Princess. They are led by Chareos the Blademaster. Among them is Beltzer of the Axe – also the bowmen of legend, Finn and Maggrig.'

'The heroes of Bel-azar? What interest can they have in a peasant woman?'

'What, indeed?'

'How did you hear of this?' Tanaki asked.

'They bragged about their mission in a village. The whole of the area is alive with the story.'

'But there is something you are not telling me,' she said, a trace of a smile on her face.

'You are quite correct, Princess,' he replied, opening his arms to her. She stepped in to him and he kissed her; then she pulled away.

'Later,' she told him. 'First tell me all.'

'Oh, no,' he said, sweeping her from her feet and carrying her into the square bedroom at the rear of the hall.

They made love for more than an hour; finally he lay back on the bolster and closed his eyes.

'Now tell me,' she said, raising herself on one elbow and looking down at him.

'You know that if I was the sort of man to fall in love, it would be with you, Princess. You are strong, intelligent, courageous and quick-witted. And in bed . . .'

'Yes, yes. I compliment you also. But tell me!'

'And you are so single-minded. I admire that.' Her face darkened. 'All right, all right,' he said, smiling. 'The Earl has commissioned me to kill Chareos.'

'And you would like me to do it for you?'

'Well, I am getting old and tired.'

'I noticed that,' she said, sitting up. 'And now I have work to do.'

'Why was Tsudai here?' he asked and she turned back to him, wondering if the concern in his eyes was genuine. Deciding it was not, she merely shrugged and stood.

129

'How is it that you hear everything, Harokas? Are you a seer?'

'No, I am a listener. And when Jungir Khan's general rides across the Steppes I know it is not for exercise.'

'He came to buy women, that was all.'

'Now it is your turn to hold something back. Would you like him dead, Princess?'

'No!' she said sharply.

'As you wish. But he hates you – you know that?'

'He says he loves me.'

Harokas grunted and rolled from the bed. 'He wouldn't know the meaning of the word.'

'And you do?' she asked, slipping into her tunic.

'Sometimes I think I do. What will you do about Chareos?'

'I will send out riders today.'

'Send the best, Princess.'

'The heroes of Bel-azar will be dead by the end of the week.'

'Perhaps,' he said softly.

Despite its bleak appearance, the land leading to the Steppes was teeming with life and Kiall found himself fascinated by the wonder of the wild. He had spent his life in the valley and knew of the habits of deer and wild sheep, but out here there were creatures of rare beauty and their behaviour was sometimes both mystic and comical.

High above them on the fourteenth day of their journey he saw great birds with long, rectangular wings, swooping and spiralling in the sky. Recognising them as vultures – but of a type he had not seen before – he spurred his horse to ride alongside Finn, who was some half a mile ahead of the group.

Finn reined in and waited for the young man. 'Is there a problem?' asked the hunter.

'No. I was watching the vultures. Does it mean something is dying?'

'Not death,' answered Finn, smiling. 'Life. They circle like that to find a mate. Watch them closely and you will see the males gliding around the females. Gradually their actions will become like mirror images.'

The vultures soared and wheeled in breathtaking displays.

'Such beauty from creatures of ugliness,' whispered Kiall.

'Why ugliness?' countered Finn. 'Because they feed on carrion? They clean the land, Kiall. In many ways they keep it beautiful.'

'Why do they mate in winter? Does the cold not threaten the eggs?'

'No,' Finn replied. 'When the female lays, she will sit upon the eggs for two months. After they hatch she will feed the young for a further four months. It is a long period for a bird.'

The questors rode on, crossing streams that rippled down from the mountains, swollen now with melted snow. Finn caught three large trout which they cooked for supper on the sixteenth day. He caught them with his hands, which impressed Kiall. The hunter shook his head. 'No great skill, Kiall. Even for them it is the mating season,' he said. 'They settle down in grooves on the shallow stream-bed to lay their eggs. They remain still and, if a man is quick and certain, he can ripple his fingers against their sides and flick them from the water.'

As the days passed more and more wildlife was seen – great crested grebes on shallow lakes; coots; herons in their comical mating dances, leaping on stick-like legs to attract the females; huge black kites swooping, diving, meeting in the air.

Okas withdrew ever more into himself, often riding with his eyes closed, lost in thought. Once he almost fell from the saddle, but Beltzer caught him.

On the afternoon of the seventeenth day Okas moved his pony alongside Chareos. 'We must find a hiding place,' he said.

'Why? Are there enemies close?'

'Yes, those too. But this will be the night of the demons.'

Chareos nodded and rode to Finn. The hunter galloped off towards the west, where rearing rock-faces rose from the snow-speckled ground. By dusk the questors were camped in a deep cave on the side of a hill.

They ate in silence seated around a small, flickering fire. Okas forbade any meat to be eaten and sat with head bowed, eyes closed. At last his head came up and he looked at Chareos.

'This is a night of great peril,' he said softly. 'The forces that will come against you are strong in their evil, powerful in their malice. They have been fed with the deaths of many, many people.'

'Tell us of the old man we are to protect,' invited Chareos. Sweat shone on his face and he could feel the cool breeze of the night on his skin. Watching the swordsman, Kiall felt his fear. Beltzer too remained silent, his small round eyes peering intently at Okas.

'His name is Asta Khan and for many years he was shaman to Tenaka Khan, Lord of the Wolves. When Tenaka . . . died . . . he left tribe and travelled – eventually – to Mountains of Moon. Tenaka's son, Jungir, and his own shaman, have decided it is time for Asta to die. They have sacrificed forty of Asta's blood kin to feed the spirits and weaken the old man. Tonight the demons will fly.'

'Why is he such a threat to Jungir?' Finn enquired.

'He knows a secret which Jungir wishes kept silent. Jungir Khan murdered his father.'

'And that is all?' asked Beltzer.

'Not all,' admitted Okas, 'but all I know for certain.'

'Can we defeat these demons?' asked Beltzer. 'Can my axe cut them?'

'We shall be entering their world. In that place, yes, they can die.

131

But their powers are very great. You are strong, fat Beltzer, but where we travel it is not strength of body but strength of heart which is important. It is a place of faith and miracles, a place of Spirit.'

'How do we go there?' Finn asked.

'You do not go there,' replied Okas. 'Two must remain to protect the fleshly forms of those who fly. You, Finn, are best man for this.'

Kiall's breathing became shallow and he could feel his heart fluttering like a caged moth. But he remained silent.

'I will go,' declared Chareos, 'as will Beltzer.' He looked at Maggrig, then at Kiall. The blond hunter smiled at Kiall, reading his terror.

'I will come with you,' stated Maggrig.

'No,' said Okas. 'You will remain. There are enemies who have discovered our trail and they will come in the night. Your skills with the bow are needed here.'

'Then,' said Kiall, his voice shaking, 'I must come?'

'There is no *must*, my friend,' answered Okas with a gentle smile. 'This is a task for *ghosts-yet-to-be*. Perhaps we can win with only Beltzer, Chareos and myself.'

'I . . . I will come,' said Kiall. 'I began this quest and I will walk where the dangers lie.' He swallowed hard.

Chareos reached over and patted his shoulder. 'Well said, Kiall.'

'You stick close to me, boy,' Beltzer told Kiall, hefting his axe. 'I'll see you safely home.'

'It is time,' said Okas. 'Finn, when we have departed put out fire and watch trails. With good fortune we return by dawn.' He rose and led the three companions deeper into the cave, where they sat in a circle. Okas began to chant in a hissing tongue which the others could not understand. Listening to the chant, Kiall found his mind spinning. Stars swam before his eyes and the roar of rushing rivers filled his ears. Then a darkness fell, a darkness so complete that all sense of being departed from him.

He came to awareness with a sudden blaze of light and found himself standing, with the others, before a fire in another cave. The body of an old man lay there, seemingly asleep. The man's spirit rose from the still form and approached them.

Asta Khan said nothing, but bowed deeply to Okas. The Tattooed Man knelt and traced a large circle in the dust of the cave floor, then rose and took Asta's hand, leading him to the centre of the circle. Asta Khan sat while Chareos, Beltzer, Kiall and Okas grouped themselves around him. Black smoke billowed from the cave walls, closing in on the questors. Beltzer lifted his axe and Chareos and Kiall drew their sabres. A sibilant hissing began from within the smoke.

Okas began to chant and was joined by the voice of Asta Khan. White light shone in the circle, blazing from the blades of the questors.

The smoke parted and a tall figure in black armour came into view.

He was wearing a dark, winged helm with the visor down, and his arms were folded across his chest.

'It is time to die, Asta Khan,' he declared.

Finn knelt beside the still forms of the departed questors, staring silently at the motionless bodies. Then he took up his bow and moved to the cave mouth where Maggrig joined him.

For some time the two men sat in silence there, watching the moonlight on the swaying branches of the trees.

'Anything?' whispered Maggrig.

Finn shrugged. 'You take the trail to the left; I'll watch over the right. But do not move too far from the cave mouth.' Maggrig nodded, and smiled. Notching an arrow to the string, he moved swiftly out into the open and vanished into the undergrowth. Finn waited for several minutes with eyes closed, allowing the darkness to concentrate his hearing. The sounds of the night were many, hidden within the whistling of the wind, the sibilant whispering of the leaves. He opened his eyes and slowly scanned the trail. Satisfied at last, he slipped out into the moonlight and moved to the right. Hiding places were many, but Finn needed somewhere which would supply a killing ground. The bow was not a good night weapon. Distances were hard to judge under moonlight, added to which a good defensive position could prove a death-trap unless there was also a second, safe way out.

He crouched behind a screen of bushes and tried to locate Maggrig. There was no sign of the blond hunter, and Finn smiled. At last he was learning something! An hour passed . . . then another.

Finn closed his eyes and pushed his concentration through the sounds of the night – flattening them, flowing with the rhythms of the land, seeking the discordant. There was nothing – and this worried him. Okas was rarely wrong, and if he said there were enemies close then enemies were close. Finn licked his lips and felt his heartbeat quicken. If he could not hear them or see them, there were only two options to consider: either Okas was wrong, or the men hunting them were as skilled as the defenders. Keeping his actions slow and smooth, Finn dropped lower to the ground and glanced back at the cave mouth. There was no movement that he could see. He stared at the rock-face, allowing his peripheral vision into play. Nothing. Just rocks, and grass, and dark scattered bushes.

Easing himself back, Finn strung his bow and notched an arrow. If the enemy were skilled, then perhaps they had seen him and Maggrig move from the cave. The thought of danger to Maggrig almost made him panic, but he quelled the feeling savagely. If they *had* seen them, then they would now be moving into place to make the kill. Yet Finn had chosen his route with care and his position was a good one. Boulders protected his right flank, there was killing ground ahead and to the left. Behind him was a narrow trail which cut to the right back to the rock-face. Bellying down, he moved on his elbows until he was screened by the undergrowth. He had now lost the advantage of the killing ground on the left, but was protected from immediate attack and knew his enemies could no longer see him.

'This is nonsense,' he told himself. 'There is no one there. You are being frightened by shadows.'

Think, man, think! He put himself in the place of the hunters. You have seen the quarry. What now must you do?

You must make him show himself for a killing shot.

How?

Give him a target. Let him see you. Finn risked a glance to the killing ground now ahead to the right. Yes, that is where I would order a man to walk. Which would mean that Finn would have to rise in order to aim. He flicked his gaze back to the undergrowth behind him. There were only two possible places for an assassin to wait: by the gnarled beech, behind the thick silver trunk, or behind the rounded boulder leading to the cave mouth. Or perhaps both? Finn began to sweat.

The only sensible course was to retreat. The enemy had all the advantages. But to give ground would mean fleeing to the cave and that would bring him into the open. Even if he made it to the rock-face, he would then be trapped inside. And Maggrig would be stranded. Gently placing his bow on the ground, he raised his hands to his face with thumbs pressed together and gave out the low hoot of a night owl four times.

The grunting cough of a badger came from ahead.

Maggrig was still safe. Better still, he knew the danger and had spotted one of the enemy.

Finn dropped below the bushes and edged back, making no sound.

A man carrying a bow moved out into the open ahead of him. For Finn to make the shot he would have to stand. The man angled towards his hiding place and Finn took a deep breath and rose, drawing back on his bowstring. Suddenly he swivelled. Another attacker appeared from behind the boulder twenty paces to the rear; Finn sent an arrow which hammered into the man's skull, then dived to the earth. Two shafts sliced the air where he had been standing. Pushing his knees under him Finn sprinted from his hiding place, hurdling bushes and boulders to drop behind a fallen tree. From here he could see the body of the man he had killed.

Now the game was more to his liking. They had hunted him with great skill, arrogantly confident of their talents. Now one was dead and the others would be nervous. Dropping to his belly once more he crawled back from the tree and, staying flat, notched a second arrow to his bow.

134

The hunters had to attack from the front now. Was there an edge? They had seen Finn was right-handed; therefore they should come from his right. It would give them an extra fraction of a second in which to make the kill. He angled his body to the right and waited.

A warrior carrying a long spear hurdled the fallen tree and Finn shot him in the chest. The man staggered. A second attacker came from the left . . . discarding his bow Finn rolled, came up with his hunting-knife, swerved away from the lunging spear and rammed his blade home into the man's belly. He held the dying man to him and scanned the undergrowth. He could see no one. With a curse he let the body drop and ran to his bow, scooping it into his hand. Just as he straightened he saw a bowman rear up. Finn was dead, and he knew it . . .

An arrow from Maggrig took the bowman high in the shoulder. The man screamed and loosed his own shaft, but it flew to the left of Finn who scrambled back into the bushes.

'The cave, Finn!' shouted Maggrig, breaking all the rules. Finn swung to see three men running across the open ground. He sent an arrow after them, but the distance was too great and his shot was high and wide. Hurling aside his bow, he drew his knife and raced after them.

But they vanished within the cave, and he knew he would be too late.

'Stand firm, or we are all lost,' said Okas. Kiall took a deep breath and watched the swirling smoke.

It vanished to reveal a glittering landscape of stark mountains and tall, skeletal trees devoid of leaves. There were six scaled creatures, their huge mouths rimmed with sharp pointed fangs. They shuffled towards him with arms extended and Kiall recoiled in horror. They had no hands or paws. Instead bloated faces hung from the ends of their arms, sharp teeth gnashing and clicking inside the hollow flesh. Each of the demons was more than seven feet tall, and their horned skin appeared impervious to Kiall's own slender sabre. He glanced to his right, seeking encouragement from Chareos.

But there was no one there.

Alone, Kiall looked to his left. An open door stood there, and through it he could see a green field carpeted with spring flowers. Children played there, and the sounds of their laughter rippled through the beckoning doorway.

The clicking of teeth made him spin. The demons were closer now. He had only to run through the doorway to be safe.

'*Stand firm or we are all lost,*' came the voice of Okas in the halls of his memory.

He thought of Ravenna. If he died here, there would be no one to rescue her. He heard a voice from the doorway.

'Quick, Kiall, run! It is safe here!' He risked a glance and saw his mother, her sweet face smiling, her hand waving.

'I can't!' he screamed. His sword came up. The doorway vanished . . . the demons closed in.

Beltzer blinked in surprise. He had no idea where the others had gone, only that he stood alone before six armed men. They wore black armour, and they carried long swords. There was nothing demonic about them as they waited to attack; their faces were grim, but human.

The giant found his axe feeling heavy in his hands and allowed the head to rest against the ground. Looking down at his hands, he saw that they were wrinkled and covered with dark brown liver spots. His arms were scrawny and thin, his legs just bone and wasted muscle. A cool breeze touched his back and he turned slowly and peered at the land behind him. It rose sharply into a towering mountain. Fresh streams flowed there and the sun shone in glory.

'Go back to the mountain,' said one of the warriors. 'We have no wish to slay an old man who cannot raise his axe. Go back.'

'Chareos?' whispered Beltzer. He licked his gums; there were no teeth there, and he felt a terrible weariness.

'You will be young again on the mountain,' said the warrior. 'Then you will be able to face us. Take a single step back and feel the strength in your limbs.'

Beltzer moved back a pace. It was true. He felt a quickening of his muscles and his eyes cleared a little. All he needed to do was move back on to the mountain and then he would find the strength to face these warriors.

'*Stand firm or we are all lost,*' came the voice of Okas in the halls of his memory.

It needed all of Beltzer's strength to lift the axe. He looked at the grim warriors. 'Come on, then,' he said. 'I'll move no further.'

'Fool!' hissed the leading warrior. 'Do you think to stand against us? We could kill you in an instant. Why not be strong again, and at least give us a good fight?'

'Will you talk all day?' roared Beltzer. 'A good fight? Come on, my boys, earn your pay.'

The warriors bunched together – and charged. Beltzer roared his defiance. His axe was suddenly light in his hands and he countered their charge with his own. His limbs were powerful once more, and his axe smashed and sliced into their ranks. Their swords cut him, but no deep thrust slowed him. Within seconds the warriors were dead, their bodies vanished. Beltzer looked back to the mountain. It was gone and in its place was a deep, yawning pit that vanished into the depths of the earth. He stood with his back to it.

And waited for more foes.

Chareos stood once more on the shadowed walls of Bel-azar, moonlight streaming on the mountain slopes and glistening on the grass of the valley. The dwellers in the dark were moving up the stairwell – and there was no Tenaka Khan to help him.

'This way,' came a soft, female voice and he turned to see a second stairway which led down into the valley. A woman stepped into the moonlight; her beauty made him gasp.

'Tura? Sweet Heaven, Tura?'

'It is I, my love. I cannot bear to see you die. Come with me.'

'I cannot. I must help my friends.'

'What friends, Chareos? You are alone; they have left you. Come with me. I love you, I always loved you. I was such a fool, Chareos, but it can be right again. It can be beautiful again.'

He groaned and his soul yearned for her.

A huge taloned hand smashed the stairwell door to shards.

'Come quickly!' yelled the woman.

'No!' shouted Chareos. He leapt forward and lanced his sword into the beast's gaping mouth, up through the cartilage beyond and into the brain.

'Help me!' Chareos turned and saw a second creature had come from the staircase behind her and was hauling her back into the darkness.

'*Stand firm or we are all lost,*' came the voice of Okas in the halls of his memory.

He screamed in his anguish, but remained where he was. Two more creatures lunged at him; he sidestepped and killed the first with a thrust to the heart, the second with a slashing sweep that cut through its neck.

The sound of laughter came to him and he saw the woman locked in an embrace with the monster at the stairwell. Her face turned to Chareos – it was white as a shroud, the eyes staring, the pupils slitted like those of a cat. Slowly she lifted her leg, stroking it against the demon's thigh.

'You never were much of a man,' she said. 'Why do you think I needed so many lovers?'

He swung away from her, but her words continued to taunt him. 'I slept with them all, Chareos. With Finn, with Beltzer. With all of your friends. I told them all what you were like. I told them how you cried on the first night we made love . . . they laughed at that.'

'Leave me alone!'

Another beast came through the doorway but Chareos ducked under the sweep of its talons and slashed his sabre through its belly. It fell back into the darkness.

Her voice came closer, but the words were softer now. 'I said that to hurt you,' she whispered. 'I am sorry . . . I am so sorry.' Closer she came and Chareos moved back a step. 'Through all that I did,' she continued, 'all the terrible wrongs I did you, you never hurt me. You could never hurt me.' Her arm flashed up. Chareos' sabre slashed through her throat and the head flopped to the floor, the body toppling beside it. The small, curved knife dropped from her fingers.

'No,' said Chareos, 'I could never hurt Tura. But you were not Tura.'

Kiall hacked and slashed at the monsters around him. The fang-lined jaws ripped at his skin and pain flooded him, yet still his sword lanced out to force them back. He slipped and fell and the demons loomed over him. Just then a warrior in black, armed with two short swords, leapt to stand over him, driving the monsters away. Kiall struggled to his feet and watched the warrior. The man's skill was breathtaking; he spun and whirled like a dancer, yet at each move his glittering blades flickered out against the demons. The last beast died and the man walked to Kiall and smiled.

'You fought well,' said the man. Kiall looked into the slanted violet eyes and the hard cruel face.

'Who are you?' he asked.

'I am a friend to Asta Khan.'

Darkness loomed before Kiall's eyes and he blinked . . .

He was back before the fire in the cave. Okas and Asta were sitting together, Beltzer and Chareos standing guard over them.

'Will they come again?' enquired Beltzer.

'I do not know,' answered Okas wearily.

'They will not,' said Asta Khan, his dark eyes glittering. 'Now it is time for my enemies to see *my* power.' He closed his eyes . . . and vanished.

Three hundred miles away Shotza screamed. The first of twelve acolytes, deep in a trance, fell back with his chest ripped open, his heart exploding. Shotza tried to run from the room, but all the doors were barred by a mist that formed like steel. One by one his acolytes died silently, until only the shaman was left.

A figure formed in the mist and Shotza backed away. 'Spare me, mighty Asta,' he begged. 'I was acting under orders from the Khan. Only spare me, and I will help you to destroy him.'

'I do not need your help for that,' said Asta, floating close to the trembling shaman. Asta's spirit hand shot out, the fingers extending

138

into long talons which slid into Shotza's chest. A terrible pain clamped the shaman's heart and he tried to cry out – but died before the scream could sound.

9

Beltzer awoke first. His body was stiff and he stretched. At that moment he saw the attackers running into the cave. He rolled to his knees and came up with his axe. The fire was dead, the light poor. Beltzer bellowed a warcry and charged. Two of the men ran at him, the third ducking and sprinting past the axeman. Beltzer ignored the runner and hammered his axe into the first of the attackers. A sword plunged through his jerkin, narrowly missing the flesh on his hip. Dragging his axe clear of the falling warrior, he backhanded a cut into the second man's ribs, the blade cleaving through to the lungs. Then he spun, ready for an attack from the rear. But the third man was dead, killed by Chareos.

Finn raced into the cave, his knife raised. He stopped as he saw Beltzer and Chareos standing over the three bodies.

'Some watchman you turned out to be,' said Beltzer.

Finn slammed the knife back into the sheath by his side. 'We killed three and wounded a fourth,' he said, 'but they doubled back on us.'

'How many more are there?' asked Chareos, wiping the blood from his blade.

'I don't know,' answered Finn.

'Find out,' Chareos told him. Finn nodded, turned on his heel and ran from the cave.

Beltzer sat down and chuckled. 'A night to remember, eh, Blade-master?'

'Yes,' agreed Chareos absently, turning to where Kiall and Okas still slept. Kneeling, he shook Kiall's shoulder.

The young man opened his eyes and flinched. 'Oh,' he whispered. 'Are we safe?'

'We are back at the cave,' replied Chareos. 'How safe we are remains to be seen. You did well back there.'

'How do you know?' Kiall asked.

'You are alive,' said Chareos simply.

'Shouldn't we be out there helping Maggrig and Finn?' queried Beltzer.

'No. The game being played is theirs. We would be a hindrance.'

Chareos took his tinder-box from his pack, cleared the ash from the fire and started a new blaze. The three men settled around it, enjoying the warmth. A scream sounded from beyond the cave and Kiall jumped.

'That could be Finn or Maggrig,' he said.

'Could be,' agreed Beltzer. 'What about some food?'

'A good idea,' pronounced Chareos and he turned to Kiall. 'Prepare some oats. My stomach is starting to think my throat has been cut.'

'What about Finn?' demanded Kiall.

'He can eat when he gets here,' replied Beltzer, grinning.

Kiall moved back to the packs and took a hide sack of oats. He glanced at Okas. 'He's still sleeping,' he said.

'I doubt that,' said Chareos.

The three questors sat in silence as the oats bubbled and thickened in a copper pot hung over the fire. The thin grey light of pre-dawn brightened the sky as Kiall ladled the food into two wooden platters.

'Not eating?' asked Beltzer as Kiall sat back.

'No, I lost my appetite,' answered the younger man, flicking his gaze to the bloodied corpses. 'How can you think of food with a stench like that in the air?'

Beltzer shrugged. 'It's only meat, boy, and bowels and guts.'

Finn entered the cave moments later and sat down, his eyes red-rimmed and weary. Maggrig followed a few minutes after. Both men ate in silence.

'Well?' asked Chareos, as the meal was finished.

'There were four more of them.'

'Did you get them all?' enquired Beltzer.

'Yes, but it was close. They were skilled, very skilled. What do we do now?'

'We wait for Okas,' answered Chareos. 'You should get some sleep.' Finn nodded and moved to the far corner of the cave, wrapping his lean frame in a blanket and settling down with his head on his saddle.

'They almost took us,' said Maggrig. 'At least one of them had a better position. His shot missed Finn's head by a finger's width.'

'Did you find their horses?' Chareos asked.

'Yes. We stripped the saddles and turned them loose. Finn thinks they were outriders for a larger force – probably the same group that took Ravenna.'

'Then they were hunting us,' said Chareos.

'Of course they were hunting us,' snapped Beltzer.

'That's why there are bodies everywhere.'

'I think Chareos means us specifically,' put in Maggrig. 'They weren't just trying to rob a small travelling party; they were looking for *us*.'

'How did you reach that conclusion?' Beltzer asked Chareos.

'Tell him, Maggrig,' said Chareos.

'First their skill. They were extra careful, which suggests to Finn and me that they knew our strengths. Second, they were prepared to take losses and still keep coming. If we were just a travelling party they would have no way of knowing how much we were carrying – and a few supplies and horses are not worth dying for.'

'So,' said Beltzer, 'the word is out already.'

'It would appear so,' Chareos agreed.

'It is most curious,' said Chien-tsu. 'The Nadir shaman no longer watches over us.' Sukai reined in his grey and gazed down at the camp-site below.

'Perhaps it is because they intend to attack tonight, lord,' said the soldier, dismounting. Chien-tsu lifted his left leg over the pommel of his saddle and jumped to the ground.

'No. They will attack tomorrow at dusk – at least that is the plan the man, Kubai, spoke of when he rode out to meet the killers last night.' Chien would long remember the ugly sound of Kubai's laughter as he spoke with the two Nadir outriders about the massacre of the 'yellow men'. His spirit had floated just above the trio and he had heard himself dismissed as an 'effeminate fool', a 'painted doll' man.

'It is galling,' said Sukai.

'Galling? I am sorry, my mind was wandering.'

'To be forced to meet one's death at the hands of such barbarians.'

'Ah yes, indeed so,' Chien agreed.

'It would have been pleasant to have had a secondary option.' Below them the twenty soldiers had prepared three camp-fires. From his position on the hill-top Chien could see the scout, Kubai, sitting apart from the men. Chien unbuttoned the brocaded red silk coat and scratched at his armpit. 'I shall not be sorry to say farewell to this garment,' he said. 'It is beginning to stink.'

'It was part of your plan, lord,' said Sukai, smiling broadly.

'Indeed it was, but it is dreadfully uncomfortable. Who will wear it tomorrow?'

'Nagasi, lord. He is your height and build.'

'I must apologise to him; it is one thing to die in service to your lord – but quite another to be forced to die in a dirty coat.'

'It is an honour for him, lord.'

'Of course it is, but good manners should be paramount. I will see him this evening. Would it be too great a privilege if we asked him to dine with us?'

'I fear that it would, lord.'

'I think you are correct, Sukai. You and I will dine together – though "dine", I fear, is too fine a description for a meal of broiled hare. However I have some good wine, which we will finish.'

Chien stepped into the saddle and waited for Sukai. The officer mounted his gelding and cursed softly.

'What concerns you, my friend?' asked Chien.

'The man, Kubai. I would dearly like to separate his head from his neck.'

'A thought I can appreciate – and share. However, it is vital that the soldiers of Kiatze commit no crime while in Nadir lands. All we can do is react.'

'As you wish, lord,' muttered Sukai, touching spurs to his mount and guiding the beast down the hill to the camp.

At noon the following day the Nadir scout, Kubai, announcing that he was riding off to hunt, galloped away to the south-west. Sukai watched him go, then turned his horse and halted the column.

Chien-tsu rode alongside him. 'We have four, perhaps five, hours,' said Chien. 'It is time to begin.' Sukai signalled the twenty guards to dismount and they tethered their horses and stood to attention. Chien walked the line in silence, stopping only to admonish a soldier whose bronze and silver hilt-guard showed a trace of tarnish. The man reddened.

'You all know,' said Chien, standing at the centre of the line, 'that treachery awaits us. The Nadir will attack at dusk. It is imperative that they believe they have surprised us, therefore you will be sitting around fires when they come. You may leave your horses saddled. Once the attack begins you may fight as your hearts desire. The Nadir greed and lust for battle shows us that one day they will march on the kingdom of Kiatze itself. With this in mind, it is vital that you account for yourselves well. I would not expect any man to die until he has dispatched at least four of the enemy. There will be no retreat; you will die here.' Chien turned away, then swung round again. 'It would not normally be necessary to add to what I have said, but we are standing under an alien sky and far from home. So let me say this: you are the best warriors, the finest of men. If it were otherwise, you would not now be with me. I shall watch the battle from the hill yonder; then I will ascertain whether Mai-syn lives. After that, I will find Jungir Khan and cut the head from his shoulders. That is all.'

Chien removed his brocaded coat of red silk and called Nagasi to him. The warrior shrugged out of his breastplate and pulled on the garment, then bowed to Chien.

'I will see that Oshi arranges your hair in a more regal fashion,' Chien told Nagasi, then walked away to where Sukai stood close to the wagon. The warrior was staring up at the storm-threatened sky.

'How many will they send against us, lord?'

'I do not know. Why does it concern you?'

142

'If it is less than one hundred we might win, and that would not be in keeping with the plan you have so carefully considered.'

'That is true,' said Chien gravely, 'but I would imagine – following your exhibition at the banquet – that they will want to be certain of the outcome. One hundred would be the barest minimum Jungir Khan would send.'

'And what if we win?' Sukai asked.

'Then you win – and we will think again,' said Chien. 'Now would you be so kind as to cut my hair?'

'The men will see you,' protested Sukai. 'It is not fitting.'

Chien shrugged. 'It is important that I pass for a Nadir nomad. A gentleman of the Kiatze has no hope of survival in this barbarous land. Come now, Sukai,' and he sat on the ground. Sukai took a long pair of brass scissors and began to cut away at the heavily lacquered hair, leaving only a top-knot on the crown. Chien stood and removed his shirt and trousers of blue silk, and his high boots. He lifted the canvas from the back of the wagon and pulled out a Nadir jerkin of goatskin, leather breeches and an ugly pair of high riding moccasins.

'This has been cleaned, I take it?' he asked, holding the goatskin at arm's length.

Sukai smiled. 'Three times, lord. Not a louse nor a single flea remains alive in it.'

'It stinks of woodsmoke,' muttered Chien, shrugging his arms into the garment. He clambered into the pair of ill-fitting breeches and tied the rawhide belt. Lastly he tugged on the moccasins.

'How do I look?' he enquired.

'Please do not ask,' said Sukai.

The warrior summoned Oshi, who brought two horses which were unsaddled and re-equipped with Nadir saddles of rough cut leather. There were no stirrups. 'Bury the other saddles,' instructed Chien.

The warrior nodded. 'Also,' Chien added, 'it would be better if Nagasi died having suffered facial injuries.'

'I have already explained that to him,' said Sukai.

'Then it is time for farewells, my friend.'

'Indeed. May your paths be straight, and your days long.'

Chien bowed. 'Look down on me from Heaven, Sukai.'

The warlord took hold of his horse's mane and vaulted into the saddle. Oshi scrambled to the back of his own mare and the two riders galloped from the camp-site.

Chien and Oshi rode high into the hills, hiding the horses in a thick stand of poplar. Then they sat in silence for an hour, Chien praying, Oshi – looking ludicrous in the clothes of a Nadir warrior – wrestling with the problem of how to look after his lord in the midst of this barren, uncivilised land.

His prayers concluded, Chien rose and moved to a rocky outcrop overlooking the valley below. As ordered Sukai had cook-fires burning, the men relaxing around them. Chien allowed anger to wash over his emotions. It was intolerable that a warrior like Sukai should be sacrificed in such a manner; there was no honour here, in this land of treachery and barbarism. With good fortune his secret messages to the Emperor, carried by his most trusted concubine, would mean no further gifts to the Khan. Perhaps also the news would encourage the Emperor to build up his army.

Oshi crept alongside Chien. 'Should we not put distance between ourselves and the action, lord?' asked the old servant.

Chien shook his head. 'It would be most unbecoming to allow them to die unobserved. If there is a small risk to us, then so be it.'

The sun began its slow descent and Chien saw the dust-cloud to the south-west. His heartbeat quickened and he fought for calm. He wanted to see, with a cool eye, the last moments of Sukai's life. It was his hope – albeit a faint one – that one day he could write a poem about it, and deliver it in person to Sukai's widow.

As the Nadir force topped the hills around the campsite, Chien's trained eye swept over them. There were almost three hundred men in the attacking group and his pride swelled. Here, at last, was a compliment from the barbarians: three hundred against twenty. Chien could almost feel Sukai's joy, watching as the twenty men ran to their horses. Sukai took up his position in the centre, drawing both his swords. Nagasi, in Chien's red coat, was beside him.

Screaming their battle cries the Nadir charged. Sukai, forming the point of a wedge, kicked his horse into a gallop to meet them. Dust swirled under the horses' hooves. Chien made to stand, but Oshi tugged nervously at his jerkin and reluctantly Chien sat. He could see Sukai cutting and cleaving a path through the Nadir ranks, and could just make out the features of the traitor Kubai at the rear. Sukai almost reached him, but a spear was thrust through his throat; he killed the wielder, plunged his second blade into the body of a Nadir warrior and fell from the saddle. The battle was brief, but Chien waited until he could count the Nadir fallen. Almost ninety of the enemy had been killed or wounded.

Kubai rode through the Nadir ranks and dismounted alongside Sukai's body, which he kicked three times. Then he hacked the head from the neck and raised it by the hair, swinging round and finally hurling it away to roll in the dust.

Chien backed away to the horses, Oshi following.

'They fought well, lord,' said Oshi.

Chien nodded and vaulted to the saddle. 'The Khan will pay dearly for Sukai's death. I swear this on the souls of my ancestors.'

Turning his horse to the south-east, Chien led the way towards the

144

distant mountains. His sword on his back, his hunting bow in his hand, he flicked the reins and let the stallion run. The wind was cold on his shaved head, but his blood was hot with the memory of the battle.

The distant mountains rose jagged against the sky, awesome in their size, clouds swirling about their peaks.

'Will we cross them, lord?' asked Oshi fearfully.

'There is a narrow pass that does not offer perils to the traveller. We will go there.'

'Do they have a name, these mountains? Do spirits wander there?'

'They are the Mountains of the Moon . . . and spirits wander everywhere, Oshi. Do not concern yourself.'

'I am concerned only for you, lord. Where will I find food to prepare for you? Where will you bathe? How can I clean your clothes?'

Chien smiled and hauled back on the reins, allowing the stallion to walk. He turned to Oshi. 'I did not bring you with me so that you could serve me. I brought you because you are an old man and a friend, Oshi. You served my father with diligence and loyalty, and me with loyalty and affection. I still remember sitting upon your knee and listening to fanciful tales of dragons and heroes. I remember you letting me drink *seichi*, and eat rice-cakes by your fireside. It was you, Oshi, who cured me of my childhood fears: my nightmares. Do not call me lord any longer. Call me Chien, as you used to when I was a child.'

'You have decided to die then, lord?' whispered Oshi, blinking back tears.

'I do not think that even I can hope to take on the Nadir nation and survive, Oshi. I am pledged to kill Jungir Khan. If necessary I will walk into his palace and do it before all of his generals. Do you believe I can walk away from such a deed?'

'You could kill him with an arrow,' ventured Oshi.

'Indeed. But then he would not know for what crime he is slain. No, it will be with a sword. But first we must ascertain the fate of Mai-syn. Once that is accomplished, we will find a ship for you to return home.'

'I could not leave you, lord . . . Chien. What would I do? What would you do without me? We will kill the Khan together.'

'Someone must take the news back to the Emperor. I will also give you letters to my wives. You will execute my will.'

'You have it all planned then?' asked Oshi softly.

'As much as can be considered at this time. It is all subject to change. Now let us ride, and seek a good camping-site.'

They made camp in a old, dry river-bed, lighting a fire against the vertical bank and eating a light meal of dried fruit. Chien was in no mood for conversation. Unrolling the blanket from behind his saddle, he wrapped it around his shoulders and settled down.

'No, lord, here,' said Oshi. 'I have pushed aside the pebbles and there is soft sand beneath. I have bunched some for a pillow. You will be more comfortable.'

Chien moved to the place Oshi had prepared; it was indeed softer, and away from the cold wind. He settled down to sleep. He dreamt of home in the ivory-white palace, with its terraced gardens and landscaped streams and waterfalls. It was a place of tranquillity. But he awoke sharply when he heard the sound of boots on the pebbles of the river-bed. Rolling from his blanket, he rose. The moon was high, full and bright. Kubai stood staring at him with a wide smile on his face, beside him four Nadir warriors. Oshi awoke and huddled against the rocks.

'Did you think I could not count?' asked Kubai. 'I searched for you among the bodies. You know why?'

'Pray tell me,' said Chien, folding his hands across his chest.

'Because of him,' he replied, pointing at Oshi. 'His body was nowhere. So I examined the corpse we took to be yours. There was a gash on the face, but not enough to fool me.'

'Your intelligence staggers me,' said Chien. 'You are quite correct. I took you for an evil-smelling, stupid, treacherous barbarian. I was wrong; you are not stupid.'

Kubai laughed. 'You cannot make me angry, yellow man. You know why? Because tonight I will hear you scream. I will take your skin an inch at a time.' Kubai drew his sword and advanced but Chien stood waiting, arms still folded. 'Are you not even going to fight, yellow man?'

Chien's arm flicked out and Kubai stopped in his tracks, the ebony handle of the throwing-knife jutting out from his throat. Chien leapt and his foot cracked against Kubai's head, cartwheeling him from his feet. The other Nadir rushed in. Ducking under a sweeping blade Chien stabbed his hand, fingers extended, to the man's midriff. The warrior doubled over, all breath gone from his lungs. Sidestepping a thrust, Chien hammered the edge of his palm into a second warrior's throat. Hurling himself forward, he rolled to his shoulder on the pebbles and came to his feet in one smooth motion. The remaining two Nadir came at him more carefully. Chien's hand snaked out and one of them crumpled to the ground with a dagger through his eye. The last warrior backed away, but Oshi reared up behind him, plunging a thin dagger through his heart.

'You must not take risks,' Chien told him. 'You are too old.'

'I am sorry, lord.'

Kubai had pulled the blade from his throat and was kneeling on the stream-bed, blood gushing to his goatskin jerkin. Chien knelt before him and gathered his blade.

'In case it is of any interest,' he said, 'your lungs are filling with blood. It is said that a man can experience the most delightful visions at such a time. You, on the other hand, deserve no such joy.'

Chien slammed the blade into Kubai's heart and pushed the body on to its back.

'I was having the most wonderful dream,' said Chien. 'I was in the gardens at home, and – you recall the plant we tried to train by the dry stone wall at the south gate?' Oshi nodded. 'Well, it was in bloom, and the flowers were quite the most exquisite shades of purple. And there was a fragrance I recall that put my roses to shame. I wonder if that purple plant ever took root?'

'I would imagine so, lord. You have a fine touch with flowers.'

'It pleases me to think so.'

A groan came from the Nadir Chien had winded and the Kiatze warrior stood and hammered a kick to the man's temple. His neck cracked and Oshi winced.

'What was I saying? Oh yes, flowers. This land could do with more flowers. Perhaps then the Nadir would become interested more in poetry than war. Saddle the horses, Oshi. This ugly place is making me melancholy.'

For three weeks the questors travelled only by night, hiding by day in woods or jagged hollows which stretched across the land. The journey in darkness was taken with great care, as the land descended in giant steps from rocky plateau to rocky plateau. The trails were scree-covered and treacherous, and the questors were often forced to dismount and lead their horses.

Four times Okas warned them of hunters, and twice the hidden questors saw bands of Nadren riders searching for sign. But Finn had obscured their trail and the hunters passed on.

Water was scarce on the Steppes and they were compelled to take wide detours to seek rock pools in the plateaux. Most of these were guarded and many times the questors were forced to move on, their throats dry. What little water they carried was used to rinse the dust from the nostrils and mouths of their mounts.

'Our enemies have all the advantages,' said Finn, as they made their third dry camp in as many days. 'They know we cannot travel without water, and they have stopped trying to track us. Now they guard all the wells and pools.'

'Not all,' said Okas. 'There is rock tank an hour's ride from here. The water is shallow, but good to drink.'

'Why is it not guarded?' Chareos asked.

'It is, but not by men.'

'If there are more demons,' croaked Beltzer, 'I'd just as soon suck grass for another day.'

'Not demons,' said Okas. 'Lions. But do not fear; I have a way with beasts.'

With a half moon to guide them the questors set off across the plateau, their horses' hooves muffled by cloth shoes. The trail wound down at first, then cut to the right, rising steeply. The horses grew increasingly nervous as the smell of lion droppings filled the air. Okas led the way on foot and the trail opened to a wide bowl-shaped arena. They saw eight lions by the pool – one male, three females and four cubs. The females rose first, baring their fangs. Okas began to chant softly; he walked slowly towards the beasts and sat some ten paces from them. The sound of his rhythmic song echoed in the rocks and a lioness padded towards him, circling him, her tail thrashing. She pushed her face against Okas' shoulder and head, then settled down beside him. The other lions ignored the old man.

Okas' voice sounded inside Chareos' mind: *'Lead the horses to the pool. Let them drink their fill. You do likewise and fill the water-sacks. Then withdraw. Let no one speak.'* Chareos turned to the others and lifted his fingers to his lips. Finn nodded, and silently they made for the water.

The song of Okas continued as the questors led the frightened horses to the pool. The need for water overcame their fear and they dipped their heads and drank. Chareos dropped to his belly and filled his mouth with the cool liquid. For some moments he held the water there, then he allowed it to trickle into his dry throat. Finally he drank until he felt he could contain no more. Only then did he fill the water-sacks. The others followed suit.

Kiall ducked his head under the surface of the pool. 'That was good,' he said as he sat up.

The lion roared. The horses reared and Beltzer almost lost grip of the reins. The lion rose and padded across towards Kiall.

'Make no move!' came the voice of Okas in Kiall's mind. *'Sit still. Absolutely still.'*

The lion prowled around Kiall, baring its yellow fangs. The song of Okas came louder now, hypnotic in its rhythm. The lion's face loomed before Kiall's eyes, the fangs brushed his skin and he could smell the creature's fetid breath. Then the lion padded back to the pride and settled down. Kiall rose unsteadily. Chareos had gathered the reins of Kiall's mount and passed them to him silently; slowly the group retreated from the pool, down the long slope and out on to the plateau.

Okas joined them and the party rode on for an hour, camping just before daybreak in a shallow lava ditch.

Finn clapped Kiall's shoulder. 'Not many men have been kissed by a lion,' he said. 'It will be something to tell your children.'

'I thought he was going to tear my head off,' said Kiall.

'I thought of doing the same,' snapped Chareos. 'Did you not see the sign for silence? Did you take lessons in stupidity, or does it come naturally?'

'Leave him be, Blademaster,' said Finn. 'You were young once. Do you know why the lion nuzzled you, Kiall?'

'No.'

'He has scent glands in his mouth. Lions often mark their territory with them. You were lucky – mostly they urinate to establish the borders of their domain.'

'In that case I feel doubly lucky,' said Kiall, smiling. He turned to Okas. 'How long before we reach the Nadren settlement?'

'Tomorrow . . . the day after.' The old man shrugged. 'The hunters are everywhere. We must continue to move with care.'

'Will Ravenna still be there, do you think?' Kiall asked Chareos.

'I would doubt it. But we'll find out where she went.'

'I'm sorry for that mistake,' apologised Kiall, seeing that Chareos was still angry.

The older man smiled. 'Finn was right, we were all young once. Do not allow mistakes to become a habit. But there is something we must talk about. There is no way we can rescue all the women who may be held by the Nadren – we are not strong enough – so prepare yourself for disappointment, Kiall. It will be wonderful if we can establish where Ravenna was sent, but there is no more than that to be gained. You understand?'

'But if they are there, we must make the attempt, surely?'

'What purpose would it serve? You have seen yourself the difficulty we are experiencing just getting to the settlement. Can you imagine what chance we would have of getting out?'

Kiall wanted to argue, to find some compelling reason why Chareos was wrong. But he had seen the arid lands of the Steppes and knew that they would have no chance to escape, encumbered by perhaps twenty freed captives. Yet he could not bring himself to answer Chareos. He looked away and stared at the stars.

'I know that you made a promise, Kiall,' continued Chareos. 'I know what that means to you. But it was a foolhardy promise. All life is compromise, and a man can do only his best.'

'As you say, I made a promise,' returned Kiall. 'And, yes, it was foolish. But perhaps I can buy them back? I have gold.'

'And they would sell them to you – and a day later, or even before, they would ride after you, kill you and take back what they sold. We are not dealing with men of honour.'

'We shall see,' said Kiall. 'It may all be as you say. But let us not decide until the day comes.'

'When the sun rises, the day has come,' said Chareos.

Kiall settled down to sleep, but his thoughts were many. He had dreamt of riding off like a knight in pursuit of his love; he had pictured her returning beside him, her gratitude and love sustaining him. But it was almost four months now since she had been taken and he was as likely to find her wed to a savage, or dead. As for the other women, many of them he had not known too well. He had always been shy in female company, and they had laughed at his blushes. Lucia, the baker's daughter, had always been kind to him. But what could he offer her now? Her father was dead, her home burned. If he took her back she would have nowhere to live, and would probably be forced to find employment in Talgithir. Then there was Trianis, the niece of Paccus the seer. Again there were no living relatives. He ran the names of the captives through his mind: Cascia, Juna, Colia, Menea . . . so many.

Chareos was right. How could they attempt to rescue twenty or more young women and then spirit them across the Steppes?

Yet, if they did not at least try, then Kiall would have branded himself both a liar and a braggart.

Kiall slept fitfully into the day. Soon after dusk the questors set off, avoiding skylines, keeping to the low ground. At last Okas led them up a winding deer trail and halted within a clearing surrounded by poplar trees. There he dismounted and moved off to the brow of a low hill. Chareos and the others joined him there and found themselves overlooking a large settlement. A tall stockade wall was built around the town, with four wooden turrets at each corner. Inside there were some sixty dwellings and a long hall. Guards paced the battlements, and lanterns were hung over the gates.

'It's more like a cursed fortress,' said Beltzer.

'We're not here to attack it,' Chareos told him.

'Thank the gods for that,' said Beltzer.

Chareos studied the layout of the buildings and the movements of the people within the town. It was just after dawn and few of the town dwellers could be seen. Two women carrying wooden buckets on yokes walked to the rear of the stockade and out through a side exit. Chareos focused his attention on this; it was shaped as a portcullis, with a heavy metal block that was raised by turning two spoked wooden wheels situated on the battlements.

Chareos eased his way back from the skyline and joined the others.

'I can see no way for us to gain entry without being seen,' he told them, 'unless we have someone on the inside.'

'Who?' asked Beltzer.

'I'll go myself,' proposed Chareos.

'No,' said Kiall. 'It makes no sense to send our leader into peril. What would the rest of us do if you were taken? No, I will go.'

'What will you tell them, boy?' chortled Beltzer. 'That you've come for your lady and they'd better surrender her or else?'

'Something like that,' said Kiall. He pushed himself to his feet and walked to his horse. Swiftly he emptied his saddlebag of gold, keeping only a single red gold ring, then he returned to the group. 'I shall tell their leader, whoever he is, that I am willing to buy back the women taken. If he is agreeable, I will signal you from the ramparts; I will raise my right arm and wave. If I think there is treachery in the air, I will raise my left.'

'What are we supposed to do then, general?' sneered Beltzer. 'Storm the citadel?'

'Be silent, you oaf!' snapped Chareos. 'So far the plan is sound. At midnight Finn and I will be at the southern wall. If you have not signalled in that time, we will come in and look for you. Be careful, Kiall. These men are killers. Life means nothing to them.'

'I know,' Kiall replied. As he walked to his horse and mounted, Okas' voice came into his mind.

'*I will be with you, seeing through your eyes.*'

He smiled at the Tattooed Man and touched heels to his horse.

The sun was bright as he headed down the grass-covered slope towards the settlement. Looking up at a sentry who had notched an arrow to his bow, Kiall waved and smiled. The gates loomed and he rode through. Sweat trickled to his back and he could not bring himself to look up at the archer. He guided the mount to a hitching-rail and dismounted. There was a well nearby and he hauled up the bucket and drank from a rusty iron ladle.

He heard the sound of moving men and turned slowly to see four guards approaching him with swords drawn. He spread his hands. 'There is no need for violence, my friends. I am here to buy a woman – maybe two.'

'Let's feel the weight of your gold,' answered a tall man.

Kiall dipped his hand into his pocket and came up with the ring. He tossed it to the man, who examined it closely.

'Very nice,' he said. 'And the rest?'

'Hidden until we complete our business.'

'Hidden eh? Well, I know a few tricks that always make a man sing out his secrets.'

'I am sure that you do,' said Kiall. 'Now take me to whoever is the leader here.'

'How do you know it's not me?' the man asked, sneering.

Kiall's temper flared. 'I do not. I merely assumed the leader would have more than half a brain.'

'You cowson!' The man's sword came up and Kiall leapt to the right, drawing his sabre.

'Leave him be!' roared a voice and the men froze. A tall man, dressed in black, came walking through the crowd which had gathered beyond the group.

'What's this to do with you?' asked the swordsman.

'I know this man,' he answered, 'and I do not want to see him killed.' Kiall looked closely at the speaker. He was hawk-faced and lean, and a jagged scar showed on his cheek; his nose was hooked, his features dark and hard. But Kiall had never seen him before.

'Why push that long nose of yours into another man's business, Harokas?' sneered the swordsman.

The man smiled coldly and drew his own sabre. 'You brainless dolt, Githa! You never saw the day dawn when you could best me with a blade.'

Githa swallowed nervously and backed away, aware that he had gone too far.

'Enough!' bellowed Kiall, doing his best to copy the authoritative tone used by Chareos. Both men froze. 'You,' said Kiall, moving forward to stand before Githa. 'Hand me the ring and go back to the ramparts.' The man blinked sweat from his eyes and happily obliged. He did not look at Harokas, but sheathed his sword and hurried away. With the excitement over, the crowd dispersed. Harokas grinned and shook his head.

'Not bad for a farm boy,' he said. 'Not bad at all. I see that Chareos has trained you well. Is he close by?'

'Perhaps. Are you a friend of his?'

'No, but I need to see him. I have been looking for you for almost four months.'

'Why?'

'I have a message from the Earl,' said Harokas. He lifted a ladle of water from the bucket and sipped it. 'But what are you doing here, Kiall, so far from home?'

'If you are from the Earl, then you must know already. This is where the women from my village were taken.'

'And you have come to win them back? How noble of you. A shame, though, that you have arrived too late. The last of them was sold off months ago. This is only a market town, Kiall. Every three months or so Nadir merchants and princes come here to buy slaves.'

Kiall swallowed back his frustration. 'How is it then that you – an Earl's man – are welcome here?'

'I am welcome in many strange places. Come, I will take you to the leader you enquired about. Perhaps then you will find answers.'

Kiall followed the tall man through the alleyways and out into the main square. Here was the hall he had seen from the hill. Harokas entered the building and led Kiall to a curtained area at the rear.

A woman rose from a satin-covered divan and strode to meet them. Her hair was short-cropped and dark, her eyes wide and slanted, her lips full. She wore a black tunic belted at the waist, and her long legs were bare. Kiall blinked and tried not to stare at her. She stood before him, too close, and he shifted his feet, trying to put more distance between them. He looked into her eyes, noting that they were blue tinged with purple.

'Well,' said Harokas, 'you have your wish, Kiall. Here is the leader you asked to meet.'

Kiall bowed, aware that he was blushing. 'I am pleased to . . . that is . . . I . . .'

'Is he retarded?' she enquired of Harokas.

'I do not believe so, Princess.'

'What do you want here?' she asked Kiall.

He took a deep breath. 'I am seeking a woman.'

'Does this look like a brothel?' she snapped.

'No. Not at all. I meant that I was seeking a special woman. She was taken from my village and I want to buy her back.'

'To buy? Our prices here are high. Can you afford her?'

'I believe that I can. How high?'

'That would depend,' said the woman, 'on how beautiful she is.'

'Her name is Ravenna. She is the most beautiful . . .' He stumbled to a halt and found himself staring into her eyes. In that moment he realised that Ravenna could never be called beautiful, not when compared with the woman before him. He felt like a traitor even to think such thoughts. 'She is . . . I think she is . . . beautiful,' he stammered, at last.

'You are riding with the heroes of Bel-azar?' she asked. Her words sent a cold chill through him. For a moment only he hesitated, considering the lie.

'Yes,' he answered.

She nodded. 'It is always better to be truthful with me, Kiall,' she told him, taking his arm and leading him back to the divan. With a wave of her hand she dismissed Harokas; leaving Kiall standing, she stretched herself out on the couch, her head resting on a blue silk-covered cushion. 'Tell me of the heroes,' she said.

'What would you have me say? They are strong men, courageous, skilful in the ways of war.'

'And why would they be interested in this . . . this girl?'

'Merely to see her safe and restored to her . . . loved ones.'

'And you are a loved one?'

'No. Well . . . yes.'

'Is it no or yes? Sit by me and explain it.' He perched on the edge of the divan, feeling the warmth of her leg against his. He cleared his throat and told her of his love for Ravenna and her decision to marry the farmer Jarel.

'I don't blame her. She was right, of course. I was . . . am a dreamer.'

'And you have no other woman?' she asked.

153

'No.'

'No stolen kisses in high meadows, no soft touches during secret trysts?'

'No.'

She moved up to sit alongside him, her arm draped over his shoulder. 'One last question, Kiall, and be sure to answer it honestly. Much depends on it. This quest of yours – have you told me the whole truth? All you seek is the girl, Ravenna?'

'I have told you the whole truth,' he said. 'I swear it.'

For several seconds she looked into his eyes, then she nodded and smiled. Her hand slipped from his shoulder and she replaced the small dagger in its hiding place behind the cushion.

'Very well, I will consider what you have said. But I make no promises. Go out into the square and find Harokas. He will see that you are fed.' He rose and bowed awkwardly. As he turned to leave, she suddenly spoke. 'Tell me, Kiall, do you trust me?'

'I would like to, my lady. It ought to be that a man could put his faith in beauty.'

She rose smoothly and moved in to him, her body pressing against him, her arms on his shoulders and her mouth only inches from his. 'And can you put your faith in beauty?'

'No,' he whispered.

'You are quite correct. Go now.'

10

'I am growing tired of sitting up here,' declared Beltzer. 'What is he doing? Why does he not signal?'

'He has met the leader,' said Okas, moving in to sit by Beltzer. 'It was interesting meeting.' The old man chuckled. 'It will be more interesting yet.'

'Why?' asked Chareos. 'Who is he?'

'It is not a *he*, Blademaster. It is a she.'

'Then he is in no danger at present?' enquired Chareos. The smile faded from Okas' face.

'Of that I am not certain. There was a moment when he spoke with her when his danger was great. I felt she would kill him. But something stayed her hand.'

'We shouldn't have sent him,' said Maggrig. 'He does not have the experience.'

154

'Not so,' said Okas, 'I believe it is lack of experience which keeps him alive down there. The woman is hard, very hard. But, whatever else, she finds Kiall . . . of interest.'

'She wants him in her bed, is that what you're saying?' put in Beltzer.

'Perhaps; she is certainly a predatory woman and it is often the way that such people find innocence attractive. But there is more, I can feel it. She questioned him about all of you.'

'And he told her?' Beltzer hissed.

'He did. That is what, I believe, saved his life.'

'But if she is the leader,' said Chareos, 'then it is she who has been sending out the hunters to kill us.'

'Exactly,' replied Okas. 'Curious, is it not?'

'There is something missing here,' said Chareos.

'Yes,' Okas agreed. 'There is something else also. There is a man in the settlement who saved Kiall. His name is Harokas and he told Kiall he wishes to talk with you, Chareos.'

'Harokas? The name is not familiar to me.'

'He says he has a message from the Earl, whatever that may mean.'

'Nothing good, I'll wager,' muttered Beltzer. 'So, what do we do?'

'We wait,' said Chareos.

'She could have armed men moving in on us,' argued Beltzer.

'Indeed she could,' agreed Chareos. 'Even so – we wait.'

'I do not know why you are still alive, farm boy,' said Harokas, as he and Kiall sat at a bench table in the crowded eating-house. 'Tanaki is not usually so gentle with enemies.'

'I am not her enemy,' Kiall told him, spooning the last of the hot broth to his mouth.

'Are you not?'

'Why should I be?'

'It was here that your beloved was dragged to the auction block. Does that not make you angry?'

Kiall sat back and stared into the cold eyes of the scarred man. 'Yes, it does. Are you saying it was . . . Tanaki . . . who led the raid?'

'No,' answered Harokas. 'Tanaki merely controls the auctions. Nadren raiders travel here from all over the Steppes. You should see this place at market time; it's a revelation.'

'I still do not understand how an Earl's man is welcome here,' said Kiall.

Harokas chuckled. 'That is because you do not . . . yet . . . understand the ways of the world. But I see no harm in instructing you. You will learn soon enough. You know, of course, that the Lord Regent outlawed the slave trade a decade ago?'

'Yes. And ended the serf laws. It was good policy.'

155

'That depends on your viewpoint. If you were a slave or a serf, indeed yes. But not if you were a nobleman. The wealth of the nobility used to depend on land. Not any more – not with the fear of Nadir invasion. Crops bring profits, to be sure, but then the Gothir lands are rich and food is cheap. No, the real profit was always in slaves. The Lord Regent did not take this into account with his new laws. Are you beginning to understand me?'

'No,' admitted Kiall.

'So slow? I took you for an intelligent man – but then you are also a romantic and that must cloud your reason.' Harokas leaned forward. 'The nobility never gave up the trade; they merely found another way of continuing. The raid on your village was sanctioned by the Earl. He takes a share of the profits and I am here to make sure his share is just.'

Kiall felt the taste of bile in his mouth. He swallowed hard and took a sip of the ale Harokas had purchased. 'We pay him taxes. We look to him for protection. And he sells us out to line his pockets?'

'It is not a nice world, is it, farm boy?'

'Why tell me this? Why?'

Harokas shrugged. 'Why not? Your chances of leaving here alive are negligible. And anyway, perhaps I am sick of it too.' He rubbed his eyes. 'I am getting old. There was a time when I believed in heroes – when I was young, like you. But there are no heroes – at least not the ones we want to see. Every man has his own reason for every deed. Usually it is selfish. Take your friends. Why are they with you? You think they care about Ravenna? No, they seek to recapture lost glories, lost youth. They want to hear their names in song again.'

'I do not believe that,' said Kiall. 'Chareos and the others have risked their lives for me – and for Ravenna. And you cheapen them, merely by speaking their names. Thank you for the meal.'

Kiall rose and left the table. The air outside was crisp and fresh, and he strode to the battlements. The two sentries ignored him as he gazed out over the land. He did not look in the direction of the camp, but waited until the voice of Okas sounded in his mind.

'What do you have to tell us?' asked Okas.

'Nothing,' replied Kiall. 'Tell Chareos not to come to the wall. I am waiting to see the woman, Tanaki.'

'Be careful in her company. She has killed before, and will kill again.'

'I will be careful. But she . . . disturbs me.'

He felt Okas drift from him and returned to the central square. The auction platform was large, supported by six piers of round stone. He pictured Ravenna standing upon it, surrounded by Nadir men ogling her, desiring her. He closed his eyes and tried to imagine her. But all he could see were the eyes of Tanaki, wide and slanted.

A man tapped his shoulder, making him jump.

'I thought it was you,' said Chellin. For a moment Kiall did not recognise the stocky warrior, then he smiled.

'You are a long way from the mountains, Chellin. I am pleased to see you made it safely.'

The man sat down on a bench seat and scratched at his black and silver beard. 'It wasn't easy. You came a long way. How are your friends?'

'Alive,' answered Kiall.

'No mean feat, considering the number of men sent out to kill them.'

'I'm glad you were not with them,' said Kiall.

'I was. We got back this morning. Still, with luck you'll sort out your difference with the Princess and we won't have to meet on a battlefield.'

'The Princess?'

'Tanaki. Did you not know she was Nadir royalty?'

'No, I did not.'

'She's the youngest child of Tenaka Khan.'

'What is she doing here?' asked Kiall, amazed.

Chellin laughed. 'You don't know much about the Nadir, do you? To them women are nothing, worth less than horses. Tanaki had some sort of falling out with her brother, Jungir; he had her banished here.'

'She is very beautiful,' said Kiall.

'She is that – and the most desirable piece I ever saw. A man could die happy if he bedded her.'

Kiall reddened and cleared his throat. 'Where will you go from here?' he asked.

Chellin shrugged. 'Who knows? North again. Maybe not. I'm tired of this life, Kiall. I may head south, to Drenai lands. Buy a farm, raise a family.'

'And have raiders descend on you to steal your daughters?'

Chellin nodded and sighed. 'Yes. Like all dreams, it doesn't bear close examination. I hope matters work well with you and the Princess. I like you; I hope they don't ask me to kill you.' Chellin rose and wandered away but Kiall sat where he was for another hour. Then a warrior came seeking him.

'You are wanted,' said the man. Kiall stood and followed him back to the long hall.

Tanaki waited, as before, on the divan. She was dressed now in a short tunic of white linen, her legs and feet bare. She wore no jewellery or ornament, save for the silver buckle on her wide black belt.

As he approached she rose. 'Welcome to my hearth, Kiall. Sit and talk with me.'

'What would you have me say, lady?'

'Very little. Just give me a compelling reason why I should not have you killed.'

'Do you kill for no reason?' he asked.

'Sometimes,' she told him. 'Is that so surprising?'

'I am becoming inured to surprises, Princess. Tell me, will you help me find Ravenna?'

She took his hand and led him to the divan, sitting beside him with her arm resting on his shoulder. 'I am not sure that I will. You know I sent men out to kill you?'

'Yes,' he whispered, aware of her breath warm on his cheek and neck.

'I did that because I heard that a group of heroes was riding out to revenge a raid. I thought you were coming to kill me.'

'That was never our intention.'

'And then I find a tall, handsome young innocent, seeking a woman who does not care for him. This man intrigues me.' Her lips touched his neck and her right hand moved across his chest, sliding down over the tense muscles of his stomach. His face felt hot, his breathing shallow. 'And I wondered,' she went on, her voice low and dreamy, 'how it was that a man who has never known love could risk so much.' Her hand slid lower.

His fingers clamped to her wrist. 'Do not toy with me, lady,' he whispered, turning in towards her. 'You know that I find your beauty . . . irresistible. But I have little . . . self-worth as it is. Just tell me where Ravenna is – and let me leave you.'

For some time she held his gaze, then she pulled back. 'How delightfully you turn me away – not with strength, but with admitted weakness. You put the decision in my hands. Very well, Kiall. But you do not wish to know where she is. I mean that, almost tenderly. I asked you to trust me this morning and now I ask it again. Leave this quest, and return to your home.'

'I cannot, lady.'

'You will die. Your friends will die. And it will be for nothing.'

He lifted her hand and gently kissed the palm. 'Then that is as it must be. But tell me.'

She sat up. 'The girl Ravenna was bought by a man named Kubai. She was sent to a city not far from here and given as a gift to another man. Then she was taken far across the Steppes to Ulrickham.'

'I shall go there. And find her.'

'She was given to Jungir Khan.' The words struck Kiall like knife-blades and he closed his eyes, his head bowing. 'So you see,' she said tenderly, 'there is no point to this quest. Ulrickham is a fortress city. No one could enter the Khan's harem and spirit away one of his brides. And even if you did – where could you go to escape his vengeance? He is the Great Khan; he has half a million men under his command. Where in all the world could you be safe from him, or his shamen?'

Kiall looked at her and smiled. 'Still I must make the attempt. And somehow it is worse now – not because of Jungir, but because of you.'

'I do not understand you.'

He stood and shook his head. 'I cannot say it. Forgive me. Do I have your permission to leave?'

For a moment it seemed as if she would speak, but she merely nodded her head. He bowed and walked from the hall.

His thoughts were many as he rode from the town and a great sadness filled him. He knew now that he did not love Ravenna; she was the dream of an adolescent, the unattainable beauty. But what could he do? He had made his promise. And, though it cost him his life, he would keep it.

He heard the sound of hoof-beats and turned in the saddle.

Harokas cantered alongside him and drew rein. 'May I ride with you?' he asked.

Kiall reined in his horse. 'I do not desire your company, sir. But if you wish to meet with Chareos, then I will not stop you.'

'Then that must suffice,' said Harokas. Kiall spurred his horse into a run and the beast was blowing hard by the time they reached the hilltop. Harokas followed at a more sedate pace. Chareos, Beltzer and Okas were seated in the clearing, but of Maggrig and Finn there was no sign. Kiall dismounted and he started to tell Chareos about Ravenna, but the Blademaster waved him to silence. 'I know,' he said, his gaze fixed on the rider following Kiall.

Harokas slid from the saddle and bowed to Chareos. 'I have searched for you for a great length of time,' he said. 'I have a message from the Earl. You have been cleared of all charges – and would be welcome at any time in the city of Talgithir. Captain Salida told the Earl of your valiant assistance at the Tavern Town.'

'Is that all?' asked Chareos coldly.

'Indeed it is. Now will the bowmen show themselves?'

'I find it hard to believe in the Earl as a forgiving man,' said Chareos, 'and I am wondering why he should send a warrior in search of me. Could it be that you are an assassin?'

'All things are possible, Chareos,' replied Harokas, smiling.

'I think we should kill him,' said Beltzer. 'I don't like the look of him.'

'And I do not like the look of you, you fat oaf!' snapped Harokas. 'Now keep silent before your betters.'

Beltzer pushed himself to his feet and chuckled. 'Let me break his back, Chareos. Just say the word.'

159

Finn emerged from the undergrowth. 'Chareos!' he called. 'You'd better see this: there's an army of Nadir warriors moving towards the town – I don't think they're here to visit.'

Tanaki watched the young man leave the hall and then rose, stretching her arms over her head, and arching her back. Her feelings were mixed as she wandered back into her living area. Kiall's innocence was both appealing and surprising – like finding a perfect flower growing on the edge of a cess-pit. She poured herself a goblet of wine and sipped it. A young man in search of his love; a dreamer. Her eyes narrowed.

'The world has some savage shocks in store for you,' she whispered. A cold breeze rustled the heavy hangings, touching the bare flesh of her legs. She shivered.

'I miss you, Father,' she said, picturing again the tall lean warrior, seeing his slow smile, watching it soften his cruel face. Tanaki had been his favourite – despite her birth being responsible for the death of her mother, Renya. Tenaka Khan had lavished all his love on his only daughter, while his sons fought for a kind word – or even a nod which might be interpreted as praise. She thought of her eldest brother, Jungir. How he had longed to be accepted by his father.

Now Jungir was the Khan, Tanaki's other brothers murdered, and she was merely living out her life awaiting the inevitable.

She smiled as she remembered her last meeting with Jungir. He so wanted her dead. But the Khan's generals would never accept the complete obliteration of Tenaka Khan's blood-line and, as everyone knew, Jungir Khan was sterile. Not one of his forty wives had conceived. Tanaki chuckled. Poor Jungir. He could ride the wildest horse, and fight with lance or sword. But in the eyes of the Nadir he was suspect, because his seed was not strong.

Tanaki pressed her hands to her belly. She had no doubt that she could conceive. And one day, perhaps, when Jungir grew desperate, she could be back in favour and wed to one of the generals. The face of Tsudai leapt into her mind and she recoiled. Not him! Never him. His touch was like the feel of lizard skin, and the memory of his tomb-dark eyes made her shiver. No, not Tsudai.

She pushed him from her mind and thought of Jungir as she had last seen him, sitting on the throne and staring down at her. 'You are safe, bitch – for the moment. But know this . . . one day I will see you humbled. Live for that day, Tanaki.'

So instead of death Tanaki was banished here, in the desolate wastelands of the south. There were few pleasures to be found in this land, save for the heady joys of alcohol and the succession of young men she took to her bed. Yet even these pleasures soon palled. Bored with her life, she had watched the inefficiency of the slave trade – alternating between glutted markets, with the price low, or no trade at

160

all. Added to this, there was no central point where slaves could be auctioned and prices guaranteed. It had taken Tanaki less than four months to establish the market town, and within a year she also coordinated all raids into Gothir territory. Prices had stabilised, the new, improved, market was buoyant and enormous profits were being made. The gold meant little to Tanaki, who had spent her childhood surrounded by the wealth of conquered nations. But the trade kept her agile mind busy, and away from thoughts of Jungir's revenge.

No matter how great the pressure from the generals, she knew there would come a time when Jungir would feel strong enough to have her killed. So strange, she realised, that she did not hate him for it. It was so easy to understand what drove him. He had yearned for his father's affection and, failing to win it, had come to hate that which his father loved.

Tanaki pulled aside a velvet curtain and gazed out of a narrow window.

'He left you nothing, Jungir,' she whispered. 'He conquered most of the world; he united the tribes; he founded an empire. What is there left for you?'

Poor Jungir. Poor sterile Jungir!

Her thoughts turned to the young man, Kiall. His face loomed in her mind, the grey eyes gentle, yet with a hint of steel. And there was passion there too, raw and unmined, volcanic and waiting.

'It would have been pleasant to swallow your innocence.' She smiled, and her expression softened. 'No, it would not,' she realised with sadness.

'Princess! Princess!' yelled Chellin, running the length of the hall. 'Nadir warriors!'

She stepped out to meet him. 'What of it?' she enquired. 'There are always Nadir warriors near here.'

'Not the Royal Wolves, Princess,' said Chellin. 'And Tsudai is leading them.'

Tanaki felt her mouth go dry. 'Is the gate shut?'

'It is, lady. But there are three hundred of them, and we have less than fifty. And most of those will run, given the chance.'

Tanaki moved to a chest of dark oak and lifted the heavy lid. She took out a wide belt, from which hung two short swords. 'We cannot fight them, lady. Why are they here?'

She shrugged and did not reply. So, she thought, the day has come. No more to see the blue of the sky, the eagle riding the wind currents over the mountains. No more men to possess her, and in possessing her to give away their souls. Anger flared. Ignoring Chellin she walked from the hall and on to the wall, climbing to the ramparts to watch the approach of the Khan's Wolves. As Chellin had said, there were more than three hundred warriors, their pointed silver helms ringed with

161

wolfskin, their silver breastplates edged with gold. They rode seemingly without formation and yet, at a single order, they could wheel and charge in a flying wedge or break into three units. Their discipline was incredible. Tenaka Khan had formed the royal guard a quarter of a century before, and trained them to a degree never before experienced among the Nadir. Among the tribesmen it was still regarded as a badge of honour to be accepted into the Wolves. For every hundred applicants, only one was given the helm and the Wolfhead embossed breastplate.

And there at the centre rode Tsudai, a fighting man without equal, a general without peer.

Men gathered around Tanaki. 'What shall we do?' asked one.

'Why are they here?' asked another.

'They are here to kill me,' said Tanaki, surprised that her voice remained calm.

'Will they want to kill the rest of us?' asked a burly warrior.

'Shut your damned mouth!' roared Chellin.

Tanaki raised her hands for silence. 'Get your horses and leave by the iron gate. Do it swiftly! They will kill all they find here.' Some of the men ran from the ramparts but Chellin stood firm.

'I'll not let them take you while I live.'

She smiled and placed her hands on the old warrior's bearded cheeks. 'And you cannot stop them. But it would please me to see you survive, Chellin. Now go!'

For a moment only he stood, then he cursed and ran for his horse.

The Nadir were closer now and the face of their general could be clearly seen by Tanaki. Tsudai was smiling. He raised his hands and riders swept out on either side of him in a skirmish line.

'What do you want here?' Tanaki shouted.

'We want you, whore!' called back Tsudai. 'You are to be brought to Ulrickham for trial.'

Tanaki's anger rose, but she fought for calm. 'By what right do you call a daughter of the Great Khan a whore, you who were suckled by a scabrous goat?'

Tsudai chuckled. 'I have here three hundred warriors, *Princess*. Each one of them will use your body between here and Ulrickham. Now the journey will be sixty days. Even my simple mind tells me that five men a day will get to enjoy the pleasures you bestow so freely on the foreigners and scum you surround yourself with. Think of it, *Princess*, three hundred men!'

'Why warn me, you foul-mouthed whoreson?'

'It could be that you will not wish to suffer such humiliation. Surely someone of the blood of the Great Khan would sooner take her own life?'

Through her fear Tanaki forced a laugh. 'My esteemed brother would like that, would he not? No, Tsudai. Come and take me. I'll survive. And when the generals hear of my treatment at your hands, I will live to see the skin flayed from your foul body.'

He spread his hands. 'As you wish, *Princess*, but do not expect too much support from the other khans. The Lord Jungir will shortly be celebrating the birth of an heir. All the omens say it will be a boy.'

'You lie! Jungir is sterile.'

'I never lie, Tanaki! You know that. One of the Khan's wives is pregnant.'

'Then she had a lover,' snapped Tanaki, before she could stop herself. But her heart sank. The Khan's concubines and wives were kept in a walled palace, patrolled by eunuchs. There was no way a man could infiltrate such a fortress. And even if by some miracle he did, the scores of spies among the concubines would carry word to the Khan.

'Will you come out – or will we come in after you?' shouted Tsudai.

'Come in!' she yelled. 'Why not come yourself?'

Tsudai chuckled and waved his arm and twenty riders raced for the walls, hurling ropes which looped over the pointed stockade timbers. As the Nadir leapt from their saddles and swiftly clambered up the walls, Tanaki drew her swords. The first man to show himself died, his throat ripped open. The second fell, his lung pierced. As the others came in sight Tanaki waited, blood dripping from her silver blades as they advanced from left and right. She leapt and spun, killing a man with a reverse sweep across the neck, then jumped from the battlement into a wagon loaded with sacks of wheat. Scrambling clear, she ran for the hall. Four men moved to cut her off but she swerved into an alley, then doubled back and waited. Six warriors raced into view. She charged into them, cutting and cleaving, breaking through their line.

On the battlements knelt a warrior holding a sling. He whirled it round his head and let fly, the small round stone cracking into Tanaki's temple. She staggered and almost fell. A man ran at her . . . spinning, she hurled her right-hand sword. It punched into his chest and he fell back, scrabbling at the blade. A second stone screamed past her. Ducking she stumbled to a barn, pushing her back against the door. Her head was swimming and a terrible dizziness overcame her. Two more Nadir warriors came into view. She half fell and they leapt at her. Her sword came up, part severing a man's arm. A fist cracked against her skull and her swords were torn from her grasp. Twice more the fist pounded at her face. She fell to her knees. Men were all around her now, tearing at her clothes. They dragged her into the barn, hurling her naked to the straw-covered floor.

'Well, well, we do not look like a princess now,' came Tsudai's voice, cold and mocking. She struggled to stand but a foot was pushed against her face and she fell back. 'I said five men a day, but these twelve warriors have at least fought for you, Princess. I will leave you in their tender care.'

She gazed up through swollen eyes and watched the men untying their rawhide belts, saw the lust in their faces. Something inside her quivered and snapped. Tears ran to her cheeks.

'Make her scream a little,' said Tsudai, 'but do not mark her unduly. There are many more men waiting.'

The general walked out into the sunlight, where he stood for a while listening to the sounds of grunting men and the low moans which came from the once proud princess. Then she screamed, long and piercing. Tsudai allowed himself a smile. He had waited a long time for this moment. Four years since the haughty Princess Tanaki had first spurned his offer of marriage. He had given her a second chance mere months before. Now she would begin to understand the depth of his hatred. The scream sounded again. More animal than human, he thought. Curious how so much despair could be carried in a sound with no words . . .

The screams drifted on the breeze, carrying high into the mountains. 'Dear Gods, what are they doing to her?' said Kiall.

'What the Nadir always do,' hissed Beltzer. 'They're raping her. My guess is they'll kill her soon after.'

'Shame,' commented Harokas. 'Good-looking woman.'

'We must do something,' said Kiall, pushing himself to his feet. Chareos grabbed his belt, hauling him back.

'Good idea,' agreed Beltzer. 'Why don't we saddle up and charge all three hundred of them? Grow up, Kiall. She's finished.'

'Kiall is right,' said Okas softly.

Beltzer turned to him, his jaw dropping. 'You think we *should* charge them?'

'No, my friend. But she is part of this . . . this quest. I know it. I feel it.'

'We're here to rescue a farm girl,' said Beltzer.

'Not any more,' said Okas.

'What do you mean?' asked Chareos.

Okas rubbed his tired eyes. 'It is coming together now, my friends. All the threads. And I can see them. The girl Ravenna was sold to Jungir Khan. He has bedded her, and it is she who now carries his child. He has made her the Kian of Wolves, the Queen. You are seeking to steal the Nadir Queen.'

Beltzer began to laugh. 'Better and better. In that case we *should* charge them. It'll be good practice for when we take on the entire Nadir army!'

'The woman down there is Tenaka Khan's daughter, Jungir's sister. She will know the palace. She will be of great help to us,' Okas said.

'Help?' said Chareos. 'We can't go on with this. It is madness now to even consider it.'

'There is more to this quest than you realise, Chareos Blademaster,' Okas continued. 'Far more. Can you not see it? The dream of Belazar, the ghost of Tenaka Khan? It is all part of a great whole.'

'What part?' asked Finn, kneeling by the Tattooed Man.

'The child,' answered Okas. 'He will be born early . . . twelve weeks from now. The stars show that he will be great king, perhaps greatest who ever lived. He will be blood-line of Ulric and Tenaka Khan, and of Regnak, Earl of Bronze. He will be warrior and statesman. As Nadir Khan, he will take his armies across the world.'

'Are you saying we should kill the babe?' Beltzer asked.

'No. I am saying you should continue with this quest – and see where it leads.'

'It will lead to death – for all of us,' declared Chareos. 'We are no longer talking of buying or stealing back a farm girl. We are talking about the Nadir Queen!'

'Let me speak,' said Kiall softly. 'You are right, Chareos, it is all too . . . too overpowering. May I then suggest we take one step at a time? Let us first think of a way to rescue Tanaki. After that we can decide what to do.'

Chareos sighed and shook his head. 'We are six men in an alien land. And you want us to consider a plan to steal a prisoner from three hundred of the fiercest warriors in the Nadir nation? Well, why not? How many ways can a man die?'

'You don't even want to consider that question,' said Harokas. 'In Nadir hands a prisoner could be killed slowly over a score of days, with each painful day worse than the last.'

'What a sack of comforts you are,' snapped Beltzer.

'The sun is going down,' said Finn. 'If we are going to get the girl, then tonight will be our best chance. Especially if the main force camps outside the walls. Then all we have to do is get down there, sneak past them, climb the walls, kill anyone inside and carry the girl out.'

'Oh, that's all?' Beltzer sneered. 'And I know who gets to carry the bitch? It's me, isn't it?'

'Correct,' admitted Finn.

'I'll come with you,' said Harokas. 'I rather like the woman. You don't mind if I stick close to you, do you, Chareos?'

'Not at all. But stay in front of me, Harokas.'

Chareos knelt on the hillside as the sun faded into dusk. The Nadir warriors had dragged the girl out into the open and dropped her naked body in the dust of the square. She was limp as a doll. Two of the men then hauled her up, lifting her on to the auction platform and bending her over the block. Chareos averted his eyes and switched his gaze to the riders beyond the town. They had settled down in the open, setting camp-fires. The general and four of his men had entered the long hall, which left seventeen men inside the town.

Too many . . .

Kiall brought Chareos a meal of dried meat and fruit, then sat in silence beside him.

What am I doing here? thought Chareos. What is this madness? The woman means nothing to me, this quest is of no consequence. What will it matter to the world in a thousand years if another Nadir Khan is born? He gazed down at the still, white form draped over the auction block and the men bearing down on her.

'Do you have a plan?' whispered Kiall. Chareos turned to the pale-faced young man.

'Do you think me some god of war, Kiall? We can get in – possibly without being observed. But then there will be seventeen against seven – six if you discount Okas, who is no warrior. Now, let us assume we could defeat all seventeen, could we do it silently? No. Therefore the other warriors outside would be alerted. Can we defeat three hundred? Even you will know the answer to that.'

'Then what do you suggest?'

'I don't know, boy!' snapped Chareos. 'Go away and let me think!'

The sky darkened, the moon shone bright. Idea after idea drifted into Chareos' mind, there to be examined, dissected, discarded. Finally he called Finn to him and outlined his thoughts. The hunter listened, his face impassive.

'Is this the only way?' he asked, at last.

'If you can think of a better plan, I'll go along with it,' answered Chareos.

Finn shrugged. 'Whatever you say, Blademaster.'

'I say we should all go home and forget this nonsense,' said Chareos, forcing a smile.

'That would win my vote,' admitted Finn. 'So why don't we?'

Chareos shrugged and pointed down to the moonlit town, where the naked form of Tanaki was tied to the auction block.

'We don't know her,' said Finn softly.

'No, we do not. But we have seen her suffering. Do I sound as naïve and romantic as Kiall?'

'Yes, but that is no bad thing, my friend. I share your view. Evil will never be countered while good men do nothing.'

'Then we are a pair of fools,' declared Chareos, and this time the smile was genuine. Finn reached out his hand and Chareos took it.

'Win or lose, we achieve nothing that the world would understand,' said Finn.

'But then the world does not matter,' answered Chareos, rising.

'Indeed it does not,' Finn replied. 'It is good to understand that.'

166

It was close to midnight when Finn and Maggrig rode from the camp. Chareos, Harokas, Kiall and Beltzer slowly made their way down the slope towards the stockaded town. Okas remained in the woods, squatting cross-legged, his eyes closed. He began to chant softly and a mist rose from the grass, swirling out to cloak the four warriors as they moved into the open.

11

The mist rolled on and down like a ghostly blanket, shimmering in the moonlight. Chareos reached the rear wall of the stockade and located the iron portcullis. Beltzer moved alongside.

'What now?' whispered the giant.

'We raise it?'

The iron grille was four feet wide and seven feet high. Beltzer handed his axe to Kiall and gripped the lowest bar. The muscles on his neck and shoulders swelled as he applied pressure: the gate creaked and rose an inch. Harokas and Chareos joined him: the gate rose another foot. 'That is enough,' hissed Kiall, dropping to his back and sliding under the gate.

Chareos turned to Beltzer. 'Can you hold it there?'

The giant grunted. Chareos ducked down and rolled under to rise beside Kiall. The two men climbed the rampart steps; there were no sentries posted. Together Kiall and Chareos turned the wheel above the gate, tightening the rope and relieving Beltzer of his burden. Swiftly they returned to the gateway, where Beltzer struggled through followed by Harokas.

'Now we wait,' whispered Chareos.

From beyond the town came the sound of galloping hooves.

Finn rode headlong into the Nadir camp, scattering two fires. Warriors surged up from their blankets as his horse thundered by them. Finn swung the horse to a stop. Notching an arrow to his short hunting-bow, he sent a shaft slicing into a man's throat.

From the other side of the camp came a wild yell and Maggrig galloped into sight through the mist. The Nadir swarmed for their horses. Finn shot a second man, then kicked his mount into a gallop and headed off towards the south. The camp was in an uproar as warriors seized their swords and ran to saddle their mounts. Within minutes the camp-site was deserted.

Inside the town Tsudai ran from the hall, mounting the ramparts to watch his soldiers splitting into two groups to hunt down the attackers. He swung to an aide who was running towards him.

'Get out there and find out what is happening!'

The man darted to his horse, vaulted into the saddle and galloped through the gates.

Chareos and Beltzer climbed through the window at the rear of the long hall and crept forward. Four Nadir officers were sitting around a table, playing with dice.

Chareos sprang into the hall, slashing his sword through the throat of the nearest man. Beltzer leapt into action beside him, his axe killing two men before they could rise. The fourth man tried to run and made it to the door, wrenching it open. Harokas' knife plunged into his chest.

Harokas stepped into the doorway, grabbing the man's corpse and lowering it to the floor.

Outside Kiall, keeping close to the shadows, crept towards the auction block where Tanaki lay unconscious. Three men ran into the square and he ducked behind two water barrels and waited.

The men climbed to the ramparts where Tsudai watched the chase. Kiall could not hear their conversation. He moved carefully out into the open and climbed to the auction platform, where he knelt by Tanaki and cut the ropes binding her wrists. She moaned as she felt his touch.

'No more,' she pleaded. Her eyes were dark and swollen, her lips cut, her body bruised and bleeding. Kiall gritted his teeth and waited. The men on the ramparts came down to the square and he heard one of them laugh. Hidden behind the block he saw a Nadir warrior point to Tanaki, then turn towards her. The others hooted and swung to Tsudai.

'It is still your day,' he told them.

The first man clambered to the platform, loosening his belt and dropping his troos. Kiall reared up and plunged his sword into the man's groin.

Tsudai's eyes widened. 'Wolves to me!' he yelled and from the barn came a further nine men, swords in their hands. 'Take him!' shouted Tsudai.

The warriors surged forward, but just as they reached the platform Beltzer came hurtling into them, his axe cleaving and cutting. Chareos and Harokas joined him. Kiall leapt from the platform, cannoning into three men and bearing them down. A sword sliced the skin of his upper arm, but then he was up, his own blade slashing at the men beneath him. Harokas ducked under a wild cut and skewered the man before him. His blade sprang clear in time to block a second thrust from another warrior. Chareos despatched two Wolves, then swung to aid Harokas. Beltzer fought like a man berserk. Within seconds the last Nadir fighting man was cut down.

168

Tsudai ran along the ramparts and jumped to the ground, rolling to break his fall. He seized the reins of his horse and vaulted to the beast's bare back. Chareos ran to block his escape, but the horse galloped clear.

'Get the girl!' Chareos shouted.

Beltzer tossed his axe to Kiall and climbed to the platform. Lifting Tanaki, he draped her over his shoulder.

Chareos led the group back to the iron gate and out into the mist-filled night. Slowly they made their way clear, judging their path by the rising ground. Within minutes they heard the sound of horses' hooves. 'Down!' hissed Chareos. The group dropped to their bellies. Horsemen passed them by within a few paces. Chareos rose.

'Which way?' whispered Beltzer. They could hear the calling of the Nadir, but the mist had thickened into a deep fog and the sounds were distorted, muffled and eerie. As Chareos led them up the slope Beltzer was breathing heavily, his face red with exertion.

'I'm not as young as I was,' he said, stopping for a moment to get his breath.

A glowing sphere formed in the air before Chareos. 'Thank the Source!' he whispered. The sphere floated away to the right. Chareos and the others followed it and soon climbed above the mist into the relative safety of the trees. Okas was still squatting on the grass, but he opened his eyes as the questors entered the clearing. 'Sit around me in a circle,' he said. 'Place the girl at the centre.' Beltzer gently laid the unconscious Tanaki to the grass and they formed a circle. Okas closed his eyes and began to chant once more, his voice low and rhythmic. Beltzer looked closely at him. The old man was painfully thin and his face was streaked with grey, his lips as blue as the tattooes on his chin.

Beltzer nudged Chareos and pointed to Okas. Chareos nodded. Whatever magic the old man was working was taking a terrible toll.

Nadir horsemen rode into the clearing and Beltzer jerked, and reached for his axe, but Chareos gripped his arm. The horsemen seemed insubstantial, like ghosts, They rode slowly past the questors.

Kiall shivered and watched the wraith riders as they passed. Okas opened his eyes and sagged sideways to the grass. Chareos and Kiall moved to him, but the old man waved them away and curled up to sleep. Chareos covered him with a blanket as Kiall turned to the girl. Under the bright moonlight he could see her face was swollen and bruised. Her left eye was closed tight, the right darkened and dis-coloured. Carefully he lifted the blanket from her body. Her legs and buttocks were also badly bruised and scratched, and there was dried blood on her thighs.

Beltzer knelt on the other side of Tanaki. 'You want some help?' he asked Kiall.

'No. There is nothing we can do. But a fire would help; we could keep her warm.'

'We cannot risk that,' said Chareos. 'I don't know how powerful the magic is, nor how long it will last.'

'I do not know why she is still unconscious,' said Kiall. 'The bruising is severe, but no bones seem to be broken.'

'I have seen this before,' Chareos told him. 'It is not the injury to the body, but to the spirit. This is an ugly business, Kiall.'

Tanaki moaned softly and Kiall lay alongside her, stroking her face. 'You are well now,' he whispered into her ear. 'You are with friends. Sleep, lady. Rest.' Chareos covered her with his own blanket, while Beltzer removed his jerkin and rolled it for a pillow beneath her head. She turned to one side, her hand outside the blanket. The fingers clenched into a fist, then opened and dug into the earth. Kiall took her hand gently and held it. Tanaki's breathing eased, and she slept.

Three times ghostly Nadir riders entered the clearing. Once a man dismounted within three paces of the questors, and knelt to examine the tracks. He looked puzzled and spoke to his companions, but the questors could hear no words. Then he mounted and rode away through the trees.

The night passed slowly. Kiall slept fitfully alongside Tanaki, while Chareos and Beltzer sat talking in low whispers. Harokas moved away to the edge of the trees and slept alone.

Dawn found Chareos and Beltzer on the hillside, scanning the horizon for signs of Finn or Maggrig. The Nadir camp was deserted, the town silent.

'They're canny men,' remarked Beltzer. 'They'll be all right.'

'I wish I could be sure,' said Chareos. 'The risk was too great; I should never have asked them to go.'

'They're grown men; they could have refused. And we did get the girl.'

Chareos was tired. His back ached and he stretched out on the grass. 'You should sleep for a while,' said Beltzer. 'I'll stand watch for Finn.'

Chareos nodded. 'Keep an eye on the Earl's man also. Don't let him move behind you.'

'You think he's an assassin?'

'I just think he needs watching.' Chareos closed his eyes and drifted off to sleep.

The sun climbed higher as Beltzer sat beside Chareos, his axe in his lap, his mind on the mountain. He felt alive now, almost young again. Almost. Carrying the girl had sapped his strength, as had the battle in the town. His huge hand curled around the axe haft. 'There's still a skirmish or two left in us, eh?' he said.

Far off to the west he saw a rider, keeping to the low hollows.

170

Beltzer shaded his eyes and tried to identify the man; it looked like Finn. Scanning the hills and hollows, he could see no pursuers. He thought of waking Chareos, but hesitated. The Blademaster was bone-weary, he needed rest. Slowly the rider made his way up the slope. It *was* Finn. He dismounted and led the horse into the clearing, then walked back to Beltzer.

'Where is Maggrig?' Finn asked.

'He's not back yet,' Beltzer told him.

Finn sank to the ground. 'I didn't think I'd make it; they almost had me. I killed two of them and then rode into a swirling river. I lost my bow. I thought the horse would drown and I hung on to the pommel. But he's a good beast. He swam well – and found solid ground.'

'Get some rest,' Beltzer advised him.

Finn shook his head. 'I've got to find Maggrig.'

'Don't be a fool! The Nadir are everywhere. Maggrig is probably holed up in some cave. He'll wait till nightfall, then make it back. If you ride out there, you'll lead them to him.'

Finn sighed. 'You are right. I'll sleep for a while. Wake me if he comes.'

Beltzer nodded. 'We got the girl,' he said. 'It went well.'

Finn did not reply but lay on the grass and closed his eyes. Beltzer sat with his back to a tree and dozed in the morning sunshine. He awoke to see Harokas kneeling beside Chareos. The hawk-nosed warrior was staring intently at the face of the sleeping man; his expression was hard to read, but Beltzer could see he was troubled.

'Don't wake him,' said Beltzer softly and Harokas looked up.

'I was sent here to kill him.'

'I know,' said Beltzer. 'So does he.'

'But there is no need, is there? You have all decided to die. And I am glad to be relieved of the task.'

Harokas rose and walked away to his horse. Beltzer watched him mount and ride away.

At the centre of the clearing Kiall awoke. He sat up and looked down at Tanaki. Her colour was better. Opening his pack, he took out some comfrey leaves which he mixed with cold water. It was good for swellings and he laboured over the poultice for some time. Satisfied at last, he touched Tanaki's hand and she awoke with a start.

'You are with friends,' he told her, his voice soothing. 'It is me, Kiall. I have a poultice here for your eyes. Lie still.' She said nothing as he placed the cool cloth over her eyelids. He took her hand and patted it gently.

'The Wolves?' she whispered.

'Gone.'

'How did . . .?'

'Do not talk, lady. Rest. We came into the town last night and slew the men who . . . attacked you. Then we carried you here. You are safe.'

'Why?'

'Rest now. Let the poultice do its work.' He tried to release her hand, but her fingers gripped his.

'Why?' she asked again.

'Because you were in need,' he said lamely. He sat with her for several minutes; then her fingers relaxed their grip and he saw she was asleep once more. He stood and stretched. Beltzer was asleep by a tree on the crown of the hill, Chareos and Finn lying close by. Of Harokas and Maggrig there was no sign.

The voice of Okas sounded in his mind. *'Kiall, can you hear me?'*

'Yes,' he answered aloud, looking down at the old man's sleeping form. The voice was like a whisper through time, impossibly distant and yet clear. 'I can hear you.'

'Tell Chareos to travel to the Mountains of the Moon. Tell him to seek out Asta Khan. Tell him I am sorry.'

The voice faded. Kiall moved to Okas and knelt by the body. It was stiff and cold.

The Tattooed Man was dead.

They buried the old man on the crown of the hill and stood silently around the grave. 'The first of us to die,' whispered Beltzer, his words hanging in the air. He walked back to the camp-site and sat staring at the blades of his axe, twirling the haft in his hands.

'I am sorry,' Kiall told Chareos. 'I wish I had never asked you to help me. It all seems so futile now. I don't know why.'

'We are free men, Kiall. We make our own choices.'

'I know that,' said the young man. 'It is just . . . there is so much savagery. Look at Tanaki. How could men do that to her? I don't understand.'

'Be glad that you do not.'

'Do you?'

Chareos turned away, staring out over the Steppes. 'Yes, sadly I do. I would never contemplate such a deed – but, yes, I understand it. It is connected with war, Kiall, and the nature of the warrior. He is competitive, and his desire is to dominate and destroy his enemies. But the word to remember is *dominate*. There is another word to consider also; *arousal*. A man can be aroused to anger as easily as he is aroused to rut. The two emotions are closely linked. Anger and lust. So the warrior is aroused in battle and fights to dominate. Tanaki, and others like her, are the victims of that. Dominated, abused, humiliated.'

'They are evil,' said Kiall. 'Simply that.'

'Would that it were so simple. Some of those men will have had wives and children. They might have been good family men; they knew love and compassion in their lives.'

'I would show them no compassion. I am glad we killed them.'

'Glad? Never be glad another man has died. Not *ever*. Just be relieved that you are alive. I had a teacher once, a great man called Attalis. He told me that the path to evil often begins with righteous anger. A Nadir band raid a Gothir village; they rape and kill. A group of Gothir soldiers set out for revenge; they want to hurt the enemy, so *they* rape and kill. It never ends. Never . . . ever . . . be glad to kill.'

Chareos walked away and stood at the graveside. Kiall left him there and wandered over to Beltzer who was sitting alone. The giant's face was set, but a muscle twitched in his cheek. His eyes were red-rimmed and he was blinking rapidly.

Kiall sat opposite him. 'Are you all right?' asked the younger man.

'Me? I'm fine. I was just thinking we haven't eaten. I'm starved.' His mouth trembled, but he clamped his jaws tight. 'Stupid old fool,' he said. 'Stupid! He killed himself to protect us. Stupid.' Beltzer sniffed, then hawked and spat. 'Damned if I'm not getting a chill. It's this weather; cold winds and dust. Only the Source knows how people live out here. Give me a city any time . . . and taverns. What are you staring at?'

'I'm sorry,' said Kiall. 'I didn't mean to stare. He had a message for you, you know. He said to say farewell to old Beltzer.'

'Did he? Truly?'

'Yes,' said Kiall, continuing the lie. 'He didn't sound unhappy.'

'You know what the worst thing is, boy? Do you?'

'No.'

'He liked me. For myself. Not because I could swing an axe, or kill a few tribesmen. But for *me*. There's not much to like, but he found it. And I'll tell you something – laugh if you like – but I loved that old man. "Old Beltzer". That's something, isn't it? I loved him.'

'Why would I laugh?'

Tears welled in Beltzer's eyes, flowing to his cheeks and into the red and silver beard. He bowed his head and wept. Kiall reached out and laid a hand on his shoulder.

'Get away!' said Beltzer. 'Leave me alone. Can't a man even grieve in private?'

Kiall rose and backed away. Tanaki was awake and sitting in the centre of the camp-site, a blanket round her shoulders. Her eyes were still swollen, but she could see.

Kiall sat beside her. 'How are you feeling?'

'You wouldn't want to know,' replied Tanaki. 'Did you kill them all?'

'Yes. No. There was one man – the leader, I think – he escaped.'

'Good.'

Kiall was surprised, but he did not press the point. 'Do you wish to be alone?' he asked.

She smiled, then winced as her lip split and a tiny drop of blood formed. 'No. You sit close by, I like your company. Why did you rescue me?'

'Does it matter?'

'It does to me.'

'Is it not enough that you were alone and needed help?'

'This is not a song or a fable, Kiall. I am not one of your yellow-haired ladies trapped in a tower.'

'But you are a princess,' he said, smiling. 'One should always rescue a princess.' She ignored the smile, and annoyance showed in her eyes.

'What about the others? Why did they help?'

'The Tattooed Man asked them to – he said you were part of our quest. Does that satisfy you?'

She nodded. 'I will repay you all.'

'There is no need.'

'I will judge that. I want no debts hanging over me. Where will you go now?'

'To find a man named Asta Khan.'

She looked at him, but he could not read her expression through the bruises she bore. 'He still lives? Surprising. My father set great store by him.'

'He does still,' said Kiall.

'What madness are you speaking? My father is dead; he has been for years.'

'It is hard to explain.'

'Try!' she snapped. 'I may be bruised, but there is nothing wrong with my brain.'

As best he could, Kiall outlined the duel with the demons, and the violet-eyed warrior who had come to his assistance. 'Okas told me it was the spirit of Tenaka Khan.'

'How did he fight?'

'With two short swords. He spun like a dancer; I have never seen anything like it.'

She nodded. 'That is one of the names he carried: Bladedancer. He was also the Prince of Shadows.'

'Chareos and Beltzer both knew him,' said Kiall, 'as did Maggrig and Finn. They are the heroes of Bel-azar; he sat with them on the last night of the battle.'

'I know. My father told me. They are the *ghosts-yet-to-be*.'

'What does that mean?'

She shrugged. 'I do not know. My father was a secretive man. He

174

told me of the warriors of the Gothir; he said one of them was blood kin – a Drenai prince. I would guess that to be Chareos. It is inconceivable that it could be the bald, fat one.'

'I know what you mean. Beltzer is not exactly cultured.'

The sound of a walking horse came to them and Beltzer leapt up, his axe in his hands. Kiall stood, drawing his sabre, as Harokas guided his mount into the camp and stepped down.

'I thought you had gone for good,' said Beltzer.

'So did I,' answered Harokas, wearily, 'but I found your friend.'

'Maggrig?' Beltzer whispered.

'Yes.'

Finn lurched to his feet and ran forward. 'Where is he?' he shouted, grasping Harokas' black jerkin.

Harokas put his hand on Finn's shoulder. 'The Nadir took him.'

'Oh, no! Oh, please no!' cried Finn, stumbling back. He ran to his horse, but Chareos cut him off, grabbing his arms and holding him tight.

'Wait!' said Chareos softly. 'We will all go. Calm yourself, my friend.'

Finn seemed to sag in Chareos' arms, his head falling to rest on the swordman's shoulder. Chareos turned to Kiall. 'Wait here with the woman. We'll be back.'

'There's no point,' said Harokas. 'The Nadir are everywhere. It's madness.'

'Even so,' replied Chareos, 'will you take us to the body?'

'It means that much to you? You'll risk your lives for a corpse?'

'Yes.'

Harokas shook his head in disbelief. 'Follow me then, but ride warily.'

Trees were sparse as the questors rode in single file behind Harokas, and the land spread out before them in a series of folds and gullies, like a giant's cloak carelessly tossed from Heaven.

They moved with care for more than an hour, coming at last to a rocky rise. Harokas dismounted and led his horse up the hill, the questors following his lead. He tethered his mount to a skeletal poplar and waited. Chareos joined him. No one had spoken since they rode from the camp. Finn stood by, white-faced, expressionless, his eyes tormented. Beltzer was beside him.

'Follow me,' whispered Harokas, 'and please . . . no heroics?'

He led them to a rock-face, and on into a narrow fissure which wound down to a ledge. There he squatted in the fading light and pointed to the Nadir camp below. The greater part of the three hundred Wolves were there, and six camp-fires had been set. At the centre of the camp, staked out naked on the ground was Maggrig, his body covered in cuts and burns. Finn groaned and Beltzer's hand gripped the hunter's shoulder.

'Have you seen enough?' whispered Harokas. 'It does not take a warrior's eye to know the man is dead.' Chareos nodded. Maggrig had been tortured, his skin partially flayed, his eyes put out.

'They are still searching for you,' said Harokas, 'so he could have told them nothing. He had courage. Great courage.'

'Yes, he did,' agreed Chareos, glancing at Finn. 'He was a fine man.'

'I think his horse broke a leg,' continued Harokas. 'It was just bad luck. He almost made it to the slopes.'

'There's nothing more to see,' said Chareos softly. He touched Finn's arm. 'Let us go, my friend.'

'Yes,' murmured Finn.

Harokas backed away from the rim of the ledge and the questors clambered back through the fissure. As they reached the horses, it was Beltzer who first noticed Finn's absence.

'No!' he cried. Turning, he ran back for the fissure, Chareos and Harokas behind him. They came to the ledge in time to see Finn walking slowly down the scree-covered slope towards the Nadir camp. Beltzer made as if to follow him, but Chareos grabbed the neck of his jerkin, hauling him from his feet.

Beltzer hit the ground hard. He stared up into Chareos' face. 'Leave it be,' said Chareos. 'He wouldn't want you there; you know that.'

Beltzer tried to speak, but no words came. He rolled to his knees, gathered his axe and stumbled back through the fissure. Harokas knelt beside Chareos.

The Blademaster ignored him, his eyes fixed on the small, dark figure closing on the Nadir camp. It would be so easy, thought Harokas, his hand on the hilt of his dagger . . . just slip the blade through his ribs, sliding it up into the heart. So easy. Then he could return to the Earl, claim his gold and get on with his life. But that would mean leaving Tanaki. He cursed inwardly and took his hand from the hilt.

Below them Finn reached the bottom of the slope and walked forward, back straight, head high. There was a roaring in his ears, like the distant sea, and his eyes were misted. So many years together, years of joy and fear. It never paid to love too much, he'd always known that. All life was balance. There was always a reckoning. Better by far not to have loved at all. He walked past two Nadir warriors who were honing their swords; they stared at him for a moment, then rose behind him. Steadily Finn walked on. He could see Maggrig now, and the terrible cruelty they had unleashed upon him. A man seized Finn's arm. Almost absently, Finn plunged his hunting-knife into the warrior's throat.

There had been that time when Maggrig went down with the Red

176

Plague. No one survived that, but Finn had sat with him, begging him to live. The fever had burned all the flesh from Maggrig's body, leaving translucent skin stretched tightly over the bones. But Finn had nursed him to health. He remembered the day he had first realised Maggrig was going to live. The sky had been grey and overcast, the mountains covered with mist. Moisture dripped from the trees and yet the day had been beautiful – so incredibly beautiful that Finn had been unable to look upon it without tears.

A second warrior came at him. Finn killed him, but the man's sword plunged into Finn's side. There was little pain. He staggered on. Something struck him in the back, but he ignored it. Close to the body now, he fell to his knees and slashed his knife through the ropes binding Maggrig's arms to the stakes. Dropping his knife, he lifted Maggrig's head. Blood gushed into Finn's throat but he spat it clear.

'You are nothing but trouble to me, boy,' he said, struggling to lift the stiffening corpse.

A spear hammered into his back, smashing through his ribs and exiting from the chest. He felt Maggrig slipping from his hands and tried, so hard, to lower the body gently to the earth.

Slowly he toppled, his head resting on Maggrig's chest.

If he could just get Maggrig to the mountains, all would be well. The sky would be grey and overcast, the mist clinging to the trees.

If he could just . . .

Swords and knives plunged into Finn's body, but he did not feel them.

High on the ledge Chareos watched it all. His hands were trembling and he tore his eyes from the scene, staring down at the ground. He sucked in a deep breath, then leaned back. For several minutes he sat in silence, remembering Finn and Maggrig as they had been back at Bel-azar. Then he turned to Harokas. 'You had your chance,' he said softly. 'It will not come again. Why did you not kill me?'

Harokas spread his hands and said nothing. Chareos backed away from the ledge and returned to the horses. Beltzer was sitting on a rock, his axe on the ground beside him.

'Did he die well?' asked the giant.

'Yes . . . whatever that means,' answered Chareos. He stepped into the saddle. 'Let's get back.'

'What are we going to do, Blademaster?' Beltzer asked. 'Yesterday seems so far away now. Okas is dead. Finn and Maggrig are dead. Do we go on?'

'What do we have to go back to? We go on.' Touching heels to the grey, Chareos rode out of the clearing. Beltzer gathered his axe, mounted and followed him.

For some time Harokas waited. Finally he vaulted into the saddle and rode after them. Chareos heard him coming and reined in as the assassin came alongside.

'Well?' asked Chareos.

'You can't take on the Nadir army with three men,' said Harokas.

'What do you suggest?'

'Four would even the odds.'

12

Chien-tsu opened his eyes. Around him the mountains reared like the spears of the gods, looming and threatening. An icy wind howled through the crags. His servant, Oshi, was huddled by a small fire, his face blue with cold. Chien shivered.

'She is dead,' he said, picturing Mai-syn as he had last seen her, radiant and happy, her dress of yellow silk shining in the sunlight.

'As always then, lord, you were correct,' said Oshi.

'I had hoped to be wrong. Come, let us find a cave.' Oshi was reluctant to leave even the illusory warmth of the small fire, but he rose without complaint and the two men led their horses along the winding mountain path. There were no trees at this height, only an occasional stunted shrub cloaked in snow. The walls of the mountains rose sheer to the left and right of the travellers, and there was no sign of a cave or shelter of any kind beyond shallow depressions in the rock-face. Oshi was convinced they would die here. It was three days since they had eaten – and that had been a stringy hare brought down by an arrow from Chien's bow.

They walked on. Chien did not feel the cold; he closed his mind to it, and thought instead of the beautiful Mai-syn. He had spirit-searched the land, seeking her soul, listening for the music of her spirit.

His mood was dark now, and colder than the mountain winds.

The trail dropped into a narrow valley, then rose again. For a while they rode, but it seemed colder to sit immobile on a saddle and they dismounted. Oshi stumbled and fell and Chien turned. 'Are you weary, old man?'

'A little, lord,' he admitted.

Chien moved on. He could not stop the servant from addressing him with his title, and had long since given up the effort.

They rounded a bend in the trail and saw an elderly man sitting cross-legged on a rock. He seemed incredibly ancient, the skin of his face weathered like sandstone. He was wearing only a loin-cloth of

178

pale skin and a necklace of human teeth; his body was emaciated, the bones sharp and jutting, like knife-blades under leather. Snow had settled on his skeletal shoulders.

'Good evening, old father,' greeted Chien, bowing.

The old man looked up and as Chien met his gaze he shuddered inwardly. The eyes were blacker than night, and cold with an ancient malice. The man smiled, showing several blackened teeth.

His voice whispered out like a breeze across tombstones. 'Mai-syn angered Jungir Khan. He threw her to his Wolves, who used her and threw her back. In her despair she cut her throat with a pair of silver scissors. It happened less than a month after her arrival.'

Chien felt his stomach heave, but he fought to keep all expression from his face.

'A simple "good evening" would have been sufficient to open the conversation, old father. But thank you for the information.'

'I do not have the time for pleasantries, Chien-tsu, nor the elaborate and inane rituals of the Kiatze.' The old man laughed. 'Look around you – this is Nadir land. It is cold, inhospitable. Only the strong survive. Here there are no green fields, no verdant pastures. A warrior is old by the time he is thirty. We have no energy to spend on pretty words.' He waved one hand. 'But that is of no matter. It is important only that you are here, and that your desire for vengeance is strong. Follow me.' Nimbly he leapt from the rock and walked away into the snow.

'He is a demon,' wailed Oshi. 'That loin-cloth is human skin.'

'I do not care for his lack of sartorial elegance,' said Chien. 'If he is a demon I will deal with him, but let us hope he is a demon with a warm cave.'

They followed the old man to what seemed a sheer rock-face. He disappeared and Oshi began to tremble, but Chien walked to the rock wall and found a narrow opening, almost invisible from the outside. He led his horse within and Oshi followed him.

Inside it was dark and cold. From somewhere in the shadows Chien heard a soft chanting. Torches sprang to life in rusted brackets on the walls. His horse reared but he calmed the beast, stroking its neck and whispering soothing words. The travellers moved on into a torch-lit tunnel that branched out into a deep cave where a fire was burning without wood.

'Sit,' said Asta Khan. 'Warm yourselves.' He turned to Oshi. 'I am not a demon; I am worse than demons. But you have no need to fear me.'

'Thank you, sir. Thank you,' said Oshi, bowing deeply.

Asta Khan ignored him, locking his gaze to Chien. 'And you do not fear me at all, man of Kiatze. That is good. I am not comfortable around fearful men. Sit! Sit! Make yourselves comfortable. It is long since I had visitors.'

179

'How long have you been here?' Chien asked, settling himself by the magical fire.

'I came when my lord was murdered. He was Tenaka Khan, the Khan of Wolves, the Prince of Shadows,' related the old man, his eyes shining with pride. 'He was the Great One, the heir of Ulric.'

'I believe I have heard the name,' said Chien. Anger flashed in Asta's eyes, but he masked it and smiled thinly.

'All men have heard it, even the soft-bellied Kiatze. But let it pass. Your people are renowned for cynicism – but I watched you fight, Chien-tsu. I saw you kill Kubai and the others. You are skilful – and fast. Very fast.'

'And you have need of my skills, old father?'

'I see your mind works as swiftly as your body. Yes, I have need of you. And you have need of me. It makes for an interesting debate, I think. Which of us needs the other more?'

'Not at the moment,' replied Chien. 'As matters stand I need you not at all.'

'Then you know how to get into the Khan's palace?' asked Asta.

'Not yet. But I will find a way.'

'No,' said Asta, 'you will not. But I can take you on a path which leads to the throne room. Alone you would not survive, for there are the Dwellers in the Dark to stop you. I will give you Jungir Khan. I will give you the means of vengeance.'

'And in return, old father?'

'You will aid the *ghosts-yet-to-be*.'

'Explain further.'

Asta shook his head. 'First we will eat. I can hear your servant's belly rumbling. Take your bow and walk from the cave. A deer is waiting there – kill it.'

Chien rose and walked back to the cave entrance. The old man was right for a doe stood trembling near the entrance, her eyes open and unblinking. Chien notched an arrow and stood for a moment looking at the beast, then he turned and retraced his steps.

'Oshi, take a knife and despatch the beast. There is no sport there.'

Asta Khan cackled loudly, rocking back and forth on his haunches.

Chien ignored him. 'Tell me of Tenaka Khan,' he said and the old man took a deep breath.

'He was the sun and moon of the Nadir people – but he was cursed with tainted blood. Half Drenai, half Nadir, he allowed himself to love a woman. I do not mean to take her for his own – although he did this. But he surrendered his soul to her. She died giving birth to his daughter Tanaki, and in dying she took part of the Khan's soul to Hell or Heaven. He ceased to care about his life, allowing the years to drift by. His son, Jungir, poisoned him. That is Tenaka Khan. What more do you wish to know?'

180

'You were his shaman?'

'I was and I am. I am Asta Khan. I placed the Helm of Ulric on his head. I rode beside him when he conquered the Drenai, and the Vagrians, when the armies of the Nadir rode into Mashrapur and Lentria. He was the fulfilment of our dreams. He should never have died. He should have lived for ever, like a god!'

'And what do you seek, Asta Khan?' asked Chien. 'Not merely vengeance?'

Asta's eyes shone for a moment, then he looked away. 'What I desire is of no concern to you. It is enough that I can give you that which you desire.'

'At this moment I desire nothing more than a hot bath.'

'Then you shall have one,' said Asta, rising. 'Follow me.' The old man rose and walked to the back of the cave, where a shallow pool had filled with melted snow from a fissure above. Asta knelt by it, dipping his hand to the water. He closed his eyes and spoke three harsh-sounding words which were lost on Chien. The water began to bubble and hiss, steam rising.

'A hot bath for the Kiatze lord,' said Asta, standing. 'Is there anything else you require?'

'A young concubine to read me the works of Lu-tzan?'

'Make do with the hot bath,' Asta told him, striding away.

Chien stripped his clothes and slid into the pool. The water was hot but not uncomfortable, despite having reached boiling point. He recalled the story of Hai-chuan, a young man accused of stealing a royal gem. Hai-chuan had pleaded innocence, and was sentenced to trial by ordeal. He had to place his hands in a pot of boiling water. If he was innocent, the gods would protect his flesh; if guilty, his skin would blister and burst. He was from the mountains and he begged the magistrate to allow him to suffer his ordeal directly under the gaze of the All-father in Heaven. Touched by his piety, the magistrate agreed and Hai-chuan was taken to the top of a high mountain. There they boiled a pot of water and he placed his hands within it. There was not a mark upon him – and he was freed. Later he sold the gem and lived like a prince. Chien smiled. It was due to the altitude, he knew. Water boiled at a much lower temperature in the mountains.

He lazed for a while in the water, then climbed out and returned to the fire to sit, naked, by the flames.

Oshi had cut the best pieces from the loins of the doe, and the smell of cooking meat filled the cave.

'Now tell me of the *ghosts-yet-to-be*,' said Chien.

Tanaki watched the men ride away, then eased herself to her feet, stifling a groan as pain roared through her. Unsteadily she rose and

181

straightened her back. Nausea threatened to swamp her, but she forced her stomach to remain calm.

'You should rest,' said Kiall, who had moved alongside her, one hand held out.

She made no reply. Bending to one side, she gently stretched the muscles of her waist and hips. Lifting her arms over her head, she eased the tension in her neck and shoulders. Her father had taught her these exercises many years before. 'The warrior's body,' he had said, 'must always be supple.' More confident now, she spun on her heel and leapt, twisting in the air. She landed clumsily.

'Can I help?' asked Kiall.

'Yes. Hold out your hands.' He did so and her long leg swung up, her heel resting on his palms. She bent forward, grasping the back of her ankle, holding the position for a while and then switching to the other leg. Finally she lifted the blanket from her shoulders and stood naked before Kiall. He blushed and cleared his throat. 'Place your hands on my shoulders,' she said, turning her back on him, 'and gently press at the muscles with your thumbs. Where they are rounded and supple, move on. Where they are knotted and tense, ease them.'

'I do not know how,' he told her, but tentatively his hands touched her skin. She sat down on her blanket with Kiall kneeling behind her. Her skin was smooth and white, the muscles beneath strong and firm, as his fingers moved over her.

'Relax, Kiall. Close your eyes. Think of nothing. Let your hands search.'

His fingers slid down over the shoulder-blades. The muscles on the right side felt as if pebbles had been inserted into them. With great care he rubbed at them, growing more confident as the tautness faded. 'That is good,' she told him. 'You have fine hands – healing hands.'

He could feel himself becoming aroused, and hated himself for it. After what she had been through, it was wholly wrong for a man to react to her in this way. His hands losing their sureness, he stood and walked away. Tanaki covered herself with the blanket cloak and lay back on the ground. The pain of her body was less now, but she would never forget the abject humiliation she had suffered. The memory of the sweating men, the stink of them, the pawing and the pain would remain with her always. She shivered and rolled to her feet. Kiall's horse stood tethered nearby; she saddled him and stepped into the stirrup, easing herself to his back. Kiall saw her and ran forward. 'Where are you going?' he asked, his voice full of concern.

'I cannot start the rest of my life dressed like this,' she said. 'My clothes are down there in the hall. And I will need weapons.'

'I'll come with you,' he offered, holding out his hand. She took it and he vaulted to the saddle behind her. 'This is not wise, Tanaki.'

'The merits cannot be decided until we are done,' she told him.

182

The bodies had been removed from the settlement, but dried blood still stained the ground and the wood of the auction platform. Tanaki slid from the saddle and entered the hall. Kiall tethered his horse and moved to the ramparts, keeping watch for Nadir warriors. As the minutes passed, he felt his tension rise. Hearing the sound of booted feet on the steps he whirled, scrabbling for his sabre. Tanaki laughed at him. She was clad now in trousers of soft oiled leather and high riding-boots. Her upper body was clothed in a matching hooded tunic, and two short swords were belted at her hips. Over her shoulder was slung a fur-lined cloak of black leather, and in her hand she carried a canvas pack.

'You have all you need?' he asked.

'Not quite. I need the head of Tsudai – but that will come to me.'

They rode back to the camp-site and tethered the horse. Tanaki drew her swords. 'Come,' she said to Kiall, 'show me your skill.'

'No. I . . . I'm not very good. I am not a warrior, you see.'

'Show me.'

Embarrassed, he drew his sabre and dropped into the stance Chareos had taught him. As she leapt forward his sabre blocked her thrust, but she spun, her second sword-blade falling to touch his neck. 'You are too stiff,' she told him.

'I loosen up when I am afraid,' he said, with a smile.

'Then be afraid!' she said, her voice low and chilling. Her sword swept towards his head and he jumped back, but she followed him in. He blocked one thrust, then a second . . . she spun, but he dropped to his knees, her blade slashing the air where his head had been. As her sword sliced down, he dived to his left and rolled. 'That is better,' she said, 'but unless you are a master – which you are not – you should fight with sabre and knife. That would double your killing power.'

Sheathing her blades she walked to the brow of the hill, staring out over the land.

Kiall joined her. 'You still intend to rescue your lady?' she asked him.

'Yes, if I can. But she is not my lady, she never was. I know that now.'

'You blame me for that, Kiall.'

'I blame you for nothing, Princess. I was foolish. I had a dream, and I thought that dream was real.'

'We are full of dreams,' she said. 'We long for the unattainable. We believe in the nonsense of fables. There is no pure love; there is lust and there is need.'

'I do not believe that, Princess.'

'Another dream you think is real?'

'I hope not. There is so much sadness and hate in the world. It would be a terrible thing if love was an illusion.'

183

'Why did you walk away from me earlier, when you were touching me?'

'I . . . I don't know.'

'You lie, Kiall. I could feel the growing warmth in your hands. You wanted to bed me, did you not?'

'No!' he replied instinctively, then looked away, reddening. 'Yes, I did,' he said angrily. 'And I know it was wrong.'

'Wrong? You are a fool, Kiall. It was honest lust – do not be ashamed of it, but do not write poems about it either. I have had fifty lovers. Some were gentle, some were cruel, and some I even grew fond of. But love? If it existed, I would have found it by now. Oh, Kiall, do not look so shocked. Life is short. Joy is everything. To deny that is to deny life.'

'You have the advantage of me,' he said softly. 'I do not have your experience of life. I was raised in a village, where we farmed and we raised cattle and sheep. But there were people there who had been together for half a lifetime. They were happy; I believe they loved one another.'

She shook her head. 'A man and a woman are drawn together by animal passions; they stay together for security. But if a better, perhaps richer man comes along, or a younger, more beautiful woman, then – and only then – can you test their *love*. Look at you, Kiall. Three days ago you loved a woman enough to risk death for her. Now you say you did not love her after all. And why? Because I appeared. Does that not prove my point?'

He remained silent for several seconds, staring out over the horizon. Finally he spoke. 'It proves only that I am a fool. That is not hard to do.'

Tanaki moved to him. 'I am sorry, I should not say these things. I thank you for rescuing me. I will be grateful to you all the days of my life. It was noble of you – and courageous. And I thank you also for walking away back there; that was considerate. But give me a few days and I will teach you joy.'

'No!' he said. 'I do not want to learn that kind of joy.'

'Then remain a fool,' she snapped, turning and stalking away to sit alone.

For almost three weeks the questors journeyed more deeply into the lands of the Nadir, moving across the desolate Steppes towards the far, grey mountains. Occasionally they stayed in small Nadir tent settlements, but mostly they camped in hidden gulleys, caves or hollows. There was no sign of pursuit, and they saw nothing of the soldiers of Tsudai.

Chareos said little during their journey. His face was set and grim, his eyes haunted. Beltzer too had little to say. Harokas proved adept with the bow and twice brought down deer. But mostly their food came from the land in the shape of long, twisted roots, purple in colour, which made a thin but nourishing soup.

Tanaki recovered well and often entered into bantering conversations with Harokas, but Kiall saw the fear in her eyes when any of the questors came too close, watched her flinch at a touch. For some days he said nothing of it. He treated her with courtesy, though she ignored him for most of the time; he guessed she was still angry at what she saw as his rejection of her.

But one night she awoke screaming, rolling from her blankets and scrabbling for her swords. Beltzer was up instantly, his silver axe in his hands. Chareos and Kiall moved to her.

'It is all right,' said Chareos, reaching out. 'It was only a dream.'

'Get back! Don't touch me!' screamed Tanaki. Her sword snaked out and Chareos leapt back, the blade missing him by a finger's breadth.

'Tanaki?' said Kiall softly. 'All is well. You were dreaming. You are with friends. Friends.'

She stepped back, her breathing ragged, her violet eyes wide and frightened. Gradually her breathing grew more calm. 'I am sorry,' she whispered, and turning on her heel, she walked from the camp-site. Beltzer returned to his blankets, grumbling. Kiall walked after Tanaki, coming upon her sitting on a flat rock. Her moonlit face was pale as ivory, and he was struck anew by her beauty. For a moment he said nothing, then he sat beside her.

She swung to face him. 'They must think me weak,' she said.

'No one thinks that,' he assured her. 'But I do not know how to help you, Tanaki. I can heal bruises, stitch wounds, prepare herbs that will bring down fevers. But I cannot deal with your pain.'

'I have no pain,' she said. 'I am healed.'

'I do not think so. Every night you toss and turn. Often you cry out, and sometimes you even weep. It hurts me to see you in pain.'

Suddenly she laughed and stood with hands on hips, facing him. 'I know what you want,' she said. 'You want what those soldiers wanted. Admit it. Be a man! Do not come to me with your, "It hurts me to see you in pain." You don't care for me. And why should you? As far as you are concerned I'm just another Nadir bitch, to be used when you desire it.'

'That's not how I see you,' he said. 'Yes, you are beautiful. Yes, any man would desire you. But I was talking of friendship – and I do care.'

'Well, I don't want your pity either,' she snapped. 'I'm not some colt with a broken leg, or a blind puppy.'

'Why are you so angry with me? If I have said – or done – anything to upset you, then I apologise.'

She seemed about to speak, but her breath came out in a long sigh and she sagged back to the stone beside him. 'I am not angry with you, Kiall.' She closed her eyes and leaned forward, her elbows resting on her knees. 'It is not you,' she repeated. 'I cannot put it behind me. Every time I close my eyes I can see their faces, feel their hands, their . . . Every time. When I sleep, they come for me. And in my dreams I think that the rescue was the dream, and *this* is the reality. I keep thinking about it. It isn't the rape itself, or the beating, it is . . .'

Her voice faded for a moment and Kiall said nothing, allowing the silence to grow. 'I have always known about such atrocities, but until you suffer you cannot understand the enormity of it. And worse, you cannot explain it. Two of those men were once palace guards at Ulrickham. One of them used to carry me on his shoulders when I was a child. So I ask myself, how could he do that to me? And why would he want to? I feel as if the world was never how I saw it – as if a gossamer veil hung before my eyes which they ripped away, leaving me to see the vileness that is reality. Only a few weeks ago I would see that look in Harokas' eye, and I would take it as a compliment. It would make me feel good. Now? Now it is like the look a fox gives a chicken, and it terrifies me.' She looked up at him. 'Do you understand any of this?'

'I understand *all* of it,' he told her. He held out his hand but she backed away from it. 'Fear,' he said gently, 'is usually good. It stops us from being reckless; it gives us caution. But Chareos says that fear is a servant who longs to be the master. And he is a terrible master who must be fought, held in thrall. You are strong, Tanaki. You are iron. You are proud. Take my hand.'

'I don't think that I can,' she said.

'Think back to the woman I first met. You are still her. You have suffered, but you are still the Princess Tanaki, daughter of Tenaka Khan. In you is the blood of greatness.'

He held out his hand and her fingers lifted towards it, fell away, then rose swiftly to hold tightly to his.

Tears welled in her eyes and she sank forward against him. He put his arm around her and sat with her for some time, neither of them speaking. At last she pulled away.

'Then we are friends?' she asked.

'Always,' he told her, smiling.

Together they walked back to the camp where Chareos was sitting alone, staring up at the eastern sky. He did not seem to notice them and Kiall wandered over to him.

'How are you faring?' he asked.

Chareos looked up. 'I do not need to be comforted,' he said, with a wry smile. 'You did well by her. You are a good man.'

'You followed me?'

'Yes. But I did not stay long. She's a fine woman, Kiall. Strong and beautiful.'

'I know that,' said the younger man, uncomfortable.

'If you were to ask me for advice – which you won't – I would tell you to take her away from here. Return to the lands of the Gothir, marry and raise tall sons.'

'And what would you do?' asked Kiall.

'I would continue this mad quest,' answered Chareos.

'Yes, I know. You cannot stop now,' said Kiall sadly. 'Now that it has cost the lives of three of your friends.'

'You are a gifted young man, Kiall. Intuitive and intelligent.'

'I wish I had never asked you for aid. I mean that truly.'

'I know. Sleep well, boy.'

During the weeks which followed Tanaki found herself constantly watching Kiall – enjoying his hesitant, nervous smile, the tilt of his head as he spoke. She had not completely lost her nervousness with the others, but Kiall's friendship had given her strength to battle her fears. During the long evenings Tanaki would walk away from the others and sit with her back to a rock, or a tree, and watch the men. They talked little, but in their movements there was much to read. Beltzer was a bear, a great ambling powerhouse filled with a bitterness he could not voice. Yet his actions were sure and confident, and his speed belied his bulk. Chareos was the timber-wolf, lean and canny, always checking the back-trail, always thinking, always aware. Harokas was the leopard, sleek and yet savage.

And Kiall?

He was the strongest of them all, confident enough to be gentle, humble enough to be wise. His was the strength born of caring, where the others had built their fortresses upon their talent for violence.

But what animal, she wondered? She sat back and closed her eyes, allowing her mind to relax into memories. She was back in the cold palace of Ulrickham. Jungir was playing with a set of carved soldiers, setting them out in battle formation, while she was sitting on a bearskin rug snuggled up against Nameas, the huge warhound. He had been a gift to Tenaka from the Gothir regent, and he followed the Khan on every hunt. Nameas was a killer in war, his terrible jaws rending and tearing, yet in the palace he was soft and gentle, turning his great head every now and then to lick at the infant curled up beside him.

Yes, that was Kiall. The warhound.

Often Tanaki would smile and beckon Kiall to her and they would

187

sit long into the evening talking. She would reach out her hand and he would take it, and they would sit beneath the stars.

One evening, in the third week of travel, she was sitting alone when a shadow fell across her. She thought it was Kiall and looked up, smiling.

'May I join you, Princess?' asked Harokas, sitting down beside her.

She swallowed hard and held the smile in place. 'I did not expect you to join this quest,' she said. 'I have always thought of you as a man who looks out only for himself.'

'As always you are correct, Tanaki,' he said. 'The quest means nothing to me.'

'Then why are you with us?'

'That should be obvious,' he told her, reaching out to touch her arm. She shrank back instinctively and his face darkened.

'You were not so coy back in the settlement, as I recall. Many was the time you invited me to your bed on cold winter evenings.'

'That was then,' she said, holding her back stiff against the tree.

'And what has changed? We were good together, Tanaki. You were the best I ever had. And did I not satisfy you?'

'Yes, you did. You are an unselfish lover, Harokas. You know how to wait. But I have changed.'

He laughed and shook his head. 'Changed? No, not you. You are a lusty wench, and in any civilised land you would be the king's courtesan. No, don't fool yourself. You will never change.' He moved back from her, his dark eyes scanning her face. 'At first I thought it was the rape, but it's not, is it? It's the farm boy. Tanaki of the Blades has fallen for a virgin!' He chuckled. 'There's a story to liven a dull evening.'

'Be careful, Harokas,' she warned him. 'My patience is not much spoken of – and with good reason. Leave me alone.'

He shook his head and his face grew grave. 'I could never do that, Princess. You are in my blood. I want you more than I ever wanted anything.'

For a moment she said nothing, then she rose. 'What we had was good. It was more than good. But it is in the past; there is no more to be said.'

He pushed himself to his feet and bowed elaborately. 'I think you are wrong, Tanaki. But I will not push myself at you; I will be here when you come to your senses. The farm boy is not for you, he never could be. What does he know? I have seen you holding hands. Sweet! But take him to your bed and he'll rut like the peasant he is. And without his innocence what will he be, save yet another farmer? You know what the attraction is for you, don't you? It has been the same since the beginning of time, my love: the desire of the experienced for the innocent, the magnetic lure of virginity. There is an excitement

188

there, you become the first and therefore unforgettable. But what then? No, Tanaki, it has not all been said yet. Good night to you.'

Chien-tsu watched the small group as they angled their horses across the pass. He noted that the lead rider paused often to study the trail: left and right, front and back. A careful man, then. Chien nodded in appreciation. He stood, beckoned Oshi and walked out to meet the riders as they reined in. A huge man on a swaybacked gelding lifted a double-headed axe in both hands and slid from the saddle, but Chien ignored him. He reached the lead rider and gave a bow which was a fraction lower than required.

'You would be Chareos the Blademaster,' said Chien, looking up into the man's dark eyes.

'And you are from Kiatze,' responded Chareos, stepping down to stand before the small warrior.

Chien was both gratified and annoyed. It was good to be recognised as a superior human being, but the man had not returned his bow and that spoke of ill-breeding. 'Yes, my name is Chien-tsu. I am the ambassador from the court of Kiatze. The shaman, Asta Khan, asked me to guide you to him.'

'I don't like the look of him, Blademaster,' said Beltzer, moving alongside Chareos.

'And I am not overly impressed with you,' remarked Chien. 'Save for the smell, which is truly awe-inspiring.'

'You have a large mouth for such a little man,' Beltzer hissed.

'Better that than to be a giant with a brain the size of a pebble,' replied Chien, stepping back and dropping into a hand-fighting stance.

'Be silent, Beltzer,' said Chareos, 'we have enough enemies without adding more.' He turned to Chien and bowed deeply. 'It is a pleasure to meet you, ambassador. You will forgive, I hope, the words of my companion. We have been riding for weeks, with little food, and we have lost three of our comrades. We are short on provisions, on stamina, and on courtesy.'

Chien nodded. 'A graceful apology, sir. Perhaps you would follow me, and then we can see to the introductions? There is venison and a warm fire in the cave.'

Chien spun on his heel and marched off, followed by Oshi. Beltzer grinned. 'Plucky little game-cock, isn't he? I'm damned if I don't like him.'

'That is just as well,' said Chareos softly. 'Had you attacked him he would have killed you.' Without another word Chareos stepped into the saddle and touched his heels to the grey.

At the cave the questors finished the venison with a speed that, to Chien at least, was more gorging than dining. Still, they were barbarians after all, and little more could be expected of them.

189

'Where is Asta Khan?' asked Chareos, wiping the fat from his fingers on to the front of his shirt.

'Sleeping,' answered Chien. 'He will join us this evening. Perhaps we could complete the introductions?'

'Of course. Well, that is Beltzer.' The giant grinned and thrust out a hand. Chien looked down at it with some distaste. It had all the aesthetic appeal of a shovel: the fingers were thick and short, ingrained with dirt, and there were grease stains on the skin. Chien sighed and gripped the hand briefly. Harokas merely nodded, as did Tanaki, but Kiall also offered his hand. This one at least was clean.

'So why is an ambassador from the east dressed as a Nadir rider?' asked Chareos.

Chien told him of the bridal gift, and of the attack upon his party. 'Unfortunately treachery is a way of life among the Nadir,' he said.

'Not only the Nadir,' put in Tanaki, her face blushing. 'The Gothir too have a long history of betrayal and broken promises.'

'I am sorry, Princess,' said Chareos. 'You are of course correct; it was a discourteous comment. But tell me, ambassador, what are your plans? Why have you not tried to reach a port for a ship home?'

'All in its own time, Chareos,' answered the warrior. 'But for now I have offered my aid to Asta Khan, and he is willing to help you. That, I believe, makes us companions.'

'You are more than welcome to travel with us, but I would appreciate knowing your purpose. It does not sit well with me to have a comrade whose plans are a mystery.'

'That I can understand. But I will follow your lead and even your instructions as leader of the group. You need know no more. When my own plans are more stone than smoke, I will inform you – and we will part company.'

Chien moved to the rear of the cave and settled down alongside a second fire, built for him by Oshi. He was more relaxed now. Chareos was almost civilised, and a thinking man. Beltzer was obviously no great thinker, but he wielded the huge axe as if it was no weight at all. The woman was unusual – great facial beauty, but with a body too stringy and boylike for Chien's taste. Yet her eyes radiated strength and purpose. Chien could identify no weak point within the group, and that pleased him.

He settled down to sleep.

Chareos wandered to the cave-mouth, looking up at the stars. There were few clouds and the vault of Heaven was enormous, breathtaking in its scale.

'Welcome to my hearth,' said a sibilant voice and Chareos felt the hairs at the nape of his neck stiffen. He turned slowly. Squatting in the shadows was an old man, wearing a thin loin-cloth of skin and a necklace of human teeth.

'Thank you, Asta Khan,' replied Chareos, moving to sit opposite the old man. 'I am glad to see you well.'

'Your aid was vital. I will not forget it.'

'Okas is dead,' said Chareos.

'I know. Protecting me was a great trial for him and he had little strength left. Now I shall aid you. I know a way into the city – into the bowels of the palace. There you can rescue the woman.'

'Why would you do this, shaman? And do not tell me about paying a debt: that is not the Nadir way. What do you hope to gain?'

'What does it matter?' asked Asta, his face a mask, his eyes cold and impenetrable.

'I do not enjoy playing another man's game.'

'Then let me say this – I have no interest in the woman. You may take her. That is what you want, is it not? There is nothing else you desire?'

'That is true enough,' answered Chareos, 'but now I have two men with their own secret plans.'

Asta cackled and the sound made Chareos shiver. 'The Kiatze? He wishes only to kill Jungir Khan. No more. When the time is right, he will leave you. Now you have only one man to concern yourself with.'

Chareos was uneasy, but he said nothing. He did not like Asta Khan and knew there was more to be said. Yet he could find no words. The old man watched him, his eyes unblinking. Chareos had the feeling his mind was being read.

'You must rest tonight,' said Asta. 'Tomorrow we walk the Path of Souls. It will not be an easy journey but, with luck and courage, we will pass through.'

'I have heard of this Path,' whispered Chareos. 'It is between worlds and it is said to be inhabited by evil creatures. Why must we walk it?'

'Because even as we speak the general Tsudai is riding towards us. He will be in the mountains by dawn. But, of course, you may prefer to fight three hundred men . . .'

'Three of our party are dead already. I wish to see no more die.'

'Sadly, Chareos, such is the fate of the *ghosts-yet-to-be*.'

13

Beltzer could not sleep. He lay back in the flickering torchlight and closed his eyes, but all he could see were the faces of Finn, Maggrig and Okas. Rolling to his side, he opened his eyes. His axe was resting against the cave wall beside him and he looked at his reflection in the broad blades.

You look like your father, he told himself, remembering the grim-faced farmer and his constant, unrelenting battle against poverty. Up an hour before dawn, in bed at midnight, day in day out, engaged in a war he could never hope to win. The farmland was rocky, near barren, but somehow his father had fought the sterile environment, producing enough food to feed Beltzer and his five brothers. By the time Beltzer was fourteen three of the brothers had gone, run away in search of an easier life in the city. The other two had died with his mother during the Red Plague. Beltzer stayed on, working alongside the bitter old man until at last, while guiding the plough-horses, his father had clutched his chest and sagged to the ground. Beltzer had been felling trees in the high meadow and had seen him fall. He had dropped his axe and sprinted down to him, but when he arrived the old man was dead.

Beltzer could not remember one kind word from his father, and had seen him smile only once, when he was drunk one midwinter evening.

He had buried him in the thin soil and had walked from the farmhouse without a backward glance.

Of his brothers he heard nothing. It was as if they had never been.

His mother was a quiet woman, tough and hardy. She too had rarely smiled, but when he thought back he realised she had had little to smile about. He had been beside her when she died. Her face had lost its perennial weariness; she had been almost pretty then.

Beltzer sat up, feeling melancholy. Looking around, he saw Chareos asleep by the dying fire. He rose and took his axe, wanting to see the stars, feel the night wind on his face.

He missed Finn. That night on the gate-tower when the Nadir dragged the bowman from the walls Beltzer had leapt in among them, cleaving and killing. He was amazed to find Chareos and Maggrig beside him. Stooping, he had lifted Finn to his back and run for the gate.

Later, when Finn recovered consciousness, his gashed brow bandaged, Beltzer had gone to him.

'How do you feel?' he had asked.

'I'd be a damn sight better if you hadn't rapped my head against that door-post,' grumbled Finn.

By all the gods in Heaven, that was a time to be alive!

Beltzer felt the breeze on his face and strolled into the last tunnel. He stopped in his tracks . . .

There before him were scores of Nadir warriors, creeping in through the entrance. They had not seen him and quickly he stepped back into the shadows.

He thought of his friends, sleeping peacefully some thirty paces away. The Nadir would be upon them in seconds.

But if he stayed where he was, he could be safe. He could live. He had the gold he had buried near Finn's cabin; that would keep him for years.

Sweet Heaven, I don't want to die!

He stepped out to stand before the Nadir, the torchlight glinting on his red and silver beard, his axe shining crimson.

'Nadir!' he bellowed, the sound echoing through the tunnels. They drew their swords and charged. Never one to wait he lifted his axe, shouted a war-cry and ran to meet them. The blades sliced down and wounded warriors screamed in agony as the giant cut and clove them aside in the narrow tunnel. Swords pierced his flesh, but he felt no pain. A man loomed before him and Beltzer slammed the axe forward, the tips of the butterfly blades skewering his chest. The Nadir fell back. Beltzer staggered, but remained upright.

'Well, my boys,' he said. 'You want to be on my mountain? You want to see the sky?'

A warrior drew his bow and let loose a shaft. Beltzer's axe came up and the arrow glanced from the blades, ripping the skin of Beltzer's temple. The Nadir charged once more, but in the narrow tunnel they could only come at him three abreast. He roared his anger and lifted the bloodied axe. Four more died, then another three, before they fell back again.

Back in the chamber Chareos had gathered his sword and was sprinting back towards the tunnels, Harokas and the others behind him.

Asta Khan stepped into his path. 'You can do nothing!' hissed the old man.

'He is my friend,' protested Chareos, reaching out to brush the shaman aside.

'I know!' whispered Asta. 'That is why he is dying for you: to give you a chance. Don't let him down now. It would break his spirit if you were to die also. Can't you understand that?'

Chareos groaned. He knew it was true, and the pain of that knowledge was too much.

'Follow me!' said Asta, moving off into the darkness. He took the questors to a second chamber, smaller than the first; there he knelt and raised his hands, palms outwards. No words were spoken, but the chamber grew cold, and colder still. Tanaki shivered and leaned in close to Kiall, who lifted his cloak around her shoulders. A deeper darkness formed before the old man and he rose. 'Follow,' he commanded. He stepped into the black doorway.

And disappeared . . .

For a moment the questors stood rooted to the spot; then Harokas walked after Asta, followed by Chien and the trembling Oshi.

'Now you,' said Chareos to Kiall.

The younger man looked at Chareos, reading the intent in his eyes.

'No, Chareos. We will go through together – or back together.'

'I don't want you to die, boy!'

'Nor I you – but the shaman is right. Beltzer would not want you there. This is his victory – that we escape.'

Tears stung Chareos' eyes as he leapt through the doorway. Tanaki and Kiall followed.

The darkness closed around them.

In the tunnel Beltzer found his strength slowly fading. A dagger was jutting from his belly, and blood was pouring from a terrible wound in his upper left arm. The limb hung uselessly at his side and he knew the bone was smashed. Yet still he hefted the axe in his right hand, defying the warriors before him. The tunnel floor was slippery with blood, and the moans of the dying echoed around him.

Again they charged, forcing him back. A sword plunged into his side, breaking his ribs. His axe hammered back to smash a warrior from his feet. Blades licked out at his flesh, piercing him. He roared at the enemy and fell to his knees. They swarmed over him, but he surged up, scattering them. Blood was gushing from his throat and chest, and one eye was closed and bleeding.

The Nadir fell back again – but not in fear.

The giant was dying. No warrior needed to die now to clear the path. They stood, staring at the axeman, their dark eyes reflecting both hatred and respect.

'Had enough, have you?' croaked Beltzer, spitting blood from his mouth. 'You don't want old Beltzer's mountain? Come on? What are you afraid of? It's only . . . death.'

He looked up at the men before him and realised he was on his knees, his axe fallen from his hands. He tried to reach for it but the floor rose up to meet him and he lay quietly for a second or two, trying to gather his strength. Then his arm stretched towards the axe. It was too far away.

But it meant so much. A Nadir warrior knelt beside him, took the axe and placed it in Beltzer's hand.

Beltzer looked up at the man.

'Watch for me on the mountain,' he said.

The man nodded. The last breath rattled from Beltzer's throat and the Nadir rose and loped off down the tunnel, leaving Beltzer with the eighteen men he had killed.

The shock of Beyond brought a scream from Kiall. It was as if black ink had been poured into his eyes, penetrating his skull, covering his brain and his soul with a dark, dark shroud. On the verge of panic he felt Tanaki's hand gripping his, warm and alive.

Then a golden light grew, emanating softly from the hands of Asta

194

Khan, and Kiall saw that they stood on a narrow pathway of shining silver. The light did not penetrate far into the blackness around them, and it seemed to Kiall that they stood in a spherical cave whose walls pressed down with the weight of worlds.

'Do not stray from the path,' whispered Asta. 'This is a place of consummate evil. Those who stray . . . die! No rescue. The only safe way is the Silver Path. Follow me.'

Asta moved carefully forward, Chien and Oshi following and behind them Harokas, Chareos, Kiall and Tanaki.

At first the journey was uneventful, but soon a sibilant whispering grew out of the darkness, closing in on them, and hundreds of shining eyes glinted from all around. The path was too narrow for Kiall to keep holding Tanaki's hand, but he kept glancing back to see her face, drawing strength from her presence.

To the right of the trail white wolves loped into view and sat staring at the travellers. They were monstrous beasts, as large as ponies.

Suddenly the creatures howled and hurled themselves forward and Kiall started to back away, but Tanaki grabbed his jerkin. 'Stay on the path,' she hissed. The beasts came closer – but stopped, fangs bared, inches from the Silver Pathway.

The party moved on into the endless dark. From close by came a scream, then the sound of laughter, manic and shrill. But they saw nothing. The rustle of wings came from above, but when Kiall looked up he saw only darkness.

Then there was silence for a while.

Chareos walked on, oblivious to his surroundings. Beltzer was dead. Maggrig and Finn were slain. His mind reeled back from the tragedies, seeking solace in memories of better times as he followed Harokas blindly, unthinking.

A voice sounded from the left of the path. 'Chareos, help me.' The Blademaster glanced to his left where Beltzer was staggering towards them, wounded but alive. As Chareos stepped from the path the skin peeled back from Beltzer's frame and a scaled creature leapt at the swordsman.

Chareos did not move.

Kiall dived at him, hooking an arm around his waist and hurling him from his feet. But the scaled beast moved with terrifying speed, twisting and looming over them. The small figure of Chien-tsu hurdled the fallen men, his silver sword slicing through the creature's neck. Harokas and Tanaki pulled Chareos back on to the path, Kiall scrambling after them, as Chien backed slowly to join them.

Asta stared down at Chareos and shook his head. These fools would never learn, he thought. Their judgements, their reason, were built on emotions: love, honour, duty, friendship. The Nadir also understood the value of all four, but viewed them differently. Instead of love of the individual, there was love of tribe. Honour and duty were not abstracts but realities, earned by serving the chosen leader. And friendship, forged in war, was the least of all. On the word of a khan one friend would cut the head from another. There would be regret, but not a moment's hesitation. No Nadir warrior would have stepped from the Silver Path. Asta walked on.

The darkness closed in around them, then Asta's voice sounded. 'Stand very still, and wait until you see the light once more. Then move swiftly, for I cannot hold the Gateway for long.'

Silence followed, broken only by the rustling of wings above and the stealthy padding of claws on the rocky ground beside the path. A shaft of dim grey light lit the scene, stretching, widening.

'Now!' yelled Asta and the little shaman ran through the opening. Chien, Oshi and Harokas ran after him. Chareos stumbled through, followed by Kiall. Tanaki ran forward, but her foot strayed from the path and instantly a hairy hand grabbed her ankle, tripping her. She rolled, drawing her sword and hacking at the limb. The hand slid away, but she saw the giant wolves bearing down on her. Bunching her legs beneath her, she hurled herself at the shrinking Gateway.

She hit the ground hard, rolled and came to her knees. The Gate had vanished, and she was kneeling on a ledge high above the city of Ulrickham.

Kiall helped her to her feet. 'I would not wish to walk that path again,' he said. Unable to speak, she merely nodded. Chareos was sitting by himself, staring down at the ground. He looked older, more weary than Kiall had ever seen him.

Kiall walked to him. 'He was a strong man. A good friend,' he said.

'He was a fool. We are all fools,' whispered Chareos. 'But I will see out the game.' He turned his gaze on the city. 'What do you think, Kiall? Shall we surround it and demand they release Ravenna?'

'Whatever you say, Chareos.'

Chareos rose and stretched his back. He smiled and clapped his hand to Kiall's shoulder. 'Life goes on, boy. Do not be too concerned for me.'

Asta Khan walked over to them, squatting to sit before Chareos. 'There is an underground river, below Ulrickham. The great Tenaka knew of it, and linked the city's sewers to it. He also strengthened the side tunnels so that there would be a means of escape if the city was surrounded.'

'Is it guarded?' Kiall asked.

'Not by men. It would not be much of a secret if all the soldiers in Ulrickham knew of its existence. No, the prisoners who laboured to strengthen the tunnels were slain.'

'But it is guarded by something,' said Chareos and Asta looked up, his dark eyes hooded.

'Yes, Blademaster. By something. The blood of the slain was used by me to weave a dark spell. I merged the tunnel with the Void.'

'The Void?' queried Kiall.

'You have just passed through it,' Asta told him. 'Only below Ulrickham there is no Silver Path.'

'We must pass through it again? I couldn't!' said Tanaki.

'You can!' hissed Asta. 'It is not long – a mere twenty paces. I will lead you.'

'And once we are through?' asked Chareos. 'How do we reach Ravenna?'

Tanaki stepped forward. 'You cannot, Chareos. Asta knows this. No man could enter the Palace of Women – but I could.'

'No,' protested Kiall. 'No, I won't have that. It is . . .'

Tanaki chuckled. 'Do not say *too dangerous*, Kiall. It is your only hope.'

'She is right,' said Asta, his eyes shining now. 'She is truly of the blood of the Great Tenaka.' Chien-tsu and Harokas joined the group, listening as Tanaki outlined her plan.

'The question is when,' said Chareos.

'The time is now,' declared Asta. 'The journey through the Void took many weeks, though it felt like hours. Ravenna is only a few days from giving birth.'

'Should we not wait until after the birth?' Harokas asked.

'No!' said Asta. 'Jungir will take the Queen and the heir around the kingdom. They will be surrounded by warriors, and there would be no way to approach them. No, it must be now. Tonight.'

Chien said nothing, but his eyes locked to the face of the shaman. There was much here that was not being said. He did not like Asta Khan, but this quest meant nothing to the Kiatze. He would aid the questors, and then demand his payment. He stood and moved back to Oshi. The old man's face was grey, his eyes wide and staring. The walk through the Void had terrified him.

'Sleep for a while, Oshi,' said Chien, but the old man shook his head. 'I would dream of that place, and I would never wake.'

Nodding, Chien took a sharp knife from the sheath in his sleeve. 'Then be so kind as to make yourself useful. Shave me.'

The little servant smiled. 'Yes, lord.'

The sun sank beyond the distant, mist-shrouded horizon and Chareos stood alone, staring down at the city below, where the first lanterns of evening had been lit. He thought of his boyhood, and the dream of Attalis that one day Chareos would return to the lands of the Drenai and find the hidden Armour of Bronze.

'You will be a great leader, my boy. I know. I can see it in you.'

How little you knew me, thought Chareos. You saw me through the eyes of hope. A great leader? I have brought my greatest friends on a quest of death, and they lie unburied and far from home.

And what did we achieve, he wondered? How has the world been changed by their deaths?

'*It is not over yet*,' whispered a voice in his mind.

'Okas?' he said aloud. But there was no response, and he wondered if he had imagined the old man's voice in the whispering of the dusk breeze. He shivered.

Beltzer had saved them all, standing alone in the dark of the mountain. Chareos smiled, and a weight lifted from him. He looked up at the sky. 'You were a cantankerous, foul-smelling, evil-minded whoreson, Beltzer. But you never let down a friend. May the Source take you. May you drink your fill in the Hall of Heroes.'

He turned away and saw Harokas standing close by, half hidden in the shadows. The assassin stepped forward.

'I am sorry, Chareos, I did not mean to eavesdrop on your farewell.'

The swordsman shrugged. 'It does not matter. What did you want?'

'You intend to go into the city?'

'Yes.'

Harokas nodded. 'It strikes me that we shall have a serious problem if you succeed. We have no horses. Even if you bring the woman out – how will we get away?'

'The wizard will think of something,' said Chareos uneasily.

'Yes, I'm sure,' answered Harokas, dropping his voice, 'but he is playing his own game – and I don't like to think what it might be. But every time I have heard of Nadir shamen it is to do with death and human sacrifice. Is that why he wants the woman, do you think?'

When Chareos said nothing Harokas nodded, understanding the silence. 'Yes, I thought you were worried about that. Look, I will not come with you. I will walk down into the city and buy ponies. I am not known there, and we are not yet at war with the Nadir. Once I have bought them I will ride south, then turn and meet you beyond that bluff, near the stand of poplar.'

Chareos looked deeply into the man's eyes. 'Will you betray us, Harokas? Will you sell us for Nadir gold?'

The assassin's face darkened, but he bit back an angry response. Instead he said, 'I say this for your ears only, Blademaster; I love Tanaki. I would die for her. You understand me? I would sell you in an instant, but not her. *Never* her.'

'I believe you,' said Chareos. 'We will meet as you say.'

Harokas eased past the Blademaster and climbed down the ridge. Chareos watched him, but the dark-garbed figure was soon lost among the shadows.

'Far be it from me to criticise a leader's decision,' said Chien-tsu, bowing low, 'but I do not believe he is to be trusted.'

'You move silently, ambassador.'

'Sometimes it is better so to do. Will we truly meet him at the place you agreed?'

'No. To get there he must pass the trail to the south. We will wait there.'

'Excellent. It may be, Chareos, that I will not be accompanying you. If that proves to be true, would you be so kind as to look after my servant, Oshi? See him safely to a port. I will leave him coin to pay his passage to Kiatze.'

'You intend to kill Jungir Khan? Alone?'

'Such is my intention. The barbarian mistreated the daughter of my Emperor. Quite rightly she took her own life. Now, I must take his. It is a question of harmony and balance.'

Chareos looked down at the small warrior, noting the steadiness of his gaze and the proud, stern set of his features.

'It seems to me, ambassador, that the life of a man like Jungir Khan would not compensate for the loss of Chien-tsu.'

'A graceful compliment,' said the Kiatze, surprised. He bowed low. 'And yet the deed must be done. I will journey with you into the bowels of the earth, and I will wait until the woman is rescued. After that, I shall seek out the Khan.'

Asta Khan led the questors down to the edge of a fissure, a jagged tear in the land's surface. Kiall leaned over and gazed down into the inky depths.

'This is the entrance,' said Asta. 'Now we climb.' The old man nimbly dropped to his haunches and slithered over the edge. Kiall shook his head and looked to Chareos.

The Blademaster unbuckled his sword-belt and hung it over his shoulders before bellying down and following the shaman.

'Wait here, Oshi,' said Chien-tsu. 'And if I do not return, take note of the man Chareos. Serve him as you would me. You understand?'

'Yes, lord,' answered the servant miserably.

Tanaki and Kiall were the last to begin the dark climb. The hand-and foot-holds were good, and the descent less perilous than first appeared. Asta Khan reached the lowest level, raised his arms, and a soft yellow light glowed on the walls of the cavern.

'A heavily pregnant woman will not be able to make that climb,' said Chareos.

'Nor will she need to,' Asta told him. 'I have made preparations.' Moving to the wall, he reached down behind a jutting rock and lifted a coil of hemp rope. 'When we have her, we will climb back to the surface and then haul her up.'

Draping the rope over the rock, he set off across the dimly glowing cavern. The others followed him through a honeycomb of tunnels until, after about half an hour, they reached a point where the glowing light did not penetrate.

Asta pointed to the forbidding wall of darkness. 'You all know what is beyond this point: it is the Void. I shall pass through, with the woman Tanaki and the warrior Chien-tsu. You, Chareos, and your friend, will remain here.'

'What purpose will that serve?' asked Chareos.

'If we are pursued, you will cover our retreat. Many of them will be killed in the Void, but others might get through. Also, much could go wrong for us beyond this barrier. You will be able to hear us – and give us aid if necessary.'

'You said there was no Silver Pathway,' said Kiall. 'How then will you cross safely?'

'I am not without power, child,' snapped Asta. 'But all life is perilously fragile. A man cannot live without danger, no matter how much he may desire it.' He turned to Chien and Tanaki. 'Draw your swords and be ready to use them.'

Kiall touched Tanaki's arm. 'Be careful,' he said, knowing the words were ludicrous but unable to find others. She smiled, leaned forward and kissed his cheek.

'Now stand close to me,' ordered Asta, 'placing your hands on my shoulders.' Chien stood on the shaman's left, Tanaki on his right. Slowly they moved into the darkness.

Once inside, a circle of fire leapt around them like a wall. The heat was incredible and the light burned at their eyes.

'I can hold this for moments only,' said Asta. 'Be ready!' He began to run, the others loping alongside him. The circle of fire remained constantly with them, no matter their speed.

From beyond the silent flames came the sounds of padding feet, talons on stone and the chilling cries of hunting beasts. Still Asta ran on, seemingly tireless.

The flames grew thinner and Tanaki began to see shapeless forms beyond the fire, keeping pace with them. When she glanced at Chien his dark eyes met her gaze and he gave a tight smile.

A scaled arm lashed at the flames. The skin shrivelled and a ghastly scream sounded.

'Almost there!' called Asta.

Suddenly the fire flared – and died.

Asta screamed. A huge creature swooped down from above them, its leather wings knocking him from his feet. Tanaki plunged a sword into the beast's belly and pulled Asta to his feet; he tore clear of her grasp and sprinted away.

A scaled monster leapt from the darkness. Chien's sword flashed out and down and the beast fell writhing to the ground.

'As you value your lives, RUN!' came the voice of Asta. Risking a glance back, Chien saw giant white wolves bearing down on them. The small warrior took to his heels. He saw Asta vanish ahead of him, followed by Tanaki. For a moment Chien experienced panic, feeling the hot breath of a beast upon his neck.

A great weight landed on his back and he fell and rolled. As the wolf beast scrambled up, twisting to attack, Chien's sword slashed through its throat. The pack howled and charged. Chien spun on his heel and flung himself forward through the opening – falling to his knees before Tanaki and the shaman.

Tanaki offered a hand and Chien accepted it, pulling himself to his feet. He glanced back. 'How is it the creatures do not follow us?' he asked.

'They cannot pass through. Think of it as a lake,' said Asta. 'We can dive through the surface, but the fish cannot leave; that is their world. It is possible to make a Gateway for them, but the power needed is great and would require many hundreds of souls.'

'I would not wish to sound defeatist, shaman,' said Chien, 'but upon our return I cannot see the woman Ravenna sprinting away from those wolves. It would be a great pity to rescue her, only to see her die in the Void.'

'She will not die there,' said Asta. 'But my power is finite and I gave you all I could spare. With her I will hold the circle. Now let us move on.'

The tunnel widened, and for the first time it was possible to see the works of men here – the walls smoothed, reinforced with timbers. There was a stairway carved into the rock and Asta mounted it, moving up to squat beneath a low ceiling. He signalled for silence and called Chien and Tanaki to him.

'Above us,' he whispered, 'is the throne room. It is now almost midnight. There should be no one there. Are you ready, Princess?'

'Yes.'

'If the throne room is not empty – we are doomed,' said Asta, for once seeming nervous and unsure.

Chien chuckled softly. 'No life is without peril, shaman,' he reminded him. Asta muttered an obscene curse and lifted the flagstone above his head. It creaked and juddered. Chien helped him with the weight and they twisted the stone to lay it alongside the opening. Tanaki levered herself up into the darkness of the throne room and Chien followed her.

'I will wait here,' said Asta.

Tanaki ran to the main doors, pressing her ear to the crack. Chien moved alongside.

'There should be no guards in the corridor,' Tanaki said. 'The Khan's sleeping quarters are on the other side of the palace. But the women's quarters will have sentries on the outside and eunuch swordsmen within.'

201

Chien nodded. 'I will come with you – and wait.'

She eased open the door and stepped into the torch-lit corridor. All was silent. Keeping to the shadows they moved on, cutting left through a narrow doorway and out into a side street. Tanaki led the warrior through the deserted streets until at last they came to a broad square beyond which was a high wall; three sentries patrolled the outside of the wall.

'How will you get in?' whispered Chien.

Tanaki smiled. 'Distract the guards,' she said. Removing her sword-belt but keeping a curved dagger, she waited until the sentries had passed and then ran to the wall, crouching in the shadows.

Digging into the pocket of his breeches, Chien came up with four golden coins. Tucking them into his belt he waited for the sentries, took a deep breath and then began to sing. He staggered out into the open, belched, half fell and then ambled on towards the men.

'Good evening, my brothers,' he said.

'What are you doing here, fool?' asked one of the sentries, moving forward and touching the point of his spear to Chien's chest.

'Fool?' repeated Chien, giggling and swaying sideways. 'You think I am a fool? Not me, brothers. I . . .' he looked left and right, as if fearing to be overheard. 'I have discovered the Great Secret. I learned it from a shaman. And never will I be poor again. Fool? No brothers, I am celebrating riches beyond your dreams.'

'Riches?' said another. 'What nonsense is this? Be off with you!'

Chien glanced over the man's shoulders. Tanaki had begun to climb the wall behind them.

'Nonsense? You don't believe me.' He waved his hand. 'Give me a copper coin and I will prove it to you. I will turn it into gold before your eyes. Then we'll see. Oh, yes. We'll see.'

The men chuckled. One of them laid his spear on the ground and fished into the pocket of his jerkin. He handed Chien a rough stamped copper coin bearing the head of Tenaka Khan.

Chien rolled the coin in his fingers and flicked it into the air. He caught it deftly and held up his fist, then he began to chant. The words were in an obscure Kiatze dialect.

'Get on with it,' said one of the sentries, losing patience.

'It is done,' said Chien. 'Here is your coin.' He opened his hand, and the gleam of gold was caught by the moonlight. The man took it, his mouth dropping open.

'Do one for me,' said the second sentry.

Tanaki was almost at the top of the wall.

'Why is it always you first?' retorted the third. 'Do mine!'

'I will do them both together,' Chien told them. He accepted their coins, and repeated his chant.

Tanaki clambered over the wall. 'There!' said Chien, handing them the gold coins.

'More! Do us more,' urged the first.

'Tomorrow, when I have rested,' promised Chien. 'Where shall we meet?'

'You know the Clay Pony, behind the Wolves' barracks?'

'Of course,' said Chien. 'But it must be only you. I could not do this for everyone; it would exhaust me. Just you three.'

'Yes, yes, just us. Be there at noon, yes?'

'Oh yes,' agreed Chien. 'I will be there. And now I am for bed. And you should be at your duties.'

He walked away, back into the shadows.

The Princess was inside, and that was a victory.

But getting out would not be so simple, he knew.

14

Tanaki rolled to the ramparts, dagger ready. There were no sentries. Swiftly she moved to the steps and ran down to the courtyard below. To her left was the guardhouse; she could see lantern light through the shuttered windows, and hear the sounds of men talking and laughing – these would be the eunuch guards. Straight ahead was the garden walkway and, to the right, the long, elaborately furnished rooms where the Khan's women spent their days. Here would be the baths and the pools. Beyond these were the sleeping quarters. Many of the concubines slept in dormitories, only the privileged few having rooms of their own.

Tanaki crept across the courtyard and into the darkened day room. Keeping to the wall she walked to the far end of the chamber, opening a door which led to a curtain-hung corridor. Several cats were sleeping here. She moved on past the dormitory rooms to a set of stairs, which she ascended swiftly.

Knowing the layout of the women's quarters, she tried to decide in which of the major rooms Ravenna would be housed. Not the nearest to the Khan's secret corridor – that would be reserved for his latest concubine. No, Ravenna would have been moved closer to the mid-wives' quarters in the east. She padded on, coming at last to a narrow door which led, she knew, to a suite of rooms overlooking the eastern Steppes. Here sunlight bathed the rooms, bringing heat in the morning but staying cool in the afternoon. Opening the door, she slipped inside. The bed had been moved to the window and Tanaki could see a young woman lying on her back. As she crept closer, it was obvious she was pregnant. Tanaki moved to the bedside and sat down, touching the woman's arm.

'Ravenna,' she whispered. 'Ravenna, wake up!'

The woman's eyes opened. 'What is it?' she asked sleepily.

'Kiall sent me.'

'Kiall?' Ravenna yawned. 'Is this a dream?'

'No. Listen to me. I am here to take you from the city. Your friend Kiall has crossed the Steppes to rescue you. For pity's sake, wake up and listen to me!'

The woman eased herself to a sitting position. 'Kiall? The dreamer?'

'The very same.'

'We could never get away from here,' whispered Ravenna. 'There are guards everywhere.'

'I got to you,' argued Tanaki.

Ravenna winced and put a hand to her distended belly. 'He kicks hard,' she said, smiling. She was an attractive girl, Tanaki realised, but no beauty. Her chinline was too strong, her eyes too small. But her smile was radiant.

'Get dressed, Ravenna. I will take you to Kiall.'

'Why has he come for me? I don't understand.'

'Neither does he. Do you want to leave?'

'You have no idea how much I want to leave. I hate this place, I hate these people. But most of all I loathe the Khan. May a thousand curses fall on his blood-line!'

'Be careful what you wish for,' snapped Tanaki. 'Your babe is of that line.'

Ravenna looked instantly contrite. 'I didn't mean . . .'

'Just get dressed,' said Tanaki. Ravenna slipped into a long robe of soft blue-dyed wool and some silk shoes. 'You have no cloak or walking shoes?' Tanaki asked.

'Why would I need a cloak in here? They never let us out.'

'Follow me,' said Tanaki, leading the woman out into the corridor. Ravenna moved slowly and Tanaki glanced back, her irritation growing, but there was nothing to be done. The pregnancy was well advanced, the swelling huge.

When they reached the door to the courtyard, Tanaki opened it a fraction and looked out. Two sentries were now patrolling the ramparts and she cursed.

'What is it?' asked Ravenna.

'Guards. Two of them.'

'Can we get past them?'

'Not at the speed you move.' She opened the door once more, watching the men, counting the seconds as the sentries passed by one another. Their only chance lay in moving as the warriors reached the angle of the walls, before they turned back. She watched them repeat the manoeuvre three times, then seized Ravenna's arm. 'Now!' she hissed.

They moved from the doorway on to open ground and crept across the courtyard to the wall. 'We'll never get out,' Ravenna whispered.

Keeping to the shadows, the two women edged closer to the postern gate. The sentries were directly above them now as Tanaki ran her hands over the gate-bolts. They were rust-covered and she cursed softly – and eased back the bolt. It moved no more than an inch, then creaked. Tanaki froze. But the guards had not heard and she moved it again. This time the bolt slid clear. Tanaki swallowed hard, took a deep breath and pulled open the gate. Glancing outside, she saw three guards were standing no more than twenty feet away. There was no way past them, and she could not kill them all.

Then she saw Chien-tsu. He walked across the open ground towards the guards and one of them turned and raised his spear. Suddenly the little warrior spun and launched a kick which cannoned against the sentry's temple to send the man catapulting from his feet. A second guard fell with a knife in his throat. The third rushed at the Kiatze warrior, but Chien-tsu stepped aside from the thrust of the spear and rammed the blade of his hand into the man's neck.

'Swiftly now!' said Tanaki, leading Ravenna into the open.

A sentry on the wall shouted an alarm as Chien raced to Ravenna, taking her arm and urging her to run. The trio made it to the first alleyway, ducking into the shadows. Ravenna was breathing heavily, her face deeply flushed. 'I am sorry,' she said, sagging against a wall. 'I cannot run any further.'

They could hear the sounds of pounding feet in a parallel street, and the calls of the soldiers.

The trio moved on. Chien drew his curved sword and took the lead. The sound of the pursuing warriors faded away. 'They are trying to cut us off from the main gates,' said Tanaki. 'That's good.'

Chien felt there was little *good* in this entire adventure, but he held his tongue. They reached the palace corridor and ran into the throne room.

Warriors raced from the shadows but Chien cut the first from his feet, ducked under a wild slice and skewered another. Tanaki hurled her dagger into the face of a charging warrior – then saw Tsudai. All thoughts of the quest vanished as she dived to the floor, scooping up the sword of a fallen warrior and rolling to her feet. Tsudai ran to meet her, screaming a battle cry. She blocked his cut, spun and rammed her sword through his chest.

'Rot in Hell!' she hissed as he sagged to the floor.

Chien was surrounded now, and Tanaki wrenched the sword clear of Tsudai's body and ran to his aid. There were six warriors against him, but she could hear more running in the corridor outside. She stabbed one man in the back and slashed her blade across the face of another. They all fell back briefly.

Asta Khan rose from the opening in the floor and uttered a weird howl. An icy wind blew across the throne room and the Nadir staggered back, screaming. The first three warriors stumbled to their knees with blood streaming from their eyes.

Tanaki grabbed Ravenna's arm and dragged her back to the hole in the floor. 'Down!' she ordered.

Ravenna clambered into the hole and Tanaki followed her, leading her down the steps, Chien bringing up the rear.

'Swiftly,' said Asta. 'The spell will not hold them long.' Ravenna staggered, but stayed upright, and Chien took her arm.

Behind them they could hear the Nadir pounding down the steps . . .

They reached the darkness. Asta took Ravenna's hand and she flinched away from the shaman, but he held her tight. 'Now is the time for courage, woman,' he said, and pulled her into the Void.

As before a circle of flames sprang up around them, and they moved across the darkness. Behind them the Nadir ran – unsuspecting – into the Void. Their screams were terrible.

The circle of fire began to fade and the dwellers in the dark closed in. Sweat shone on Asta's brow as he struggled on. Taloned hands reached out for them, but the flames held them back. At last they reached the outer limit – and passed through. Asta collapsed to the stone floor. Seeing Ravenna, Kiall ran forward to take her in his arms. Tanaki watched the scene and turned away, her thoughts confused.

Chareos helped Asta to his feet.

The old man shrugged clear of his aid. 'We must get out of here,' he said. 'Help the woman. Carry her if you must.'

Back they went through the honeycomb of tunnels, arriving at last at the fissure. Kiall, Chareos, Tanaki and Chien climbed to the surface, Kiall carrying the rope. They lowered it down and Asta made a loop in which Ravenna sat. Slowly the three men pulled her to the top.

Then they began to walk towards the hills. Chareos glanced back to see that half a mile away the city gates had opened and a column of riders was galloping out towards them.

The sound of hoofbeats came from the left. Chareos drew his sabre and spun . . . Harokas dragged his horse to a halt, behind him a string of ponies.

'You had better mount,' said the assassin. They helped Ravenna into the saddle of the first, then the others mounted.

'There is only one place we can reach,' said Asta Khan. 'Follow me.' He kicked his pony into a run and set off towards the west. The questors followed him, cutting to the right through a series of narrow passes. After an hour's hard riding, with the Nadir closing on them, they emerged at last into a narrow valley.

The moon was high and Chareos groaned as he saw the broken tower and the stretch of battlements silhouetted against the sky. 'No!' he whispered.

But they rode on into the ghostly fortress of Bel-azar.

The eastern gates lay open and the questors rode their weary mounts inside. Chareos and Kiall dismounted and ran back to the gates, forcing them shut. Harokas found a thick beam which he and Tanaki wedged into the great bolt-plates. Then they mounted the rampart steps and watched from the battlements as the thirty Nadir riders drew rein outside. Asta Khan joined them. He leapt nimbly to the wall and stood looking down at the riders, letting them see him.

'Will they attack?' asked Kiall. Chareos said nothing.

Asta Khan began to dance on the precarious footing, twisting and leaping. He howled like a wolf, the sound eerie and chilling as it echoed in the mountains. Three Nadir riders turned their mounts and rode back towards the city, but the others dismounted and sat on the rocks. Asta turned and jumped back to the ramparts, his dark eyes gleaming.

'They are frightened,' he said. 'This is a haunted place. They know dark spirits walk here.'

In the open ground below Ravenna cried out and clutched her belly. Kiall and Tanaki ran down to her, helping her into a ruined guard-house where there was a dust-covered bed. Tanaki pulled aside a rotted blanket and placed her own on the mattress; then they lowered Ravenna to it.

'It's coming,' cried Ravenna. 'I can feel it.'

Kiall heard a movement behind him and saw Asta Khan standing in the doorway. The shaman's face was shining and the glint of triumph was in his eyes. It chilled Kiall.

'Leave us,' Tanaki told Kiall and gladly he obeyed, easing past the shaman and moving out into the dawn light. Chareos was still on the ramparts, below the ruined gate-tower. Chien-tsu and Oshi had lit a fire near the main barracks building, and were sitting together talking in low voices. Harokas had led the ponies back to a paddock section, where he had unsaddled them and was brushing their lathered frames. Kiall walked to the steps and climbed to where Chareos sat watching the Nadir.

'We did it,' said Kiall. 'Whatever happens now, we did what we set out to do.'

Chareos looked up and smiled. 'Yes, we did it. We found your lady, and we brought her back to Gothir lands. That is a feat in itself. But do not hold out any great hopes, Kiall. I do not wish to sound defeatist, but I do not believe five warriors and a shaman can hold off the Nadir nation.'

Kiall chuckled. 'I cannot explain it, Chareos, but I don't care any more. All my life I've been a dreamer. Now I feel that a dream has been achieved. I'm not even frightened of dying.'

'I am,' admitted Chareos. 'Especially here.' He pointed to the gate-tower. 'There it is, boy – the scene of great deeds. From there Beltzer leapt to win back the standard. There we sat talking with Tenaka Khan. And it was here we were dubbed the *ghosts-yet-to-be*. It is not a good feeling to be sitting here waiting for death.'

'And birth,' said Kiall. 'Okas told us the child would be a great king – perhaps the greatest who ever lived. That's something, isn't it?'

Chareos nodded and turned away. The fortress loomed around him, grim and threatening, and he could feel its memories in the cold stone, hear again the screams of the dying and the clash of iron blades.

Tanaki joined them. 'It was a false alarm,' she said. 'She is resting now. Is there any sign?'

'No,' answered Kiall. 'They just sit there and wait – I don't know what for.'

'They are waiting for Jungir Khan,' she said. 'They don't know why we took their queen, but they dare not risk anything that might cause her harm. Jungir will decide what to do.'

She walked off to the gate-tower door and pushed it open. Kiall followed her, mounting the cracked steps to the tower itself, where she sat down and leaned her back against the wall.

'Well,' she said, 'you have seen your woman once more.'

He looked down at her and then knelt, taking her hand. 'She is not my woman, Tanaki. It was like seeing an old friend. I am not skilled in these matters, but I . . . I want you to know, before . . .' He stumbled to silence.

'Before we die?' she prompted.

'Yes, before we die. I want you to know that I love you. I know you do not believe in love, but I would sooner hold your hand here for a night than live a hundred years without you. Does that sound foolish?'

'Yes,' she said, reaching out and stroking his face, 'but it is wonderfully foolish. It is beautifully foolish.' She drew him towards her, brushing her lips against his. His arms circled her. 'Would you like to make love?' she whispered.

He drew back. 'Yes, but we will not – not in this cold stone place, which reeks of death and misery. Can we just sit together, close?'

'For a man of little experience, you so often say exactly the right words,' she told him.

The sun climbed high behind them, the sky cloudless and streaked with red. 'It will be a fine day,' he said.

She did not reply.

Harokas saw them from the courtyard and sighed. Then he caught sight of Asta Khan, moving furtively from the main barracks building; he was carrying something. As Harokas squinted against the sunlight, he saw that the shaman was holding a bleached skull which he carried to the room where Ravenna lay. Harokas watched him slip inside.

The assassin strolled up to where Chareos sat. 'This would be a good time to ride off deep into Gothir lands,' he said.

Chareos shook his head. 'The woman would lose the babe. She is close to giving birth.'

Harokas sighed. 'If we stay, we will all die. And women can conceive a second time, Chareos. It would not cause the world to fall in darkness were she to lose this one child?'

'The child is special,' insisted Chareos. 'But more than that, I am meant to be here. I cannot explain it – but I have known for many years that my destiny lay here.'

'I think Asta Khan feels the same way. I have just seen him carrying an old skull into the woman's room. Truly the ways of shamen are beyond me – I am happy to say.'

'A skull?' The words of Okas came flooding back to him: '*Why are Tenaka Khan's bones buried at Bel-azar?*' Chareos pushed himself to his feet and descended the broken steps, crossing the courtyard and opening the door to the old guardhouse. Ravenna was sleeping but at the foot of the bed was Asta Khan, sitting cross-legged, a skull in his lap.

'What are you doing here?' asked Chareos.

The shaman glanced up. 'Nothing that will harm the woman, Chareos. You have my word.'

'And the child?'

'The child was not part of the bargain – but she will give birth to a healthy babe.'

'What is it that you are not telling me, Asta? What foulness are you planning with those . . . those relics?'

'Relics? If you had any idea of what these bones . . .' He stopped and forced a smile. 'I have kept my bargain with you, Blademaster. You cannot fault me. But I too have a quest – and it is worth more than my life.'

'You promise me you do not mean to harm Ravenna – or the child?'

'The child will be born,' said Asta with a secretive smile. 'He will be born strong and grow fast. He will be the Great Khan. No harm will come to him – or to the mother of his flesh.'

'Chareos!' came Kiall's voice. 'Come quickly!' The Blademaster turned from the shaman and ran back to the wall. Beyond, on the open plain, a horde was galloping towards the fortress. Leading them was a warrior dressed in black, riding a grey stallion.

'The whoreson is riding to kill me on my own horse,' exclaimed Chareos.

'See who rides beside him,' said Harokas. 'Now there is a surprise!'

On a bay stallion, his blond hair glinting in the sunlight, rode the Earl of Talgithir.

The Nadir halted some two hundred yards from the fortress and dismounted, while the Earl kicked his horse into a canter and rode up to the walls.

'Open the gate!' he called.

Chareos leaned over the ramparts. 'For what purpose?' he asked.

'Because I demand it!' roared the Earl, his face reddening. Then he recognised Chareos. 'Oh, it is you, is it, Blademaster? I should have guessed. Now open the gate – and you will all live.'

'I asked you for your purpose,' said Chareos.

'I do not need to answer to you, swordsman. I am the Earl of Talgithir, appointed by the Lord Regent.'

'And you have no jurisdiction at Bel-azar,' said Chareos. 'Talgithir is far from here.'

The Earl leaned back in his saddle and laughed. 'You have been gone for some time, Chareos. I am now the Regent's envoy to the Nadir and, as such, my orders are to be obeyed anywhere in the realm. Now will you open that gate?'

'I do not think that I will,' said Chareos. 'I care not what appointment you have received. You are a slave trader and a traitor to your people. When the Lord Regent hears of your dealings, you will hang.'

'You are hardly in a position to threaten me. But I will wait.' Swinging his horse's head, he cantered back to the Nadir.

'I don't understand this,' said Harokas. 'Why is he so calm?'

Chareos shrugged. 'I have an uncomfortable feeling we are going to find out.'

Throughout the morning the Nadir remained where they were, but as the sun reached noon and the shadows disappeared there came from the west the sound of walking horses. Chareos and Kiall ran to the western gate, dragging it open. Three hundred lancers were riding to the fortress, led by Salida.

Kiall cursed. 'That's why the Earl was so calm – his soldiers have come to meet him. Now we are truly trapped.'

'Do not be so sure,' whispered Chareos. 'Salida is no lickspittle.'

'He's unlikely to take on a Nadir army – and his own Earl,' said Kiall.

Chareos moved out before the riders. Salida drew rein and stepped from the saddle. 'Well met,' greeted the officer. 'You do turn up in the most unlikely places.' He lifted the water canteen from his saddle and drank deeply.

'The Earl is outside the fortress,' said Chareos softly. 'He is with Jungir Khan and a thousand Nadir warriors.'

'There is a treaty being negotiated. It does not concern you,' said Salida.

'There is a *slight* problem,' Chareos told him.

Salida walked to a boulder and sat down. 'Somehow, I did not doubt it,' he said wearily. Chareos joined him and swiftly outlined the journey into Nadir lands, and the secrets they had discovered concerning the Earl's dealings with the Nadren. Lastly he told of the rescue of Ravenna and the imminent birth.

'What is it you have against me, Chareos?' asked Salida. 'Why must you turn up like a bad smell, just when life is looking good? I have had a rise in pay and I now command three hundred men. We have a treaty in prospect and my career is golden. Now you tell me the Earl is a traitor – and you have kidnapped the Nadir Queen. Excellent!'

'What will you do?'

'What would you have me do?' snapped Salida. 'The Lord Regent is expecting a treaty – a treaty he believes will safeguard the Gothir nation. Do you think he will risk a war because of a stolen peasant girl?'

'It is your decision, my friend,' said Chareos softly. 'All Jungir Khan wants is my life, and the lives of my friends. Such a small price to pay for peace, is it not?'

'For the guarantee of peace I would pay more than that,' hissed Salida. The Captain stood and looked to his men. 'Dismount!' he called. 'Take the horses inside. Beris!' A young officer came forward. 'Twenty groups to the wall, eight groups in reserve. Let the others look to the horses and prepare some food.'

'Yes, sir. Sir?'

'What is it?'

'Are we here to fight? I thought we were to accompany the Earl back to New Gulgothir with the treaty.'

'So did I, my boy. Isn't life full of nice surprises?' He turned back to Chareos. 'I assume you have the proof to back up your accusations?'

'Of course: the finest proof of all, the word of the Nadir Queen and the man who collected the Earl's profits. And lastly, the Nadir Princess who dealt with him.'

'This is insane, Chareos. You know that, don't you?'

'I know that you're a better man than the one you serve.'

'You can forget the compliments,' snapped Salida, marching into the fortress and ascending the battlement steps. Seeing Harokas, he scowled.

'Welcome, Salida, old friend,' greeted Harokas. The soldier grunted and watched his men fan out along the wall.

211

The Nadir rose as the line of armoured men took up their positions. Once more the Earl mounted his bay and galloped to the wall.

'Good to see you, Salida,' he called. 'Arrest those people and open the gate.' Behind him the Nadir had mounted and were riding slowly forward.

'You have been named as a traitor,' answered Salida. 'I ask you now to surrender yourself to me. You will be taken to New Gulgothir for trial before the Lord Regent.'

'Are you mad?' stormed the Earl. 'Who accuses me? Chareos? A man I forgave for murder?'

'I do,' said Harokas. 'You trafficked in slaves – and I collected your gold. The Princess Tanaki is also here. Answer that – *my lord*.'

'I need not answer to you. Come, Salida, think of your position. You have three hundred men. There are a thousand here – and a thousand thousand still to be called upon. You cannot prevail. Open the gates – and we will ignore this . . . this insubordination.'

'I ask you again, my lord, to surrender yourself.'

'I'll see you dead, you miserable cur!' the Earl shouted.

Jungir Khan spurred the grey alongside the nobleman. 'Why are they not opening the gate to you?' he asked mildly.

'They are traitors,' snarled the Earl. 'Kill them all!'

'You cannot even control your own captain,' said Jungir. 'How then can you serve me?'

The Earl started to answer, but Jungir's hand flashed up – and the curved dagger blade plunged into the Earl's heart. Slowly he slid from the saddle. Jungir rode the grey stallion forward.

'Who commands this castle?' he called.

'I, Salida.'

'I am Jungir Khan. Come down, I wish to speak with you. It is not fitting that two commanders should negotiate in this manner.'

On the wall Harokas turned to Salida. 'Don't listen to him; it is a trick. Once the gate is open, they will storm through.'

'These broken walls would not stop them,' answered Salida. He strode down the rampart steps and ordered the gate to be opened. Chareos walked with him and waited in the gateway.

As Salida walked on to the open ground Jungir touched his heels to the grey – which suddenly reared up, almost toppling him from the saddle. He clung on grimly as the stallion ducked its head and bucked. Jungir wrenched the beast's head and the horse fell – the Khan leaping from the saddle and falling to the dust. The stallion – ears flat to its skull, eyes rolling – lashed out at the Nadir leader, who fell back. The horse reared above him, hooves ready to smash his skull, as Chareos ran forward. 'Be calm, Grey One,' he called. 'To me!' The stallion swung to the sound of his voice and trotted away from the fallen Khan. Chareos stroked the beast's long neck.

212

Jungir rose and brushed the dust from his breeches. He was acutely aware that his men would be avidly watching what followed. The Khan had lost face. Worse, he had been rescued by the enemy.

'Are you all right, my lord?' Salida asked.

'I am well. You!' called the Khan to Chareos. 'You may keep the horse. It is a gift.' He swung back to Salida. 'Now, Captain, you say the dead man was a traitor. I have dealt with him. Now I ask you to return to me my property. To refuse will be taken as an act of war against the Nadir people. Is this what you wish, Captain?'

'No, Highness, it is not,' answered Salida. 'But you are standing on Gothir lands and Bel-azar is a Gothir fortress. Will you be so kind as to wait for me to seek orders from my superiors in Gulgothir? I will send a rider – and an answer will be forthcoming within the day?'

'I could take this ruin within an hour,' said Jungir.

'The Nadir are indeed a ferocious enemy,' Salida agreed. 'But allow me the day.'

For a moment Jungir was silent. He walked away, as if considering the request, and glanced at his warriors. The incident with the stallion had worried them. The tribesmen put great weight on omens; the horse had unseated the Khan and now stood in the gateway, allowing itself to be petted by the tall, dark-eyed warrior there. A good shaman would find a positive omen, even in this bizarre circumstance, but Shotza was dead and Asta Khan was standing on the ramparts in full view of the Nadir. If Jungir gave the order his men would attack, but they would do so less willingly, fearing bad omens. And if they should fail to take the walls swiftly there was a chance that – believing the gods were against them – they would turn on their leader. Jungir thought it through. The risk of failure was remote – but on a day like this? He swung back to Salida. 'Men should have time to consider their actions,' he said. 'I give you your day. But hear this: not one person is to leave the fortress – save for your messenger. And all who are not soldiers will be handed over to me. Otherwise I will destroy you all. Let that message be carried to the Lord Regent.'

The Khan strode back through his lines, the Nadir flowing after him. They stopped and made camp a half-mile from the wall.

'You are a man with nerve,' Harokas told Salida.

'And you will need to be,' said Salida, 'if the Lord Regent sends the message I expect him to.'

The day wore on, dusk shadows stretching across the valley. The Nadir lit camp-fires and Salida ordered most of the men back from the ramparts. The soldiers started their own cook-fires and Salida brought a bowl of thick soup to where Chareos sat on the wall.

The Blademaster accepted it and put it aside to cool. 'I am sorry, Salida. Once more I seem to have caused trouble for you.'

213

Salida shrugged. 'I am a soldier, Chareos. Trouble is what I am paid for. But – and I hope you will not take this amiss – when this is over I do not want to see you again.'

'In the circumstances that is understandable,' agreed Chareos with a wry smile. He looked down on the body of the Earl. 'Strange, he was a man of many talents and yet he always told me he envied my role at Bel-azar. He often said he would like to have had the chance to fight here. And he did . . . on the wrong side.'

'*That* is a question of perspective, Chareos. The wrong side is the losing side. We have yet to see which side we are on.'

'What do you think the Lord Regent will decide?'

'Let us wait and see,' said Salida, looking away.

'My thoughts exactly,' agreed Chareos. 'He will sell us out. Better that, I suppose, than a costly war he cannot win.'

An ululating chant began in the guardhouse and Salida shivered. 'I do not like that man,' he said. 'Like all Nadir shamen, he reeks of death.'

Tanaki joined them on the battlements, Kiall beside her. 'That is a birth chant,' she said. 'I'll go down and help.'

Chareos yawned and stretched out on the battlements. He was weary and his bones ached. Rolling his blanket for a pillow, he lay down in the shadows and tried to sleep.

'*Defend the babe, Blademaster*,' came the voice of Okas.

Chareos awoke with a start. Salida had returned to his men and only six sentries walked the walls. Chareos sat up. Asta Khan had promised him the mother and the babe would be safe. What then was the danger? He recalled again the words of Okas back in Tavern Town.

'*Why do the bones of Tenaka Khan lie buried at Bel-azar?*'

Tenaka Khan – The King Beyond the Gate, the Prince of Shadows. A man Asta believed should never have died. Now the shaman sat in the birth room, holding to the skull of the Great Khan. Chareos' mouth was dry and the thoughts tumbled together. What had Asta said? 'No harm will come to the mother of his flesh.'

What of his spirit, his soul?

He glanced down at the guardhouse. In there, at this very moment, Asta Khan was waiting to slay the child's soul. Chareos rose and ran down the rampart steps.

He had reached the guardhouse door and was about to enter when he heard a sound from behind and swivelled, but too late. Asta's dagger slashed out to nick the skin of his face. As the little shaman jumped back Chareos tried to draw his sabre, but his limbs were sluggish and heavy.

'I knew,' whispered Asta Khan, 'that you would divine my purpose. But it is too late for you, Chareos. Die in peace.'

The poison flooded his veins. His legs gave way, and he did not feel himself hit the ground.

Asta pulled the body to the side of the building, then returned to his place at the bedside. He sat on the cold floor and closed his eyes, his spirit soaring free.

Ravenna was moaning with the pain of the contractions, Tanaki beside her. Kiall was asleep by the far wall, but he awoke and sat up. 'What is happening?' he asked.

'Her water's broken. The babe will be born any time now,' answered Tanaki.

'What can I do?'

'What all men do at this time – nothing,' she answered, a smile robbing the words of venom. Kiall rose and walked from the room. Outside the night was fresh and clear. Most of the soldiers were asleep, save the guards on the walls. He looked around for Chareos, but there was no sign of the Blademaster. Seeing Chien-tsu rise from his blankets, Kiall strolled over to him.

The little warrior stretched and lifted his sword-belt into place, the long blade hanging between his shoulder-blades. His servant slept on, snoring softly.

'Where is Chareos?' asked Chien.

'On the wall, I think.'

'Let us hope so,' said Chien, trotting towards the rampart steps. They searched the wall and the gate-tower. Chien seemed anxious now. He turned to stare back into the fortress, his eyes alighting on the still figure by the guardhouse wall. Both men ran to the body and Chien turned it over, feeling for a pulse.

'What happened to him?' asked Kiall.

'I do not know. I heard his soul cry out. It woke me.'

'Look, there is a cut to his face.'

'It could have happened when he fell,' said Chien. 'We must get him to a fire. His body is cold, but the heart still beats.'

Chareos awoke to a bleak landscape – the sky a pitiless grey, the land devoid of life. A dead tree stood like a skeleton on the brow of a distant hill, and a light shone there. Chareos shook his head. He had no recollection of travelling to this barren land. As he walked towards the light wolves howled in the distance, the sound eerie and hollow. Chareos climbed the hill and sat by the light, which was emanating from a point just above the ground. He reached out to touch it, but a voice stopped him.

'It is fragile, Chareos, and pure,' said Okas and Chareos turned. The Tattooed Man smiled and held out his hand. Chareos took it.

'What is the light?' asked the Blademaster.

'There are two lights,' said Okas. 'They are the souls of the twins Ravenna carries.'

'They are beautiful,' Chareos whispered.

215

'All children have bright souls, but these two are special. They will change the world, Chareos. For good or ill.'

'How did you come here? For that matter, how did I come here?'

'Asta Khan poisoned your body. Even now you are dying in the world beyond. He plans to kill what he sees as the soul of the child.'

'I remember,' said Chareos. 'He wants to bring Tenaka Khan back to life. Can he do it?'

'Yes, if his timing is right. That is why the bones were at Bel-azar. That is also why Jungir placed a thousand spells on the Tomb of Ulric – not to stop robbers from getting in, but to stop Tenaka Khan from getting out. But Asta fooled him; he substituted the Khan's bones, and carried them to Bel-azar – to await the *ghosts-yet-to-be*.'

'So we fulfilled his dreams?'

'We kept him alive when he was weak. But now he is strong again.'

'What can we do?'

Okas shrugged. 'We can defend the child.'

'Can we succeed?'

'No, Chareos. But when has that ever been important?'

A cold wind blew across the hill-top and a dark mist formed. The mist hardened to become a horde of demons with dull red eyes and long talons. In their midst stood Asta and beside him Tenaka Khan, the King Beyond the Gate.

Chareos stood and drew his sabre. It shone with a silver light.

'Still you oppose me?' sneered Asta Khan. 'It will avail you nothing. Look now upon my army!' As far as the eye could see there were creatures of darkness, and Chareos could sense their lust for blood like a physical force pushing him back.

'Step aside, Chareos,' said Tenaka Khan. 'You have done all that you were intended to do. The *ghosts-yet-to-be* have fulfilled their quest – they have given me a second chance at life.'

'No, Great Khan,' replied Chareos. 'You had your life, and it ended. This child deserves to see the sky and live his own life. And I do not believe that my friends and I died for your glory. If anything, it was for the babe.'

'Enough of this!' shouted Asta. 'You think to stop us alone?'

'But he is not alone,' said Beltzer, walking to stand beside Chareos. When the Blademaster looked at his friend, Beltzer was no longer old and fat, no longer bald. Red hair framed his face in a lion's mane, and his silver axe blazed with light.

Maggrig and Finn appeared on his left, white bows in their hands.

Chareos felt a swelling in his throat and tears formed in his eyes. He brushed them away with the sleeve of his shirt.

'Now you know, Tenaka,' he said, 'the meaning of the *ghosts-yet-to-be*. Bring on your demons. We defy you all!' Beltzer hefted his axe, Maggrig and Finn drew back on their bows. Asta raised his arm, but

Tenaka held to it. The Khan walked forward, his violet eyes sad and thoughtful.

'I thought you were created for me,' he said. 'I knew you had some purpose – it is why I let you live, why I scarred my life of victories with that one defeat.' He gazed down at the light and sighed. 'But you are right, Chareos. My day has passed. Let the child see the sky.'

He turned away and walked back to the demon horde. A path opened before him and he vanished from sight.

Asta walked towards Chareos, but the Blademaster blocked his way to the light.

The shaman looked old now, wretched and desolate as he looked up at Chareos, blinking and confused.

'You must let me have the babe,' he said.

'No.'

'I do not mean to kill it. I cannot now – not without Tenaka's blessing. But the Nadir must have a Khan. You see that, do you not? He is of the blood of kings. Let me have him.'

'What do you offer, Asta Khan?'

'I have an antidote to the poison. You will live.'

'You misunderstand me. What do you offer the child?'

'My life. I will defend him all the days of my life. I will teach him to be the Khan.'

'Then you may have him.'

Asta's surprise was genuine. 'Let me see his spirit.'

'No. Return to Bel-azar and give me your antidote. You will see the babe when he is born.'

'Can I trust you, Chareos?'

'I am afraid that you can,' said the Blademaster.

Asta turned and vanished and the mist formed about the demons once more. The wind howled, the mist swirling away into the grey sky.

And the heroes of Bel-azar were alone on the hill-top. The light from the twin spirits grew, touching the dead tree. Leaves sprang from the branches, blossoms of pink and white flowered into life and fragile petals fell like snowflakes around the souls.

15

For sixteen hours Chareos lay close to death, scarcely breathing. Asta Khan stayed by his side, pouring a foul-smelling potion between his lips and rubbing his limbs, forcing the blood to circulate. Chien-tsu offered his help, but Asta waved him away.

'Is he doing any good?' Kiall asked the Kiatze warrior.

'I have never seen anyone work harder. I could almost believe he actually cares whether Chareos lives or dies. Almost.'

Kiall returned to the guardhouse where Ravenna had given birth to twin boys, healthy and strong. Tanaki was still at the bedside, but both women were asleep. Kiall was about to leave her there when Tanaki opened her eyes; she smiled wearily and stood, moving in to his embrace.

'What now?' she asked, looking up at him.

'Now we wait for the Lord Regent's answer.'

One of the babes began to cry and Tanaki went to where he lay with his brother in a makeshift crib, lifting him clear. She carried him to Ravenna, pulled back the blanket and held him to Ravenna's breast. The mother did not stir from her sleep.

Tanaki rubbed the babe's back and returned him to the crib. The other babe awoke but did not cry. Tanaki lifted him also and carried him to Ravenna. He too drank lustily.

'It is a pity Ravenna was not the woman of Chareos,' said Tanaki.

'Why?'

'He could have challenged Jungir Khan to single combat for her. It is the Nadir custom and the Khan could not have refused. That way, we could have avoided a war.'

'I could challenge him,' said Kiall.

Fear flashed into Tanaki's eyes. 'You will do no such thing! I have seen you in action and you are not one half as skilful as Jungir. He would cut you into pieces.'

'I could strike a lucky blow,' he argued.

'Luck does not enter into a contest of that nature. Put the idea from your mind.'

He paused in the doorway. 'I do love you,' he said. 'You know that?'

'Yes. I know.'

He left her then and walked to the ramparts where Salida was standing with Harokas and Chien-tsu. Glancing back at the unconscious Chareos, he saw the shaman was still beside him.

'I think his heart gave out,' said Harokas.

'He is not a young man,' Salida said, 'but I hope he pulls through.'

The Nadir began to stir, rising from their camp-fires and saddling their horses. Salida glanced at the sky. It was almost time.

A rider came galloping through the western gate, leaping from the saddle of his lathered mount. He ran to Salida, handing him a scroll of parchment sealed with green wax and stamped with the Lord Regent's seal. Salida walked away from the others, removed his battle gauntlets and opened the scroll. He sniffed loudly and read the document slowly; then he rolled it once more and tucked it into his belt.

Pulling on his gauntlets, he returned to the others.

The Nadir began to ride forward with Jungir Khan at their head.

They halted below the battlements and Jungir looked up.

'You have your answer, Captain Salida?'

'I do, Highness. I am instructed to hold this fortress in the name of the Gothir people, and to deny access to any foreign power.'

'Then it is war,' said Jungir, drawing his sword.

'Wait!' shouted Kiall. 'May I speak, Highness?'

'Who are you, boy?' called Jungir.

'I am Kiall. Ravenna was my woman, stolen from my village. We were betrothed. Now I demand the right of combat to decide what happens to her.'

Jungir leaned back in the saddle, his dark eyes fixed on Kiall. 'You wish to challenge me directly?'

'It is my right, and the Nadir custom so to do.'

Jungir glanced to his left, watching the men around him. Each of them knew the custom and he felt, with certainty, that the boy's daring appealed to them.

'And when you lose?' called Jungir Khan. 'What then? I get my woman back – and what else?'

'I can speak only for Ravenna, sire.'

'Very well. Come down – and we will fight, man to man. And I promise not to kill you slowly, for you have followed your woman as a man should.' A grunt of approval came from the Nadir warriors around him.

Inside the fortress Asta Khan heard the exchange. As Kiall descended the rampart steps Asta ran to him, grabbing his arm.

'What do you want?' asked Kiall, trying to pull away.

'Listen to me, fool, there is no need to die! I will help you in this battle, if you trust me.'

'I want no trickery, or magic,' said Kiall.

'No tricks,' Asta assured him. 'Just say these words after me. Will you do that?'

Kiall shrugged. 'What are they?'

'Merely a good luck charm which will open you to a friend. Trust me, Kiall. Can you not see I am with you? I am fighting to save the life of Chareos. Does that mean nothing? I am your friend.'

'Speak the words,' said the former villager.

Asta Khan closed his eyes, and began to chant:

Nadir we
Youth born,
Blood letters,
Axe wielders
Victors still.

Kiall spoke the words. 'What do they mean?'

'Life,' whispered a cool voice inside his mind and Kiall reeled back.

219

'Do not be afraid,' said the voice of Tenaka Khan. 'I am the warrior who aided you against the demons and I will aid you now. I want you to relax, to allow me to live – for but a brief moment. It is all I ask, in return for the aid I gave you.'

Kiall could feel the rising tension in him, like a pressure building. 'Give way, Kiall. And let me save your friends.'

'It is my fight,' he argued weakly.

'Jungir Khan poisoned me,' said Tenaka. 'He poisoned his own father. You must allow me my hour of revenge.'

'I . . . I don't know.'

'Trust me. Relax,' said Tenaka and Kiall felt himself give, felt the power of Tenaka Khan flow through his veins. Their memories merged, and Kiall felt the thrill of countless battles – saw the fall of the mighty Dros Delnoch, experienced the great love the Khan had known for Renya, the Joining Child. But more than this, he felt the confidence of the warrior born. He tried to will himself forward, but found to his terror that he could no longer control his limbs. His arms stretched out, his lungs filled with air.

'Oh,' came his voice, 'oh, it is good to breathe again!'

Tenaka Khan moved to the postern gate. At that moment Tanaki ran from the guardhouse. 'Kiall!' she screamed, 'oh, please don't do this.'

She flung herself into his arms and Tenaka kissed the top of her head.

'I will come back,' he said softly. 'He cannot beat me.'

'But he *can*. He is the greatest swordsman since my father. There is not a man alive – save perhaps Chareos – who could best him.'

'Did you love your father?' he asked.

'You know that I did. More than anything.'

'And do you love me?' he asked. Trapped behind his own eyes, Kiall despaired of the answer.

'Yes,' she said simply. 'I am for you, Kiall. Now and always.'

'Your father loved you,' he said. 'You were the joy Renya left . . . him. Watch from the battlements – and fear nothing. Kiall will come back to you. I promise, Naki.'

He turned to the gate, opened the bolts and walked towards the waiting horde. For a moment Tanaki was stunned. He had seemed so different, and he had used her pet name – the name she carried as a child. She swung to Asta Khan.

'What have you done?' she shouted. The old man said nothing, but returned to the still form of Chareos. The Blademaster opened his eyes.

'I kept my bargain,' whispered Asta. 'Will you keep yours?'

'I will,' answered Chareos. 'What is happening?'

'Kiall has gone outside to battle with Jungir Khan.'

'By the Source, no,' groaned Chareos. 'Help me to the battlements.' The wiry shaman pulled Chareos to his feet and half carried him to the steps. Painfully Chareos eased his way up to the ramparts.

Out on the valley floor Tenaka Khan strode out confidently to meet his son. Jungir carried the jewelled blade given to him by Chien-tsu. Tenaka drew the cavalry sabre, tested it for weight and then hurled it aside. He walked past the surprised Jungir, halting before an old man on a grey pony.

'They told me on the battlements that you were Subodai, the oldest friend of Tenaka Khan,' he said.

The grim-eyed old man nodded his head.

'Would you loan me one of the short swords Tenaka gave you on your last meeting.'

The old man looked closely at the figure of Kiall, at the stance and the tilt of the head, at the grey eyes that fixed to his own. He shivered and drew his sword, reversing it and handing it to the young man without a word.

Tenaka turned and swung the blade twice. He returned to Jungir Khan.

'When you are ready, Highness,' he said.

Jungir launched a lightning thrust. Tenaka parried it – and stepped in close. 'Did you think the poison would keep me from you, my son?' he whispered.

Jungir blanched. His face darkened and he attacked again – and again. But each time the dazzling blade of Tenaka Khan blocked his approach. As the battle moved further from the watching warriors, Jungir aimed a wild cut. Tenaka blocked it, and stepped inside once more.

'Asta smuggled my bones here years ago. Yet I can still taste the poison from your cup.'

'Stop it!' screamed Jungir. His sword lowered a fraction and Tenaka Khan leapt forward, twisting the blade from his grasp. It fell in the dirt ten paces away.

'Pick it up,' ordered Tenaka. Jungir scrambled for the blade and ran at Tenaka, offering no defence. Before he could stop himself Tenaka instinctively rammed his sword home into his son's chest. Jungir sagged against him.

'I loved you, Father,' he said, 'and you never cared for me. Not once.'

Tenaka seized his son and sank with him to the earth, tears filling his eyes. 'Oh, my son! I was so proud of you. But I wanted you to be a strong man – a Nadir man. And I never showed my feelings – save for Tanaki. Yet I loved you – and your brothers. Jungir . . . Jungir!'

But the Khan was dead.

Tenaka stood with head bowed by the body. He wrenched the sword clear and flung it from him, then he knelt by his dead son.

The old general rode forward and dismounted. He walked now with a limp, but he was the same man Tenaka Khan had rescued all those years before.

'Who are you?' hissed the general. '*Who?*'

'I am merely a man,' said Tenaka, turning to stare at the battlements and his only daughter. The foolish boy had given him life, and he had used it to kill the last of his sons. And he knew, in that moment, that he could not rob his daughter of her love. No, better finally to accept death and fly in search of Jungir. 'Kiall, come forth,' he said softly.

Kiall found the tension lifting from him. He stretched and turned back to the general. 'I thank you for the use of your sword, sir. The spirit of Tenaka Khan bade me ask for it.'

'Just for a moment . . .' said the general. He shook his head. 'It doesn't matter. Return to your fortress; you will die soon enough.'

Asta Khan leapt to the battlements. 'Subodai!' he called.

'What is it, warlock?'

'The son of the Khan is born!'

'Is this true?' Subodai hissed at Kiall.

'Yes. In the night.'

'I will bring him to you,' shouted Asta. 'Do not attack.'

Kiall walked back to the fortress, where two soldiers opened the postern gate. Asta was moving towards the gatehouse when Chareos stopped him.

'Wait,' he said. 'I will bring out the child.'

Chareos walked into the guardhouse, where Ravenna was awake with one child at her breast, the other sleeping.

He sat beside her. 'I do not know how to say this, my lady. But, to avert the war, I promised one of your sons would be Khan. And now I am trapped by that promise.'

She looked at the anguish in his eyes and reached out a hand to him.

'One of them is born to be Khan. The other would be slain – it is the Nadir way,' she said. 'Let Asta have what he wants. I will raise the other.' She lifted the babe from her breast and kissed him tenderly. 'Take him before I change my mind.'

'I will help you raise him, I swear it.' He took the babe. 'Now let there be no sound. Asta must not know there are twins.'

He walked to the door and out into the sunlight. Asta ran forward, holding out his thin arms for the child.

'A new Great Khan,' he said gleefully. Chareos passed the babe to him and it began to howl, but Asta leaned down and whispered in his ear. The babe quietened, and fell asleep.

'I did what I had to do,' said Asta. 'But I am grateful to you,

222

Blademaster.' Chareos nodded, and watched the shaman walk out to the waiting army.

Within minutes they had departed the valley. As Chareos sat down in the sunshine and sagged back against the wall, Salida joined him.

'I would not have believed the Lord Regent could be so heroic,' said Chareos.

'No,' said Salida, lifting the parchment from his belt and tossing it to Chareos' lap. The Blademaster opened it. The message was simple.

Give Jungir Khan all he asks for.

'I think we did that, don't you?' observed Salida.

Epilogue

Kiall and Tanaki did not wait to be wed in the Gothir fashion. They cut their palms after the Nadir way, and pledged their troth before witnesses at Bel-azar. Then they rode from the fortress, back to the Steppes and out of the pages of Nadir history.

Chien-tsu and Oshi journeyed back to the Empire of the Kiatze, where the ambassador was covered with garlands and given lands of great wealth and greater beauty.

Harokas journeyed with Salida to New Gulgothir, where the Lord Regent grudgingly gave the Captain a fine award and a promotion.

Seven years later three riders halted before the first great gates of Castle Tenaka.

'Once, my son,' said Chareos, 'this was Dros Delnoch, the mightiest of the Drenai fortresses. In those days it was ruled by the Earl of Bronze. One day that title will be yours.'

The boy turned his violet eyes on the six massive walls rearing back along the pass. 'I will take it from the other side,' he said softly.

Chareos smiled and turned to his wife, Ravenna. 'Do you have regrets?' he asked.

'None,' she said, taking his hand. The boy twisted in his saddle and stared back over the northern steppes.

A thousand miles away another violet-eyed child stood, staring south.

'What are you looking at?' asked Asta Khan.

'The enemy,' whispered the boy.

WAYLANDER II

This novel is dedicated with great affection to Jennifer Taylor, and her children Simon and Emily, for sharing the joy of the American adventure, and to Ross Lempriere who walked the dark woods once more in search of the elusive Waylander.

Acknowledgements:
My thanks to my editor Oliver Johnson, to Justine Willett, and to proof readers Jean Maund and Stella Graham, test readers Tom Taylor and Edith Graham, and to Mary Sanderson, Alan Fisher, Stan Nicholls, and Peter Austin.

Introduction

Most authors I have met talk of favourite characters. These are not just heroes who leap off the page. Mostly they are characters who don't need to be *written*. They write themselves. They make the author's job a joy. Their dialogue and their actions move from the author's mind to the page so swiftly that no apparent effort is needed. Set up a scene, introduce the hero and watch what happens.

I have three favourites: Druss the Legend, Jon Shannow, and Waylander.

Waylander was a dream to write. But when he rode off with Danyal, and the twin children, Krylla and Miriel, at the end of the novel I felt there was no more to be said about this enigmatic assassin. He had found true love, and a form of redemption. Family life beckoned.

I have said before that all my characters are based on real people. It is one of the elements that has so far helped to keep my work successful.

In 1991 I saw someone who I knew would make a great character in the right novel. I had first seen her in 1976 as a gangly child, moving past my house on roller skates. It was heart in the mouth stuff as this dark haired nine-year-old tottered and weaved along the street. You just knew a fall was coming but strangely, despite the laws of gravity, she stayed upright. Her family moved abroad and she continued her upbringing in Papua New Guinea for a number of years.

When she returned to Hastings she was a tall, athletic young woman, newly qualified as a sports massage therapist. She was also a runner of genuine talent. She had – and still has – a bubbly personality and an enquiring mind. But what made her ideal as a character in a fantasy was a complex mix of stunning naivete, keen intelligence and real grit. Her teenage years had been spent in Papua, and she had experienced few of the usual pressures on young people in the materialistic West. Fashion bored her. She was happiest in running gear. Her idea of fun was to take part in a muddy cross-country race, or to run alone across the Hasting's Fire Hills.

I knew if I could capture a fraction of her personality in a novel the character would captivate readers.

One morning I received from my publishers a parcel of letters sent by fans. There were around twenty letters. Several of them talked about Waylander, but one stuck in my mind. It was from a woman

231

who said that, although she loved the character, just what kind of parent would he make to two young girls? How on earth could they have a normal upbringing when raised by a master assassin? And what kind of adults would they grow to be?

This was a good question. Raised in the wilderness by a man of violence, they would be quite unlike other children. Their world view, their recreational interests, even their dreams, would be worlds apart from others of their age.

With just this thought in mind I wrote a scene where a tall, athletic young woman was running through the hills. I had no idea where the story would take me.

As always it drew me into an adventure that was a joy to write.

I discovered that Waylander was not the greatest parent in the world.

But he raised kids you just didn't want to mess with.

Prologue

The man called Angel sat quietly in the corner of the tavern, his huge gnarled hands cupped around a goblet of mulled wine, his scarred features hidden by a black hood. Despite the four open windows, the air in the sixty-foot room was stale, and Angel could smell the smoke from the oil-filled lanterns, merging with the combined odours of sweating men, cooked food and sour ale.

Lifting his goblet Angel touched his lips to the rim, taking just a sip of the wine and rolling it around his mouth. The Spiked Owl was full tonight, the drinking area crowded, the dining-hall packed. But no one approached Angel as he nursed his drink. The hooded man did not like company, and such privacy as a man could enjoy in a tavern was accorded to the scarred gladiator.

Just before midnight an argument began between a group of labourers. Angel's flint-coloured eyes focused on the group, scanning their faces. There were five men, and they were arguing over a spilled drink. Angel could see the rush of blood to their faces, and knew that despite the raised voices, none of them was in the mood to fight. When a battle is close the blood runs from the face, leaving it white and ghostly. Then his gaze flickered to a young man at the edge of the group. This one was dangerous! The man's face was pale, his mouth set in a thin line, and his right hand was hidden within the folds of his tunic.

Angel looked back towards Balka, the tavern-owner. The burly former wrestler stood behind the serving shelf, watching the men. Angel relaxed. Balka had seen the danger and was ready.

The row began to die down – but the pale young man said something to one of the others and fists suddenly flew. A knife flashed in the lantern light, and a man shouted in pain.

Balka, a short wooden club in his right hand, vaulted the serving shelf and leapt at the white-faced knife-wielder, cracking the club first against the man's wrist, forcing him to drop the blade, then hammering a blow to the temple. He dropped to the sawdust-covered floor as if poleaxed.

'That's it, my lads!' roared Balka. 'The night is done.'

'Oh, one more drink, Balka?' pleaded a regular.

'Tomorrow,' snapped the tavern-keeper. 'Come on, lads. Let's clear away the mess.'

The drinkers downed the last of their ale and wine, and several took hold of the unconscious knifeman, dragging him into the street. The man's victim had been stabbed in the shoulder; the wound was deep, his arm numb. Balka gave him a large tot of brandy before sending him on his way to find a surgeon.

At last the tavern-owner shut the door, dropping the lock-bar into place. His barmen and serving girls began gathering tankards, goblets and plates, and righting tables and chairs knocked over in the brief fight. Balka slipped his club into the wide pocket of his leather apron and strolled to where Angel sat.

'Another quiet evening,' he muttered, pulling up a chair opposite the gladiator. 'Janic!' he called. 'Bring me a jug.'

The young cellar boy emptied a bottle of the finest Lentrian red into a clay jug, sought out a clean pewter goblet, and carried both to the table. Balka looked up at the boy and winked. 'Good lad, Janic,' he said. Janic smiled, cast a nervous glance at Angel and backed away. Balka sighed and leaned back in his chair.

'Why don't you just pour it from the bottle?' asked Angel, his grey eyes staring unblinking at the tavern-keeper.

Balka chuckled. 'It tastes better from clay.'

'Horse dung!' Angel reached across the table, lifting the jug and holding it below his misshapen nose. 'It's Lentrian red . . . at least fifteen years old.'

'Twenty,' said Balka, grinning.

'You don't like people knowing you're rich enough to drink it,' observed Angel. 'It would tarnish the image. Man of the people.'

'Rich? I'm just a poor tavern-keeper.'

'And I'm a Ventrian veil-dancer.'

Balka nodded and filled his goblet. 'To you, my friend,' he said, draining the drink in a single swallow, wine overflowing to his forked grey beard. Angel smiled and pushed back his hood, running his hand across his thinning red hair. 'May the gods shower you with luck,' said Balka, pouring a second drink and downing it as swiftly as the first.

'I could do with some.'

'No hunting parties?'

'A few – but no one wants to spend money these days.'

'Times are hard,' agreed Balka. 'The Vagrian Wars bled the treasury dry and now that Karnak's upset the Gothir and the Ventrians I think we can expect fresh battles. A pox on the man!'

'He was right to throw out their ambassadors,' said Angel, eyes narrowing. 'We're not a vassal people. We're the Drenai and we shouldn't bend the knee to lesser races.'

'Lesser races?' Balka raised an eyebrow. 'This may surprise you, Angel, but I understand that non-Drenai people also boast two arms, two legs and a head. Curious, I know.'

'You know what I mean,' snapped Angel.

'I know – I just don't happen to agree with you. Here, enjoy a little quality wine.'

Angel shook his head. 'One drink is all I need.'

'And you never finish that. Why do you come here? You hate people. You don't talk to them and you don't like crowds.'

'I like to listen.'

'What can you hear in a tavern, save drunkards and loud-mouths? There is little philosophy spoken here that I've ever heard.'

Angel shrugged. 'Life. Rumours. I don't know.'

Balka leaned forward, resting his massive forearms on the table. 'You miss it, don't you? The fights, the glory, the cheers.'

'Not a bit,' responded the other.

'Come on, this is Balka you're talking to. I saw you the day you beat Barsellis. He cut you bad – but you won. I saw your face as you raised your sword to Karnak. You were exultant.'

'That was then. I don't miss it. I don't long for it,' Angel sighed, 'but I remember the day, right enough. Good fighter was Barsellis, tall, proud, fast. But they dragged his body across the arena. You remember that? Face-down he was, and his chin made a long, bloody groove in the sand. Could have been me.'

Balka nodded solemnly. 'But it wasn't. You retired undefeated – and you never went back. That's unusual. They all come back. Did you see Caplyn last week? What an embarrassment. He used to be so deadly. He looked like an old man.'

'A dead old man,' grunted Angel. 'A dead old fool.'

'You could still take them all, Angel. And earn a fortune.'

Angel swore and his face darkened. 'I'd bet that's what they told Caplyn.' He sighed. 'It was better when we fought hand to hand, no weapons. Now the crowd just want to see blood and death. Let's talk about something else.'

'What – politics? Religion?'

'Anything. Just make it interesting.'

'Karnak's son was sentenced this morning: one year in exile in Lentria. A man is murdered, his wife falls to her death, and the killer is exiled for a year to a palace by the coast. There's justice for you.'

'At least Karnak put the boy on trial,' said Angel. 'The sentence could have been worse. And don't forget, the murdered man's father pleaded for leniency. Quite a moving speech, I understand – all about high spirits and accidents and forgiveness.'

'Fancy that,' observed Balka drily.

'What is that supposed to mean?'

'Oh, come on, Angel! Six men – all nobles – all drunk, snatch a young married woman and try to rape her. When her husband attempts to rescue her he is cut down. The woman runs and falls over a cliff-edge. High spirits? And as for the murdered man's father, I understand Karnak was so moved by his pleas that he sent a personal gift of two thousand Raq to the man's village, and a huge supply of grain for the winter.'

'Well, there you are,' said Angel. 'He's a good man.'

'I don't believe you sometimes, my friend. Don't you think it odd that the father should suddenly make that plea? Gods, man, he was coerced into it. People who criticise Karnak tend to have *accidents*.'

'I don't believe those stories. Karnak's a hero. He and Egel saved this land.'

'Yes, and look what happened to Egel.'

'I think I've had enough of politics,' snapped Angel, 'and I don't want to talk about religion. What else is happening?'

Balka sat silently for a moment, then he grinned. 'Oh, yes, there's a rumour that a huge sum has been offered for the Guild to hunt down Waylander.'

'For what purpose?' asked Angel, clearly astonished.

Balka shrugged. 'I don't know. But I heard it from Symius, and his brother is the clerk at the Guild. Five thousand Raq for the Guild itself, and a further ten thousand to the man who kills him.'

'Who ordered the hunt?'

'No one knows, but they've offered large rewards for any information on Waylander.'

Angel laughed and shook his head. 'It won't be easy. No one has seen Waylander in . . . what . . . ten years? He could be dead already.'

'Someone obviously doesn't think so.'

'It's madness – and a waste of money and life.'

'The Guild are calling in their best men,' offered Balka. 'They'll find him.'

'They'll wish they hadn't,' said Angel softly.

1

Miriel had been running for slightly more than an hour. In that time she had covered around nine miles from the cabin in the high pasture, down to the stream path, through the valley and the pine woods, up across the crest of Axe Ridge, and back along the old deer trail.

She was tiring now, heartbeat rising, lungs battling to supply oxygen to her weary muscles. But still she pushed on, determined to reach the cabin before the sun climbed to noon high.

The slope was slippery from last night's rain and she stumbled twice, the leather knife-scabbard at her waist digging into her bare thigh. A touch of anger spurred her on. Without the long hunting knife and the throwing-blade strapped to her left wrist she could have made better time. But Father's word was law, and Miriel did not leave the cabin until her weapons were in place.

'There is no one here but us,' she had argued, not for the first time.

'Expect the best – prepare for the worst,' was all he said.

And so she ran with the heavy scabbard slapping against her thigh, the hilt of the throwing-blade chafing the skin of her forearm.

Coming to a bend in the trail she leapt the fallen log, landing lightly and cutting left towards the last rise, her long legs increasing their pace, her bare feet digging into the soft earth. Her slim calves were burning, her lungs hot. But she was exultant, for the sun was at least twenty minutes from noon high and she was but three from the cabin.

A shadow moved to her left – talons and teeth flashing towards her. Instantly Miriel threw herself forward, hitting the ground on her right side and rolling to her feet. The lioness, confused at having missed her victim with the first leap, crouched down, ears flat to her skull, tawny eyes focusing on the tall young woman.

Miriel's mind was racing. *Action and reaction. Take control!*

Her hunting knife slid into her hand and she shouted at the top of her voice. The lioness, shocked by the sound, backed away. Miriel's throat was dry, her heart hammering, but her hand was steady on the blade. She shouted once more and jumped towards the beast. Unnerved by the suddenness of the move the creature slunk back several more paces. Miriel licked her lips. It should have run by now. Fear rose, but she swallowed it down.

Fear is like fire in your belly. Controlled, it warms you and keeps you alive. Unleashed, it burns and destroys you.

Her hazel eyes remained locked to the tawny gaze of the lioness and she noted the beast's ragged condition, the deep angry scar to its right foreleg. No longer fast it could not catch the swift deer, and it was starving. It would not – could not – back away from this fight.

Miriel thought of everything Father had told her about lions: *Ignore the head – the bone is too thick for an arrow to penetrate. Send your shaft in behind the front leg, up and into the lung.* But he had said nothing about fighting such a beast when armed with but a knife.

The sun slid from behind an autumn cloud and light shone from the knife-blade. Instantly Miriel angled the blade, directing the gleam into the eyes of the lioness. The great head twisted, the eyes blinking against the harsh glare. Miriel shouted again.

But instead of fleeing the lioness suddenly charged, leaping high towards the girl.

For an instant only Miriel froze. Then the knife swept up. A black crossbow bolt punched into the creature's neck, just behind the ear, a second slicing into its side. The weight of the lioness struck Miriel, hurling her back, but the hunting knife plunged into the beast's belly.

Miriel lay very still, the lioness upon her, its breath foul upon her face. But the talons did not rake her, nor the fangs close upon her. With a coughing grunt the lioness died. Miriel closed her eyes, took a deep breath, and eased herself from beneath the body. Her legs felt weak and she sat upon the trail, her hands trembling.

A tall man, carrying a small double crossbow of black metal, emerged from the undergrowth and crouched down beside her. 'You did well,' he said, his voice deep.

She looked up into his dark eyes and forced a smile. 'It would have killed me.'

'Perhaps,' he agreed. 'But your blade reached its heart.'

Exhaustion flowed over her like a warm blanket and she lay back, breathing slowly and deeply. Once she would have sensed the lioness long before any danger threatened, but that Talent was lost to her now, as her mother and her sister were lost to her. Danyal killed in an accident five years ago, and Krylla wed and moved away last summer. Pushing such thoughts from her mind she sat up. 'You know,' she whispered, 'I was really tired when I came to the last rise. I was breathing hard, and my limbs felt as if they were made of lead. But when the lioness leapt, all my weariness vanished.' She gazed up at her father.

He smiled and nodded. 'I have experienced that many times. Strength can always be found in the heart of a fighter – and such a heart will rarely let you down.'

She glanced at the dead lioness. 'Never shoot for the head – that's what you told me,' she said, tapping the first bolt jutting from the creature's neck.

He shrugged and grinned. 'I missed.'

'That's not very comforting. I thought you were perfect.'

'I'm getting old. Are you cut?'

'I don't think so . . .' Swiftly she checked her arms and legs, as wounds from a lion's claws or fangs often became poisonous. 'No. I was very lucky.'

'Yes, you were,' he agreed. 'But you made your luck by doing everything right. I'm proud of you.'

'Why were you here?'

'You needed me,' he answered. Rising smoothly to his feet he reached out, drawing her upright. 'Now skin the beast and quarter it. There's nothing quite like lion meat.'

'I don't think I want to eat it,' she said. 'I think I'd like to forget about it.'

'Never forget,' he admonished her. 'This was a victory. And you are stronger for it. I'll see you later.' Retrieving his bolts the tall man cleaned them of blood, returning them to the leather quiver at his side.

'You're going to the waterfall?' she asked him softly.

'For a little while,' he answered, his voice distant. He turned back to her. 'You think I spend too much time there?'

'No,' she told him sadly. 'It's not the time you sit there. Nor the effort you put into tending the grave. It's you. She's been . . . gone . . . now for five years. You should start living again. You need . . . more than this.'

He nodded, but she knew she had not reached him. He smiled and laid his hand on her shoulder. 'One day you'll find a love and then we can talk on equal terms. I do not mean that to sound patronising. You are bright and intelligent. You have courage and wit. But sometimes it is like trying to describe colours to a blind man. Love, as I hope you will find, has great power. Even death cannot destroy it. And I still love her.' Leaning forward he drew her towards him, kissing her brow. 'Now skin that beast. And I'll see you at dusk.'

She watched him walk away, a tall man moving with grace and care, his black and silver hair drawn back into a tightly-tied ponytail, his crossbow hanging from his belt.

And then he was gone – vanished into the shadows.

The waterfall was narrow, no more than six feet wide, flowing over white boulders in a glittering cascade to a leaf-shaped bowl thirty feet across and forty-five long. At its most southern point a second fall occurred, the stream surging on to join the river two miles south. Golden leaves swirled on the surface of the water, and with each breath of breeze more spiralled down from the trees.

Around the pool grew many flowers, most of them planted by the man who now knelt by the graveside. He glanced up at the sky. The

239

sun was losing its power now, the cold winds of autumn flowing over the mountains. Waylander sighed. A time of dying. He gazed at the golden leaves floating on the water and remembered sitting here with Danyal and the children, on another autumn day ten lifetimes ago.

Krylla was sitting with her tiny feet in the water, Miriel swimming among the leaves. 'They are like the souls of the departed,' Danyal had told Krylla. 'Floating on the sea of life towards a place of rest.'

He sighed again and returned his attention to the flower-garlanded mound beneath which lay all he had lived for.

'Miriel fought a lion today,' he said. 'She stood and did not panic. You would have been proud of her.' Laying his ebony-handled crossbow to one side he idly dead-headed the geraniums growing by the headstone, removing the faded, dry red blooms. The season was late and it was unlikely they would flower again. Soon he would need to pull them, shaking dry the roots and hanging them in the cabin, ready for planting in the spring.

'But she is still too slow,' he added. 'She does not act with instinct, but with remembered learning. Not like Krylla.' He chuckled. 'You remember how the village boys used to gather around her? She knew how to handle them, the tilt of the head, the sultry smile. She took that from you.'

Reaching out he touched the cold, rectangular marble head-stone, his index finger tracing the carved lines.

Danyal, wife of Dakeyras,
the pebble in the moonlight

The grave was shaded by elms and beech, and there were roses growing close by, huge yellow blooms filling the air with sweet fragrance. He had bought them in Kasyra, seven bushes. Three had died as he journeyed back, but the remainder flourished in the rich clay soil.

'I'm going to have to take her to the city soon,' he said. 'She's eighteen now, and she needs to learn. I'll find a husband for her.' He sighed. 'It means leaving you for a while. I'm not looking forward to that.'

The silence grew, even the wind in the leaves dying down. His dark eyes were distant, his memories solemn. Smoothly he rose and, taking up the clay bowl beside the headstone, he moved to the pool, filled the bowl and began to water the roses. Yesterday's rain had been little more than a shower and the roses liked to drink deep.

Kreeg crouched low in the bushes, his crossbow loaded. How easy, he thought, unable to suppress a smile.

Find Waylander and kill him. He had to admit that the prospect of

240

such a hunt had frightened him. After all, Waylander the Slayer was no mean opponent. When his family were slain by raiders, he roamed the land until he had hunted down every one of the killers. Waylander was a legend among the Guild, a capable swordsman, but a brilliant knife-fighter and a crossbowman without peer. More than this he was said to possess mystical abilities, always sensing when danger was near.

Kreeg sighted the crossbow at the tall man's back. Mystical abilities? Pah. In one heartbeat he would be dead.

The man at the graveside picked up a clay bowl and moved towards the pool. Kreeg shifted his aim, but his intended victim crouched down, filling the bowl. Kreeg lowered his bow a fraction, slowly letting out his held breath. Waylander was side-on now, and a sure killing shot would have to be to the head. What was he doing with the water? Kreeg watched the tall man kneel by the roses, tipping the bowl and splashing the contents around the roots. He'll go back to the grave, thought Kreeg. And once there I'll take him.

So much in life depended on luck. When the kill order came to the Guild, Kreeg had been out of money and living off a whore in Kasyra, the gold he had earned from killing the Ventrian merchant long since vanished in the gambling dens of the city's south side. Now Kreeg blessed the bad luck that had dogged him in Kasyra. For all life, he knew, was a circle. And it was in Kasyra that he had heard of the hermit in the mountains, the tall widower with the shy daughter. He thought of the message from the Guild.

Seek out a man named Dakeyras. He has a wife Danyal and a daughter Miriel. The man has black and silver hair, dark eyes, and is tall, close to fifty years of age. He will be carrying a small double crossbow of ebony and bronze. Kill him and bring the crossbow to Drenan as proof of success. Move with care. The man is Waylander. Ten thousand in gold is waiting.

In Kasyra Kreeg had despaired of earning such a fabulous sum. Then – blessed be the gods – he had told the whore of the hunt.

'There's a man with a daughter called Miriel who lives in the mountains to the north,' she said. 'I've not seen him, but I met his daughters years ago at the Priests' School. We learned our letters there.'

'Do you remember the mother's name?'

'I think it was something like Daneel . . . Donalia . . .'

'Danyal?' he whispered, sitting up in bed, the sheet falling from his lean, scarred body.

'That's it,' she said.

Kreeg's mouth had gone dry, his heart palpitating. Ten thousand!

241

But Waylander? What chance would Kreeg have against such an enemy?

For almost a week he toured Kasyra, asking about the mountain man. Fat Sheras the miller saw him about twice a year, and remembered the small crossbow.

'He's very quiet,' said Sheras, 'but I wouldn't like to see his bad side, if you take my meaning. Hard man. Cold eyes. He used to be almost friendly, but then his wife died – five . . . six years ago. Horse fell, rolled on her. There were two daughters, twins. Good-looking girls. One married a boy from the south and moved away. The other is still with him. Shy child. Too thin for my taste.'

Goldin the tavern-keeper, a thin-faced refugee from the Gothir lands, also remembered him. 'When the wife was killed he came here for a while and drank his sorrows away. He didn't say much. One night he just collapsed and I left him lying outside the door. His daughters came and helped him home. They were around twelve then. The city elders were talking of removing them from his care. In the end he paid for places at the Priests' School and they lived there for almost three years.'

Kreeg was uplifted by Goldin's tale. If the great Waylander had taken to drinking heavily then he was no longer to be feared. But his hopes evaporated as the tavern-keeper continued.

'He's never been popular. Keeps to himself too much,' said Goldin. 'But he killed a rogue bear last year, and that pleased people. The bear slaughtered a young farmer and his family. Dakeyras hunted it down. Amazing! He used a small crossbow. Taric saw it – the bear charged him and he just stood there, then, right at the last moment, as the bear reared up before him he put two bolts up through its open mouth and into the brain. Taric says he's never seen the like. Cold as ice.'

Kreeg found Taric, a slim blond hostler, working at the Earl's stables.

'We tracked the beast for three days,' he said, sitting back on a bale of hay and drinking deeply from the leather-bound flask of brandy Kreeg offered him. 'Never saw him break sweat – and he's not a young man. And when the bear reared up he just levelled the bow and loosed. Incredible! There's no fear in the man.'

'Why were you with him?'

Taric smiled. 'I was trying to pay court to Miriel, but I got nowhere. Shy, you know. I gave up in the end. And he's a strange one. Not sure I'd want him for a father-in-law. Spends most of his time by his wife's grave.'

Kreeg's spirits had soared anew. This was what he had been hoping for. Hunting a man through a forest was chancy at best. Knowing his victim's habits made the task slightly less hazardous, but to find there

242

was one place the victim always visited . . . that was a gift from the gods. And a graveside at that. Waylander's mind would be occupied, full of sorrow, perhaps, and fond memories.

So it had proved. Kreeg, following Taric's directions, had located the waterfall soon after dawn this morning, and found a hiding place which overlooked the headstone. Now all that was left was the killing shot. Kreeg's gaze flickered to the ebony crossbow, still lying on the grass beside the grave.

Ten thousand in gold! He licked his thin lips and carefully wiped his sweating palm on the leaf-green tunic he wore.

The tall man walked back to the pool, collecting more water, then crossed to the furthest rose bushes, crouching once more by the roots. Kreeg switched his gaze to the headstone. Forty feet away. At that distance the barbed bolt would punch through Waylander's back, ripping through the lungs and exiting through the chest. Even if he missed the heart his victim would die within minutes, choking on his own blood.

Kreeg was anxious for the kill to be over and his eyes sought out the tall man.

He was not in sight.

Kreeg blinked. The clearing was empty.

'You missed your chance,' came a cold voice.

Kreeg swung, trying to bring the crossbow to bear. He had one glimpse of his victim, arm raised, something shining in his hand. The arm swept down. It was as if a bolt of pure sunlight had exploded within Kreeg's skull. There was no pain, no other sensation. He felt the crossbow slipping from his hands, and the world spinning.

His last thought was about luck.

It had not changed at all.

Waylander knelt by the body and lifted the ornate crossbow the man had held. The shoulder-stock of ebony had been expertly crafted, and embossed with swirling gold. The bow itself was of steel, most likely Ventrian, for its finish was silky smooth and there was not a blemish to be seen. Putting aside the weapon he returned his scrutiny to the corpse. The man was lean and tough, his face hard, the chin square, the mouth thin. Waylander was sure he had never seen him before. Leaning forward he dragged his knife clear of the man's eye-socket, wiping the blade across the grass. Drying the knife against the dead man's tunic he slipped it once more into the black leather sheath strapped to his left forearm.

A swift search of the man's clothing revealed nothing, save four copper coins and a hidden knife, hanging from a thong at his throat. Taking hold of the leaf-green tunic Waylander hauled the corpse upright, hoisting the body over his right shoulder. Foxes and wolves would fight over the remains, and he wanted no such squabbles near Danyal's grave.

Slowly he made his way to the second waterfall, hurling the body out over the rim and watching it plummet to the rushing stream below. At first the impact wedged the corpse against two boulders, but slowly the pull of the water exerted itself and Kreeg's lifeless form floated away, face-down towards the distant river. Retrieving his own cross-bow, and taking up the assassin's weapon, Waylander made his way back to the cabin.

Smoke was lazily drifting up from the stone chimney and he paused at the edge of the trees, staring without pleasure at the home he had crafted for Danyal and himself. Built against the base of a rearing cliff, protected from above by an overhang of rock, the log cabin was sixty feet long, with three large, shuttered windows and one door. The ground before it had been cleared of all trees, bushes and boulders, and no one could approach within a hundred feet without being seen.

The cabin was a fortress, and yet there was beauty also. Danyal had covered the corner joints with mottled stones of red and blue, and planted flowers beneath the windows, roses that climbed and clung to the wooden walls, pink and gold against the harsh, ridged bark.

Waylander scanned the open ground, searching the tree line for any second assassin who might be hidden. But he could see no one. Carefully keeping to cover he circled the cabin, checking for tracks and finding none, save those made by his own moccasins and Miriel's bare feet. Satisfied at last, he crossed to the cabin and stepped inside. Miriel had prepared a meal of hot oats and wild strawberries, the last of the season. She smiled as he entered, but the smile faded as she saw the crossbow he carried.

'Where did you find that?' she asked.

'There was a man hidden near the graveside.'

'A robber?'

'I don't believe so. This bow would cost perhaps a hundred gold pieces. It is a beautifully crafted weapon. I think he was an assassin.'

'Why would he be hunting you?'

Waylander shrugged. 'There was a time when I had a price on my head. Perhaps I still have. Or maybe I killed his brother, or his father. Who knows? One thing is certain, he can't tell me.'

She sat down at the long oak table, watching him. 'You are angry,' she said at last.

'Yes. He shouldn't have got that close. I should have been dead.'

'What happened?'

'He was hidden in the undergrowth some forty paces from the graveside, waiting for the killing shot. When I moved to get water for the roses I saw a bird fly down to land in the tree above him, but it veered off at the last moment.'

244

'It could have been a fox or any sudden movement,' she pointed out. 'Birds are skittish.'

'Yes, it could have been,' he agreed. 'But it wasn't. And if he'd had enough confidence to try for a head shot I would now be lying beside Danyal.'

'Then we've both been lucky today,' she said.

He nodded, but did not answer, his mind still puzzling over the incident. For ten years they had lived without his past returning to haunt him. In these mountains he was merely the widower Dakeyras. Who, after all this time, would send an assassin after him?

And how many more would come?

The sun was hanging over the western peaks, a blazing copper disc of fire casting a last, defiant glare over the mountainside. Miriel squinted against the light.

'It's too bright,' she complained.

But his hand swept up, the wooden chopping board sailing into the sky. Smoothly she brought the crossbow to her shoulder, her fingers pressing the bronze trigger. The bolt leapt from the weapon, missing the arcing wood by little more than a foot. 'I said it was too bright,' she repeated.

'Picture failure and it will happen,' he told her sternly, recovering the wooden board.

'Let me throw it for you, then.'

'I do not need the practice – you do!'

'You couldn't hit it, could you? Admit it!'

He gazed into her sparkling eyes, and noted the sunlight glinting red upon her hair, the bronzed skin of her shoulders. 'You ought to be married,' he said suddenly. 'You are far too beautiful to be stuck on a mountainside with an old man.'

'Don't try to evade the issue,' she scolded, snatching the board from him and walking back ten paces. He chuckled and shook his head, accepting defeat. Carefully he eased back the steel string of the lower bow arm. The spring-loaded hook clicked and he inserted a short black bolt, gently pressing the notch against the string. Repeating the manoeuvre with the upper bow arm, he adjusted the tension in the curved bronze triggers. The weapon had cost him a small fortune in opals many years ago, but it had been crafted by a master and Waylander had never regretted the purchase.

He looked up and was about to ask Miriel to throw when she suddenly hurled the board high. The sunlight seared his eyes but he waited until the spinning board reached its highest point. Extending his arm he pressed the first bronze trigger. The bolt flashed through the air, hammering into the board, half splitting it. As it fell he released the second bolt. The board exploded into shards.

'Horrible man!' she said.

He made a low bow. 'You should feel privileged,' he told her, holding back his smile. 'I don't usually perform without payment.'

'Throw again,' she ordered him, restringing the crossbow.

'The wood is broken,' he pointed out.

'Throw the largest piece.'

Retrieving his bolts he hefted the largest chunk of wood. It was no more than four inches across and less than a foot long. 'Are you ready?'

'Just throw!'

With a flick of his wrist he spun the chunk high into the air. The crossbow came up, the bolt sang, plunging into the wood. Waylander applauded the shot. Miriel gave an elaborate bow.

'Women are supposed to curtsey,' he said.

'And they are supposed to wear dresses and learn embroidery,' she retorted.

'True,' he conceded. 'How do you like the assassin's bow?'

'It has good balance, and it is very light.'

'Ventrian ebony, and the stock is hollowed. Are you ready for some swordplay?'

She laughed. 'Is your pride ready for another pounding?'

'No,' he admitted. 'I think we'll have an early night.' She looked disappointed as they gathered their weapons and set off back to the cabin. 'I think you need a better swordmaster than I,' he told her as they walked. 'It is your best weapon and you are truly skilled. I'll think on it.'

'I thought you were the best,' she chided.

'Fathers always seem that way,' he said drily. 'But no. With bow or knife I am superb. With the sword? Only excellent.'

'And so modest. Is there anything at which you do not excel?'

'Yes,' he answered, his smile fading.

Increasing his pace he walked on, his mind lost in painful memories. His first family had been butchered by raiders, his wife, his baby girls and his son. The picture was bright in his mind. He had found the boy lying dead in the flower garden, his little face surrounded by blooms.

And five years before, having found love a second time, he had watched helplessly as Danyal's horse had struck a hidden tree root. The stallion hit the ground hard, rolling, trapping Danyal beneath it and crushing her chest. She had died within minutes, her body racked with pain.

'Is there anything at which you do not excel?'

Only one.

I cannot keep alive those I love.

246

2

Ralis liked to tell people he had been a tinker since the stars were young, and it was not far from the truth. He could still remember when the old king, Orien, had been but a beardless prince, walking behind his father at the Spring Parade on the first road called the Drenai Way.

Now it was the Avenue of Kings, and much wider, leading through the triumphal arch built to celebrate victory over the Vagrians.

So many changes. Ralis had fond memories of Orien, the first Battle King of the Drenai, wearer of the Armour of Bronze, victor in a hundred battles and a score of wars.

Sometimes, when he was sitting in lonely taverns, resting from his travels, the old tinker would tell people of his meeting with Orien, soon after the Battle at Dros Corteswain. The King had been hunting boar in Skultik Forest and Ralis, young then and dark-bearded, had been carrying his pack towards the fort town of Delnoch.

They had met at a stream. Orien was sitting on a boulder, his bare feet submerged in the cold water, his expensive boots cast aside. Ralis had released the straps of his pack and moved to the water's edge, kneeling to drink.

'The pack looks heavy,' said the golden-haired King.

'Aye, it is,' Ralis had agreed.

'A tinker, are you?'

'Aye.'

'You know who I am?'

'You're the King,' said Ralis.

Orien chuckled. 'You're not impressed? Good for you. I don't suppose you have any ointment in that pack. I have blisters the size of small apples.'

Ralis shook his head and spread his arms apologetically. At that moment a group of young noblemen arrived on the scene, surrounding the King. They were laughing and shouting, bragging of their skills.

Ralis had left unnoticed.

As the years passed he followed the King's exploits, almost as if gathering news of an old friend. Yet he doubted if the memory of their meeting had survived for more than a moment or two with the King himself. It was all different now, he thought, as he hitched his pack for the walk up to the cabin. The country had no king – and that wasn't right. The Source would not look kindly upon a country without a prince.

Ralis was breathing heavily as he topped the last rise and gazed down on the flower-garlanded cabin. The wind died down and a beautiful silence settled over the forest. Ralis took a deep breath. 'You can both step out here,' he said softly. 'I may not be able to see you, but I know you're close by.'

The young woman appeared first. Dressed in leggings of oiled black leather and a tunic of grey wool she rose from the undergrowth and grinned at the old man. 'You're getting sharper, Ralis,' she observed.

He nodded and turned to his right. The man stepped into view. Like Miriel he wore leggings of black leather and a tunic shirt, but he also sported a black, chain-mail shoulder-guard and a baldric, from which hung three throwing knives. Ralis swallowed hard. There was something about this quiet mountain man that always disturbed the ancient tinker, and had done ever since they met on this same mountainside ten years before. He had thought about it often. It was not that Dakeyras was a warrior – Ralis had known many such – nor was it in the wolf-like way that he moved. No, it was some indefinable quality that left Ralis thinking of mortality. To stand close to Dakeyras was somehow to be close to death. He shuddered.

'Good to see you, old man,' said Dakeyras. 'There's meat on the table, and cold spring water. Also some dried fruit – if your teeth can manage it.'

'Nothing wrong with my teeth, boy,' snapped Ralis. 'There may not be so many as once there were, but those that are left can still do their job.'

Dakeyras swung to the girl. 'You take him down. I'll join you presently.'

Ralis watched him move silently back into the trees. 'Expecting trouble, are you?' he asked.

'What makes you ask that?' replied the girl.

'He's always been a careful man – but he's wearing chain mail. Beautifully made, but still heavy. I wouldn't think he'd wear it in these mountains just for show.'

'We've had trouble,' she admitted.

He followed her down to the cabin, leaving his pack by the door and stretching out in a deep horsehair-padded leather chair. 'Getting too old for this life,' he grunted.

She laughed. 'How long have you been saying that?' she asked him.

'About sixty years,' he told her. Leaning back he rested his head against the chair and closed his eyes. I wonder if I'm a hundred yet, he wondered. I'll have to work it out one day – find a point of reference.

'Water or fermented apple juice?' she asked him.

248

Opening the pouch at his side he removed a small packet, handing it to her. 'Make a tisane of that,' he requested. 'Just pour boiling water on it and leave it for a little while.'

'What is it?' she enquired, lifting the packet to her nose and drawing in the scent.

'A few herbs, dill and the like. Keeps me young,' he added with a wide grin.

She left him then and he sat quietly, drinking in his surroundings. The cabin was well built, the main room long and wide, the hearth and chimney solidly constructed of limestone. The south wall had been timbered, and a bearskin hung there. Ralis smiled. It was neatly done, but he had walked these mountains before Dakeyras was born, and he knew about the cave. Had sheltered there a time or two. But it was a clever idea to build a cabin against a cave mouth, then disguise the entrance. A man should always have an escape route.

'How long should I leave it brewing?' came Miriel's voice from the back room.

'Several minutes,' he replied. 'When the shredded leaves start to sink it'll be ready.'

The weapons rack on the wall caught his eye: two longbows, several swords, a sabre, a Sathuli tulwar and half a dozen knives of various lengths and curves. He sat up. A new crossbow lay upon the table. It was a nice piece and Ralis levered himself from his chair and picked up the weapon, examining the gold embossing.

'It is a good bow,' said Miriel, striding back into the room.

'It's better than the man who owned it,' he told her.

'You knew him?'

'Kreeg. A cross between a snake and a rat. Good Guild member, though. Could have been rich if he wasn't such a bad gambler.'

'He tried to kill my father – we don't know why.'

Ralis said nothing. Miriel moved to the kitchen, returning with his tisane, which he sipped slowly. They ate in comfortable silence, the old man devouring three helpings of lion meat. Dipping a slab of freshly-baked bread into the rich gravy he looked up at Miriel and sighed. 'They don't eat as well as this in the palace at Drenan,' he said.

'You are a flatterer, Ralis,' she chided him. 'But I like it.'

Wandering to his pack he untied the flap and delved deep into the interior, coming up at last with a corked metal flask and three small silver cups. Returning to the table he filled the cups with amber liquid. 'The taste of heaven,' he said, savouring the moment.

Miriel lifted her cup and sipped the spirit. 'It's like swallowing fire,' she said, reddening.

'Yes. Good, isn't it?'

'Tell me about Kreeg.'

'Not much to tell. He was from the south, a farmboy originally.

Fought in the Vagrian Wars, and then joined Jonat for the rebellion. When Karnak smashed the rebel army Kreeg spent a year or two in Ventria. Mercenary, I think. He joined the Guild three years ago. Not one of their best, you understand, but good enough.'

'Then someone paid him to kill my father?'

'Yes.'

'Why?'

The old man shrugged. 'Let's wait until he gets back.'

'You make it sound like a mystery.'

'I just don't like repeating myself. At my age time is precious. How much do you remember of your childhood?'

'What do you mean?'

'I mean, Dakeyras . . . where did you meet him?' He could see that the question surprised her, and watched her expression change from open and friendly to guarded and wary.

'He's my father,' she said softly.

'No,' he told her. 'Your family were killed in a raid during the Vagrian Wars. And Dakeyras, riding with a man named Dardalion, found you and your sister . . . and a brother, I believe, in the care of a young woman.'

'How do you know this?'

'Because of Kreeg,' he said, refilling his cup.

'I don't understand.'

The voice of Dakeyras cut in from the doorway. 'He means he knows who Kreeg was sent to kill.' The tall man untied the thong of his black leather cloak and draped it over the chair. Taking up the third silver cup he tossed back the contents.

'Fifteen thousand in gold,' said Ralis. 'Five for the Guild, ten for the man who brings your crossbow to the Citadel. There are said to be more than fifty men scouring the country for news of you. Morak the Ventrian is among them, as are Belash, Courail and Senta.'

'I've heard of Morak and Courail,' said Dakeyras.

'Belash is Nadir and a knife-fighter. Senta is a swordsman paid to fight duels. He's very good – old noble family.'

'I expect there is also a large reward for information regarding my whereabouts,' said Dakeyras softly.

'I wouldn't doubt it,' said Ralis, 'but then it would be a brave man who betrayed Waylander the Slayer.'

'Are you a brave man?' The words were spoken gently, but the undercurrent was tense and the old man found his stomach knotting.

'More guts than sense,' admitted Ralis, holding the man's dark gaze.

Waylander smiled. 'That's as it should be,' he said, and the moment passed.

'What will we do?' asked Miriel.

'Prepare for a long winter,' said Waylander.

Ralis was a light sleeper, and he heard the creaking of leather hinges as the main door opened. The old man yawned and swung his legs from the bed. Although it was almost dawn thin shafts of moonlight were still seeping through the cracks in the shutters of the window. He rose and stretched. The air was cool and fresh with the threat of approaching winter. Ralis shivered and pulled on his warm woollen leggings and tunic.

Opening his bedroom door he stepped into the main room and saw that someone had fanned the embers of last night's fire, laying fresh kindling on the hungry flames. Waylander was a courteous host, for there would not normally have been a fire this early on an autumn day. Moving to the shuttered window he lifted the latch and pushed at the wooden frame. Outside the moon was fading in a greying sky, the stars retreating, the pale pink of the dawn showing above the eastern peaks.

Movement caught his eye and Ralis squinted, trying to focus. On the mountainside, at least a quarter of a mile distant, he thought he saw a man running. Ralis yawned and returned to the fire, easing himself down into the deep leather chair. The kindling was burning well and he added two seasoned logs from a stack beside the hearth.

So, he thought, the mystery is solved at last. What was surprising was that he felt in such low spirits now. For years he had known Dakeyras and his family, the beautiful wife, the twin girls. And always he had sensed there was more to the mountain man. And the mystery had occupied his mind, perhaps even helping to keep him active at an age when most – if not all – of his youthful contemporaries were dead.

A fugitive, a nobleman having turned his back on wealth and privilege, a refugee from Gothir tyranny . . . all these he had considered as backgrounds for Dakeyras. And more. But the speculation was now over. Dakeyras was the legendary Waylander – the man who killed King Orien's son, Niallad. But he was also the hero who had found the hidden Armour of Bronze, returning it to the Drenai people, freeing them from the murderous excesses of the invading Vagrians.

The old man sighed. What fresh mysteries could he find now to exercise his mind, and blot out the passing of time and the inevitable approach of death?

He heard Miriel rise from her bed in the far room. She wandered in, tall and slim and naked. 'Good morning,' she said brightly. 'Did you sleep well?'

'Well enough, girl. You should put some clothes on.' His voice was gruff, the words said in a sharper tone than he had intended. It wasn't that her nakedness aroused him; it was the opposite, he realised. Her

251

youth and her beauty only made him feel the weight of his years, looming behind him like a mountain. She returned to her room and he leaned back in his chair. When had arousal died? He thought back. It was in Melega that he had first noticed it, some fifteen years before. He had hired a whore, a buxom wench, but had been unable to perform despite all her expert ministrations.

At last she had shrugged. 'Dead birds cannot rise from the nest,' she told him cruelly.

Miriel returned, dressed now in grey leggings and a shirt of creamy white wool. 'Is that more to your liking, sir tinker?'

He forced a smile. 'Everything about you, my dear, is to my liking. But naked you remind me of all that there once was. Can you understand that?'

'Yes,' she said, but he knew she was humouring him. What did the young ever understand? Pulling a tall chair to the fireside she reversed it and sat astride it opposite him, her elbows resting on the high back. 'You mentioned some of the men who are hunting my father,' she said. 'Can you tell me of them?'

'They are all dangerous men – and there will be those among them I do not know. But I know Morak the Ventrian. He's deadly, truly deadly. I believe he is insane.'

'What weapons does he favour?' she asked.

'Sabre and knife, but he is a very skilled bowman. And he has great speed – like a striking snake. He'll kill anyone – man, woman, child, babe in arms. He has a gift for death.'

'What does he look like?'

'Medium height, slim. He tends to wear green, and he has a ring of heavy gold, set with a green stone. It matches his eyes, cold and hard.'

'I will watch out for him.'

'If you see him – kill him,' snapped Ralis. 'But you won't see him.'

'You don't think he'll come here?'

'That's not what I said. You would both be best advised to leave here. Even Waylander cannot defeat all who are coming against him.'

'Don't underestimate him, tinker,' she warned.

'I don't,' he replied. 'But I am an old man, and I know how time makes dotards of us all. Once I was young, fast and strong. But slowly, like water eating at stone, time removes our speed and our strength. Waylander is not a young man. Those hunting him are in their prime.'

She nodded and looked away. 'So you advise us to run?'

'Another place, under another name. Yes.'

'Tell me of the others,' she said.

And he did, relating all he had heard of Belash, Courail, Senta and many more. She listened, mostly in silence, but occasionally interrupting him with pertinent questions. At last satisfied she had drained his knowledge, she stood.

'I will prepare you some breakfast,' she said. 'I think you have earned it.'

'What did you gain from my stories?' he asked her.

'It is important to know your enemy,' she answered him. 'Only with knowledge can you ensure victory.'

Ralis said nothing.

Waylander sat quietly on the rough-hewn platform, high in the oak, staring out to the west, over the rolling plains towards the distant towers of Kasyra. Some four miles to his left he could see the Corn Road, a ribbon of a trail leading from the Sentran Plain south towards Drenan. There were few wagons now, the corn having been gathered and stored, or shipped to markets in Mashrapur or Ventria. He saw several horsemen on the road, all riding towards Kasyra and the surrounding villages.

A cool breeze rustled the leaves around him and he settled back, his mind drifting through the libraries of memory, sifting, seeking. His early training as a soldier in the Sathuli Wars told him that a static enemy was one facing defeat. The forest and mountains of Skeln boasted many caves and hiding places, but a persistent enemy would find him, for a man had to hunt to eat, and in hunting he left tracks. No, the soldier he had been knew only one way to win – attack!

But how? And where? *And against whom?*

The hunt-geld had been placed in the Guild. Even if he were to find the man who had ordered the kill, and slay him, the hunt would go on.

The wind picked up, and Waylander pulled his fur-lined cloak more tightly around his frame. The run had been hard, his ageing muscles complaining at the severity of the exercise, his lungs on fire, his heartbeat a pounding drum. Stretching out his right leg he rubbed at the still-burning muscles of his calf, and thought of all he knew of the Guild.

Fifteen years ago the Guild had approached Waylander, offering to broker his contracts. He had refused them, preferring to work alone. In those days the Guild had been a mysterious, shadowy organisation, operating in secret. Its rules were simple. Firstly, all killings were to be accomplished with blade, shaft or knotted rope. Murder by poison or fire was not allowed – the Guild wished for no innocent victims to be slain. Secondly, all monies were paid direct to the Guild and a signed document was placed with the Patriarch, giving reasons for the contract. Such reasons could not include matters of the heart, or religious quarrels.

In theory a cuckolded husband could not hire an assassin to murder his wife, her lover, or both. In practice, of course, such niceties never applied. As long as the contractor declared his reasons as being business or political, no questions were asked. Under Karnak the

trade had become – if not morally acceptable – at least more legitimate. Waylander smiled. By allowing the Guild to operate openly, the
financially-beleaguered Karnak had found yet one more source of
taxable income. And in times of war such income was vital to pay
soldiers, armourers, merchants, ship-builders, masons . . . the list was
endless.

Waylander stood and stretched his aching back. How many would
come against him? The Guild would have other contracts to meet.
They could not afford to send all their fighters scouring the country
for news of him. Seven? Ten? The best would not come first. They
would sit back and watch, while lesser men began the hunt, men like
Kreeg.

And were they already here, hidden, waiting?

He thought of Miriel and his stomach tightened. She was strong and
lithe, skilled with all weapons. But she was young, and had never
fought warriors, blade to blade.

Removing his cloak Waylander rolled it and looped it over his
shoulder, tying it to his knife-belt. The cold wind bit into his naked
chest, but he ignored it as he climbed down the tree. His eyes scanned
the undergrowth, but there was nothing to be seen. Swiftly he leapt
from the lowest branch, landing lightly on the moss-covered earth.

The first move would have to be left to the enemy. The fact galled
him but having accepted it, he pushed it from his mind. All he could do
now was prepare himself. You have fought men and beasts, demons
and Joinings, he told himself. And you are still alive while your
enemies are dust.

I was younger then, came a small voice from his heart.

Spinning on his heel he swept a throwing blade from its forearm
sheath and sent it flashing through the air, to plunge home into the
narrow trunk of a nearby elm.

Young or old, I am still Waylander.

Miriel watched the old man make his way slowly towards the north-
west and the distant fortress of Dros Delnoch. His pack was high on
his shoulders, his white hair and beard billowing in the breeze. He
stopped at the top of a rise, turned and waved. Then he was gone.
Miriel wandered back through the trees, listening to the birdsong,
enjoying the leaf-broken sunlight dappling the path. The mountains
were beautiful in the autumn, leaves of burnished gold, the last fading
blooms of summer, the mountainsides glowing green and purple; all
seemingly created just for her pleasure.

Coming to the brow of a hill she paused, her eyes scanning the trees
and the paths wending down to the Sentran Plain. A figure moved into
sight, a tall man, wearing a cloak of green. The cold of a remembered
winter touched her skin, making her shiver, her hand moving to the

254

hilt of the shortsword at her side. The green cloak identified him as the assassin Morak. Well, this was one killer who would not live to attack her father.

Miriel stepped into sight and stood waiting as the man slowly climbed towards her. As he approached she studied his face – his broad, flat cheekbones and scarred and hairless brows, a nose flattened and broken, a harsh gash of a mouth. The chin was square and strong, the neck bulging with muscle.

He paused before her. 'The path is narrow,' he said, politely enough. 'Would you be so kind as to move aside?'

'Not for the likes of you,' she hissed, surprised that her voice remained steady, her fear disguised.

'Is it customary in these parts to insult strangers, girl? Or is it that you rely on gallantry to protect you?'

'I need nothing to protect me,' she said, stepping back and drawing her sword.

'Nice blade,' he said. 'Now put it away – lest I take it from you and spank you for your impudence.'

Her eyes narrowed, anger replacing fear, and she smiled. 'Draw your sword – and we'll see who suffers,' she told him.

'I do not fight girls,' he replied. 'I am seeking a man.'

'I know whom you seek, and why. But to get to him you must first pass me. And that will not be easy with your entrails hanging to your ankles.' Suddenly she leapt forward, the point of her blade stabbing towards his belly. He swayed aside, his arm flashing up and across, the back of his hand cannoning against her cheek. Miriel stumbled and fell, then rolled to her feet, her face burning from the slap.

The man moved to the right, slipping the thong from his green cloak and laying the garment over a fallen tree. 'Who taught you to lunge like that?' he asked. 'A farmer, perhaps? Or a herdsman? That is not a hoe you are holding. The thrust should always be disguised, and used following a riposte or counter.' He drew his own sword and advanced on her. Miriel did not wait for his attack, but moved in to meet him, thrusting again, this time at his face. He blocked the blow and spun on his heel, his shoulder thudding into her chest, hurling her from her feet.

She sprang up and rushed in, slashing the blade towards his neck. His own sword swept up, blocking the blow, but this time she spun and leapt, her booted foot cracking against his chin. She expected him to fall but he merely staggered, righted himself, and spat blood from his mouth. 'Good,' he said softly. 'Very good. Swift and in perfect balance. Perhaps there is something to you after all.'

'You'll never know,' she told him, launching an attack of blistering speed, aiming cuts and thrusts to face and body. Each one he blocked, and never once made the riposte. At last she fell back, confused and dismayed. She could not breach his defences, but what was more galling was that he made no attempt to breach hers.

'Why will you not fight me?' she asked him.

'Why should I?'

'I mean to kill you.'

'Do you have a reason for this hostility?' he enquired, the ugly gash of a mouth breaking into a smile.

'I know you, Morak. I know why you are here. That should be enough.'

'It would . . .' he started to say, but she attacked again, and this time he wasn't quite fast enough, her blade slicing past his face and cutting his earlobe. His fist lashed out and up, thundering against her chin. Half-stunned, Miriel lost her grip on her sword and fell to her knees. The newcomer's blade touched her neck. 'Enough of this nonsense,' he said, moving away from her and picking up his cloak.

Gathering her sword she faced him again. 'I will not let you pass,' she said grimly.

'You couldn't stop me,' he told her, 'but it was a game effort. Now where is Waylander?' She advanced again. 'Wait,' he said, sheathing his sword. 'I am not Morak. You understand me? I am not from the Guild.'

'I don't believe you,' she said, her blade now resting on his throat.

'Then believe this: had I wished to kill you I would have. You know that is true.'

'Who are you?'

'My name is Angel,' he answered, 'and a long time ago I was a friend to your family.'

'You are here to help us?'

'I don't fight other men's battles, girl. I came to warn him. I see now it was unnecessary.'

Slowly she lowered her sword. 'Why are they hunting him? He has harmed no one.'

He shrugged. 'Not for many a year, I'll grant you that, but he has many enemies. It is one of the drawbacks of an assassin's life. Did he teach you to use a sword?'

'Yes.'

'He ought to be ashamed of himself. Swordfighting is heart and mind in perfect harmony,' he said sternly. 'Did he not tell you that?'

'Yes he did,' she snapped.

'Ah, but like most women you only listen when it suits you. Yes, I can see that. Well, can you cook?'

Holding back her temper she gave her sweetest smile. 'I can. I can also embroider, knit, sew, and what else? Ah yes . . .' Her fist cracked against his chin. Standing alongside the fallen tree he had no time to move his feet and steady himself, and a second blow sent him

256

sprawling across the trunk to land in a mud-patch on the other side. 'I almost forgot,' she said. 'He taught me to fight with my fists.'

Angel pushed himself to his knees and slowly rose. 'My first wife was like you,' he said, rubbing his chin. 'A dreadful woman, soft as goosedown on the outside, baked leather and iron inside. But I'll say this, girl – he did a better job of teaching you to punch than he did to thrust. Can we have a truce now?'

Miriel chuckled. 'Truce,' she agreed.

Angel rubbed his swollen jaw as he walked behind the tall mountain woman. A kick like an angry horse and a punch almost as powerful. He smiled ruefully, his eyes watching the way she moved, graceful and yet economical. She fought well, he conceded, but with too much head and too little instinct. Even the punches she had thrown had been ill-disguised, but Angel had allowed them to land, sensing she needed some outlet for frustration at having been so easily defeated.

A proud woman. And attractive, he decided, somewhat to his surprise. Angel had always favoured big-breasted women, buxom and comfortable, warm between the sheets. Miriel was a mite thin for his taste and her legs, though long and beautifully proportioned, were just a little too muscular. Still, as the saying went, she was a woman to walk the mountains with.

He chuckled suddenly, and she turned. 'Something is amusing you?' she asked, her expression frosty.

'Not at all, Miriel. I was just remembering the last time I walked these mountains. You and your sister would have been around eight, maybe nine. I was thinking that life goes by with bewildering speed.'

'I don't remember you,' she said.

'I looked different then. This squashed nose was aquiline, and my brows boasted hair. It was long before the mailed gloves of other fist-fighters cut and slashed at the skin. My mouth too was fuller. And I had long red hair that hung to my shoulders.'

She leaned in close, peering at him. 'You were not called Angel then,' she announced.

'No. I was Caridris.'

'I remember now. You brought me a dress – a yellow dress, and a green one for Krylla. But you were . . .'

'Handsome? Yes, I was. And now I am ugly.'

'I did not mean . . .'

'No matter, girl. All beauty passes. I chose a rough occupation.'

'I don't understand how any man would wish to pursue such a way of life. Causing pain, being hurt, risking death – and for what? So that a crowd of fat-bellied merchants can see blood flow.'

'I used to think there was more to it,' he said softly, 'but now I will not argue with you. It was brutal and barbaric, and mostly I loved it.'

257

They walked on to the cabin. After he had eaten Angel sat down by the dying fire and pulled off his boots. He glanced at the hearth. 'A little early for fires, isn't it?'

'We had a guest – an old man,' said Miriel, seating herself opposite him. 'He feels the cold.'

'Old Ralis?' he enquired.

'Yes. You know him?'

'He's been plying his trade between Drenan and Delnoch for years – decades. He used to make knives the like of which I've never seen since. Your father has several.'

'I'm sorry I struck you,' she said suddenly. 'I don't know why I did it.'

'I've been struck before,' he answered, with a shrug. 'And you were angry.'

'I am not usually so . . . short-tempered. But I think I am a little afraid.'

'That is a good way to be. I've always been careful around fearless men – or women. They have a tendency to get you killed. But take some advice, young Miriel. When the hunters come don't challenge them with the blade. Shoot them from a distance.'

'I thought I was good with a sword. My father always tells me I am better than him.'

'In practice, maybe, but in combat I would doubt it. You think out your moves and that robs you of speed. Sword-play requires subtle skills and a direct link between hand and mind. I'll show you.' Leaning to his right he lifted a long twig from the tinderbox and stood. 'Stand opposite me,' he ordered her. Then, holding the stick between his index fingers he said: 'Put your hand over the stick and, when I release it, catch it. Can you do that?'

'Of course, it is . . .' As she was answering him he opened his fingers. The twig dropped sharply. Miriel's hand flashed down, her fingers closing on air, and the twig landed at her feet. 'I wasn't ready,' she argued.

'Then try again.'

Twice more she missed the falling twig. 'What does it prove?' she snapped.

'Reaction time, Miriel. The hand should move as soon as the eye sees the twig fall – but yours doesn't. You see the twig. You send a message to your hand. Then you move. By this time the twig is falling away from you.'

'How else can anyone catch it?' she asked him. 'You have to tell your hand to move.'

He shook his head. 'You will see.'

'Show me,' she demanded.

'Show her what?' asked Waylander from the doorway.

'She wants to learn to catch twigs,' said Angel, turning slowly.

'It's been a long time, Caridris. How are you?' asked the mountain man, the small crossbow pointing at Angel's heart.

'Not here looking for a kill, my friend. I don't work for the Guild. I came to warn you.'

Waylander nodded. 'I heard you retired from the arena. What do you do now?'

'I sold hunting weapons. I had a place in the market square, but it was sequestered against my debts.'

'Ten thousand gold pieces would buy it back for you,' said Waylander coldly.

'Indeed it would – five times over. But as I have already told you, I do not work for the Guild. And do not even think of calling me a liar!'

Waylander pulled the bolts clear of the weapon then released the strings. Dropping the bow to the table he turned back to the scarred fighter. 'You are no liar,' he said. 'But why would you warn me? We were never close.'

Angel shrugged. 'I was thinking of Danyal. I didn't want to see her widowed. Where is she?'

Waylander did not reply, but Angel saw the colour fade from his face, and a look of anguish that was swiftly masked. 'You may stay the night,' said Waylander. 'And I thank you for your warning.' With that he took up his crossbow and left the cabin.

'My mother died,' whispered Miriel. 'Five years ago.' Angel sighed and sank back in his chair. 'You knew her well?' she asked.

'Well enough to be a little in love with her. How did she die?'

'She was riding. The horse fell and rolled on her.'

'After all she'd been through . . . battles and wars . . .' He shook his head. 'There's no sense to such things, none at all. Unless it be that the gods have a grim sense of humour. Five years, you say. Gods! He must have adored her to stay alone this long.'

'He did. He still does, spending too much time by her grave, talking to her as if she can still hear him. He does that here sometimes.'

'I see it now,' said Angel softly.

'What do you see?'

'Isn't it obvious, Miriel? The killers are gathering – assassins, hunters, stalkers of the night. He cannot kill them all, he knows that. So why is he still here?'

'You tell me.'

'He's like the old stag hunted by wolves. It takes to the high ground, knowing it is finished, and then it turns and waits, facing the enemy for one last battle.'

'But he's not like that stag. He's not old! He's not! And he's not finished, either.'

259

'That's not how he sees it. Danyal was what he lived for. Perhaps he thinks that in death they will be reunited, I don't know. What I *do* know – and so does he – is that to stay here means death.'

'You are wrong,' said Miriel, but her words carried no conviction.

3

Floating on a sea of pain Ralis knew he was dying; his arms were tied behind him, the skin of his chest was seared and cut, his legs broken. All his dignity had been stripped from him in the screams of anguish the knives and hot irons had torn from his soul. There was nothing of the man left, save one small flickering spark of pride.

He had told them nothing. Cold water drenched him, easing the pain of the burns and he opened his one remaining eye. Morak knelt before him, an easy smile on his handsome face.

'I can free you from this pain, old man,' he said. Ralis said nothing. 'What is he to you? A son? A nephew? Why do you suffer this for him? You have walked these mountains for what . . . fifty, sixty years? He's here and you know where he is. We will find him anyway, eventually.'

'He . . . will . . . kill you . . . all,' whispered Ralis.

Morak laughed, the others following his lead. Ralis smelt the burning of his flesh moments before the pain seared into his skull. But his throat was hoarse and bleeding from screaming and he could only utter a short, broken groan.

And suddenly, wonderfully, the pain passed, and Ralis heard a voice calling to him.

He rose from his bonds and flew towards the voice. 'I did not tell them, Father,' he shouted triumphantly. 'I did not tell them!'

'Old fool,' said Morak, as he stared at the corpse sagging against the ropes. 'Let's go!'

'Tough old man,' put in Belash as they left the glade. Morak rounded on the stocky Nadir tribesman.

'He made us waste half a day – and for what? Had he told us at the start, he would have walked off with ten, maybe twenty gold pieces. Now he's dead meat for the foxes and the carrion birds. Yes, he was tough. But he was also stupid!'

Belash's jet-black eyes stared up into Morak's face. 'He died with honour,' muttered the Nadir. 'And great will be his welcome in the Hall of Heroes.'

Morak's laughter welled out. 'The Hall of Heroes, eh? They must be getting short of men if they need to rely on elderly tinkers. What stories will he tell around the great table? How I sold a knife for twice its worth, or how I mended a broken cookpot? I can see there'll be some merry evenings ahead for all of them.'

'Most men mock what they can never aspire to,' said Belash, striding on ahead, his hand on his sword-hilt.

The words cut through Morak's good humour, and his hatred of the little Nadir welled anew. The Ventrian swung to face the nine men who followed him. 'Kreeg came to these mountains because he had information that Waylander was here. We'll split up and quarter the area. In three days we'll meet at the foot of that peak to the north, where the stream forks. Baris, you go into Kasyra. Ask about Kreeg, who he stayed with, where he drank. Find out where he got his information.'

'Why me?' asked the tall, sandy-haired young man. 'And what happens if you find him while I'm gone? Do I still get a share?'

'We all get a share,' promised Morak. 'If we find him and kill him before you get back I will see that the gold is held for you in Drenan. Can I be fairer than that?'

The man seemed unconvinced, but he nodded and walked away. Morak cast his eyes over the remaining eight men. All were woodsmen and proven warriors, men he had used before, tough and unhindered by morals. He despised them all, but was careful to keep his thoughts to himself. No man needed to be wakened by a saw-edged blade rasping across his jugular. But Belash was the only one he hated. The tribesman was fearless and a superb killer with knife or bow. He was worth ten men on a hunt such as this. One day, though, Morak thought with grim relish, one day I will kill you. I will slide a blade into that flat belly, and rip out your entrails.

Organising the men in pairs he issued his instructions. 'If you come upon any dwellings, ask about a tall man and a young daughter. He may not be using the name Dakeyras, so seek out any widower who fits the description. And if you find him make no move. Wait until we are all together. You understand?'

The men nodded solemnly, then departed.

Ten thousand Raq in gold was waiting for the man who killed Waylander, but the money meant little to Morak. He had ten times that amount hidden away with merchants in Mashrapur and Ventria. What mattered was the hunt and the kill – to be the man who slew a legend.

He felt the sharp rise of anticipated pleasure, as he considered all he might do to fill Waylander's last hours with exquisite pain. There was the girl, of course. He could rape and kill her before Waylander's eyes. Or torture her. Or give her to the men, to use and abuse. Be calm, he told himself. Let the anticipation build. First you have to find him.

Swinging his leaf-green cloak about his shoulders he walked off in pursuit of Belash. The Nadir had made camp in a sheltered hollow and was kneeling upon his blanket, hands clasped in prayer, several old fingerbones, yellowed and porous, lying before him. Morak sat down on the other side of the fire. What a disgusting practice, he thought, carrying the bones of your father in a bag. Barbarians! Who would ever understand them? Belash finished his prayer and returned the bones to the pouch at his side.

'Your father have anything interesting to tell you?' asked Morak, his green eyes alight with amusement.

Belash shook his head. 'I do not speak with my father,' he said. 'He is gone. I speak to the Mountains of the Moon.'

'Ah yes, the mountains. Do they know where Waylander dwells?'

'They know only where each Nadir warrior rests.'

'Lucky them,' observed Morak.

'There are some matters you should not mock,' warned Belash. 'The mountains house the souls of all Nadir, past and future. And through them, if I am valiant, I will find the home of the man who killed my father. I shall bury my father's bones in that man's grave, resting on his chest. And he will serve my father for all time.'

'Interesting thought,' said Morak, keeping his voice neutral.

'You *kol-isha* think you know everything. You think the world was created for your pleasure, but you do not understand the land. You, you sit there and you breathe air and feel the cold earth beneath you, and you notice nothing. And why? Because you live your lives in cities of stone, building walls to keep at bay the spirit of the land. You see nothing. You hear nothing. You feel nothing.'

I can see the boil starting on your neck, you ignorant savage, thought Morak. And I can smell the stench from your armpits. Aloud he said: 'And what is the spirit of this land?'

'It is female,' answered Belash. 'Like a mother. She nourishes those who respond to her, giving them strength and pride. Like the old man you killed.'

'And she talks to you?'

'No, for I am the enemy of this land. But she lets me know she is there and watching me. And she does not hate me. But she hates you.'

'Why would that be true?' asked Morak, suddenly uncomfortable. 'Women have always liked me.'

'She reads your soul, Morak. And she knows it is full of dark light.'

'Superstition!' snapped Morak. 'There is no woman. There is no force in the world save that which is held in ten thousand sharp swords. Look at Karnak. He ordered the assassination of the great hero Egel, and now he rules in his place, revered, even loved. He is the force in the Drenai world. Does the lady love him?'

Belash shrugged. 'Karnak is a great man – for all his faults – and he fights for the land, so maybe she does. And no man truly knows whether Karnak ordered Egel's killing.'

I know, thought Morak, remembering the moment when he stood over the great man's bed and plunged the dagger into his right eye.

Oh yes, I know.

It was close to midnight when Waylander returned. Angel was sitting beside the fire, Miriel was asleep in the back room. Waylander lifted the lock-bar into place on the iron brackets of the door then unclipped the quiver from his belt, laying it on the table beside his ebony crossbow. Angel glanced up. The only light in the room came from the flickering fire, and in its glow Waylander seemed an eldritch figure surrounded by dancing demon shadows.

Silently, Waylander lifted clear his black leather baldric, with its three throwing knives, then untied the two forearm sheaths, placing the weapons upon the table. Two more knives came from hidden scabbards in his knee-length moccasins. At last he walked to the fire and sat down opposite the former gladiator.

Angel sat back, his pale eyes watching the warrior, observing his tension.

'I see you fought Miriel,' said Waylander.

'Not for long.'

'No. How many times did you knock her down?'

'Twice.'

Waylander nodded. 'The tracks were not easy to read. Your footprints were deeper than hers, but they overlaid one another.'

'How did you know I knocked her down?'

'The ground was soft, and I found where her elbow struck the earth. You beat her easily.'

'I defeated thirty-seven opponents in the arena. You think a girl should best me?'

Waylander said nothing for a moment. Then: 'How good was she?'

Angel shrugged. 'She would survive against an unskilled swordsman, but the likes of Morak, or Senta? She'd be dead within seconds.'

'She's better than me,' said Waylander. 'And I would survive against them for longer than that.'

'She's better than you when you *practise*,' replied Angel. 'You and I both know the difference between that and the reality of combat. She is too tense. Danyal once told me of the test you set her. You recall?'

'How could I forget?'

'Well, were you to try it with Miriel she would fail. You know that, don't you?'

'Perhaps,' admitted Waylander. 'How can I help her?'

'You can't.'

'But you could.'

'Yes. But why would I?'

Waylander threw a fresh chunk of wood to the coals, remaining silent as the first yellow flames licked at the bark. His dark gaze swung to Angel. 'I am a rich man, Caridris. I will pay ten thousand in gold.'

'I notice you don't live in a palace,' remarked Angel.

'I choose to live here. I have merchants looking after my investments. I will give you a letter to one of them in Drenan. He will pay you.'

'Even after you are dead?'

'Even then.'

'I don't intend to fight for you,' said Angel. 'Understand? I will be a tutor to your daughter, but that is all.'

'I need no one to fight for me,' snapped Waylander. 'Not now. Not ever.'

Angel nodded. 'I accept your offer. I will stay and teach her, but only so long as I believe she is learning. When the day comes – as it will – when I can teach her no more, or she cannot learn, then I leave. Is that agreeable?'

'It is.' Waylander rose and moved to the rear wall. Angel watched him press his palm against a flat stone, then reach inside a hidden compartment. Waylander turned and tossed a heavy pouch across the room. Angel caught it, and heard the chink of metal within. 'There is a part-payment,' said Waylander.

'How much?'

'Fifty gold Raq.'

'I'd have undertaken the task for this alone. Why pay so much more?'

'You tell me?' countered Waylander.

'You set the price at the same level as the hunt-geld upon you. You are removing temptation from my path.'

'That is true, Caridris. But not the whole truth.'

'And what is the whole truth?'

'Danyal was fond of you,' replied Waylander, rising to his feet. 'And I wouldn't want to kill you. Now I'll bid you goodnight.'

Waylander found sleep elusive, but he lay still, eyes closed, resting his body. Tomorrow he would run again, building his strength and stamina, preparing for the day when the assassins would come.

He was pleased Angel had chosen to stay. He would be good for Miriel, and when the killers finally tracked him down he would ask the gladiator to take the girl to Drenan. Once there she would inherit all his wealth, choose a husband and enjoy a life free from peril.

Slowly he relaxed and faded into dreams.

Danyal was beside him. They were riding by a lakeside, and the sun was bright in a clear blue sky.

'I'll race you to the meadow,' she shouted, digging her heels into the grey mare's flanks.

'No!' he shouted, his panic growing. But she rode away. He saw the horse stumble and fall, watched as it rolled across Danyal, the pommel of the saddle crushing her chest. 'No!' he screamed again, waking, his body bathed in sweat.

All was silent. He shivered. His hands were trembling and he rose from the bed and poured himself a goblet of water. Together he and Danyal had crossed a war-torn land, enemies all around them. Werebeasts had hunted them, Nadir warriors had tracked them. But they had survived. Yet in peace-time, beside a still lake, Danyal had died.

Forcing back the memories he focused instead upon the dangers he faced, and how best to tackle them. Fear settled upon him. He knew of Morak. The man was a torturer who revelled in the pain of others – unhinged, perhaps even insane, yet he never failed. Belash was unknown to him, but he was Nadir, and that meant he would be a fearless fighter. A warrior race, the Nadir had little time for weaklings. Constantly at war the tribesmen fought one another with pitiless ferocity, and only the very strong survived to manhood.

Senta, Courail, Morak, Belash . . . how many more? And who had paid them? The last question he pushed aside. It didn't matter. Once you have killed the hunters you can find out, he told himself.

Once you have killed the hunters . . .

A great weariness of spirit settled upon him. Taking up his tinderbox he lifted a bronze lantern from the hook on the wall above his bed and struck a flame, holding it to the wick. A golden light flickered. Rehanging the lantern, Waylander sat down upon the bed and gazed at his hands.

Hands of death. The hands of the Slayer.

As a young soldier he had fought for the Drenai against Sathuli raiders, protecting the farmer and the settlers of the Sentran Plain. But he hadn't protected them well enough, for a small band of killers had crossed the mountains to raid and pillage. On the return journey they stopped at his farmhouse, raped and murdered his wife and killed his children.

On that day Dakeyras changed. The young soldier resigned his commission and set out in pursuit of the killers. Coming upon their camp he had slain two of them, the rest fleeing. But he tracked them and, one by one, hunted them down. Each man he caught he tortured, forcing information on the names and likely destinations of the remaining raiders. It took years, and on the endless journey the young officer named Dakeyras died, to be replaced by the empty killing-machine known as Waylander.

By then, death and suffering meant nothing to the silent hunter and, one night in Mashrapur, his money gone, he had been approached by a merchant seeking revenge on a business rival. For forty silver pieces Waylander undertook his first assassination. He did not try to justify his actions, not even to himself. The hunt was everything, and to find the killers he needed money. Cold and heartless he moved on, a man apart, feared, avoided, telling himself that when the quest was over he would become Dakeyras again.

But when the last of the raiders had died screaming, staked out across a campfire, Waylander knew Dakeyras was gone forever. And he had continued his bloody trade, the road to Hell carrying him forward until the day he killed the Drenai King.

The enormity of the deed, and its terrible consequences, haunted him still. The land had been plunged into war, with thousands slain, widowed, orphaned.

The golden lantern light flickered on the far wall and Waylander sighed. He had tried to redeem himself, but could a man ever earn forgiveness for such crimes? He doubted it. And even if the Source granted him absolution it would mean nothing. For he could not forgive himself. Maybe that's why Danyal died, he thought, not for the first time. Perhaps he was always to be burdened by sorrow.

Pouring himself a goblet of water he drained it and returned to his bed. The gentle priest Dardalion had guided him from the road to perdition, and Danyal had found the tiny spark of Dakeyras that remained, fanning it to life, bringing him back from the dead.

But now she too was gone. Only Miriel remained. Would he have to watch her die?

Miriel would fail the test. That's what Angel had said, and he was right. Dakeyras recalled the day he himself had tested Danyal. Deep in Nadir territory assassins had come upon him, and he had slain them. Danyal asked him how it was that he killed with such ease.

He walked away from her and stooped to lift a pebble. 'Catch this,' he said, flicking the stone towards her. Her hand snaked out and she caught the pebble deftly. 'That was easy, was it not?'

'Yes,' she admitted.

'Now if I had Krylla and Miriel here, and two men had knives at their throats, and you were told that if you missed the pebble they would die, would it still be easy to catch? The onset of fear makes the simplest of actions complex and difficult. I am what I am because, whatever the consequences, the pebble remains a pebble.'

'Can you teach me?'

'I don't have the time.' She had argued, and finally he said, 'What do you fear most at this moment?'

'I fear losing you.'

He moved away from her and lifted a second pebble. Clouds partly obscured the moonlight and she strained to see his hand. 'I am going to throw this to you,' he said. 'If you catch it, you stay and I train you. If you miss it you return to Skarta.'

'No, that's not fair! The light is poor.'

'Life is not fair, Danyal. If you do not agree, then I ride away alone.'

'Then I agree.'

Without another word he flicked the stone towards her – a bad throw, moving fast and to her left. Her hand flashed out and the pebble bounced against her palm. Even as it fell her fingers snaked around it, clutching it like a prize.

She laughed. 'Why so pleased?' he asked her.

'I won!'

'No, tell me what you did.'

'I conquered my fear.'

'No.'

'Well, what then? I don't understand.'

'You must if you wish to learn.'

Suddenly she smiled. 'I understand the mystery, Waylander.'

'Then tell me what you did.'

'I caught a pebble in the moonlight.'

Waylander sighed. The room was cold, but his memories were warm. Outside a wolf howled at the moon, a lonely sound, haunting and primal. And Waylander slept.

'You move with all the grace of a sick cow,' stormed Angel, as Miriel pushed herself to her knees, fighting to draw air into her tired lungs. Angry now she surged to her feet, the sword-blade lunging at Angel's belly. Sidestepping swiftly he parried the thrust, the flat of his left hand striking her just behind the ear. Miriel hit the ground on her face.

'No, no, no!' said Angel. 'Anger must be controlled. Rest now for a while.' He walked away from her and stopped at the well, hauling up the copper-bound bucket and splashing water to his face.

Miriel rose wearily, her spirits low. For months now she had believed her sword skills to be high, better than most men, her father had said. Now she was faced with the odious truth. A sick cow, indeed! Slowly she made her way to where Angel sat on the wall of the well. He was stripped to the waist now and she saw the host of scars on the ridged muscles of his chest and belly, on his thick forearms and his powerful shoulders.

'You have suffered many wounds,' she said.

'It shows how many skilful swordsmen there are,' he answered gruffly.

'Why are you angry?'

He was silent for a moment. Then he took a deep breath. 'In the city there are many clerks, administrators, organisers. Without them Drenan would cease to run. They are valued men. But place them in these mountains and they would starve to death while surrounded by game and edible roots. You understand? The degree of a man's skill is relative to his surroundings, or the challenges he faces. Against most men you would be considered highly talented. You are fast and you have courage. But the men hunting your father are warriors. Belash would kill you in two . . . three . . . heartbeats. Morak would not take much longer. Senta and Courail both learned their skills in the arena.'

'Can I be as good?'

He shook his head. 'I don't think so. Much as I hate to admit it I think there is an evil in men like them . . . men like me. We are natural killers, and though we may not talk of our feelings yet each of us knows the bitter truth. We enjoy fighting. We enjoy killing. I don't think you will. Indeed, I don't think you should.'

'You think my father enjoys killing?'

'He's a mystery,' admitted Angel. 'I remember talking to Danyal about that. She said he was two men, the one kind, the other a demon. There are gates in the soul which should never be unlocked. He found a key.'

'He has always been kind to me, and to my sister.'

'I don't doubt that. What happened to Krylla?'

'She married and moved away.'

'When I knew you as children you had a . . . power, a Talent. You and she could talk to each other without speaking. You could see things far off. Can you still do it?'

'No,' she said, turning away.

'When did it fail?'

'I don't want to talk about it. Are you ready to teach me?'

'Of course,' he answered. 'That is why I am being paid. Stand still.' Rising he moved to stand before her, his hands running over her shoulders and arms, fingers pressing into the muscles, tracing the lines of her biceps and triceps, up over the deltoids and the joints of her shoulders.

She felt herself reddening. 'What are you doing?' she asked, forcing herself to meet his eyes.

'Your arms are not strong enough,' he told her, 'especially at the back here,' he added, squeezing her triceps. 'All your power is in your legs and lungs. And your balance is wrong. Give me your hand.' Even as he spoke he took hold of her wrist, lifting her arm and staring down at her fingers. 'Long,' he said, almost to himself. 'Too long. It means you cannot get a good grip on the sword-hilt. We'll cut more leather for it tonight. Follow!'

He strode to the edge of the tree line and walked from trunk to trunk, examining the branches. At last satisfied he stood beneath a spreading elm, a thick limb sprouting just out of reach above him. 'I want you to jump and catch hold of that branch and then slowly pull yourself up until your chin touches the bark. Then – and still slowly, mind – lower yourself until the arms are almost straight. Understand?'

'Of course I understand,' she snapped. 'It was hardly the most complex of instructions.'

'Then do it!'

'How many times?'

'As many as you can. I want to see the limits of your strength.'

She leapt upwards, her fingers hooking over the branch, and hung for a moment adjusting her grip. Then slowly she hauled herself up.

'How does it feel?' he asked.

'Easy,' she answered, lowering herself.

'Again!'

At three she began to feel her biceps stretching. At five they began to burn. At seven her arms trembled and gave way and she dropped to the ground. 'Pathetic,' said Angel. 'But it is a start. Tomorrow morning you will begin your day with seven, eight if you can. Then you can run. When you return you will do another seven. In three days I will expect you to complete twelve.'

'How many could you do?'

'At least a hundred,' he replied. 'Follow!'

'Will you stop saying *follow!* It makes me feel like a dog.'

But he was moving even as she spoke and Miriel followed him back across the clearing. 'Wait here,' he ordered, then walked to the side of the cabin where the winter wood was stored. Selecting two large chunks he carried them back to where Miriel was waiting and laid them on the ground twenty feet apart. 'I want you to run from one to the other,' he said.

'You want me to run twenty feet? Why?'

His hand snaked out, rapping against her cheek. 'Stop asking stupid questions and do as you are told.'

'You whoreson!' she stormed. 'Touch me again and I'll kill you!'

He laughed and shook his head. 'Not yet. But do as I tell you – and maybe you'll have the skill to do just that. Now move to the first piece of wood.'

Still seething she walked to the first chunk, his voice following her. 'Run to the second and stoop down, touching the wood with your right hand. Turn instantly and run back to the first, touching it with your left hand. Am I going too fast for you?'

Miriel bit back an angry retort and started to run. But she covered the distance in only a few steps and had to chop her stride. Feeling both ungainly and uncomfortable she ducked down, slapped her fingers against the wood then turned and ran back. 'I think you have the idea,' he said. 'Now do it twenty times. And a little faster.'

For three hours he ordered her through a series of gruelling exercises, running, jumping, sword-work, endless repetition of thrusts and cuts. Not once did she complain, but nor did she speak to him. Grimly she pushed herself through all of his exercises until he called a break at midday. Tired now, Miriel strode back to the cabin, her limbs trembling. She was used to running, inured to the pain of oxygen-starved calves and burning lungs. In truth she even enjoyed the sensations, the sense of freedom, of speed, of power. But the weariness and aches she felt now were all in unaccustomed places. Her hips and waist felt bruised and tender, her arms leaden, her back aching.

To Miriel strength was everything, and her faith in her own skills had been strong. Now Angel had undermined her confidence, first with the consummate ease of his victory in the forest, and now with the punishing routines that exposed her every weakness. She had been awake when Waylander made his offer to the former gladiator, and had heard his response. Miriel believed she knew what Angel was trying to do, force her to refuse his training, humiliate her into quitting. Then he would claim his fortune from her father. And, because Dakeyras was a man of pride and honour, he would pay the ten thousand.

You will not find it easy, Angel, she promised. No, you will have to work for your money, you ugly whoreson!

Angel was well satisfied with the day's training. Miriel had performed above his expectations, fuelled no doubt by anger at the slap. But Angel cared nothing for the motivation. It was enough that the girl had proved to be a fighter. At least he would have something to work with. Given the time, of course.

Waylander had left just after dawn. 'I will be back in four days. Perhaps five. Make good use of the time.'

'You can trust me,' Angel told him.

Waylander smiled thinly. 'Try to stop her attacking anyone else. She should be safe then. The Guild has a rule about innocent victims.'

Morak follows no rules, thought Angel, but he said nothing as the tall warrior loped away towards the north.

An hour before dusk Angel called a halt to the work, but was surprised when Miriel announced she was going for a short run. Was it bravado, he wondered? 'Carry a sword,' he told her.

'I have my knives,' she answered.

'That's not what I meant. I want you to *carry* a sword. To hold it in your hand.'

'I need this run to loosen my muscles, stretch them out. The sword will hamper me.'

'I know. Do it anyway.'

She accepted without further argument. Angel returned to the cabin and pulled off his boots. He too was tired, but would be damned before letting the girl know. Two years out of the arena had seen his stamina drain away. He poured himself a drink of water and slumped down in front of the dead fire.

Given a month, possibly two, he could make something of the girl. Increase her speed, lower her reaction time. The side sprints would help with balance, and the work to build her arms and shoulders add power to her lunges and cuts. But the real problem lay within her heart. When angry she was fast but wild, easy meat for the skilled swordsman. When cool her movements were stilted, her attacks easy to read and counter. The end result of any combat, therefore, would be the same.

She had been gone perhaps an hour when he heard her light footfalls on the hard-packed clay of the clearing. He looked up as she entered, her tunic drenched in perspiration, her face red, her long hair damp. The sword was still in her hand.

'Did you carry it all the way?' he asked softly.

'Yes. That's what you told me.'

'You did not drop it on the trail and pick it up on your return?'

'No!' she answered, offended.

He believed her, and swore inwardly. 'Do you always do as you are told?' he snapped.

'Yes,' she told him, simply.

'Why?'

Throwing the sword to the table top she stood before him, hands on hips. 'Are you now criticising me for obeying you? What do you want from me?'

He sighed. 'Merely your best – and you gave that today. Rest now. I will prepare supper.'

'Nonsense,' she said sweetly. 'You are an old man, and you look weary. You sit there and I'll bring you some food.'

'I thought we had a truce,' he said, following her to the kitchen, where she took down a large ham and began to slice it.

'That was yesterday. That was before you set out to cheat my father.'

His face darkened. 'I have never cheated anyone in my life.'

She swung on him. 'No? What would you call ten thousand in gold for a few days' work?'

'I did not ask for the sum – he offered it. And if you were eavesdropping – a womanly skill, I've found – then you will have heard me tell him I'd do it for fifty.'

'You want cheese with this ham?' she asked.

'Yes, and bread. Did you hear what I said?'

'I heard you, but I don't believe you. You were trying to force me to fail. Admit it!'

'Yes, I admit it.'

'Then that's all there is to say. There's your food. When you have finished it, clean your plate. And then do me the kindness of spending the evening in your room. I've had enough of your company today.'

'The training doesn't stop just because the sun's gone down,' he said softly. 'Today we worked your body. This evening we work your mind. And I will go to my room when it pleases me. What are you going to eat?'

'The same as you.'

'Do you have any honey?'

'No.'

'Dried fruit?'

'Yes – why?'

'Eat some. I learnt a long time ago that sweetmeats and cakes sit more easily on a tired stomach. You'll sleep better and wake more refreshed. And drink a lot of water.'

'Anything else?'

'If I think of anything I'll tell you. Now let us finish this meal and start to work.'

Having finished his meal Angel cleared away the ash of the previous night's fire, laid fresh kindling, and struck a spark to the tinder. Miriel had eaten in the kitchen, and had then walked through the cabin and out into the night. Angel was angry with himself. You are no teacher, he thought. And the girl was right – he wanted her to quit. But not for the reasons she believed. He sighed and leaned back on his haunches, watching the tiny flames devouring the kindling, feeling the first soft waves of heat from the fire.

He had tried to train the boy, Ranuld, showing him the moves and defences he would need in his new career, but Ranuld had died from a disembowelling cut in his first fight. Then there was Sorrin, tall and athletic, fearless and fast. He had lasted for seven fights – had even become a favourite with the crowd. Senta had killed him – heelspin and reverse thrust to the throat. Good move, beautifully executed. Sorrin was dead before he knew it.

That was the day Angel retired. He had fought a dull Vagrian, whose name he couldn't recall. The man was tough, but slowed by a recent wound. Even so he had almost taken Angel, cutting him twice. After the battle Angel had sat in the arena surgery, the doctor stitching his wounds, while on the table opposite lay Sorrin's bloody corpse. Beside it sat Senta, a bandage soaked in honey and wine being applied to a shallow cut in his shoulder.

'You trained him well,' said Senta. 'He almost took me.'

272

'Not well enough,' answered Angel.

'I look forward to meeting the master.'

Angel had looked into the young man's eager eyes, seeing the mocking expression on the handsome face, the smile that was almost a sneer. 'It won't happen, boy,' he had said, the words tasting like acid in his mouth. 'I'm too old and slow. This is your day. Enjoy it.'

'You are leaving the arena?' whispered Senta, astonished.

'Yes. That was my last fight.'

The young man nodded, then cursed as the orderly tied the knot in the bandage on his shoulder. 'You dolt!' snapped Senta.

'I'm sorry, sir!' said the man, moving back, his face twisted in fear.

Senta returned his gaze to Angel. 'I think you are wise, old man, but for myself I am disappointed. You are a favourite with the crowds. I could have made my fortune by defeating you.'

Angel added wood to the fire and stood. Senta had only fought for one more year, then he had joined the Guild, earning far more as an assassin than a gladiator.

The door opened behind him, and he felt a cold draught. Turning he saw Miriel walking towards her room. She was naked and carrying her clothes, her body wet from a bath in the stream. His gaze took in her narrow back and waist, the long muscular legs and firm, rounded buttocks. Arousal touched him and he swung back to the fire.

After a few minutes Miriel joined him, her body clothed in a loose woollen robe of grey wool. 'What work did you have in mind?' she asked him, seating herself in the chair opposite.

'You know why I slapped you?'

'You wanted to dominate me.'

'No. I wanted to see you angry. I needed to know how you reacted when your blood was high.' Idly he stabbed at the fire with an iron poker. 'Listen to me, girl, I am not a teacher. I have only trained two people – young men I loved. Both died. I am . . . was . . . a fine fighter, but just because I have a skill does not mean I can pass it on. You understand?' She remained silent, her large eyes staring at him, expressionless. 'I was a little in love with Danyal, I think, and I have respect for your father. I came here to warn him, so that he would leave the area, travel to Ventria or Gothir. And yes, I could use the gold. But that's not why I came, nor is it why I agreed to stay. If you choose not to believe me then I will leave in the morning – and I will not claim the fortune.'

Still she said nothing.

'I don't know what else I can say to you.' He shrugged and sat back.

'You told me we were going to work,' she said softly. 'On my mind. What did you mean?'

He spread his hands and stared into the fire. 'Did your father ever tell you about the test he set Danyal?'

273

'No. But I heard you say I would fail it.'

'Yes, you would.' And Angel told her of the pebble in the moonlight, and talked on of the warrior's heart, the willingness to risk everything, but the confidence to believe the risk was calculated.

'How do I achieve this?' she asked.

'I don't know,' he admitted.

'The two men you trained – did they have it?'

'Ranuld believed he did, but he tied up in his first fight, his muscles tense, his movements halting. Sorrin had it, I think, but he met a better man. It comes from an ability to close off that part of the imagination that is fuelled by fear. You know, the part that pictures terrible wounds and gangrene, pumping blood and the darkness of death. But at the same time the mind must continue to function, seeing the opponent's weaknesses, planning ways through his defences. You have seen my scars. I have been cut many times – but always I won. And I beat better men, faster men, stronger men. I beat them because I was too obstinate to give up. And their confidence would begin to fail, and the windows of their minds would creep open. Their imagination would seep out, and they would begin to doubt, to fear. And from that moment it did not matter that they were better, or faster or stronger. For I would grow before their eyes and they would shrink before mine.'

'I will learn,' she promised.

'I doubt it can be learned. Your father became Waylander because his first family were butchered by raiders, but I don't believe the atrocity *created* Waylander. He was always there, beneath the surface of Dakeyras. The real question is, what lies beneath the surface of Miriel?'

'We will see,' she said.

'Then you wish me to stay?'

'Yes. I wish you to stay. But answer me one question honestly.'

'Ask.'

'What is it *you* fear?'

'Why would you think I fear anything?' he hedged.

'I know that you did not want to stay, and I sense you are torn between your desire to help me and a need to leave. So what is it?'

'The question is a fair one. Let us leave it that you are right. There *is* something I fear, but I am not prepared to talk about it. As you are not prepared to speak of the loss of your Talent.'

She nodded. 'There is one – or more – among the assassins that you do not wish to meet. Am I close?'

'We must thicken the grip on your sword,' he said. 'Cut some strips of leather – thin, no wider than a finger's width. You have glue?'

'Yes. Father makes it from fishbones and hide.'

'First bind the hilt until the size feels comfortable. When curled

274

around it your longest finger should just touch the flesh below your thumb. When you are satisfied, glue the strips into place.'

'You did not answer me,' she said.

'No,' he replied. 'Cut and bind the strips tonight. It will give the glue time to dry. I will see you in the morning.' He rose and strode across the room.

'Angel!'

His hand was on the door latch. 'Yes.'

'Sleep well.'

4

Dardalion swung away from the window and faced the two priests standing before his desk.

'The argument,' he said, 'is of intellectual interest only. It is of no real importance.'

'How can that be, Father Abbot?' asked Magnic. 'Surely it is central to our beliefs?'

'In this I must agree with my brother,' put in the forked-bearded Vishna, his dark eyes staring unblinking at the Abbot. Dardalion beckoned them to be seated and leaned back in his wide leather chair. Magnic looked so young against Vishna, he thought, his pale face, soft-featured and unlined, his blond, unruly hair giving him the appearance of a youth some years from twenty. Vishna, tall and stern, his black forked beard carefully combed and oiled, looked old enough to be Magnic's father. Yet both were barely twenty-four.

'The debate is of worth only because it makes us consider the Source,' said Dardalion at last. 'The pantheistic view that God exists in everything, every stone and every tree, is an interesting one. We believe the Universe was created by the Source in a single moment of blinding energy. From Nothing came Something. What could that Something be, save the body of the Source? That is the argument of the pantheists. Your view, Magnic, that the Source is separate from the world, and that only the Chaos Spirit rules here, is also widely held. The Source, in a terrible War against His own rebellious angels, sent them hurtling to the earth, there to rule, as He rules in Heaven. This argument makes Hell of our world. And I would agree that there is strong evidence to suggest that sometimes it is.

'But in all these debates we are trying to imagine the unimaginable, and therein lies a great danger. The Source of All Things is beyond us.

His actions are timeless, and so far above our understanding as to make them meaningless to us. Yet still we try to force our minds to comprehend. We struggle to encompass His greatness, to draw Him in and place Him in acceptable compartments. This leads to dispute and disruption, discord and disharmony. And these are the weapons of the Chaos Spirit.' Dardalion rose and walked around the oak desk to stand beside the two priests, laying a hand on each of them. 'The important point is to know that He exists, and to trust His judgment. You see, you could both be right, and both be wrong. We are dealing here with the Cause of All Causes, the one great truth in a universe of lies. How can we judge? From what perspective? How does the ant perceive the elephant? All the ant sees is part of the foot. Is that the elephant? It is to the ant. Be patient. When the Day of Glory arrives all will be revealed. We will find the Source together – as we have planned.'

'That day is not far off,' said Vishna quietly.

'Not far,' agreed Dardalion. 'How is the training progressing?'

'We are strong,' said Vishna, 'but we have problems still with Ekodas.'

Dardalion nodded. 'Send him to me this evening, after meditation.'

'You will not talk him round, Father Abbot,' ventured Magnic diffidently. 'He will leave us rather than fight. He cannot overcome his cowardice.'

'He is not a coward,' said Dardalion, masking his annoyance. 'I know this. I once walked the same road, believed the same dreams. Evil can sometimes be countered with love. Indeed, that is the best way. But sometimes evil must be faced with steel and a strong arm, yet do not call him a coward for holding to high ideals. It lessens you as much as it insults him.'

The blond priest blushed furiously. 'I am sorry, Father Abbot.'

'And now I am expecting a visitor,' said Dardalion. 'Vishna, wait for him at the front gate and bring him straight to my study. Magnic, go to the cellar and fetch a bottle of wine and some bread and cheese.' Both priests stood. 'One more thing,' said Dardalion, his voice little more than a whisper. 'Do not shake hands with the man, or touch him. And do not try to read his thoughts.'

'Is he evil, then?' asked Vishna.

'No, but his memories would burn you. Now go and wait for him.'

Dardalion returned to the window. The sun was high, shining down on the distant Delnoch peaks, and from this high window the Abbot could just see the faint grey line of the first wall of the Delnoch fortress. His eyes tracked along the colossal peaks of the mountains, traversing west to east towards the distant sea. Low clouds blocked the view, but Dardalion pictured the fortress of Dros Purdol, saw again the dreadful siege, heard the screams of the dying. He sighed.

The might of Vagria was humbled before the walls of Purdol, and the history of the world changed in those awful months of warfare. Good men had died, iron spears ripping into their bodies . . .

The first Thirty had been slaughtered there, battling against the demonic powers of the Brotherhood. Dardalion alone had survived. He shivered, as he relived the pain of the spear plunging into his back, and the loneliness as the souls of his friends flew from him, hurtling towards the eternal serenity of the Source. The Thirty had fought on the astral plane alone, refusing to bear weapons in the world of flesh. How wrong they had been!

The door opened behind him, and he stiffened, his mouth suddenly dry. Swiftly he closed the gates of his Talent, shutting out the swelling violence emanating from his visitor. Slowly he turned. His guest was tall, wide-shouldered and yet lean, dark-eyed and stern of appearance. He was dressed all in black and even the chain-mail shoulder-guard was stained with dark dye. Dardalion's eyes were drawn to the many weapons, the three knives sheathed to the man's baldric, the throwing blades in scabbards strapped to his forearms, the short sabre and crossbow bolt quiver at his side. Two more knives were hidden, he knew, in the man's knee-length moccasins. But the weapon of death that drew his gaze was the small ebony crossbow the man held in his right hand.

'Good day, Dakeyras,' said Dardalion, and there was no welcome in his voice.

'And to you, Dardalion. You are looking well.'

'That will be all, Vishna,' said the Abbot, and the tall, white-robed priest bowed and departed. 'Sit you down,' Dardalion told his visitor, but the man remained standing, his dark eyes scanning the room, the shelves packed with ancient tomes, the open cupboards bursting with manuscripts and scrolls, the dust-covered rugs and the decaying velvet hangings at the high, arched window. 'I study here,' said Dardalion.

The door opened and Magnic entered, bearing a tray on which stood a bottle of wine, two loaves of black bread and a hunk of blue-veined cheese. Placing them on the desk the blond priest bowed and departed.

'They are nervous of me,' said Waylander. 'What have you told them?'

'I told them not to touch you.'

Waylander chuckled. 'You don't change, do you? Still the same priggish, pompous priest.' He shrugged. 'Well, that is your affair. I did not come here to criticise you. I came for information.'

'I can offer you none.'

'You don't know yet what I am going to ask. Or do you?'

'You want to know who hired the assassins and why.'

'That's part of it.'

'What else?' asked Dardalion, filling two goblets with wine and offering one to his guest. Waylander accepted it, taking the drink with his left hand, politely sipping the contents and then replacing the goblet on the desk top, there to be forgotten. The sound of clashing sword-blades rose up from the courtyard below. Waylander moved to the window and leaned out.

'Teaching your priests to fight? You do surprise me, Dardalion. I thought you were against such violence.'

'I am against the violence of evil. What else did you want to know?'

'I have not heard from Krylla since she moved away. You could . . . use your Talent and tell me if she is well.'

'No.'

'That is it? A simple *no* – not a word of explanation?'

'I owe you no explanations. I owe you nothing.'

'That's true,' said Waylander coldly. 'I saved your life, not once but many times, but you owe me nothing. So be it, priest. You are a fine example of religion in action.'

Dardalion reddened. 'Everything you did was for your own ends. I used all my powers to protect you. I watched my disciples die while I protected you. And yes, for once in your life you did the decent deed. Good for you! You don't need me, Waylander. You never did. Everything I believe in is mocked by your life. Can you understand that? Your soul is like a blazing torch of dark light, and I need to steel myself to stand in the same room as you, closing off my Talent lest your light corrupt me.'

'You sound like a windy pig, and your words smell about as fine,' snapped Waylander. 'Corrupt you? You think I haven't seen what you are doing here? You had armour made in Kasyra, and helms bearing runic numbers. Knives, bows, swords. Warrior priests: isn't that a contradiction, Dardalion? At least my violence is honest. I fight to stay alive. I no longer kill for hire. I have a daughter I am trying to protect. What is your excuse for teaching priests to kill?'

'You wouldn't understand!' hissed the Abbot, aware that his heartbeat was rising and that anger was threatening to engulf him.

'You are right again, Dardalion. I don't understand. But then I am not a religious man. I served the Source once, but then He discarded me. Not content with that He killed my wife. Now I see His . . . Abbot, isn't it? . . . playing at soldiers. No, I don't understand. But I understand friendship. I would die for those I love, and if I had a Talent like yours I would not deny it to them. Gods, man, I would not even deny it to a man I disliked.' Without another word the black-garbed warrior strode from the room.

Dardalion slumped back in his chair, fighting for calm. For some time he prayed. Then he meditated before praying again. At last he

278

opened his eyes. 'I wish I could have told you, my friend,' he whispered. 'But it would have been too painful for you.'

Dardalion closed his eyes once more and let his spirit free. Passing through flesh and bone as if his body had become water he rose like a swimmer seeking air. High now above the Temple he gazed down on the grey castle and the tall hill upon which it stood, and he saw the town spread out around the foot of the hill, the narrow streets, the wide market square and the bear-pit beyond it, stained with blood. But his spirit eyes sought out the man who had been his friend. He was moving easily down the winding path towards the trees and Dardalion felt his sorrow, and his anger.

And the freedom of the sky could not mask the sadness which swept through the Abbot.

'You could have told him,' whispered the voice of Vishna in his mind.

'The balance is too delicate.'

'Is he so important, then?'

'Of himself? No,' answered Dardalion, 'but his actions now will change the future of nations – that I know. And I must not – will not – attempt to guide him.'

'What will he do when he finds out the truth?'

Dardalion shrugged. 'What he always does, Vishna. He will look for someone to kill. It is his way – a law made of iron. He is not evil, you know, but there is no compromise in him. Kings believe it is their will that guides history. They are wrong. In all great events there are men like Waylander. History may not recall them, but they are there.' He smiled. 'Ask any child who won the Vagrian War and they will tell you it was Karnak. But Waylander recovered the Armour of Bronze. Waylander slew the enemy general Kaem.'

'He is a man of power,' agreed Vishna. 'I could feel that.'

'He is the deadliest man I ever met. Those hunting him will find the truth of that, I fear.'

Waylander found his anger hard to control as he followed the winding hill path that led down to the forest. He paused and sat at the edge of the path. Anger blinds, he told himself. Anger dulls the senses! He took a deep, slow breath.

What did you expect of him?

More than I received.

It was galling, for he had loved the priest. And admired him – the gentleness of his soul, the bottomless well of forgiveness and understanding he could bring to bear. What changed you, Dardalion, he wondered. But he knew the answer, and it lay upon his heart with all the weight only guilt can muster.

Ten years ago he had found the young Dardalion being tortured by robbers. Against his better judgement he had rescued him, and in so doing had been drawn into the Vagrian War, helping Danyal and the children, finding the Armour of Bronze, fighting werebeasts and demonic warriors. The priest had changed his life. Dardalion had been pure then, a follower of the Source, unable to fight, even in order to survive, unwilling to eat meat. He could not even hate the men who tortured him, nor the vile enemy that swept across the land bringing blood and death to thousands.

Waylander had changed him. With the priest in a trance, his spirit hunted across the Void, Waylander had cut his own arm, holding it above Dardalion's face. And the blood had splashed to the priest's cheek, staining his skin and lips, flowing into his mouth. The unconscious Dardalion had reacted violently, his body arching in an almost epileptic spasm.

And he killed the demon spirit hunting him.

To save Dardalion's life, Waylander had sullied the priest's soul.

'You sullied me too,' whispered Waylander. 'You touched me with your purity. You shone a light on the dark places.' Wearily he pushed himself to his feet. From here he could see the town below, the small church a stone's throw from the bloodstained bear-pit, the timber-built homes and stables. He had no wish to journey there. South lay his home; south was where Danyal waited, silent among the flowers and the glittering falls.

Once under cover of the trees he relaxed a little, feeling the slow, eternal heartbeat of the forest all around him. What did these trees care for the hopes of Man? Their spirits were everlasting, born into the leaf, carried back to the ground, merging with the earth, feeding the tree, becoming leaves. An endless passive cycle of birth and rebirth through the eons. No murders here, no guilt. He felt the weight of his weapons, and wished he could cast them all aside and walk naked in the forest, the soft earth beneath his feet, the warm sun upon his back.

A shout of pain came from some way to his left, followed by the sound of cursing. Stepping swiftly, knife in hand, he pushed back a screen of bushes and saw four men standing close to the mouth of a shallow cave some fifty paces away, at the foot of a gentle slope. Three were carrying wooden clubs, the fourth a shortsword which, even at this distance, Waylander could see was part-rusted.

'Bastard damn near took my arm off,' complained a burly balding man, blood dripping from a shallow wound in his forearm.

'We need a bow, or spears,' said another.

'Leave the beast. It's a demon,' said a third, backing away, 'and it's dying anyway.'

One by one they moved back from the cave mouth, but the last man stopped and threw a large stone into the dark recesses of the cave. A deep growl was heard and a huge hound appeared in the entrance, blood on its fangs. The men suddenly panicked and ran back up the slope. The first of them, the balding fat man with the injured arm, saw Waylander standing there and paused.

'Don't go down there, friend,' he said. 'The dog is a killer.'

'Rabid?' queried Waylander.

'Nah. It was one of the pit dogs. There was a bear-fight this morning, damn fine one at that. But one of Jezel's hounds got loose. Worst of them too, part-wolf. We thought the bear had killed it and we were hauling the bodies out, but it wasn't dead. Bastard reared up and tore Jezel's throat away. Terrible thing. Terrible. Then it ran. The gods alone know how it managed it. Ripped up by the bear and all.'

'Not many dogs would turn on their owners that way,' observed Waylander.

'Pit dogs will,' said a second man, tall and skeletally thin. 'It's the training you see, the beatings and the starving and the like. Jezel is . . . was . . . a damn fine trainer. The best.'

'Thanks for the warning,' said Waylander.

'Not at all,' replied the thin man. 'You looking for lodgings for the night? I own the inn. We've a good room.'

'Thank you, no. I have no coin.'

The man's interest died instantly; with a swift smile he moved past Waylander and, followed by the others, strode off in the direction of the town. Waylander transferred his gaze to the hound, which had slumped exhausted to the grass and was now lying on its right side breathing hoarsely, its blood-covered flanks heaving.

Waylander moved slowly down the slope, halting some ten feet from the injured animal. From here he could see that its wounds were many, and its grey flanks carried other, older scars from claw and fang and whip. The hound gazed at him through baleful eyes, but its strength was gone, and when Waylander rose and moved to its side it managed only a weary growl.

'You can stop that,' said Waylander, gently stroking the hound's huge grey head. From the gashes and cuts he could see the dog had attacked the bear at least three times. There was blood seeping from four parallel rips in the hide, the skin peeled back exposing muscle and bone. Judging by the size of the clawmarks, the bear must have been large indeed. Sheathing his knife Waylander examined the injuries. There were muscle tears, but no broken bones that he could find.

Another low growl came from the hound as Waylander eased a flap of skin back into place, and the beast struggled to turn its head, baring its fangs. 'Lie still,' ordered the man. 'We'll see what can be done.' From a leather pouch at his belt Waylander removed a long needle and a thin length of twine, stitching the largest of the wounds, seeking to stem the flow of blood. At last satisfied he moved to the head, stroking the beast's ears. 'You must try to rise,' he said, keeping his voice low, soothing. 'I need to see your left side. Come on. Up, boy!' The hound struggled, but sank back to the earth, tongue lolling from its gaping jaws.

Waylander rose and moved outside to a fallen tree, cutting from it a long strip of bark, which he twisted into a shallow bowl. Nearby was a slender stream and he filled the bowl, carrying it back to the stricken hound, and holding it beneath the creature's mouth. The hound's nostrils quivered, and once more it struggled to rise. Waylander pushed his hands beneath the huge shoulders, helping it to its feet. The head drooped, the tongue slowly lapping at the water. 'Good,' said Waylander. 'Good. Finish it now.' There were four more jagged cuts on the hound's left side, but these were matted with dirt and clay, which had at least stopped the flow of blood.

Having finished drinking the exhausted hound sank back to the earth, its great head resting on its huge paws. Waylander sat beside the beast, which gazed up at him unblinking, and noted the many scars, old and new, which crisscrossed its flanks and head. The right ear had been ripped away some years before and there was a long, thick scar which ran from the hound's shoulder to the first joint of its right leg. 'By the gods, you're a fighter, boy,' said the man admiringly. 'And you're no youngster. What would you be? Eight? Ten? Well, those cowards made a mistake. You're not going to die, are you? You won't give them the satisfaction, will you?'

Reaching into his shirt the man pulled clear a wedge of smoked meat, wrapped in linen. 'This was to have lasted me another two days,' said Waylander, 'but I can live without a meal for a while. I'm not sure that you can.' Unfolding the linen he took his knife and cut a section of meat which he laid before the hound. The dog merely sniffed at it, then returned its brown gaze to the man. 'Eat, idiot,' said Waylander, lifting the meat and touching it to the hound's long canines. Its tongue snaked out and the man watched as the dog chewed wearily. Slowly, as the hours passed, he fed the rest of the meat to the injured hound. Then, with the light fading, he took a last look at the wounds. They were mostly sealed, though a thin trickle of blood was seeping from the deepest cut on the rear right flank.

'That's all I can do for you, boy,' said Waylander, rising. 'Good luck to you. Were I you, I wouldn't stay here too long. Those oafs may decide to come back for some sport – and they could bring a bowman.' Without a backward glance the man left the hound and made his way back into the forest.

The moon was high when he found a place to camp, a sheltered cave where his fire could not be seen, and he sat long into the night, wrapped in his cloak. He had done what he could for the dog, but there was little chance it would survive. It would have to scavenge for food, and in its wounded state it would not be able to move far. If it had been stronger he would have encouraged it to follow him, taken it to the cabin. Miriel would have loved it. He recalled the orphaned fox cub she had mothered as a child. What was the name she gave it? Blue. That was it. It stayed near the cabin for almost a year. Then, one day, it just loped off and never returned. Miriel had been twelve then. It was just before . . .

The memory of the horse falling, rolling, the terrible scream . . .

Waylander closed his eyes, forcing the memories back, concentrating on a picture of little Miriel feeding the fox cub with bread dipped in warm milk.

Just before dawn he heard something moving at the cave entrance. Rolling to his feet he drew his sword. The grey wolfhound limped inside and settled down at his feet. Waylander chuckled and sheathed his sword. Squatting down he reached out to stroke the beast. The dog gave a low, warning growl and bared its fangs.

'By Heaven, I like you, dog,' said Waylander. 'You remind me of me.'

Miriel watched the ugly warrior as he trained, his powerful hands clasped to the branch, his upper body bathed in sweat. 'You see,' he said, hauling himself smoothly up, 'the movement must be fluid, feet together. Touch your chin to the wood and then lower – not too fast, mind. No strain. Let your mind relax.' His voice was even, no hint of effort in his actions.

He was more powerfully built than her father, his shoulders and arms ridged with massive bands of muscle, and her eyes caught a trickle of sweat flowing over his shoulder and down his side. Like a tiny stream over the hills and valleys of his body. Sunlight gleamed on his bronzed skin, and the white scars shone like ivory on his chest and arms. Her gaze moved to his face, the smashed nose, the gashed, deformed lips, the swollen damaged ears. The contrast was chilling. His body was so beautiful.

But his face . . .

He dropped to the ground and grinned. 'Was a time I could have completed a hundred. But fifty's not bad. What are you thinking?'

Caught offguard she blushed. 'You make it look so simple,' she said, averting her gaze.

In the three days she had been practising she had once struggled to fifteen. He shrugged. 'You are getting there, Miriel. You just need more work.' Moving past her he picked up a towel and draped it over his neck.

'What happened to your wife?' she asked suddenly.

'Which one?'

'How many have you had?'

'Three.'

'That's a little excessive, isn't it?' she snapped.

He chuckled. 'Seems that way now,' he agreed.

'What about the first one?'

He sighed. 'Hell-cat. By Heaven she could fight. Half-demon – and that was the gentle half. The gods alone know where the other half came from. She swore her father was Drenai – I didn't believe it for a moment. Had some good times, though. Rare good times.'

'Did she die?'

He nodded. 'Plague. She fought it, mind. All the swellings had gone, the discolouration. She'd even begun to get her hair back. Then she caught a chill and had no strength left to battle it. Died in the night. Peaceful.'

'Were you a gladiator then?'

'No. I was a merchant's book-keeper.'

'I don't believe it! How did you meet her?'

'She danced in a tavern. One night someone reached up and grabbed her leg. She kicked him in the mouth. He drew a dagger. I stopped him.'

'Just like that? A book-keeper?'

'Do not make the mistake of judging a man's physical courage, or his skills, by the work he is forced to do,' he said. 'I knew a doctor once who could put an arrow through a gold ring at forty paces. And a street cleaner in Drenan who once held off twenty Sathuli warriors, killing three, before he carried his injured officer back to camp. Judge a man by his actions, not his occupation. Now let's get back to work.'

'What about the other wives?'

'Don't want to work yet, eh? All right. Let's see, what can I tell you about Kalla? She was another dancer. Worked in the south quarter in Drenan. Ventrian girl. Sweet – but she had a weakness. Loved men. Couldn't say no. That marriage lasted eight months. She ran off with a merchant from Mashrapur. And lastly there was Voria. Older than me, but not much. I was a young fighter then, and she was the patron of the Sixth Arena. She took a fancy to me, showered me with gifts. Married her for her money, have to admit it, but I learned to love her, in my own way.'

'And she died, too?'

'No. She caught me with two serving maids and threw me out. Made my life Hell. For three years she kept trying to have me killed in the arena. Spiked my special wine with a sleeping-draught once. I was almost dead on my feet when I went out to fight. Then she hired two assassins. I had to leave Drenan for a while. I fought in Vagria, Gothir, even Mashrapur.'

'Does she still hate you?'

He shook his head. 'She married a young nobleman, then died suddenly leaving him all her money. Fell from a window – accident, they said, but I spoke to a servant who said he'd heard her having a terrible row with her husband just before she fell.'

284

'You think he killed her?'

'Sure of it.'

'And now he lives fat off her wealth?'

'No. Curiously he fell from the same window two nights later. His neck was broken in the fall.'

'And you wouldn't have had anything to do with that?'

'Me? How could you think it? And now let's work, if you please. Swords, I think.'

But just as Miriel was drawing her sword she saw movement in the undergrowth to the north of the cabin. At first she thought it was her father returning, for the first man who came into sight was dressed all in black. But he carried a longbow and was darkly bearded. He was followed by a shorter, stockier man in a tan leather jerkin.

'Follow my lead,' whispered Angel. 'And say nothing, even if they speak to you.'

He turned and waited as the men approached. 'Good day,' said the black-garbed bowman.

'And to you, friend. Hunting?'

'Aye. Thought we might find a stag.'

'Plenty south of here. Boar too, if you like the meat.'

'Nice cabin. Yours?'

'Yes,' said Angel. The man nodded.

'You'd be Dakeyras then?'

'That's right. This is my daughter, Moriae. How do you know of us?'

'Met some people in the mountains. They said you had a cabin here.'

'So you came to visit?'

'Not exactly. Thought you might be an old friend of mine. His name was Dakeyras, but he was taller than you and darker.'

'It's not an uncommon name,' said Angel. 'If you kill a stag I'll buy some of the meat. Game will be pretty scarce once winter comes.'

'I'll bear that in mind,' said the bowman.

The two men walked off towards the south. Angel watched them until they were out of sight.

'Assassins?' asked Miriel.

'Trackers, huntsmen. They'll be in the employ of Senta or Morak.'

'You took a risk claiming to be Dakeyras.'

'Not really,' he said. 'They were likely to have been given a description of Waylander – and I certainly don't fit it.'

'But what if they hadn't? What if they had merely attacked you?'

'I'd have killed them. Now, let's work.'

Kesa Khan stared gloomily into the green flames, his jet-black eyes unblinking. He hawked and spat into the fire, his expression impassive, his heart beating wildly.

285

'What do you see, shaman?' asked Anshi Chen. The wizened shaman waved a hand, demanding silence, and the stocky chieftain obeyed. Three hundred swords he could call upon, but he feared the little man as he feared nothing else in life, not even the prospect of death.

Kesa Khan had seen all he needed to, but still his slanted eyes remained locked to the dancing flames. Reaching a skeletal hand into one of the four clay pots before him he took a pinch of yellow powder and flicked it into the fire. The blaze flared up, orange and red, shadows leaping to the cave wall and cavorting like demons. Anshi Chen cleared his throat and sniffed loudly, his dark Nadir eyes flickering nervously left and right.

Kesa gave a thin smile. 'I have seen the dragon in the dream,' he said, his voice a sibilant whisper.

The colour fled from Anshi's face. 'Is it over, then? We are all dead?'

'Perhaps,' agreed Kesa, enjoying the fear he felt emanating from the warrior.

'What can we do?'

'What the Nadir have always done. We will fight.'

'The Gothir have thousands of warriors, fine armour, swords of steel that do not dull. Archers. Lancers. How can we fight them?'

Kesa shook his head. 'I am not the Warlord of the Wolves, you are.'

'But you can read the hearts of our enemies! You could send demons to rip open their bellies. Or is Zhu Chao mightier than Kesa Khan?' For a moment there was silence then Anshi Chen leaned forward, bowing his head. 'Forgive me, Kesa. I spoke in anger.'

The shaman nodded sagely. 'I know. But there is truth in your fear. Zhu Chao *is* mightier. He can call upon the blood of many souls. The Emperor has a thousand slaves and many hearts have been laid upon the altar of the Dark God. And what do I have?' The little man twisted his body and pointed at the three dead chickens. He gave a dry laugh. 'I command few demons with those, Anshi Chen.'

'We could raid the Green Monkeys, steal some children,' offered Anshi.

'No! I will not sacrifice Nadir young.'

'But they are the enemy.'

'This day they are the enemy, but one day all Nadir will unite – this is written. This is the message Zhu Chao has carried to the Emperor. This is why the dragon is in the dream.'

'You cannot help us, then?'

'Do not be a fool, Anshi Chen. I am helping you now! Soon the Gothir will come against us. We must prepare for that day. Our winter camp must be close to the Mountains of the Moon, and we must be ready to flee there.'

'The Mountains?' whispered Anshi. 'But the demons . . .'

'It is that, or die. Your wives and your children, and the children of your children.'

'Why not flee south? We could ride hundreds of leagues from Gulgothir. We could merge with other tribes. How would they find us?'

'Zhu Chao would find you,' said Kesa. 'Be strong, warlord. From one among us will come the leader the Nadir have longed for. Can you understand that? The Uniter! He will end Gothir rule. He will give us the world.'

'I will live to see this?'

Kesa shook his head. 'But neither will I,' he told the chieftain.

'It will be as you say,' pledged Anshi. 'We will move our camp.'

'And send for Belash.'

'I don't know where he is.'

'South of the new Drenai fortress, in the mountains they call Skeln. Send Shia to bring him.'

'Belash has no love for me, shaman. You know this.'

'I know many things, Anshi. I know that in the coming days we will rely on your steady judgement, and your calm skills. You are known and respected, as the Wily Fox. But I know we will need the power of Belash, the White Tiger in the Night. And he will bring another: he will give us the Dragon Shadow.'

Ekodas paused outside the Abbot's study, composing his thoughts. He loved life at the temple, its calm and camaraderie, the hours of study and meditation, even the physical exercises, running, archery and sword skills. In every way he felt a part of The Thirty.

Bar one.

He tapped at the door then pushed the latch. The room was lit by the golden light of three glass-sided lanterns and he saw Dardalion sitting at his desk, poring over a goatskin map. The Abbot looked up. In this gentle light he seemed younger, the silver highlights in his hair gleaming gold.

'Welcome, my boy. Come in and sit.' Ekodas bowed then strode to a chair. 'Shall we share thoughts, or would you like to speak out loud?' asked Dardalion.

'To speak, sir.'

'Very well. Vishna and Magnic tell me you are still troubled.'

'I am not troubled, Father. I know what I know.'

'You do not see this as arrogance?'

'No. My beliefs are only those that you enjoyed before your adventures with the killer, Waylander. Were you wrong then?'

'I do not believe that I was,' replied Dardalion. 'But then I no longer believe that there is only one road to the Source. Egel was a man of vision, and a believer. Three times a day he prayed for guidance. Yet

287

he was also a soldier, and through him – aye, and Karnak – the lands of the Drenai were saved from the foe. He is dead now. Do you think the Source refused to take his soul to paradise?'

'I do not know the answer to that question,' said the young man, 'but what I do know is that I have been taught, by you and others, that love is the greatest gift of the Source. Love for all life, for all His Creation. Now you are saying that you expect me to lift a sword and take life. That cannot be right.'

Dardalion leaned forward, resting his elbows on the desktop, his hands clasped together as if in prayer. 'Do you accept that the Source created the lion?'

'Of course.'

'And the deer?'

'Yes – and the lion slays the deer. I know this. I do not understand it, but I accept it.'

'I feel the need of flight,' said Dardalion. 'Join me.'

The Abbot closed his eyes. Ekodas settled himself more comfortably in the chair, resting his arms upon the padded wings then took a deep breath. The release of spirit seemed effortless to Dardalion, but Ekodas mostly found it extraordinarily difficult, as if his soul had many hooks into the flesh. He followed the lessons he had learned for the last ten years, repeating the mantras, cleansing the mind.

The dove in the temple, the opening door, the circle of gold upon the field of blue, the spreading of wings in a gilded cage, the loosing of chains on the temple floor.

He felt the first loosening of his hold upon his body, as if he was floating in the warm waters of the womb. He was safe here, content. Feeling drifted back to him, his spine against the hard wood of the chair, his sandalled feet on the cold floor. No, no, he chided himself. You are losing it! His concentration deepened once more. But he could not soar.

Dardalion's voice whispered into his mind, 'Take my hand, Ekodas.'

A light shone golden and warming and Ekodas accepted the merging. The release was instant and his spirit broke clear of the temple of his body, soaring up through the second temple of stone to float high in the night sky above the land of Drenai.

'Why is it so difficult for me?' he asked the Abbot.

Dardalion, young again, his face unlined, reached out and touched his pupil's shoulder. 'Doubts are fears, my boy. And dreams of the flesh. Small guilts, meaningless but worrisome.'

'Where are we going, Father?'

'Follow and observe.' East they flew, across the glittering, star-dappled Ventrian Sea. A storm raged here, and far below a tiny trireme battled the elements, great waves washing over her flat decks. Ekodas saw a sailor swept overboard, watched him fall below the waves, saw the gleaming spark of his soul float up and vanish.

The land appeared dark below them, the mountains and plains of Ventria stretching to the east, while here on the coast, brightly-lit towns and ports shone like jewels on a cloak of black. Dardalion flew down, down . . . The two priests hovered some hundred feet in the air and Ekodas saw the scores of ships harboured here, heard the pounding of the armourers' hammers in the town.

'The Ventrian battle fleet,' said Dardalion. 'It will sail within the week. They will attack Purdol, Erekban and Lentrum, landing armies to invade Drenai. War and devastation.'

He flew on, crossing the high mountains and swooping down over a city of marble, its houses laid out in a grid pattern of wide avenues and cluttered streets. There was a palace upon the highest hill, surrounded by high walls manned by many sentries in gold-embossed armour of white and silver. Dardalion flew into the palace, through the walls and drapes of silk and velvet, coming at last to a bedchamber where a dark-bearded man lay sleeping. Above the man hovered his spirit, formless and vague, unaware and unknowing.

'We could stop the war now,' said Dardalion, a silver sword appearing in his hand. 'I could slay this man's soul. Then thousands of Drenai farmers and soldiers, women and children, would be safe.'

'No!' exclaimed Ekodas, swiftly moving between the Abbot and the formless spirit of the Ventrian king.

'Did you think I would?' asked Dardalion, sadly.

'I . . . I am sorry, Father. I saw the sword and . . .' His voice tailed away.

'I am no murderer, Ekodas. And I do not know the complete Will of the Source. No man does. No man ever will, though there are many who claim such knowledge. Take my hand, my son.' The walls of the palace vanished and with bewildering speed the two spirits crossed the sea once more, this time heading north-east. Colours flashed before Ekodas' eyes and, if not for the firm grip of Dardalion's hand, he would have been lost in the swirling lights. Their speed slowed and Ekodas blinked, trying to adjust his mind.

Below him was another city with more palaces of marble. A huge amphitheatre to the west and a massive stadium for chariot races at the centre marked it as Gulgothir, the capital of the Gothir empire.

'What are we here to see, Father?' asked Ekodas.

'Two men,' answered Dardalion. 'We have crossed the gates of time to be here. The scene you are about to witness happened five days ago.'

Still holding to the young priest's hand Dardalion floated down over the high palace walls and into a narrow room behind the throne hall. The Gothir Emperor was seated on a silk-covered divan. He was a young man, no more than twenty, with large protruding eyes and a receding chin, which was partly hidden by a wispy beard. Before him, seated on a low stool, was a second man, dressed in long dark robes of shining silk, embroidered with silver. His hair was dark and waxed flat to his skull, the sideburns unnaturally long and braided, hanging to his shoulders. His eyes were slanted beneath high flared brows, his mouth a thin line.

'You say the empire is in danger, Zhu Chao,' spoke the Emperor, his voice deep, resonant and strong, belying the weakness of his appearance.

'It is, sire. Unless you take action your descendants will be overthrown, your cities vanquished. I have read the omens. The Nadir wait only for the day of the Uniter. And he is coming, from among the Wolfshead.'

'And how can I change this?'

'If wolves are killing one's sheep, one kills the wolves.'

'You are talking of an entire tribe among the Nadir.'

'Indeed, sire. Eight hundred and forty-four savages. They are not people as you and I understand the term. Their lives are meaningless, but their future sons could see an end to Gothir civilisation.'

The Emperor nodded. 'It will take time to gather sufficient men for the task. As you know, the Ventrians are about to invade the lands of the Drenai and I have plans of my own.'

'I understand that, sire. You will wish to reclaim the Sentran Plain as part of Gothir, which is only just and right, but that will take no more than ten thousand men. You have ten times that many under your command.'

'And I need them, wizard. There are always those who seek the overthrow of monarchs. I can spare you five thousand for this small task. In one month you will have the massacre you desire.'

'You misjudge me, sire,' put in Zhu Chao, bowing deeply and spreading his hands like a supplicant. 'I am thinking only of the future good of Gothir.'

'Oh, I believe in the prophecy, wizard. I have had other sorcerors and several shamen telling me similar stories, though none named a single tribe. But you have other reasons for wanting the Wolves destroyed, otherwise you would have traced the line of this Uniter back to one named man. Then the task would have been made so much more simple: one knife in the night. Never take me for a fool, Zhu Chao. You want them all dead for your own reasons.'

'You are all-wise, sire, and all-knowing,' whispered the wizard, falling to his knees and touching his forehead to the floor.

'No, I am not. And knowing that is my strength. But I will give you the deaths you desire. You have been a good servant to me, and never played me false. And as you say, they are only Nadir. It will sharpen the troops, give a cutting edge to the soldiers before the invasion of Drenan. I take it you will send your Brotherhood knights into the fray?'

'Of course, sire. They will be needed to combat the evil powers of Kesa Khan.'

The scene faded and Ekodas felt again the warm prison of his body. He opened his eyes to find Dardalion staring at him. 'Am I supposed to have learned something, Father Abbot? I saw only evil men, proud and ruthless. The world is full of such.'

'Yes, it is,' agreed Dardalion. 'And were we to spend our lives travelling the earth and slaying such men there would still be more of them at the end of our journey than there were at the beginning.'

'But surely that is *my* argument, Lord Abbot,' said Ekodas, surprised.

'Exactly. That is what you must consider. I appreciate your argument, and accept the premise on which it is made, and yet I still believe in the cause of The Thirty. I still believe we must be a Temple of Swords. What I would like you to do, Ekodas, is to lead the debate tomorrow evening. I will present your arguments as if they were my own. You will deliver mine.'

'But . . . that makes no sense, Father. I do not even begin to understand your cause.'

'Do the best that you can. I will make this debate an open vote. The future of The Thirty will depend upon the outcome. I will do my utmost to sway our brothers to your argument. You must do no less. If I win then the swords and armour will be returned to the storerooms and we will continue as an order of prayer. If you win we will await the guidance of the Source and ride to our destiny.'

'Why can I not argue my own beliefs?'

'You believe I will do them less than justice?'

'No, of course not, but . . .'

'Then it is settled.'

5

Morak listened to the reports as the hunters came in, his irritation growing. Nowhere was there any sign of Waylander, and the man Dakeyras had proved to be a balding redhead with a face that looked as if it had seen a stampede of oxen from underneath.

I hate forests, thought Morak, sitting with his back to the trunk of a willow, his green cloak wrapped tightly around him. I hate the smell of mould, the cold winds, the mud and the slime. He glanced at Belash, sitting apart from the others sharpening his knife with long sweeping strokes. The grating noise of the whetstone added to Morak's ill-humour.

'Well, somebody killed Kreeg,' he said at last. 'Somebody put a knife or an arrow through his eye.' No one spoke. They had found the body the previous day, wedged in the reeds of the River Earis.

'Could have been robbers,' said Wardal, a tall, thin bowman from the Forest of Graven, far to the south.

'Robbers?' sneered Morak. 'Hell's teeth! I've had lice with more brains than you! If it was robbers don't you think a fighter like Kreeg would have had more wounds? Don't you think there would have been a fight? Someone very skilful sent a missile through his eyeball. A man with rare talent is killed – that suggests to me he was slain by someone with *more* talent. Is my reasoning getting through to you?'

'You think it was Waylander,' muttered Wardal.

'A giant leap of the imagination. Many congratulations. The question is, where in Hell's name is he?'

'Why should he be easy to find?' asked Belash, suddenly. 'He knows we are here.'

'And what mighty spark of logic leads you to that conclusion?'

'He killed Kreeg. He knows.'

Morak felt a chill breeze blowing and shivered. 'Wardal, you and Tharic take the first watch.'

'What are we watching for?' enquired Tharic.

Morak closed his eyes and took a deep breath. 'Well,' he said at last, 'you could be watching for enormous elephants that will trample all over our supplies. But were I you, I would be alert for a tall man, dressed in black, who is rather good at sending sharp objects through eyeballs.' At that moment a tall figure stepped from the undergrowth. Morak's heart missed a beat, but then he recognised Baris. 'The normal procedure is to shout "Hallo the camp",' he observed. 'You took your time.'

The blond forester settled down by the fire. 'Kasyra is not a small place, but I found the whore Kreeg was living with. She told him about a man called Dakeyras who lives near here. I've got directions.'

'Wrong man,' said Morak. 'Wardal and Tharic already met him. What else did you find?'

'Little of interest,' answered Baris, pulling the remains of a loaf of bread from the pouch at his side. 'By the way, how long has Angel been a member of the Guild?'

'Angel? I've not heard that he is,' said Morak. 'Why?'

'He was in Kasyra a week or so back. Tavern-keeper recognised

292

him. Senta is there, too. He said to tell you that when he finds your body he'll be sure to give it a fine burial.'

But Morak wasn't listening. He laughed and shook his head. 'Wardal, have you ever been to the arena?'

'Aye. Saw Senta fight there. Beat a Vagrian called . . . called . . .'

'Never mind! Did you ever see Angel fight?'

'Oh yes. Tough. Won some money on him once.'

'Would you remember his face at all?'

'Red hair, wasn't it?' answered Wardal.

'Correct, numbskull. Red hair. And a face his mother would disown. I wonder if the tiniest thought is trying to make its way through that mass of bone that houses your brain? If it is, do share it with us.'

Wardal sniffed loudly. 'The man at the cabin!'

'The man who said he was Dakeyras, yes,' said Morak. 'It was the right cabin, just the wrong man. Tomorrow you can return there. Take Baris and Tharic. No, that might not be enough. Jonas and Seeris as well. Kill Angel and bring the girl here.'

'He's a gladiator,' objected Jonas, a stout balding warrior with a forked beard.

'I didn't say fight him,' whispered Morak. 'I said kill him.'

'Wasn't nothing about no gladiators,' persisted Jonas. 'Tracking, you said. Find this Dakeyras. I've seen Angel fight as well. Don't stop, does he? Stick him, cut him, hit him . . . still keeps going.'

'Yes, yes, yes! I am sure he would be delighted to know you are among his greatest admirers. But he's older now. He retired. Just walk in, engage him in conversation, then kill him. If that sounds a little too difficult for you, then head for Kasyra – and kiss goodbye to any thought of a share in ten thousand gold pieces.'

'Why don't *you* kill him?' asked Jonas. 'You're the swordsman here.'

'Are you suggesting that I am frightened of him?' countered Morak, his voice ominously low.

'No, not at all,' answered Jonas, reddening. 'We all know how . . . skilled you are. I just wondered, that's all.'

'Have you ever seen the nobles hunt, Jonas?'

'Of course.'

'Have you noticed how, when chasing boar, they take hounds with them?'

The man nodded glumly. 'Good,' said Morak. 'Then take this thought into that pebble-sized brain: I am a hunting noble and you are my dogs. Is that clear? I am not being paid to kill Angel. I am paying you.'

'We could always shoot him from a distance, I suppose,' said Jonas. 'Wardal's very good with that bow.'

'Fine,' muttered Morak. 'Just so long as it is done. But bring the girl to me, safe and hearty. You understand? She is the key to Waylander.'

'That is against Guild rules,' said Belash. 'No innocents may be used . . .'

'I know the Guild rules!' snapped Morak. 'And when I want lessons in proper conduct I shall be sure to call on you. After all, the Nadir are well known for their rigid observance of civilised behaviour.'

'I know what you want from the girl,' said Belash. 'And it is not this key to her father.'

'A man is entitled to certain pleasures, Belash. They are what make living worthwhile.'

The Nadir nodded. 'I have known some men who share the same . . . pleasures . . . as you. When we catch them among the Nadir we cut off their hands and feet and stake them out over anthills. But then, as you say, we do not understand you civilised people.'

The face was huge and white as a fish belly, the eye sockets empty, the lids shaped like fangs, clacking as they closed. The mouth was lipless, the tongue enormous and cratered with tiny mouths.

Miriel took Krylla's hand, and the children tried to flee – but the demon was faster, stronger. One scaled hand closed on Miriel's arm, the touch burning.

'Bring them to me!' came a soft voice, and Miriel saw a man standing close by, his face also pale, his skin scaled like a beautiful albino snake. But there was nothing beautiful about the man. Krylla began to cry.

The monstrous creature that held them leaned over the children, touching the cavernous mouth to Miriel's face. She felt pain then, terrible pain. And she screamed.

And screamed . . .

'Wake up, girl,' said the demon, his hand once more on her shoulder. Her fingers snaked out, clawing at his face, but he grabbed her wrist. 'Stop this. It is me, Angel!'

Her eyes flared open and she saw the rafters of the cabin, the light of the moon seeping through the knife-thin gaps in the shutters, felt the rough wool of the blankets on her naked frame. She shuddered and fell back. He stroked her brow, pushing back the sweat-drenched hair. 'Just a dream, girl. Just a dream,' he whispered. She said nothing for a moment, trying to gather her thoughts. Her mouth was dry and she sat up, reaching for the goblet of water by her bedside.

'It was a nightmare. Always the same one,' she said, between sips. 'Krylla and I were being hunted across a dark place, an evil place. Valleys without trees, a sky without sun or moon, grey, soulless.' She shivered. 'Demons caught us, and terrible men . . .'

294

'It's over,' he assured her. 'You are awake now.'

'It's never over. It's a dream now – but it wasn't then.' She shivered again, and he reached out, drawing her to him, his arms upon her back, his hand patting her. Lowering her head to his shoulder she felt better. The remembered cold of the Void was strong in her mind, and the warmth of his skin pushed it back.

'Tell me about it,' he said.

'It was after Mother died. We were frightened, Krylla and me. Father was acting strangely, shouting and weeping. We knew nothing about drunken men. And to see Father stumbling and falling was terrifying. Krylla and I used to sit in our room, holding hands. We used to soar our spirits high into the sky. We were free then. Safe – so we thought. But one night, as we played beneath the stars we realised we were not alone. There were other spirits in the sky with us. They tried to catch us, and we fled. We flew so fast, and with such terror in our hearts that we had no idea where we were. But the sky was grey, the land desolate. Then the demons came. Summoned by the men.'

'But you escaped from them.'

'Yes. No. Another man appeared, in silver armour. We knew him. He fought the demons, killing them, and brought us home. He was our friend. But he does not appear in my dreams now.'

'Lie back,' said Angel. 'Have a little gentle sleep.'

'No. I don't want the dream again.'

Pulling back the woollen blanket Angel slid in beside her, resting her head on his shoulder. 'No demons, Miriel. I shall be here to bring you back if there are.' Pulling the blanket up around them both he lay still. She could feel the slow, rhythmic beat of his heart and closed her eyes.

She slept for a little over an hour and awoke refreshed. Angel was sleeping soundlessly beside her. In the faint light of pre-dawn his ugliness was softened, and she tried to picture him as he had been all those years ago when he had brought her the dress. It was almost impossible. Her arm was draped across his chest and she slowly drew it back, feeling the softness of his skin and the contrasting ridges of hard muscle across his belly. He did not wake, and Miriel felt a powerful awareness of her own nakedness. Her hand slid down, the tips of her fingers brushing over the pelt of tightly curled hair below his navel. He stirred. She halted all movement, aware now of her increased heart-beat. Fear touched her, but it was a delicious fear. There had been village boys who had filled her with longing, left her dreaming of forbidden trysts. But never had she felt like this, the onset of fear synchronised to her passion. Never had she been so aware of her desires. Her needs. His breathing deepened again. Her hand slid down, fingers caressing him, circling him, feeling him quicken and swell.

Doubt followed by panic suddenly flared within her. What if he opened his eyes? He could be angry at her boldness, might think her a whore. Which I am, she thought, with a burst of self-disgust. Releasing him she rolled from the bed. She had bathed the previous night, but somehow the thought of ice-cold water on her skin seemed not only pleasurable, but necessary. Moving carefully to avoid waking him she eased open the bedroom door and crossed the cabin floor.

Lifting the bar from its brackets she opened the main door and stepped out into the sunlit clearing before the cabin. The bushes and trees were still silvered with dew, the autumn sunlight weak upon her skin. How could she have acted so, she wondered as she strolled to the stream. Miriel had often dreamed of lovers, but never in her fantasies had they been ugly. Never had they been so old. And she knew she was not in love with the former gladiator. No, she realised, that's what makes you a whore. You just wanted to rut like an animal.

Reaching the stream she sat down on the grass, her feet dangling in the water. Flowing from the high mountains there were small rafts of ice on the surface, like frozen lilies. And it was cold.

She heard a movement behind her but, lost in thought, she was not swift enough, and as she rolled to her feet a man's hands caught her shoulder, hurling her to the grass. Ramming her elbow sharply back she connected with his belly. He grunted in pain and sagged across her. The smell of woodsmoke, greasy leather and stale sweat filled her nostrils and a bearded face fell against her cheek. Twisting she slammed the heel of her hand against the man's nose, snapping his head back. Scrambling to her feet she tried to run, but the man grabbed her ankle, and a second man leapt from hiding. Miriel's fist cracked against the newcomer's chin, but his weight carried him forward and she was knocked to the ground, her arms pinned beneath her.

'A real Hellcat,' grunted the second man, a tall blond forester. 'Are you all right, Jonas?' The first man struggled to his feet, blood seeping from his nose and streaming into his black beard.

'Hold her still, Baris. I've just the weapon to bring her to heel.' The balding warrior began to unfasten the thongs of his leggings, moving forward to stand over Miriel.

'You heard what Morak said. Unharmed,' objected Baris.

'I've never known a woman harmed by it yet,' responded Jonas.

Miriel, her arms and shoulders pinned, arched her back then sent her right foot slamming up between the forester's legs. Jonas grunted and slumped to his knees. Baris slapped her face, grabbed her hair and hauled her to her feet. 'Don't give up, do you?' he snarled, slapping her again, this time with the back of his hand. Miriel sagged against him.

'That's better,' he said. Her head came up sharply, cannoning against his chin. He stumbled back, then drew his knife, his arm arcing back for the throw. Miriel, still half-stunned, threw herself to her right, rolling to her knees. Then she was up and running.

Another man jumped into her path, but she swerved round him, and almost made the clearing before a stone from a sling ricocheted from her temple. Falling to her knees she tried to crawl into the undergrowth, but the sound of running feet behind her told her she was finished. Her head ached, and her senses swam. Then she heard Angel's voice.

'Time to die, my boys.'

Miriel awoke in her own bed, a water-soaked cloth on her brow, her head throbbing painfully. She tried to sit up, but felt giddy then sick. 'Lie still,' said Angel. 'That was a nasty strike. You've a lump the size of a goose egg.'

'Did you kill them?' she whispered weakly.

'No. Never seen men run so fast. They sent up a cloud of dust. I have a feeling they knew me – it was very gratifying.'

Miriel closed her eyes. 'Don't tell my father I went out without weapons.'

'I won't. But it was stupid. What were you thinking of – the dream?'

'No, not the dream. I just . . . I was just stupid, as you say.'

'The man who never made a mistake never made anything,' he said.

'I'm not a man!'

'I'd noticed. But I'm sure it holds true for women. Two of the men were bleeding, so I'd guess you caused them some pain before they downed you. Well done, Miriel.'

'That's the first time you've praised me. Be careful. It might go to my head.'

He patted her hand. 'I can be a mean whoreson, I know that. But you're a fine girl – tough, strong, willing. I don't want to see your spirit broken – but I don't want to see your body broken, either. And I know only one way to teach. I'm not even sure I know that very well.'

She tried to smile, but the pain was growing and she felt herself slipping into sleep.

'Thank you,' she managed to say. 'Thank you for being there.'

From his high study window Dardalion saw the troop of lancers slowly climbing the winding path, twenty-five men in silver armour, cloaked in crimson, riding jet-black horses, their flanks armoured in chain-mail. At their head rode a man Dardalion knew well. Against the sleek, martial perfection of his men Karnak should have looked comical; overweight and dressed in clothes of clashing colours – red cloak, orange shirt, green trews tied with blue leggings and below them black riding boots, edged with a silver trim. But no one laughed at his eccentric dress. For this was the hero of Dros Purdol, the saviour of the Drenai.

Karnak the One-eyed.

297

The man's physical strength was legendary, but it paled against the colossal power of his personality. With one speech he could turn a motley group of farmers into sword-wielding heroes who would defy an army. Dardalion's smile faded. Aye, and they would die for him, *had* died for him – in their thousands. They would go on dying for him.

Vishna entered the study, his spirit voice whispering into Dardalion's mind, 'Will their arrival delay the Debate, Father?'

'No.'

'Was it wise to instruct Ekodas to argue the cause of right?'

'Is it the cause of right?' countered Dardalion, speaking aloud and swinging to face the dark-bearded Gothir nobleman.

'You have always taught me so.'

'We shall see, my boy. Now go down and escort the Lord Karnak to me. And see that his men are fed, the horses groomed. They have ridden far.'

'Yes, Father.'

Dardalion returned to the window, but he did not see the distant mountains, nor the storm clouds looming in the north. He saw again the cabin on the mountainside, the two frightened children, and the two men who had come to kill them. And he felt the weight of the weapon of death in his hands. He sighed. The cause of right? Only the Source knew.

He heard the sound of booming laughter from the winding stairs beyond his room, and felt the immense physical presence of Karnak even before the man crossed the threshold.

'Gods, but it is good to see you, old lad!' boomed Karnak, striding across the room and clasping a huge hand to Dardalion's shoulder. The man's smile was wide and genuine, and Dardalion returned it.

'And you, my lord. I see your dress sense is as colourful as ever.'

'Like it? The cloak is from Mashrapur, the shirt from a little weavery in Drenan.'

'They suit you well.'

'By Heaven you are a terrible liar, Dardalion. I expect your soul will burn in Hellfire. Now sit you down and let us talk of more important matters.' The Drenai leader moved round the desk to take Dardalion's chair, leaving the slender Abbot to sit opposite him. Karnak unbuckled his sword-belt, laying it on the floor beside him, then eased his great bulk into the seat. 'Damned uncomfortable furniture,' he said. 'Now, where were we? Ah, yes! What can you tell me about the Ventrians?'

'They will sail within the week, landing at Purdol, Erekban and the Earis estuary,' answered Dardalion.

'How many ships?'

'More than four hundred.'

'That many, eh? I don't suppose you'd consider whipping up a storm to sink the bastards?'

'Even if I could – which I can't – I would refuse such a request.'

'Of course,' said Karnak, with a wide grin. 'Love, peace, the Source, morality and so on. But there are some who could, yes?'

'So it is said,' agreed Dardalion, 'among the Nadir and the Chiatze. But the Ventrians have their own wizards, sir, and I don't doubt they'll be making sacrifices and casting spells to ensure good weather.'

'Never mind their problems,' snapped Karnak. 'Could you locate a demon conjurer for me?'

Now it was Dardalion who laughed. 'You are a wonder, my lord. And I shall do you the kindness of treating that request as a jest.'

'Which of course it wasn't,' said Karnak. 'Still, you've made your point. Now, what of the Gothir?'

'They have reached agreement with the Sathuli tribes, who will allow an invading force to pass unopposed to occupy the Sentran Plain once the Ventrians have landed. Around ten thousand men.'

'I knew it!' snapped Karnak, his irritation growing. 'Which legions?'

'The First, Second and Fifth. Plus two mercenary legions made up of Vagrian refugees.'

'Wonderful. The Second and the Fifth are not a worry to me – our spies say they are mostly raw recruits with little discipline. But the First are the Emperor's finest, and the Vagrians fight like pain-maddened tigers. Still, I have a week, you say. Much can happen in that time. We'll see. Tell me of the Sathuli leader.'

For more than an hour Karnak questioned Dardalion until, satisfied at last, he rose to leave. Dardalion raised his hand. 'There is another matter to be discussed, my lord.'

'There is?'

'Yes. Waylander.'

Karnak's face darkened. 'That is none of your affair, priest. I don't want you spying on me.'

'He is my friend, Karnak. And you have ordered his killing.'

'These are affairs of state, Dardalion. Damn it all, man, he killed the King. There has been a price on his head for years.'

'But that is not why you hired the Guild, my lord. I know the reason, and it is folly. Worse folly than you know.'

'Is that so? Explain it to me.'

'Two years ago, with the army treasury empty, and a rebellion on your hands, you received a donation from a merchant in Mashrapur, a man named Gamalian. One hundred thousand in gold. It saved you. Correct?'

'What of it?'

'The money came from Waylander. Just as this year's donation of eighty thousand Raq from the merchant, Perlisis, came from Waylander. He has been supporting you for years. Without him you would have been finished.'

Karnak swore and slumped back into his seat, rubbing a massive hand across his face. 'I have no choice, Dardalion. Can you not see that? You think I want to see the man killed? You think there is any satisfaction in it for me?'

'I am sure there is not. But in having him hunted you have unleashed a terrible force. He was living quietly in the mountains, mourning his wife. He was no longer Waylander the Slayer, no longer the man to be feared, but day by day he is becoming Waylander again. And soon he will consider hunting down the man who set the price.'

'I'd sooner he tried that, than the other alternative,' said Karnak, wearily. 'But I hear what you say, priest, and I will think on it.'

'Call them off, Karnak,' pleaded Dardalion. 'Waylander is a force like no other, almost elemental, like a storm. He may be only one man, but he will not be stopped.'

'Death can stop any man,' argued Karnak.

'Remember that, my lord,' advised Dardalion.

It was the dog that found the remains of the old tinker. Waylander had been moving warily through the forest when the hound's head had lifted, its great black nostrils quivering. Then it had loped off to the left. Waylander followed and found the animal tearing rotting meat from the old man's leg.

The dog was not the first to find the body and the corpse was badly mauled.

Waylander made no attempt to call the dog away. There was a time when such a scene would have revolted him, but he had seen too much death since then: his memories were littered with corpses. He recalled his father walking him through the woods near their home in the valley, and they had come across a dead hawk. The child he had been was saddened by the sight. 'That is not the bird,' said his father. 'That is merely the cloak he wore.' The man pointed up to the sky. 'That is where the hawk is, Dakeyras. Flying towards the sun.'

Old Ralis had gone. What was left was merely food for scavengers, but cold anger flared in Waylander nevertheless. The tinker had been harmless, and always travelled unarmed. There was no need for such senseless torture. But that was Morak's way. The man loved to inflict pain.

The tracks were easy to read and Waylander left the dog to feed and set off in pursuit of the killers. As he walked he studied the spoor. There were eleven men in the group, but they had soon split up. He knelt and examined the trail. There had been a meeting. One man – Morak? – had addressed the group, and they had paired and moved off. A single set of prints headed east, perhaps towards Kasyra. The others moved in different directions. They were quartering the forest, and that meant they did not know of the cabin. The old man had told them nothing.

Identifying the track of Morak, narrow-toed boots with deep heels, he decided to follow the Ventrian. Morak would not be wandering the forest in the search. He would find a place to wait. Waylander set off once more, moving with care, stopping often to scan the trees and the lines of the hills, keeping always to cover.

Towards dusk he halted and loaded his crossbow. Ahead of him was a narrow path, wending up a gentle rise. The wind had changed and he smelt woodsmoke coming from the south-west. Squatting by a huge, gnarled oak he waited for the sun to go down, his thoughts sombre. These men had come into the forest to kill him. That he understood; this was their chosen occupation. But the torture and murder of the old man had lit a cold fire in Waylander's heart.

They would pay for that deed.

And they would pay in kind.

A barn owl soared into the night seeking rodent prey and a grey fox padded across the path directly in front of the waiting man. But Waylander did not move, and the fox ignored him. Slowly the sun set, and night changed the personality of the forest. The whispering wind became the sibilant, ghostly hiss of a serpent's breath, the gentle trees stood stark and forbidding, and the moon rose, quarter full and curved like a Sathuli tulwar. A killer's moon.

Waylander eased himself to his feet and removed his cloak, folding it and laying it over a boulder. Then he moved silently up the slope, crossbow in hand. There was a sentry sitting beneath a tall pine. As a safeguard against being surprised he had scattered dry twigs in a wide circle around the base of the tree, and was now sitting on a fallen log, sword in hand. His hair was pale, almost silver in the moonlight.

Waylander laid his crossbow on the ground and moved out behind the seated man, his moccasined feet gently brushing aside the twigs. His left hand seized the man's hair, dragging back his head, his right swept out and across, the black blade slicing jugular and vocal chords. The sentry's feet thrashed out, but blood was gouting from his throat and within seconds all movement had ceased. Waylander eased the body to the ground and walked back to where his crossbow lay. The campfire was some thirty paces to the north and he could see a group of men sitting around it. Moving closer he counted them. Seven. Three were unaccounted for. Silently he circled the camp, finding two more of the assassins standing guard. Both died before they were even aware of danger.

Closer to the fire now Waylander puzzled over the missing man. Was it the one sent towards Kasyra? Or was there a sentry he had not located? He scanned the group by the fire. There was Morak, sitting on the far side, wrapped in a green cloak. But who was missing? Belash! The Nadir knife-fighter.

Keeping low to the ground Waylander moved into the deeper

shadows of the forest, stopping only once to smear his face with mud. His clothes were black, and he merged into the darkness. Where in Hell's name was the Nadir? He closed his eyes, letting the soft sounds of the forest sweep over him. Nothing.

Then he smiled. Why worry about what you cannot control, he thought. Let Belash worry about me! He slid out from his hiding place and angled in towards the camp. A little confusion was called for.

There was a screen of low bushes to the north of the campsite. Dropping to all fours Waylander edged closer then rose, crossbow pointed. The first bolt crashed through a man's temple, the second plunged into the heart of a bearded warrior as he leapt to his feet.

Ducking, Waylander ran to the south then traversed a slope and moved north once more, coming up to the camp from the opposite side. It was, as he had expected, deserted now, save for the two corpses. Reloading the crossbow he squatted down in the shadows and waited. Before long he heard movement to his right. He grinned and dropped to his belly.

'Any sign of him?' whispered Waylander.

'No,' came the reply from close by. Waylander sent two bolts in the direction of the voice. The thudding of the impacting bolts was followed by a grunt and the sound of a falling body.

Fool! thought Waylander, easing himself back into the undergrowth.

The moon disappeared behind a thick bank of cloud. Total darkness descended on the forest. Waylander crouched low, waiting, listening. Taking two bolts from his small quiver he waited for the night breeze to rustle the leaves above him before pulling back the strings and loading the weapon, the forest sounds covering the slight noise of the bolts slipping into place. The wounded man he had shot cried out in pain, begging for help. But no one came.

Waylander crept deeper into the forest. Had they run, or were they hunting him? The Nadir would not run. Morak? Who knew what thoughts filled the mind of a torturer.

To his left was an ancient beech, its trunk split. Waylander looked at the sky. The moon was still hidden, but the clouds were breaking. Stepping up to the trunk he reached up with his left hand and swiftly hauled himself to the lowest branch, climbing some twenty feet up into the tree.

The moon shone bright, and he ducked down. Below him the forest was lit by eldritch light. He scanned the undergrowth. One man was crouched behind a section of gorse. A second was close by. This one carried a short Vagrian hunting bow, a barbed arrow notched to the string. Laying down the crossbow Waylander traversed the trunk and sought out the others. But no one else could be seen.

Returning to his original position, he watched the two hidden men for some time. Neither moved, save to glance around fearfully. And neither made any attempt to communicate with the other. Waylander wondered if each knew of the other's presence so close by.

Reaching into his pouch he pulled clear a large triangular copper coin, and this he threw into the screen of bushes close to the first assassin. The man swore and lunged up. Immediately the second man spun round and loosed an arrow which tore into the first man's shoulder.

'You puking idiot!' shouted the wounded man.

'I'm sorry!' answered the bowman, dropping the bow and moving forward to his comrade's side. 'Is it bad?'

Waylander dropped quietly to the ground on the other side of the tree.

'You damn near killed me!' complained the first man.

'Wrong,' said Waylander. 'He has killed you.'

A bolt punched through the man's skull just above his nose. The bowman leapt to his right, diving for cover, but Waylander's second bolt lanced through his neck. An arrow flashed by Waylander's face, burying itself in the trunk of the ancient beech. Ducking he ran for cover, hurling himself over a fallen tree and scrambling up a short steep bank into dense undergrowth.

Three left.

And one of these was the Nadir!

Sword in hand Morak hid behind a large boulder, listening for any signs of movement. He was alone, and filled with the fear of death.

How many were dead already?

The man was a demon! The hilt of his sword was greasy with sweat, and he wiped it on his cloak. His clothes were filthy, his hands mud-streaked. This was no place for a nobleman to die, surrounded by filth and worms and rotted leaves. He had fought men before, blade to blade, and knew he was no coward, but the dark of the forest, the hissing of the wind, the sibilant rustling of the leaves and the knowledge that Waylander was moving towards him like Death's shadow, almost unmanned him.

A movement from behind caused his heart to palpitate. He swung, trying to bring up his sword, but Belash's powerful hand gripped his wrist. 'Follow me,' whispered the Nadir, easing back into the undergrowth. Morak was more than willing to obey and the two men crept towards the south, Belash leading the way down the slope to where Waylander's cloak lay upon a boulder.

'He will come back here,' said Belash, keeping his voice low.

Morak saw that the Nadir was carrying a short hunting bow of Vagrian horn, a quiver of arrows slung across his broad shoulders. 'What about the others?' he asked.

'Dead – all except Jonas. He loosed a shaft at Waylander, but it missed. Jonas dropped his bow and ran.'

'Cowardly scum!'

Belash grinned. 'Bigger share for us, yes?'

'I didn't think you were interested in coin. I thought this was just an exercise in valiant behaviour. You know, Father's bones and all that.'

'No time for talk, Morak. You sit here and rest. I will be close by.'

'Sit here? He'll see me.'

'Of course. It is a small crossbow – he will come in close. Then I'll kill him.'

Morak uttered a foul curse. 'What if he just creeps up and lets fly before you see him?'

'Then you die,' said Belash.

'Quaint sense of humour you have. Why don't you sit here? I'll take the bow.'

'As you wish,' answered Belash contemptuously, his dark eyes gleaming with amusement. He handed Morak the weapon then folded his arms and sat, staring towards the south. Morak faded back into the undergrowth and notched an arrow to the string.

The moonlight cast spectral shadows on the small clearing where Belash waited and Morak shivered. What if Waylander were to come from a different direction? What if, even now, he was creeping silently through the forest behind him? Morak swung his head, but could see nothing untoward. But then who could see anything in this cursed gloom!

The Nadir's plan was a simple one, born of a simple mind. But they were not dealing with a simpleton. If he stayed here he could die. There was no certainty to the plan. Yet if he left the Nadir behind, then Belash would feel betrayed. And if he survived, the Nadir would then hunt him down. Morak toyed with the thought of taking the risk, of slipping away quietly, but Belash was a woodsman of almost mystical skill. He would hear him – and give chase immediately. An arrow then – straight through the back. No. The Nadir was strong. What if it failed to kill immediately? Morak knew he could best Belash sword to sword, but the Nadir's immense strength might bring him in close enough to use that wicked dagger . . . That was a thought he didn't enjoy.

Think, man!

Dropping the bow, Morak felt around the soft earth until his fingers closed on a large stone the size of his fist. This was the answer. Standing, he walked back out into the clearing. Belash glanced round.

'What is wrong?'

'I have another plan,' he said.

'Yes?'

304

'Is that him?' hissed Morak, pointing to the north. Belash's head jerked round.

'Where?'

The stone cracked against the back of the Nadir's neck. Belash fell forward. Morak hit him again. Then again. The Nadir slumped to the ground. Morak dropped the stone and drew his dagger. Always best to make sure. Then he heard movement in the undergrowth. Backing away from the sound, Morak turned and ran, sprinting down the track.

And did not see the ugly hound that emerged from the bushes.

Belash floated up from the darkness to a painful awakening. Soft earth was against his face and his head pounded. He tried to rise, but nausea swamped him. Reaching up he touched the back of his neck. The blood was beginning to congeal. His hand moved down to his belt. The knife was still in its sheath. For a while he struggled to remember what had happened. Had Waylander come upon them?

No. I would now be dead.

His mouth was dry. Something cold pushed against his face. He turned his head and found himself staring into the baleful eyes of a huge, scarred hound. Belash lay perfectly still, save for his hand which inched slowly towards his knife.

'That would not be wise,' said a cold voice.

At first he thought it was the hound that had spoken to him. A devil dog come to claim his soul?

'Here, dog!' came the voice again. The hound padded away. Belash forced himself to his knees, and saw the black-garbed figure sitting on the boulder. The man's crossbow was now hanging from his belt, his knives sheathed.

'How did you surprise me?' asked Belash.

'I didn't. Your friend – Morak? – struck you from behind.'

Belash tried to stand, but his legs were too weak and he slumped back. Slowly he rolled to his back then, taking hold of the jutting branch of a fallen tree he pulled himself to a sitting position. 'Why am I still alive?' he asked.

'You intrigue me,' the man told him.

Truly the ways of the southerners are mysterious, thought Belash, leaning his head against the rough bark of the tree trunk. 'You left me my weapons. Why?'

'I saw no reason to remove them.'

'You think I am so poor an opponent that you need not fear me?'

The man chuckled. 'I never yet met a Nadir who could be described as a poor opponent, but I have seen many head wounds – and yours will leave you weak for several days, if not longer.'

Belash did not reply. Bracing his legs beneath him he rose unsteadily and then sat back upon the tree. His head was spinning, but he preferred to be on his feet. He was only some three paces from Waylander, and he wondered if he could draw the knife and catch the man unawares. It was unlikely, but it was the only chance he had to stay alive.

'Don't even think of it,' said Waylander softly.

'You read thoughts?'

'I don't need any special skill to understand a Nadir mind, not when it comes to battle. But you wouldn't make it – trust me on that. Are you Notas?'

Belash was surprised. Few southerners understood the complex structures governing the Nadir tribes and their compositions. Notas meant no tribe, an outcast. 'No. I am of the Wolves.'

'You are a long way from the Mountains of the Moon.'

'You have walked among the Tent-people?'

'Many times. Both as friend and enemy.'

'What was the name the Nadir gave you?' enquired Belash.

The man smiled thinly. 'They called me the Soul Stealer. And an old Notas leader once gave me the name Oxskull.'

Belash nodded. 'You rode with the giant, Ice-eyes. There are songs about you – dark songs, of dark deeds.'

'And they are true,' admitted the man.

'What happens now?'

'I haven't decided. I will take you to my home. You can rest there.'

'Why do you think I would not kill you, once my strength has returned?'

'The Guild allows no Nadir members. Therefore you were to be paid by Morak. Judging by the lumps on your skull I would say that Morak has terminated your employment. What would you gain by killing me?'

'Nothing,' agreed Belash. Except the honour of being the man who slew the Soul Stealer. And surely the Mountains would look kindly upon the man who avenged the theft of the treasure? Surely they would then grant him the vengeance he sought.

Waylander moved forward. 'Can you walk?'

'Yes.'

'Then follow me.' The tall man strode away, his broad back an inviting target.

Not yet, thought Belash. First let me find my strength.

6

The table was forty feet long and three feet wide, and had once been covered by fine linens and decorated with golden plates and goblets. The finest of foods had graced the plates, and nobles had carved their meats with knives of gold. Now there was no fine linen, and the plates were of pewter, the goblets of clay. Bread and cheese lay upon the plates, cool spring water in the goblets. At the table sat twenty-eight priests in white robes. Behind each priest, glittering in the lantern light, was a suit of armour, a bright silver helm, a shining cuirass and a scabbarded sword. And against each suit of armour rested a long wooden staff.

Ekodas sat at the head of the table, Dardalion beside him.

'Let me present my own arguments,' pleaded Ekodas.

'No, my son. But I will do them justice, I promise you.'

'I did not doubt that, sir. But I cannot do justice to yours.'

'Do your best, Ekodas. No man can ever ask for more than that.' Dardalion lifted a finger to his lips, then closed his eyes. All heads bowed instantly and the union began. Ekodas felt himself floating. There was no sight, no sound, no feeling. Just warmth. He sensed Vishna, and Magnic, Palista, Seres . . . all the others flowing all around him.

'We are One,' pulsed Dardalion.

'We are One,' echoed the Thirty.

And the prayer-song began, the great hymn to the Source, mind-sung in a tongue unknown to any of them, even Dardalion. The words were unfathomable, but the sensations created by the sounds produced a sweet magic, filling the soul with light.

Ekodas was transported back to his childhood, to see again the tall, gangling dark-haired youth with the violet eyes, working behind his father in the fields, planting the seed, gathering the harvest. Those were good days, though he did not know it at the time. Shunned by the other youths of the village he had no friends, and no one to share his small joys, his discoveries. But now, as he soared within the hymn he saw the love his parents gave him, despite their fears at his Talent. He felt the warm hugs from his mother, and his father's calloused hand ruffling his hair.

And such was the power of the hymn he could even see, without hate, the Vagrian soldiers attacking his home, watch the axe that

307

dashed his father's brains to the floor, the plunging knife that snatched his mother from life. He had been in the barn when the Vagrians rode in. His parents had been slain within the first minute of the raid. Ekodas had leapt from the high hay-stall and run towards the soldiers. One turned and lashed out with a sword. It cut the boy's shoulder and neck, glancing up to slash across his brow.

When he awoke he was the only living Drenai for miles around. The Vagrians had even butchered the farm animals. All the buildings were burning, and a great pall of smoke hung over the land. He walked the two miles to the village on the third day after the raid. Bodies lay everywhere, and though the smoke was gone now, great flocks of crows circled in the sky. He gathered what food remained – a half-charred side of ham, a small sack of dried oats – and found a shovel which he carried back to his home, digging a deep grave for his parents.

For a year he had lived alone, gathering grain, edible roots and flowers that could be made into soups. And in that year he saw no one. In the day he would work. At night he would dream, dream of flying through the night sky, of soaring above the mountains in the clean light of the stars. Such dreams!

One night as he circled and soared a dark shape had materialised before him. It was a man's face, black hair waxed close to the skull, high slanted eyes, long braided sideburns that hung far below the chin.

'Where are you from, boy?' asked the man.

Ekodas had been frightened. He backed away, but the face swelled and a body appeared, long arms reaching out for him. The hands were scaled and taloned, and Ekodas fled. Other dark shapes appeared, like the crows above the village, and they called out to him. Far below he saw the little shelter he had created for himself from the unburnt timber of the barn. Down, down he flew, merging with his body and snapping awake, his heart beating wildly. In the heartbeat between dream and awakening he was sure he had heard triumphant laughter.

Two days later a traveller came by, a slender man with a gentle face. He walked slowly, and when he sat he winced with pain, for there was a stitched wound in his back.

'Good morning Ekodas,' he had said. 'I am Dardalion – and you must leave this place.'

'Why? It is my home.'

'I think you know why. Zhu Chao has seen your spirit soaring. He will send men to bring you to him.'

'Why should I trust you?'

The man smiled and reached out his hand. 'You have the Talent, the gift of the Source. Touch me. Find, if you can, a spark of evil.'

Ekodas gripped the hand, and in an instant Dardalion's memories flowed through him, the great Siege of Purdol, the battles with the

308

Brotherhood, the journey with Waylander, the terrible memories of bloodshed and death.

'I will come with you, sir.'

'You will not be alone, my boy. There are nine like you so far. There will be more.'

'How many more?'

'We will be Thirty.'

The prayer-hymn ended. Ekodas felt the coldness of separation, and the awareness of flesh and sinew, the cold breeze from the open window blowing against his bare legs. He shivered and opened his eyes.

Dardalion stood. Ekodas glanced up at the Abbot's slender, ascetic face.

'My brothers,' said Dardalion, 'behind you stands the armour of the Thirty. Beside it is the staff of the Source priest. Tonight we will decide where our destiny lies. Do we wear the armour and find the Source in a battle to the death against the forces of evil, or do we go our separate ways in peace and harmony? Tonight I speak for the latter. Ekodas will argue the former. At evening's end you will each stand and make your decisions. You will either take up the staff or the sword. May the Source guide us in our deliberations.'

He was silent then for several moments, and then he began to speak of the binding power of love, and the changes it wrought in the hearts of men. He spoke of the evil of hatred and greed and lust, pointing out, with great force, the folly of believing that swords and lances could eradicate evil. He spoke of rage and the demons that lay waiting within every human soul; demons with whips of fire that could impel a good man to rape and murder. Ekodas listened with growing astonishment. All his own arguments, and more, flowed from the Abbot.

'Yes love,' continued Dardalion, 'can heal the wounds of hatred. Love can eradicate lust and greed. Through love a man of evil can come to repentance and find redemption. For the Source abandons no man.

'Each of us here has been blessed by the Source. We have Talents. We can read minds, we can soar. Some can heal wounds with a touch. We are gifted. We could walk from here and spread our message of love throughout the realm.

'Many years ago I found myself in a terrible predicament. The Dark Brotherhood were reforming, seeking out gifted children, drawing them into their evil ways. Those who resisted were sacrificed to the forces of darkness. I decided then that I too would seek out those with talent, training them, building a new Thirty to stand against evil. While doing so I came upon two sisters, children of tragedy. They lived with a widower, a strong man, fearless and deadly. But they were lost in the soulless grey of the Void, hunted by demonic powers and by two of the Brotherhood. I fought them off and saved the spirits of these children, bringing them to their home. And then I returned to my body and I rode for their cabin. The Brotherhood killers knew where to find them, and I sought to warn their father.

'But when I arrived he was unconscious, having filled his belly with strong wine, trying to erase his grief at the death of his wife. The children were alone. While at the cabin I sensed the imminent arrival of the two men. I could feel their lust for violence and death travelling before them like a red mist. There was nowhere to run. Nowhere to hide.

'I did something then that I have always regretted. I took a small double crossbow from the unconscious man, and I loaded it. Then I stepped out to wait for the killers. During the Vagrian Wars I had killed with the sword, but I had sworn never to take another human life. As I waited I prayed they would be turned back by the very threat of the bow.

'But they came on, and they laughed at me, for I was known to them. I was a Source priest, a preacher of love. They mocked me and drew their swords. This bow I held had killed many men and it had power, dread power, in its ebony stock. The men advanced. My arm came up. And the first bolt flew. The first man died. The second man turned to run. Without thinking I shot him through the back of the neck. I felt like leaping into the air with joy. I had saved the children. Then the enormity of the deed came home to me, and I fell to my knees, hurling the crossbow from me.

'At Dros Purdol the first Thirty had fought against demons and the spirits of evil. But none of them – save myself – had ever lifted a sword against a human foe. And they died unresisting when the enemy breached the walls. Yet I, in one moment, had betrayed all we stood for.

'I had not only taken human life, I had robbed two men of any chance of redemption.

'I went back in to the children and I took them in my arms. My spirit went into both of them, closing the doorways to their Talent, robbing them of their Source-given gift so that the Brotherhood would not find them again. I put them in their bed and soothed them to sleep. Then I dragged the bodies from the clearing, burying them in a shallow grave.

'I have been haunted by that day, and not an hour of my life has passed without my thinking of it. I want none of you to face those regrets. And the surest way I know of avoiding such pain would be if each of you takes up the Source staff.' Dardalion sat down and Ekodas saw that the Abbot's hands were trembling.

The young priest took a deep breath and rose. 'Brothers, there is not a word spoken by the Abbot with which I disagree. But that alone does not make his argument true. He spoke of love generating love, and hatred breeding more hatred. We all agree with that – and if that was all there was to discuss, there would be no need for me to speak. But it is infinitely more complex. I have been asked to present an argument with which I fundamentally disagree. Is Ekodas right and his argument wrong? Is the argument a good one and Ekodas' judgement flawed? How can I know? How can any of us know? So let us examine a broader picture.

'We sit here safe, within a circle of swords held by other men. Recruits at Delnoch, lancers at the Skeln Pass, infantry at Erekban; all preparing to fight and perhaps to die to protect their families, their land and, yes, all of us. Are they evil? Will the Source deny them the gift of eternity? I would hope not. This world was created by the Source, every animal, every insect, plant and tree. But for one to live another usually dies. It is the way of all things. When the rose rises up it blocks the light that feeds the smaller plants, smothering them. For the lion to prosper the deer must die. All the world is in combat.

'Yes we sit safe. And why? Because we allow the responsibility – aye and the sin – to sit with other men.' He paused and stared at the listening priests, proud Vishna, the former Gothir nobleman, the fiery Magnic, whose eyes registered his surprise at the apparent change in the speaker, the slender, witty Palista, who was watching with a look of wry amusement.

Ekodas smiled. 'Ah, my brothers, if the argument were purely that we become warrior priests it would be the more easy to raise moral objections. But that is not the reality. We were gathered here because the Dark Brotherhood is abroad in the world, ready to bring chaos and despair to these and other lands. And we know, through the memories of our Father Abbot, what these men are capable of. We know that ordinary warriors cannot stand against their vile powers.'

He paused again and sipped water from his goblet of clay. 'The Lord Abbot talked of slaying the men who came for the children – but what was the alternative? To allow two innocent babes to be sacrificed? Whose purpose would that have served? As for the men and their redemption, who is to say where their souls travelled, and what hopes of redemption lie there?

'No, the Abbot has cause to regret only one aspect of that terrible day – the joy he felt at the killings. For that is the central point to this argument. As warrior priests we must fight – if fight we must – without hatred. We must be defenders of the Light.

'This Source-made world is in delicate balance, and when the scales of evil outweigh those of the good, what should we do? We were given gifts by the Source, gifts which enable us to stand against the Brotherhood. Do we deny those gifts? Many are the men who could take up the staff. Many are the priests who could – and will – journey the world with their gospels of love.

'But where are the Warriors of Light who can stand against the Brotherhood? Where are the Source Knights who can turn aside the spells of evil?' He spread his hands. 'Where, save for here? Not one of us can say with certainty that the path we choose is the right one. But we judge a rose by its bloom and by its fragrance. The Brotherhood seeks to rule, and by so doing, to usher in a new age of blood. We seek to see men living in peace and harmony, free to love, free to father their sons and daughters, free to sit in the evenings and watch the glory of the sunset, content that evil is far from them.

'We know where evil lies and, with pure hearts, we should stand against it. If it can be turned aside by love, so be it! But if it comes seeking slaughter and pain, then we should meet it with sword and shield. For that is our purpose. For we are the Thirty!' He sat down and closed his eyes, his emotions surging, his thoughts suddenly confused.

'Let us pray,' said Dardalion, 'and then let each man choose his path.'

For some minutes there was silence, then Ekodas saw Vishna rise and draw his silver sword, laying it on the table before him. Magnic followed, the grating rasp of steel blade on steel scabbard sawing through the silence. One by one the priests drew the swords, until only Dardalion and Ekodas were left. Dardalion waited and Ekodas smiled thinly. He stood, his eyes locked to the Abbot's level gaze.

'Did you trick me, Father?' pulsed Ekodas.

'No, my son. Did you convince yourself?'

'No, Dardalion. I still believe that to fight evil with its own weapons is folly and will lead merely to more hatred, more death.'

'Then why did you present the argument with such power?'

'Because you asked me to. And I owe you everything.'

'Then take up the staff, my son.'

'It is too late for that, Father.' Ekodas reached out and curled his fingers around the hilt of the silver longsword. The blade hissed into the air, catching the light from the many lanterns.

'*We are One!*' shouted Vishna.

And thirty swords were raised high, glittering like torches.

Karnak strode through the cheering troops, smiling and waving. Three times he stopped to exchange a few words with individual soldiers whose names he remembered. It was this common touch that endeared him to the men, and he knew it.

Behind him walked two officers of his general staff. Gan Asten, a former low-ranking officer promoted by Karnak during the civil war, was now one of the most powerful commanders in the Drenai army.

Beside him was Dun Galen, nominally Karnak's aide, but in reality the man whose network of spies kept Karnak's hand on the reins of power.

Karnak reached the end of the line and stooped to enter the tent. Asten and Galen followed him. The two guards extended their lances across the opening, signalling that the Lord Protector was not to be disturbed, and the soldiers drifted back to their campfires.

Inside Karnak's smile vanished. 'Where in the devil's name is he?' he snapped.

The skeletally thin Galen shrugged. 'He was in the palace and reportedly told his guards he would be visiting friends. That was the last they saw of him. Later, when his room was searched they found he had taken several changes of clothing and had also stolen gold from Varachek's vault – some two hundred Raq. Since then there has been no sign.'

'He was living in fear of Waylander,' said Asten. 'Every sound in the night, every banging shutter.'

'Waylander is a dead man!' roared Karnak. 'Could he not trust me with that? By Shemak's balls, he's one man. One!'

'And still alive,' pointed out Asten.

'Don't say it!' stormed Karnak. 'I know you advised me against bringing in the Guild, but how in the name of all that's holy did we arrive at this mess? One girl dies – an accident. And yet it has cost me damn near twenty thousand in gold – money I can ill-afford to lose – and seen my son scurrying away like a frightened rabbit!'

'There is a troop of lancers hunting him even as we speak, sir,' said the black-garbed Galen. 'They will bring him in.'

'I'll believe that, old lad, when I see it,' grunted Karnak.

'The Guild has proved a disappointment,' pointed out Asten, quietly.

Karnak grinned. 'Well, when the war is over I'll close them down and get the money back. One of the advantages of power.' The smile faded. 'Three wives, scores of willing women, and what do I get? Bodalen. What did I do to deserve such a son, eh, Asten?'

Wisely Gan Asten chose not to reply, but Galen stepped in swiftly. 'He has many talents, sir. He is highly thought of. He is just young and headstrong. I'm sure he didn't intend the girl to die. It was just sport, young men chasing a filly.'

'Until she fell and broke her neck,' grunted Asten, his florid face expressionless.

'An accident!' responded Galen, flashing a murderous glance at the general.

'It wasn't an accident when they killed her husband.'

'The man ran at them with a sword. They defended themselves. What else would you expect from Drenai noblemen?'

313

'I would not know of the ways of noblemen, Galen. My father was a farmer. But I expect you are correct. When drunken young nobles set off on a quest for rape one should not be surprised when they turn to murder.'

'Enough of this,' said Karnak. 'What's past is past. I'd cut off my right arm to bring the girl back – but she's dead. And her former guardian is alive. Neither of you know Waylander. I do. You would not want him hunting you – or your sons.'

'As you said yourself, sir, he is only one man,' said Galen, his voice softening, but still sibilant. 'And Bodalen is not even in the realm.'

Karnak sat down on a canvas-covered stool. 'I liked Waylander, you know,' he said quietly. 'He stood up to me.' He chuckled. 'He went into Nadir lands and fought off tribesmen, demonic beasts and the Vagrian Brotherhood. Amazing!' He glanced up at Galen. 'But he has to die. I can't let him slay my son.'

'You can rely on me, sir,' answered Galen, bowing deeply.

Karnak swung to Asten. 'What happened with the witch woman, Hewla?'

'She would not use her powers against Waylander,' answered the general.

'Why?'

'She didn't tell me, sir. But she did say she would consider raising a storm against the Ventrian fleet. I told her no.'

'No?' raged Karnak, lurching from his seat. '*No?* There'd better be a damn good reason, Asten.'

'She wanted a hundred children sacrificed. Something about paying the price for demonic assistance.'

Karnak swore. 'If we lose there'll be a lot more than a hundred children suffering. More like ten thousand.'

'You want me to go back to her?'

'Of course I don't want you to go back to her! Damn it, why does the enemy always have more power at his command? I'll wager the Ventrian King wouldn't think twice about a few scrawny brats.'

'We could use captured Sathuli children,' offered Galen. 'Make a swift raid into the mountains. After all, they have allied with Gothir against us.'

Karnak shook his head. 'Such an action would sully my reputation, turn the people against me. There's no way it could be kept secret. No, my friends, I think we'll have to rely on stout hearts and sharp swords. And luck, let's not forget that! But in the meantime, find Bodalen.'

'He probably believes he's safer in hiding,' said Asten.

'Find him and convince him otherwise,' ordered Karnak.

Waylander banked up the fire and settled back against the boulder, watching the sleeping Nadir. Belash had tried to keep up, but had

314

fallen several times, vomiting beside the trail. The blows to the head had weakened the warrior and Waylander had helped him to a sheltered hollow.

'Your skull may be cracked,' said Waylander, as the man lay shivering beside the fire.

'No.'

'It's not made of stone, Belash.'

'Tomorrow I will be strong,' promised the Nadir. In the dying light of the sun his face was grey, dark streaks colouring the skin beneath his slanted eyes.

Waylander touched the man's throat. The pulse was strong, but erratic. 'Sleep,' he said, covering the man with his cloak. The flames licked hungrily at the dry wood and Waylander reached out his hands, enjoying the warmth. The hound lay at his side, huge head on massive paws. Idly Waylander stroked the beast's ruined ears. A low rumbling growl came from its throat. 'Quiet,' said Waylander, smiling. 'You know you enjoy it, so stop complaining.'

He gazed at the sleeping Nadir. I should have killed you, he thought idly, but he did not regret allowing the man to live. There was something about Belash that struck a chord in him. A shadow flickered at the edge of his vision. Waylander glanced to his left. Sitting by the fire was a hooded old woman, her face a remarkable picture of ancient decay and ugliness, her teeth rotten, her nose swollen and blue-veined, her eyes rheumy and yellow.

'You move silently, Hewla,' whispered Waylander.

'No, I don't. I move like an old crone with my joints cracking like dry twigs.'

'I did not hear you.'

'That's because I'm not here, child,' she told him, reaching out her hand and thrusting it into the flames, which danced and flickered through suddenly transparent skin and bone. 'I am sitting by my own fire, in my own cabin.'

'What do you require of me?'

Her eyes glinted with amusement, her mouth forming the parody of a smile. 'Not impressed with my magic? How dull. You have no inkling of the concentration needed to produce this image. But do your eyes widen in wonder? Do you sit there jaw agape in amazement? No. You ask what I require. What makes you think I require anything, child? Perhaps I felt in need of company.'

'Unlikely,' he said, with a wry smile. 'But you are welcome whatever. Are you well?'

'When you are four hundred and eleven years old the question is irrelevant. I haven't been well since the old King's grandfather was a child. I'm just too stubborn to die.' She glanced at the sleeping Nadir. 'He dreams of killing you,' she said.

He shrugged. 'His dreams are his own affair.'

'You are a strange man, Waylander. Still, the dog likes you.'

He chuckled. 'He'll make a better friend than most men.'

'Aye.' The old woman fell silent, but her gaze remained on the black-garbed warrior. 'I always liked you, child,' she said softly. 'You never feared me. I was sorry to hear of the death of your lady.'

He looked away. 'Life moves on,' he said.

'Indeed it does. Morak will come again. He is no coward, but he likes to be sure. And Senta is even now approaching your cabin. What will you do?'

'What do you think?' he countered.

'You'll fight them until they kill you. Not the most subtle of plans, is it?'

'I never was a man suited to subtlety.'

'Nonsense. It's just that you have always been a little in love with death. Perhaps it would help to know why they are hunting you?'

'Does it matter?'

'You won't know unless I tell you!' she snapped.

'Then tell me.'

'Karnak has a son, Bodalen. He is allied to the Brotherhood. He and some friends were riding near a village, south of Drenan. They saw a young woman gathering herbs. The men had been drinking, and she aroused their lust. They chased her. She turned and fought, breaking one man's jaw. Then she ran. Bodalen followed her. As she fled she glanced back, lost her footing, and fell. She tumbled over the edge of a rock-face. Her neck was broken in the fall. Her husband came upon the scene. He was unarmed. The men killed him, leaving him by her body. You hear what I am saying?'

'I hear, but I don't know what it has to do with me,' he answered.

'They were seen riding from the area and Bodalen was brought to trial. He was sentenced to a year in exile, and Karnak paid a fortune in blood-geld to the dead man's father.'

Waylander's mouth was dry. 'Where was the village?'

'Adderbridge.'

'Are you saying he killed my Krylla!' hissed Waylander.

'Yes. Karnak found out that you were her guardian. He fears you will seek Bodalen. That is why the Guild hunt you.'

Waylander's mind was reeling and his unfocused eyes stared into the darkness, memories flooding him with echoes of the past, Krylla and Miriel splashing in the stream by the cabin, laughing and squealing in the sunshine, Krylla's tears when the pet goose died, her happiness when Nualin had proposed, the gaiety of the wedding and the dance that followed it. He saw her smiling face, the twin of Miriel, but with a mouth that smiled more easily and a manner that

316

won over every heart. With great effort he forced the memories back and turned his now cold eyes on the witch woman's image.

'Why did you come here, Hewla?' he asked icily.

'I told you. I like you. Always have.'

'That may or may not be true. But I ask again, why did you come?'

'Hmm, I do so admire you, child. There is no fooling you, is there?' Her malevolent eyes gleamed in the firelight. 'Yes, there is more to this than just Bodalen.'

'I did not doubt it.'

'Have you heard of Zhu Chao?'

Waylander shook his head. 'Nadir?'

'No. Chiatze. He is a practitioner of the Dark Arts. No more than that, though he would no doubt describe himself as a wizard. He is young – not yet sixty, and still has the strength to summon demons to his bidding. He has rebuilt the Brotherhood, and – nominally, mark you! – serves the Gothir Emperor.'

'And Bodalen?'

'Karnak's son reveres him. The Brotherhood is behind the coming wars. They have infiltrated many of the noble houses of Ventria, Gothir and Drenai. They seek to rule, and perhaps they will succeed – who knows?'

'And you want me to kill Zhu Chao.'

'Very astute. Yes, I want him dead.'

'I am no longer an assassin, Hewla. If the man was threatening you then I would deal with him. But I will not hunt him down for you.'

'But you will hunt Bodalen,' she whispered.

'Oh, yes. I will find him. And he will know justice.'

'Good. You will find him with Zhu Chao,' she said. 'And if the little wizard should happen to step into the path of one of your bolts, so be it.'

'He is in Gulgothir?'

'Indeed he is. I think he feels safer there. Well, I shall leave you now. It is difficult at my age to hold such a spell.' He said nothing. She shook her head. 'Not even a thank you for old Hewla?'

'Why should I thank you?' he answered. 'You have brought me only pain.'

'No, no, child. I have saved your life. Look inside yourself. You no longer wish to wait here and die alongside your lovely Danyal. No. The wolf is back. Waylander lives again.'

Angry words rose in his throat. But Hewla had vanished.

7

Miriel's head was aching, but the acute pain of the night before had faded to a dull ache as she rose and dressed, making her way through the cabin to the clearing where Angel was chopping logs. Stripped to the waist he was swinging the long-handled axe with practised ease, splitting the wood expertly.

He stopped as he saw her and thudded the axe into a log, then took up his shirt and strolled towards her. 'How are you feeling today?' he asked.

'I'm ready,' she told him.

He shook his head. 'I think you should rest this morning. Your colour is not good.'

There was a chill in the air and she shivered. 'They will come back,' she said.

He shrugged. 'There's not a blessed thing we can do about that, Miriel.'

'Except wait?'

'Exactly.'

'You don't seem concerned.'

'Oh, but I am. It is just that I learned long ago that there is little point in worrying about matters over which you have no control. We could flee, I suppose, but to where? We don't know where they are, and could run straight into them. At least here we have the advantage of home ground. And this is where your father expects to find us. Therefore we wait.'

'I could track them,' she offered.

He shook his head. 'Morak wasn't with them, nor was Belash. I wouldn't want to track either of them. They would have sentries watching from the high hills, or trees. They would see us coming. No, we wait for Waylander.'

'I don't like the thought of just sitting,' she said.

'I know,' he told her, stepping forward and laying his hand on her shoulder. 'It is always the hardest part. I was the same when I was waiting for the call into the arena. I could hear the clash of swords outside, smell the sand and the sawdust. I always felt ill.'

Miriel's eyes narrowed. 'There's someone coming,' she said.

He swung, but there was no one in sight. 'Where?' She pointed to the south, where a flock of doves had flown up from a tall pine. 'It could be your father.'

'It could,' she agreed, spinning on her heel and walking back into the cabin. Angel stood where he was, one hand on the porch-rail, the other resting on the leather-bound hilt of his shortsword. Miriel rejoined him, a sword belted to her waist, a baldric of throwing-knives hanging from her shoulder.

A tall man appeared at the edge of the clearing, saw them, and walked down the slope, sunlight glinting in the gold of his hair. He moved with animal grace, arrogantly, like a lord in his domain, thought Miriel, anger flaring. The newcomer was dressed in expensive buckskin, heavily fringed at the shoulders. He wore two swords, short sabres in black leather scabbards adorned with silver. His leggings were dark brown and tucked into thigh-length tan cavalry boots that had been folded down, exposing the lining of cream-coloured silk.

Coming closer he bowed to Miriel, his arm sweeping out in courtly style. 'Good morning, Miriel.'

'Do I know you?'

'Not yet, and the loss is entirely mine.' He smiled as he spoke and Miriel found herself blushing. 'Ah, Angel,' said the newcomer, as if noticing the gladiator for the first time. 'The princess and the troll . . . I feel as if I have stepped into a fable.'

'Really?' countered Angel. 'Seeing you makes me feel I have stepped into something altogether less pleasant.'

The man chuckled with genuine humour. 'I have missed you, old man. Nothing was the same once you left the arena. How is your . . . shop?'

'Gone, but then you knew that.'

'Yes, come to think of it someone did mention that to me. I was distressed to hear of it, of course. Well, is no one going to offer breakfast? It's a long walk from Kasyra.'

'Who is this . . . this popinjay?' asked Miriel.

'Oh yes, do introduce us, Angel, there's a good fellow.'

'This is Senta, one of the hired killers sent to murder your father.'

'Delicately put,' said Senta. 'But it should be pointed out that I am not a bowman, nor am I the kind of assassin who kills from hiding. I am a swordsman, lady, probably the best in the land.'

Miriel's fingers closed around the hilt of her sword, but Angel caught her arm. 'He may be conceited, and self-obsessed, but he is quite right,' said Angel, his eyes holding to Senta's gaze. 'He *is* a fine bladesman. So let us stay calm, eh? Prepare some food, Miriel.'

'For him? No!'

'Trust me,' he said softly, 'and do as I say.'

Miriel looked into his flint-coloured eyes. 'Is this what you want?'

'Yes,' he said simply.

Her hands were trembling as she carved the cold meat. She felt confused, uncertain. Angel's strength was prodigious, and she knew he was no coward. So why was he pandering to this man? Was he frightened?

The two men were sitting at the table when she returned. Senta stood as she entered. 'You really are a vision!' he said. Her reply was short and obscene. Senta's eyes widened. 'Such language from a lady?'

Furious and embarrassed, Miriel laid down the tray of food and bit back an angry retort.

'Seen anything of Morak?' asked Angel, breaking the bread and passing a section to Senta.

'Not yet – but I sent him a message. He's got Belash with him, did you know?'

'It doesn't surprise me. What does is that you and Morak do not travel together,' said Angel. 'You are two of a kind – the same easy smiles, the same sly wit.'

'And there the resemblance ends,' said Senta. 'His heart is rotten, Angel, and his desires are vile. It hurts me that you would link us so.' He glanced at Miriel. 'This is very fine bread. My compliments.'

Miriel ignored him, but he seemed not to notice. 'Lovely area this,' he went on. 'Close to the sea, and not yet plagued by people and their filth. One day I must find myself such a home in the mountains.' He looked around him. 'Well-built, too. A lot of love and effort.' His eyes were drawn to the weapons on the wall. 'That's Kreeg's crossbow, isn't it? Well, well! His whore was missing him in Kasyra. Something tells me he won't be going back to her.'

'He was like you,' said Miriel softly. 'He thought it would be easy, but when you face Waylander the only easy part is the dying.'

Senta laughed. 'Everyone dies, beauty. Everyone. And if he is useful with a sword it might be me.'

Now it was Angel who chuckled. 'You are a strange man, Senta. What on earth makes you think Waylander will face you blade to blade? You won't even see him. All you'll feel is the bolt that cleaves into your heart. And you won't feel that for very long.'

'Well, that wouldn't be very sporting, would it?' countered Senta, his smile fading.

'I don't think he regards this as sport,' said Angel.

'How disappointing. Perhaps I misjudged him. From all I've heard he doesn't seem to be a coward.' He shrugged. 'But then these stories do tend to become exaggerated, don't they?'

'You have a curious sense of what denotes cowardice,' said Miriel. 'When a snake comes into the house a man does not lie down on his belly to fight it fang to fang. He just stamps on its head, then throws the useless carcass out into the night. One does not deal with vermin in the way one deals with men!'

Senta clapped his hands, slowly and theatrically, but anger showed in his blue eyes.

'Finish your breakfast,' said Angel softly.

'And then I am to leave, I suppose?' Senta responded, slicing a section of meat then lancing it with his knife and raising it towards his mouth.

'No, Senta, then you will die.'

The knife froze. Senta shook his head. 'I'm not being paid to kill you, old man.'

'Just as well,' said Angel. 'You wouldn't be there to collect it. I'll wait for you outside.'

The former gladiator stood and left the room. Senta glanced up at Miriel. 'It's a good breakfast. May I stay on for supper?'

'Don't kill him!'

'What?' Senta seemed genuinely surprised. 'I have no choice, beauty. He has challenged me.' He stared at her. 'Are you and he . . . ? No, surely not.' He stood. 'I'm sorry. Truly. I quite like the old boy.'

'He's not that old.'

'He's twice my age, Miriel, and as a swordsman that makes him older than the mountains.'

'If you kill him you'll have to kill me. I'll come for you. I swear it.'

Senta sighed, then bowed. There was no hint of mockery in his eyes. Swinging on his heel the assassin stepped out into the light. Angel was standing some thirty feet from the door, sword in hand.

'Arena rules?' called Senta.

'As you like.'

'Are you sure about this, Angel? There is no need for us to fight. And you know well enough you will lose.'

'Don't tell me, boy, show me!'

Senta drew his sabre and advanced.

Waylander emerged from the trees and saw the two swordsmen circling one another.

'Ho Angel!' he called. The two warriors paused, glancing up towards him as he made his way down the slope, the stocky Nadir following. From Ralis' description Waylander guessed the swordsman was Senta.

'Leave him to me!' said Angel, as the gap closed.

'No one fights for me,' replied Waylander, his eyes fixed on Senta, noting the man's balance and his condescending smile. There was no fear here, only a cold confidence bordering on the arrogant. Waylander came closer. Still he had not drawn a weapon and he saw Senta's eyes glance down at the scabbarded sword. 'You are hunting me?' asked Waylander, moving ever closer. Only a few paces separated them.

321

'I have a commission from the Guild,' replied Senta, taking a step back.

Waylander kept moving. Senta was tense now, for Waylander had halted immediately before him. 'Arena rules?' enquired the assassin.

Waylander smiled. His head snapped forward, butting the blond swordsman on the bridge of the nose. Senta staggered back. Waylander stepped in and hammered his elbow into the man's jaw. Senta hit the ground hard, his sword falling from his fingers. Waylander grabbed the man's long golden hair, hauling him to his knees. 'I don't duel,' he said, drawing a razor-sharp knife from his baldric.

'Don't kill him!' shouted Angel.

'As you wish,' answered Waylander, releasing his hold on the half-conscious swordsman. Senta slumped back to the ground. Waylander sheathed his knife and walked into the cabin.

'Welcome back, Father,' said Miriel, stepping into his embrace. His arms swept round her, stroking her back, his face pressed against her hair.

'We have to leave,' he whispered, his voice trembling. 'We're going north.'

'What has happened?' she asked him.

He shook his head. 'We'll talk later. Prepare two packs – food for three days, winter clothing. You know what is needed.' She nodded and looked past him. He glanced back to see the Nadir warrior standing in the doorway. 'We met in the mountains,' said Waylander. 'This is Belash.'

'But he's . . .'

'Yes, he was. But Morak betrayed him. Left him to die.' Waylander waved the man forward. 'This is my daughter, Miriel.' Belash's face showed no expression, but his eyes were drawn to the weapons she wore. The Nadir said nothing, but walked into the kitchen where he helped himself to a hunk of bread and some cheese.

'Can you trust him?' whispered Miriel.

Waylander's smile was broad. 'Of course not. But he will be valuable where we are going.'

'Into Gothir?'

'Yes.'

'What changed your mind?'

'There's a man there I must find. Now prepare the packs.'

She half-turned, then looked back at him. 'Why did you spare Senta?'

He shrugged. 'Angel asked me to.'

'Hardly a good reason.'

'It's as good as any other.'

Miriel walked away. Waylander moved to the dead fire and sat down in the broad leather chair. Angel entered, half-carrying Senta.

Blood was streaming from the man's broken nose, and his eyes were swollen half-shut. Angel lowered him to the bench-seat at the table. Senta sagged forward, blood dripping to the wood. Angel found a cloth, which he passed to the man. Senta held it to his face.

Angel moved in close to Waylander and whispered, 'Why is Belash still among the living?'

'A whim,' answered Waylander.

'Whims like that can kill you. They're not like people, they're savages spawned by demons. I think you have made a bad mistake.'

'I've made mistakes before. Time will tell about this one.' He stepped alongside Senta. 'Lie back along the bench,' he ordered. 'The blood will stop faster that way.'

'I thank you for your concern,' muttered the swordsman thickly.

Waylander sat beside him. 'Be advised. Do not come against me again.'

Senta dropped the blood-covered cloth and sniffed loudly. 'You taught me a valuable lesson,' he said, forcing a smile. 'I shall not forget it.'

Waylander stood and strode from the cabin. Angel followed him. 'You have not asked me why I wanted him alive.'

'I don't care,' replied Waylander, kneeling and patting the hound, which had stretched out in the shade. The dog gave a low growl and arched its neck. Waylander rubbed its muzzle. 'It is not important, Angel.'

'It is to me. I am in your debt.'

'How is Miriel progressing?'

'Better than she was. And I don't want your ten thousand.'

Waylander shrugged. 'Take it. I won't miss it.'

'That's not the point, damn you!'

'Why so angry?'

'Where are you going from here?' countered Angel.

'North.'

'May I come with you?'

'Why?' asked Waylander, genuinely surprised.

'I have nowhere else to go. And I can still train Miriel.'

Waylander nodded, and was silent for several moments. 'Did anything happen while I was away – between the two of you, I mean?'

Angel reddened. 'Nothing! Gods, man, my boots are older than her!'

'She could do worse, Angel. And I must find her a husband.'

'That won't take long. She's a lovely girl, and I guess it will be good to know she's safe like her sister.'

'Her sister is dead,' said Waylander, fighting to remain calm, his voice barely above a whisper. Once more Krylla's face came back to him, and he felt a cold, berserk rage building. 'That's why they are hunting me,' he went on. 'Karnak's son killed her. The Lord Protector paid the assassins because he fears I'll hunt down the boy.'

'Gods of Mercy! I didn't know it was Krylla,' said Angel. 'There was a trial, but the victim was not even named. Bodalen was exiled for a year.'

'A harsh punishment indeed.'

'But you're not going after him?'

Waylander took a deep calming breath. 'I am heading north,' he answered. 'Travelling to Gothir.'

'It's probably wise,' agreed Angel. 'You cannot go against the whole Drenai army. But you do surprise me – I thought you would have put vengeance above everything else.'

'Perhaps age is making me mellow.'

Angel grinned. 'You didn't look too mellow when you downed Senta. And where in Hell's name did you find that dog? It's the ugliest beast I've ever seen. Look at those scars!'

'Bear-fighter,' said Waylander. 'Retired – just like you.'

Senta, his nose swollen, his nostrils stained with blood, moved out into the sunlight, just as Angel knelt to pet the dog.

'You know, Angel,' said the swordsman, 'the resemblance is striking. If your own mother were to appear in our midst she wouldn't know which of you to call in for dinner.'

'The nose is an improvement – and it's bleeding again,' replied Angel, turning away and reaching out to the hound. Its fangs showed and a low snarl sounded. Angel drew back and stood.

Senta sniffed and spat blood to the dust, then walked past the two men and retrieved the sabre that was still lying in the dust. With the weapon in his hand he strolled back to Waylander. 'Mercy is a rare beast,' he said. 'You think it was wise to let me live?'

'If it proves a mistake I'll kill you,' Waylander told him.

'You are an unusual man. How did you know I wouldn't gut you as soon as you closed in on me?'

Waylander shrugged. 'I didn't.'

The swordsman nodded. 'I think I will travel with you,' he said. 'I heard you tell Angel you were heading north. I've always wanted to return to Gothir. I had some fine times there.'

'I may not want your company,' said Waylander.

'I can see that might be so. But there was something else you told Angel that interested me greatly.'

'I'm listening.'

'You're looking for a husband for Miriel.'

'You know where I might find one?'

'Very droll. I am a rich man, and not – despite your efforts – unhandsome. And my father continues to berate me for not supplying him with a grandson. I'll take her off your hands.'

'Shemak's balls, but you've got nerve!' stormed Angel.

'I like a man with nerve,' said Waylander. 'I'll think on it.'

'You're not serious!' exclaimed Angel. 'A few minutes ago this man was trying to kill you for money. He's an assassin.'

'Which of course puts me lower on the social scale than an arena-killer,' observed Senta.

'Madness!' muttered Angel, stalking back into the cabin.

Senta sheathed his sabre. 'Why are we heading north?' he asked.

'There's someone I must find in Gulgothir.'

Miriel carried a bowl of heated water and a clean cloth to where Senta sat. She had not heard his conversation with her father, but she saw he now had his sabre once more. The blond warrior looked up through swollen eyes. He smiled. 'Merciful care for the fallen hero?'

'You are not a hero,' she told him, dipping the cloth in the water and gently sponging away the blood staining Senta's face. Reaching up he took hold of her wrist.

'He stamped on my head, but he did not throw the useless carcass out into the forest.'

'Be grateful for that,' she said, pulling her hand free.

'Interesting man. He read me well. He knew I wouldn't kill him before he'd drawn a weapon.'

'What will you do now?' she asked.

He grinned, then winced as pain flared through his broken nose. 'I shall enter a monastery and devote my life to good works.'

'It was a serious question.'

'And you are a serious woman, beauty. Too serious. Do you laugh much? Do you dance? Do you make assignations with young men?'

'What I do is none of your affair! And stop calling me beauty. I don't like it.'

'Yes, you do. But it makes you uncomfortable.'

'Do you still plan to kill my father?'

'No.'

'Am I expected to believe that?'

'You are free to believe or disbelieve, beauty. How old are you?'

'I will be eighteen next summer.'

'Are you a virgin?'

'You'll never know!' she told him. Taking up the bowl, she walked back to the kitchen where Belash was still eating. Most of the ham had gone, and half of the cheese. 'Is this your first meal in a month?' she snapped.

The Nadir looked up, his dark eyes expressionless. 'Fetch me water,' he ordered.

'Fetch it yourself, bowel-brain!' His face darkened and he rose from his seat. Miriel's dagger swept up. 'One wrong move, you Nadir dog-

eater, and the breakfast you've just eaten will be all over the floor.'
Belash grinned and walked to the water jug, filling a clay goblet.
'What is so amusing?' she demanded.

'You *kol-isha*,' answered Belash, drawing his own knife and cutting
the last slice of ham from the bone. He shook his head and chuckled.

'What about us?' persisted Miriel.

'Where are your babies?' countered Belash. 'Where is your man?
Why are you garbed for war? Knives and swords – such foolishness.'

'You think a woman cannot use these weapons?'

'Of course they can. You should see my Shia – knife, sword,
handaxe. But it is not natural. War is for men, for honour and glory.'

'And death,' she pointed out.

'Of course death. That is why women must be protected. Many
babies must be born to replace the dead warriors.'

'It might be better just to stop the wars.'

'Pah! It is always useless to talk to women. They have no understanding.'

Miriel took a deep breath, but refrained from further argument.
Leaving the Nadir to his endless breakfast she walked to her room and
began to pack.

8

Hewla eased her frame up from the wicker chair and winced as pain
flared in her arthritic hip. The fire was dying down and she slowly bent
to lift a log on to the glowing coals. There was a time when her fires
needed no fuel, when she had not been forced to walk the forest
gathering twigs and sticks.

'Curse you, Zhu Chao,' she whispered. But the words only made her
the more angry, for once such a curse would have been accompanied
by the beating of demon wings and the harsh raucous cries of the
Vanshii as they flew to their victim.

How could you have been so stupid? she asked herself.

I was lonely.

Yes, but now you are still lonely, and the *grimoires* are gone.

She shivered and added another thick stick to the fire, which
hungrily devoured it. It was small consolation that the Books of
Spellfire would be virtually useless to Zhu Chao. For the spells
contained in them had given Hewla life, long after her skin should
have turned to dust, had held at bay the mortal pain of her inflamed

joints. The six books of Moray Sen. Priceless. She remembered the day she had shown them to him, opening the secret compartment behind the firestone. She had believed in him then, the young Chiatze. Loved him. She shuddered. Old fool.

He had taken the *grimoires* she had schemed for, killed for, sold her soul for.

Now the Void beckoned.

Waylander will kill him, she thought with grim relish.

The room was becoming warmer and Hewla was at last feeling some comfort from the heat. But then an icy blast of freezing air touched her back. The old woman turned. The far wall was shimmering and a cold, cold wind was blowing through it, scattering scrolls and papers. A clay goblet on the table trembled and fell, rolling to the floor, shattering. The wind grew stronger. Hewla's shawl flew back, falling across the fire, and the old woman stumbled against the power of the demon wind.

A dark shape appeared by the wall, silhouetted against icy flames.

Hewla's hand came up and a bright light blazed from her fingers, surrounding the demon. The wind died down, but she felt the creature's elemental power pushing back against the light. A taloned hand clawed through. Flames burst around it and it withdrew.

A flickering figure appeared to her left, and she saw Zhu Chao's image forming.

'I have brought an old friend to see you, Hewla,' he said.

'Rot in Hell,' she hissed.

He laughed at her. 'I see you retain some vestiges of power. Tell me, hag, how long do you think you can hold him from you?'

'What do you want from me?'

'I cannot master the first of the Five Spells. Something is missing from the *grimoires*. Tell me and you shall live.'

Once again the taloned hand tore through the light. Flames seared it, but not as powerfully as before. Fear swelled in Hewla's heart and, had she believed Zhu Chao's promise, she might have told him. But she did not.

'What is missing is something you will never find – courage!' she said. 'You will grow older, your powers fading. And when you die your soul will be carried screaming to the Void.'

'You foolish old crone,' he whispered. 'All the books speak of the Mountains of the Moon. The answers lie there. I shall find them.'

Talons ripped at the light, and it parted like a torn curtain. The dark shape loomed in the room. As swiftly as she could, Hewla drew the small curved dagger from the sheath at her waist.

'I will wait for you in the Void,' she promised.

Holding the dagger blade beneath her left breast she plunged it home.

Senta sat quietly on the wall of the well, watching Waylander and Miriel some distance away. The man had his hand on the girl's shoulder. Her head was bowed. Senta did not need to guess at the subject of their conversation. He had heard Waylander telling Angel of the death of Miriel's sister.

Senta looked away. His broken nose was sending shafts of pain behind his eyes and he felt sick. In his four years in the arena he had not felt pain like this. Minor cuts, and once a twisted ankle, were all the swordsman had suffered. But then those fights had been governed by rules. With a man like Waylander there were no rules. Only survival.

Despite his pain Senta felt relieved. He had no doubt that he would have killed the older man in a duel, though if he had, there would still have been Angel to face. And it would have saddened him to slay the old gladiator. But, more than that, it would have wrecked any chance with Miriel.

Miriel . . .

His first sight of her had shocked him, and he still didn't know why. The noblewoman, Gilaray, had a more beautiful face. Nexiar was infinitely more shapely. Suri's golden hair and flashing eyes were far more provocative. Yet there was something about this mountain girl that had fired his senses. But what?

And why marriage? He could hardly believe he'd made the offer. How would she take to life in the city? He focused on her once more, picturing her in a gown of silver satin, pearls laced through her dark hair. And chuckled.

'What is amusing you?' asked Angel, strolling to where he sat.

'I was thinking of Miriel at the Lord Protector's Ball, in a flowing dress and with her knives strapped to her forearms.'

'She's too good for the likes of you, Senta. Far too good.'

'That's a matter of opinion. Would you sooner see her standing behind a plough, old before her time, her breasts flat, like two hanged men?'

'No,' admitted Angel, 'but I'd like to see her with a man who loved her. She's not like Nexiar, or any of the others. She's like a colt – fast, sleek, unbroken.'

Senta nodded. 'I think you are right.' He glanced up at the gladiator. 'How very perceptive of you, my friend. You do surprise me.'

'I surprise myself sometimes. Like asking Waylander not to kill you. I'm regretting it already.'

'No, you're not,' said Senta, with an easy smile.

Angel grunted a short obscenity and sat beside the swordsman. 'Why did you have to talk of marriage?'

'You think I'd have been better advised to suggest rutting with her under a bush?'

'It would have been more honest.'

'I don't think it would,' said Senta softly. He became aware of Angel staring at him and felt himself blushing.

'Well, well,' said Angel. 'That I should live to see the great Senta smitten. What would they say in Drenan?'

Senta grinned. 'They'd say nothing. The entire city would be swept away under an ocean of tears.'

'I thought you were going to marry Nexiar. Or was it Suri?'

'Beautiful girls,' agreed Senta.

'Nexiar would have killed you. She damn near did for me.'

'I heard the two of you were close once. Is it true that she was so repulsed by your ugliness that, when in bed, she insisted you wore your helmet?'

Angel laughed. 'Close. She had a velvet mask made for me.'

'Ah, but I like you, Angel. Always did. Why did you ask him to spare me?'

'Why didn't you kill him when he approached you?' countered Angel.

Senta shrugged. 'My great-grandfather was a congenital idiot. My father was convinced I took after him. I think he was right.'

'Answer the question, damn you!'

'He had no weapon in his hand. I have never killed an unarmed man. It's not in me. Does that satisfy you?'

'Aye, it does,' admitted Angel. His head came up, nostrils flaring. Without a word he strode back to the cabin, emerging moments later with his sword strapped to his waist. The sound of walking horses came to Senta and he loosened his sabres in their scabbards, but remained where he was at the well. Belash came into sight, stepping from the cabin doorway, knife in his right hand, whetstone in his left. Waylander said something to Miriel, and she vanished into the cabin, then the black-garbed warrior lifted his double crossbow from the hook on his belt, swiftly drawing back the strings and notching two bolts into place.

The first of the horsemen came into view. He wore a full-faced helm of gleaming black metal, a black breast-plate and a blood-red cloak. Behind him came seven identical warriors, each riding black geldings, none less than sixteen hands high. Senta stood and strolled to where Waylander and the others were standing.

The horsemen reined in before the cabin, the horses forming a semi-circle around the the waiting men. No one spoke and Senta felt his skin crawl as he scanned the black knights. Only their eyes could be seen, through thin rectangular slits in the black helms. The expressions were all the same – cold, expectant, confident.

Finally one of them spoke. Senta could not tell which one, for the voice was muffled by the helm.

'Which of you is the wolfshead Dakeyras?'

'I am,' replied Waylander, addressing the rider directly before him.

'The Master has sentenced you to death. There is no appeal.'

The knight reached a black gauntleted hand to his sword-hilt, drawing the blade slowly. Waylander started to lift the crossbow – but his hand froze, the weapon still pointing at the ground. Senta looked at him, surprised, and saw the muscles of his jaw clench, his face redden with effort.

Senta drew the first of his sabres and prepared to attack the horsemen, but even as the blade came clear he saw one of the horsemen glance towards him, felt the man's cold stare touch him like icy water. Senta's limbs froze, a terrible pressure bearing down on him. The sabre sagged in his hand.

The black knights dismounted and Senta heard the whispering of steel swords being drawn from scabbards. Something bounced at his feet, rolling past him. It was the whetstone Belash had been carrying.

He struggled to move, but his arms felt as if they were made of stone.

And he saw a black sword rising towards his throat.

Inside the cabin Miriel lifted Kreeg's crossbow from the wall, flicking open the winding arms and swiftly rotating them, drawing the string back to the bronze notch. Selecting a bolt she pressed it home and swung back towards the door.

A tall knight stepped into the doorway, blocking out the light. For a moment only she froze. Then the bow came up.

'No,' whispered a sibilant voice in her mind.

A terrible lethargy flowed into her limbs and she felt as if a stream of warm, dark water was seeping through the corridors of her mind, drawing out her soul, emptying her memories. It was almost welcome, a cessation of fear and concern, a longing for the emptiness of death. Then a bright light flared, deep within her thoughts, holding back the black tidal wave of warm despair. And she saw, silhouetted against the light, the silver warrior who had rescued her as a child.

'Fight them!' he ordered. 'Fight them, Miriel! I have opened the doorways to your Talent. Seek it! And live!'

She blinked, and tried to aim the crossbow, but it was so heavy, so terribly heavy . . .

The black knight walked further into the room. 'Give me the weapon,' he said, his voice muffled by the helm. 'And I will give you joys you have not yet even dreamed of.' As he approached Miriel saw Waylander on his knees in the dust of the clearing, a black bladed sword raised above his head.

'*No!*' she shouted. The crossbow tilted to the right. She squeezed the bronze trigger. The bolt slashed through the air, plunging into the black helm and disappearing up to the flights. The black knight toppled forward.

Outside, Waylander, suddenly free of the spell, threw himself to the left as the sword hissed down. Hitting the ground on his shoulder he rolled and let fly the first of his bolts. It took the swordsman under the right armpit, cleaving through to the lungs.

A dark shadow fell across him. Waylander rolled again – but not swiftly enough! A black sword flashed for his face. The hound sprang across the fallen man, its great fangs closing on the swordsman's wrist. Belash took one running step then launched himself feet-first at the knight, cannoning the man from his feet. The Nadir landed lightly and hurled himself on the assailant, driving his knife under the chinstrap of the black helmet and up into the man's brain.

The hound's angry growling panicked the horses. They reared, and – save for one gelding – bolted.

Free of the spell, Senta brought up his sabre, barely blocking the blade thrusting for his throat. He parried a second cut and, twisting his wrist, sent a vicious return that clanged against the knight's neck gorget of reinforced chain mail. Senta shoulder-charged the warrior, spinning him from his feet. A second man attacked, but this time Senta swayed aside from the killing thrust and rammed his sabre up under the man's helmet, the point slicing through the soft skin beneath the chin, and on up through his mouth. The knight fell back. Senta lost hold of the sabre and drew his second blade.

Angel, his back to the cabin wall, was battling against two knights, the former gladiator desperately blocking and parrying. Waylander sent a bolt through the thigh of the first assailant. The man grunted in pain and half-turned. Angel's sword smashed against the knight's helm, cutting through the chinstrap. The helm fell loose. Waylander's sword clove through the man's skull. Angel sidestepped a lunge from the second knight, grabbed the man's arm and hauled him, head-first, into the wall. Dropping to the man's back Angel took hold of the helm, dragging it back and sharply to the left. The knight's neck snapped with a stomach-wrenching crack.

'Look out!' yelled Senta. Waylander dropped to one knee. A sword-blade sliced the air above him. Waylander flung himself backwards, hammering into his attacker and hurling the man from his feet. Senta leapt at the man. His opponent reared to his feet, then lunged. Senta swayed aside, ramming his elbow into the man's helm. The knight staggered. Senta leaned back and kicked out, his booted foot cracking against the knight's knee. The joint gave way. The knight screamed in

331

pain as he fell. Belash threw himself on the fallen warrior, pulling back the neck-guard and driving his knife deep into the knight's throat.

Miriel, the crossbow loaded once more, stepped from the cabin. The last knight ran to the one horse that had not bolted and leapt for the saddle, grabbing the pommel. The horse reared and began to run, dragging the knight with it. The hound bounded after it. Miriel brought the crossbow to her shoulder and sighted the weapon. The bolt sang clear and flashed across the clearing to punch home into the knight's helm. For several seconds he clung to the pommel, but as the horse reached the rise the man's fingers loosened and he fell to the earth. Instantly the dog was upon him, fangs ripping at the dead man's throat, but unable to pierce the chain mail. Waylander called to the hound and it loped back across the clearing, standing close, its flanks pressing against Waylander's leg.

Slowly the swirling dust in the clearing settled back to the earth.

One knight moaned, but Belash sprang upon him, ripping the man's helmet clear and cutting his throat. Another – the first to attack Senta – reared up and ran for the trees. The hound set off in pursuit, but Waylander called out to it and it paused, staring back at its master.

Miriel slowly turned the winding arms of the crossbow then, with the weapon strung, walked back into the cabin to fetch a bolt.

'He's getting away!' shouted Senta.

'I don't think so,' said Waylander softly.

Miriel reappeared and offered the bow to Waylander. He shook his head. The knight had reached the rise and was scrambling up the slope.

'Allow for the fact that you are shooting uphill,' advised Waylander.

Miriel nodded. The bow came up and, apparently without sighting, she loosed the bolt. It took the knight low in the back. He arched up, then tumbled down the slope. Belash, his bloody knife in hand, ran across to the fallen man, wrenching off the helm and preparing for the killing thrust.

'Dead!' he called back.

'Nicely done,' said Waylander.

'What in Hell's name were they?' asked Angel.

'The Brotherhood,' Waylander told him. 'They have hunted me before. Sorceror knights.'

Belash strolled back to where the others stood. He glanced at Miriel. 'One damn fine archer,' he said. 'For a *kol-isha*,' he added, after a pause. 'I'll fetch the horses.' Sheathing his knife he strolled away to the south.

Miriel dropped the crossbow and rubbed her eyes. All around her she could hear the buzzing of angry insects, but she could see nothing. She tried to concentrate on the sounds, separating them.

'. . . *do that . . . witch . . . powers . . . Brotherhood . . . Kai . . . pain . . . escape . . . Durmast . . . Danyal . . .*' And she realised she was hearing the fragmented thoughts of the men around her. Belash thought her possessed, Waylander was reliving his last battle with the Brotherhood when the giant Durmast had died to save him. Senta was staring at her, his passion aroused.

She felt Angel move behind her, and a wave of emotion swept over her, warm and protective, strong, enduring. His hand touched her shoulder.

'Do not concern yourself. I am not injured,' she said. She felt his confusion, and turned towards him. 'You remember my Talent, Angel?'

'Yes.'

'It is back!'

'You have very powerful enemies,' said Senta, as Waylander retrieved his bolts from the two dead knights.

'I'm still alive,' Waylander pointed out, moving past him and into the cabin, where he slumped down in the wide leather chair. His head was pounding and he rubbed at his eyes. There was no relief. Miriel joined him.

'Let me help you,' she said softly. Her hand touched his neck. Instantly all pain flowed away from him. He sighed, his dark eyes looking up to meet her gaze.

'You saved us. You destroyed their spell.'

'It broke their concentration when I killed the leader,' she said. Miriel knelt before him, her hands resting on his knees. 'Why did you lie to me?' she asked him.

'What lie?' he replied, averting his eyes.

'You said we were going north to escape the assassins.'

'And we are.'

'No. You are seeking Bodalen. Hewla told you where to find him.'

'What else do you know?' he asked wearily.

'Too much,' she answered.

He sighed. 'You found your Talent. I thought it was gone forever.'

'It was given back to me by the man who stole it. You remember when Mother died and you began to drink strong wine? And how you woke up one morning and there were bloodstains in the clearing, and a shallow grave with two corpses? You thought you'd killed them while drunk. You couldn't remember. You asked Krylla and me about them. We said we didn't know. And we didn't. It was your friend, Dardalion. The men were coming to capture us, perhaps to kill us, because we had the Talent. Dardalion stopped them – killed them with your crossbow.'

'He swore never to kill again,' whispered Waylander.

'He had no choice. You were drunk and unconscious, and the weapon carried so much death and violence that it swamped him.' Waylander hung his head, wishing to hear no more, but unwilling to stop her. 'He closed off our Talent. And he took away the memories of the demons and the man who tried to capture our souls. He did it to protect us.'

'But now you remember it all?'

'Yes.'

'I did my best, Miriel . . . Do not read my thoughts . . . my life.'

'It is too late.'

He nodded and stood. 'Then do not hold me in too great a contempt.'

'Oh, Father!' Stepping forward she embraced him. 'How could I hold you in contempt? I love you. I always have.'

Relief washed over him, and he closed his eyes as he held her. 'I wanted you to be happy – like Krylla. I wanted a good life for you.'

'I have had a good life. And I have been happy,' she told him. She drew back from him and smiled, lifting her hand to stroke his cheek. 'The packs are ready, and we should move.' She closed her eyes. 'Belash has found the horses and will be here soon.'

Taking hold of her shoulders he drew her in to him once more. 'You could head south with Angel,' he said. 'I have money in Drenan.'

She shook her head. 'You need me.'

'I do not want to see you . . . hurt.'

'Everyone dies, Father,' she said. 'But this is no longer just a private war between you and Karnak. I wonder if it ever was.'

'What is it, then?'

'I don't know yet, but Karnak did not send the Brotherhood. When I killed the last man he had an image in his mind. He was thinking of a tall man, with black hair, greased to his skull. Slanted eyes, long robes of dark purple. He it was who sent them. And he is the same man who tried to hurt Krylla and me; the man who summoned the demons.'

'From where did the Dark Knights come?'

'Dros Delnoch, and before that Gulgothir.'

'Then that is where the answers lie,' he said.

'Yes,' she agreed, sadly.

Angel watched the Nadir leading the five horses across the clearing. Disgusting little savage, he thought! Everything about Belash sickened him, the slanted, soulless eyes, the cruel mouth, the man's barbaric method of killing. It made Angel's skin crawl. He glanced north at the distant mountains. Beyond these the Nadir bred like lice, living their short, violent lives engaged in one bloody war after another. There had never been a Nadir poet, nor an artist nor a sculptor. And never would be! What a vile people, thought Angel.

'Uses that knife well,' observed Senta.

'Bastard Nadir,' grunted Angel.

'I thought your first wife was part-Nadir?'

'She was not!' snapped Angel. 'She was . . . Chiatze. They're different. The Nadir are not human. Devils, all of them.'

'Canny fighters, though.'

'Talk about something else!' demanded Angel.

Senta chuckled. 'How did you know they were coming? You walked away and fetched your sword from the cabin.'

Angel frowned, then smiled, his mood clearing. 'I smelt horse dung – the breeze was blowing from the south. I thought they might be more assassins. I wish they had been. Shemak's balls, but I was frightened when that spell fell upon me. I'm still not over it. To just stand, unable to move, while a swordsman approached me . . .' He shuddered. 'It was like my worst nightmare.'

'Not something I'd like to repeat,' agreed Senta. 'Waylander said they were the Brotherhood. I thought they were wiped out in the Vagrian Wars.'

Angel's pale eyes scanned the bodies. 'Well, they obviously weren't.'

'What do you know of them?'

'Precious little. There are legends of a sorceror who founded the order, but I can't remember his name, nor where they began. Ventria, I think. Or was it further east? They were called the Blood Knights at one time, because of the sacrifices. Or was it the Crimson Knights?'

'Forget it, Angel. I think "precious little" covered it.'

'I never was much of a history student.'

Belash approached them. 'They are the Knights of Blood,' he said. 'The first of their temples was built in Chiatze three hundred years ago, founded by a wizard named Zhi Zhen. They became very powerful and tried to overthrow the Emperor. Zhi Zhen was captured after many battles and impaled on a golden spike. But the Order did not die out. It spread west. The Vagrian General Kaem used Brotherhood priests at the Siege of Purdol. Now they have reformed in Gothir, under a wizard named Zhu Chao.'

'You are well-informed,' said Senta.

'One of them killed my father.'

'Well, they can't be all bad,' said Angel.

Belash stood for a moment, his flat features expressionless, his dark eyes locked to Angel's face. Then he nodded slowly and walked away.

'That shouldn't have been said,' chided Senta.

'I don't like him.'

'That's no excuse for bad manners, Angel. Insult the living, not the dead.'

'I speak my mind,' muttered Angel, but he knew Senta was right, and the insult left a bad taste in his mouth.

'Why do you hate them so?'

'I witnessed a massacre. Sixty miles north of the Delnoch Pass. My father and I were travelling from Namib. We were in the hills, and we saw the Nadir attack a convoy of wagons. I'll never forget it. The torture went on long into the night. We slipped away, but the screams followed us. They follow me still.'

'I lived in Gulgothir for a while,' said Senta. 'I have relatives there, and we used to ride to the hunt. One day, high summer it was, the hunting party spotted three Nadir boys, walking beside a stream. The huntmaster shouted something and the riders broke into a gallop, spearing two of the boys as they stood there. The third ran. He was chased and cut a score of times, not enough to bring him down, but enough to keep him running. Finally he fell to the ground, exhausted and, I would guess, dying. The huntsmen, Gothir nobles all, leapt from their horses and hacked him to pieces. Then they cut off his ears for trophies.'

'There is a point to this tale?' enquired Angel.

'Savagery breeds savagery,' said Senta.

'That's today's sermon, is it?'

'By Heaven but you are in a foul mood, Angel. I think I'll leave you to enjoy it alone.'

Angel remained silent as Senta moved back into the cabin.

Soon they would be heading north. Into Nadir country. Angel's mouth felt dry and the flames of fear grew in his belly.

9

Ekodas loved the forest, the majestic trees living in quiet brotherhood, the plants and flowers cloaking the earth, and the serenity born of eternal life. When the world was young, the earth still warm, the first trees had grown here, living, breathing. And their descendants were still here, endlessly watching the small, fleeting lives of men.

The young priest, his white robes now stained with mud, moved alongside a huge oak, reaching out to lay his hand upon the rough bark. He closed his eyes. The tree had no heart to hear, yet there was still the pulsing beat of life within the trunk, the slow flowing of sap through the capillaries, the stretching of growth in new wood.

Ekodas was at peace here.

He walked on, his mind open to the sounds of the forest, the late birdsong, the skittering of small animals in the undergrowth. He sensed the heartbeat of a fox close by, and smelt the musky fur of an old badger. He stopped. And smiled. The fox and the badger were sharing a burrow.

An owl hooted. Ekodas glanced up. The light was fading, the sun dipping into the western sea.

He turned and began the long climb towards the temple. The debate came back to him then and he sighed, regretting the weakness which had driven him to betray his principles. Deep down he knew that Dardalion himself was now unsure of the path on which they stood. The Abbot had *almost* wanted to be free of the destiny he had planned for so long. Almost.

Yet if love had won the day then everything Dardalion had striven for would have seemed as nothing. A tragic waste of life and Talent. I could not do that to you, Dardalion, thought Ekodas. I could not make a mockery of your life.

The young priest drew in a deep breath, seeking to feel once more the calm of the forest. Instead there came a sharp, jagged stab in his mind. Anger. Fear. Arousal. Lust. Focusing his Talent, he scanned the trees. And sensed two men . . . and . . . yes, a woman.

Pushing his way through the bushes at the side of the track, he traversed the hill until he came to a deer-trail leading down into a deep gulley. He heard the sound of a man's voice.

'Be sensible, woman. We're not going to hurt you. We'll even pay!'

Another voice cut in, harsh and deep. 'Enough talk! Take the bitch!'

Ekodas rounded the final bend and saw the two men, foresters by their garb, standing with knives drawn and facing a young Nadir woman. She also held a knife and was waiting, poised, her back to a rock-face.

'Good evening, friends,' said Ekodas. The first of the men, tall and slim, wearing a green tunic of homespun wool and brown leather leggings and boots, swung towards him. He was a young man, with sandy hair tied in a pony-tail.

'This is no place for a priest,' he said.

Ekodas walked on, halting immediately before the man. 'The forest is a wonderful place for meditation, brother.' He sensed the man's confusion. There was little that was evil in him, but his lusts were aroused and they had clouded his reason. He wanted the woman, and his mind was seething with erotic thoughts and images.

The second man pushed forward. He was shorter and stockier, his eyes small and round. 'Go back where you came from!' he ordered. 'I'll not be turned aside by the likes of you!'

'What you are planning is evil,' said Ekodas softly. 'I cannot permit it. If you continue along this gulley you will find the road to Estri. It is a small village and there is, I understand, a woman there who has a special smile for men with coin.'

'I know where Estri is,' hissed the second man. 'And when I want your pigging advice I'll ask for it. You know what this is?' The knife-blade came up, hovering before Ekodas' face.

'I know what it is, brother. What is your purpose in showing it to me?'

'Are you a halfwit?'

The first man took hold of his friend's arm. 'Leave it, Caan. It doesn't matter.'

'Matters to me. I want that woman.'

'You can't kill a priest!'

'Pigging watch me!' The knife swept up. Ekodas swayed aside, caught the man's wrist and twisted the arm up and back. His foot snaked out, hooking behind the knifeman's knee. The forester fell back. Ekodas released his grip and the man tumbled to the earth.

'I have no wish to cause you pain,' said Ekodas. The man scrambled up and charged. Ekodas brushed aside the knife-arm and sent his elbow crashing into the man's chin. He dropped as if poleaxed. Ekodas turned to the first man. 'Take your friend to Estri,' he advised. 'And once there bid him goodbye. He brings out the worst in you.' Stepping past the man he approached the Nadir woman. 'Greetings, sister. If you will follow me I can take you to lodgings for the night. It is a temple, and the beds are hard, but you will sleep soundly and without fear.'

'I sleep without fear wherever I am,' she said. 'But I will follow you.'

Her eyes were dark and beautiful, her skin both pale and yet touched with gold. Her lips were full, the mouth wide and Ekodas found himself remembering the images in the forester's mind. He reddened and began the long climb.

'You fight well,' she said, drawing alongside him, her knife now sheathed in a goatskin scabbard, a small pack slung across her shoulders.

'Have you travelled far, sister?'

'I am not your sister,' she pointed out.

'All women are my sisters. All men my brothers. I am a Source priest.'

'Your brother down there has a broken jaw.'

'I regret that.'

'I don't. I would have killed him.'

'My name is Ekodas,' he said, offering his hand. She ignored it and walked on ahead.

'I am Shia.' They reached the winding path to the temple and she gazed up at the high stone walls. 'This is a fortress,' she said.

'It was once. Now it is a place of prayer.'

338

'It is still a fortress.'

The gates were open and Ekodas led her inside. Vishna and several of the other priests were drawing water from the well. Shia stopped and stared at them. 'You have no women for this work?' she asked Ekodas.

'There are no women here. I told you, we are priests.'

'And priests have no women?'

'Exactly so.'

'Only sisters?'

'Yes.'

'Your little tribe won't last long,' she said, with a deep throaty chuckle.

The screams died down and a hoarse, choking death-rattle came from the slave. His arms relaxed, sagging into the chains and his legs spasmed. Zhu Chao slashed the knife into the ribcage, sawing through the arteries of the heart and ripping the organ clear. He carried it to the centre of the circle, stepping carefully over the chalk lines that marked the stones, zig-zagging between the candles and the wires of gold that linked the chalice and the crystal. Laying the heart in the chalice he drew back, placing his feet within the twin circles of Shemak.

The Fourth Grimoire lay open on a bronze lectern and he turned the page and began to read aloud in a language lost to the world of men for a hundred millennia.

The air around him crackled, and fire ran along the wires of gold, circling the chalice in rings of flame. The heart bubbled, dark smoke oozing from it, billowing up to form a shape. Massive rounded shoulders appeared, and a huge head with a cavernous mouth. Eyes flickered open, yellow and slitted. Long arms, bulging with muscle, sprouted from the shoulders.

Zhu Chao began to tremble, and felt his courage waning. The creature of smoke threw back its head and a sibilant hissing filled the room.

'What do you want of me?' it said.

'A death,' answered Zhu Chao.

'Kesa Khan?'

'Exactly so.'

A sound issued from the creature of smoke – slow, volcanic hissing that Zhu Chao took to be laughter. 'He wants your death also,' said the demon.

'Can he pay in blood and pain?' countered Zhu Chao, aware that sweat was trickling down his face and that his hands were trembling.

'He has served my master well.'

'As have I.'

339

'Indeed. But I will not grant your request.'

'Why?'

'Look to the lines of your life, Zhu Chao.'

The smoke dispersed, as if a clean wind had swept through the room. The chalice was empty, the heart vanished without trace. Zhu Chao turned to where, moments before, the body of the young slave had hung in chains. It too was gone.

The sorceror stumbled from the circle, uncaring now about the lines of chalk which his sandalled feet smeared and scattered. Taking up the Third Grimoire he carried it to a leather-topped desk and searched through the pages. The spell he needed was a small one, needing no blood. He spoke the words then traced a pattern in the air. Where his finger passed a shining line appeared, a spider's web forming. At last satisfied he pointed to various intersections. Small spheres sprang into being at each spot, some blue, others green, one gold, two black. Zhu Chao drew in a deep breath, focusing his concentration. The web began to shift and move, the spheres spinning, circling the golden globe at the centre. The sorceror took up a quill pen, dipping it into a small well of ink. He found a large sheet of papyrus and began to write, occasionally glancing up at the swirling pattern in the air.

After an hour he had filled the page with symbols. Tired, he rubbed his eyes and stretched his back. The swirling web disappeared. Taking the sheet he walked back to the chalice, said the Six Words of Power and dropped the papyrus into the golden bowl.

It burst into flames, which reared up forming a burning sphere, a great globe which rose from the chalice, hanging in the air before his face. The sphere stretched and flattened, the flames dying down, and Zhu Chao saw a man dressed in black moving along the high walls of his palace. In the man's hand was a small crossbow.

The scene flickered and changed. There was an ancient fortress, with high twisted walls and tilted turrets. An army was gathered there, scaling-ladders and ropes at the ready. Upon the wall, on the highest turret, stood Kesa Khan. Beside him was a woman, also dressed in black.

The vision shimmered and Zhu Chao saw a dragon high in the sky, circling above the fortress. But then it turned and flew straight towards Gulgothir, passing over the quiet homes and flying like an arrow towards Zhu Chao's own palace. Its shadow swept over the land, like a black demon, flowing over the palace walls and into the courtyard. There the shadow froze on the flagstones, blacker than night, rising up and becoming a man.

The same man, carrying the crossbow.

Faint now, the image swirled once more and Zhu Chao found himself gazing at a cabin in the mountains. The man was there again – as were the bodies of the nine knights. The sorceror was shocked. How

340

had Waylander overcome his knights? He knew no spells. Fear flickered in Zhu Chao's heart. The dragon in the dream had flown to his palace, promising death and despair.

Not mine, thought Zhu Chao, fighting down the beginnings of panic. No, not mine.

His weariness was forgotten as he moved up the winding stair to the upper rooms. Bodalen was there, lounging on a couch, his booted feet upon a silver-topped table.

'What is there that you have not told me about Waylander?' demanded the sorceror.

Bodalen rolled to his feet. He was a tall man, wide-shouldered, lantern-jawed, his eyes blue beneath thick brows, his mouth large and full-lipped. He was the image of the younger Karnak and his voice had the same resonant power. 'Nothing, my lord. He is an assassin – that is all.'

'The assassin has slain nine of my knights. You understand? Men of great power.'

Bodalen licked his lips. 'I can't explain it, my lord. My father talked of him often. He said nothing about magic.'

Zhu Chao fell silent. What reason would Waylander have for coming to his palace, save to kill Bodalen? If Karnak's son were no longer here . . . He smiled at the young Drenai. 'He will not thwart us,' he said. 'Now there is something you can do for me, my boy.'

'Gladly, my lord.'

'I want you to ride into the Mountains of the Moon. I will give you a map to follow. There is a fortress of great antiquity there, a curious place. There are many tunnels below it, and chambers filled with gold and jewels, so it is said. Take ten men, and plentiful supplies, and move into the fortress. Find a hiding place in the underground caverns. Within the next few weeks Kesa Khan will journey there. When he does, you can emerge and kill him.'

'There will be many Nadir warriors with him,' objected the younger man.

Zhu Chao smiled thinly. 'Life offers many dangers, Bodalen, and a brave man can overcome them all. It would please me if you agreed to undertake this small quest.'

'You know I would give my life for the cause, my lord. It is just . . .'

'Yes, yes,' snapped Zhu Chao, 'I understand. You were born with the looks of your father and none of his courage. Well, know this, Bodalen: at his side you were of great use to me. Here, as a runaway, you are valueless. Do not make the mistake of displeasing me.'

Bodalen paled. 'Of course not, my lord. I . . . I would be happy to . . . a map, you say?'

'You shall have a map, and ten trustworthy men. Very trustworthy.

341

And if you do this successfully, Bodalen, you will be rewarded beyond your desires. You will become King over all the Drenai.'

Bodalen nodded and smiled. 'I will serve you well, my lord. And you are wrong: I do not lack courage. I will prove it to you.'

'Of course, my boy. Forgive me, I spoke in anger. Now go and prepare for the journey.'

Ekodas led Shia through the dining-hall and up through the second and third levels to where Dardalion sat in his study. The young priest tapped at the door.

'Enter,' called the Abbot. Ekodas opened the door, ushering the young Nadir woman into the room.

Dardalion rose and bowed. 'Welcome, my dear. I am sorry that your visit to Drenai lands should have had so unsettling a beginning.'

'Did I say it was unsettling?' countered Shia, walking forward and scanning the study, her mocking gaze drifting over the burdened shelves and open cupboards stacked with scrolls, parchments and books.

'Do you read?' asked Dardalion.

She shook her head. 'What would be the purpose?'

'To understand our own needs and desires we must first understand the needs and desires of our ancestors.'

'I do not see that as true,' she answered. 'The desires of our ancestors were obvious – that is why we are here. And those desires do not change, which is why we have children.'

'You think that history can teach us nothing?' asked Ekodas.

'History can,' she admitted, 'but these are not history, they are merely writings. Are you the leader here?' she asked, turning to Dardalion.

'I am the Abbot. The priests you have seen are my disciples.'

'He fights well,' she said, smiling and pointing at Ekodas. 'He should not be here among prayer-men.'

'You use the term as an insult,' accused Ekodas, blushing.

'If you feel insulted by it, then that is what it must be,' she told him.

Dardalion chuckled and moved around his desk. 'You are welcome here, Shia, daughter of Nosta Vren. And in the morning we will direct you to your brother, Belash.'

Her dark eyes sparkled and she laughed. 'Your powers do not surprise me, Silver-hair. I knew you were a mystic.'

'How?' enquired Ekodas.

Dardalion moved alongside the bewildered priest, laying a hand on the younger man's arm. 'How else would I know about the . . . unsettling, did I say? . . . attack,' Dardalion told him. 'You have a keen mind, Shia. And you are a brave woman.'

She shrugged. 'I do not need you to tell me what I am. But it pleases me to hear the compliment. I would like to sleep now. The fighting prayer-man offered me a bed.'

'Ekodas, take our guest to the western wing. I have had a fire prepared in the south-facing dormitory.' Swinging back to Shia he bowed again. 'May your dreams be pleasant, young lady.'

'They will or they won't,' she answered, her eyes still faintly mocking. 'Is your man allowed to sleep with me?'

'I fear not,' Dardalion told her. 'We are celibate here.'

She shook her head in disbelief. 'Why do men play such games?' she asked. 'Lack of good lovemaking causes diseases of the belly and back. And bad headaches.'

'But set against that,' said Dardalion, barely suppressing a smile, 'is that it frees the spiritual mind to heights rarely found in more earthly pleasures.'

'Do you know that for certain, or is it only in writings?' she countered.

'It is only in writings,' he agreed. 'But faith is an integral part of our life here. Sleep well.'

Ekodas, his face burning, led the Nadir woman along the western corridor, his discomfiture increased by the sound of the Abbot's laughter echoing behind them.

The room was small, but a bright fire was burning in the hearth and fresh blankets had been laid on the narrow bed.

'I hope you will be comfortable here,' he said stiffly. 'I will wake you in the morning with a little breakfast – bread and cheese and the juice of summer apples.'

'Do you dream, prayer-man?'

'Yes. Often.'

'Dream of me,' she said.

10

They were camped in a sheltered hollow within a wood, and a small fire flickered in a circle of stones. Senta, Angel and Belash were sleeping, Waylander taking the third watch. He was sitting on the hilltop, his back to a tree, his black clothing merging him into the night shadows. Beside him lay the hound, which he had named Scar.

Miriel lay wrapped in her cloak, her back to the fire, her shoulders warm, her feet cold. Autumn was fading fast, and the smell of snow was in the air. She could not sleep. The ride from the cabin had been made in near silence, but Miriel had linked into the thoughts of the riders. Belash was thinking of home and vengeance, and whenever his thoughts turned to Waylander he pictured a bright knife. Angel was confused. He did not want to travel north, yet he did not want to leave them. His thoughts of Miriel were equally contrasting. He was fond of her, by turns paternal and yet aroused by her. Senta suffered no confusion. His thoughts were filled with erotic images which both stimulated and frightened the young mountain girl.

Waylander she left alone, fearing the new-found darkness within him.

Sitting up, she added several sticks to the fire, then shifted her position so that her legs and feet could bathe in the warmth of the small blaze. A voice whispered into her mind, so faint she thought at first she had imagined it. It came again, but she could make no sense of the words. Concentrating her Talent she focused all her power on the whispers. Still nothing. It was galling. Lying down she closed her eyes, her spirit drifting up from her body. Now the whisper was clearer, but still seeming to come from an impossible distance.

'Who are you?' she called.

'Trust me!'

'No.'

'Many lives depend on your trust. Women, children, old ones.'

'Show yourself!' she commanded.

'I cannot – the distance is too great, my power stretched.'

'Then what would you have me do?'

'Return to the flesh and awake Belash. Tell him to hold his left hand over the fire and cut his palm. Let the blood fall into the flames. Tell him Kesa Khan commands this.'

'And then what?'

'And then I will come to you and we will talk.'

'Whose lives depend on this?' she asked. Immediately she sensed his agitation.

'I can talk no more. Do this swiftly or the link will be broken. I am nearing exhaustion.'

Miriel returned to her body and rose, moving to Belash. As she neared the Nadir warrior he rolled to his feet knife in hand, his eyes wary. She told him the message she had received from Kesa Khan and expected him to question her, or express his doubts. But the Nadir instantly moved to the fire, slicing his knife-blade across his open palm. Blood spilled instantly from the wound, splashing into the flames.

The voice of Kesa Khan boomed inside her mind, causing her to reel back. 'Now you may come to me,' he said.

'Can I trust this Kesa Khan?' she asked Belash.

'Does he say that you can?' he answered.

'Yes.'

'Then obey him,' advised the Nadir. Miriel did not rely on the words, but read the images beyond them. Belash feared Kesa Khan, but there was no doubt that he also admired him, and would trust him with his life.

Miriel lay back and let her spirit drift clear. Instantly she was swept into a bewildering maze of light and colour. Her senses reeled and she lost control of her flight, spinning wildly through a thousand bright rainbows and into a darkness deeper than death. But before fear could turn to panic the darkness lifted, and she found herself sitting by a lakeside village. There were houses here, rough-crafted but secure against the winter wind and snow. Children were playing at the water's edge, and she recognised herself and Krylla. Sitting beside them on an upturned boat was a man, tall and slim, with wide staring eyes and tightly curled hair.

Miriel's heart leapt, and for the first time in twelve years she remembered her real father's face. This was the winter just before the Vagrians had invaded, just before her parents and all her friends had been butchered. It was a peaceful time, full of quiet joy.

'Are you comfortable with this illusion?' asked the wizened old man sitting beside her.

'Yes,' she told him. 'Very.' She turned her attention to him. He was no more than four and a half feet tall, bird-boned ribs pressing against the taut skin of his chest. His head was too large for his body and his wispy hair hung lank to his shoulders. His two front teeth were missing and his words were sibilant as a result. He was wearing ragged leggings and knee-length moccasins tied with strips of black leather.

'I am Kesa Khan.'

'That means nothing to me.'

'It will,' he assured her. 'We share the same enemy. Zhu Chao.' He almost spat the name.

'I do not know this man.'

'He sent the Dark Knights to kill your father, just as he sends the Gothir army to wipe out my people. And you do know him, Miriel. Look.' The scene flickered, the village disappearing. Now they sat on a high wall overlooking a flower garden. A man sat there, his robes dark, his hair waxed to his head, his sideburns braided and hanging to his chin. Miriel tensed. This was the scaled hunter who had tried to capture her and Krylla five years ago, before the silver knight rescued them. But here he had no scales. He was merely a man sitting in a garden.

'Do not be misled,' warned Kesa Khan. 'You are gazing upon evil.'

'Why does he seek to kill my . . . father?' She hesitated as she spoke, the image of her real father strong in her mind.

345

'Bodalen serves him. He thought it would be a simple matter to hunt down Waylander and slay him. Then he could have returned Bodalen to the Drenai, awaiting the moment the son betrayed the father.' The old man chuckled, the sound dry and unpleasant. 'He should have known Waylander as I knew him. Ha! I tried to hunt him down once. I sent six great merged beasts to destroy him, and twenty hunters of rare skill. None survived. He has a gift for death.'

'You are my father's enemy?'

'Not now!' he assured her. 'Now I wish him for a friend.'

'Why?'

'Because my people are in peril. You can have no conception of what it is to live under the Gothir yoke. We have no rights under their laws. We can be hunted down like vermin. No one will raise a hand to object – that is bad enough. But now Zhu Chao has convinced the Emperor that my tribe – the oldest of the Tent-people – needs to be eradicated. Exterminated! Soon the soldiers will march against us.'

'How can my father help you? He is only one man.'

'He is the Dragon Shadow, the hope of my people. And he has with him the White Tiger in the Night and old Hard-to-kill. Also there is Senta. And, more importantly perhaps, there is you.'

'That is still only five. We are not an army.'

'We shall see. Ask Waylander to come to the Mountains of the Moon. Ask him to help us.'

'Why should he? You are a man who tried to kill him.'

'Tell him we are outnumbered ten to one. Tell him we are doomed. Tell him we have more than two hundred children who will be slaughtered.'

'You don't understand . . . these are not his children. You are asking him to risk his life for people he does not know. Why would he even consider it?'

'I cannot answer that, Miriel. Just tell him what I have said.'

The colours swirled once more and Miriel felt a sickening lurch as her spirit was united with her body. Waylander was beside her, and the sun was high in the sky.

Waylander felt a surge of relief as Miriel opened her eyes. He stroked her hair. 'What happened?' he asked.

Taking hold of his arm she eased herself into a sitting position. Her head was throbbing with dull pain, her mouth dry. 'A little water,' she croaked. Pulling free the cork, Angel passed her a leather-bound canteen and she drank greedily. 'We need to speak,' she told Waylander. 'Alone.'

Angel, Belash and Senta withdrew and she recounted her meeting with Kesa Khan. Waylander listened in silence until she had finished.

'You believed him?'

'Yes. He did not tell me all he knew, but what he said was true. Or at least he believed it to be true. His people face annihilation.'

'What did he mean by calling me the Dragon Shadow?'

'I don't know. Will you go?'

He smiled. 'You think I should?'

She looked away. 'When we were young Krylla and I used to love the stories that Mother . . . Danyal . . . told. You know, of heroes crossing seas of fire to rescue princesses.' She smiled. 'We felt like princesses because you had rescued us. You were the man who helped save the Drenai. We loved you for that.'

'It wasn't for the Drenai,' he said. 'It was for me.'

'I know that now,' she told him. 'And I don't want to sway you. I know you would die for me, as you would have risked all for Mother or Krylla. And I know why you are heading north. You want vengeance.'

'I am what I am, Miriel.'

'You were always better than you knew,' she said, reaching up and stroking his lean face. 'And whatever choice you make I will not condemn you.'

He nodded. 'Where do you wish to go?'

'With you,' she answered simply.

'Tell me what he said again.' She repeated the words of Kesa Khan. 'A cunning old man,' said Waylander.

'I agree. But what makes you say so?'

'The children. He wanted me to know about the children. He knows me too well. By heaven I hate sorcerors!' Waylander took a long, deep breath. And saw again the flowers in bloom around the dead face of his son. How old would he have been now? A little older than Senta, perhaps?

He thought of Bodalen. And Karnak.

Senta, Belash and Angel were standing by the tethered horses. Summoning them to him he asked Miriel to tell the story for a third time.

'He must think we are insane,' said Angel, as Miriel concluded her tale.

'No,' said Senta softly, 'he knows us better than that.'

'What's that supposed to mean?'

'Oh come on, Angel, don't you just love the thought of impossible odds?' asked Senta, grinning.

'No, I don't. I leave that sort of idiocy for young men like you. Talk sense to him, Dakeyras.'

'You are free to ride where you please,' said Waylander. 'There is nothing holding you here.'

'But you are not going to go to the Mountains?'

'Indeed I am,' said Waylander.

'How will you stop the killing? Will you ride out on a tall horse and face the Gothir army? Tell them you're Waylander the Slayer and you're not going to allow them to butcher a few Nadir?'

'As I said, you are free to go where you will,' repeated Waylander.

'What about Miriel?' asked Angel.

'She can speak for herself,' said Miriel. 'And I shall ride to the Mountains of the Moon.'

'Just tell me why,' pleaded Angel. 'Why are you all doing this?'

Waylander was silent for a moment. Then he shrugged. 'I don't like massacres,' he said.

Vishna's voice was calm, but Dardalion could sense the tension in the priest as he spoke. 'I do not see how we can be sure that the woman is sent by the Source. We have all agreed to risk our lives in the battle against evil. I have no qualms concerning that decision. To stand upon the walls of Purdol against the Ventrians would help Karnak maintain the defence of the Drenai, as would offering our assistance to the General at Delnoch. But to ride into the steppes and risk our lives for a small Nadir tribe . . . ?' He shook his head. 'What purpose would it serve, Father?'

Dardalion did not answer, but turned to the others, the blond Magnic, the slender Palista and the silent, reserved Ekodas. 'What is your view, brother?' he asked Magnic.

'I agree with Vishna. What do the Nadir offer the world? Nothing. They have no culture, no philosophy, save that of war. To die for them would be meaningless.' The young priest shrugged. 'But I will follow your orders, Father Abbot.'

Dardalion nodded towards Palista. 'And you, my boy?'

'It is a difficult question,' answered Palista, his voice deep, incongruously so, issuing as it did from his small slender frame. 'It seems to me the answer depends on how we view the arrival of the woman. If the Source directed her to us then our way is clear. If not . . .' He spread his hands.

Ekodas spoke. 'I agree with Palista. The woman's arrival is the central issue. For, although I respect Vishna and Magnic, I believe the argument they use is flawed. Who granted us the right to judge the worth or otherwise of the Nadir? If our actions should save a single life, only the Source can know what that life is worth. The saved one could be a future Nadir prophet, or his son may become one, or his grandson. How can we know? But is the woman directed by the Source? She has asked us for nothing. Surely that is the key?'

'I see,' said Dardalion. 'You believe that she should have received wisdom in a dream perhaps, and approached us directly for help?'

'There are many examples of such happenings,' said Ekodas.

348

'If such was the case here, where would faith begin?' countered the Abbot.

'I do not understand, Father.'

'My dear Ekodas, we are talking about faith. Where is the need for faith, if we have proof?'

'Surely another flawed argument,' put in Palista. 'By this token anyone who came and said they were sent by the Source would have to be disbelieved.'

Dardalion laughed aloud. 'Excellent, my dear Palista! But this moves us from one extreme to another. What I am saying is that there must always be an element of faith. Not proof, but faith. If she had come and claimed to be Source-directed we would have read her thoughts and known the truth. Then there would have been no faith. We would have acted thereafter in sure knowledge. Instead, we have prayed for a sign. Where should the Thirty ride? And what was our answer? Ekodas rescued a Nadir woman. Why is she here? To find her brother and bring him home to help face a terrible enemy. Who is that enemy? None other than Zhu Chao, the man whose evil led me to gather the Thirty together. Do these facts not speak to you? Can you not feel the threads of destiny drawing together?'

'This is difficult for me,' said Vishna, with a sigh. 'I am the only Gothir present among the Thirty. My family and friends are high in the council of the Emperor. It is likely that old friends will be riding against these same Nadir. It does not make me feel comfortable to know that I may have to draw a sword against these men.'

'I understand that,' said Dardalion. 'But it is my belief that Shia is sent to us, and that the Mountains of the Moon beckon. What else can I say?'

'I think we all need more prayer – and more guidance,' observed Ekodas. The others nodded in agreement.

'Faith is essential,' added Vishna. 'But there must be another sign.'

'It is unlikely to come with letters of fire in the sky,' said Dardalion softly.

'Even so,' put in Ekodas, 'if it is our destiny to die in Nadir lands then the Source will lead us there.'

Dardalion looked to each of the young men before him, then he rose. 'Very well, my brothers, we will wait. And we will pray.'

Ekodas slept fitfully, Shia's words haunting him like a curse. And he did dream of her, and woke often, his body tense with suppressed passion. He tried prayer, and when that failed he repeated the longest, most complex meditation mantras. For a while his concentration held. Then he would picture her ivory skin, tinged with gold, her dark almond-shaped eyes . . .

He rose silently from his bed in the hour before dawn, moving with care so as not to awaken the five brothers who shared the small dormitory. Taking a clean white robe from the chest beneath his bed he dressed swiftly and made his way down to the kitchens.

Fat Merlon was already there, removing the rough linen from several large rounds of cheese. In the far corner Glendrin was supervising the baking, and the smell of fresh bread filled the room.

'You are awake early,' said Merlon, as Ekodas entered.

'I couldn't sleep,' he admitted.

'I would dearly love another hour, brother,' said Merlon expectantly.

'Of course,' Ekodas told him. 'I will take your duty.'

'I will say ten blessings for you, Ekodas,' beamed Merlon, embracing the smaller man and patting his back. Merlon was a large man, balding already at twenty-six, and his strength was prodigious. The other priests gently mocked him for his vast appetite, but in truth there was little fat upon him, save for his belly, and Ekodas felt himself being crushed by the man.

'Enough, Merlon!' he gasped.

'I'll see you at breakfast,' yawned Merlon, ambling away towards the sleeping area.

Glendrin glanced back. 'Fetch me the tray and pole, Ekodas,' he called, flicking the latch on the oven doors. The two-pronged pole was hanging upon hooks on the far wall. Ekodas lifted it clear, attached the prongs to a ridged metal plate and passed the implement to Glendrin. Using a cloth to protect his hands Glendrin opened wide the oven doors then pushed the pole inside, the plate sliding under three golden crusted loaves. These he withdrew and Ekodas, slipping on gloves of white wool, removed the bread, placing it on the long kitchen table. There were twelve loaves in all and the smell made Ekodas feel as if he had not eaten for a week.

'Merlon churned the butter,' said Glendrin, sitting down at the table. 'But I'll wager he ate half of it.'

'You have flour in your beard,' Ekodas pointed out. 'It makes you look older than time.'

Glendrin grinned and rubbed his hand across the red trident beard. 'You think the woman was sent?' he asked.

Ekodas shrugged. 'If she was she came to haunt me,' he answered.

Glendrin chuckled. 'You'll need those ten blessings Merlon promised you,' he said, wagging a finger at his friend. 'Carnal thoughts are a sin!'

'How do you deal with them?' asked Ekodas.

Glendrin's smile faded. 'I don't,' he admitted. 'Now let us get on.'

Together they prepared the cheese, drew fresh water from the well, and carried the food through to the dining-hall, setting out the plates and cutlery, jugs and goblets.

350

Then Ekodas prepared a tray of bread and cheese for Shia, feeling his excitement rise at the prospect of seeing her once more. 'I cannot find the apple juice,' he told Glendrin.

'We finished it yesterday.'

'But I promised her some.'

Glendrin shook his head. 'Then I would imagine she will despise you for the rest of your life,' said the red-headed priest.

'Fool!' replied Ekodas, placing a jug of water and a clay goblet upon the tray.

'Do not be too long with her,' advised Glendrin. Ekodas did not reply.

Leaving the heat of the kitchen he climbed the cold stone stairwell and made his way to Shia's room. Balancing the tray on his left arm he opened the door. The Nadir woman was asleep on the floor before the dead fire, her head resting on her elbow, her legs drawn up, her body bathed in the last of the moonlight.

'Good morning,' said Ekodas. She gave a low groan, stretched, then sat. Her hair was unbraided now, hanging dark and lustrous to her shoulders. 'I have some breakfast for you.'

'Did you dream of me?' she asked, her voice husky from sleep.

'There is no apple juice,' he told her. 'But the water is fresh and cold.'

'Then you did, prayer-man. Were they good dreams?'

'You should not speak this way to a priest,' he admonished her.

She laughed at him, and his face reddened. 'You *kol-isha* are a strange people.' Rising smoothly she walked to the bed, sitting cross-legged upon it. Taking the loaf she tore off a chunk and tasted it. 'Needs salt,' she said. He poured her a goblet of water and passed it to her. Her hand reached out, her fingers stroking his skin. 'Soft hands,' she whispered. 'Soft skin. Like a child.' Then she took the goblet and sipped the water.

'Why did you come here?' he asked.

'You brought me,' she told him, dipping her finger into the bowl of butter and licking it.

'Were you sent?'

'Yes. By my shaman, Kesa Khan. To fetch my brother home. But you know this.'

'Yes, but I just wondered . . .'

'Wondered what?'

'Ah, it does not matter. Enjoy your breakfast. The Abbot will see you before you leave. He will tell you where to find Belash.'

'There is still time, prayer-man,' she whispered, reaching out and taking his hand. He snatched it back.

'Please do not speak like this,' he pleaded. 'I find you . . . very unsettling.'

'You desire me.' It was a statement, accompanied by a smile.

Ekodas closed his eyes for a moment, struggling to compose his thoughts. 'Yes. But that in itself is not a sin, I believe.'

'Sin?'

'A wrong action . . . like a crime.'

'Like stealing the pony of your brother?' she enquired.

'Yes, exactly. That would be a sin. Indeed any theft, or lie, or malicious action is a sin.'

She nodded slowly. 'Why then is lovemaking a sin? Where is the theft? The lie? Or the malice?'

'It does not have to be just these actions,' he said, his voice close to a stammer. 'It is also the breaking of rules, or oaths. Each of us here made a promise to the Source. It would be breaking that promise.'

'Did your god ask you to make this promise?'

'No, but . . .'

'Then who did?'

He spread his hands. 'It is a part of our tradition. You understand? Rules made by holy men many centuries ago.'

'Ah, it is in the writings, then.'

'Exactly so.'

'We have no writings,' she said brightly. 'So we live and laugh, we make love and we fight. No diseases of the belly, no head pains, no bad dreams. Our god speaks to us from the land, not in writings.'

'It is the same god,' he assured her.

She shook her head. 'No, prayer-man, I don't think so. Our god is strong.'

'Will he save your people from the Gothir?' snapped Ekodas, before he could stop himself. 'I'm sorry! It was a thoughtless question. Please forgive me.'

'There is nothing to forgive, for you do not understand, Ekodas. Our god *is* the land, and the land makes us strong. We will fight. And we will either conquer or die. It does not matter to the land whether we win or lose, for alive or dead we are at one with it. The Nadir *are* the land.'

'Can you win?' he asked softly.

'Will you be sorry when I am dead?' she countered.

'Yes,' he told her, without hesitation.

Smoothly she rolled to her feet and moved in close to him, her arm circling his neck. Her lips brushed his cheek. 'Foolish Ekodas,' she whispered. Then she released him.

'Why am I foolish?' he asked.

'Take me to the Abbot. I wish to leave now.'

Waylander reined in the black gelding and dismounted, walking the last few paces to the crest of the hill where he bellied down and studied the line of mountains stretching from west to east across the great Sentran Plain. The hound Scar padded up the hill, stretching out alongside him.

There were three routes to the north, but which one should they take? North-east lay the Delnoch Pass, with its new six-walled fortress. That was the direct road to Gulgothir and the Mountains of the Moon, but would the commanding officer have been warned to watch for Waylander?

He sighed and swung his gaze to the north and the high lonely passes inhabited by Sathuli tribesmen, long-time enemies of the Drenai. No wagons passed through their lands, no convoys, no travellers. Ferocious fighters, the Sathuli lived their lives in isolation from the civilisations of both Gothir and Drenai.

Lastly there was Dros Purdol, the harbour fortress, far to the east. But beyond that was the great desert of Namib. Waylander had crossed it before. Twice. He had no wish to see it again.

No. He would have to risk Delnoch.

Just as he was about to push back from the skyline he caught a glint of light to the east. Remaining where he was he waited, eyes focused on the distant tree line. A column of riders appeared, lances held to the vertical, sunlight gleaming from the polished iron helms and weapons. There were some thirty lancers, moving slowly, conserving the strength of their mounts.

Waylander eased back from the crest then rose and walked to where the others waited. Scar followed, keeping close to Waylander's side. 'We'll wait here for an hour,' he said, 'then we'll make for Delnoch.'

'You see anything?' asked Angel.

'Lancers. They are riding for the fortress.'

'You think they might be looking for us?' put in Senta.

Waylander shrugged. 'Who knows? Karnak is anxious to see me dead. By now my description could be with every army unit within fifty miles.'

Miriel rose and strolled to the hilltop, crouching behind a screen of gorse to gaze down on the lancers. For some minutes she remained motionless, then returned to the group. 'The officer is Dun Egan,' she told Waylander. 'He is tired and hungry, and thinking about a woman he knows in a tavern by Wall Two. And yes, he has your description. Twenty of his men are behind us, to the south-west. They have orders to apprehend you.'

'What now?' asked Angel.

Waylander's expression was grim. 'Across the mountains,' he said at last.

'The Sathuli are fine fighters, and they don't like strangers,' Senta pointed out.

353

'I've been through before. To kill me they have to catch me.'

'You intend going alone?' asked Miriel softly.

'It is best,' he replied. 'You and the others make for Delnoch. I will find you beyond the mountains.'

'No. We should be together. My Talents can keep us safe.'

'There's truth in that,' Angel observed.

'Perhaps there is,' agreed Waylander, 'but against that, five riders raise more dust than one. Five horses make more noise than one. The high passes exaggerate every sound. A falling stone can sometimes be heard half a mile away. No. I go alone.' Miriel started to speak, but he touched a finger to her lips. 'No more argument, Miriel,' he said with a smile. 'I have hunted alone for more than half my life. I am at my strongest alone. Go to Delnoch, and once through the fortress head due north. I will find you.'

'I will be with you,' she whispered, leaning in close and kissing his cheek.

'Always,' he agreed.

Moving to his mount, Waylander swung into the saddle and touched heels to the gelding's side. The hound loped alongside as the black-garbed rider crested the hill. The lancers were tiny dots in the distance now and Waylander gave them not a moment of thought as he angled towards the rearing Delnoch peaks.

Alone.

His spirits soared. Much as he loved Miriel he felt a great release, a sense of freedom from the burdens of company. Glancing down at the hound he chuckled. 'Not entirely alone, eh Scar?' The dog cocked its head to one side and ran on, sniffing at the ground, seeking rabbit spoor. Waylander drew in a deep breath. The air was fresh and cold, blowing down from the snow-topped peaks. The Sathuli would be building their winter stores now, their thoughts far from raiding and war. With skill, and a little luck, he should be able to ride the high passes and the echo-haunted canyons without their knowledge.

A little luck? He thought of the route ahead – the narrow, ice-covered trails, the treacherous slopes, the frozen streams, the realms of the wolf, the bear and the mountain lion.

Fear touched him – and he laughed aloud. For with the onset of fear he felt the pounding of his heart, the rushing of blood in vein and muscle, the strength in his arms and torso. Right or wrong he knew this was what he had been born for, the lonely ride into danger, enemies all around. For what was fear if not the wine of life, and the taste of it thrilled him anew.

I have been dead these last five years, he realised. A walking corpse, though I did not know it. He thought of Danyal, and found himself remembering the joys of their life, without the sharp, jagged bitterness at her passing. The mountains loomed, grey and threatening.

And the man rode on.

Miriel sat silently in the garden of the tavern staring down over the colossal walls of Dros Delnoch. The journey to the fortress had passed without incident, save for the bickering between Angel and Belash. At first Miriel found it hard to understand the hatred festering within the gladiator, then she used her Talent. She shivered at the memory, and switched her line of thought. Her father would now be travelling through the lands of the Sathuli. A fiercely independent people, they had crossed the sea from the deserts of Ventria three hundred years before, settling in the Delnoch mountains. She knew little of their history, save that they believed in the words of an ancient prophet, and were persecuted for their beliefs in their home country. They were a solitary race, hardy and ferocious in battle, and permanently at war with the Drenai.

She sighed. Waylander would not cross their lands without a fight, she knew, and she prayed he would come through safely.

Behind the three tavern buildings, the ancient keep reared between the narrows of the Delnoch Pass. Impressive and strong, the keep was dwarfed by the new fortress which now filled the valley. Miriel scanned the immense structure, with its crenellated battlements of reinforced granite, its massive gate-towers and turrets.

'They call it Egel's Folly,' said Angel, moving alongside her and handing her a goblet of watered wine. Senta and Belash followed him from the tavern and sat on the grass with Miriel. 'Each of the walls is more than sixty feet high, and the barracks can accommodate thirty thousand men. Some of them have never been used. Never will be.'

'I have never seen anything like it,' she whispered. 'The sentries on the first wall seem as small as insects from here.'

'A magnificent waste of money,' said Senta. 'Twenty thousand labourers, a thousand stone-masons, fifty architects, hundreds of carpenters. And all built for a dream.'

'A dream?' inquired Miriel.

Senta chuckled and turned to Belash. 'Yes. Egel said he saw a vision of Belash and a few of his brothers – a veritable ocean of warriors gathering against the Drenai. Hence this monstrosity.'

'It was built to keep out the Nadir?' asked Miriel, disbelieving.

'Indeed it was, Miriel,' said Senta. 'Six walls and a keep. The largest fortress in the world, to thwart the smallest enemy. For not one Nadir tribe numbers more than a thousand warriors.'

'But there are more than a thousand tribes,' pointed out Belash. 'The Uniter will bring them all together. One people. One king.'

'Such are the dreams of all poor peoples,' said Senta. 'The Nadir

355

will never unite. They hate each other as much – if not more – than they hate us. They are always at war. And they take no prisoners.'

'That's not true,' hissed Angel. 'They do take prisoners – and then they torture them to death. Men, women and children. They are the most despicable race.'

'No true Nadir would torture children,' said Belash, his dark eyes angry. 'They are killed swiftly.'

'I know what I saw!' snapped Angel. 'And do not think to call me a liar!'

Belash's hand moved to his knife. Angel's fingers curled around the hilt of his sword. Miriel stepped between them. 'We will not fight amongst ourselves,' she said, laying her hand on Angel's arm. 'There is evil in all races, but only a foolish man condemns an entire people.'

'You did not see what I saw!' he told her.

'But I have seen it,' she said softly. 'The overturned wagons, the looting and the deaths. And I can see your father with his arm around you, holding his cloak before your eyes. It was an evil day, Angel, but you must let it go. The memory is poisoning you.'

'Stay out of my head!' he roared suddenly, pulling back from her and striding towards the tavern.

'He carries demons in his soul,' said Belash.

'We all carry them,' added Senta.

Miriel sighed. 'He was only nine years old when he saw the attack, and the screams have been with him ever since. But he no longer sees the truth – perhaps he never did. His father's cloak blocked the most savage of the sights, and he does not remember that there were others in the attack who were not Nadir. They wore dark cloaks, and their weapons were of blackened steel.'

'Knights of Blood,' said Belash.

Miriel nodded. 'I believe so.'

Belash rose. 'I shall stroll and look at this fortress. I wish to see these walls my people inspired.'

He wandered away and Senta moved alongside Miriel. 'It is nice to be alone,' he said.

'You are picturing me on a bed covered with sheets of satin. It does not please me.'

He grinned. 'It is not courteous to read a man's thoughts.'

'It does not concern you that I know what you are thinking?'

'Not at all. There is nothing to shame me. You are a beautiful woman. No man could sit with you for long without thinking of satin sheets, or soft grass, or summer hay.'

'There is more to life than rutting!' she told him, aware that she was blushing.

'How would you know, beauty? You have no experience of such things.'

'I'll never marry you.'

'You cut me to the quick, beauty. How can you make that judgement? You don't know me yet.'

'I know enough.'

'Nonsense. Take my hand for a moment.' Reaching out he gently clasped her wrist, his fingers sliding down over hers. 'Never mind my thoughts. Feel my touch. Is it not gentle? Is it not pleasing?'

She snatched back her hand. 'No, it is not!'

'Ah ha! Now you lie, beauty. I may not have your Talents, but I know what you felt. And it was far from unpleasant.'

'Your arrogance is as colossal as these walls,' she raged.

'Yes, it is,' he agreed. 'And with good reason. I am a very talented fellow.'

'You are conceited and see no further than your own desires. So tell me, Senta, what is it that you offer me? And please, no boasts about the bed-chamber.'

'You say my name so beautifully.'

'Answer my question, damn you. And do remember that I shall know if you are lying.'

He smiled at her. 'You are for me,' he said softly, 'as I am for you. What would I offer you? Everything I have, beauty,' he whispered, his eyes holding to hers. 'And everything I will ever have.'

For a moment she was silent. 'I know that you believe the words as you say them,' she said. 'But I do not believe you have the strength to live by them.'

'That may be true,' he admitted.

'And you were prepared to kill Angel and my father. You think I can forgive that?'

'I hope so,' he told her. And in that moment she saw within his thoughts a flickering image, a remembrance that he was struggling to keep hidden. It shocked her.

'You weren't planning to kill Angel! You were ready to die.'

His smile faded and he shrugged. 'You asked me to spare him, beauty. I thought perhaps you loved him.'

'You didn't even know me – you don't know me now. How could you be prepared to lay down your life in that way?'

'Do not be too impressed. I like the old man. And I would have tried to disarm him, wound him maybe.'

'He would have killed you.'

'Would you have been sorry?'

'No – not then.'

'But you would be now?'

'I don't know . . . yes. But not because I love you. You have had many women – and you have told them all that you loved them. Would you have died for them?'

'Perhaps. I have always been a romantic. But with you it is different. I know that.'

'I do not believe love can strike that swiftly,' she said.

'Love is a strange beast, Miriel. Sometimes it leaps from hiding and strikes like a sudden spear. At other times it can creep up on you, slowly, skilfully.'

'Like an assassin?'

'Indeed so,' he agreed with a bright smile.

11

Jahunda notched an arrow to his bowstring and waited for the rider to emerge from the trees. His fingers were cold, but his blood ran hot with the hunt. The Drenai had chosen his route with care, avoiding the wide, much-used paths, and holding to the narrow deer-trails. But even so Jahunda had spotted him, for the Lord Sathuli had ordered him to watch the south from Chasica Peak, and no one could enter Sathuli lands from the Sentran Plain without being observed from Chasica. It was a great honour to be so trusted – especially for a fourteen-year-old with no blood kills to his name. But the Lord Sathuli knows I will be a great warrior and hunter, thought Jahunda. And he chose me for this task.

Jahunda had sent up a signal smoke then clambered down from the peak, making his way carefully to the first ambush site. But the Drenai had cut to the right, angling up into the high pass. Hooking his bow over his shoulder Jahunda ran to the second site, overlooking the deer-trail. The Drenai must emerge here. He chose his arrow with care, and hoped he could make the kill before the others arrived. Then the horse would be his by right, and a fine beast it looked. He closed his eyes and listened for the soft clopping of hooves in the snow. Sweat was seeping from under his white burnoose and fear made his mouth dry. The Drenai was no merchant. This one was a careful man who knew where he was riding and the danger he was in. That he travelled here at all spoke well of his bravery, and his confidence. Jahunda was anxious that the first shaft should strike a mortal blow.

There was no sound from the snow-shrouded trees and Jahunda risked a glance around the boulder.

Nothing.

But the man had to be close. There was no other route. Jahunda inched his way to the left and leaned out. Still nothing. Perhaps the rider had doubled back. Maybe he should have waited by the first site. Indecision rippled through him. The Drenai could be relieving himself against a tree, he told himself. Give it time! His heart was beating fast and he tried to calm himself. But the horse was magnificent! He could sell it and buy Shora a shawl of silk, and one of those bangles with the blue stones that Zaris sold at ridiculously high prices. Oh, how Shora would love him if he arrived at her father's house bearing such gifts. He would be an acclaimed warrior, a hunter, a defender of the land. It would hardly matter then that he could not yet grow a beard.

He heard the clop of hooves and swallowed hard. Wait! Be patient. He drew back on the string and glanced up at the sun. It would cast a shadow from high and to the right of the rider and from his hiding place behind the boulder Jahunda could time his attack perfectly. He licked his lips and watched for the shadow of the horse. As it drew alongside the boulder he stepped out, bow raised.

The saddle was empty. There was no rider.

Jahunda blinked. Something hard struck the back of his head and he fell to his knees, his bow falling from his fingers. 'I am dying!' he thought. And his last thoughts were of beautiful Shora.

He felt rough hands shaking him and slowly came to consciousness.

'What happened, boy?' asked Jitsan, the Lord Sathuli's chief scout.

He tried to explain, but one of the other hunters came up, tapping Jitsan's shoulder. 'The Drenai sent his horse forward then moved around behind the boy and clubbed him. He is heading for Senac Pass.'

'Can you walk?' Jitsan asked Jahunda.

'I think so.'

'Then go home, child.'

'I am ashamed,' said Jahunda, hanging his head.

'You are alive,' pointed out Jitsan, rising and moving off swiftly, the six hunters following him.

There would be no horse for the young Sathuli warrior now. No bangle. No shawl for Shora.

He sighed and gathered up his bow.

Waylander dismounted, leading the gelding up the steep slope. Scar padded alongside him, not liking the cold snow under his paws. 'There's worse to come,' said the man.

He had seen the signal smoke and watched, with grim amusement, the antics of the young Sathuli sentry. The boy could not have been more than fourteen. Callow and inexperienced, he had run too swiftly for the ambush site, leaving footprints easily seen leading to the boulder behind which he hid. There was a time Waylander would have killed him. 'You're getting soft,' he scolded himself. But he did not regret the action.

At the top of the slope he halted, shading his eyes from the snow glare and seeking out the route to Senac Pass. It was twelve years since he had come this way, and that had been summer-time, the slopes of the mountains green and verdant. The wind was biting through his jerkin and he untied his fur-lined cloak from behind his saddle and unrolled it, fastening it into place with a brooch of bronze and a leather thong.

He studied the trail behind him then walked on, leading the gelding. The trail was narrow, wending its way down a snow-covered slope of scree and on to a long, twisting ledge no more than four feet wide. To the right was the mountain, to the left a dizzying drop into the valley some four hundred feet below. In summer the journey across the ledge had been fraught enough but now, ice-covered and treacherous . . .

You must be insane, he told himself. He started to walk, but the gelding held back. The wind was whistling across the mountain face and the horse wanted no part of such a venture.

'Come on, boy!' urged Waylander, tugging on the reins. But the gelding would not move. Behind the horse Scar let out a deep, menacing growl. The gelding leapt forward, almost sending Waylander over the edge. He swayed on the brink, but his hold on the reins saved him and he pulled himself back to safety. The ledge wound on around the mountain face for almost a quarter of a mile until, just beyond a bend, it was split by a steep scree slope leading down into the valley.

Waylander took a deep breath, and was just about to step on to the scree, when Scar growled again. The horse lurched forward, pulling the reins from Waylander's hand. The beast hit the scree head-first, and tumbled down the slope. An arrow flashed past Waylander's head. Spinning, he drew two knives. Scar leapt to attack the first Sathuli to come into sight around the bend behind them. The hound's great jaws snapped at the archer's face. Dropping his bow the warrior threw himself back, cannoning into a second man, who fell from the ledge, his scream echoing away. Scar hurled himself upon the first man, fangs locking to the man's forearm.

Waylander moved closer to the rock-face as a third Sathuli edged into sight. The warrior raised his tulwar over the hound. Waylander's arm snapped forward, the black-bladed knife slicing between the man's ribs. With a grunt he dropped the tulwar and fell to his knees, before toppling to his face in the snow.

'Here, Scar!' shouted Waylander. For a moment only the dog continued to rip and tear at the first Sathuli, but when Waylander called again it released its grip and backed away. Unhooking the small crossbow from his belt Waylander loaded it and waited. The man with the injured arm was lying on the brink of the precipice, breathing hoarsely. The other warrior was dead.

360

'Who is leader here?' called Waylander, in halting Sathuli.

'Jitsan,' came the reply. 'And I speak your tongue better than you do mine.'

'Do you like to wager?'

'On what?'

'On how long your friend there lives if you do not come for him and bind his wounds.'

'Speak plainly, Drenai!'

'I am passing through. I am no danger to the Sathuli. Nor am I a soldier. Give me your word the hunt will cease and I will leave here now. You can rescue your friend. If not, I wait. We fight. He dies.'

'If you wait you die,' shouted Jitsan.

'Even so,' answered Waylander. The injured man groaned and tried to roll himself from the ledge to certain death on the rocks below. It was a brave move, and Waylander found himself admiring the warrior. Jitsan called out to him in Sathuli and the man ceased his struggle.

'Very well, Drenai, you have my word.' Jitsan stepped into sight, his sword sheathed.

Waylander flicked the bolts from the crossbow and loosed the strings. 'Let's go, dog,' he said, and leapt to the scree, sliding down the slope on his haunches. Scar followed him instantly, tumbling and rolling past his master.

But Waylander had misjudged the speed of the descent and he lost his grip on the crossbow as he struck a hidden rock which catapulted him into the air, spinning and cartwheeling. Relaxing his muscles he rolled himself into a ball and prayed he would not strike a tree or a boulder.

At last the dizzying fall slowed and he came to a stop in a deep drift of snow. His body was bruised and aching, and two of his knives had fallen from their sheaths. Curiously his sword was still in its scabbard. He sat up. His head was spinning, and he felt a rush of nausea. After it had passed he pushed himself to his knees. As well as the two knives, his crossbow quiver was empty, his leggings were torn and his right thigh was gashed and bleeding.

To his right lay the gelding, its neck broken in the fall. Waylander took a long, deep breath, his fingers probing at his bruised ribs. Nothing seemed broken. Scar padded over to him, licking his face. The stitches on the dog's side had opened and a thin trickle of blood was oozing from the wound.

'Well, we made it, boy,' said Waylander. Slowly and with great care he stood. Several of his crossbow bolts and one of his knives lay nearby, close to the dead gelding. Gathering the weapons he searched around the snow for his knife, but could not find it. Scar ran back up the slope and returned with the crossbow in his jaws.

361

A second search left Waylander with twelve bolts and one knife recovered. The gash in his leg was not deep, requiring no stitches, but he bound the wound with a bandage taken from his saddlebag and then sat on a jutting rock and shared some dried meat with the hound.

High above him he saw the signal smoke. Reaching down he stroked Scar's huge head. 'You just can't trust the Sathuli,' he said. The hound twisted its head and licked the man's hand.

Waylander stood and surveyed the valley. The snow was deep here, but the way to Senac Pass lay open.

Lifting the food sack from the dead horse he set off towards the north.

Slowly the six hundred black-cloaked warriors filed into the huge hall, forming twenty ranks before the dais on which stood Zhu Chao and his six captains. Red lanterns glowed with crimson light and shadows flickered across the great curving beams of the high ceiling.

All was silent. Zhu Chao spread wide his arms, his caped gown arching down from his shoulders like the wings of a demon. 'The day is here, comrades!' he shouted. 'Tomorrow the Ventrians attack Purdol and the pass at Skeln. Gothir troops will then march on the Sentran Plain. And five thousand soldiers will obliterate the Nadir wolves, bringing us the treasures of Kar-Barzac.

'Within the month all three great nations will be ruled by the Brotherhood. And we will have the power our strength and our faith deserves.

'The Days of Blood are here! The days when, for us, the only law will be to do as we will, wherever we choose.' A thunderous roar rose up from the ranks, but he quelled it with a swift wave of his hand. 'We are talking about power, comrades. The Elder Races did not understand the power they held. The oceans drank their cities, and their culture is all but lost to us.

'But there is one great centre of their might, named in all the *grimoires*. In the Mountains of the Moon lies the citadel of Kar-Barzac. The arcane strength of the Elders still flows there, and with it we will find not only the instruments to maintain our rule, but the secret of immortality. Win this war and we will live forever, our dreams made true, our lusts sated, our desires fulfilled.' This time he let the cheering mount, and stood arms folded, drinking in the adulation. Gradually the sound died away. Zhu Chao spoke again.

'To those who are chosen to ride against the Wolves I say this: kill them all, and their whores and their brats. Leave nothing alive. Burn their bodies and grind their bones to powder. Consign their dreams to the ashes of history!'

As the renewed cheering died down he strode from the dais, exiting the hall through a small side door. Followed by his captains

362

he made his way to a suite of rooms in the western wing of the palace. Here he stretched himself out on a couch and bade his officers sit around him.

'The plans are all set?' he asked the first of his officers, Innicas, a wide-shouldered albino in his mid-forties, with a forked white beard and a jagged scar across his brow. His long hair was braided and his pink eyes, unblinking, shone with a cold light.

'Yes, lord. Galen will see Karnak delivered to us. He has convinced him to meet with the Sathuli chieftain. He will be captured and delivered alive to Gulgothir. But tell me, lord, why do we need him? Why not just slit his throat and be done with it?'

Zhu Chao smiled. 'Men like Karnak are rare indeed. They have power, deep elemental strength. He will be a worthy gift to Shemak, as will the Emperor. Two lords beneath the sacrificial knife. When has our master known such a sacrifice? And I shall enjoy watching both men beg for their lives.'

'And the Source priests?' enquired a second officer, a slim man with thinning, shoulder-length grey hair.

'Dardalion and his comical troop?' Zhu Chao gave a dry laugh. 'Tonight, Casta. Use sixty men. Destroy their souls as they sleep.'

'I am concerned, lord,' said Innicas, 'about the man, Waylander. Was he not allied with Dardalion many years ago?'

'He is a killer. No more, no less. He has no understanding of the mystic arts.'

'He slew nine of our warriors,' pointed out Casta.

'He has a step-daughter, Miriel. It is she who has Talent. And with him were two arena warriors named Senta and Angel. Also there was the renegade Belash. The timing of the attack was unfortunate, but they will not survive a second assault – that I promise you.'

'I mean no disrespect, sir, but this Waylander does seem to show a spectacular talent for survival,' said Innicas. 'Do we know where he is?'

'At this moment he is being pursued through Sathuli lands. He is wounded, alone – save for a mangy hound – and has little food and no water. The hunters are closing in. We shall see how far his talent for survival can be stretched.'

'And the girl?' asked the grey-haired Casta.

'At Dros Delnoch. But she will join Kesa Khan. She will be at Kar-Barzac.'

'You want her taken alive?' asked Melchidak.

'It matters not to me,' answered Zhu Chao, 'but if she is then give her to the men. Let them amuse themselves. When they are done, sacrifice her to the master.'

'You spoke, lord, of the power of the Elders and immortality,' said Casta. 'What awaits us at Kar-Barzac?'

Zhu Chao smiled. 'One day at a time, Casta. When the Nadir wolves are dead I will show you the Crystal Chamber.'

Ekodas lay in his pallet bed listening to the sounds of the night, the flapping of bats' wings beyond the open window, the sibilant sighing of the winds of winter. It was cold, and the single blanket did little to retain body heat.

In the next bed Duris was snoring. Ekodas lay awake, ignoring the cold, his thoughts focused on the Nadir woman, Shia. He wondered where she was, and whether she had found her brother. He sighed and opened his eyes. Moonlight was casting deep shadows from the rafters of the rough-wrought ceiling and a winter moth was flitting between the beams.

Closing his eyes once more Ekodas sought the freedom of flight. As usual this proved difficult, but at last he soared free of his body and floated alongside the moth, gazing down on his sleeping comrades. The moon was shining in a cloudless sky as he flew from the temple, and the countryside was bathed in spectral light.

'Are you restless, brother?' asked Magnic, appearing alongside him.

'Yes,' he answered.

'As am I. But it is silent here, and we are free of the flesh.' It was true and Ekodas acknowledged it. The world was a different place when viewed through spirit eyes, tranquil and beautiful, eternal and almost sentient. 'You spoke well, Ekodas. You surprised me.'

'I surprised myself,' he admitted. 'Though, as I am sure you are aware, I am not totally convinced – even by my own arguments.'

'I think none of us are truly sure,' said Magnic softly, 'but there must be balance. Without it harmony cannot be found. I fear the Brotherhood, and I loathe and despise all they stand for. You know why?'

'Tell me.'

'Because I long for such pleasures myself. Deep in me I can see the attraction of evil, Ekodas. We are stronger than normal men. Our Talents could earn us fame, riches and all the pleasures known to man. And in my quiet moments I know that I lust for these things.'

'You are not responsible for your desires,' said Ekodas. 'They are primal, a part of being human. Only if we act upon them do we sin.'

'I know that, but it is why I could not take up the staff. I could never be a priest of love, never. At some time in the future I would succumb to my desires. This is why the Thirty is for me. I have no future, save with the Source. You are different, my friend. You are strong. Like Dardalion once was.'

'You thought me a coward,' pointed out Ekodas.

Magnic smiled. 'Yes, but I was seeing only my own lack of courage. Transferring it to you.' He sighed. 'Now that our way is set I see

364

everything differently. And now I must continue my watch.' Magnic vanished and Ekodas floated alone in the night sky. The temple below was grey and forbidding, its turrets rearing against the sky like upraised fists.

'It is still a fortress,' Shia had said. And so it was. Just like us, Ekodas realised. Prayer within, might without. There was comfort in the thought, for a fortress, no matter how many spears, swords and arrows were contained within it, could never be an offensive weapon.

He soared higher and to the north, through thin, misty clouds that were forming above the mountains. Below him now the mighty fortress of Dros Delnoch spanned the pass.

He floated down. On the last wall he saw a tall, dark-haired woman, sitting beside a handsome golden-haired man. The man reached out to take the woman's hand, but she drew back, turning her head to gaze up at Ekodas.

'Who are you?' she asked him, her spirit voice loud as thunder within him. Ekodas was astonished and suddenly disconcerted. Swiftly he flew high and away from the fortress. Such power! His mind reeled.

Just then a terrible scream filled his ears. Brief, agonising, and then terminated. He sped for the temple.

A man appeared alongside him, a blade of fire in his hand. Ekodas twisted in the air, the sword hissing by him. He reacted without conscious thought, the long years of his training and Dardalion's endlessly patient tuition, coming together in an instant to save his life. 'In spirit form,' Dardalion had told them, 'we are naked and unarmed. But I will teach you to craft armour from faith, swords from courage and shields made from belief. Then you will stand against the demons of the dark, and the men who aspire to be like them.'

Ekodas armoured himself with a shining breastplate of silver, a glimmering shield appearing on his left forearm. He parried the next blow with his own sword of silver light.

His opponent was protected by black armour and a full-faced helm. Ekodas blocked a thrust then sent his own blade cleaving into the man's neck. The sword of light flashed through the dark armour like sunlight piercing a storm cloud. There was no blood. No scream of pain. His assailant merely disappeared without a sound. But Ekodas knew that wherever the man's body lay the heart had stopped beating, and only a silent, unmarked corpse would lie witness to the battle beneath the stars.

Ekodas flew on to the temple. 'Dardalion!' he pulsed, using all his power. '*Dardalion!*'

Three opponents appeared around him. The first he slew with a slashing cut across the belly, the silver sword slicing through the dark armour with terrible ease. The second he killed with a riposte to the head. The third loomed behind him, blade raised.

Vishna appeared, lancing his sword through the man's back. More warriors appeared above the temple, and the Thirty gathered, silver against black, swords of light against blades of fire.

Ekodas fought on, his sword forming glittering arcs of white light as it clove into the enemy. Beside him Vishna battled with controlled fury. All around them the battle raged in an awful silence.

And then it was over.

Weary beyond anything he had ever experienced, Ekodas returned to his body and sat up. He reached over to Duris, but the man was dead. So too was Branic in the far bed.

Ekodas stumbled from the room, down to the hall. One by one the members of the Thirty gathered there. Twenty-three priests had survived the attack, and Ekodas looked from face to face, seeking out those to whom he was closest. Glendrin was alive. And Vishna. But Magnic was gone. It seemed only moments before he had been talking with the blond priest about life and desire. Now there was only a body to be buried, and they would never, in this world, speak again.

The full weight of sorrow descended upon Ekodas and he sank to the bench-seat, resting his elbows on the table. Vishna moved alongside him, placing a hand on his shoulder.

'Your warning saved us, Ekodas,' he said.

'My warning?'

'You woke Dardalion. He made the Gather.'

Before Ekodas could respond Dardalion spoke up from the far end of the hall. 'My brothers, it is time to pray for the souls of our departed friends.' One by one he named them and many tears were shed as he talked of them. 'They are with the Source now, and are blessed. But we remain. Some days ago we asked for another sign. I think that we have just seen it. The Brotherhood are preparing to ride against the Nadir. It is my belief that we should be in the Mountains of the Moon to receive them. But that is only my view. What is the view of the Thirty?'

Ekodas rose. 'The Mountains of the Moon,' he said.

Vishna echoed the words, as did Glendrin, Palista, fat Merlon and all the surviving priests.

'Tomorrow then,' said Dardalion. 'And now let us prepare the bodies of our friends for burial.'

12

Angel's head was pounding, and his anger flowed unabated as Miriel paid the fine to the master-at-arms.

'We don't like troublemakers here,' the man told Miriel. 'Only his reputation prevented him from receiving the flogging he deserves.'

'We are leaving Delnoch today,' she said, smiling sweetly as the man counted out the twenty silver coins.

'I mean, who does he think he is?' the soldier persisted.

'Why not ask me, you arrogant whoreson?' stormed Angel, his hands gripping the bars of the cell door.

'You see?' said the man, shaking his head.

'He is not usually quarrelsome,' replied Miriel, casting a warning glance at the former gladiator.

'I think he should have been flogged,' put in Senta, with a broad grin. 'What a mess. The tavern looks as though a tidal wave flowed through it. Disgraceful behaviour.'

Angel merely glared. The master-at-arms slowly rose and lifted a huge ring of keys from a hook by the door. 'He is to be taken straight from Delnoch. No stopping. Are your horses outside?'

'They are,' said Miriel.

'Good.' He unlocked the cell door and the glowering Angel stepped into the room. One eye was blackened and half-closed, and his lower lip was split.

'I'd say it was an improvement,' said Senta.

Angel pushed past him, striding out into the sunlight. Belash was waiting, his dark eyes inscrutable.

'Don't say a word!' warned Angel, snatching the reins of his mount from the tethering post and climbing into the saddle. Miriel and Senta emerged into the sunlight, the master-at-arms behind them.

'Straight out, no stopping,' repeated the soldier.

Miriel swung into the saddle and led the group down to the gate-tunnel below the fifth wall. Sentries examined the passes Miriel had obtained and waved them through, across the open ground to the next tunnel, and the next. At last they rode out into the pass itself.

Senta moved his horse alongside Angel's mount. 'How are you feeling?' he asked.

'Why don't you go . . .' He closed his mouth on the words as Miriel reined back, swinging her horse alongside.

'What happened, Angel?' she asked.

'Why don't you read my mind and find out?' he snapped.

'No,' she said. 'You and Senta are right – it *is* bad manners. I'll not do it again, I promise. So tell me how the fight started.'

'It was just a fight,' he answered with a shrug. 'Nothing to tell.'

Miriel turned to Belash. 'You were there?'

The Nadir nodded. 'A man asked old Hard-to-Kill what it is like to have a face that a cow has trampled on.'

'Yes? And then?'

'He said, "Like this!" Then he broke the man's nose.' Belash mimicked the blow, a straight left.

Senta's laughter pealed out, echoing in the pass. 'It is not something to laugh at,' insisted Miriel. 'One man with a broken nose and jaw, two others with broken arms. One even fractured his leg.'

'That was the man he threw out of the window,' said Belash. 'And it was not even open.'

'Why were you so angry?' Miriel asked Angel. 'Back at the cabin you were always so . . . so controlled.'

He relaxed and sat slumped in the saddle. 'That was then,' he told her, touching his heels to the gelding and riding ahead.

Senta glanced at Miriel. 'You don't see a great deal without your Talent, do you?' he observed, urging his horse into a canter and coming alongside Angel once more.

'What now?' asked the gladiator.

'You took out six men with your bare hands. That's impressive, Angel.'

'Is there a joke coming?'

'No. I'm sorry I missed the fight.'

'It wasn't much. A bunch of town-dwellers. Not a single muscle in sight.'

'I'm glad you decided to stay with us. I'd have missed your company.'

'I'd not miss yours, boy.'

'Oh yes, you would. Tell me, how long have you been in love with her?'

'What kind of a stupid question is that?' stormed Angel. 'I'm not in love. Shemak's balls, Senta, look at me! I'm almost as old as her father and my face would curdle milk. No, she'll be better off with a younger man. Even you, may my tongue turn black for saying it.'

Senta was about to speak when he saw a rider emerging from the rocks to the left. It was a young Nadir woman with jet-black hair, wearing a goatskin tunic and tan leggings. Belash galloped past them and leapt from the saddle. The woman dismounted and embraced him. Miriel, Senta and Angel sat their mounts quietly as the two Nadir conversed in their own tongue. Then Belash led the girl to the waiting trio.

'This is Shia, my sister. She was sent to find me,' he told them.

'It is good to meet you,' said Senta.

'Why? You do not know me.'

'It is a traditional greeting,' he explained.

'Ah. What is the traditional response?'

'That depends on the circumstances,' said Senta. 'And this is Miriel.' Shia glanced at the tall mountain woman, seeing the knives on the black baldric and the sabre at her side.

'What a strange people,' she said. 'Men who live like women and women who arm themselves like men. Truly it is beyond understanding.'

'And this is Angel.'

'Yes,' she said. 'Old Hard-to-Kill. It-is-good-to-meet-you.' Angel shook his head and grunted. Tugging his reins he moved off down the pass. 'Was the greeting incorrect?' Shia asked Senta.

'He's having a bad day,' observed the swordsman.

Bodalen tried to blame his trembling on the cold wind hissing down from the high passes of the Mountains of the Moon, but he knew better. Seven days from Gulgothir, and deep into Nadir territory his fear was almost uncontrollable. The eleven riders had skirted three small tent villages and encountered no hostile action, but Bodalen's mind was filled with images of torture and mutilation. He had heard many stories of the Nadir, and the thought that the tribesmen were close was unmanning him.

What am I doing here, he asked himself. Riding into a hostile land with scum like Gracus and his men. It's your fault, Father. Always pushing, cajoling, forcing! I'm not like you. I never was, nor would I wish to be! But you made me what I am.

He recalled the day Galen had first approached him, bringing with him the refined Lorassium leaf, and remembered with pleasure the taste of it upon his tongue, bitter and numbing. And with it the exquisite thrill that ran through his veins. All his fears vanished, all his dreams grew. Joy beyond reckoning flooded his senses. Oh, yes. The memories of the orgies that had followed aroused him even now, as his horse slowly trudged along the mountain trail. Passion, and the daring excitement of pain inflicted on willing – aye and unwilling – partners, the slender whips, the begging screams.

Then Galen had introduced him to the Lord Zhu Chao. And the promises began. When Karnak – that bloated, self-obsessed tyrant – was dead it would be Bodalen who would rule the Drenai. And he could fill his palace with concubines and slaves. A lifetime of pleasure, free from restraint. What price those promises now?

He shivered and swung to see the dark, hawk-like Gracus riding just behind him, the other riders following in a silent line. 'Almost there, Lord Bodalen,' said Gracus, unsmiling.

Bodalen nodded, but did not reply. He knew he lacked his father's physical courage, but he lacked nothing of his intelligence. Zhu Chao no longer saw him as a person of value. He was being used as an assassin.

Where had it all gone wrong? He licked his lips. That was easy to answer. When that damned girl had died.

Waylander's daughter.

What a cursed trick of fate!

His horse reached the crest of the trail and Bodalen gazed down on a green valley, with sparkling streams. It was some two miles across and perhaps four deep, and at the centre reared an ancient fortress with four turrets and a portcullis gate. Bodalen blinked and rubbed his eyes. The turrets were leaning and twisted, the walls uneven, as if the earth had reared up below the structure. And yet it still stood.

Gracus drew alongside. 'Kar-Barzac,' he said.

'It looks like something fashioned by a drunken man,' said Bodalen.

Gracus shrugged, unconcerned. 'We can shelter there,' he answered.

Slowly the eleven riders filed down into the valley. Bodalen could not take his eyes from the citadel. The windows, archers' slits, were not straight but crooked, each a different height, some canted, others stretched. 'It couldn't have been built like that, surely?' he asked Gracus. One of the towers leaned out at an impossible angle, and yet there were no cracks in the great stones. As they grew closer Bodalen remembered a visit to an armoury when he was a child. Karnak had showed him a great furnace. They had thrown an iron helm into the fire and the boy had watched as it slowly melted. Kar-Barzac was like that helm.

They rode across the valley and Gracus pointed at a nearby tree. The trunk was split and had curled around itself, forming a weird knot. And the leaves were sharp and long, five-pronged and red as blood. Bodalen had never seen a tree like it.

As they neared the citadel they saw the half-eaten carcass of a bighorn sheep. Gracus angled his mount to ride close to the body. Bodalen followed him. The sheep's eyes were gone, but the head remained, mouth wide open.

'By the blood of Missael!' whispered Bodalen. The sheep had short, pointed fangs.

'This valley is bewitched!' said one of the men.

'Be silent!' roared Gracus, dismounting. He knelt by the carcass. 'It looks as if it has been chewed by rats,' he said. 'The bite-marks are small.' He stood and swung into the saddle.

Bodalen felt his unease growing. Everything in this valley seemed unnatural. Sweat rolled down his back. He glanced at Gracus, noting the beads of perspiration on his brow. 'Is it just fear, or is it hotter here?' he asked the warrior.

'It's hotter,' answered Gracus. 'But that's often the way with mountain valleys.'

'Not this hot, surely?'

'Let's get to the castle,' said Gracus.

A horse screamed and reared, unseating the rider. Instantly a host of rat-like creatures swarmed from the long grass, leaping on the man, covering him in a blanket of grey striped fur. Blood spouted from a score of wounds. Gracus swore and kicked his horse into a gallop, Bodalen following him.

No one even looked back.

The ruined gates of the castle loomed before them and the ten remaining riders galloped into the courtyard beyond. This too was uneven, but showed no cracks, nor breaks in the marble. Bodalen swung down from the saddle and ran to a rampart stair, climbing swiftly to the crooked battlements. Out on the valley floor all was still, save for the writhing, grey fur mounds where once had been horse and man.

'We can't stay here!' said Bodalen, as Gracus joined him at the battlements.

'The master has ordered it. That is an end to the matter.'

'What were those things?'

'I don't know. Some kind of small cat, perhaps.'

'Cats don't hunt like that,' insisted Bodalen.

'Rats! Cats! What difference does it make? The master says to hide here and kill Kesa Khan. That we will do.'

'But what if there are creatures like that living below the castle? What then, Gracus?'

'We will die,' answered the warrior, with a grim smile. 'So let us hope there are none.'

Waylander lay flat, he and Scar part-covered by his cloak, reversed now so that the sheepskin lining merged with the snow around him. His right arm was stretched out over the dog and he stroked the broad head.

'Stay silent, boy,' he whispered. 'Our lives depend on it.'

No more than sixty paces back down the trail seven Sathuli warriors were examining tracks in the snow. The gash in Waylander's leg was healing fast, but the wound in his upper left arm nagged at him. They had almost surprised him two days before, laying an ambush in a narrow pass. Four Sathuli had died in the attack, a fifth left mortally wounded, his lifeblood gushing from a tear in the great artery at the groin. Scar had killed two, but had it not been for a sudden change in the direction of the wind which alerted the hound, Waylander would now be dead. As it was his arm ached, the wound constantly leaking blood. It was too far back for him to stitch the tear, and too close to the shoulder joint to bandage. A low rumbling growl began in Scar's throat, but he patted the dog, whispering soothing words.

The seven Sathuli were trying to make sense of the tracks leading up the hill. Waylander knew what they were thinking. The human footprints were leading north, but the tracks of the hound went both up and down the hill. The Sathuli were confused. At the top of the slope the trail narrowed, a huge boulder by the trees making an ideal hiding-place. Not one of the warriors wanted to walk that slope, fearing a hidden crossbowman. Waylander could not hear their arguments, but he saw two of them gesticulating, pointing to the east. Waylander had taken a chance, moving carefully up the slope, then retracing his steps, walking backwards, placing his feet in the tracks he had made during the climb. Then he had lifted Scar, hurling the yelping hound into a snow drift to the left of the trail. A long branch overhung the slope here and Waylander had leapt to grasp it, moving hand over hand until he dropped to the ground by the trunk. Then, the huge hound beside him, he had hunkered down to wait for the Sathuli.

He was cold and wet. Reversing the cloak made him almost invisible in the snow, but it also countered the heat-retaining qualities of the sheepskin and he began to shiver.

The Sathuli concluded their discussions. Three men moved up the slope, two heading to the right of the trail and two to the left.

Waylander winced as he pulled his crossbow into position, the wound in his arm seeping fresh blood. Silently he eased himself back, moving behind a snow-covered screen of bushes, then traversing the slope and climbing to where several fallen trees had created a latticed wall on the hillside. Scar padded behind him, tongue lolling from his massive jaws.

The two Sathuli came in sight. Both carried short hunting bows, arrows notched. Waylander laid his hand on Scar's shoulder, gently pushing him down. 'Quiet now!'

The white-robed warriors drew alongside the tree wall. Waylander rose, arm extended. The first bolt flew, punching through the leading warrior's temple. He dropped without a sound. The second swung, dropped his bow and drew his tulwar.

'Face me like a man, blade to blade!' he demanded.

'No,' replied Waylander. The second bolt slashed through the man's robe, cleaving into his heart. His mouth opened. The tulwar dropped from his hand. He took two tottering steps towards Waylander, then pitched to his face in the snow.

Retrieving his bolts Waylander stripped the white robes from the first corpse and the burnoose from the second. Within moments he

372

became a Sathuli warrior. Scar padded out and stood before him, head cocked to one side, nostrils quivering. 'It is still me,' said the man, kneeling down and extending his hand. Scar edged cautiously forward, sniffing at the outstretched fingers. Satisfied, the hound sat back on its haunches. Waylander patted its head.

'Time to move,' said the man. Reloading the crossbow he carefully traversed the slope.

By now the other hunters would have found where the tracks stopped, and they would be regrouping, rethinking their strategy. Then it would become apparent that two of their number were missing, and they would know Waylander was behind them. They would have two choices: wait for him to come to them, or continue the hunt.

Waylander had fought the Sathuli before, both as a soldier leading troops, and as a lone traveller. They were a patient people, yet also ruthless and courageous. But he did not think they would wait for him. Trusting in the advantage of numbers they would set out to find their missing companions and then follow his tracks. Therefore, since he could not disguise his trail, he would have to render it useless to them.

Reaching the top of the slope he moved silently into the snow-shrouded pine wood. There were few sounds here, the gentle sighing of the mountain breeze, the occasional groaning of a branch weighed down with snow. Drawing in a deep breath he let it out slowly then rose, moving back towards the east in a wide circle until he came to the high point of the slope above where he had earlier lain in wait for the two Sathuli. Kneeling behind a boulder he gazed down to where the bodies lay. The corpses were still there, but had been turned to their backs, arms folded across their chest, their tulwars in their hands.

'Wait here, Scar,' he told the dog and moved to the edge of the slope. The hound trotted after him. Twice more he tried to make the dog obey. At last he gave up. 'You need training, you ugly whoreson!'

Carefully Waylander made his way down to the tree wall until he came to the tracks he had made not an hour before. They were overlaid now by the footprints of the hunters. Waylander smiled. The tracks now formed a great ring, with no beginning and no end. Calling the hound to him he knelt and, with a groan, lifted Scar to his shoulder. 'You are a troublesome ally, boy!' he said. Hauling himself to the tree wall he inched his way back along it, clambering down by the base of the largest fallen tree, where the snow-covered roots clawed uselessly at the sky. Here, his tracks hidden by thick bushes, he climbed back to the crest of the slope and settled down to wait.

It was nearing dusk when the first of the trackers came into sight. Waylander hunkered down behind a boulder and waited until he heard the men slithering down the slope. At the bottom, by the bodies, they began to argue among themselves. He could not follow the debate, but at least one of the men used the Sathuli word for circle. They were angry and tired, and one sat down on the tree wall, flinging down his bow.

Waylander watched them dispassionately. Once more they had two choices: either continue to follow the circle towards the south, or retrace their steps back up the slope. If they moved south he would chance the open valleys to Gothir lands.

If north he would have to kill them.

They talked on for almost an hour. The light was beginning to fail. The warrior who had flung down his bow cleared away a section of snow and built a fire. The others hunkered down around it. Once the flames were high they added wet pine needles to the blaze, a thick, oily smoke rising to the darkening sky.

Waylander cursed and eased back from the crest. 'They're calling for more help,' he told the uncomprehending hound. 'But from where – north or south? Or both?' Scar cocked his head and licked at Waylander's hand. 'We'll have to run for it, boy, and take our chances.'

Rising, he moved silently towards the south, the hound beside him.

'It makes no sense,' said Asten, his voice trembling despite his attempts to remain calm.

Karnak chuckled and thumped the angry General on the shoulder. 'You worry too much, old lad. Look, the Gothir are ready to invade as soon as the Ventrians land. They are not going to risk attacking Delnoch – they've made a deal with the Sathuli Lord. Well, I can make deals too. And if we stop the Gothir then we can use all our forces against the Ventrians and crush them in a single battle.'

'That's all well and good, Karnak, but why does it have to be you that rides into Sathuli lands? It's madness!'

'Galen assures me we have safe conduct.'

'Pah!' sneered Asten. 'I wouldn't believe that walking snake if he told me the sun shines in the summer-time. Why can't you see it?'

'See what?' countered Karnak. 'See that you and he are not exactly bosom friends? It matters nothing. You are a fine leader of men, while his talent for duplicity and deceit is invaluable. I don't need my officers to like one another, Asten, but you carry your dislike to extremes that affect your judgement.'

Asten reddened, but took a deep breath before he replied. 'As you say, I am a good leader – no false modesty – but I am not, and never will be, a charismatic leader. I cannot raise morale to the heights you can. You are vital to us, and now you are planning to ride into Sathuli lands with a mere twenty men! They hate us, Karnak – you most of all. Before the Vagrian War you led two legions into their territory and crushed their army. Kashti's teeth, man, you killed the present lord's father!'

'Ancient history!' snapped Karnak. 'They are a warrior race. They understand the nature of battle.'

'The risk is too great,' said Asten wearily, knowing he had lost.

Karnak grinned. 'Risk? Gods, man, that's what I live for! To look into the eye of the beast, to feel its breath upon my face. What are we if we face no dangers? Frail flesh and bone to live and age and die. I'll ride into those mountains with my twenty men, I'll beard the Sathuli lord in his own den, *and* I'll win him over. The Gothir will not reach the Sentran Plain, and the Drenai will be secure. Isn't that a risk worth taking?'

'Aye,' stormed Asten. 'It's a risk I would willingly take. But then the Drenai can afford to lose old Asten, the farmer's son. There are many capable officers who could take *his* place. But who will take yours when the Sathuli betray you and nail your head to a palace post?'

Karnak was silent for a moment. 'If I do . . . die,' he said softly, 'you'll win for us, Asten. You're a survivor, old lad. The men know that.'

'Then know this, Karnak. If for any reason Galen comes back without you, I intend to cut his throat.'

Karnak chuckled. 'You do that,' he said, the smile fading. 'You do exactly that!'

13

Black and grey vultures, their bellies distended, hobbled on the plain. Some still squabbled over the carcasses that lay around the ruined tents. Crows had also gathered, and these darted in among the vultures, their sharp beaks pecking at unresisting flesh. Smoke spiralled lazily from the burning tents, creating a grey pall that hung over the scene of the massacre.

Angel guided his horse down on to the plain. The glutted vultures closest to the horsemen waddled away, the others ignoring the newcomers.

Belash and Shia rode alongside Angel. 'These were Green Monkey tribe,' said Belash. 'Not Wolves.' Vaulting from the saddle he moved among the bodies.

Angel did not dismount. To his left was a small circle of bodies, the men on the outside, women and children within. Obviously the last of the warriors had died defending their families. One woman had covered her baby's body with her own, but the broken lance that jutted from her back had thrust through the infant she shielded.

'Must be more than a hundred dead,' said Senta. Angel nodded. To his right the bodies of five infants lay where they had been thrown against a wagon, their heads crushed. Blood stained the rim of the wagon-wheel, and it was all too obvious how the babes had been killed.

Belash walked back to where Angel sat his mount. 'More than a thousand soldiers,' he said. 'Heading for the mountains.'

'Wanton slaughter,' whispered Angel.

'Yes,' agreed Belash. 'So they can't be all bad, eh?'

Angel felt a piercing stab of shame as he heard his own words repeated back to him, but he said nothing and tugged on the reins, galloping his horse back up the hillside to where Miriel waited.

Her face was the colour of wood-ash and she was gripping the pommel of her saddle, her knuckles bone-white. 'I can feel their pain,' she said. 'I can feel it, Angel. I can't close it out!'

'Then don't try,' he told her.

She let out a shuddering sigh, and huge tears formed, spilling to her cheeks. Dismounting, Angel lifted her from the saddle, holding her close as wracking sobs shuddered her frame. 'It is all in the land,' she said. 'All the memories. Soaked in blood. The land knows.'

He rubbed her back and stroked her hair. 'It's seen blood before, Miriel. And they can't be hurt any more.'

'What kind of men could do this?' she stormed, anger replacing her sorrow.

Angel had no answer. To kill a man in battle he understood, but to lift a baby by its heels and . . . he shuddered. It passed all understanding.

Belash, Shia and Senta rode up the hill. Miriel wiped her eyes and looked up at Belash. 'The soldiers are between us and the mountains,' she said. 'This is your land. What do you advise?'

'There are paths they will not know,' he told her. 'I will lead you – if you still wish to go on.'

'Why would I not?' she countered.

'There will be no time for tears, woman, where we shall ride. Only swords and true hearts.'

She smiled at him then, a cold smile, and mounted her horse. 'You lead, Belash. We will follow.'

'Why are you doing this?' asked Shia. 'We are not your people, and old Hard-to-Kill hates the Nadir. So tell me why.'

'Because Kesa Khan asked me,' said Miriel.

'I will accept that,' the girl said, after a moment. 'But what of you?' She turned her gaze to Angel and Senta.

Senta chuckled and drew his sword. 'This blade,' he said, 'was specially made for me by a master armourer. It was a gift, lovely. He came to me one day and presented it. No man has ever bested me with a sword. I'm rather proud of that. But, you know, I didn't ask the armourer about the quality of the steel, or the amount of care that went into its crafting. I just accepted the gift and thanked him for it. You understand?'

'No,' she answered. 'What has that to do with my question?'

'Like trying to teach mathematics to a fish,' said Senta, shaking his head.

Angel edged his horse forward and leaned close to Shia. 'Let's put it this way, lady. He and I are the finest swordsmen you'll ever see, but our reasons for being here are none of your damned business!'

Shia nodded solemnly. 'That is true,' she admitted, no trace of rancour in her voice.

Senta laughed aloud. 'You should have been a diplomat, Angel.' The gladiator merely grunted.

Belash led the way to the east and the distant mountains, Miriel riding behind with Shia, Angel alongside Senta bringing up the rear. Dark clouds loomed above the peaks and lightning flashed like a jagged spear from earth to sky. The sound of thunder followed almost instantly.

'The mountains are angry,' Belash told Miriel.

'So am I,' she replied. A howling easterly wind blew sheets of rain across the barren, featureless land, and soon the riders travelled hunched in their saddles, drenched through.

For several hours they rode, until at last the sheer walls of the Mountains of the Moon loomed above them. The rain died down and Belash rode on ahead, angling back towards the south, scanning the forbidding peaks and the open steppes to the north. They had seen no soldiers, but now, with the clouds clearing, the smoke of many campfires could be seen in the distance, drifting up to merge with the grey sky.

'This is the secret path,' said Belash, pointing to the mountain face.

'There's no way through,' said Angel, gazing up at the black, basaltic wall of rock. But Belash rode up a short scree slope – and vanished. Angel blinked. 'Shemak's balls!' he whispered.

Miriel urged her mount up the slope, the others following. Virtually invisible from the outside there was a wide crack in the face, some four feet wide, leading to a shining tunnel. Miriel rode in, Angel behind her. There was scarcely a finger's breadth of space between thigh and wall on both sides, and several times the riders had to lift their legs up on to the saddle in order for their mounts to squeeze through. The walls loomed around them and Angel felt his heartbeat quickening. Above

377

them huge boulders were clustered, having fallen and wedged together precariously.

Senta spoke. 'If a butterfly were to land on that mass it would all come tumbling down.' His voice echoed up into the crack. A low groan came from above them and black dust filtered down through the rocks.

'No speaking!' whispered Shia.

They rode on, emerging at last on a wide ledge overlooking a bowl-shaped crater. More than a hundred tents were pitched there. Belash touched heels to his horse and galloped down the slope.

'I think we're home,' said Senta.

From this high vantage point Angel could see the vastness of the steppes beyond the mountains, brown and arid, great folds across the land, rippling hills, humped-back ridges, as far as the eye could see. It was a hard, dry land and yet, as the sun dipped below the storm clouds, Angel saw in the steppes a relentless beauty that spoke to his warrior's heart. It was the beauty of a sword-blade, strong and unyielding. There were no fields or meadows, no silver streams. Even the hills were sharp and unwelcoming. And the voice of the land whispered to him.

Be strong or die, it said.

The mountains reared around him like a jagged black crown, the tents of the Nadir seeming fragile, almost insubstantial against the eternal power of the rocks on which they stood.

Angel shivered. Senta was right.

They were home.

Altharin was angry. He had been angry since the Emperor had given him this command. Where was the glory in wiping out vermin? Where was the advancement? Within days the main body of the army would be filing through Sathuli lands to invade the Drenai, sweeping across the Sentran Plain, meeting the Drenai sword to sword, lance to lance.

But no. Not for Altharin. He gazed up at the looming black peaks and wrapped his fur-lined cloak more tightly about his long, lean frame.

What a place!

Basaltic rocks, jagged and sharp. No horses could ride here – the lava beds cut their hooves to ribbons. And men on foot had to make long, lung-bursting climbs before reaching the enemy. He glanced to his left where the hospital tents had been erected. Eighty-seven dead so far, in five miserable days.

Turning he strolled back to his own tent, where an iron brazier glowed with hot coals. Loosening his cloak he cast it over a canvas-backed chair. His manservant, Becca, bowed low.

'Mulled wine, sir?'

'No. Send for Powis.' The man scurried from the tent.

Altharin had suspected this assignment would not be as easy as the Emperor believed. Surround and exterminate a few hundred Nadir, then rejoin the main army at the southern camp. Altharin shook his head. The first attack had gone well. The Green Monkeys had sat and watched as the Gothir lancers rode in, and only when the killing began did they recognise that death was upon them. But when the scouts reached the camp of the Wolves they found it deserted, the tracks leading off into these cursed mountains.

Altharin sighed. Tomorrow the Brotherhood would arrive, and his every move would be watched and reported back, his actions questioned, his strategies derided. I cannot win here, he thought.

The tent-flap opened and Powis ducked into the interior. 'You called for me, sir?'

Altharin nodded. 'You have gathered the reports?'

'Not quite all of them, sir,' answered the young man. 'Bernas is with the surgeons. He has a nasty wound to his face and shoulder. And Gallis is still on the peak, trying to force a path through from the north.'

'What have you learned from the others?'

'Well, sir, we have found only three routes through to the interior. All are defended by archers and swordsmen. The first is narrow and the men can move only two abreast. This makes them easy targets, not just for arrows, but rocks hurled from above. The second is some three hundred paces north. It is fairly wide, but the Nadir have moved rocks and boulders across it, making a rough, but effective wall. We lost fourteen men there this morning. The last route is the one Gallis is trying to force. He has three hundred men with him. I don't know yet what success he has enjoyed.'

'Numbers?' snapped Altharin.

'Twenty-one killed today, slightly more than forty wounded.'

'Enemy losses?'

'Difficult to say, sir.' The young man shrugged. 'Men tend to exaggerate such matters. They claim to have killed a hundred Nadir. I would guess the figure is less than half, perhaps a quarter of that.'

The manservant, Becca, ducked inside the tent and bowed. 'The Lord Gallis is returning, sir.'

'Send him to me,' ordered Altharin.

Moments later a tall, wide-shouldered man entered. He was around forty years of age, dark-eyed and black-bearded. His face was streaked with sweat and smeared with black, volcanic dust. His grey cloak was slashed and grime-covered, and there were several dents in his embossed iron breastplate.

'Make your report, Cousin,' said Altharin.

Gallis cleared his throat, removed his white plumed iron helm, and moved to the folding table on which sat a wine jug and several goblets of copper and silver. 'With your permission?' he croaked.

'Of course.'

The officer filled a goblet and drained it at a single swallow. 'The cursed dust is everywhere,' he said. He took a deep breath. 'We lost forty-four men. The pass is narrow at the base, flaring out above. We forced our way some two hundred paces towards their camp.' He rubbed at his eyes, smearing black ash across his brow. 'Resistance was strong, but I thought we would get through.' He shook his head. 'Then, at the narrowest point, the renegades struck.'

'Renegades?' queried Altharin.

'Aye, Cousin. Drenai or Gothir traitors. Two swordsmen, unbelievably skilful. Behind them, above and to the right, was a young woman with a bow. She was dressed in black. Every arrow found its mark. Between her and the swordsmen I lost fifteen men in that one place. And high above us, on both sides, the Nadir sent rocks and boulders down upon us. I ordered the men to pull back, to prepare for a second thrust. Then Jarvik lost his temper and ran at the swordsmen, challenging them. I tried to stop him.' Gallis shrugged.

'They killed him?'

'Yes, Cousin. But I wish they had shot him. As it was one of the swordsmen, the ugliest fellow I've ever seen, stepped out and accepted his challenge.'

'You're not telling me he defeated Jarvik in single combat?'

'That's exactly what I *am* saying, Cousin. Jarvik cut him, but the man was unstoppable.'

'I can't believe it!' said Powis, stepping forward. 'Jarvik won the Silver Sabre contest last spring.'

'Believe it, boy,' snapped Gallis. Turning to Altharin the officer shook his head once more. 'No one was in a mood to continue the attack after that. I left a hundred men to hold the position and brought the rest back.'

Altharin swore, then moved to a second folding table on which maps were spread. 'This is largely unexplored territory,' he said, 'but we do know there are few sources of food within the mountains – especially in winter. Normally we would starve them out, but that is not what the Emperor has ordered. Suggestions, gentlemen?'

Gallis shrugged. 'We have the numbers to eventually wear them down. We must just keep attacking on all three fronts. Eventually we must break through.'

'How many will we lose?' asked Altharin.

'Hundreds,' admitted Gallis.

'And how will that look back in Gulgothir? The Emperor sees this as a short, punitive raid. And we all know who arrives tomorrow.'

'Send the Brotherhood in when they get here,' said Gallis. 'Let's see how far their sorcery will carry them.'

'I have no control over the Brotherhood, more's the pity. What I do know, however, is that our reputations and our futures are in the balance here.'

'I agree with that, Cousin. I'll order the attacks to continue throughout the night.'

'Stop grumbling,' said Senta, as the curved needle once more pricked under the flesh of Angel's shoulder, bringing together the flaps of the wound.

'You are enjoying this, you bastard!' retorted Angel.

'How cruel!' Senta chuckled. 'But fancy letting a Gothir farmboy fool you with a riposte counter.'

'He was good, damn you!'

'He moved with all the grace of a sick cow. You should be ashamed of yourself, old man.' Senta completed the last of ten stitches, and bit off the twine. 'There. Better than new.'

Angel glanced down at the puckered wound. 'You should have been a seamstress,' he muttered.

'Just one of my many talents,' replied Senta, rising and moving out of the cave and staring down over the mountainside. From the cave mouth he could hear the distant screams of wounded men, the echoing clash of war. The stars were bright in a clear sky and a cold wind was hissing over the peaks and crags. 'We can't hold this place,' he said, as Angel moved alongside him.

'We're doing well enough so far.'

Senta nodded. 'There are too many of them, Angel. And the Nadir are relying on the wall across the centre pass. Once the soldiers breach that . . .' He spread his hands.

Two Nadir women made their way across the open ground bearing bowls of clotted cheese. They stopped before the Drenai warriors, eyes averted, and laid the bowls on the ground before them, departing as silently as they had come.

'Really welcome here, aren't we?' observed Senta.

Angel shrugged. There were more than a hundred tents dotted around the giant crater and from the high cave the two men could see Nadir children playing in the moonlight, running and sending up clouds of black, volcanic dust. To the left a line of women were moving into the deep caves carrying wooden buckets, gathering water from artesian wells deep below the mountains.

'Where tomorrow?' asked Angel, sitting down with his back to the rocks.

'The wall, I think,' said Senta. 'The other two passes are easily defended. They'll come at the wall.' A shadow moved to the right. Senta chuckled. 'He's back, Angel.'

The gladiator swore and glanced around. A small boy of around nine years of age was squatting on his haunches watching them. 'Go away!' roared Angel, but the child ignored him. 'I hate the way he just stares,' snapped Angel. The boy was thin, almost skeletal, his clothes threadbare. He wore an old goatskin tunic from which most of the hair had long since vanished, and a pair of dark leggings, torn at the knees and frayed at the waist. His eyes were slanted and black, and they stared unblinkingly at the two men. Angel tried to ignore him. Lifting the bowl of cheese he dipped his fingers into the congealed mass and ate. 'Horse droppings would taste better than this,' he said.

'It is an acquired taste,' agreed Senta.

'Damned if I can eat it.' He swung to the boy. 'You want some?' He did not move. Angel offered him the bowl. The child licked his lips, but remained where he was. Angel shook his head. 'What does he want?' he asked, placing the bowl on the ground.

'I've no idea – but he's obviously fascinated by you. He followed you today, mimicking your walk. Quite funny, really. I hadn't noticed it before, but you move like a sailor. You know, rolling gait.'

'Any more of my habits you'd like to criticise?'

'Too many to mention.'

Angel stood and stretched. The child immediately imitated him. 'Stop that!' said Angel, leaning forward, hands on hips. The tiny figure adopted the same stance. Senta's laughter pealed out. 'I'm going to get some sleep,' said Angel, turning his back on the boy and re-entering the cave.

Senta remained where he was, listening to the faint sounds of battle. The boy edged closer and snatched the bowl, backing away to the shadows to eat. For a while Senta dozed, then he heard movement on the mountainside. He was instantly awake. Belash climbed to the cave mouth.

'They have pulled back,' he said, squatting down beside the swordsman. 'No more now until the dawn, I think.' Senta glanced to where the boy had been, but only the empty bowl remained. 'We killed many,' said Belash, with grim satisfaction.

'Not enough. There must be more than three thousand of them.'

'Many more,' agreed Belash. 'And others are coming. It will take time to kill them all.'

'Ever the optimist.'

'You think we cannot win? You do not understand the Nadir. We are born to fight.'

'I have no doubts concerning the skills of your people, Belash. But this place is ultimately indefensible. How many fighters can you muster?'

382

'This morning there were three hundred and seventy . . . three,' he said, at last.

'And tonight?'

'We lost maybe fifteen.'

'Wounded?'

'Another thirty . . . but some of these can fight again.'

'How many altogether – during the last four days?'

Belash nodded glumly. 'I understand what you are saying. We can hold for maybe eight . . . ten more days. But we will kill many before then.'

'That's hardly the point, my friend. We must have a secondary line of defence. Further into the mountains perhaps.'

'There is nowhere.'

'When we rode down here I saw a valley to the west. Where does it lead?'

'We cannot go there. It is a place of evil and death. I would sooner die here, cleanly and with honour.'

'Fine sentiments, I'm sure, Belash. But I'd as soon not die anywhere quite yet.'

'You do not have to stay,' pointed out Belash.

'True,' agreed Senta, 'but, as my father so often points out, stupidity does tend to run in our family.'

High above the mountains, linked to the spirit of Kesa Khan, Miriel floated beneath the stars. Below her, on the moonlit plain were the tents of the Gothir, erected in five lines of twenty, neat and rectangular, evenly spaced. To the south were a score of picket lines where the horses were tethered, and to the east a latrine pit, exactly thirty feet long. One hundred camp fires were burning brightly, and sentries patrolled the camp's perimeter.

'A methodical people,' pulsed the voice of Kesa Khan. 'They call themselves civilised because they can build tall castles and pitch their tents with geometrical precision, but from here you can see the reality. Ants build in the same way. Are they civilised?'

Miriel said nothing. From this great height she could see both the tiny camp of the Nadir and the might of the Gothir attackers. It was dispiriting. Kesa Khan's laughter rippled out. 'Never concern yourself with despair, Miriel. It is always the weapon of the enemy. Look at them! Even from here you can feel their vanity.'

'How can we defeat them?'

'How can we not?' he countered. 'There are millions of us, and but a few of them. When the Uniter comes they will be swept away like grass-seeds.'

'I meant *now*.'

'Ah, the impatience of youth! Let us see what there is to be seen.'

The stars spun and Miriel found herself looking down at a small campfire in a shallow cave on a mountainside. She saw Waylander sitting hunched before the flames, the hound, Scar, stretched out beside him. Waylander looked tired and she sensed his thoughts. He had been hunted, but had eluded the trackers, killing several. He was clear of Sathuli lands now, and was thinking about stealing a horse from a Gothir town some three leagues to the north.

'A strong man,' said Kesa Khan. 'The Dragon Shadow.'

'He is weary,' said Miriel, wishing she could reach out and hug the lonely man by the campfire.

The scene shifted to a city of stone set in the mountains, and a deep dungeon where a large man was chained to a dank, wet wall. 'You treacherous cur, Galen,' said the prisoner.

A tall, thin warrior in the red cloak of a Drenai lancer stepped forward, taking hold of the prisoner's hair and wrenching back the head. 'Enjoy your insults, you whoreson! Your day is over, and harsh words are all you have now. Yet they will avail you nothing: tomorrow you travel in chains to Gulgothir.'

'I'll come for you, you bastard!' swore the prisoner. 'They won't hold me!' The thin warrior laughed, then bunched his fist and struck the helpless man three times in the face, splitting his lip. Blood flowed to his chin and his one pale eye focused on the red-cloaked soldier. 'I suppose you'll tell Asten we were betrayed, but you managed to escape?'

'Yes. Then, when the time is right, I'll kill the peasant. And the Brotherhood will rule in Drenan. How does that make you feel?'

'It should be an interesting meeting. I'd like to be there to see you telling Asten how I was captured.'

'Oh, I shall tell it well. I shall speak of your enormous bravery, and how you were slain. It will bring a tear to his eye.'

'Rot in hell!' said the prisoner.

Miriel felt the close presence of Kesa Khan and the old shaman's voice whispered into her mind. 'You know who this is?'

'No.'

'You are gazing upon Karnak the One-Eyed, Lord Protector of the Drenai. He does not look mighty now, chained in a Sathuli dungeon. Can you feel his emotions?'

Miriel concentrated, and the warm rush of Karnak's anger swept over her. 'Yes. I can feel it. He is picturing his tormentor being killed by a soldier with red hair.'

'Yes. But there is something else to consider, girl. There is no despair in Karnak, yes? Only anger and the burning desire for revenge. His conceit is colossal, but so is his strength. He has no fear of the chains, or the enemies around him. Already he is planning, building his hopes. Such a man can never be discounted.'

'He is a prisoner, unarmed and helpless. What can he do?' asked Miriel.

'Let us return to the mountains. I am tiring. And tomorrow the real enemy will show himself. We must be ready to face the evil they will unleash.' All light faded in an instant and Miriel opened the eyes of her body and sat up. The fire in the cave had burned low. Kesa Khan added wood to the dying flames and stretched, the bones of his back creaking and cracking. 'Aya! Age is no blessing,' he said.

'What is this evil you spoke of?' asked Miriel.

'In a moment, in a moment! I am old, child, and the transition from spirit to flesh takes a little time. Let me gather my thoughts. Talk to me!'

She looked at the wizened old man. 'What do you wish me to talk about?'

'Anything!' he snapped. 'Life, love, dreams. Tell me which of the two men you wish to bed!'

Miriel reddened. 'Such thoughts are not for idle chatter,' she scolded.

He cackled and fixed her with a piercing gaze. 'Foolish girl! You cannot make up your mind. The young one is witty and handsome, but you know his love is fickle. The older one is like the oak, powerful and enduring, but you feel his lovemaking would lack excitement.'

'If you already know my thoughts, why ask me?'

'It entertains me. Would you like my advice?'

'No.'

'Good. I like a woman who can think for herself.' He sniffed and reached for one of the many clay pots beside the fire, dipping his finger into the contents and scooping a pale grey powder into his mouth. He closed his eyes and sighed. 'Yes . . . yes . . .' He took a deep breath and opened his eyes. Miriel leaned forward. His pupils had all but disappeared and the irises had changed from dark brown to pale blue. 'I am Kesa Khan,' he whispered, his voice lighter, friendlier. 'And I am Lao Shin, the spirit of the mountains. And I am Wu Deyang, the Traveller. I am He Who Sees All.'

'The powder is narcotic?' asked Miriel softly.

'Of course. It opens the window of worlds. Now listen to me, Drenai girl. You are brave, of that there is no question. But tomorrow the dead will walk again. Do you have the heart to face them?'

She licked her lips. 'I am here to help you,' she answered.

'Excellent. No false bravado. I will show you how to armour yourself. I will teach you to summon weapons as you need them. But the greatest weapon you possess is the courage in your heart. Let us hope that the Dragon Shadow has taught you well, for if he has not

385

you will bed neither of those fine warriors. Your soul will wander the Grey Paths for eternity.'

'He taught me well,' said Miriel.

'We shall see.'

With the hound loping off ahead Waylander moved on to the boulder-strewn plain. There were few trees here, and the land sloped gently downward towards a white stone village by a river bank. A horse pasture was fenced off at the north of the village and to the south sheep grazed on the last of the autumn grass. It was a small settlement, built without walls, evidence of the longstanding agreement between Gothir and Sathuli. There were no raids here. It struck Waylander as strange that the Gothir could treat the Sathuli so well and the Nadir so badly. Both were nomadic tribes which had moved slowly down from the north and east. Both were warrior races, who worshipped different gods from the Gothir, and yet they were perceived as opposites. The Sathuli, in Gothir tales, were proud, intelligent and honourable. The Nadir, on the other hand, were seen as base, treacherous and cunning. All his adult life Waylander had moved among the tribes and could find no evidence to support the Gothir view.

Save, perhaps, for the sheer numbers of Nadir who roamed the steppes. The Sathuli posed no threat, whereas the Nadir, in their millions, were a future enemy to be feared.

He shrugged away such considerations and looked for the hound. It was nowhere to be seen. He stopped and scanned the slopes. There were many boulders and the dog was probably scratching at a rabbit burrow. Waylander smiled and walked on. It was cold, the weak sunshine unable to counter the biting wind. He pulled his fur-lined cloak more tightly around his shoulders.

The Sathuli would remember the chase as they sang the Songs of Passing over the hunters who would not return. He thought back to the boy who had first tried to ambush him, and was pleased that he had not killed him. As to the others, well, they had made their choices and he regretted their deaths not at all.

He could see people moving in the village below, a shepherd with a long crook striding up the hill, a dog at his side, several women at the main well, drawing buckets of cool water, children playing by the horse pasture fence. It was a peaceful scene.

He strode on, the path winding down between two huge boulders that jutted from the earth of the mountainside. In the distance a horse whinnied. He paused. The sound had come from the east. He turned and gazed up at the thin stand of trees on the slope. There were bushes growing there and he could not see a horse. Flicking back his cloak he lifted his crossbow, stringing it and sliding two bolts into place. There should be nothing to fear now, he chided himself. The Sathuli were unlikely to venture so far north. But he waited.

Where was Scar?

Moving forward more cautiously he approached the boulders. A figure stepped into sight, green cloak fluttering in the breeze, a bent bow in his hands. Waylander threw himself to the right as the arrow leapt from the string, slicing past his face. He struck the ground on his shoulder, the impact making his hand contract, loosing the bolts on the crossbow, which hammered into the soft earth of the slope. Rolling to his feet he drew his sabre.

The man in the green cloak hurled aside his bow, drawing his own blade. 'This is how it should be, sword to sword,' he said, smiling.

Waylander pulled free the thongs that held his cloak in place, allowing it to drop to the earth. 'You would be Morak,' he said softly.

'How gratifying to be recognised,' answered the swordsman, angling himself towards the waiting Waylander. 'I understand you are not at your best with a sabre, therefore I will give you a short lesson before killing you.'

Waylander leapt to the attack. Morak blocked and countered. The ringing of steel on steel echoed on the mountainside, the two sabres shining in the sunlight. Morak, in perfect balance fended off every attack, his blade licking out to open a shallow cut on Waylander's cheek. Waylander swayed back and sent a vicious slashing blow towards Morak's belly. The green-clad swordsman neatly sidestepped.

'I'd say you were better than average,' he told Waylander. 'Your balance is good, but you are a little stiff in the lower back. It affects the lunge.'

Waylander's hand snapped forward, a black-bladed throwing knife flashing towards Morak's throat. The assassin's sabre swept up, deflecting the knife which clattered against one of the boulders. 'Very good,' said Morak. 'But you are dealing with a master now, Waylander.'

'Where is my dog?'

'Your dog? How touching! You stand at the point of death and you are concerned for a flea-bitten hound? I killed it, of course.'

Waylander said nothing. Backing away to more level ground he watched the swordsman follow. Morak was smiling now, but the smile did not reach the gleaming green eyes. 'I shall kill you with a remarkable lack of speed,' he said. 'A few cuts here and there. As the blood runs so your strength will fail. Do you think you will beg me for life?'

'I would doubt it,' said Waylander.

'All men beg, you know. Even the strongest. It depends only upon where the knife enters.' Morak leapt. Waylander's sabre parried the thrust, the blades clashing again and again. A second small cut appeared on Waylander's forearm. Morak laughed. 'There is no panic in you – not yet. I like that. What happened to that daughter of yours? By Heavens I'll yet enjoy her. Long legs, firm flesh. I'll make her squeal. Then I'll open her up from neck to belly!'

Waylander edged back and said nothing.

'Good! Good! I can't make you angry. That's rare! I shall enjoy finding your breaking point, Waylander. Will it come when I cut off your fingers? Or will it be when your manhood is sizzling on a fire?'

He lunged again, the blade slicing the leather of Waylander's tunic shirt just above the left hip. Waylander hurled himself forward, hammering his shoulder into the assassin's face. Morak fell awkwardly, but rolled to his feet before Waylander could bring his sword to bear. The blades clashed again. Waylander aimed a thrust at Morak's head, but the swordsman swayed aside, blocking the lunge and sending a riposte that flashed past Waylander's neck. Waylander backed away towards the boulders. Morak attacked, forcing his opponent further down the trail. Both men were sweating freely, despite the cold.

'You are game,' said Morak. 'I did not expect you to prove this resilient.'

Waylander lunged. Morak parried, then attacked in a bewildering series of thrusts and cuts that Waylander fought desperately to counter. Twice Morak's sabre pierced the upper chest of Waylander's tunic, the blade being turned aside by the chain-mail shoulder-guard. But the older man was tiring now, and Morak knew it. He stepped back. 'Would you like a little time to get your breath?' he asked, with a mocking grin.

'How did you find me?' said Waylander, grateful for the respite.

'I have friends among the Sathuli. After our . . . unfortunate . . . encounter back in the mountains I came here, seeking more warriors. I was with the Lord Sathuli when news of the hunt came in. The Lord Sathuli is most anxious to see you dead. He feels your journey across his lands is an insult to tribal pride. He would have sent more men – but he has other matters on his mind at the moment. Instead he paid me. By the way, would you like to know who hired the Guild to hunt you?'

'I already know,' Waylander told him.

'Oh, how disappointing. Still, I am by nature a kind-hearted man, so I will at least give you a little good news before I kill you. Even as we speak the Lord Protector of the Drenai lies chained in a Sathuli dungeon, ready to be delivered to the Emperor of the Gothir.'

'That's impossible!'

'Not at all. He was persuaded to meet with the Lord Sathuli, in a bid to prevent Gothir troops crossing tribal lands. He travelled with a small party of loyal soldiers and one, rather disloyal, officer. His men were slaughtered and Karnak taken alive. I saw him myself. It was quite comical. Unusual man – offered me a fortune to help him escape.'

'He obviously doesn't know you too well,' said Waylander.

'On the contrary, I have worked for him before – many times. He paid me to kill Egel.'

'I don't believe it!'

'Yes, you do – I can see it in your eyes. Ah well, recovered your breath? Good. Then let us see some blood!' Morak advanced, his blade lancing out. Waylander blocked, but was forced back, past the jutting boulders. Morak laughed. 'The lesson is now over,' he said. 'Time for the enjoyment to begin.'

A dark shadow moved behind him and Waylander saw the hound, Scar, pulling himself painfully forward on his front paws, his back legs limp and useless. An arrow had pierced his ribs and blood was dribbling from the huge jaws. Waylander edged to the left. Morak moved right. He had not seen the dying hound. Waylander leapt forward, sending a wild cut towards Morak's face. The assassin moved back a step – and Scar's huge jaws snapped shut on his right calf, the fangs sinking through skin, flesh and sinew. Morak screamed in pain. Waylander stepped in and rammed his sabre into the assassin's belly, ripping it up through the lungs.

'That's for the old man you tortured!' hissed Waylander. Twisting the blade he tore it free, disembowelling the swordsman. 'And that's for my dog!'

Morak fell to his knees. 'No!' he moaned. Then toppled sideways to the earth.

Casting aside his sword Waylander knelt by the hound, stroking its head. There was nothing he could do to save the beast. The arrow had pierced its spine. But he sat with it, cradling the huge head in his lap, speaking softly, his voice soothing, until the juddering breathing slowed and finally stopped.

Then he stood, gathered his crossbow, and walked to the stand of trees where Morak had hidden his horse.

14

The wall was rough-built, but bound with a mortar composed of the volcanic black dust of the mountains. Once tamped down and doused with water it set to the hardness of granite. From the south the enemy faced a structure ten feet high, but on the defensive side there was a rampart which allowed the defenders to lean out and send volley after volley of arrows into the ranks of the attackers, then duck down out of sight of any enemy archers.

So far the wall had held. In several places the Gothir had rolled boulders to the foot of it trying to find a way of scaling the defence and later, the front ranks had carried crudely-built ladders. Others used ropes with iron hooks to gain purchase, but the defenders fought with tribal ferocity, hacking and killing all who reached the top.

Once the Gothir had almost formed a fighting wedge, six men forcing their way on to the rampart, but Angel, Senta and Belash had charged into them – and the Gothir warriors died within moments. Again and again the Gothir charged, wave after wave, seeking to overwhelm the Nadir by sheer force of numbers. It had not succeeded.

Yet.

But now something had changed and each defender felt the stirrings of a terrible fear. Angel noticed it first – a coldness in the pit of the belly. His hands began to tremble. The Nadir warrior alongside him dropped his sword, a low, keening moan coming from his lips. Angel glanced at Senta. The swordsman was leaning on the wall and staring out over the narrows of the pass. The Gothir had fallen back, but instead of regrouping they had retreated out of sight. At first the fifty Nadir warriors manning the rough-built wall had jeered and shouted. But now an uncomfortable silence settled on the defenders.

Angel shivered. The black walls of the mountains loomed around him, and he felt as if he were standing inside the gaping jaws of an enormous monster. The trembling worsened. He tried to sheath his sword, but it clattered against the scabbard. He swore and laid the blade against the wall.

Three Nadir warriors turned and ran back up the pass, leaving their weapons behind them. The voice of Belash roared out. The fleeing men halted and turned, sheepishly. But the fear was growing.

Angel made his way to Senta's side. His legs felt they had no strength, and he leaned on the wall for support. 'What the devil is happening?' he asked Senta. The other man, his face pale, his eyes wide, did not reply. Movement came from the mouth of the pass. Angel swung his head and saw a line of black-cloaked, black-armoured men moving towards the wall.

'The Knights of Blood!' whispered Senta, his voice shaking.

A Nadir beside him cried out and fell back, his bladder loosening, urine soaking his leggings. Angel saw Belash sheath his sword and snatch a bow from a warrior's hand. Notching an arrow the stocky Nadir climbed to the top of the wall and drew back on the string. Angel heard him groan – and cry out. Then Belash slowly began to turn.

Angel hurled himself at Senta, dragging him back just as the arrow was loosed. It flashed past them, ricocheting from a rock and plunging into the shoulder of a crouching warrior.

Silently the Knights of Blood advanced.

The Nadir seemed powerless to stop them. Angel scrambled to his feet and took up his sword. The trembling was now so great he knew he would not be able to use it. The defenders began to stream back from the wall – even Belash.

A tiny man in ragged clothes moved into sight, Miriel beside him. He was wizened and ancient, but Angel felt a sudden surge of elation, cutting through the fear, firing his blood. The Nadir paused in their flight. The little shaman ran to the wall, climbing nimbly to the top. The Knights of Blood were less than twenty paces from the wall.

Kesa Khan raised his hands and flashes of blue fire leapt from palm to palm. Angel felt all fear lifting from him; anger replaced it. The shaman's hands swept out, bony fingers pointing at the marching, black-cloaked warriors. Blue fire lanced into the line, rippling over breastplates and helms. The man at the centre of the line stumbled. Blue fire became red as his hair burst into flames. Cloaks and leggings blazed – and the advancing line broke, men beating at the tongues of flame licking at their clothing.

The Nadir defenders returned to the wall, taking up bow and spear and sending shaft after shaft into the milling men.

The Knights of Blood broke and ran.

The little Nadir leapt down from the wall and walked away without a word.

Miriel approached Angel. 'You should sit down. Your face is the colour of snow.'

'I've never known such a fear,' he admitted.

'But you didn't run,' she pointed out.

Ignoring the compliment he gazed after the Nadir shaman. 'I take it that was Kesa Khan. He doesn't waste a lot of time on conversation, does he?'

She smiled. 'He's a tough old man, but he's exhausted. That spell will have weakened him more than you could possibly know.'

Senta joined them. 'We can't hold this place,' he said. 'They almost broke through this morning, twice. Only the Source knows how we held them off.'

A cry went up from one of the defenders. Senta swung to see hundreds of Gothir warriors charging into the pass. Drawing his swords he ran back to the wall.

'He's right,' said Angel. 'Talk to the old man! We must find another place.' Then he too ran to join the defenders.

Bodalen followed the torch-carrying Gracus deep into the bowels of the castle, through endless corridors and down stairways of metal.

Everything was twisted, unnatural, and a low humming filled the air, causing Bodalen's head to pound.

Behind the tall Drenai came the other eight Brotherhood warriors, grim silent men. The ninth had taken the horses into the mountains, and now all hope of fleeing this sorcerous place was gone from Bodalen.

Down, down they journeyed, through five levels, the humming growing ever more loud. The walls of the castle were no longer of stone, but sleek, shining metal, bulging and cracked in places. Beyond the cracks were wires of copper and iron, gold and silver, wound together, braided.

Bodalen hated the castle, and feared the secrets it might contain. But even through his cowardice his fascination grew. On one level there was a set of steel doors, which Gracus and two other men forced open. Within was a small room. There was no furniture, but one wall carried a small ornament, like a carving table, twelve round stones set in brass, each stone bearing a symbol that Bodalen could not decipher.

There was little of interest save for the ornament and the warriors moved on, seeking stairs.

At last they came to a great hall that was lit as if by sunlight, bright and cheerful. Yet there were no windows, and Bodalen knew they were hundreds of feet below ground. Gracus dropped the spluttering torch to the metal floor and gazed around him. There were tables and chairs, all of metal, and huge iron cabinets, ornately decorated with bright gems that sparkled, the light dancing from them.

Panels of opaque glass were set all around the hall, and these glowed with white light. Gracus drew his sword and struck one of them, which shattered, spilling fragments to the hall floor. Beyond the panel was a long, gleaming cylinder. A second warrior strode forward, thrusting his sword into it. There was a flash and the knight was lifted from his feet and hurled twenty feet across the floor. Half the lights in the hall dimmed and died.

Gracus ran to the fallen man, kneeling beside him. 'Dead,' he said, rising and turning to the others. 'Touch nothing. We will await the master. The spells are mightier than we can understand.'

Bodalen, the humming so loud it made him nauseous, moved across the hall to an open doorway. Beyond it he saw a huge crystal, some three feet in circumference, floating between two golden bowls. Tiny bolts of lightning flickered and shone all around it as it spun. Bodalen stepped into the room. The walls here were all of gold, save for the far wall, which had been partly stripped, exposing carved blocks of granite, twisted far beyond their original squares.

But it was not the crystal, nor the walls of gold that caused the breath to catch in his throat.

'Gracus!' he shouted. The Brotherhood knight entered the room – and gazed down at the immense skeleton stretched out by the far wall.

'What in the name of Hell is it?' whispered Bodalen.

Gracus shook his head. 'Hell is where it came from,' he answered, kneeling beside the two skulls, his fingers tracing the twin lines of vertebrae leading to the massive shoulders. The beast, whatever it was, had boasted three arms, one of which sprouted from below the enormous ribs. One of the knights tried to lift the thigh bone, but the rotted sinew held it in place.

'I cannot even get my hands around this bone,' said the man. 'The creature must have been twelve feet tall, maybe more.'

Bodalen glanced back at the doorway, which was no more than three feet wide and six feet tall. 'How did it get in here?' he asked. Gracus moved to the doorway. There were great tears in the metal around the frame, exposing the stone beneath.

'I don't know how it got in,' said Gracus softly, 'but it tore its fingers to the bone trying to get out. There must be another entrance. Hidden.'

For some time they searched the walls, seeking a disguised doorway. But there was nothing. Bodalen felt a great weariness settling on him and his headache worsened. He started for the doorway, but his legs gave way and he slumped to the floor. Fatigue overwhelmed him, and he saw Gracus stumble to his knees before the spinning crystal.

'We must . . . get out,' said Bodalen, trying to drag himself across the gleaming golden floor. But his eyes closed and he fell into a deep, and at first dreamless, sleep.

Awareness came to him slowly. He could see a cottage, built by a stream, a cornfield beyond it, blue mountains, hazy in the distance behind it. There was a man walking behind a team of oxen. He was ploughing a field.

Father.

No, not Father. Father is Karnak. He never ploughed a field in his life. *Father*.

Confusion flowed over him like a fog, swirling, unreal. He looked up at the sun, but there was no sun, just a spinning crystal high in the sky, humming like a thousand bees.

The man with the plough turned towards him. 'Don't spend your day lazing, Gracus!' he said.

Gracus? I'm not Gracus. I am dreaming. That's it! A dream. Wake up!

He felt himself rising from sleep, felt the awareness of flesh and muscle. He tried to move his arm, but it seemed lodged, trapped. He opened his eyes. Gracus was lying beside him. Close beside him. He must be lying on my arm, thought Bodalen. He tried to roll, but Gracus moved with him, his head lolling, his mouth open. Bodalen struggled to rise. He felt an unaccustomed weight on his right side and swung his head. There was another man lying there.

And he had no head.

I am lying on his head, thought Bodalen, panic gripping him. He surged up. The body on the right rose with him. Bodalen screamed. The headless body was part of him, the shoulders bonded to Bodalen's flesh.

Sweet Heaven! Calm down, he told himself. This is still a dream. Just a dream.

His left arm had disappeared, embedded into and merging with Gracus' shoulder. He tried to pull it clear, but the limp body of the Brotherhood knight merely moved closer. Their legs touched – and bonded.

The crystal continued to spin.

Across the room Bodalen saw the bodies of the other knights, melding together, twisting as if involved in some silent, unnatural orgy. And between them, lying still on the golden floor, was the huge skeleton.

Bodalen screamed again.

And passed out.

It awoke with no memory, but stretched its huge muscles and rolled to its belly, its three legs levering it upright, its two heads striking the golden ceiling. Rage suffused the beast, and one of the heads roared in anger. The other remained silent, grey eyes blinking at the light from the crystal.

Two other beasts were still asleep.

The crystal spun, blue lights dancing between the golden bowls.

The beast shuffled towards it, reaching out with its three great arms. A massive finger touched the flickering blue fire. Pain swept along the immense limbs, burning the creature. Both heads roared now. One arm swept out, striking the crystal, dislodging it, sending it hurtling towards the far wall. The blue flames died.

And all the lights dimmed and faded.

The near-darkness was comfortable, reassuring. The beast slumped down to its haunches. It was hungry. The smell of burnt meat came from the hall beyond. It moved to the doorway, and saw a small dead creature lying on the floor. The corpse was part-clothed in hide and metal. The meat was still fresh and the beast's hunger swelled. It tried to move forward but its great bulk could not pass through the doorway. Rearing up, it began to tear at the exposed blocks above the metal frame. The other beasts joined it, adding their strength.

And slowly the great rocks began to crack and give.

Kesa Khan opened his eyes and smiled. Miriel was watching him, saw the gleam of triumph in his eyes. 'We can move now,' he said, with a dry laugh. 'The way is made smooth.'

'But you said there was nowhere else!'

'There wasn't. Now there is. It is a fortress – very old. It is called Kar-Barzac. Tomorrow we will make the journey.'

'There is much that you are not telling me,' pointed out Miriel.

'There is much you do not need to know. Rest, Miriel, you will need your strength. Go – sit with your friends. Leave me. I will call you when the time comes.' Miriel wanted to question him further, but the little man had once more closed his eyes and sat, arms folded before the small fire.

She rose and wandered out into the night. Senta was asleep when she reached the small cave, but Angel was sitting under the stars, listening to the distant sounds of battle coming from the pass. A small boy was close by him. Miriel smiled. The two figures were in an identical position some twenty feet apart, Angel and the child both sitting cross-legged. The gladiator was sharpening his sword with a whetstone, the boy, holding a piece of wood, copying him.

'I see you have made a friend,' said Miriel. Angel grunted something inaudible. Miriel sat beside him. 'Who is he?'

'How should I know? He never speaks. He just mimics.'

Miriel's Talent reached out, then drew back. 'He's totally deaf,' she said. 'An orphan.'

Angel sighed. 'I didn't need to know that,' he said, sheathing his sword. The ragged child slid his stick into his belt.

Miriel reached out and stroked the gladiator's face. 'You are a good man, Angel. It means you have no real skill when it comes to harbouring hate.'

He caught her wrist and held to it. 'You shouldn't be touching me,' he said softly. 'The man for you is in there. Young. Handsome. With a disgusting lack of scars.'

'I will choose my own man when the time comes,' she told him. 'I am not some Drenai noblewoman whose marriage brings an alliance between warring factions. Nor do I have to concern myself with a dowry. I will marry a man I like, a man I respect.'

'You didn't mention love,' he pointed out.

'I have heard great talk of it, Angel, but I don't know what it is. I love my father. I love you. I loved my sister and my mother. One word. Different feelings. Are we talking of lust?'

'Partly,' he agreed. 'And there's nothing wrong with that, though many would have us believe otherwise. But it is more than that. I had an affair with a dark-haired woman once. Unbelievable. In bed she could raise more passion in me than any of my wives. But I didn't stay with her. I didn't love her, you see. I adored her. But I didn't love her.'

'There's that word again!' chided Miriel.

He chuckled. 'I know. It's just a short way of describing someone who is your friend, bed-mate, sister, aye even mother sometimes. Someone who will arouse your passion and your admiration and your respect. Someone, who when the whole world turns against you, is still standing by your side. You look for someone like that, Miriel.' He released her hand and looked away.

She leaned in close. 'What about you, Angel? Would you be a friend, a lover, a brother and a father?'

He turned his scarred features towards her. 'Aye, I would.' He hesitated and she sensed his indecision. At last he smiled and, taking her hand, kissed it. 'My boots are older than you, Miriel. And you may think it makes no difference now, but it does. You need a man who can grow with you, not grow senile on you.' He took a deep breath. 'It's hard to admit this, you know.'

'You are not old,' she admonished him.

'Don't you like Senta?' he countered.

She looked away. 'I find him . . . exciting . . . frightening.'

'That's good,' he said. 'That's how life should be. Me, I'm like an old armchair. Comfortable. A girl like you needs more than that. Give him a chance. There's a lot of good in him.'

'Why do you like him so much?'

He grinned. 'I knew his mother,' he said. 'A long time ago. Before he was born.'

'You mean . . . ?'

'I have no idea, but he could be. He certainly doesn't take after the husband. But that's between you and me now! Understand?'

'And yet you would have fought him back at the cabin?'

He nodded, his face solemn. 'I wouldn't have won. He's very good. The best I've ever seen.' Suddenly she laughed. 'What's so amusing?' he asked.

'He wasn't going to try to kill you. I read that in his thoughts. He was looking to disarm or wound you.'

'That would have been a bad mistake.'

She looked into his eyes and her smile faded. 'But you might have been killing your own son!'

'I know. Not very uplifting, is it? But I am a warrior, Miriel, and when swords are drawn there is no emotion. Merely survival or death.' He glanced at the Nadir boy, who was sleeping now against a rock, his head resting on his stick-thin arms, his knees drawn up to his belly. Rising silently, Angel moved across to the lad, covering him with his cloak. Then he returned to Miriel. 'What is the old man planning?'

'I don't know, but we will be moving – tomorrow. To an old fortress in the mountains.'

'That is good news. We cannot hold here for much longer. You should get some sleep.'

'I can't. He will need me soon.'

'For what?'

'For when the dead walk,' she answered.

Kesa Khan sat by his fire, his ancient body shivering as the night winds fanned the flames. He was beyond tiredness now, a mortal weariness settling on him. It was all so complex, so many lines of destiny to be drawn together. Why, he wondered idly, had this not come to pass when he was young and in full strength? Why now, when he was old and weary and ready for the grave? The gods were indeed capricious at best.

Plans, ideas, strategies flowed through his mind. And each was dependent upon another for success. The journey of a thousand leagues begins with a single step, he told himself. Concentrate only on the step before you.

The demons would come, and with them the souls of the dead. How best to combat them? The Drenai woman was strong, stronger than she knew, but she alone could not guarantee success. Closing his eyes he mentally summoned Miriel. The time was close.

He reached for the clay pot and the grey powder, but his hand drew back. He had taken too much already. Ah, but the gods do love a reckless man! Dipping his finger into the powder he scooped a small amount to his mouth. His heart began to beat erratically, and he felt strength flowing into his limbs. The fire burned yellow, then gold, then purple, and the shadows on the walls became dancers, spinning and turning.

The Drenai woman entered the cave. My, but she was ugly, he thought. Too tall and stringy. Even in his youth he could not have found her attractive. The Drenai warrior with the scarred face moved in behind her. Kesa Khan's dark eyes focused on the man. 'This is no place for those with no power,' he said.

'I told him that,' said Miriel, seating herself opposite the shaman, 'but he came anyway.'

'She said there would be demons and the undead. Can they be slain with a sword?' asked Angel.

'No,' answered the shaman.

'With bare hands, then?'

'No.'

'How then will Miriel fight them?'

'With her courage and her Talent.'

'Then I shall stand beside her. No one has yet doubted my courage.'

'You are needed here, to man the wall, to stop the human enemy. It would be the worst folly to allow you to enter the Void. It would be a waste.'

'You do not control my life,' roared Angel. 'I am here because of her. If she dies I leave. I care nothing for you lice-infested barbarians. You understand? So if she is in danger – I go with her.'

Kesa Khan's eyes became hooded and wary as he gazed on the towering Drenai. How I hate them, he thought. Their casual arrogance, their monumental condescension. Lifting his eyes he met Angel's pale gaze, and Kesa Khan allowed his hatred to transmit to the warrior. Angel smiled and nodded slowly. Kesa Khan rose. 'As you wish, Hard-to-Kill. You will journey with the woman.'

'Good,' said the gladiator, sitting beside Miriel.

'No,' she said. 'This is not wise. If I am to fight then I cannot look after Angel.'

'I need no looking after!' he protested.

'Be quiet!' she snapped. 'You have no conception of the journey – or the perils, or what is needed even to protect yourself. You will be like a babe in arms. And I will have no time to suckle you!'

He reddened and pushed himself to his feet. Kesa Khan stepped forward. 'No, no!' he said. 'I think you misjudge the situation, Miriel, as did I at first. The Void is a deadly place, but a man with courage is not to be lightly dismissed. I will send you both. And I will arm Hard-to-Kill with weapons he understands.'

'Where will you be?'

'Here. Waiting. But I will be linked to you.'

'But this is where the demons will come, surely?'

'No. They will not be hunting me. Did you not realise? That is why I needed you. They will be seeking out your father. Zhu Chao knows he is a terrible danger to him. He has tried to kill him in this world, and failed. Now he will seek to lure his soul into the Void. He must be protected.'

'He also has no Talent,' said Miriel, fear rising.

'There you are wrong,' whispered Kesa Khan. 'He has the greatest talent of all. He knows how to survive.'

15

Kasai and his men had been hunting for more than three hours when they saw the southerner on the giant red stallion. Kasai reined in his hill pony. It was a fine beast, fourteen hands tall, but the southerner's horse was sixteen hands, maybe more. Kasai's cousin Chulai reined in alongside him. 'Do we kill him?' he asked.

'Wait,' ordered Kasai, studying the approaching rider. The man was dressed in black, a dark fur-lined cloak slung across his shoulders. There was dried blood on his face. The rider saw them and angled his horse towards the waiting group. Kasai saw no sign of fear in the man.

'Fine horse,' said Kasai, as the man pulled back on the reins.

'Better than the man I killed to get him,' said the rider, his dark eyes scanning the group. He seemed amused, which angered Kasai.

'It is a horse worth killing for,' he said pointedly, hand on his sword-hilt.

'True,' agreed the rider. 'But the question you must ask yourself is, whether he is worth dying for.'

'We are five, you are one.'

'Wrong. One and one. You and I. For when the action begins I will kill you within the first heartbeat.' The words were spoken with a quiet certainty that swept over Kasai's confidence like a winter wind.

'You dismiss my brothers so easily?' he said, trying to re-establish the fact that they outnumbered the southerner.

The rider laughed and swung his gaze over the other men. 'I never dismiss any Nadir lightly. I've fought too many in the past. Now it seems you have two choices; you can fight, or we can ride to your camp and eat.'

'Let us kill him,' said Chulai, slipping into the Nadir tongue.

'It will be the last move you make, dung-brain,' said the rider, in perfect Nadir.

Chulai half-drew his sword, but Kasai ordered him back. 'How do you know our tongue?' he enquired.

'Do we eat or fight?' countered the man.

'We eat. We offer you the hospitality of the tent. Now, how do you know our tongue?'

'I have travelled among the Nadir for many years, both as friend and enemy. My name is Waylander, though I have other names among the people of the tents.'

Kasai nodded. 'I have heard of you, Oxskull – you are a mighty warrior. Follow me, and you will have the food you desire.' Kasai wheeled his pony and galloped towards the north. Chulai cast a murderous glance at the Drenai and then followed.

Two hours later they were seated around a burning brazier within a tall, goatskin tent. Waylander was sitting cross-legged upon a rug, Kasai before him. Both men had dined from a communal bowl of curdled cheese and shared a clay goblet of strong spirit.

'What brings you to the steppes, Oxskull?'

'I seek Kesa Khan of the Wolves.'

Kasai nodded. 'His death has been long overdue.'

Waylander chuckled. 'I am not here to kill him, but to help him survive.'

'It cannot be true!'

'I assure you that it is. My daughter and my friends are with him now – or so I hope.'

Kasai was amazed. 'Why? What are the Wolves to you? We still talk of Kesa Khan's magic and the werebeasts he sent to kill you. Why would you help *him*?'

'The enemy of my enemy is my friend,' answered Waylander. 'There is a man who serves the Emperor. He is the enemy I wish to see slain.'

'Zhu Chao! May the gods curse his soul until the stars burn out! Aye, a good enemy, that one. But you are too late to help the Wolves. The Gothir have already begun their attack upon the mountain stronghold. There is no way through.'

'I will find a way.'

Kasai nodded and drained the last of the spirit, refilling the goblet from a jug beside him. He offered it to Waylander, who drank sparingly. 'My people are the Tall Spears. We are enemies of the Wolves. Lifelong – and before that. But I do not want to see the Gothir destroy them. I wish to be the man who drives a blade into Anshi Chen. I wish to cut the head from Belash. I wish to drag out the heart of Kesa Khan. Such pleasures are not for some round-eyed, stone-dwelling pig to enjoy.'

'How many men do you have here?'

'Fighting men? Six hundred.'

'Perhaps you should consider aiding the Wolves.'

'Pah! My tongue would turn black and all my ancestors turn their backs upon me when I entered the Vale of Rest. No, I shall not aid them, but I will aid you. I will give you food and, if you wish, a guide. There are other routes into the Mountains.'

'I thank you, Kasai.'

'It is nothing. If you do find Kesa Khan, tell him why I helped you.'

'I'll do that. Tell me, do you dream of the day the Uniter will come?'

'Of course, what Nadir does not?'

'How do you see him?'

'He will be of the Tall Spears, that is certain.'

'And how will he unite the Nadir?'

Kasai smiled. 'Well, first he will obliterate the Wolves, and all other treacherous tribes.'

'Suppose the Uniter is not of the Tall Spears. Suppose he is of the Wolves?'

'Impossible.'

'He'll need to be a rare man,' said Waylander.

'Let's drink to that,' said Kasai, passing the goblet.

Wrapped in his cloak, his head resting on his saddle, Waylander lay on the rug, listening to the night winds howling outside the tent. On the far side of the brazier Kasai was sleeping, his two wives on either side of him, his children close by. Waylander was tired, but sleep would not come. Rolling on to his back he gazed up at the smoke drifting through the hole in the tent roof, watching the wind swirl it away. He could see three stars, high in the night sky. He closed his eyes.

And remembered the day he had fought to protect the Armour of Bronze. The Nadir had come for him, but these he had slain. Then the last of the wolf-beasts had stalked him. Two bolts through the brain had finally ended the terror. Wounded and alone he had dragged himself from the cave – only to face the Knights of the Brotherhood. These he could not defeat, but Durmast the giant, treacherous Durmast, had arrived to save him, giving his life for a man he had planned to betray.

Waylander sighed. So many dead. Durmast, Gellan, Danyal, Krylla . . . And always the wars – conquest and battle, defeat and despair. Where does it end, he thought. With the grave? Or do the battles go on?

Kasai was snoring now. Waylander heard him grunt as one of his wives nudged him. Opening his eyes he gazed across the tent. The brazier was burning low, a soft red glow filling the interior. Kasai had a family. He had made a gift to the future. He was loved.

Waylander turned to his side, facing away from the Nadir leader. Once more he tried for sleep, but this time he saw Dardalion, tied to the tree, his flesh sliced and bleeding, the men around him laughing and mocking.

That was the day Waylander's world had changed. He had rescued the priest, then been drawn into the eternal battle, Light against Dark, Harmony against Chaos. And he had met Danyal. He groaned and rolled again, his body weary, muscles aching.

Stop dwelling on the past, he told himself. Think about tomorrow. Just tomorrow. He would find a way into the Mountains of the Moon. He would stand beside Miriel and Angel and do that which he did best. He would fight.

He would kill.

Sleep took him by surprise, and his soul drifted into darkness.

The walls were clammy, the corridor dark and claustrophobic. Waylander blinked and tried to remember how he had come here. It was so hard to concentrate. Was he looking for something? Someone?

There were no doors or windows, just this endless tunnel. Cold water was soaking through his boots as he waded on.

I am lost, he thought.

There was no source of light, and yet he could see.

Stairs. Must look for stairs. Fear touched him, but he suppressed it ruthlessly. Stay calm! Think! He moved on. Something white caught his eye on the far wall. There was an alcove there. Splashing across the streaming water he saw a skeleton, rusty chains holding it to the wall. The ligaments and tendons had not yet rotted and the thing was intact, save for the left leg, which had parted at the knee. Something moved within the ribcage and Waylander saw two rats had made a nest there.

'Welcome,' said a voice. Waylander stepped back in shock. The head was no longer a skull but a handsome face, framed in golden hair. It smiled at him. Waylander's heart was beating wildly and he reached for his crossbow. Only then did he realise he was weaponless. 'Welcome to my home,' said the handsome head.

'I am dreaming!'

'Perhaps,' agreed the head. A rat pushed its way through the gaping ribcage and sprang to a nearby shelf of stone.

'Where is this place?' asked Waylander.

The head laughed, the sound echoing away into the tunnel. 'Well, let us think . . . Does it look to you like paradise?'

'No.'

'Then it must be somewhere else. But one mustn't complain, must one? It is pleasant to have a visitor after so long. The rats are company, of course, but their conversation is rather limited.'

'How do I get out of here?'

The head smiled, and Waylander saw the pale eyes widen, a gleam of triumph showing there. Waylander spun. A sword lunged for his throat. Swaying aside he slammed his fist into a face out of nightmare. His assailant fell back into the water, but rose swiftly. He looked like a man, save that his skin was scaled, his eyes huge and set, like a fish, on either side of his head. He had no nose, merely slits in the skin of his face, and his mouth was shaped like an inverted V, lipless and rimmed with fangs.

The creature leapt forward. Waylander reached out, his fingers curling around one of the skeleton's ribs, and snapping it clear. The sword slashed down. Waylander sidestepped the blow and rammed the broken rib into the creature's chest. Dropping the sword it let out a terrible howl. And disappeared.

Waylander scooped up the sword and swung back to the skeleton. The handsome head was no longer visible. The rotting skull sagged against the vertebrae and toppled into the murky water.

Sword in hand Waylander moved on, every sense alert.

The tunnel widened and he saw an arch of stone and a path leading to a stairwell. An old man was sitting on the first stair. His robes were old and covered in mildew and mould. In his hands was a sphere of transparent crystal, a white light shining at the centre.

Waylander approached him.

'This is your soul,' said the old man, holding up the crystal. 'If I drop it, or break it, or crush it, you will never leave here. You will wander these tunnels for eternity. Go back the way you have come.'

'I wish to climb those stairs, old man. Step aside.'

402

'One step towards me and your soul perishes!' warned the old man, holding the crystal high. Waylander sprang forward, his sword smashing through the crystal, sending glittering shards to the water. The old man fell back. 'How did you know?' he moaned.

'My soul is my own,' answered Waylander. The old man vanished. And the stairs beckoned.

Waylander edged forward. The stairwell walls shimmered with a faintly green light, the stairs glistening as if oiled. He took a long deep breath then ventured on to the first step. Then the second. Arms swept out from the walls, hooked fingers and talons reaching for him. The sword slashed down, hacking through a scaled wrist. Fingers grabbed at his black leather tunic. Tearing himself free he forced his way up the stairwell, the sword-blade hacking a path through the writhing, questing limbs.

At the top of the stairs was a square landing. There were two doors, one edged with gold and part-open, the other guarded by a huge three-headed serpent, whose coils rose up around the frame. The part-open door showed a shaft of sunlight, warm and welcoming, beckoning the man. Waylander ignored it, his eyes fixed to the serpent. Its mouths were cavernous, each showing twin fangs more than a foot long. Venom dripped from them, splashing to the stone of the landing, bubbling and hissing.

A figure in a robe of light appeared at the part-open door. 'Come this way. Quickly!' said the figure, a friendly-faced man with white hair and kindly blue eyes. 'Come to the light!' Waylander moved towards him, as if to comply, but once close enough he reached out, pulling the man forward by his robes, then hurling him at the serpent. Two of the heads darted forward, the first closing on the man's shoulder, the second sinking its fangs into his leg. The victim's screams filled the air.

As Waylander leapt past the struggling man the third head lunged down. Waylander's sword smote it in the eye. Black blood bubbled from the wound and the head withdrew. Throwing his shoulder against the door Waylander felt the wood give way, and he fell into a wide hall. Rolling to his feet he saw a man waiting for him, sword in hand.

It was Morak.

'No dying dog to save you now!' said the dead assassin.

'I don't need help for the likes of you,' Waylander told him. 'You were nothing then. You are less than nothing now.'

Morak's face twisted and he ran to the attack. Waylander side-stepped, parried the lunge then sent a riposte that almost tore Morak's head from his neck. The assassin staggered then righted himself, his head hanging at an obscene angle.

'How do you kill a dead man?' he mocked. Morak attacked again.

403

Waylander parried and once more chopped at the gashed neck. The head fell to the floor, but the body continued its assault. Waylander blocked two thrusts, slashing his blade into the already open ribcage. It did not even slow the headless opponent. Laughter came from the air. 'Are you beginning to know fear?' Morak's voice echoed in the hall, the air filled with screaming obscenities.

Ducking under a wild cut Waylander ran to the head, lifting it by the hair. Spinning round he hurled it towards the doorway. It bounced and rolled through the gap. A serpent lunged, the great mouth snapping shut. The screams stopped instantly.

The headless body collapsed.

Waylander whirled, awaiting the next attack.

'How did you know which door to take?' asked another voice. Waylander searched for the source of the sound, but could see no one.

'It was not difficult,' he answered, holding his blade at the ready.

'Yes, I can see that. The sunlight and the white robe was a little too obvious. I won't make that mistake again. I must say Morak was a disappointment. He gave you a much greater battle while alive.'

'He had more to fight for,' said Waylander. 'Who are you? Show yourself!'

'Of course, how impolite of me.' A figure shimmered into being on the far side of the hall, a tall man wearing purple robes. His hair was waxed flat to his skull, save for two braided sideburns that hung to his slender shoulders. 'I am Zhu Chao.'

'I have heard the name.'

'Of course you have. Now, let us see what we can conjure for our pleasure. Something from your past, perhaps?' Zhu Chao extended his arm, pointing at a spot midway into the hall. Black smoke swirled there, forming into a beast more than eight feet high. It had the head of a wolf, the body of a giant man. 'Such a shame you do not have your little bow with you,' said Zhu Chao.

Waylander backed away as the beast advanced, its blood-red eyes focused on its prey. A silver arrow lanced across the hall, spearing into the creature's neck. A second followed it, piercing the great chest. The beast slumped to its knees then fell headfirst to the flagstones.

Waylander spun. Miriel, bow in hand, Angel beside her, was standing by the doorway. Angel ran forward.

'Get back!' ordered Waylander, sword raised.

'What the Hell is the matter with you?' asked Angel.

'Nothing is as it seems in this place,' Waylander told him. 'And I'll not be fooled by a demon just because he looks like a friend.'

Miriel advanced. 'Judge by actions, Father,' she said. Waylander's crossbow materialised in his hand, a full bolt quiver appearing at his belt.

'How did you come here?' he asked, still wary.

'Kesa Khan sent us. Now we must get out of this place.'

404

Loading his crossbow, Waylander swung back to where Zhu Chao had been standing.

But the wizard had gone.

There were many doors on both sides of the hall. Miriel ran towards the nearest, but Waylander called her back.

'What is this place?' he asked her.

'It exists in the Void. The castle was created by Zhu Chao as a trap for you. We must get out, move beyond his power.' Once more she started for the door, but he grabbed her arm, his dark eyes showing his anger.

'Stop and think!' he snapped. 'This is *his* creation, so none of the doorways will lead to freedom. Beyond them is only more peril.'

'What do you suggest?' asked Angel. 'Do we just wait here?'

'Exactly. His powers are not inexhaustible. We stand, and we fight. Whatever comes we kill.'

'No,' insisted Miriel. 'You have no conception of what exists in the Void. Demons, monsters, spirits – creatures of colossal evil. Kesa Khan warned me of them.'

'If Zhu Chao had the power to conjure such creatures I would already be dead,' said Waylander softly. 'But whatever surprises he has for us are waiting beyond those doors. There or here. Those are our only choices. And here we have space. Tell me of the Void,' he ordered Miriel.

'It is a place of spirit,' she told him, 'of wandering. It is the Great Emptiness between what was and what is.'

'Nothing is real here?'

'Real and yet not real. Yes.'

'This crossbow is not ebony and steel?'

'No. It is a thing of spirit – *your* spirit. An extension of your will.'

'Then I need not load it?'

'I . . . don't know.'

Waylander levelled the bow and loosed the triggers. The bolts flashed across the hall, hammering into a black door. He gazed down at the weapon, the strings hanging slack. Then he raised it again. Instantly two bolts slashed through the air. 'Good,' he said. 'Now let them come. And I will have my knives.' A baldric appeared on his chest, three knives in sheaths hanging from it. His chain-mail shoulder-guard materialised, not black, but of shining silver. 'What of you, Angel?' he asked, with a wide grin. 'What do you desire?'

The gladiator smiled. 'Two golden swords and armour, encrusted with gems.'

'You shall have them!'

A golden helm appeared, a white-crested plume arcing back from brow to nape of neck. And a breastplate and greaves, glittering with rubies and diamonds. Two scabbarded swords shimmered into place at his side.

All the doors in the hall swept open and a host of shadow shapes swarmed towards the waiting warriors.

'I'll have light also!' yelled Waylander. The ceiling disappeared and sunlight filled the hall, spearing through the dark horde, which vanished like mist in a morning breeze.

Then a black cloud formed above them, obliterating the light, and a cold voice hissed from all around them. 'You learn swiftly, Waylander, but you do not have the skill to oppose me.'

Even as the echoes died away nine knights in black armour appeared, long triangular shields upon their arms, black-bladed swords in their hands. Waylander spun and sent two bolts at the first. They thudded into the knight's shield. Miriel loosed a shaft, but this also was turned aside. And the knights advanced.

'What do we do?' whispered Angel, drawing both his swords.

Waylander aimed his crossbow above the advancing warriors and let fly. The bolt swept over the advancing men then turned, plunging into the back of the closest. 'Anything is possible here,' said Waylander. 'Let your mind loose!'

The knights charged, holding their shields before them. A white shield appeared on Waylander's arm, his crossbow becoming a sword of light. He leapt forward, crashing his shield into the first knight, hurling him back off-balance, then moved into the gap, slashing his blade to the left, cleaving it through the ribs of an advancing warrior.

Angel took two running steps then threw himself towards the ground, rolling into the charging knights. Three tumbled over him, their shields clattering to the flagstones. He reared up and killed the first two, one with a disembowelling lunge, the second with a reverse thrust. Miriel slew the third with an arrow through the eye.

Two knights converged on Miriel. Instantly her bow became a shining sabre. Ducking under a wild cut she leapt high, her foot hammering into the first man's chin. He was catapulted back. The second slashed his sword towards her face. She swayed and sent her sabre in a wicked slash that tore through the chain-mail at the knight's throat. He fell and she plunged her sword into his unprotected back.

The three remaining knights backed away. Angel ran at them. 'No!' bellowed Waylander. 'Let them go!'

Angel backed to where Waylander and Miriel were standing. 'I can't think of any magic,' he grumbled.

'You will need none,' said Waylander, pointing to the fading castle walls. 'It is over.'

Within a heartbeat they were standing on a wide grey road, the castle a memory.

'You risked your life for me, Miriel,' said Waylander, taking his daughter in his arms. 'You came into Hell for me. I'll never forget that, as long as I live.' Releasing her he turned to Angel. 'And you too my friend. How can I thank you?'

'You could start by letting Miriel take me away from here,' answered Angel, casting nervous glances at the slate-grey sky and the brooding hills.

Waylander laughed. 'So be it. How do we leave, Miriel?'

She moved alongside him and laid her hands over his eyes. 'Think of your body, and where it sleeps. Then relax, as if drifting to sleep. And we will see you in the mountains very soon.'

Reaching up he pulled clear her hands, holding to them. 'I won't be coming to the mountains,' he said softly.

'What do you mean?'

'I will just be another sword there. I must go where my talents can be used at their best.'

'Not Gulgothir?' she pleaded.

'Yes. Zhu Chao is the cause of all this. When he is dead maybe it will be over.'

'Oh Father, he is a wizard. And he will be guarded. Worse, he knows you will come – that is why he laid this trap for you. He will be waiting. How can you succeed?'

'He's Waylander the Slayer,' said Angel. 'How can he not?'

'What a fool!' cackled Kesa Khan, leaping to his feet and capering about the cave, his weariness forgotten. Miriel looked on in astonishment. Angel merely shook his head. 'To think,' continued the shaman, 'that he tried to kill Waylander by direct action. It is almost bliss! Like trying to choke a lion by forcing your head into its mouth. Bliss!'

'What are you talking about?' asked Miriel.

Kesa Khan sighed and settled down by the fire. 'You are his daughter and you do not see it? He is like a fire. Left to his own devices he burns down to low, glowing embers. But to attack him is to throw twigs and branches to the flames. Can you understand that? Look!' Kesa Khan waved his hand above the flames, which flattened into a mirror of fire. Within it they saw Waylander moving slowly through the Void tunnel, water drenching his boots. 'Here he was afraid, for there were no enemies, only darkness. He was lost. No memory. No weapons.' They watched the tiny figure reach the skeleton, saw the golden-haired head materialise. 'Now observe!' ordered Kesa Khan.

The scaled creature reared up behind Waylander, who snatched the rib and rammed it into the beast's chest. 'Now,' said the shaman, 'he has a sword. Now, he has a purpose. Enemies are all around him. His talents are focused. See how he moves, like a wolf.'

407

Silently they sat as the tiny figure destroyed the sphere and battled his way up the staircase of hands. 'This I loved,' cackled the shaman, as Waylander threw the white-robed priest into the jaws of the serpent. 'He knew, do you see? In the dark, surrounded by foes, he knew there was no succour. The doorway he chose was the guarded one. Oh, it is so perfect. He must have Nadir blood! And to summon sunshine into the Void! Beautiful. Perfect! Zhu Chao must be trembling now. By all the gods, I would be.'

'I do not know if he is trembling,' said Miriel, 'but I do know my father is riding for Gulgothir. And there will be no sunshine to summon there. Zhu Chao will surround himself with armed guards: he will be waiting.'

'As the gods will,' said Kesa Khan, with a wave of his hand. The fire flared once more. 'Tomorrow we must move the women and children to Kar-Barzac. I have sent a message to Anshi Chen. He will leave a small rearguard to hold the passes. Fifty men will remain here until dark to defend the wall. It should be enough.'

'What about my father?' insisted Miriel.

'His fate is in the hands of the gods,' answered Kesa Khan. 'He will live or die. There is nothing we can do.'

'Zhu Chao will use magic to locate him,' said Miriel. 'Can you shield him?'

'No, I do not have the power. There are deadly beasts in the valley of Kar-Barzac. I need all my strength to send them into the mountains, clearing the path for my people to the fortress.'

'Then what chance will my father have?'

'That we will see. Do not underestimate him.'

'There must be something we can do!'

'Yes, yes. We fight on. We make Zhu Chao concentrate his energies on Kar-Barzac. That is what he wants. His dreams lie in that old castle.'

'Why?' asked Angel.

'The Elders built it. They cast great spells there, creating living demons known as Joinings to fight their wars. Beasts merged with men: the magic was colossal. So great that it ultimately destroyed them, but in Kar-Barzac the magic lived on, radiating out. You will see. The valley is twisted by it, deformed trees, carnivorous sheep and goats. I even saw a rabbit there with fangs. Nothing could live in that valley without being corrupted, twisted out of shape. Even the castle is now a monstrosity, the granite blocks reshaped as if they were wet clay.'

'Then how the Hell can we go there?' said Angel.

Kesa Khan smiled, and his dark eyes gleamed. 'Someone was kind enough to stop the magic,' he said. He looked away from them, staring into the fire.

'What is it you are not telling us?' asked Miriel.

'A great deal,' admitted the shaman. 'But there is much you do not need to know. Our enemies reached Kar-Barzac before us. They removed the source of magic – aye, and died for it. Now it is safe. We shall defend its walls, and there the line of the Uniter will be continued.'

'How long can we hold this fortress?' enquired Angel.

'We shall see,' answered Kesa Khan, 'but for now I need to drive the beasts from the valley. Leave me.'

16

Zhu Chao's image floated before Altharin as the General stood in his tent, his aide Powis beside him, the albino Brotherhood captain, Innicas, to his left.

'You have failed your Emperor,' said Zhu Chao. 'He set you a simple task and you have behaved like an incompetent. A few Nadir to kill and you baulk at the test.'

'Those few Nadir,' said Altharin coldly, 'have boxed themselves behind three narrow passes. I have lost more than two hundred men trying to force a way through them, and your famed Brotherhood have enjoyed no more success than I. One old man broke their attack.'

'You dare to criticise the Brotherhood?' hissed Zhu Chao. 'You are worse than incompetent. You are a traitor!'

'I serve the Emperor – not you, you puffed up . . .' He groaned and sagged into the arms of Powis, a long-handled knife jutting from his ribs.

Eyes wide with shock, Powis took the dying General in his arms, lowering him to the floor. He looked up at the white-haired figure of Innicas. 'You have killed him!' he whispered.

Altharin tried to speak, but blood bubbled from his lips and his head sagged back. Innicas leaned down and dragged the knife clear, wiping it clean on the dead General's tunic of silk. Powis rose, hands trembling.

'Do nothing rash, boy!' said the image of Zhu Chao. 'The order for his death came from the Emperor himself. Go and fetch Gallis. Tell him the Emperor has promoted him.'

Powis stepped back then gazed down at the corpse upon the floor. 'Do it now!' ordered Innicas.

Powis stumbled back and ran from the tent.

'There is another pass, Lord, thirty miles to the north,' said Innicas.

'Take one hundred men – the best we have. The Nadir will try to reach Kar-Barzac. Catch them in the valley. They will be stretched thin, some already at the fortress, others trying to fight a rearguard. The women and children will be in a column on open ground. Destroy them! We'll see how well the Nadir fight when there is nothing left to fight for.'

'As you order it, Lord, so will it be,' said Innicas, bowing.

'Have you reached Gracus and the others?'

'No, Lord. But Zamon is waiting in the mountains with their horses. He said they arrived safely. They are planning to move below ground. Perhaps the magic of Kar-Barzac prevents communication.'

'They are there – that is what matters,' said Zhu Chao. 'All is as we planned it. The Ventrians have landed in the south. The Drenai, without Karnak, have fallen back in disorder. Our own troops are waiting to sweep down on to the Sentran Plain. But much of what we need for future control lies in Kar-Barzac. Do not fail me, Innicas!'

'You may rely on me, my lord.'

'Let it be so.'

The Gothir, dragging and carrying their wounded with them, fell back as the sun drifted low behind the mountains. Senta slumped to the ground, Belash beside him. 'I hate to admit it, but I'm getting tired,' said the swordsman.

'I also,' admitted Belash. The Nadir leaned his head back against the black rock of the wall. 'The attacks were more fierce today.' He rubbed his tired eyes. 'We will fall back in two hours.'

'How far is it to this fortress?'

'We will be in the valley by the dawn,' said Belash glumly.

'You don't sound too enthusiastic, my friend.'

'It is a place of much evil.' Belash opened the pouch at his side and removed the bones, which he held pressed between his palms. He sighed. 'I think Belash will die there,' he said.

'What are those things?' asked Senta, seeking to change the subject.

'The right hand of my father. He was killed, a long time ago now, and still I am no closer to avenging him.'

'What happened?'

'He had ponies to sell and rode to the market at Namib. A long way. He went with my brother and Anshi Chen. Only Anshi survived the attack. He was behind the herd, and when the raiders struck, Anshi fled.'

'That's why there is such anger between you? Because he was a coward?'

'He is no coward!' snapped Belash. 'There were too many of the raiders, and it would have been stupid to fight. No, Anshi and I loved

410

the same woman. She chose him. But he is a fine chieftain, may my tongue turn black for admitting it. I tried to track the raiders. I found my father's body, took these bones and buried the rest. But the tracks were too old. Anshi watched as my father was struck down. He saw the man who dealt the death blow; he described him to me. I have lived since then in the hope of finding him – a white-haired warrior, with eyes the colour of blood.'

'There's still time,' said Senta.

'Maybe.' Belash levered himself to his feet, and wandered away along the wall, speaking to the defenders, kneeling beside the wounded and the dying.

Senta stretched himself out, lying back with his head on his hands, watching the stars appear in the darkening sky. The air was fresh and cool, the bonded rocks below his back feeling almost soft. He closed his eyes. When he opened them again Miriel was beside him. He smiled, 'I fell asleep,' he said. 'But I dreamt of you.'

'Something lascivious, I have no doubt.'

He sat up and stretched. 'No. We were sitting in a field by a stream, beneath the branches of a willow. We were holding hands. Like this.' Reaching out he took her hand, raising it to his lips.

'You never give in, do you?' she said, pulling back from his touch.

'Never! Why don't you kiss me, beauty? Just the once. To see if you like it.'

'No.'

'You cut me to the bone.'

'I think you'll survive.'

'You are frightened, aren't you? Frightened of giving. Frightened of living. I heard you with Angel last night, offering yourself to him. It was a mistake, beauty, and Angel was right to say no. Insane, but right. What is it you fear?'

'I don't want to talk about this,' said Miriel, making to rise. Reaching out he lightly touched her arm.

'Talk to me,' he said softly.

'Why?' she whispered.

'Because I care.'

She sank back and for a while, said nothing. He did not press her, but sat beside her in silence. At last she spoke. 'If you love someone you open all the doors into your heart. You let them in. When they die you have no defences. I saw my father's pain when . . . when Mother was killed. I don't want that pain. Ever.'

'You can't avoid it, Miriel. No one can. We are like the seasons – we grow in spring, mature in summer, fade in the autumn and die in the winter. But it is foolish to say, "It is springtime but I will grow no flowers for they must fade." What is life without love? Perpetual winter. Cold and snow. It's not for you, beauty. Trust me.'

411

His hand stroked her hair and he leaned in close, his lips brushing her cheek. Slowly she turned her head and his mouth touched hers.

An arrow sailed over the wall, and the sound of pounding feet echoed in the pass.

'The Gothir have immaculate timing,' he said, rising up and drawing his sword.

Angel was uneasy as he stood on the rim of the valley, looking out over the moonlit grassland and the gentle hills. In the distance he could see the turrets and walls of Kar-Barzac, close to a wide flat lake the colour of old iron. Nadir women and children were moving down into the valley in a long, shuffling line, many of them dragging carts piled high with their possessions. Angel switched his gaze to the rearing mountains that circled the valley, scanning the twisted peaks. This was all open ground, and he thought of the defenders manning the three passes, and prayed the rearguard would hold. For if the Gothir forced their way through any one pass . . .

He closed his mind to the pictures of carnage.

Most of the Nadir warriors had ridden ahead to the fortress, the majority of those remaining defending the passes. Only thirty men rode with the women and children, shepherding them towards Kar-Barzac. Angel swung into the saddle and rode down the hill, his mood lifting as he saw the mute Nadir boy marching beside an overloaded cart, Angel's cloak upon his scrawny shoulders and in his right hand a length of wood, shaped like a sword. The cloak was dragging in the dust. Angel rode alongside the boy and leaned down, lifting him in the air and perching him on the saddle behind him. The boy grinned and waved his wooden sword in the air.

Touching heels to the gelding Angel galloped the horse towards the front of the line where Belash rode beside the Nadir war chief, Anshi Chen. The two warriors were deep in conversation. Anshi looked up as Angel approached. He was a stocky man, running to fat, and his dark eyes showed only hostility as the Drenai reined in.

'We are moving too slowly,' said Angel. 'It will be dawn soon.'

Belash nodded. 'I agree, but many are old. They can move no faster.'

'They could if they left those carts behind.'

Anshi Chen sniffed loudly, then hawked and spat. 'Their possessions are their lives,' he said. 'You would not understand that, Drenai, for yours is a land of plenty. But each of those carts carries far more than you see. A lantern of bronze may be just a light in the dark to you, but it might have been made by a great-grandfather a century ago, and prized ever since. Every item has a value far greater than you can comprehend. Leaving them behind would be a knife in the soul to any family here.'

412

'It is not a knife in the soul that concerns me,' said Angel. 'It is a knife in the back. But this is your war.' Swinging the horse's head he rode back along the line.

There were more than three hundred people filing on to the valley floor, and he guessed it would be another two hours before the last of them reached the fortress. He thought of Senta and Miriel back at the wall, and Waylander on his lonely journey to Gulgothir.

The stars were fading now, the sky lightening.

And his unease grew.

The white-haired Innicas moved back from the shelter of the boulder to where his brother knights waited. 'Now,' he told them. 'The moment is here.' Gathering the reins of his black stallion he vaulted into the saddle, drawing the black sword from the scabbard at his side. One hundred warriors mounted their horses and waited for his order. Innicas closed his eyes, seeking the Communion of Blood. He felt the flowing of the souls, tasted their anger and their need, their bitterness and their desires. 'Let not one Nadir live,' he whispered. 'All dead. Gifts to the Lord of All Desires. Let there be pain. Let there be fear and anguish. Let there be despair!' The souls of his knights fluttered in his mind like black moths, circling the dark light of his hatred. 'What do we need?' he asked them.

'Blood and death,' came the reply, hissing in his mind like a host of snakes.

'Blood and death,' he agreed. 'Now let the spell grow. Let fear flow out over our enemies like a flood, a raging torrent to drown their courage.'

Like an invisible mist the spell rolled out, drifting over rock and shale, down on to the valley, swelling, growing.

The one hundred Knights of Blood ended the communion and rode from their hiding-place, fanning out into a fighting line, swords at the ready.

Angel felt the cold touch of fear, his mind leaping back to the day at the cabin when the Brotherhood had first appeared. Dragging on the reins he swung the horse to face the south, and saw the enemy silhouetted against the sky, their black cloaks flowing in the breeze, their swords raised high. Belash saw them at the same time, and shouted to Anshi Chen.

As the spell of fear rolled over them women and children began to wail and run, scattering across the valley. Some threw themselves to the ground, covering their heads with their hands. Others merely stood, frozen in terror. Shia was walking in the centre of the column when the spell struck. With trembling hands she lifted her bow from her shoulder and clumsily notched an arrow to the string.

413

Angel felt the mute boy's arms tighten around him. Swinging in the saddle he lifted the child, lowering him to the ground beside a hand-drawn cart. The child looked up at him, his eyes wide and fearful. Angel drew his sword and forced a smile. The child pulled his stick from his belt and waved it in the air.

'Good lad!' said Angel.

The thirty Nadir outriders galloped their mounts to where Belash and Anshi Chen were waiting. Angel joined them. 'Their spell of fear will not hold once the killing starts!' said Angel. 'Trust me!'

'There are too many of them,' muttered Anshi Chen, his voice trembling.

'There'll be less before long,' snarled Angel. 'Follow me!' Kicking his horse into a gallop he charged at the black line.

The Brotherhood swept forward, and the thunder of hoofbeats echoed in the valley like the drums of doom. Anger swept through Angel. Behind him were women and children and if, as was most likely, the Brotherhood did break through he did not want to be alive to see the slaughter. He did not glance back to see if the Nadir were with him. He did not care. Battle fever was strong upon him.

The black line came closer, and Angel angled his horse towards their centre. Belash came galloping alongside, screaming a Nadir war cry.

Three horsemen closed on Angel. Ducking under one wild cut he slashed his sword into the helm of a second knight. The man was catapulted from the saddle. Belash's horse went down, but the Nadir leapt clear and rolled to his feet. A sword-blade glanced from his shoulder. He leapt and dragged the rider from the saddle, plunging his own blade deep into the man's belly.

The small wedge of Nadir riders was surrounded now, and the wings of the Brotherhood line, some forty men, swept on towards the women and children.

Shia watched them come, fear surging inside her, and drew back on her bowstring. Her first shaft pierced the neck of the leading horse. It fell and rolled, hurling its rider clear, but bringing down two following horses. Other knights swerved to avoid colliding with the fallen. A second shaft sank into the neck of a knight. He swayed in the saddle for a moment, before toppling to the ground.

Shia notched a third arrow – then heard the thunder of hooves from behind her! So close! Spinning she saw a score of riders in silver armour, white cloaks fluttering behind them. They galloped through the refugee line and bore down on the Brotherhood. Shia could not believe what she was seeing. Like silver ghosts they had come from nowhere, and in their wake the spell of fear vanished, like ice under sunlight.

414

On the far side of the field Angel cut his way clear of the mass and saw the white knights hammer into the Brotherhood. Exultant now he turned again and drove his mount back into the mêlée. Swords clashed all around him, but he was oblivious to danger. His horse went down and he hit the ground hard, a hoof clipping his temple. Losing his grip on his sword Angel rolled. A blade slashed down at him, but he ducked under it, then hurled his weight at the rider's horse. Off-balance the beast fell, tipping the knight to the earth. Angel scrambled across the fallen horse. The knight was struggling to rise when Angel's boot cracked into his helm. The chinstrap ripped and the helm fell clear. The knight tried in vain to stab his attacker, but Angel's fist smashed into his face, spinning him round. Angel's hands closed on his throat like bands of iron. Dropping his sword the knight grabbed at the fingers. But all strength fled from him.

Angel dropped the corpse and gathered up the knight's sword.

Anshi Chen hacked his blade towards the neck of an attacker, but the man part-blocked the blow, the sword striking the side of the helm and dislodging the visor. As it came clear, hanging from the helm like a broken wing, Anshi recognised the albino face. 'Belash!' he cried. 'It is him, Belash!'

Innicas' sword swept out, the blade plunging into Anshi's belly. Belash, hearing the cry, swung and saw Innicas deliver the death blow. All reason fled from the Nadir, and he let out a terrible scream of hate. A horse reared alongside him. Belash leapt at the rider, dragging him from the saddle. Not stopping to slay the man Belash took hold of the pommel and vaulted to the beast's back. Innicas saw him, felt his rage, and quickly scanned the battle line.

The Brotherhood were broken.

Panic rose in his heart. With a savage kick he pushed his horse into a gallop and rode for the south and the hidden pass. Belash set after him, leaning low over the stallion's neck, cutting down wind resistance. Innicas, in full armour, was the heavier man and his stallion tired as it pounded up the hillside. Innicas glanced back. The Nadir was closing.

The knight's stallion, almost at the point of exhaustion, stumbled upon the shale and half-fell. Innicas jumped clear. Belash bore down upon him. The shoulder of Belash's stallion cannoned into the knight, punching him from his feet. Dragging on the reins Belash leapt lightly to the shale.

'You killed my father,' he said. 'Now you will serve him for eternity.'

Innicas, sword in hand, gazed upon the stocky Nadir. The man had no armour, and carried only a short sabre.

The albino's courage returned. 'You cannot stand against me, vermin!' he sneered. 'I'll cut you into pieces.'

Belash attacked, but Innicas' sword blocked the blow and a murderous riposte saw the black blade bury itself in Belash's side, cleaving under the ribs. With the last of his strength Belash dropped his sword and drew his curved dagger. Innicas wrenched at his blade, trying to drag it clear. Belash reached out, his left hand clawing at Innicas' helm, fingers hooking around the broken visor. Innicas felt himself being drawn into a deadly embrace. 'No!' he shouted. Belash's knife plunged into Innicas' left eye, piercing him to the brain. Both men fell.

Innicas twitched and was still. Belash, with trembling hands, opened the blood-drenched pouch at his side, tipping the fingerbones on to the chest of the dead knight. 'Father,' he whispered, blood bubbling from his lips. 'Father . . .'

In his panic Innicas had misread the battle. Despite being surprised by the arrival of the white knights, the Brotherhood still had the advantage of numbers. Only seven of the Nadir warriors remained now and, despite being joined by the twenty white-cloaked knights, they were outnumbered by more than two to one.

Angel, bleeding from several wounds, could feel the battle was ready to turn against the Brotherhood. Their leader had fled, and the arrival of the white knights had stunned them. But the enemy could yet win, he knew.

Not while I live, he thought.

A sword slashed past his face, the flat of the blade slamming against his chin. He went down and struggled to rise. Hooves pounded on the earth all around him. Rearing up he pushed a booted foot from the stirrups and propelled the rider to the ground. Taking hold of the pommel he tried to mount the horse, but it reared, throwing him to the ground once more.

With a curse Angel gathered up his fallen sword. A blade lashed down. Angel blocked the blow and, as the rider rode past him, reached up and grabbed the man's cloak, hauling him from the saddle. The knight hit the ground hard. The point of Angel's sword slid between visor and helm and with all his weight Angel drove the weapon deep into the man's skull. The blade snapped. Angel swore.

There was a fallen sword close by. Dodging between the milling horses Angel reached for it, but a rearing hoof smashed into his head and he fell face down on to the grass.

He awoke to silence and a terrible pounding in his skull.

'I always seem to be stitching your wounds,' said Senta.

Angel blinked and tried to focus on the ceiling above him. It was twisted at a crazy angle, and the window below it was canted absurdly. 'There's something wrong with my eyes,' he muttered.

'No. It's this place – Kar-Barzac. Nothing is as it should be here. Kesa Khan says it has been corrupted over the centuries by sorcery.'

Angel struggled to sit, but his head swam and he fell back. 'What happened?' he groaned.

'I arrived to save you.'

'Single-handed, I suppose.'

'Close. We waited until just after midnight then, when the Gothir had fallen back for the fifth time, we ran for our horses. There were only thirty of us left, but it was enough to send the Brotherhood fleeing from the field.'

'I don't remember that,' said Angel. 'In fact, my thoughts are hazy. I seem to recall ghosts riding to our rescue, in white armour.'

'Priests,' said Senta. 'Source priests.'

'In armour?'

'An unusual Order,' said Senta. 'They call themselves the Thirty, although there are only eleven of them now. They are led by an Abbot named Dardalion.'

'He was at Purdol. He helped Karnak. Get me up!'

'You should lie back. You've lost a lot of blood.'

'Thank you for your concern, Mother. Now help me up, damn you!'

'As you wish, old fool.' Senta's hand slid under Angel's shoulder, levering him to a sitting position. Nausea gripped him but he swallowed it down and sucked in a deep breath. 'I thought we were finished. Where's Miriel?'

'She's safe. She's with Dardalion and Kesa Khan.'

'And the Gothir?'

'Camped all around us, Angel. They've been reinforced. Must be seven, eight thousand men in the valley.'

'Wonderful. Is there any good news?'

'None that I can think of, but you do have a visitor. Charming little fellow. He's sitting in the hallway now – I'll send him to you in a while. I found him sitting by what we thought was your body. He was crying. Very touching it was. Brought a tear to my eye, I can tell you.' Angel swore. Senta chuckled. 'I knew you weren't dead, Angel. You're too stubborn to die.'

'How many did we lose?'

Senta's smile faded. 'Belash is dead, and Anshi Chen. There are some three hundred warriors left, but many of those are youngsters, untried. I don't think we can hold this place for long.'

'They've not attacked yet?'

'No. They're busy chopping down trees, making scaling ladders and the like.'

417

Angel lay back and closed his eyes. 'Just let them give me a day or two. Then I'll be ready. I'm a fast healer, Senta.'

'In that case we'll try not to start the war without you.'

Senta found Miriel on the inner rampart, leaning on the twisted wall and staring out over the camp-fires of the enemy. Nadir warriors were standing close by, sharpening their weapons. The swordsman moved past the Nadir and halted beside the tall mountain girl. 'Angel's fine,' he said. 'A few minor cuts and a large lump on that thick skull. I sometimes think if the world ended in fire and flood he would walk out of the cinders with singed hair and wet boots.'

She smiled. 'He does appear so wonderfully indestructible.'

'Come and see what I have found,' said Senta, walking away to a set of stairs which led down to a narrow corridor and a large suite of rooms. The windows were distorted, shaped now like open, screaming mouths, and the walls were crooked. But the large bedchamber was empty and in its centre was a golden four-post bed, beautifully proportioned, rectangular and solid. There were pillows of silk and a coverlet filled with goose down.

'How could such a bed survive when a fortress of stone is corrupted?' she asked.

The swordsman shrugged. 'There are other objects of gold that are apparently not affected by the sorcery. I found two goblets downstairs, exquisitely carved.'

She moved towards the bed, then angled away to the first of the three windows. From here the valley could be seen. 'There's another column of cavalry moving down,' she told him.

'I don't care about the cavalry,' he said.

She swung towards him, her back to the window, her face blushing crimson. 'You think I will let you bed me?'

'I think you should seriously consider it,' he told her, with a wide smile.

'I don't love you, Senta.'

'You don't know that yet,' he said reasonably. 'Here's where you can find out.'

'You think love springs from the loins?'

He laughed aloud. 'Mine always has – until now.' He shook his head, the smile fading. 'You are frightened, beauty. Frightened to live. Well, here we are, trapped in a decrepit fortress, our futures measured in days. This is no time to be frightened of life. You owe me a kiss, at least. The Gothir stole the last one.'

'One kiss is all you will have,' she promised, moving forward.

He opened his arms to her and she stepped inside. Reaching up he pushed his fingers into her long dark hair, easing it back from her face, stroking the high cheekbones, his hand curling round to the nape of her neck. He could feel his heart pounding as he kissed her brow and her cheek. She tilted her head, her lips brushing against his skin. Their lips met, and he felt her body pressing against him. Her mouth tasted sweet, warm, and his passion soared. But he made no move to pull her to the bed. Instead he ran his hands down her back, halting at the slender waist, feeling the curve of her hips. And he kissed her neck and shoulder, revelling in the scent of her skin.

She was wearing a black leather tunic, laced at the front with slender thongs. Slowly he moved his right hand to her breast, his fingers hooking to the first knot.

'No,' she said, moving back from him. Swallowing his disappointment he took a deep breath. She smiled. 'I'll do it.' Unfastening the knife-belt at her waist she lifted the tunic over her head, and stood before him naked. His eyes drank her in, the long sun-bronzed legs, the flat belly, the high, full breasts.

'You're a vision, beauty. No question of it.'

He stepped towards her, but she stopped him. 'What about you?' she asked. 'Do I not get a chance to admire?'

'Every chance,' he told her, pulling free his shirt and unhooking his belt. He almost stumbled as he struggled to remove his leggings, and her laughter was infectious.

'You'd think you'd never removed leggings before,' she said.

Reaching out he took her arm and gently pulled her to the bed. A cloud of dust rose as they fell upon it, causing him to cough. 'Such romance,' she giggled. He joined in her laughter and they lay quietly together for a few moments, staring into each other's eyes. His right hand stroked the skin of her shoulder and arm, moving down until his forearm brushed across her nipple. She closed her eyes and slid in towards him. The hand moved on, over the flat belly and on to the thigh. Her legs were closed, but now she parted them. He kissed her again. Her arm hooked around his neck, pulling him into a fierce embrace.

'Gently, beauty,' he whispered. 'There is no need for haste. Nothing beautiful is ever crafted at speed. And I want this first time to be special.'

She moaned as his palm pressed gently against her pubic mound, and for some time he slowly caressed her. Her breathing quickened, her body moving into spasm. She cried out, again and again. Finally he rose above her, lifting her long legs over his hips and guiding himself into her. He kissed her again, then drove into her, releasing the self-imposed chains of his own passion.

He tried to keep his movements slow, but his needs were greater than his wish to make the moment last, and when Miriel cried out again, in a series of rhythmic, almost primal groans, he succumbed at last. His body spasmed, his arms pulling her into a tight embrace.

Then he moaned and lay still. He sighed and his body relaxed as he lay upon her, feeling his own heartbeat and hers together, pounding against the warm skin of his chest.

'Oh,' she whispered. 'Was that love?'

'By all the gods I hope so, beauty,' he answered her, rolling to his back. 'For nothing else in my life has given me so much pleasure.'

Raising herself on her elbow she gazed down at his face. 'It was . . . wonderful. Let's do it again!'

'In a while, Miriel,' he answered.

'How long?'

He chuckled and drew her into his embrace. 'Not long. I promise you!'

17

Dardalion opened his eyes, his spirit returning to the flesh, feeling the weight of his body and the silver armour upon it. It was cold in the room, despite the log fire burning in the hearth.

'They will not attack today – and perhaps not tomorrow,' he told Kesa Khan. 'Their General Gannis is a careful man. He has sent work parties to the woods to cut trees and make scaling ladders. He intends one great attack which will swamp us.'

The little Nadir shaman nodded. 'We will hold them for one, maybe two assaults. After that . . .' He spread his hands.

Dardalion rose from the gold lacquered chair and moved to the fire, extending his hands to the flames, enjoying the sudden warmth. 'What I do not understand – and neither does the Gothir General – is why the Emperor has chosen this course. The coming Uniter will not be stopped. It is written that the Nadir will rise. There is nothing he can do to change the future. Nothing.'

'It is not the Emperor, but Zhu Chao who seeks our destruction,' said Kesa Khan, with a dry laugh. 'Twin needs spur him on: his hatred for the Wolves, and his desire for absolute power.'

'Why does he hate you so?'

Kesa Khan's eyes glittered and his smile was cruel. 'Many years ago he came to me, seeking to understand the nature of magic. He is a Chiatze, and he was studying the Dark Arts and the origins of the Knights of Blood. I turned him away. He had the wit, but not the courage.'

'And for this he hates you?'

'No, not just for this. He crept back to my cave, and I caught him trying to steal . . .' the shaman's eyes were hooded now '. . . objects of value. My guards took him. They wanted to kill him, but I decided to be merciful. I merely cut something from him, gave him a wound to remember me by. He still had his life, but he would never sire life. You understand?'

'Only too well,' answered Dardalion coldly.

'Do not judge me, priest,' snapped Kesa Khan.

'It is not for me to judge. You planted the seed of his hatred, and now you are gathering the harvest.'

'Pah, it is not that simple,' said the shaman. 'He was always a creature of evil. I should have killed him. But his hatred I can bear. This fortress, and what it contains, is the second of his desires. There is more powerful sorcery here than has been seen in the world for ten millennia. Zhu Chao wants it . . . needs it. Once upon a distant time the Elders here performed miracles. They learned how to merge flesh. A man who had lost a leg could grow a new one. Organs riddled with cancer could be replaced, without use of a knife. Bodies could be regenerated, rejuvenated. Here was the secret of immortality. The force was contained within a giant crystal, encased in a covering of pure gold. It radiated power, and only gold and to a lesser extent lead, could imprison it. You saw the valley?'

'Yes,' said Dardalion. 'Nature perverted.'

'Fifty years ago, a group of robbers came to this place. They found the Crystal Chamber and stripped the gold from its walls, removing the covering from the crystal itself.' He laughed. 'It was not a wise action.'

'What happened to them? Why did they not steal the crystal?'

'The power they unleashed killed them. The Elders knew how to control it, to focus the forces. Without their skill it has become merely a corrupting, violent, haphazard sorcery.'

'I sense no power emanating from here,' said Dardalion.

'No. Zhu Chao sent men here. They removed the crystal from its setting. It sits now upon a golden floor some two hundred feet below us.'

'Did these men also die?'

'I think you could call it a kind of death.'

Dardalion felt cold as he looked into the shaman's malevolent eyes. 'What is it that you are not telling me, Kesa Khan? What secret strategies have yet to be unveiled?'

'Do not be impatient, priest. All will be revealed. Everything is in a delicate state of balance. We cannot win here by might or guile – we must rely on the intangibles. Your friend Waylander, for example. He now hunts Zhu Chao, but can he enter his palace, fight his way through a hundred guards and overcome the sorcery at Zhu Chao's command? Who knows? Can we hold here? And if not, can we find a way to escape? Or should we use the power of the crystal?'

'You know the answer to the last question, shaman – no. Else you would have come here years ago. No one knows what destroyed the Elders, save that there are areas of great desolation where once were mighty cities. Everything we know of them speaks of corruption and greed, enormous evils and terrible weapons. Even the wickedness within you recoils at their misdeeds. Is it not so?'

Kesa Khan nodded. 'I have walked the paths of time, priest. I know what destroyed them. And yes, I wish to see no return to their foul ways. They raped the land and lived like kings while fouling the rivers and lakes, the forests – aye, even the air they breathed. They knew everything and understood nothing. And they were destroyed for it.'

'But their legacy lives on here,' said Dardalion softly.

'And in other secret places, yet to be found.'

Dardalion knelt by the fire, adding several logs to the blaze. 'Whatever else, we must destroy the crystal. Zhu Chao must not possess it.'

Kesa Khan nodded. 'When the time comes we will seek it out.'

'Why not now?'

'Trust me, Dardalion. I am far older than you, and I have walked paths that would burn your soul to ashes. Now is not the time.'

'What would you have me do?'

'Find a quiet place and send out your spirit to seek Waylander. Cloak him – as you did once before – protect him from the sorcery of Zhu Chao. Give him his chance to kill the beast.'

On the highest tower Vishna sat upon the ramparts, Ekodas beside him. The forked bearded Gothir nobleman sighed. 'My brothers could be down there,' he said.

'Let us pray that is not the case,' said Ekodas.

'I think we were wrong,' said Vishna softly, 'and you were right. This is no way to serve the Source. I killed two men in that charge yesterday. I know they were evil, I felt it radiating from them, but I was lessened by the deed. I can no longer believe the Source wishes us to kill.'

Reaching out, Ekodas laid a hand upon his friend's shoulder. 'I do not know what the Source requires, Vishna. I only know that yesterday we protected a column of women and children. I do not regret that, but I regret bitterly that it was necessary to kill.'

'But why are we here?' cried Vishna. 'To ensure the birth of a child who will ultimately destroy all that my family have spent generations building? It is madness!'

Ekodas shrugged. 'Let us hope there is some greater purpose. But I believe it will be enough to thwart the Brotherhood.'

Vishna shook his head. 'There are only eleven of us left. You think we can achieve some great victory?'

'Perhaps. Why don't you seek out Dardalion? Pray together. It will help.'

'No, it won't. Not this time, brother,' said Vishna sadly. 'I have followed him all my adult life, and I have known the great joy of comradeship – with him, with you all. I never doubted until now. But this is a problem I must solve alone.'

'For what it is worth, my friend, I think it is better to be unsure. It seems to me that most of the problems of this world have been caused by men who were too sure; men who always knew what was right. The Brotherhood chose a path of pain and suffering. Not their own, of course. They rode into that valley to butcher women and babes. Remember that!'

Vishna nodded. 'You are probably right, Ekodas. But what when one of my brothers climbs this wall, sword in hand. What do I do? He is obeying the orders of his Emperor, as all good soldiers must. Do I kill him? Do I hurl him to his death?'

'I don't know,' admitted Ekodas. 'But there are enough real perils facing us, without creating more.'

'I wish to be alone, my friend. Do not be insulted, I beseech you.'

'I am not insulted, Vishna. May your deliberations bring you peace.' Turning, Ekodas ducked under the crumbling lintel and descended the undulating stairs. He came out into a narrow corridor leading to a long hall. Within it fat Merlon was helping the Nadir women to prepare food for the warriors. Ekodas saw Shia kneading dough close by. She looked up and smiled at him.

'How are you, lady?' he asked.

'I am well, prayer-man. Your arrival was a surprise most pleasant.'

'I did not think we would be in time. We first journeyed west into Vagria and then south in order to avoid the besiegers. The ride was long.'

'And now you are here. With me.'

'I was sorry to hear of your brother's death,' he said swiftly, as she rose from the table.

'Why? Did you know him?'

'No. But it must have caused you pain. For that I am sorry.'

Leaving the table she moved in close to him. 'There is a little pain, but it is my own. Yet I am also proud, for the man he slew was the same knight who killed our father. That is a blessing for which I thank the gods. But Belash is now in the Hall of Heroes. He has many beautiful maidens around him, and his cup is full of fine wine. Rich meats are cooking, and he has a hundred ponies to ride when he wishes. My pain is only that I will not see him again. But I am happy for him.'

423

Ekodas could think of no reply, so he bowed and backed away. 'You look like a man now,' said Shia approvingly, 'And you fight like a warrior. I watched you kill three and maim a fourth.'

He winced and walked swiftly from the hall. But she followed him out on to the lower rampart above the courtyard. The stars were bright and he drew in several deep, cool breaths.

'Did I insult you?' she asked.

'No. It is . . . just . . . that I do not like to kill. It does not please me to hear that I maimed a man.'

'Do not concern yourself. I cut his throat.'

'That is hardly an uplifting thought.'

'They are our enemies,' she said, speaking as if to a simpleton. 'What else would you do with them?'

'I have no answers, Shia. Only questions that no one can answer.'

'I could answer them,' she assured him brightly.

He sat back on the rampart wall and looked into her moonlit face. 'You are so confident. Why is that?'

'I know what I know, Ekodas. Ask me one of your questions.'

'I hate to kill, I know that. So why, during yesterday's battle, did I feel exultant with each sword-stroke?'

'I thought your questions would be hard,' she chided. 'Spirit and Flesh, Ekodas. The Spirit is immortal. It loves the Light, it worships beauty, of thought and deed. And it has Eternity to enjoy, Time to contemplate. But the Flesh is Dark. For the Flesh knows it has not long to live. Against the time of the Spirit the life of the Flesh is like a lightning flash. So it has little time to know pleasure, to taste the richness of life; lust, greed, gain. It wants to experience everything, and it cares for nothing save existence. What you felt was the surging joy of the Flesh. Nothing more. And certainly nothing to cause you self-loathing.' She chuckled, a rich, throaty sound that touched him like fire in the blood.

'What is so amusing?'

'You should feel sorry for the part of you that is Flesh, Ekodas. For what do you offer him in his brief existence? Rich food? No. Strong wines? Dances? Lust in the firelight?' She laughed again. 'No wonder he takes such pleasure from combat, eh?'

'You are a provocative woman,' he scolded.

'Thank you. Do I arouse you?'

'Yes.'

'But you fight it?'

'I must. It is the way I have chosen to live.'

'Do you believe the Spirit is eternal?'

'Of course.'

'Then do not be selfish, Ekodas. Does the Flesh not deserve a day in the sun? Look at my lips. Are they not full and pleasing? And is my

424

body not firm where it should be, and yet soft where it needs to be?'

His throat was dry, and he realised she had moved in very close. He stood and reached out, holding her at arms' length. 'Why do you torment me, lady? You know that I cannot give you what you desire.'

'Would you if you could?'

'Yes,' he admitted.

'We have our own priests,' she said. 'Kesa Khan is one. He also forbears from lovemaking, but it is a choice. He does not condemn it as wrong. Do you believe the gods created us?'

'The Source, yes.'

'And did they . . . He, if you like . . . not create men and women to desire one another?'

'I know where this is leading, but let me say this: there are many ways to serve the Source. Some men marry and beget children. Others choose different paths. What you said about the Flesh has great merit, but in subjugating the desires of the Flesh the Spirit becomes stronger. I can, in my Spirit form, fly through the air. I can read minds. I can heal the sick, removing cancerous growths. You understand? I can do these things because the Source has blessed me. And because I abstain from earthly pleasures.'

'Have you ever had a woman?' she countered.

'No.'

'How does your Source feel about killing?'

He smiled ruefully. 'His priests are pledged to love all living things, and harm none.'

'So you have chosen to break one of His commandments?'

'I believe that we have.'

'Is lovemaking a greater sin than killing?'

'Of course not.'

'And you still have your Talents?'

'Yes, I do.'

'Think on that, Ekodas,' she said, with a sweet smile. Then, spinning on her heel she returned to the hall.

The deaths of Belash and Anshi Chen created a void in the battle leadership of the Nadir, and the mood in the fortress was sullen and fatalistic. Nadir wars were fought on horseback on the open steppes and despite the transient security offered by the warped citadel, they were ill at ease manning the crooked battlements of Kar-Barzac.

They viewed the silver knights with disquiet, and rarely spoke to Senta or Miriel. But Angel was different. His transparent hostility towards them made him a force they could understand and feel at ease with. No patronising comments, no condescension. Mutual dislike and respect became the twin ties that allowed the remaining warriors to form a bond with the former gladiator.

425

He organised them into defence groups along the main wall, ordering them to gather rocks and broken masonry for hurling down on an advancing enemy. He chose leaders, issued orders, and lifted their spirits with casual insults and coarse humour. And his open contempt for the Gothir soldiers helped the tribesmen to overcome their own fears.

As the sun rose on the third day of the siege he gathered a small group of leaders around him and squatted down among them on the battlements. 'Now none of you beggars have ever seen a siege, so let me make it plain for you. They will carry forward stripped tree trunks as scaling ladders and lean them against the walls. Then they will climb the broken branches. Do not make the mistake of trying to push the ladders *away* from the wall. The weight of wood and armed men will make that impossible. Slide them left or right. Use the butt-end of your spears, or loop ropes over the top of the trunks. Unbalance them. Now we have around three hundred men to defend these walls, but we need a reserve force, ready to run and block any gaps that appear in the line. You, Subai!' he said, pointing to a short, wide-shouldered tribesman with a jagged scar on his right cheek. 'Pick forty men and hold back from the battle. Wait in the courtyard, watching the battlements. If our line breaks anywhere, reinforce it.'

'It will be as you order,' grunted the tribesman.

'Make sure it is, or I'll rip out your arm and beat you to death with the wet end.' The warriors smiled. Angel rose. 'Now, follow me to the gate.' The gates themselves had long since rotted, but the Nadir had managed to lower the portcullis, almost two tons of rusted iron, to block the entrance. Carts and wagons had been overturned at the base and thirty bowmen stood by. Angel moved to the archway. 'They will attempt to lift the portcullis. They will fail, for it is wedged above. But it is badly rusted and they will bring up saws and hammers to force an opening. You, what's your name again?'

'How many times must you ask, Ugly One?' countered the Nadir, a hook-nosed, swarthy man, taller than the average tribesman. Angel guessed he was a half-breed.

'All you beggars look alike to me,' said Angel. 'so tell me again.'

'Orsa Khan.'

'Well, Orsa Khan, I want you to command this defence. When they break through – as they will eventually – set fire to the carts. And hold them back to allow the men on the walls to retreat to the keep.'

'They will not break through while I live,' promised Orsa.

'That's the spirit, boy!' said Angel. 'Now, are there any questions?'

'What else do we need to ask?' put in Borsai, a young warrior of sixteen, still beardless. 'They come, we kill them until they go away. Is that not so?'

'Sounds a good strategy to me,' agreed Angel. 'Now, when some of them reach the ramparts – as they will – don't stab for their heads. Slash your blades at their hands as they reach for a hold. They'll be wearing gauntlets, but good iron will cut through those. Then, when they fall, they'll probably take two or three others with them. And that's a fair drop, my boys. They won't get up again.'

Leaving the warriors to their duties, Angel toured the walls. According to the Thirty, the Gothir would attack first by the main gate of the southern wall, a direct frontal assault to overwhelm the defenders. Therefore they had concentrated their manpower here, leaving only fifty warriors spread thin around the other walls. Angel had wanted to arm some of the younger women, but the Nadir would have none of the plan. War was for men, he was told. He did not argue. They would change their minds soon enough.

Striding across the courtyard he saw Senta and Miriel walking out towards him. Anger touched him then, for he could see by their closeness, the way she leaned in to him, that they had become lovers. The knowledge tasted of bile in his mouth, but he forced a smile. 'Going to be a cold day,' he said, indicating the gathering snow clouds above the mountains.

'I dare say the Gothir will warm it up for us,' Senta pointed out, draping his arm around Miriel's shoulder. She smiled, and leaned in to kiss his cheek.

Angel looked at them, the tall mountain girl, her smile radiant, and the handsome swordsman, golden-haired and young, dressed now in a buckskin shirt beneath a breastplate of glittering iron, and tan leggings of polished leather. Angel felt old as he watched them, the weight of his years and his disappointments hanging upon him like chains of lead. His own leather tunic was ragged and torn, his leggings filthy, and the pain of his wounds was only marginally less than the pain in his heart.

He moved away from them towards the keep, aware that they had not noticed his departure. He saw the mute child sitting on the keep steps, his wooden sword thrust into his belt. Angel grinned and clapped his hands. The boy copied him and rose smiling.

'You want some food, boy?' he said, lifting his fingers to his mouth and mimicking the act of chewing. The boy nodded and Angel led the way up to the main hall, where cook fires were burning in the hearths. A fat knight, wearing a leather apron, was stirring soup. He glanced at the child.

'He needs some weight on those bones,' he said, smiling and ruffling the boy's hair.

'Not as much as you're carrying, brother,' said Angel.

'It is a curious fact,' said the knight, 'but I only have to look at a honeycake and I feel the weight pile on.' Sitting the boy at the table he ladled soup into a bowl and watched with undisguised pleasure as the child enjoyed it. 'You should ask Ekodas to look at the boy,' said the knight softly. 'He has a real gift for healing. The child was not always deaf, you know. It faded slowly when he was a baby. And there is little wrong with his vocal chords. It is just that hearing no sound he makes no sound.'

'How do you know all this?' asked Angel.

'It is a talent fat people have, thin man.' He chuckled. 'My name is Merlon.'

'Angel,' responded the former gladiator, extending his hand. He was surprised to feel the strength in Merlon's grip, and he swiftly reappraised the priest. 'I think you're carrying a lot more muscle than fat,' he said.

'I have been blessed with a physique as strong as my appetite,' the other replied.

The child ate three bowls of the soup and half a loaf of bread while Angel sat and talked with the huge warrior priest. Shia approached them and sat on the bench seat alongside Angel.

'I told you they would not let us fight,' she said, anger showing in her eyes.

Angel grinned. 'That you did. But things will change, if not tomorrow, then the day after – as soon as they try an attack from all four sides. We have not the numbers of men to stop them. Make sure the women gather all the surplus . . . weapons.'

'By surplus you mean the weapons of our dead?'

'Exactly,' he admitted. 'And not just weapons, breastplates, helms, arm-guards. Anything to protect.'

At that moment a young woman ran into the hall. 'They are coming! They are coming!' she shouted.

'So it begins,' said Merlon, removing the leather apron and striding across the hall to where his breastplate, helm and sword were laid by the hearth.

Miriel stood to the left of the wall, almost at the corner, a crazily-angled turret leaning out above her. Her mouth was dry as she saw the Gothir line surge forward, and she ceased to notice the biting winter wind.

Twenty trees had been cut down and stripped of branches, and these were carried forward by heavily-armed men. Behind them marched two thousand foot-soldiers, shortswords and shields held at the ready. Miriel glanced to her right. At the centre of the ramparts stood Angel, grim and powerful, his sword still sheathed. Further along was Senta, a wide grin on his face, his eyes gleaming with the thrill of the coming battle. She shivered, but not with the cold.

More than a thousand men carried the tree trunks, and the pounding of their feet on the hard valley floor was like a roll of thunder. Two

Nadir beside Miriel hefted large rocks, laying them on the battlement. Archers sent shafts down into the charging ranks, but wounds were few among the armoured men, though Miriel saw a handful of soldiers reel back or fall as iron points lanced into unprotected thighs and arms.

The first trunk was raised and fell against the battlement with a booming thud. A Nadir hurled a rope over the top and began to pull.

'Wait until there are men on it!' bellowed Angel.

More trees crashed against the wall. A section of battlement gave way and a Nadir was hurled screaming to the courtyard forty feet below. Miriel swung and saw the man struggle to rise, but his leg was smashed. Several women ran forward, lifting the injured man and carrying him into the keep.

Notching an arrow to her bow Miriel leaned out over the wall. Thousands of men were swarming up the ladders, using the stubs of sawn-off branches for hand and footholds. Sighting her bow she sent an arrow through the temple of a soldier who had almost reached the top. He sagged back, and fell into the man behind him, dislodging him.

Angel hefted a large boulder and hurled it over the wall. It struck an attacker on his upraised shield, smashing the man's arm and shoulder. Amazingly he managed to hold on to the branch, but the boulder hit the man below on the helm, sweeping him from the tree. Stones and rocks rained down on the attackers, but still they came on, a score of men reaching the battlements.

Senta leapt forward, spearing his blade through the throat of the first man to reach the ramparts. Miriel dropped her bow and gathered up the trailing rope the Nadir had looped over the first trunk. 'Help me!' she shouted at the nearest warriors. Three men turned at her cry and ran to her aid. Together they hauled on the rope and, just as the first Gothir appeared, they succeeded in moving the ladder a foot to the right. Top-heavy now, the wood groaned – and slid sideways. A Gothir soldier jumped for the battlement, but lost his footing and fell screaming to the valley floor. The tree collided with a second ladder and, for a moment only, was held. Then both began to move.

'Let go the rope,' shouted Miriel, as the overburdened ladder fell away. The rope hissed and cracked like a whip as it was dragged over the battlements. The falling ladders struck a third, which was also dislodged from the wall. Miriel ran along the battlements to where Senta stood. 'The scaling ladders are too close together,' she shouted. 'Move that one and you'll bring down three, maybe four more.'

He looked to where she was pointing and nodded. Ropes had been placed along the wall and he lifted one, shaking out the loop. While the Nadir battled to keep the Gothir from the battlements Senta hurled a loop over the closest ladder and started to pull. It would not budge. Miriel joined him – but to no avail. Angel saw them and sent four men to assist.

Gothir warriors were scrambling over the battlements now, and one of them threw himself at Senta. The swordsman saw the blow almost too late, but let go the rope and lashed out with his foot, kicking the oncoming warrior in the knee. The man fell. Drawing his sword Senta sent a crashing blow to the soldier's helm. The Gothir struggled to rise. Senta ran in and shoulder-charged him, hurling him from the ramparts to the courtyard below.

Miriel and the others were still trying to pull the tree clear, but it was wedged into one of the crenellations of the battlement wall. Angel picked up a fallen axe, ducked under the rope and delivered a thunderous blow to the crumbling stone of the battlement. Twice more he struck. The granite shifted. Dropping to his haunches he lifted his feet and kicked out. The granite blocks fell away. The tree slid clear, struck the next crenellation – and snapped.

The rope-wielders were thrown back – Miriel, still holding the rope, tumbling from the ramparts. As the tree snapped Angel saw Miriel fall and dived for the snaking rope. The hemp tore the flesh from his fingers and Miriel's falling weight hauled him to the edge of the rampart. But he held on, regardless of pain or the peril of the drop. Just as he was being pulled over the edge a Nadir warrior threw himself across the fallen gladiator. Then Senta grabbed Angel's legs.

Miriel was dangling fifteen feet below the rampart. With the rope now steady she climbed and hooked her foot over the stone. A Nadir hauled her to safety. Angel climbed wearily to his feet, blood dripping from his torn palms.

The dislodged tree had toppled seven more, killing more than a hundred soldiers. Fearful of a similar fate the remaining Gothir warriors scrambled down to safety and retreated out of arrow range. Gleefully the Nadir sent all the trunks crashing to the earth. Subai, leaving the reserve force, climbed to the battlements, turned his back to the Gothir and, dropping his leggings, exposed his buttocks to the enemy. The Nadir howled with delight.

Orsa Khan, the tall half-breed, lifted his sword high above his head and shouted a Nadir refrain. It was picked up along the line until all the defenders were screaming it at the uncomprehending Gothir.

'What are they saying?' asked Angel.

'It is the last verse of the battle song of the Wolves,' said Senta. 'I can't make it rhyme in translation, but it goes like this.

Nadir we,
Youth born.
Axe-wielders,
Victors still.'

'You don't see too many axes among them,' complained Angel.

'Ever the poet,' said Senta, laughing. 'Now go and get those hands bandaged. You're dripping blood everywhere.'

18

The passing of the years, and with them the fading of his powers, was a source of intense irritation to Kesa Khan. As a young man in his physical prime, he had sought to master the arcane arts, to command demons, to walk the paths of mist, scouring the past, exploring the future. But when young, though strong enough, his skills were not honed to the perfection needed for such missions of the spirit. Now that his mind burned with power, his aged frame could not support his desires.

Even while acknowledging the manifest unfairness of life he found himself chuckling at the absurdity of existence.

He banked up his fire, not in the hearth, but in an ancient brazier he had set upon the stone floor at the centre of the small room high in the keep-tower. His precious clay pots were set around it, and from one of them he took a handful of green powder which he sprinkled on to the dancing flames. Instantly an image formed of Waylander entering the great gates of Gulgothir. He was disguised as a Sathuli trader in flowing robes of grey wool and a burnoose, bound with braided black horsehair. His back was bent under a huge pack, and he shuffled like an old man, crippled with the rheumatism. Kesa Khan smiled.

'You will not fool Zhu Chao, but no other will recognise you,' he said. The scene faded before he was ready. Kesa Khan cursed softly, and thought of the crystal lying on the golden floor below the castle. With it you could be young again he told himself. You could bide through the centuries, assisting the Uniter.

'Pah,' he said aloud. 'Were that the case would I not have seen myself in one of the futures? Do not delude yourself, old man. Death approaches. You have done all that you can for the future of your people. You have no cause to regret. No cause at all.'

'Not many can say that,' came the voice of Dardalion.

'Not many have lived as single-mindedly as I,' answered Kesa Khan. He glanced towards the doorway in which the Abbot was standing. 'Come in, priest. There is a draught, and my bones are not as young as they were.'

There was no furniture in the room and Dardalion sat cross-legged upon the rug. 'To what do I owe the pleasure of your company?' asked the old shaman.

'You are a devious man, Kesa Khan, and I lack your guile. But I do

431

not lack powers of my own. I, too, have walked the paths of mist since last we spoke. I, too, have seen the Uniter you dream of.'

The shaman's eyes glittered with malice. 'You have seen but one? There are hundreds.'

'No,' said Dardalion. 'There are thousands. A vast spider's web of possible futures. But most of them did not interest me. I followed the path that leads from Kar-Barzac, and the child to be conceived here. A girl. A beautiful girl, who will wed a young warlord. Their son will be mighty, their grandson mightier still.'

Kesa Khan shivered. 'You saw all this in a single day? It has taken me fifty years.'

'I had fifty years less to travel.'

'What else did you see?'

'What is there that you wish to know?' countered the Drenai.

Kesa Khan bit his lip, and said nothing for a moment. 'I know it all,' he lied, shrugging his shoulders. 'There is nothing new. Have you located Waylander?'

'Yes. He has entered Gulgothir in disguise. Two of my priests are watching him, seeking to divert any search spells.'

Kesa Khan nodded. 'It is almost time to retrieve the crystal,' he said, transferring his gaze to the flickering fire.

'It should be destroyed,' advised Dardalion.

'As you wish. You will need to send one of your men – a priest who is unlikely to be corrupted by its power. You have such a man?'

'Corrupted?'

'Aye. Even in its dormant state it exerts great influence, firing the senses like strong drink that removes inhibition. The man you send must have great control over his . . . passions, shall we say? Any weakness he has will be multiplied a hundred times. I will send no Nadir on such a quest.'

'As you well know there is one among my priests with the strength to overcome such evil,' said Dardalion. He leaned in close to the wizened shaman. 'But tell me, Kesa Khan, what else is down there?'

'Have you not used your great powers to find out?' countered the wizened Nadir, unable to keep a sneer from disfiguring his face.

'No spirit can penetrate the lower levels. There is a force there many times stronger than I have encountered before. But you know all this, old man, and more. I do not ask for your gratitude – it is meaningless to me. We are not here for you. But I would ask for a little honesty.'

'Ask all you like, Drenai. I owe you nothing! You want the crystal – then seek it out.'

Dardalion sighed. 'Very well, I shall do just that. But I will not send Ekodas into the Pit. I shall go myself.'

'The crystal will destroy you!'

'Perhaps.'

'You are a fool, Dardalion. Ekodas is many times stronger than you. You know this.'

The Abbot smiled. 'Yes, I know.' The smile faded and his eyes hardened. 'And now the time for pretence is over. You need Ekodas. Without him your dreams are dust. I have seen the future, Kesa Khan. I have seen more than you know. Everything here is in a state of delicate balance. One wrong strategy and your hopes will die.'

The shaman relaxed, and added fuel to the flames in the brazier. 'We are not so different, you and I. Very well, I will tell you all that you desire to know. But it must be Ekodas who destroys the evil. You agree?'

'Let us talk, and then I will decide.'

'That is acceptable, Drenai.' Kesa Khan took a deep breath. 'Ask your questions.'

'What perils wait in the lower levels?'

The shaman shrugged. 'How would I know? As you say, no spirit power can enter there.'

'Who would you send with Ekodas?' asked Dardalion softly.

'The Drenai woman and her lover.'

Dardalion caught the gleam in the shaman's eyes. 'You are transparent in your hate, Kesa Khan. You need us now, but you want us all dead, eventually. Especially the woman. Why is that?'

'Pah, she is of no consequence!'

'And still the lies flow,' snapped Dardalion. 'But we will talk again, Kesa Khan.'

'You will send Ekodas?'

Dardalion remained silent for a moment. Then he nodded. 'But not,' he said, 'for the reasons you believe.'

The Abbot stood and left the room. The shaman fought down his anger, and remained sitting cross-legged before the fire. How much more did the Drenai know? What had he said of the Uniter? Kesa Khan summoned the words from memory: '*A vast spider's web of possible futures. But most of them did not interest me. I followed the path that leads from Kar-Barzac, and the child to be conceived here. A girl. A beautiful girl, who will wed a young warlord. Their son will be mighty, their grandson mightier still.*'

Did he know the identity of the young warlord? Where he might be found? Kesa Khan cursed softly, and wished he had the strength to walk the paths of mist once more. But he could feel his heart beating within the cage of his ribs, fluttering weakly like a dying sparrow. His dark eyes narrowed. He had no choice. He must go on with his plans. Let the Drenai destroy the crystal – it was not important to the future of the Nadir. What *was* vital was that Ekodas should journey to the chamber, and with him the woman, Miriel.

433

The merest moment of regret touched him then. She was a strong woman, proud and caring.

It was, he admitted, a shame she had to die.

Angel looked down at the perfectly-healed skin of his torn palms, then up into the face of the young priest. 'There is no mark,' he said. 'No scab or scar!'

The young man smiled wearily. 'I merely accelerated your own healing processes. I have also removed a small growth from one of your lungs.'

'A cancer?' whispered Angel, fear rising in his throat.

'Yes, but it is gone.'

'I felt no pain from it.'

'Nor would you until it was much larger.'

'You saved my life, then? By all the gods, priest, I don't know what to say. My name is Angel.' He thrust out his newly-healed hand.

The priest took it. 'Ekodas. How goes it on the wall?'

'We're holding them. They'll not try scaling the battlements again. Next time it will be the portcullis.'

Ekodas nodded. 'You are correct. But it will not be until tomorrow. Get some rest, Angel. You are no longer a young man and your body is very tired.' The priest glanced over Angel's shoulder. 'The boy is with you?' he asked.

Angel looked round. The deaf child was standing close, Angel's green cloak draped over his shoulders. 'Yes. Your large friend – Merlon? – suggested I ask you to look at him. He's deaf.'

'I am very weary. My powers are not inexhaustible.'

'Another time, then,' said Angel, rising.

'No,' insisted Ekodas. 'Let us at least examine him.'

Angel waved the boy to him, but he shied away when the priest reached out. Ekodas closed his eyes. The child immediately slumped into Angel's arms, deeply asleep. 'What did you do?'

'He will come to no harm, Angel. He will merely sleep until I wake him.' Ekodas placed his open palms over the child's ears and stood, stock still, for several minutes. At last he stepped back and sat down opposite the gladiator. 'He had a severe infection when very young. It was not treated, and spread through the bones around the ears. This damaged the eardrums, making them incapable of relaying vibrations to the brain. You understand?'

'Not a word of it,' admitted Angel. 'But can you heal him?'

'I have already done so,' said Ekodas. 'But you must stay with him for a while. He will be frightened. Every noise will be new to him.'

Angel watched the young priest move away across the hall. The boy stirred in his arms. His eyes opened.

'Feel better?' asked Angel. The boy stiffened, his eyes flaring with shock. Angel grinned and tapped his own ear. 'You can hear now.' A woman moved past them, behind the child. He swivelled and stared at her feet as they padded across the stone floor. Angel touched the boy on the arm, gaining his attention, then began to rhythmically tap at the table at which they sat, making small drumming sounds. The child scrambled from his lap and ran from the hall.

'What a great teacher you are,' muttered Angel. Weariness flooded him and he rose and walked through the hall, finding a small unoccupied room in a corridor beyond it. There was no furniture here, but Angel lay down on the stone floor, his head pillowed on his arm.

And he slept without dreams.

Miriel woke him and he sat up. She had brought him a bowl of weak broth and a chunk of bread. 'How are your hands?' she asked him.

'Healed,' he told her, turning them palms upwards. 'By one of the priests – Ekodas. He has a rare Talent.'

She nodded. 'I have just met him.' He took the soup and began to eat. Miriel sat silently beside him. She seemed preoccupied, and continually tugged at a long lock of hair by her temple.

'What is wrong?'

'Nothing.'

'Lying doesn't suit you, Miriel. Are we not friends?'

She nodded, but did not meet his eyes. 'I feel ashamed,' she said, her voice barely above a whisper. 'People are dying here. Every day. And yet I have never been happier. Even on the wall, when the Gothir were advancing I felt alive in a way I have never known before. I could smell the air – so sweet and cold. And with Senta . . .' She blushed and looked away.

'I know,' he told her. 'I have been in love.'

'It seems so stupid, but a part of me doesn't want this to end. Do you know what I mean?'

'Everything ends,' he said, with a sigh. 'In a curious way it is what makes life so beautiful. I knew an artist once, who could craft flowers from glass – fabulous items. But one night, as we were drinking in a small tavern, he told me he had never once fashioned anything with the beauty of a genuine rose. And he knew he never would. For the secret of its beauty is that it must die.'

'I don't want it to die. Ever.'

He laughed. 'I know that feeling, girl. But Shemak's balls! You're young – not yet twenty. Draw every ounce of pleasure you can from life, savour it, hold it on your tongue. But don't waste time with thoughts of loss. My first wife was a harridan. I adored her, and we fought like tigers. When she died I was bereft but, given the chance, I would not go back and live differently. The years with her were golden.'

435

She smiled at him sheepishly. 'I don't want the pain my father suffered. I know that sounds pathetic.'

'There's nothing pathetic about it. Where is the man himself?'

'Gathering torches.'

'For what?'

'Kesa Khan has asked me to lead Ekodas through the lower levels. We are to seek out a crystal.'

'I'll come with you.'

'No,' she said firmly as he started to rise. 'Ekodas says you are more tired than you will admit. You don't need a walk in the dark.'

'There could be danger,' he objected.

'Kesa Khan says not. Now you rest. We'll be back within a couple of hours.'

For the merchant, Matze Chai, sleep was a joy to be treasured. Each night, no matter what pressures his ventures loaded upon him, he would sleep undisturbed for exactly four hours. It was Matze Chai's belief that it was this blissful rest that kept his mind sharp while dealing with treacherous Gothir tradesmen and wily nobles.

So it was with some surprise that when he was awakened by his manservant, Luo, he noticed the dawn was still some way off, and that the night stars could still be seen through the balcony window.

'I am sorry, master,' whispered Luo, bobbing and bowing in the moonlight, 'but there is a man to see you.'

Matze Chai absorbed this information, and much more. No ordinary man could have prevailed upon Luo to disturb his rest. Nor would anyone of Matze's acquaintance leave the servant in such a state of fear.

He sat up and removed the net of silk that covered his waxed and gleaming hair. 'Light a lantern or two, Luo,' he said softly.

'Yes, master. I am sorry, master. But he was insistent that you should be awakened.'

'Of course. Think no more of it. You did exactly the right thing. Fetch me a comb.' Luo lit two lanterns, placing them on the desk beside the bed. Then he brought a bronze mirror and an ivory comb. Matze Chai tilted his head and Luo carefully combed his master's long beard, parting it at the centre and braiding it expertly. 'Where did you leave this man?' he asked.

'In the library, master. He asked for some water.'

'Ah, water!' Matze Chai smiled. 'I will dress myself. Be a good fellow and go to my study. In the third cabinet from the garden window you will find, wrapped I believe in red vellum and tied with blue twine, a set of parchments and scrolls. Bring them to the library as soon as you can.'

'Should I summon the guard, master?'

'For what purpose?' inquired Matze Chai. 'Are we in danger?'

'He is a rough and violent man. I know these things.'

'The world is full of rough and violent men. And yet I am still rich and safe. Do not concern yourself, Luo. Merely do as I have bid you.'

'Yes, master. Red vellum. Third cabinet from the window.'

'Tied with blue twine,' reminded Matze Chai. Luo bowed and backed from the room. Matze Chai stretched and rose, moving to his wardrobe and selecting an openfronted robe of shimmering purple, which he belted to his waist with a golden sash. In slippers of softest velvet he moved down the curving staircase into the long, richly-carpeted hall and across into the library.

His guest was seated upon a silk-covered couch. He had discarded a filthy Sathuli robe and burnoose and his clothes of black leather were travel-stained and dusty. A small black cross-bow lay beside him.

'Welcome to my home, Dakeyras,' said Matze Chai, with a wide smile.

The man smiled back. 'I'd say you were investing my money well – judging from the antiquities I see around me.'

'Your wealth is safe and growing apace,' Matze told him. He sat down on the couch opposite the newcomer, having first lifted the foul-smelling Sathuli robe between index finger and thumb and dropping it to the floor. 'I take it you are travelling in disguise.'

'Sometimes it is advisable,' admitted his guest.

Luo appeared, carrying the scrolls and ledgers. 'Put them on the table,' said Matze. 'Oh . . . and remove these items,' he added, touching the robes with the toe of his velvet slipper. 'Prepare a hot scented bath in the lower guest-room. Send for Ru Lai and tell her there is a guest who will require a hot-oil massage.'

'Yes, master,' answered Luo, gathering up the Sathuli robes and backing from the room.

'Now, Dakeyras, would you like to examine the accounts?'

The man smiled. 'Ever one step ahead, Matze. How did you know it was me?'

'A midnight guest who frightens Luo and asks for a glass of water? Who else would it be? I understand there is a price on your head once more. Who have you offended now?'

'Just about everyone. But Karnak set the price.'

'Then it should please you to know he is currently languishing in the dungeons of Gulgothir.'

'So I understand. What other news is there?'

'The price of silk is up. And spices. You have investments in both.'

'I didn't mean the markets, Matze. What news from Drenai?'

'The Ventrians have had some success. They stormed Skeln but were pushed back at Erekban. But without Karnak they are set to lose the war. At present there is a cessation of hostilities. The Ventrians are holding the ground they have taken, and a Gothir force is camped in the Delnoch mountains. The fighting has ceased temporarily. No one knows why.'

'I could hazard a guess,' said the newcomer. 'There are Brotherhood knights in all three camps. I think there is a deeper game being played.'

Matze nodded. 'You could be right, Dakeyras. Zhu Chao has become more powerful in these last few months: only yesterday a decree from the Emperor was published bearing the royal seal, but Zhu Chao's signature. Worrying times. Still, that should not affect business. Now how can I help you?'

'I have an enemy in Gulgothir who desires my death.'

'Then kill him and be done with it.'

'I intend to. But I will need information.'

'Everything is available in Gulgothir, my friend. You know that. Who is this . . . unwise person?'

'A countryman of yours, Matze Chai. We have already spoken of him. He has a palace here and is close to the Emperor.'

Matze Chai licked his lips nervously. 'I do hope this is merely a bad jest.' The newcomer shook his head. 'You realise his home is guarded by men and demons, and that his powers are very great. He could even now be watching us.'

'Aye, he could. But there's nothing I can do about that.'

'What do you need?'

'I need a plan of the palace, and an estimate of the numbers of guards and their placements.'

Matze sighed. 'You are asking a great deal, my friend. If I aid you and you are captured – and confess – then my life would be forfeit.'

'Indeed it would.'

'Twenty-five thousand Raq,' said Matze Chai.

'Drenai or Gothir?' countered the newcomer.

'Gothir. The Drenai Raq has suffered in recent months.'

'That is close to the sum I have invested with you.'

'No, my friend, that is *exactly* the sum you have invested with me.'

'Your friendship carries a high price, Matze Chai.'

'I know of a man who was once a member of the Brotherhood, but he became overly addicted to Lorassium. He is a former captain of Zhu Chao's guard. And there are two others who once served the man we speak of and will be helpful with information as to his habits.'

'Send for them in the morning,' said Waylander, rising. 'And now I shall take the bath – and the massage. Oh, one small point. Before I visited you I went to another merchant who invests for me. I left him with sealed instructions. If I do not collect them tomorrow by noon he will open them and act upon the contents.'

'I take it,' said Matze, with a tight smile, 'we are talking about a contract for my death?'

438

'I have always liked you, Matze. You have a sharp mind.'

'This speaks of a certain lack of trust,' said Matze Chai, aggrieved.

'I trust you with my money, my friend. Let that be sufficient.'

The Gothir attacked three times in the night, twice trying to scale the walls but the third time launching their assault on the portcullis. The Nadir sent volley after volley of arrows into the attackers, but to little effect. Hundreds of soldiers clustered around the portcullis making a wall of shields against the rusted iron, while other men hacked and sawed at the metal bars.

Orsa Khan, the tall half-breed, threw lantern-oil over the barricade of carts and wagons and set fire to the base. Thick black smoke swirled around the gateway, and the attackers were driven back. On the walls Dardalion and the last of the Thirty battled alongside Nadir warriors, repelling assaults.

By dawn the last of the attacks had ceased and Dardalion made his way back through the hall, leaving Vishna and the others on the ramparts. He tried to commune with Ekodas, but could not break through the wall of power emanating from below the castle. He found Kesa Khan alone in his high room, the old shaman standing by the crooked window staring out over the valley.

'Three more days is all we have,' said Dardalion.

Kesa Khan shrugged. 'Much can happen in three days, Drenai.'

Dardalion unbuckled his silver breastplate, pulling it clear. Removing his helm he sat down on the rug by the glowing brazier.

Kesa Khan joined him. 'You are tired, priest.'

'I am,' admitted Dardalion. 'The paths of the future drained me.'

'As they have me on many occasions. But it was worth it to see the days of Ulric.'

'Ulric?'

'The Uniter,' said Kesa Khan.

'Ah yes, the First Uniter. I am afraid I spent little time observing him. I was more interested in the Second. An unusual man, don't you think? Despite his mixed blood and his torn loyalties he still drew the Nadir together and accomplished all that Ulric failed to do.'

Kesa Khan said nothing for a moment. 'Can you show me this man?'

Dardalion's eyes narrowed. 'But you have seen him, surely? He is the Uniter you spoke of.'

'No, he is not.'

Dardalion sighed. 'Take my hand, Kesa Khan, and share my memories.' The shaman reached out, gripping hard to Dardalion's palm. He shuddered, and his mind swam. Dardalion summoned his concentration, and together they witnessed the rise of Ulric Khan, the merging of the tribes, the great hordes sweeping across the

439

steppes, the sacking of Gulgothir and the first siege of Dros Delnoch.

They watched the Earl of Bronze turn back the Nadir host, and saw the signing of the peace treaty, and the honouring of the terms; the marriage between the Earl's son and one of Ulric's daughters, and the birth of the child, Tenaka Khan, the Prince of Shadows, the King Beyond the Gate.

Dardalion felt Kesa Khan's pride swell, followed immediately by a sense of despair. The separation was swift, and brought a groan from the Drenai. He opened his eyes and saw the fear on Kesa Khan's face. 'What is it? What is wrong?'

'The woman, Miriel. From her will come the line of men leading to this Earl of Bronze?'

'Yes – I thought you understood that? You knew that a child would be conceived here.'

'But not to her, Drenai! I did not know about her! The line of Ulric begins here also.'

'So?'

Kesa Khan's breathing was shallow, his face distorted. 'I . . . I believed Ulric was the Uniter. And that Miriel's descendants would seek to thwart him. I . . . she . . .'

'Out with it, man!'

'There are beasts guarding the crystal. There were three, but their hunger was great and they turned upon one another. Now there is only one. They were men sent by Zhu Chao to kill me. Karnak's son, Bodalen, was one of them. The crystal merged them.'

'You could breach the power all along! What treachery is this?' stormed Dardalion.

'The girl will die down there. It is written!' The shaman's face was pale and stricken. 'I have destroyed the line of the Uniter.'

'Not yet,' said Dardalion, surging to his feet.

Kesa Khan lunged out, grabbing the priest's arm. 'You don't understand! I have made a pact with Shemak. She will die. Nothing can alter it now.'

Dardalion tore himself clear of Kesa Khan's grip. 'Nothing is inalterable. And no demon will hold sway over me!'

'If I could change it I would,' wailed Kesa Khan. 'The Uniter is everything to me! But there must be a death. You cannot stop it!'

Dardalion ran from the room, down the winding stair to the hall, and on to the deep stairwell leading to the subterranean chambers. Just as he was entering the darkness Vishna pulsed to him from the ramparts. 'The Brotherhood are attacking, brother. We need you!'

'I cannot!'

'Without you we are lost! The castle will fall!'

Dardalion reeled back from the doorway, his mind whirling.

Hundreds of women and children would be slain if he deserted his post. Yet if he did not, then Miriel was doomed. He fell to his knees in the doorway, desperately seeking the path of prayer, but his mind was lost in thoughts of the coming chaos. A hand touched his shoulder. He looked up. It was the scarred, ugly gladiator.

'Are you ill?' asked the man. Dardalion rose and took a deep breath. Then he told all to Angel. The man's face was grim as he listened. 'A death, you say? But not necessarily Miriel's?'

'I don't know. But I am needed on the wall. I cannot go to her.'

'I can,' said Angel, drawing his sword.

19

Zhu Chao stood on the balcony, leaning on the gilded rail and staring at the battlements of his palace. There were no vulgar crenellations here, but sweeping flutes and curves as befitted a Chiatze nobleman. The gardens below were filled with fragrant flowers and trees, with elaborate walkways curving around ponds and artificial streams. It was a place of quiet, tranquil beauty.

Yet it was still strong. Twenty men, armed with bow and sword, walked the four walls, while four others – keen-eyed and watchful – manned the mock towers at each corner. The gates were barred, and six savage hounds patrolled the gardens. He could see one of them now, lying on all fours beside an ornate path. Its black fur made it almost invisible.

I am safe, thought Zhu Chao. Nothing can harm me.

Why then am I so afraid?

He shivered and drew his sheepskin-lined robe of purple wool more closely about his slender frame.

Kar-Barzac was becoming a disaster. Kesa Khan still lived, and the Nadir were defending the walls like men possessed. Innicas was dead, the Brotherhood all but destroyed. And Galen had been inexplicably murdered upon his return to the Drenai forces. He had walked into the tent of General Asten, and told the man about the tragic betrayal that had seen the death of Karnak. Asten had listened quietly, then stood and approached the Brotherhood warrior. Suddenly he reached out, grabbing Galen by the hair and wrenching back his head. A knife-blade flashed. Blood gouted from Galen's throat. Zhu Chao had seen it all, the dying warrior falling to the floor, the stocky General looming above him.

Zhu Chao shivered. It was all going wrong.

And where was Waylander?

Three times he had cast the search spell. Three times it had failed. But tonight all will be made well, he assured himself. Midwinter's Eve, and the great sacrifice. Power will flow into me, the gift of Chaos will be mine. Then I shall *demand* Kesa Khan's death. Tomorrow the Ventrian King will be dead. His troops will turn to the Brotherhood for leadership, as will the Drenai soldiers. Galen was not the only loyal knight among them. Asten would die, as the Emperor would die.

Three empires become one.

Not for me the petty titles of King or Emperor. With the crystal in my hands I shall be the Divine Zhu Chao, Lord of All, King of Kings. The thought pleased him. He glanced at the nearest wall, watching the soldiers marching along the parapet. Strong men. Faithful. Loyal. I am safe, he told himself once more.

He glanced up at the mock tower to the left. The soldier there was sitting with his back to the outside. Sleeping! Irritation flared. Zhu Chao pulsed a command to him, but the man did not move. The sorceror mentally summoned Casta, the Captain of the Guard.

'Yes, Lord,' came the response.

'The guard on the eastern tower. Have him brought to the court-yard and flogged. He is sleeping.'

'At once, Lord.'

Safe? How safe can I be with men such as these guarding me? 'And Casta!'

'Yes, Lord.'

'After he is flogged, cut his throat.' Turning on his heel Zhu Chao returned to his apartments, his good mood in tatters. He felt the need of wine, but held back. Tonight the sacrifice must be conducted without error. He thought of Karnak in chains, the curved sacrificial knife slowly slicing into the Drenai's chest. His mood brightened.

This is my last day as the servant of others, he thought. From tomorrow's dawn I shall be the Lord of Three Empires.

No, not until the crystal is in your power. For only then will you know immortality. Only then will you be whole again. A muscle at his jaw twitched and he saw again the unholy fire and the sharp little dagger in Kesa Khan's hand. Hate suffused him, and shame rose like acid in his throat.

'You will watch your people die, Kesa Khan,' he hissed. 'Every man, woman and babe. And you will know who is to blame. That is the price for what you stole from me!'

His memories echoed the remembered pain, and the months of terrible suffering that followed the mutilation. But the crystal would change everything. The Third Grimoire told of it. An ancient knight had been carried into the chamber, his arm cut away by a weapon of light. They had laid him upon a bed, and unleashed the power of the crystal. Within two days a new arm had sprouted from the severed limb.

But better even than this, according to the Fourth Grimoire, leaders of the Elder Races had been transformed by the crystal, their aging bodies made young again. Zhu Chao's throat was dry, and this time he succumbed to a small goblet of wine.

'Lord! Lord!' pulsed Casta, fear radiating in his spirit voice.

'What is it?'

'The sentry is dead, Lord! A crossbow bolt through the heart. And there is the mark of a grappling hook on the turret.'

'He's here!' screamed Zhu Chao, aloud. 'Waylander is here!'

'I cannot hear you, Lord,' pulsed Casta.

Zhu Chao fought for calm. 'Get the men from the walls. Search the gardens. Find the assassin!'

The oil-dipped torch sent crazed shadows across the rippled walls of the stairwell, and black smoke swirled in Angel's nostrils as he descended the stairs. There was a fear in him greater than any he had experienced. It was a fear of death. Not his own – that he was prepared for. But his terror grew as he considered Miriel and the monster, her young body broken, her dead eyes staring up, seeing nothing.

Angel swallowed hard, and moved on. He could not afford the security of stealth, but blundered on down the stairs, ever down. Dardalion had said the crystal chamber was on the sixth level, but the beast could be anywhere. Angel hawked and spat, vainly trying to dampen his dry mouth. And he prayed to any god that might be listening, Dark or Light, or any shade in between.

Let her live!

Take me instead. I've had a life, a good life. He missed a step and stumbled against the wall, sparks showering down from the torch, burning his bare forearm. 'Concentrate, you fool!' he told himself, his words echoing along the silent corridors.

Where now, he wondered as the stairwell joined a long, flat hallway. There was a dim light here, glowing from panels in the walls. He gazed around him. Everything was made of metal – walls, ceiling, floor. Shining and rust-free, the metal everywhere was crumpled and ripped, as if it had no more strength than rotted linen.

Angel shivered. The corridors were damp and cold and his muscles ached with it. Ekodas had pointed out how tired he was, and he felt it now. His limbs seemed leaden, his energy waning. Drawing in a deep breath he thought of Miriel and pushed on.

A large, arched doorway loomed before him. He entered it, sword raised. A movement sounded from behind. He swung, his sword

443

arcing down. At the last moment he dragged the blade aside – just missing the child dressed in his own cloak of green. 'Shemak's balls, boy! I could have killed you!'

The boy shrank back against the doorway, his lip trembling, his eyes wide and frightened. Angel sheathed his sword and forced a smile. 'Followed me, did you?' he said, reaching out and drawing the child to him. 'Ah well, no harm done, eh?'

He knelt down beside the boy. 'You take the torch,' he said, holding it out for the lad. In truth he no longer needed its light, for the panels cast an eerie glow over the hall. There were metal beds here and rotted mattresses. Angel stood and drew his sword once more. Signalling to the boy he moved out into the corridor, seeking stairs.

Despite the danger he was pleased the boy was with him. The silence and the endless corridors were unnerving him. 'Stay close,' whispered the man. 'Old Angel will look after you.'

Not understanding, the boy nodded and grinned up at the gladiator.

'Have you the faintest idea of where we are?' Senta asked Ekodas, as the silver-armoured priest rounded yet another bend in the labyrinth of corridors on the seventh level.

'I think we are close,' said Ekodas, his face eerily pale in the faint yellow light.

Senta saw that he was sweating heavily. 'Are you all right, priest?'

'I can feel the crystal. It is making me nauseous.'

Senta turned to Miriel. 'You do take me to some romantic places,' he said, putting his arm around her and kissing her cheek. 'Volcanic caves, sorcerous castles, and now a trip in the dark a hundred miles below the earth.'

'No more than three hundred feet,' said Ekodas.

'Allow for poetic overstatement,' snapped Senta.

Miriel laughed. 'You needn't have come,' she chided.

'And miss this?' he cried, in mock astonishment. 'What sort of a man refuses a walk in the dark with a beautiful woman?'

'And a priest,' she pointed out.

'That is a flaw, I grant you!'

'Be silent!' hissed Ekodas. Genuinely surprised, Senta was about to fire back an angry reply when he saw that Ekodas was listening intently, his dark eyes narrowing to scan the gloom at the end of the corridor.

'What is it?' whispered Miriel.

'I thought I heard something – like breathing. I don't know, perhaps I imagined it.'

'It is unlikely there'd be anything living down here,' said Miriel. 'There is no food source.'

'I cannot use my Talent here,' said Ekodas, wiping sweat from his face. 'I feel so . . . so limited. Like a man suddenly blind.'

'Happily you do not need your Talent,' said Senta, still irritated by the priest's outburst. 'This is hardly the most . . .' He halted in mid-sentence, for now he could also hear stentorian breathing. Silently he drew his sword.

'It could be a trick of the earth,' whispered Miriel. 'You know, like wind whistling through a crack in the rocks.'

'There's not usually a great deal of wind at this depth,' said Senta.

They moved cautiously on, until they came to a long room, filled with metal cabinets. Most of the glowing panels had ceased to operate, but two still cast pale light across the iron floor. Miriel saw an object lying beneath an overturned table. 'Senta,' she said softly. 'Over there!'

The swordsman crossed the room and knelt. He rose swiftly and backed to where Ekodas and Miriel were standing. 'It's a human leg,' he said. 'Or what's left of it. And believe me, you don't want to know the size of the bite-marks.'

'Kesa Khan said there was no danger,' put in Miriel.

'Perhaps he didn't know,' volunteered Ekodas. 'The crystal is through that doorway. Let me find and destroy it, then we'll leave as fast as we can.'

'If we disappeared in a flash of magic it wouldn't be fast enough,' Senta told him. The priest did not smile, but moved on through what was left of the doorway. 'Look at that,' Senta told Miriel. 'The stone of the wall around the door has been torn out. You know, call me boring if you like, but at this moment I'd like to be sitting in that cabin of yours, with my feet out towards the fire, waiting for you to bring me a goblet of mulled wine.' The lightness of tone could not disguise the fear in his voice, and when Ekodas cried out, apparently in pain, Senta almost dropped his sword.

Miriel was the first to the doorway.

'Get back!' shouted Ekodas. 'Stay beyond the walls. The power is too much for you to bear!'

Senta caught Miriel by the arm and hauled her back. 'You know, beauty, I don't mind telling you that I am frightened. Not for the first time, but I've never known anything like this.'

'And me,' she agreed.

A shuffling sound came from the other end of the hall.

'I have a bad feeling about this,' whispered Senta.

And the creature moved into sight. It was colossal, almost twelve feet high, and Senta gazed in horror at the beast's two heads. Both were grotesque, with only vestigial traces of humanity; the mouths wide, almost as long as his forearm, the teeth crooked and sharp.

445

Miriel drew her sword and backed away. 'Whatever you have to do, Ekodas, do it now!' she shouted.

The creature leaned forward, part-supporting its weight on two huge arms, its three legs drawn up beneath its bloated belly. It looked to Senta like a giant white spider crouching before them. One of the heads lolled to the left, eyes opening, fastening on Miriel. A groan came from its grotesque lips, deep and full of torment. The mouth on the other head opened and a piercing scream echoed in the hall. The creature tensed and shuffled crablike towards them, groaning and screaming.

Miriel edged to the left, Senta to the right.

The beast ignored the swordsman and charged at the girl, scattering tables and chairs. The speed was not great, but its huge bulk seemed to fill the room.

Senta ran at it, hurling himself at its broad back. One of the four arms clubbed at him, smashing his ribs. He staggered and almost fell. But the creature was rearing up above Miriel. She slashed her sword across a huge forearm, slicing deep into the flesh. Then Senta attacked again, plunging his own blade into the great belly.

A fist clubbed him again and he was sent spinning to the floor, his sword torn from his grasp. He saw Miriel dive beneath the creature's grasp and roll to her feet. Senta tried to rise, but a piercing pain clove into his side, and he knew several of his ribs were broken.

'Ekodas! For the sake of all that's holy help us!'

Ekodas knelt in the golden chamber, the crystal held in his hands, his thoughts far away. The doors of his mind were all open now, and the noises from beyond the chamber held no meaning for him. His life unfolded before the eyes of memory, wasted and filled with ridiculous fears. The sanctuary of the temple now seemed more of a grey prison, holding him from the riches of life. He gazed down at the many facets of the crystal, seeing himself reflected a hundred times, and he felt the strength of his soul expanding within the frail flesh of his body.

In an instant he could see not only the battle in the hall outside, but also the grim fighting on the walls far above. And more than this he saw the man Waylander moving silently along the darkened corridors of Zhu Chao's palace.

He laughed then. What did it matter?

And he saw Shia, standing beside the tall Orsa Khan, and the hole in the portcullis gate through which Gothir soldiers were scrambling. Meaningless, he thought, though he felt a shaft of irritation that he would no longer have the opportunity of enjoying her body, his enhanced memory recalling again the smell of her skin and her hair.

'Ekodas! For the sake of all that's holy help us!'

For all that's holy! What an amusing thought. Just like the temple, the Source was created by men as a prison for the soul, to prevent stronger men from enjoying the fruits of their power. I am free of such baggage, he thought.

Dardalion had said the crystal was evil. Such nonsense. It was beautiful, perfect. And what was evil, save a name given by weak men to a force they could neither comprehend nor control?

'Now you understand,' whispered a voice in his mind. Ekodas closed his eyes, and saw Zhu Chao, sitting at a desk in a small study.

'Yes, I understand,' Ekodas told him.

'Bring me the crystal, and we shall know such power, such joy!'

'Why should I not keep it for myself?'

Zhu Chao laughed. 'The Brotherhood is already in place, Ekodas. Ready to rule. Even with the crystal it would take you years to reach such a position of power.'

'There is truth in that,' agreed Ekodas. 'It will be as you say.'

'Good. Now show me the battle, my brother.'

Ekodas stood and, the crystal in his hands, walked to the doorway. Beyond it he saw Miriel dive to the floor and roll as the beast lunged for her. Senta, one hand clutching his ribs, had drawn a dagger and was stumbling forward to the attack.

Foolish man. Like trying to kill a whale with a needle.

The injured warrior plunged his dagger into the beast's back. The beast half-turned, and a mighty fist crashed into Senta's neck. He crumpled to the floor without a sound. Miriel saw him fall. And screamed, the sound full of fury. Hurling herself forward she thrust her blade into one of the open mouths, plunging it up into what should have been a brain.

Ekodas chuckled. There was no brain there, he knew. It was situated – if brain it could be called – between the heads, in the enormous lump of the shoulders.

The beast caught hold of Miriel, lifting her from her feet. Ekodas found himself wondering whether it would tear her apart, or merely bite her head from her shoulders.

'Such confusion in the beast's mind,' said Zhu Chao. 'Part of it is still Bodalen. It recognises the girl, the twin of a maid he killed by accident. See it hesitate! And can you feel the rising anger from the souls that were once of the Brotherhood?'

'I can,' admitted Ekodas. 'Hunger, desire, bafflement. Amusing, is it not?'

A figure moved in the background.

'More entertainment,' whispered the voice of Zhu Chao. 'Sadly I cannot retain the spell, and must miss the inevitable conclusion. We will share the memory in Gulgothir.'

The sorceror faded from Ekodas, and the young priest returned his attention to the gladiator who had entered the hall.

You shouldn't have come, he thought. You are too weary for such an adventure.

Angel had heard the awful screams and was already running as he entered the hall. He saw Senta stretched out, unconscious on the floor and witnessed the monster lunge down, grabbing Miriel and dragging her into the air.

Reversing his sword, holding it now like a dagger, Angel angled his run, leaping first to a metal table and then launching himself at the beast's bloated back. He landed knees first and plunged his sword deep in the creature's flesh, driving it down with all of his weight. The monster reared up and swung. Angel was thrown clear. It still held Miriel in one huge hand, but now it turned on Angel. Half-stunned he rolled to his feet and staggered.

The boy carrying the torch ran forward, thrusting the burning brand at the beast. One of its many arms thrashed out, but the boy was nimble enough to duck and run back. Angel, his pale eyes glittering with battle fury, saw the beast charge again. Instead of running away, he hurled himself at the grotesque colossus, his hand reaching out for Senta's sword, where it jutted from the swaying belly. Massive fingers caught at Angel's left shoulder, just as his own hand curled around the sword-hilt. The beast lifted him high, the movement tearing the sword free of its prison of flesh. Blood gouted from the wound. Angel smashed the blade into the brow of the second head, splitting the skull.

The creature dropped Miriel, as pain from the awful injury flared through it. Angel struck again. And again. Another hand grabbed Angel's leg, drawing him towards the gaping mouth and the sabre-long fangs.

Miriel swung to see Ekodas, holding tightly to the crystal and leaning on the door-frame watching the drama. Running to him she pulled his sword from its scabbard and returned to the fray.

'Between the shoulders,' said Ekodas, conversationally. 'That's where the brain is located. Can you see the hump there?'

Holding the broadsword two-handed, Miriel sent a powerful cut into the beast's leg, just above the knee. Blood spurted from the wound and the creature staggered back, one hand releasing its hold on Angel's leg. The former gladiator hacked his own sword into the arm holding him. The great fingers spasmed, and he fell to the floor. Blood was pouring from the monster, gushing from both heads, and numerous wounds to the body.

Still it came on. Miriel saw Angel backing away, and knew he was trying to draw it away from her. But now Miriel felt the power of the crystal, enhancing her Talent, filling her with rage. Images flooded her mind, radiating from the beast. Confusion, anger, hunger.

448

But one image flickered above the rest. Miriel saw Krylla running through the woods, a tall wide-shouldered man pursuing her.

Bodalen.

And she knew. Locked within this loathsome beast was the man who murdered her sister.

A huge arm swept down towards her. Ducking under the clumsy lunge she ran to the left – then charged in at the beast, leaping high, her foot coming down on one massive knee joint. Using this as a foothold she propelled herself up on to its back. A hand reached for her, but she threw herself forward. Reversing the sword she stood high on the beast's shoulders. 'Die!' she screamed. The blade lanced down through the bulging hump. As it pierced the skin the sword seemed to accelerate, for there was no muscle beneath to hold it back, and the skin split like an overripe melon, brains gushing out.

The beast reared one last time, dislodging Miriel. Then it swayed and fell.

Angel ran to where Miriel had fallen, reaching out and helping her to her feet. 'Thank the Source! You're alive!'

He put his arm around her, but she stiffened and he saw her staring towards the still form of Senta. Breaking clear of his embrace she ran to the fallen swordsman, turning him to his back. Senta groaned and opened his eyes. He saw Angel and tried to smile.

'You're wounded again,' he whispered. Angel could feel the blood trickling from torn skin on the side of his face.

Angel knelt by his side, noting the blood at the corners of his mouth, and the unnatural stillness of his limbs. Gently he reached out, squeezing the man's fingers. There was no answering grip.

'Let me help you up,' said Miriel, dragging on his left arm.

'Leave him, girl!' said Angel, his voice soft. Miriel slowly let the arm down.

'Not much of a place to end one's days in, eh, Angel?' said Senta. He coughed and blood sprayed from his handsome mouth, staining his chin. 'Still, I guess I couldn't . . . be . . . in better company.'

Angel swung towards Ekodas. 'Can you do anything, priest?'

'Nothing. His neck is broken, and his spine in two places. And his ribs have pierced a lung.' The priest's tone was light, almost disinterested.

Angel returned his attention to the dying swordsman. 'Fancy letting a creature like that kill you,' he said gruffly. 'You ought to be ashamed of yourself.'

'I am.' He smiled and closed his eyes. 'There's no pain. It's very peaceful really.' His eyes flared open, and fear was in his voice. 'You'll carry me out, won't you? Don't want to spend eternity down here. I'd like to be able . . . to feel the sun . . . you know?'

449

'I'll carry you myself.'

'Miriel . . . !'

'I'm here,' she said, her voice trembling.

'I'm . . . sorry . . . I had such . . .' His eyes closed again. And he was gone.

'*Senta!*' she shouted. 'Don't do this! Get up. Walk!' Standing she dragged on his arm.

Angel rose and grabbed her. 'Let him go, princess. Let him go!'

'I can't!'

He drew her into a tight embrace. 'It's over,' he said softly. 'He's not here any more.'

Miriel pulled away from him, her face set, eyes gleaming. Spinning on her heel she walked to the dead beast, dragging her sword clear. Then she turned on Ekodas. 'You bastard! You stood by and did nothing. He would be alive but for you.'

'Perhaps,' he agreed. 'Perhaps not.'

'Now you die,' said Miriel, suddenly running forward. Ekodas raised his hand. Miriel groaned and halted so suddenly it seemed she had run into an invisible wall.

'Calm yourself,' said Ekodas. 'I didn't kill him.'

'Destroy the crystal, priest,' said Angel, 'before it destroys you.'

Ekodas smiled. 'You don't understand. No one would who had not felt its power.'

'I can feel it,' said Angel. 'At least I would guess it is the crystal that is filling me with the desire to kill you.'

'Yes, that is probably true. On a lesser mind the crystal would have that kind of effect. I should draw back. Return to the fortress.'

'No,' said Angel. 'You were sent here by those who trusted you. They believed only you had the strength to resist the . . . thing. They were wrong, weren't they? It's overpowered you.'

'Nonsense. It has merely enhanced my considerable Talents.'

'So be it. We'll wait for you at the fortress,' said Angel, with a deep sigh. He stepped forward. 'One small point, though . . .'

'Yes?'

Angel leaned back, and kicked out and up, his boot hitting the crystal, sending it spinning from the priest's hand. Ekodas tried to punch out, but the warrior rolled away from the blow and swung his elbow into the priest's face. Ekodas staggered. Angel sent a thundering left cross that cannoned into his opponent's chin. Ekodas hit the floor face-first – and did not move.

Miriel, freed from whatever spell Ekodas had cast, moved towards the still body.

'Leave him be, child,' said Angel. 'He was not responsible.' Moving to the crystal Angel felt its power reaching out to him, with promises of strength, immortality and fame. Angel reeled back. 'Give me the sword,' he told Miriel. Taking the hilt in both hands he smote the crystal with one terrible blow.

It exploded into bright, glittering fragments, and a great rush of cool air filled the hall.

Ignoring the fallen priest Angel walked wearily back to Senta's body and lifted it, letting the head fall against his shoulder.

'Let's take him back to the sunlight,' he said.

20

Zhu Chao was trembling, sweat trickling down his cheeks. He struggled for calm, but his pulse was racing and he could feel the erratic hammering of his heart.

He cannot reach you, he told himself. He is one man. I have many men. And there are the dogs. Yes, yes, the dogs. They will sniff him out! He sat down at his desk and stared at the open doorway, where the two guards waited, swords drawn.

The hounds had been shipped from Chiatze, formidable beasts with huge jaws and powerful shoulders. Hunting dogs, they had been known to drag down bears. They would rend him, tear the flesh from his bones!

The sorceror poured himself a goblet of wine, his trembling causing him to spill the liquid over several parchments lying on the oak-topped desk. He didn't care. Nothing mattered now, save that he lived through this fear-filled night.

'Lord!' pulsed Casta.

'Yes?'

'One of the dogs is dead. The others are sleeping. We found the remains of fresh meat by one of them. I think he poisoned them. Lord! Can you hear me?'

Zhu Chao was stunned, and felt his reasoning swept away on a tide of panic.

'Lord! Lord!' pulsed Casta. But Zhu Chao could not respond. 'I've ordered all the men into the main palace grounds,' continued Casta. 'And we've sealed the ground floor, and I have men guarding all three stairways.'

The sorceror drained his wine and poured a second goblet. The spirit steadied his failing courage. 'Good,' he pulsed. He stood – and swayed, catching hold of the side of the desk. Too much wine, he realised, and drunk too swiftly. Never mind. It would pass. He took several deep breaths, and felt his strength return.

Swiftly he crossed the room and stepped into the corridor. The two guards snapped to attention. 'Follow me,' he ordered, and marched towards the stairwell leading to the dungeon chambers. He made one man walk before him on the stairs, the other following sword in hand. At the foot of the stairwell they emerged into a torch-lit corridor. Three men were playing dice at the far table. They sprang to their feet as Zhu Chao stepped into the light.

'Bring the prisoners to the Inner Sanctum,' he said.

'Lord!' pulsed Casta, his voice triumphant.

'Speak!'

'He is dead. One of the guards found him scaling the roof. They fought, and the assassin was killed and hurled to the stones below.'

'Yes!' roared Zhu Chao, his fist sweeping up into the air. 'Bring his body to me. I will consign it to Hell!' Oh, how sweet life felt at that moment, the words in his mind singing like a nightingale: *Waylander is dead. Waylander is dead!*

Leaving the men he entered a small room at the end of the corridor, locking the door behind him. From a hiding place beneath a desk of oak he removed the Fifth Grimoire and studied the ninth chapter. Closing his eyes he spoke the words of power and found himself floating above the walls of Kar-Barzac. But there was no way past the pulsating force that radiated from below the fortress. Then, as suddenly as sunshine following a storm, the power faded and died. Zhu Chao was stunned. Swiftly he sent his spirit questing into the labyrinth below the citadel and found the priest Ekodas nursing the crystal. He could feel the surging of the man's Talent, his growing ambition, his burgeoning desires.

He spoke to the priest, sensing a kindred spirit, and when Ekodas said he would bring the crystal to Gulgothir, Zhu Chao knew he spoke the absolute truth. He fought hard to keep his triumph from Ekodas, and returned to his palace.

Waylander was dead. The crystal was his. And in a few short moments the souls of kings would be dedicated to Shemak.

And the son of a shoemaker would be the Lord of the Earth!

The Gothir forces had fallen back again, but the defenders manning the walls were fewer now, and desperately weary. Dardalion moved among the Thirty, pausing only at the body of fat Merlon. He had died at the ruined gateway, hurling himself into the mass of warriors surging through the ruptured portcullis. Orsa Khan and a score of Nadir warriors had joined him, and together they had forced back the attackers. But, just as the Gothir retreated to their camp, Merlon had slumped to the ground, bleeding from many wounds.

452

He died within moments. Dardalion knelt by the body. 'You were a good man, my friend,' he said softly. 'May the Source greet you.'

From the corner of his eye he saw Angel emerge from the hall, carrying the body of the swordsman, Senta. Dardalion sighed and stood. Miriel came next, a small boy beside her. The Abbot walked across to them, and waited silently as Angel laid down the body of his friend. In the presence of the silver-armoured Abbot the small boy eased back and vanished into the hall.

'Where is Ekodas?' Dardalion asked at last.

'He's alive,' said Angel. 'And the crystal is destroyed.'

'The Source be praised! I was not sure that even Ekodas would have the strength.'

He saw Miriel about to speak, but Angel cut in swiftly. 'It was a creation of great evil,' he said.

Ekodas appeared in the doorway, blinking in the fading light. Dardalion ran to him. 'You did it, my son. I am proud of you.' He reached out to embrace the priest, but Ekodas brushed him away.

'I did nothing – save let a man die,' he whispered. 'Leave me, Dardalion.' The priest stumbled away.

The Abbot swung back to Miriel. 'Tell me all,' he said. Miriel sighed and related the story of the fight with the monster, and the death of Senta. Her voice was low and spiritless, her eyes distant. Dardalion felt her pain and her sorrow.

'I am so sorry, my child. So terribly sorry.'

'People die in wars all the time,' she said tonelessly. As if in a dream she walked away towards the battlements.

Angel covered Senta with his cloak then stood. 'I'd like to kill Kesa Khan,' he hissed.

'It would achieve nothing,' replied Dardalion. 'Go with Miriel. She is fey now, and could come to harm.'

'Not while I live,' said Angel. 'But tell me, Abbot, what is it for? Why did he die down there? Please tell me it was worth something. And I don't want to hear about Uniters.'

'I cannot answer all your questions. Would that I could. But no man can know where his steps will ultimately lead, nor the results of his actions. But I will tell you this, and I will trust you to keep it in your heart and not speak of it to any living soul. There she is, sitting on the battlements. What do you see?'

Angel looked up and saw Miriel bathed in the fiery light of dusk. 'I see a beautiful woman, tough and yet gentle, strong and yet caring. What do you think I should see?'

'What I see,' whispered Dardalion. 'A young woman carrying the seed of future greatness. Even now it is growing within her, tiny, a mere spark of life, created from love. But that spark could one day, if we survive here, give birth to a flame.'

'She is pregnant.'

'Yes. Senta's son.'

'He didn't know,' said Angel, staring down at the cloak-shrouded corpse on the stones.

'But you know, Angel. You know now that she has something to live for. But she will need help. There are few men strong enough to take on the burden of another man's child.'

'That is no worry to me, Abbot. I love her.'

'Then go to her, my son. Sit with her. Share her grief.'

Angel nodded and moved away. Dardalion strode into the hall. The boy was sitting at a bench table, staring down at his hands. Dardalion sat opposite him. Their eyes met and Dardalion smiled. The boy returned it.

Kesa Khan entered the hall from the stairwell leading to the upper floors. He saw Dardalion and crossed to the table. 'I saw her on the battlements,' he said. 'I am . . . happy that she survived.'

'Her lover did not,' said Dardalion.

The shaman shrugged. 'It is not important.'

Dardalion bit back an angry reply, and shifted his gaze to the boy. 'I have something for you, Kesa Khan,' he said, still staring at the black-eyed child.

'Yes?'

'The young warlord who will wed the daughter of Shia.'

'You know where to find him?'

'You are sitting beside him,' said Dardalion, rising.

'He is a mute. Worthless!'

'By all that's holy, shaman, I do despise you!' roared Dardalion. Fighting for calm he leaned forward. 'He had an infection of the ear that made him deaf. Without being able to hear he never learned to speak. Ekodas healed him. Now all he needs is time, patience, and something that is a little beyond you, I think – love!' Without another word Dardalion spun on his heel and strode from the hall.

Vishna met him in the courtyard. 'They are massing again. We'll be hard pressed to hold them.'

Waylander crouched down on the roof, watching the men gathering round the body below. The guard had almost surprised him, but the man had been slow to bring his sword to bear, and a black-handled throwing-knife had sliced into his throat, ending his indecision – and his life. Swiftly Waylander had stripped the man, then he removed his own jerkin and leggings and dressed the corpse.

The dead man was a little shorter than Waylander, but the black breastplate and full-faced helm fitted well, though the dark woollen leggings rode high on the calf. This discrepancy was covered by the man's knee-length boots. They were tight, but the leather was soft and pliable, and the fit caused Waylander little discomfort.

Leaning out over the parapet he had seen the guards in the courtyard below. Drawing the dead man's sword and holding his own blade in his right hand he shouted. 'He's here! On the roof!' Out of sight of the men below he clashed the two swords together, the discordant noise ringing above the palace. Then he clove his own blade three times into the dead man's face, smashing the bones and disfiguring the features. Laying aside the swords he had then hauled the corpse to the parapet and sent the body plummeting to the ground.

He waited several minutes, and watched as the soldiers below carried the body inside the palace. Then he put on the full-faced helm, gathered his second rope and ran to the rear of the roof, leaning out and scanning the windows below. According to the information supplied by Matze Chai there was a stairwell at the corner of the building, winding down to the lower levels.

Looping his rope over a jutting pillar he climbed to the wall and abseiled down, past two windows, halting by a third. It was open, and no light showed within. Hooking his foot over the sill he climbed inside. It was a sleeping chamber with a narrow bed. There were no blankets or sheets upon it, and he took it to be an unused guest-room. Hiding his loaded crossbow within the folds of the dead man's black cloak he stepped out into the corridor. The stairs were to his right and he made for them. He heard sounds of footfalls on the stairs and kept moving. Two knights rounded a bend and climbed towards him.

'Who was it who killed the assassin?' the first asked him.

Waylander shrugged. 'Not me, more's the pity,' he said, continuing on his way.

'Well, who else is up there?' continued the first man, grabbing Waylander's shoulder. The assassin turned, the crossbow coming up.

'No one,' he said – and loosed a bolt which hammered into the man's open mouth and up into the brain. The second knight tried to run, but Waylander shot again, the bolt plunging into the back of the man's neck. He fell to the stairs and was still.

Reloading the crossbow with his last two bolts the assassin moved on.

As his chains were unlocked Karnak tensed, but a knife-blade touched his throat, and he knew his struggles would be useless. The huge Drenai general glared at the men holding his arms. 'By all the gods I'll remember your faces,' he told his captors.

One of them laughed. 'You won't have long to remember them,' he said.

They dragged him out of the dungeon and along the torch-lit

corridor. He saw Zhu Chao standing by a doorway. 'A pox on you, you yellow-faced bastard!' he shouted.

The Chiatze did not reply, but stood aside as Karnak was led into the Inner Sanctum. A pentagram had been chalked on the stone floor, and gold wires had been stretched between candle-holders of stained iron, forming a six-pointed star above the chalk. Karnak was hauled to a wall, where once more he was shackled by the wrists. He saw another prisoner already there, a tall, slender man, his bearing regal despite the bruises and cuts to his face.

'I know you,' whispered Karnak.

The man nodded. 'I am the fool who trusted Zhu Chao.'

'You are the Emperor.'

'I was,' replied the man sourly. He sighed. 'The serpent enters . . .'

Karnak swung his head to see the purple-robed figure of Zhu Chao approach them.

'Tonight, gentlemen, you will witness the supreme gift of power.' His slanted eyes glowed as he spoke and the faintest trace of a smile showed at his thin-lipped mouth. 'I do appreciate that you will not share my pleasure, even though you will be instrumental in supplying it.' Leaning forward he laid a hand on Karnak's massive chest. 'You see, I will begin by cutting out your heart and laying it upon the golden altar. This gift will summon the servant of the Lord Shemak.' He turned to the Emperor. 'That is where you enter the proceedings. You I will deliver whole, and the demon will devour you.'

'Do as you please, wizard,' snapped the Emperor. 'But do not bore me any longer.'

'I assure *Your Highness* you will not remain bored for long.' Three men entered the room, carrying a blood-drenched body. Zhu Chao swung round. 'Ah,' he said. 'My supposed nemesis. Bring it here!'

The knights carried it forward and laid the corpse on the floor. Zhu Chao smiled. 'See how puny he looks in death, his face sheared away by the sharp sword of a valiant knight? See how . . .' He faltered, his eyes staring at the right hand of the corpse. The third finger was missing, an old wound covered in a white scar. Zhu Chao knelt and lifted the man's right hand. Upon the signet finger was a ring of red gold, shaped like a coiled serpent. 'You fools!' hissed Zhu Chao. 'This is Onfel! Look, see the ring!' Zhu Chao scrambled to his feet, his composure lost. 'Waylander is alive! He is in the palace. Get out! All of you! Find him!'

The knights ran from the room. Zhu Chao pushed shut the door, and dropped a heavy lock-bar into place.

Karnak's laughter boomed out. 'He'll kill you, sorceror. You are dead!'

'Shut your stinking mouth!' screamed Zhu Chao.

'How can you make me? With what will you threaten me?' asked the giant Drenai. 'Death? I don't think so. I know this man who hunts you. I know what he is capable of. By the bones of Missael, I had men hunting him myself. The best assassins, the finest swordsmen. Yet still he lives.'

'Not for long,' said the sorceror. A slow, cruel smile curved his thin lips. 'Ah yes! You hired assassins – to protect your beloved Bodalen. He told me of it only recently.'

'You have seen my son?'

'Seen him? Oh, I saw a lot of him, my dear Karnak. He was mine, you see. He fed me all your plans, in return for a promise that when I had killed you he would rule the Drenai.'

'You lying whoreson!' stormed Karnak.

'Not so. Ask your fellow guest, the late Emperor. He has no reason to lie. He will die alongside you. Bodalen was weak, spineless, and ultimately of little use to me.' Zhu Chao laughed, a high shrill sound that echoed in the chamber. 'Even when he had the strength of ten he had difficulty completing his task. Poor, stupid, dead Bodalen.'

'Dead?' whispered Karnak.

'Dead,' repeated Zhu Chao. 'I sent him to an enchanted fortress. You would not like to see what he became. Therefore I shall show you.'

The sorceror closed his eyes and Karnak's mind reeled. He found himself staring into a dimly-lit chamber, where a creature out of nightmare was battling against a young woman and the gladiator, Senta. He watched Senta struck down, and saw a second arena warrior – Angel – leap to the attack. The scene faded.

'I would like to be able to show you more, but sadly I had to leave,' said Zhu Chao, his words ripe with malice. 'But the monster was Bodalen – and several other of my men, merged by magic.'

'I do not believe you,' said Karnak.

'I thought you might not. So, for your edification, Drenai, here is another scene I took from Kar-Barzac.'

The vision shimmered again, and Karnak groaned as he saw Bodalen and the other warriors falling asleep in the crystal chamber, the bodies beginning to writhe, and merge . . .

'No!' he screamed, and wrenched savagely at the chains which held him.

'I do so enjoy your pain, Drenai,' said Zhu Chao. 'And here is a second source of agony for you. Tomorrow Galen will kill your friend Asten, and the Drenai will come, as the Gothir already have, under the rule of the Brotherhood. As indeed will Ventria. Three empires under one Lord. Myself.'

'You are forgetting Waylander,' snarled Karnak. 'By all the gods, I would give my soul to be alive at the moment he kills you.'

'Before the night is over my powers will be so great that no blade

457

will be able to cut me. Then I will welcome this . . . Drenai savage!'

'Welcome him now,' came a cold voice from the other side of the room.

Zhu Chao spun, dark eyes narrowing as he peered into the shadows by the door. A knight stepped from behind a pillar, and lifted clear the full-faced helm he wore.

'You can't be here!' whispered Zhu Chao. 'You can't!'

'I came in with the men carrying the body. So good of you to lock the others out.'

The assassin stepped closer, crossbow raised. Zhu Chao ran to his left and leapt over the golden wires, making for the centre of the pentagram. Waylander loosed a bolt that flashed for the sorceror's neck, but Zhu Chao swung at the last instant, his hand coming up. The bolt pierced his wrist – and he screamed in pain. Waylander took aim. But the sorceror ducked behind the altar of gold and began to chant.

Black smoke oozed around the altar, swirling up to form a massive figure, with hair and eyes of green flame. Waylander sent a crossbow bolt into the huge chest, but it passed through and clattered against the far wall.

Zhu Chao rose and stood before the creature of smoke and fire. 'Now what will you do, little man!' he jeered at Waylander. 'What pitiful weapons can you bring to bear?' The assassin said nothing. He had no more bolts, and dropped the crossbow, drawing his sabre. 'Lord Shemak!' screamed Zhu Chao. 'I call for this man's death!'

The figure with eyes of flame spread its massive arms, and a voice like distant thunder rumbled in the room. 'You do not command me, human. You ask for favours, and you pay for them with blood. Where is the payment?'

'There!' said Zhu Chao, pointing to the chained men.

'They still live,' said the demon. 'The ritual is incomplete.'

'I will deliver their strength to you, Lord, I swear it! But first, I beg you, give me the life of the assassin, Waylander.'

'It would please me more to see you slay him,' said the demon. 'Shall I give you the strength?'

'Yes! Yes!'

'As you wish!'

Zhu Chao suddenly screamed in pain, his head arcing back. His body twisted and grew, stretching, swelling. His robes fell away as new muscles formed, huge and knotted. His body spasmed and a series of terrible groans came from the deformed throat. Nose and chin stretched out, and sleek velvet fur burst through his skin, covering the now colossal eight-foot frame. His mouth opened to reveal long fangs, and his fingers, treble-jointed now, boasted talons.

The creature that had been Zhu Chao stumbled forward, dislodging the delicate golden wires, scattering the black candlesticks.

Against the wall Karnak tore at his chains, using all of his mighty strength. Two of the links stretched, but did not give. Again and again the Drenai threw his weight against them.

Waylander backed away from the beast, and the smoke-demon's laughter filled the room.

Outside the Sanctum the remaining Knights of Blood were hammering on the door, calling out for their master. Waylander ran back to where he had discarded his helm. Slipping it over his head he lifted the bar on the door – and stepped aside. The door burst open, three knights tumbling inside, one falling to his knees directly before the awesome beast. The man screamed and tried to rise. The beast's talons tore into him, lifting the knight into the air, the deadly fangs ripping open his throat. Blood sprayed across the altar.

The other knights stood transfixed.

'It killed the master!' yelled Waylander. 'Use your swords!'

But the knights turned and fled. The beast leapt at Waylander. Ducking under the sweep of its talons the assassin sent a slashing cut to the creature's belly, but the blade merely sliced the surface of the skin. Waylander dived and rolled to his feet.

Karnak, with one last effort, snapped the right-hand chain, then turned and used both hands to rip loose the left. Spinning on his heel he swung the chains around above his head and charged the monster. The iron links hit the beast on the throat, whipping around the neck. It turned and reared high, dragging Karnak from his feet. Waylander darted forward and plunged his sword into the open belly, driving it home with all his weight and strength.

A great howl went up – and a taloned arm flashed down, opening the flesh of Waylander's shoulder. He fell back. Karnak dragged back on the chain, which tightened around the beast's throat. It tried to turn and rend its attacker but Karnak, despite his great bulk, moved nimbly, keeping the chain taut. Waylander ran to the fallen knight, retrieving the man's sword. Holding the blade double-handed, the assassin advanced once more, lifting the sword high and cleaving it down on the elongated skull. The blade bounced clear on the first stroke, but twice more Waylander struck. The bone of the skull parted on the third blow, the sword wedging deep into the beast's cranium. It sank to all fours, blood gushing from its mouth, talons scratching at the stone.

And died.

The smoke-demon was silent for a moment. 'You offer me good sport, Waylander,' he said softly. 'But then you always have. I think you always will.'

The smoke billowed and faded – and the demon vanished.

Karnak unwound the chain from the dead beast's throat and crossed to Waylander. 'Good to see you, old lad,' he said, with a wide smile.

'The men you sent are all dead,' said Waylander coldly. 'Now only you remain.'

Karnak nodded. 'I was trying to protect my son. No excuses. He's . . . dead. You're alive. Let that be an end to it.'

'I choose my own endings,' said Waylander, moving past the giant Drenai to where the Emperor stood, still chained to the wall. 'It has always been said that you are a man of honour,' Waylander told him.

'It is a source of pride to me,' said the Emperor.

'Good. You see I have two choices, Majesty. I can kill you, or I can let you go. But there is a price for the latter.'

'Name it, and if it is within my power you may have it.'

'I want the attack on the Nadir Wolves stopped; the army ordered back.'

'What are the Nadir to you?'

'Less than nothing. But my daughter is with them.'

The Emperor nodded. 'It will be as you say, Waylander. Is there nothing you want for yourself?'

The assassin smiled wearily. 'Nothing any man can give me,' he said.

Angel pushed the table on to the stairs, up-ending it to block the view of the enemy archers on the landing above, then sank to his haunches and stared around the hall.

The Gothir had forced the portcullis gate on the eleventh day of the siege, the defenders falling back to the transient safety of the keep. The older women and children hid in the lower levels of the fortress while, as Angel had predicted, the younger women now joined the men in the defence of the citadel.

Only eighty-five men remained, and these were desperately tired as the siege reached the thirteenth day. The barricades at the keep-gate were holding, but the Gothir had scaled the outside walls, climbing in through undefended windows, and were now in control of all the upper levels, occasionally attacking down the narrow stairwells, but more often merely loosing shafts into the packed hall below.

An arrow thudded into the upturned table. 'I know you're there, arse-face!' yelled Angel.

Miriel joined him. She had lost weight, the skin of her face taut and fleshless, her eyes gleaming unnaturally. Since Senta's death she had fought as one possessed with a lust for death. Angel had been hard-pressed to defend her, and had taken two minor cuts, one to the shoulder, the other to the forearm, hurling himself into the path of warriors closing in on her.

'We're finished here,' she said. 'The barricade will not hold them for long.'

He shrugged. There was no need to reply. The point was all too

460

obviously correct, and Angel could sense the mood of grim resignation among the Nadir. Miriel sat beside him, resting her head on his shoulder. He curled his arm around her. 'I loved him, Angel,' she said, her voice barely above a whisper. 'I should have told him, but I didn't know until he was gone.'

'That makes you feel guilty? That you didn't say the words?'

'Yes. He deserved more. And it's so hard to accept that he's . . .' She swallowed hard, unable to give sound to the word. Forcing a smile she brightened, briefly. 'He had such a zest for life, didn't he? And always so witty. Nothing grey about Senta, was there?'

'Nothing grey,' he agreed. 'He lived his life to the full. He fought, loved . . .'

'. . . and died.' She said it swiftly, and fought to hold back the tears.

'Yes, he died. Shemak's balls, we all die.' Angel sighed, then smiled. 'For myself I've no regrets. I've had a full life. But it grieves me to know that . . . you're here with me now. Everything is ahead of you – or it should be.'

She took his hand. 'We'll be together in the Void. Who knows what adventures await. And maybe he's there . . . waiting!'

Another arrow thudded into the table, then Angel heard the sound of boots upon the stairs. Surging to his feet he drew his sword. As the Gothir swarmed down Angel wrenched the table aside and leapt to meet them, Miriel just behind him.

Angel killed two, Miriel a third and the Gothir fell back. An archer loomed at the top of the stairs. Miriel hurled a knife which lanced into his shoulder, and he dived from sight. Angel backed away and wedged the table across the stairwell. 'Well,' he said, with a wide grin, 'we're not finished yet.'

Striding across the hall he saw the priest Ekodas, kneeling beside the stricken Dardalion. The Abbot was still sleeping and Angel paused. 'How is he?' he asked.

'Dying,' replied Ekodas.

'I thought you had healed the wound.'

'I did, but his heart has given out. It is almost ruptured and the valves are thinner than papyrus.' It was the first time the two men had spoken since the battle against the beast. Ekodas glanced up, then stood before the former gladiator. 'I am sorry for what happened,' he said. 'I . . . I . . .'

'It was the crystal,' put in Angel, swiftly. 'I know. It had a similar effect on me.'

'Yet you destroyed it.'

'I never had it in my hands. Don't torture yourself, priest.'

'Priest no longer. I am not worthy.'

'I'm no judge, Ekodas, but we all have weaknesses. We're made that way.'

The slender priest shook his head. 'That is generous of you. But I watched as your friend died – and I made a pact with evil. Zhu Chao came to me in that chamber. He seemed like . . . like a brother of the soul. And for that short time I had such vile dreams. I never realised there was so much . . . darkness inside me. I will walk another path now.' He shrugged. 'The crystal didn't change me, you see. It merely opened my eyes to what I am.'

Dardalion stirred. 'Ekodas!' The young priest knelt by the Abbot, taking his hand. Angel moved away towards the barricade.

'I am here, my friend,' said Ekodas.

'It . . . was all . . . done in faith, my son. And I can feel the others waiting for me. Summon the living for me.'

'There is only Vishna.'

'Ah. Fetch him then.'

'Dardalion, I . . .'

'You wish to be . . . released from your vows. I know. The woman, Shia.' Dardalion's eyes closed and a spasm of pain twisted his features. 'You are free, Ekodas. Free to wed, free to live . . . free to be.'

'I am sorry, Father.'

'You have nothing to be . . . sorry for. I sent you down there. I knew your destiny, Ekodas. From the moment she came to the temple there was a bond between you. Know peace, Ekodas . . . and . . . the joys of love.' He smiled weakly. 'You have done your duty by me, and by the others. Now . . . fetch Vishna, for time is short.'

Ekodas sent out a pulse and the tall forked-bearded warrior came running from the far side of the hall to kneel beside the dying Abbot. 'I can speak no more,' whispered Dardalion. 'Join me in communion.'

Vishna closed his eyes, and Ekodas knew their two spirits were now united. He made no attempt to join the communion, and waited patiently for it to end. He was holding Dardalion's hand when the Abbot died. Vishna jerked and groaned, then opened his dark eyes.

'What did he say?' asked Ekodas, releasing the hand.

'If we survive I am to travel to Ventria and found a new temple. The Thirty will live on. I am sorry that you will not be accompanying me.'

'I cannot, Vishna. It's gone from me. And, truth to tell, I don't want it back.'

Vishna stood. 'You know, just as he died, and flew from me, I felt the presence of the others – Merlon, Palista, Magnic. All waiting for him. It was wonderful. Truly wonderful.'

Ekodas gazed down on Dardalion's dead face, perfectly still and serene. 'Farewell, Father,' he whispered.

The silence beyond the keep was broken by the sound of distant trumpets.

'The Source be praised,' said Vishna.

'What is it?'

'That is the Gothir signal for withdrawal.' He sat down and closed his eyes, his spirit flying from the keep. Moments later he returned. 'A messenger has come from the Emperor. The siege is lifted. It is over, Ekodas! We live!'

At the barricade Angel peered into the courtyard. The Gothir were withdrawing in order, silently and in ranks of three. Angel sheathed his sword and turned to the defenders. 'I think you have won, my lads!' he shouted.

Orsa Khan leapt to the barricade and watched the departing soldiers. Swinging to Angel he threw his arms around the gladiator and kissed both his scarred cheeks. The other remaining Nadir surged forward, pulling Angel down and hoisting him to their shoulders, and a great cheer went up.

Watching the scene Miriel smiled, but the smile faded as she gazed around the hall. The dead were lying everywhere. Kesa Khan emerged from the lower stair, leading women and children back to the light. The old shaman approached her.

'Your father has slain Zhu Chao,' he said, but he did not meet her gaze. 'You have won for us, Miriel.'

'At great cost,' she told him.

'Yes, the price was not insignificant.' The small boy who had followed Angel was beside the shaman, and Kesa Khan reached out and patted his head. 'Still we have a future,' said the old man. 'Without you we could have been dust in the mountains. I wish joy for you.'

Miriel took a deep, slow breath. 'I can't believe it is over.'

'Over? No. Only this battle. There will be others.'

'Not for me.'

'For you also. I have walked the futures, Miriel. You are a child of battle. You will remain so.'

'We shall see,' she said, turning away from him to see Angel striding towards her. She looked up into his scarred, ravaged face, and the twinkling grey eyes. 'It looks as though we've a little time left after all,' she said.

'It certainly seems that way,' he agreed. Reaching down Angel hoisted the young Nadir boy to his shoulder. The child giggled happily and waved his wooden sword in the air.

'You're good with children,' said Miriel. 'He adores you.'

'He's a courageous pup. He followed me down into the depths, and then charged the beast with a burning brand. Did you see him?'

'No.'

Angel turned to Kesa Khan. 'Who will look after him?' he asked.

'I shall. As a son,' answered the shaman.

'Good. I may visit now and again. I'll hold you to that.' Lifting the boy down he watched as Kesa Khan led him away. The boy glanced back and waved his sword. Angel chuckled. 'What now?' he asked Miriel.

'I'm pregnant,' she said, looking into his pale eyes.

'I know. Dardalion told me.'

'It frightens me.'

'You? The Battle Queen of Kar-Barzac? I don't believe it.'

'I don't have any right to ask, but . . .'

'Don't say it, girl. There's no need. Old Angel will be there. He'll always be there. In any way that you want him.'

The walls of Dros Delnoch reared high into the southern sky as Waylander drew rein. Karnak heeled his mount alongside the black-clad assassin. 'The war beckons,' he said.

'I'm sure you'll conquer, General. It's what you're good at.'

Karnak laughed. 'I expect I shall.' Then his smile faded. 'What of you, Waylander? How does it stand between us?'

The assassin shrugged. 'Whatever is said here will not change a jot of what is bound to follow. I know you, Karnak, I always did. You live for power, and your memory is long. Your son is dead – you'll not forget that. And after a while you'll come to blame me – or mine – for his passing. And I too have my memories. We are enemies, you and I. We will remain so.'

The Drenai leader gave a thin smile. 'You do not think highly of me. I can't say as I blame you, but you are wrong. I *am* willing to forget the past. You saved my life – and in so doing you have probably saved the Drenai from destruction. That's what I shall remember.'

'Perhaps,' said Waylander, swinging his horse's head and riding towards the Mountains of the Moon.

Epilogue

Karnak returned to Dros Delnoch, gathered the forces there and led them against the Ventrians, smashing their army in two decisive battles at Erekban and Lentrum.

In the two years that followed Karnak took to brooding about the fear of assassination, becoming convinced that Waylander would one day seek him out and slay him. Against the advice of Asten he once more contacted the Guild, increasing the price on the assassin's head.

A veritable army of searchers was despatched, but no news of Waylander surfaced in Drenan.

Until one day three of the best hunters returned, bearing a rotting head, wrapped in canvas, and a small ebony and steel, double-bladed crossbow. Stripped of flesh, the skull and the crossbow were exhibited in the Museum at Drenan, under the inscription, cast in bronze: *Waylander the Slayer, the man who killed the King*.

One winter's day, three years later, and five after the siege of Kar-Barzac, the crossbow was stolen. In the same week, as Karnak marched at the head of the annual Victory Parade, a young woman with long dark hair stepped from the crowd. In her right hand was the stolen bow.

People in the crowd saw her speak to the Drenai leader just before she killed him, two bolts plunging into his chest. A rider, leading a second horse, galloped on to the Avenue of Kings, and the woman vaulted to the saddle just as Karnak's guards were rushing to apprehend her.

The two assassins made their escape, and many were the theories surrounding the murder: they were hired by the son of the Ventrian King, the battle monarch whose body was thrown in a mass grave after the defeat at Erekban. Or she was one of Karnak's mistresses, furious after he discarded her for a younger, prettier girl. Some in the crowd swore they recognised the male rider as Angel, a former gladiator. None knew the woman.

Karnak was given a state funeral. Two thousand soldiers marched behind the wagon bearing his body. Crowds lined the Avenue of Kings, and many were the tears shed for the man described on his tombstone as *'this greatest of Drenai heroes'*.

The skull of Waylander was sold eight years later. It was bought at auction by the Gothir merchant Matze Chai, acting on behalf of one of his clients, a mysterious noble who lived in a palace in the Gothir city of Namib. When asked why a foreigner should pay such a vast amount for the skull of a Drenai assassin, Matze Chai smiled and spread his elegant hands.

'But you must know?' insisted the curator of the museum.

'I assure you that I do not.'

'But the price . . . It is colossal!'

'My client is a very rich man. He has invested with me for many years.'

'Was he a friend to this Waylander?'

'I gather they were close,' admitted Matze Chai.

'But what will he do with the skull? Display it?'

'I doubt it. He told me he intends to bury it.'

'Why?' asked the man, astonished. 'Forty thousand Raq just to bury it?'

'He is a man who likes to choose his own endings,' said Matze Chai.

THE FIRST CHRONICLES OF
DRUSS THE LEGEND

Druss the Legend is dedicated with great love and affection to the memory of Mick Jeffrey, a quiet Christian of infinite patience and kindness. Those privileged to know him were blessed indeed. Goodnight and God bless, Mick!

Acknowledgments:
My thanks to my editor John Jarrold, copy editor Jean Maund, and test readers Val Gemmell, Stella Graham, Edith Graham, Tom Taylor, and Vikki Lee France. Thanks also to Stan Nicholls and Chris Baker for bringing Druss to life in a new way.

Introduction

Druss was really the first of my heroes. He was based on a child's idealised view of his stepfather.

Bill Woodford became my stepfather in 1954. He changed my life in so many ways. Probably the best example of this came soon after he married my mother. I was six years old and had terrible dreams of vampires coming to drink my blood. I don't know why these dreams occurred, but I still recall the terror of them. My mother took me to see specialists who assured me that vampires didn't exist, but the dreams continued.

One night, as I awoke screaming, Bill came into the room. I told him there was a vampire coming for me. He said: 'I know, son. I saw it. Broke its neck. Won't have no vampires in my house.' I never dreamt of vampires again.

Druss was Bill writ large.

After the publication of *Legend* in 1984, I wrote a prequel called *Druss the Legend*. The publishers rejected it on two counts. Firstly, as a young man, Druss was too similar to Conan, invincible and deadly, and, secondly, all of his early tales were recounted in *Legend* and this robbed the prequel of surprise.

So I moved on, writing other stories. Over the years more and more fans wrote asking for earlier tales of Druss. I talked it over with editors and test-readers. Would it sell? We couldn't decide.

Then I gave an interview to a journalist from a science fiction publication. In it I said I was considering a new Druss novel.

The response was overwhelming. Letters were coming in from all over the world asking when it would be published.

This answered the question as to whether it would sell.

Which was not enough for me. The real question was whether I could overcome the lack of surprise.

At a convention in 1990 I asked a fan, who knew *Legend* so well he could quote passages verbatim, what he could remember about Druss' early life. He said: 'He loses Rowena, sets off to track her down, finds her then takes part in the Battle of Skeln. He also becomes known as the Silver Slayer among the Sathuli and Deathwalker among the Nadir.' He then also listed other characters mentioned by Druss in *Legend* – Sieben the Poet, Ekodas, Bodasen and Gorben the prince who became a king.

My heart sank. 'No point in you reading the prequel then,' I said. 'You know it already.'

'I know *what* he did, but I'd love to read *how*,' he told me.

'I'd like to find *that* out myself,' I said.

It was a real joy to walk the hills with Druss again. So much so that some years later I added a third story to the series, *Legend of Deathwalker*. God willing there will be one more before Druss is finally laid to rest.

Book One

Birth of a Legend

Prologue

Screened by the undergrowth he knelt by the trail, dark eyes scanning the boulders ahead of him and the trees beyond. Dressed as he was in a shirt of fringed buckskin, and brown leather leggings and boots, the tall man was virtually invisible, kneeling in the shadows of the trees.

The sun was high in a cloudless summer sky, and the spoor was more than three hours old. Insects had criss-crossed the hoof-marks, but the edges of the prints were still firm.

Forty horsemen, laden with plunder . . .

Shadak faded back through the undergrowth to where his horse was tethered. He stroked the beast's long neck and lifted his swordbelt from the back of the saddle. Strapping it to his waist he drew the two short swords; they were of the finest Vagrian steel, and double edged. He thought for a moment, then sheathed the blades and reached for the bow and quiver strapped to the saddle pommel. The bow was of Vagrian horn, a hunting weapon capable of launching a two-foot-long arrow across a killing space of sixty paces. The doeskin quiver held twenty shafts that Shadak had crafted himself: the flights of goose feather, stained red and yellow, the heads of pointed iron, not barbed, and easily withdrawn from the bodies of the slain. Swiftly he strung the bow and notched an arrow to the string. Then looping the quiver over his shoulder, he made his way carefully back to the trail.

Would they have left a rearguard? It was unlikely, for there were no Drenai soldiers within fifty miles.

But Shadak was a cautious man. And he knew Collan. Tension rose in him as he pictured the smiling face and the cruel, mocking eyes. 'No anger,' he told himself. But it was hard, bitterly hard. Angry men make mistakes, he reminded himself. The hunter must be cold as iron.

Silently he edged his way forward. A towering boulder jutted from the earth some twenty paces ahead and to his left; to the right was a cluster of smaller rocks, no more than four feet high. Shadak took a deep breath and rose from his hiding-place.

From behind the large boulder a man stepped into sight, bowstring bent. Shadak dropped to his knee, the attacker's arrow slashing through the air above his head. The bowman tried to leap back behind the shelter of the boulder, but even as he was dropping Shadak

475

loosed a shaft which plunged into the bowman's throat, punching through the skin at the back of his neck.

Another attacker ran forward, this time from Shadak's right. With no time to notch a second arrow Shadak swung the bow, lashing it across the man's face. As the attacker stumbled, Shadak dropped the bow and drew his two short swords; with one sweeping blow he cut through the neck of the fallen man. Two more attackers ran into view and he leapt to meet them. Both men wore iron breastplates, their necks and heads protected by chain mail, and they carried sabres.

'You'll not die easily, you bastard!' shouted the first, a tall, wide-shouldered warrior. Then his eyes narrowed as he recognised the swordsman facing him. Fear replaced battle lust – but he was too close to Shadak to withdraw and made a clumsy lunge with his sabre. Shadak parried the blade with ease, his second sword lancing forward into the man's mouth and through the bones of his neck. As the swordsman died, the second warrior backed away.

'We didn't know it was you, I swear!' he said, hands trembling.

'Now you do,' said Shadak softly.

Without a word the man turned and ran back towards the trees as Shadak sheathed his swords and moved to his bow. Notching an arrow, he drew back on the string. The shaft flashed through the air to punch home into the running man's thigh. He screamed and fell. As Shadak loped to where he lay, the man rolled to his back, dropping his sword.

'For pity's sake don't kill me!' he pleaded.

'You had no pity back in Corialis,' said Shadak. 'But tell me where Collan is heading and I'll let you live.' A wolf howled in the distance, a lonely sound. It was answered by another, then another.

'There's a village . . . twenty miles south-east,' said the man, his eyes fixed on the short sword in Shadak's hand. 'We scouted it. Plenty of young women. Collan and Harib Ka plan to raid it for slaves, then take them to Mashrapur.'

Shadak nodded. 'I believe you,' he said, at last.

'You're going to let me live, yes? You promised,' the wounded man whimpered.

'I always keep my promises,' said Shadak, disgusted at the man's weakness. Reaching down, he wrenched his shaft clear of the man's leg. Blood gushed from the wound, and the injured warrior groaned. Shadak wiped the arrow clean on the man's cloak, then stood and walked to the body of the first man he had killed. Kneeling beside the corpse, he recovered his arrow and then strode to where the raiders had tethered their horses. Mounting the first, he led the others back down the trail to where his gelding waited. Gathering the reins, he led the four mounts back out on the trail.

'What about me?' shouted the wounded man.

Shadak turned in the saddle. 'Do your best to keep the wolves away,' he advised. 'By dark they will have picked up the scent of blood.'

'Leave me a horse! In the name of Mercy!'

'I am not a merciful man,' said Shadak.

And he rode on towards the south-east, and the distant mountains.

1

The axe was four feet long, with a ten-pound head, the blade flared, and sharp as any sword. The haft was of elm, beautifully curved, and more than forty years old. For most men it was a heavy tool, unwieldy and imprecise. But in the hands of the dark-haired young man who stood before the towering beech it sang through the air, seemingly as light as a sabre. Every long swing saw the head bite exactly where the woodsman intended, deeper and deeper into the meat of the trunk.

Druss stepped back, then glanced up. There were several heavy branches jutting towards the north. He moved around the tree, gauging the line where it would fall, then returned to his work. This was the third tree he had tackled today and his muscles ached, sweat gleaming on his naked back. His short-cropped black hair was soaked with perspiration that trickled over his brow, stinging his ice-blue eyes. His mouth was dry, but he was determined to finish the task before allowing himself the reward of a cooling drink.

Some way to his left the brothers Pilan and Yorath were sitting on a fallen tree, laughing and talking, their hatchets beside them. Theirs was the task of stripping the trunks, hacking away smaller branches and limbs that could be used for winter firewood. But they stopped often and Druss could hear them discussing the merits and alleged vices of the village girls. They were handsome youths, blond and tall, sons of the blacksmith, Tetrin. Both were witty and intelligent, and popular among the girls.

Druss disliked them. To his right several of the older boys were sawing through the larger branches of the first tree Druss had felled, while elsewhere young girls were gathering deadwood, kindling for winter fires, and loading them to wheelbarrows to be pushed downhill to the village.

At the edge of the new clearing stood the four workhorses, hobbled now and grazing, waiting for the trees to be cleaned so that chain traces could be attached to the trunks for the long haul into the valley. Autumn was fading fast, and the village elders were determined that the new perimeter wall would be finished before winter. The frontier mountains of Skoda boasted only one troop of Drenai cavalry, patrolling an area of a thousand square miles. Raiders, cattle thieves, slavers, robbers and outlaws roamed the mountains, and the ruling council in Drenai made it clear they would accept no responsibility for the new settlements on the Vagrian borders.

But thoughts of the perils of frontier life did not discourage the men and women who journeyed to Skoda. They sought a new life, far removed from the more civilised south and east, and built their homes where land was still free and wild, and where strong men did not need to tug the forelock nor bow when the nobles rode by.

Freedom was the key word, and no talk of raiders could deter them.

Druss hefted his axe, then thundered the blade into the widening notch. Ten times more he struck, deep into the base of the trunk. Then another ten smooth, powerful strokes. Three more axe-blows and the tree would groan and give, wrenching and tearing as she fell.

Stepping back he scanned the ground along the line of the fall. A movement caught his eye, and he saw a small child with golden hair sitting beneath a bush, a rag doll in her hand. 'Kiris!' bellowed Druss. 'If you are not out of there by the time I count to three I'll tear off your leg and beat you to death with the wet end! One! Two!'

The child's mouth dropped open, her eyes widening. Dropping her rag doll she scrambled clear of the bush and ran crying from the forest. Druss shook his head and walked forward to retrieve the doll, tucking it into his wide belt. He felt the eyes of the others on him, and guessed what they were thinking: Druss the Brute, Druss the Cruel – that's how they saw him. And maybe they were right.

Ignoring them, he walked back to the tree and hefted his axe.

Only two weeks before he had been felling a tall beech, and had been called away with the work almost completed. When he returned it was to find Kiris sitting in the topmost branches with her doll, as always, beside her.

'Come down,' he had coaxed. 'The tree is about to fall.'

'Won't,' said Kiris. 'We like it here. We can see for ever.'

Druss had looked around, for once hoping that some of the village girls were close by. But there was no one. He examined the huge cleft in the trunk; a sudden wind could cause the trunk to topple. 'Come down, there's a good girl. You'll be hurt if the tree falls.'

'Why should it fall?'

'Because I've been hitting it with my axe. Now come down.'

'All right,' she said, then started to climb down. The tree suddenly tilted and Kiris screamed and clung to a branch. Druss's mouth was dry.

'Quickly now,' he said. Kiris said nothing, nor did she move. Druss swore and, setting his foot to a low knot, levered himself up to the first branch. Slowly and with great care he climbed the half-felled tree, higher and higher towards the child.

At last he reached her. 'Put your arms around my neck,' he commanded. She did so, and he began the climb down.

Half-way to the ground Druss felt the tree shudder – and snap. Leaping clear he hugged the child to him, then hit the ground, landing awkwardly with his left shoulder slamming into the soft earth. Shielded by his bulk, Kiris was unhurt, but Druss groaned as he rose.

'Are you hurt?' asked Kiris.

Druss's pale eyes swung on the child. 'If I catch you near my trees again, I shall feed you to the wolves!' he roared. 'Now begone!' She had sprinted away as if her dress was on fire. Chuckling at the memory now, he hefted his axe and thundered the blade into the beech. A great groan came from the tree, a wrenching, tearing sound that drowned out the nearby thudding of hatchets and the sawing of boughs.

The beech toppled, twisting as it fell. Druss turned towards the water-sack hanging from a branch nearby; the felling of the tree signalled the break for the midday meal, and the village youngsters gathered in groups in the sunshine, laughing and joking. But no one approached Druss. His recent fight with the former soldier Alarin had unsettled them, and they viewed him even more warily than before. He sat alone, eating bread and cheese and taking long, cool swallows of water.

Pilan and Yorath were now sitting with Berys and Tailia, the daughters of the miller. The girls were smiling prettily, tilting their heads and enjoying the attention. Yorath leaned in close to Tailia, kissing her ear. Tailia feigned outrage.

Their games ceased when a black-bearded man entered the clearing. He was tall, with massive shoulders and eyes the colour of winter clouds. Druss saw his father approach, and stood.

'Clothe yourself and walk with me,' said Bress, striding away into the woods. Druss donned his shirt and followed his father. Out of earshot of the others, the tall man sat down beside a fast-moving stream and Druss joined him.

'You must learn to control that temper, my son,' said Bress. 'You almost killed the man.'

'I just hit him . . . once.'

'The *once* broke his jaw and dislodged three teeth.'

'Have the Elders decided on a penalty?'

'Aye. I must support Alarin and his family through the winter. Now I can ill afford that, boy.'

'He spoke slightingly of Rowena and I'll not tolerate that. *Ever.*'

Bress took a deep breath, but before speaking he lifted a pebble and hurled it into the stream. Then he sighed. 'We are not known here, Druss – save as good workers and fellow villagers. We came a long way to be rid of the stigma my father bequeathed our family. But remember the lessons of his life. He could not control his temper – and he became an outcast and a renegade, a bloodthirsty butcher. Now they say blood runs true. In our case I hope they are wrong.'

481

'I'm not a killer,' argued Druss. 'Had I wanted him dead, I could have broken his neck with a single blow.'

'I know. You are strong – you take after me in that regard. And proud; that I think came from your mother, may her soul know peace. The gods alone know how often I have been forced to swallow my pride.' Bress tugged at his beard and turned to face his son. 'We are a small settlement now, and we cannot have violence among ourselves – we would not survive as a community. Can you understand that?'

'What did they ask you to tell me?'

Bress sighed. 'You must make your peace with Alarin. And know this – if you attack any other man of the village you will be cast out.'

Druss's face darkened. 'I work harder than any man. I trouble no one. I do not get drunk like Pilan and Yorath, nor try to make whores of the village maids like their father. I do not steal. I do not lie. Yet they will cast *me* out?'

'You frighten them, Druss. You frighten me too.'

'I am not my grandfather. I am not a murderer.'

Bress sighed. 'I had hoped that Rowena, with all her gentleness, would have helped to calm that temper of yours. But on the morning after your wedding you half-kill a fellow settler. And for what? Don't tell me he spoke slightingly. All he said was that you were a lucky man and he'd like to have bedded her himself. By all the gods, son! If you feel you have to break a man's jaw for every compliment he pays your wife, there won't be any men left in this village to work at all.'

'It wasn't said as a compliment. And I can control my temper, but Alarin is a loud-mouthed braggart – and he received exactly what he deserved.'

'I hope you'll take note of what I've said, son.' Bress stood and stretched his back. 'I know you have little respect for me. But I hope you'll think of how Rowena would fare if you were both declared outcast.'

Druss gazed up at him and swallowed back his disappointment. Bress was a physical giant, stronger than any man Druss had ever known, but he wore defeat like a cloak. The younger man rose alongside his father.

'I'll take heed,' he said.

Bress smiled wearily. 'I have to get back to the wall. It should be finished in another three days; we'll all sleep sounder then.'

'You'll have the timber,' Druss promised.

'You're a good man with an axe, I'll say that.' Bress walked away for several paces, then turned. 'If they did cast you out, son, you wouldn't be alone. I'd walk with you.'

Druss nodded. 'It won't come to that. I've already promised Rowena I'll mend my ways.'

'I'll wager she was angry,' said Bress, with a grin.

'Worse. She was disappointed in me.' Druss chuckled. 'Sharper than a serpent's tooth is the *disappointment* of a new wife.'

'You should laugh more often, my boy. It suits you.'

But as Bress walked away the smile faded from the young man's face as he gazed down at his bruised knuckles and remembered the emotions that had surged within him as he struck Alarin. There had been anger, and a savage need for combat. But when his fist landed and Alarin toppled there had been only one sensation, brief and indescribably powerful.

Joy. Pure pleasure, of a kind and a power he had not experienced before. He closed his eyes, forcing the scene from his mind.

'I am not my grandfather,' he told himself. 'I am not insane.' That night he repeated the words to Rowena as they lay in the broad bed Bress had fashioned for a wedding gift.

Rolling to her stomach she leaned on his chest, her long hair feeling like silk upon his massive shoulder. 'Of course you are not insane, my love,' she assured him. 'You are one of the gentlest men I've known.'

'That's not how they see me,' he told her, reaching up and stroking her hair.

'I know. It was wrong of you to break Alarin's jaw. They were just words – and it matters not a whit if he meant them unpleasantly. They were just noises, blowing into the air.'

Easing her from him, Druss sat up. 'It is not that easy, Rowena. The man had been goading me for weeks. He wanted that fight – because he wanted to humble me. But he did not. No man ever will.' She shivered beside him. 'Are you cold?' he asked, drawing her into his embrace.

'*Deathwalker*,' she whispered.

'What? What did you say?'

Her eyelids fluttered. She smiled and kissed his cheek. 'It doesn't matter. Let us forget Alarin, and enjoy each other's company.'

'I'll always enjoy your company,' he said. 'I love you.'

Rowena's dreams were dark and brooding and the following day, at the riverside, she could not force the images from her mind. Druss, dressed in black and silver and bearing a mighty axe, stood upon a hillside. From the axe-blades came a great host of souls, flowing like smoke around their grim killer. *Deathwalker!* The vision had been powerful. Squeezing the last of the water from the shirt she was washing, she laid it over a flat rock alongside the drying blankets and the scrubbed woollen dress. Stretching her back, she rose from the water's edge and walked to the tree line where she sat, her right hand closing on the brooch Druss had fashioned for her in his father's workshop – soft copper strands entwined around a moonstone, misty and translucent. As her fingers touched the stone her eyes closed and her mind cleared. She saw Druss sitting alone by the high stream.

'I am with you,' she whispered. But he could not hear her and she sighed.

No one in the village knew of her Talent, for her father, Voren, had impressed upon her the need for secrecy. Only last year four women in Drenan had been convicted of sorcery and burnt alive by the priests of Missael. Voren was a careful man. He had brought Rowena to this remote village, far from Drenan, because, as he told her, 'Secrets cannot live quietly among a multitude. Cities are full of prying eyes and attentive ears, vengeful minds and malevolent thoughts. You will be safer in the mountains.'

And he had made her promise to tell no one of her skills. Not even Druss. Rowena regretted that promise as she gazed with the eyes of Spirit upon her husband. She could see no harshness in his blunt, flat features, no swirling storm-clouds in those grey-blue eyes, no hint of sullenness in the flat lines of his mouth. He was Druss – and she loved him. With a certainty born of her Talent she knew she would love no other man as she loved Druss. And she knew why . . . he needed her. She had gazed through the window of his soul and had found there a warmth and a purity, an island of tranquillity set in a sea of roaring violent emotions. While she was with him Druss was tender, his turbulent spirit at peace. In her company he smiled. Perhaps, she thought, with my help I can keep him at peace. Perhaps the grim killer will never know life.

'Dreaming again, Ro,' said Mari, moving to sit alongside Rowena. The young woman opened her eyes and smiled at her friend. Mari was short and plump, with honey-coloured hair and a bright, open smile.

'I was thinking of Druss,' said Rowena.

Mari nodded and looked away and Rowena could feel her concern. For weeks her friend had tried to dissuade her from marrying Druss, adding her arguments to those of Voren and others.

'Will Pilan be your partner at the Solstice Dance?' asked Rowena, changing the subject.

Mari's mood changed abruptly, and she giggled. 'Yes. But he doesn't know yet.'

'When will he find out?'

'Tonight.' Mari lowered her voice, though there was no one else within earshot. 'We're meeting in the lower meadow.'

'Be careful,' warned Rowena.

'Is that the advice of the old married woman? Didn't you and Druss make love before you were wed?'

'Yes, we did,' Rowena admitted, 'but Druss had already made his pledge before the Oak. Pilan hasn't.'

'Just words, Ro. I don't need them. Oh, I know Pilan's been flirting with Tailia, but she's not for him. No passion, you see. All she thinks about is wealth. She doesn't want to stay in the wilderness, she yearns for Drenan. She'll not want to keep a mountain man warm at night, nor make the beast with two backs in a wet meadow, with the grass tickling her . . .'

'Mari! You really are too frank,' admonished Rowena.

Mari giggled and leaned in close. 'Is Druss a good lover?'

Rowena sighed, all tension and sadness disappearing. 'Oh, Mari! Why is it that you can talk about forbidden subjects and make them seem so . . . so wonderfully ordinary? You are like the sunshine that follows rain.'

'They're not forbidden here, Ro. That's the trouble with girls born in cities and surrounded by stone walls and marble, and granite. You don't feel the earth any more. Why did you come here?'

'You know why,' said Rowena uneasily. 'Father wanted a life in the mountains.'

'I know that's what you've always said – but I never believed it. You're a terrible liar – your face goes red and you always look away!'

'I . . . can't tell you. I made a promise.'

'Wonderful!' exclaimed Mari. 'I love mysteries. Is he a criminal? He was a book-keeper, wasn't he? Did he steal some rich man's money?'

'No! It was nothing to do with him. It was me! Don't ask me any more. Please?'

'I thought we were friends,' said Mari. 'I thought we could trust one another.'

'We can. Honestly!'

'I wouldn't tell anyone.'

'I know,' said Rowena sadly. 'But it would spoil our friendship.'

'Nothing could do that. How long have you been here – two seasons? Have we ever fought? Oh, come on, Ro. Where's the harm? You tell me your secret and I'll tell you mine.'

'I know yours already,' whispered Rowena. 'You gave yourself to the Drenai captain when he and his men passed through here on patrol in the summer. You took him to the low meadow.'

'How did you find out?'

'I didn't. It was in your mind when you told me you would share a secret with me.'

'I don't understand.'

'I can see what people are thinking. And I can sometimes tell what is going to happen. That's my secret.'

'You have the Gift? I don't believe it! What am I thinking now?'

'A white horse with a garland of red flowers.'

'Oh, Ro! That's wonderful. Tell my fortune,' she pleaded, holding out her hand.

'You won't tell anyone else?'

'I promised, didn't I?'

'Sometimes it doesn't work.'

'Try anyway,' urged Mari, thrusting out her plump hand. Rowena reached out, her slender fingers closing on Mari's palm, but suddenly she shuddered and the colour faded from her face.

'What is it?'

Rowena began to tremble. 'I . . . I must find Druss. Can't . . . talk . . .' Rising, she stumbled away, the washed clothes forgotten.

'Ro! Rowena, come back!'

On the hillside above, a rider stared down at the women by the river. Then he turned his horse and rode swiftly towards the north.

Bress closed the door of the cabin and moved through to his work room, where from a small box he took a lace glove. It was old and yellowed, and several of the pearls which had once graced the wrist were now missing. It was a small glove and Bress sat at his bench staring down at it, his huge fingers stroking the remaining pearls.

'I am a lost man,' he said softly, closing his eyes and picturing Alithae's sweet face. 'He despises me. Gods, I despise myself.' Leaning back in his chair he gazed idly at the walls, and the many shelves bearing strands of copper and brass, work tools, jars of dye, boxes of beads. It was rare now for Bress to find the time to make jewellery; there was little call for such luxuries here in the mountains. Now it was his skills as a carpenter which were valued; he had become merely a maker of doors and tables, chairs and beds.

Still nursing the glove, he moved back into the hearth room.

'I think we were born under unlucky stars,' he told the dead Alithae. 'Or perhaps Bardan's evil stained our lives. Druss is like him, you know. I see it in the eyes, in the sudden rages. I don't know what to do. I could never convince father. And I cannot reach Druss.'

His thoughts drifted back – memories, dark and painful, flooding his mind. He saw Bardan on that last day, blood-covered, his enemies all around him. Six men were dead, and that terrible axe was still slashing left and right . . . Then a lance had been thrust into Bardan's throat. Blood bubbled from the wound but Bardan slew the lance wielder before falling to his knees. A man ran in behind him and delivered a terrible blow to Bardan's neck.

From his hiding-place high in the oak the fourteen-year-old Bress had watched his father die, and heard one of the killers say: 'The old wolf is dead – now where is the pup?'

He had stayed in the tree all night, high above the headless body of Bardan. Then, in the cold of the dawn he had climbed down and stood by the corpse. There was no sadness, only a terrible sense of relief combined with guilt. Bardan was dead: Bardan the Butcher. Bardan the Slayer. Bardan the Demon.

486

He had walked sixty miles to a settlement, and there had found employment, apprenticed to a carpenter. But just as he was settling down, the past came back to torment him when a travelling tinker recognised him: he was the son of the Devil! A crowd gathered outside the carpenter's shop, an angry mob armed with clubs and stones.

Bress had climbed from the rear window and fled from the settlement. Three times during the next five years he had been forced to run – and then he had met Alithae.

Fortune smiled on him then and he remembered Alithae's father, on the day of the wedding, approaching him and offering him a goblet of wine. 'I know you have suffered, boy,' said the old man. 'But I am not one who believes that a father's evil is visited upon the souls of his children. I know you, Bress. You are a good man.'

Aye, thought Bress, as he sat by the hearth, a good man.

Lifting the glove he kissed it softly. Alithae had been wearing it when the three men from the south had arrived at the settlement where Bress and his wife and new son had made their homes. Bress had a small but thriving business making brooches and rings and necklets for the wealthy. He was out walking one morning, Alithae beside him carrying the babe.

'It's Bardan's son!' he heard someone shout and he glanced round. The three riders had stopped their horses, and one of the men was pointing at him; they spurred their mounts and rode at him. Alithae, struck by a charging horse, fell heavily, and Bress had leapt at the rider, dragging him from the saddle. The other men hurled themselves from their saddles. Bress struck left and right, his huge fists clubbing them to the ground.

As the dust settled he turned back to Alithae . . .

Only to find her dead, the babe crying beside her.

From that moment he lived like a man with no hope. He rarely smiled and he never laughed.

The ghost of Bardan was upon him, and he took to travelling, moving through the lands of the Drenai with his son beside him. Bress took what jobs he could find: a labourer in Drenan, a carpenter in Delnoch, a bridge-builder in Mashrapur, a horse-handler in Corteswain. Five years ago he had wed a farmer's daughter named Patica – a simple lass, plain of face and none too bright. Bress cared for her, but there was no room left for love in his heart for Alithae had taken it with her when she died. He had married Patica to give Druss a mother, but the boy had never taken to her.

Two years ago, with Druss now fifteen, they had come to Skoda. But even here the ghost remained – born again, it seemed, into the boy.

'What can I do, Alithae?' he asked.

Patica entered the cabin, holding three fresh loaves in her arms. She was a large woman with a round pleasant face framed by auburn hair.

She saw the glove and tried to mask the hurt she felt. 'Did you see Druss?' she asked.

'Aye, I did. He says he'll try to curb his temper.'

'Give him time. Rowena will calm him.'

Hearing the thunder of hooves outside, Bress placed the glove on the table and moved to the door. Armed men were riding into the village, swords in their hands.

Bress saw Rowena running into the settlement, her dress hitched up around her thighs. She saw the raiders and tried to turn away but a horseman bore down on her. Bress ran into the open and leapt at the man, pulling him from the saddle. The rider hit the ground hard, losing his grip on his sword. Bress snatched it up, but a lance pierced his shoulder and with a roar of anger he twisted round and the lance snapped. Bress lashed out with the sword. The rider fell back, and the horse reared.

Riders surrounded him, with lances levelled.

In that instant Bress knew he was about to die. Time froze for him. He was the sky, filled with lowering clouds, and smelled the new-mown grass of the meadows. Other raiders were galloping through the settlement, and he heard the screams of the dying villagers. Everything they had built was for nothing. A terrible anger raged inside him. Gripping the sword, he let out the battlecry of Bardan.

'Blood and death!' he bellowed.

And charged.

Deep within the woods Druss leaned on his axe, a rare smile on his normally grim face. Above him the sun shone through a break in the clouds, and he saw an eagle soaring, golden wings seemingly aflame. Druss removed his sweat-drenched linen headband, laying it on a stone to dry. Lifting a waterskin, he took a long drink. Nearby Pilan and Yorath laid aside their hatchets.

Soon Tailia and Berys would arrive with the haul-horses and the work would begin again, attaching the chains and dragging the timbers down to the village. But for now there was little to do but sit and wait. Druss opened the linen-wrapped package Rowena had given him that morning; within was a wedge of meat pie, and a large slice of honey cake.

'Ah, the joys of married life!' said Pilan.

Druss laughed. 'You should have tried harder to woo her. Too late to be jealous now.'

'She wouldn't have me, Druss. She said she was waiting for a man whose face would curdle milk and that if she married me she would spend the rest of her life wondering which of her pretty friends would steal me from her. It seems her dream was to find the world's ugliest man.'

His smile faded as he saw the expression on the woodsman's face, and the cold gleam that appeared in his pale eyes. 'Only jesting,' said Pilan swiftly, the colour ebbing from his face.

Druss took a deep breath and, remembering his father's warning, fought down his anger. 'I am not . . . good with jests,' he said, the words tasting like bile in his mouth.

'No harm done,' said Pilan's brother, moving to sit alongside the giant. 'But if you don't mind my saying so, Druss, you need to develop a sense of humour. We all make jests at the expense of our . . . friends. It means nothing.'

Druss merely nodded and turned his attention to the pie. Yorath was right. Rowena had said exactly the same words, but from her it was easy to take criticism. With her he felt calm and the world had colour and joy. He finished the food and stood. 'The girls should have been here by now,' he said.

'I can hear horses,' said Pilan, rising.

'They're coming fast,' Yorath added.

Tailia and Berys came running into the clearing, their faces showing fear, their heads turning towards the unseen horsemen. Druss snatched his axe from the stump and ran towards them as Tailia, looking back, stumbled and fell.

Six horsemen rode into sight, armour gleaming in the sunlight. Druss saw raven-winged helms, lances and swords. The horses were lathered and, on seeing the three youths, the warriors shouted battle cries and spurred their mounts towards them.

Pilan and Yorath sprinted away towards the right. Three riders swung their horses to give chase, but the remaining three came on towards Druss.

The young man stood calmly, the axe held loosely across his naked chest. Directly in front of him was a felled tree. The first of the riders, a lancer, leaned forward in the saddle as his gelding jumped over the fallen beech. At that moment Druss moved, sprinting forward and swinging his axe in a murderous arc. As the horse landed the axe-blade hissed over its head, plunging into the chest of the lancer to splinter his breastplate and smash his ribs to shards. The blow hammered the man from the saddle. Druss tried to wrench the axe clear, but the blade was caught by the fractured armour. A sword slashed down at the youth's head and Druss dived and rolled. As a horseman moved in close he hurled himself from the ground, grabbing the stallion's right foreleg. With one awesome heave he toppled horse and rider. Hurdling the fallen tree, he ran to where the other two youths had left their hatchets. Scooping up the first he turned as a raider galloped towards him. Druss' arm came back, then snapped forward. The hatchet sliced through the air, the iron head crunching into the man's teeth. He swayed in the saddle. Druss ran forward to drag him from the horse.

489

The raider, having dropped his lance, tried to draw a dagger. Druss slapped it from his hand, delivered a bone-breaking punch to the warrior's chin and then, snatching up the dagger, rammed it into the man's unprotected throat.

'Look out, Druss!' yelled Tailia. Druss spun, just as a sword flashed for his belly. Parrying the blade with his forearm, he thundered a right cross which took the attacker full on the jaw, spinning him from his feet. Druss leapt on the man, one huge hand grabbing his chin, the other his brow. With one savage twist Druss heard the swordsman's neck snap like a dry stick.

Moving swiftly to the first man he had killed, Druss tore the felling axe clear of the breastplate as Tailia ran from her hiding-place in the bushes. 'They are attacking the village,' she said, tears in her eyes.

Pilan came running into the clearing, a lancer behind him. 'Swerve!' bellowed Druss. But Pilan was too terrified to obey and he ran straight on – until the lance pierced his back, exiting in a bloody spray from his chest. The youth cried out, then slumped to the ground. Druss roared in anger and raced forward. The lancer desperately tried to wrench his weapon clear of the dying boy. Druss swung wildly with the axe, which glanced from the rider's shoulder and plunged into the horse's back. The animal whinnied in pain and reared before falling to the earth, its legs flailing. The rider scrambled clear, blood gushing from his shoulder and tried to run, but Druss's next blow almost decapitated him.

Hearing a scream, Druss began to run towards the sound and found Yorath struggling with one raider; the second was kneeling on the ground, blood streaming from a wound in his head. The body of Berys was beside him, a blood-smeared stone in her hand. The swordsman grappling with Yorath suddenly head-butted the youth, sending Yorath back several paces. The sword came up.

Druss shouted, trying to distract the warrior. But to no avail. The weapon lanced into Yorath's side. The swordsman dragged the blade clear and turned towards Druss.

'Now your time to die, farm boy!' he said.

'In your dreams!' snarled the woodsman. Swinging the axe over his head, Druss charged. The swordsman side-stepped to his right – but Druss had been waiting for the move, and with all the power of his mighty shoulders he wrenched the axe, changing its course. It clove through the man's collarbone, smashing the shoulder-blade and ripping into his lungs. Tearing the axe loose, Druss turned from the body to see the first wounded warrior struggling to rise; jumping forward, he struck him a murderous blow to the neck.

'Help me!' called Yorath.

'I'll send Tailia,' Druss told him, and began to run back through the trees.

Reaching the crest of the hill he gazed down on the village. He could see scattered bodies, but no sign of raiders. For a moment he thought the villagers had beaten them back . . . but there was no movement at all.

'Rowena!' he yelled. 'Rowena!'

Druss ran down the slope. He fell and rolled, losing his grip on the felling-axe, but scrambling to his feet he pounded on – down into the meadow, across the flat, through the half-finished gates. Bodies lay everywhere. Rowena's father, the former book-keeper Voren, had been stabbed through the throat, and blood was staining the earth beneath him. Breathing hard, Druss stopped, and stared around the settlement square.

Old women, young children and all the men were dead. As he stumbled on he saw the golden-haired child, Kiris, beloved of all the villagers, lying sprawled in death alongside her rag doll. The body of an infant lay against one building, a bloodstain on the wall above showing how it had been slain.

He found his father lying in the open with four dead raiders around him. Patica was beside him, a hammer in her hand, her plain brown woollen dress drenched in blood. Druss fell to his knees by his father's body. There were terrible wounds to the chest and belly, and his left arm was almost severed at the wrist. Bress groaned and opened his eyes.

'Druss . . .'

'I am here, Father.'

'They took the young women. . . . Rowena . . . was among them.'

'I'll find her.'

The dying man glanced to his right at the dead woman beside him. 'She was a brave lass; she tried to help me. I should have . . . loved her better.' Bress sighed, then choked as blood flowed into his throat. He spat it clear. 'There is . . . a weapon. In the house . . . far wall, beneath the boards. It has a terrible history. But . . . but you will need it.'

Druss stared down at the dying man and their eyes met. Bress lifted his right hand. Druss took it. 'I did my best, boy,' said his father.

'I know.' Bress was fading fast, and Druss was not a man of words. Instead he lifted his father into his arms and kissed his brow, hugging him close until the last breath of life rasped from the broken body.

Then he pushed himself to his feet and entered his father's home. It had been ransacked – cupboards hauled open, drawers pulled from the dressers, rugs ripped from the walls. But by the far wall the hidden compartment was undiscovered and Druss prised open the boards and hauled out the chest that lay in the dust below the floor. It was locked. Moving through into his father's workshop, he returned with a large hammer and a chisel which he used to pry off the hinges. Then he took hold of the lid and wrenched it clear, the brass lock twisting and tearing free.

Inside, wrapped in oilskin, was an axe. And such an axe! Druss unwrapped it reverently. The black metal haft was as long as a man's arm, the double heads shaped like the wings of a butterfly. He tested the edges with his thumb; the weapon was as sharp as his father's shaving-knife. Silver runes were inscribed on the haft, and though Druss could not read them he knew the words etched there. For this was the awful axe of Bardan, the weapon that had slain men, women, and even children during the reign of terror. The words were part of the dark folklore of the Drenai.

Snaga, the Sender, the blades of no return

He lifted the axe clear, surprised by its lightness and its perfect balance in his hand.

Beneath it in the chest was a black leather jerkin, the shoulders reinforced by strips of silver steel; two black leather gauntlets, also protected by shaped metal knuckle-guards; and a pair of black, knee-length boots. Beneath the clothes was a small pouch, and within it Druss found eighteen silver pieces.

Kicking off his soft leather shoes, Druss pulled on the boots and donned the jerkin. At the bottom of the chest was a helm of black metal, edged with silver; upon the brow was a small silver axe flanked by silver skulls. Druss settled the helm into place, then lifted the axe once more. Gazing down at his reflection in the shining blades, he saw a pair of cold, cold blue eyes, empty, devoid of feeling.

Snaga, forged in the Elder days, crafted by a master. The blade had never been sharpened, for it had never dulled despite the many battles and skirmishes that filled the life of Bardan. And even before that the blade had been in use. Bardan had acquired the battle-axe during the Second Vagrian War, looting it from an old barrow in which lay the bones of an ancient battle king, a monster of Legend, Caras the Axeman.

'It was an evil weapon,' Bress had once told his son. 'All the men who ever bore it were killers with no souls.'

'Why do you keep it then?' asked his thirteen-year-old son.

'It cannot kill where I keep it,' was all Bress had answered.

Druss stared at the blade. 'Now you can kill,' he whispered.

Then he heard the sound of a walking horse. Slowly he rose.

2

Shadak's horses were skittish, the smell of death unnerving the beasts. He had bought his own three-year-old from a farmer south of Corialis and the gelding had not been trained for war. The four mounts he had taken from the raiders were less nervous, but still their ears were back and their nostrils flaring. He spoke soothingly to them and rode on.

Shadak had been a soldier for most of his adult life. He had seen death – and he thanked the gods that it still had the power to stir his emotions. Sorrow and anger vied in his heart as he gazed upon the still corpses, the children and the old women.

None of the houses had been put to the torch – the smoke would be seen for miles, and could have brought a troop of lancers. He gently tugged on the reins. A golden-haired child lay against the wall of a building, a doll beside it. Slavers had no time for children, for they had no market in Mashrapur. Young Drenai women between the ages of fourteen and twenty-five were still popular in the eastern kingdoms of Ventria, Sherak, Dospilis and Naashan.

Shadak touched heels to the gelding. There was no point in remaining in this place; the trail led south.

A young warrior stepped from one of the buildings, startling his horse which reared and whinnied. Shadak calmed it and gazed upon the man. Although of average height he was powerfully built, his huge shoulders and mighty arms giving the impression of a giant. He wore a black leather jerkin and helm and carried a fearful axe. Shadak glanced swiftly around the corpse-strewn settlement. But there was no sign of a horse.

Lifting his leg, Shadak slid from the saddle. 'Your friends leave you behind, laddie?' he asked the axeman. The young man did not speak but stepped out into the open. Shadak looked into the man's pale eyes and felt the unaccustomed thrill of fear.

The face beneath the helm was flat and expressionless, but power emanated from the young warrior. Shadak moved warily to his right, hands resting on the hilts of his short swords. 'Proud of your handi-work, are you?' he asked, trying to force the man into conversation. 'Killed many babes today, did you?'

The young man's brow furrowed. 'This was my . . . my home,' he said, his voice deep. 'You are not one of the raiders?'

'I am hunting them,' said Shadak, surprised at the relief he felt.

'They attacked Corialis looking for slaves, but the young women escaped them. The villagers fought hard. Seventeen of them died, but the attack was beaten off. My name is Shadak. Who are you?'

'I am Druss. They took my wife. I'll find them.'

Shadak glanced at the sky. 'It's getting dark. Best to start in the morning, we could lose their trail in the night.'

'I'll not wait,' said the young man. 'I need one of your horses.'

Shadak smiled grimly. 'It is difficult to refuse when you ask so politely. But I think we should talk before you ride out.'

'Why?'

'Because there are many of them, laddie, and they do have a tendency to leave rearguards behind them, watching the road.' Shadak pointed to the horses. 'Four lay in wait for me.'

'I'll kill any I find.'

'I take it they took all the young women, since I see no corpses here?'

'Yes.'

Shadak hitched his horses to a rail and stepped past the young man into the home of Bress. 'You'll lose nothing by listening for a few minutes,' he said.

Inside the building he righted the chairs and stopped. On the table was an old glove, made of lace and edged with pearls. 'What's this?' he asked the cold-eyed young man.

'It belonged to my mother. My father used to take it out now and again, and sit by the fire holding it. What did you want to talk about?'

Shadak sat down at the table. 'The raiders are led by two men – Collan, a renegade Drenai officer, and Harib Ka, a Ventrian. They will be making for Mashrapur and the slave markets there. With all the captives they will not be able to move at speed and we will have little difficulty catching them. But if we follow now, we will come upon them in the open. Two against forty – these are not odds to inspire confidence. They will push on through most of tonight, crossing the plain and reaching the long valley trails to Mashrapur late tomorrow. Then they will relax.'

'They have my wife,' said the young man. 'I'll not let them keep her for a heartbeat longer than necessary.'

Shadak shook his head and sighed. 'Nor would I, laddie. But you know the country to the south. What chance would we have of rescuing her on the plains? They would see us coming from a mile away.'

For the first time the young man looked uncertain. Then he shrugged and sat, laying the great axe on the table-top, where it covered the tiny glove. 'You are a soldier?' he asked.

'I was. Now I am a hunter – a hunter of men. Trust me. Now, how many women did they take?'

494

The young man thought for a moment. 'Perhaps around thirty. They killed Berys in the woods. Tailia escaped. But I have not seen all the bodies. Maybe others were killed.'

'Then let us think of thirty. It won't be easy freeing them.'

A sound from outside made both men turn as a young woman entered the room. Shadak rose. The woman was fair-haired and pretty, and there was blood upon her blue woollen skirt and her shirt of white linen.

'Yorath died,' she told the young man. 'They're all dead, Druss.' Her eyes filled with tears and she stood in the doorway looking lost and forlorn. Druss did not move, but Shadak stepped swiftly towards her, taking her in his arms and stroking her back.

He led her into the room and sat her at the table. 'Is there any food here?' he asked Druss. The young man nodded and moved through to the back room, returning with a pitcher of water and some bread. Shadak filled a clay cup with water and told the girl to drink. 'Are you hurt?' he asked.

She shook her head. 'The blood is Yorath's,' she whispered. Shadak sat beside her and Tailia sagged against him; she was exhausted.

'You need to rest,' he told her gently, helping her to rise and leading her through the building to a small bedroom. Obediently she lay down, and he covered her with a thick blanket. 'Sleep, child. I will be here.'

'Don't leave me,' she pleaded.

He took her hand. 'You are safe . . . Tailia. Sleep.' She closed her eyes, but clung to his hand, and Shadak sat with her until the grip eased and her breathing deepened. At last he stood and returned to the outer room.

'You were planning to leave her behind?' he asked the young man.

'She is nothing to me,' he said coldly. 'Rowena is everything.'

'I see. Then think on this, my friend: suppose it was you who had died and it was Rowena who survived hiding in the woods. How would your spirit feel if you saw me ride in and leave her alone in this wilderness?'

'I did not die,' said Druss.

'No,' said Shadak, 'you didn't. We'll take the girl with us.'

'No!'

'Either that or you walk on alone, laddie. And I do mean *walk*.'

The young man looked up at the hunter, and his eyes gleamed. 'I have killed men today,' he said, 'and I will not be threatened by you, or anyone. Not ever again. If I choose to leave here on one of your stolen horses, I shall do so. You would be wise not to try to stop me.'

'I wouldn't *try*, boy, I'd do it.' The words were spoken softly, and with a quiet confidence. But deep inside Shadak was surprised, for it was a confidence he did not feel. He saw the young man's hand snake around the haft of the axe. 'I know you are angry, lad, and concerned for the safety of . . . Rowena. But you can do nothing alone – unless of course you are a tracker, and an expert horseman. You could ride off into the dark and lose them. Or you could stumble upon them, and try to kill forty warriors. Then there'll be no one to rescue her, or the others.'

Slowly the giant's fingers relaxed, the hand moving away from the axe haft, the gleam fading from his eyes. 'It hurts me to sit here while they carry her further away.'

'I understand that. But we will catch them. And they will not harm the women; they are valuable to them.'

'You have a plan?'

'I do. I know the country, and I can guess where they will be camped tomorrow. We will go in at night, deal with the sentries and free the captives.'

Druss nodded. 'What then? They'll be hunting us. How do we escape with thirty women?'

'Their leaders will be dead,' said Shadak softly. 'I'll see to that.'

'Others will take the lead. They will come after us.'

Shadak shrugged, then smiled. 'Then we kill as many as we can.'

'I like that part of the plan,' said the young man grimly.

The stars were bright and Shadak sat on the porch of the timber dwelling, watching Druss sitting beside the bodies of his parents.

'You're getting old,' Shadak told himself, his gaze fixed on Druss. 'You make me feel old,' he whispered. Not in twenty years had a man inspired such fear in Shadak. He remembered the moment well – he was a Sathuli tribesman named Jonacin, a man with eyes of ice and fire, a legend among his own people. The Lord's champion, he had killed seventeen men in single combat, among them the Vagrian champion, Vearl.

Shadak had known the Vagrian – a tall, lean man, lightning-fast and tactically sound. The Sathuli, it was said, had treated him like a novice, first slicing off his right ear before despatching him with a heart thrust.

Shadak smiled as he remembered hoping with all his heart that he would never have to fight the man. But such hopes are akin to magic, he knew now, and all men are ultimately faced with their darkest fears.

It had been a golden morning in the Delnoch mountains. The Drenai were negotiating treaties with a Sathuli Lord and Shadak was present merely as one of the envoy's guards. Jonacin had been mildly insulting at the dinner the night before, speaking sneeringly of Drenai sword skills. Shadak had been ordered to ignore the man. But on the following morning the white-robed Sathuli stepped in front of him as he walked along the path to the Long Hall.

496

'It is said you are a fighter,' said Jonacin, the sneer in his voice showing disbelief.

Shadak had remained cool under the other's baleful stare. 'Stand aside, if you please. I am expected at the meeting.'

'I shall stand aside – as soon as you have kissed my feet.'

Shadak had been twenty-two then, in his prime. He looked into Jonacin's eyes and knew there was no avoiding confrontation. Other Sathuli warriors had gathered close by and Shadak forced a smile. 'Kiss your feet? I don't think so. Kiss this instead!' His right fist lashed into the Sathuli's chin, spinning him to the ground. Then Shadak walked on and took his place at the table.

As he sat he glanced at the Sathuli Lord, a tall man with dark, cruel eyes. The man saw him, and Shadak thought he glimpsed a look of faint amusement, even triumph, in the Lord's face. A messenger whispered something in the Lord's ear and the chieftain stood. 'The hospitality of my house has been abused,' he told the envoy. 'One of your men struck my champion, Jonacin. The attack was unwarranted. Jonacin demands satisfaction.'

The envoy was speechless. Shadak stood. 'He shall have it, my Lord. But let us fight in the cemetery. At least then you will not have far to carry his body!'

Now the hoot of an owl brought Shadak back to the present, and he saw Druss striding towards him. The young man made as if to walk by, then stopped. 'I had no words,' he said. 'I could think of nothing to say.'

'Sit down for a moment and we will speak of them,' said Shadak. 'It is said that our praises follow the dead to their place of rest. Perhaps it is true.'

Druss sat alongside the swordsman. 'There is not much to tell. He was a carpenter, and a fashioner of brooches. She was a bought wife.'

'They raised you, helped you to be strong.'

'I needed no help in that.'

'You are wrong, Druss. If your father had been a weak, or a vengeful man, he would have beaten you as a child, robbed you of your spirit. In my experience it takes a strong man to raise strong men. Was the axe his?'

'No. It belonged to my grandfather.'

'Bardan the Axeman,' said Shadak softly.

'How could you know?'

'It is an infamous weapon. Snaga. That was the name. Your father had a hard life, trying to live down such a beast as Bardan. What happened to your real mother?'

Druss shrugged. 'She died in an accident when I was a babe.'

'Ah yes, I remember the story,' said Shadak. 'Three men attacked your father; he killed two of them with his bare hands and near crippled the third. Your mother was struck down by a charging horse.'

'He killed two men?' Druss was astonished. 'Are you sure?'

'So the story goes.'

'I cannot believe it. He always backed away from any argument. He never stood up for himself at all. He was weak . . . spineless.'

'I don't think so.'

'You didn't know him.'

'I saw where his body lay, and I saw the dead men around it. And I know many stories concerning the son of Bardan. None of them speaks of his cowardice. After his own father was killed he tried to settle in many towns, under many names. Always he was discovered and forced to flee. But on at least three occasions he was followed and attacked. Just outside Drenan he was cornered by five soldiers. One of them shot an arrow into your father's shoulder. Bress was carrying an infant at the time and according to the soldiers he laid the babe behind a boulder, and then charged at them. He had no weapon, and they were all armed with swords. But he tore a limb from a tree and laid into them. Two went down swiftly, the others turned and fled. I know *that* story is true, Druss, because my brother was one of the soldiers. It was the year before he was killed in the Sathuli campaign. He said that Bardan's son was a black-bearded giant with the strength of six men.'

'I knew none of this,' said Druss. 'Why did he never speak of it?'

'Why should he? Perhaps he took no pleasure for being the son of a monster. Perhaps he did not relish speaking of killing men with his hands, or beating them unconscious with a tree branch.'

'I didn't know him at all,' whispered Druss. 'Not at all.'

'I expect he didn't know you either,' said Shadak, with a sigh. 'It is the curse of parents and children.'

'You have sons?'

'One. He died a week ago at Corialis. He thought he was immortal.'

'What happened?'

'He went up against Collan; he was cut to pieces.' Shadak cleared his throat and stood. 'Time for some sleep. It'll be dawn soon, and I'm not as young as I was.'

'Sleep well,' said Druss.

'I will, laddie. I always do. Go back to your parents and find something to say.'

'Wait!' called Druss.

'Yes,' answered the swordsman, pausing in the doorway.

'You were correct in what you said. I wouldn't have wanted Rowena left in the mountains alone. I spoke in . . . anger.'

Shadak nodded. 'A man is only as strong as that which makes him angry. Remember that, laddie.'

Shadak could not sleep. He sat in the wide leather chair beside the hearth, his long legs stretched out before him, his head resting on a

498

cushion, his body relaxed. But his mind was in turmoil – images, memories flashing into thoughts.

He saw again the Sathuli cemetery, Jonacin stripped to the waist, a broad-bladed tulwar in his hands and a small iron buckler strapped to his left forearm.

'Do you feel fear, Drenai?' asked Jonacin.

Shadak did not answer. Slowly he unstrapped his baldric, then lifted clear his heavy woollen shirt. The sun was warm on his back, the mountain air fresh in his lungs. *You are going to die today*, said the voice of his soul.

And then the duel began. Jonacin drew first blood, a narrow cut appearing on Shadak's chest. More than a thousand Sathuli onlookers, standing around the perimeter of the cemetery, cheered as the blood began to flow. Shadak leapt back.

'Not going to try for the ear?' he asked conversationally. Jonacin gave an angry growl, and launched a new attack. Shadak blocked a thrust, then thundered a punch to the Sathuli's face. It glanced from his cheekbone, but the man staggered. Shadak followed up with a disembowelling thrust and the Sathuli swayed to his right, the blade slashing the skin of his waist. Now it was Jonacin's turn to jump backwards. Blood gushed from the shallow wound in his side; he touched the cut with his fingers, staring down amazed.

'Yes,' said Shadak, 'you bleed too. Come to me. Bleed some more.'

Jonacin screamed and rushed forward but Shadak side-stepped and clove his sabre through the Sathuli's neck. As the dying man fell to the ground Shadak felt a tremendous sense of relief, and a surging realisation. He was alive!

But his career was ruined. The treaty talks came to nothing, and his commission was revoked upon his return to Drenan.

Then Shadak had found his true vocation: Shadak the Hunter. Shadak the Tracker. Outlaws, killers, renegades – he hunted them all, following like a wolf on the trail.

In all the years since the fight with Jonacin he had never again known such fear. Until today, when the young axeman had stepped into the sunlight.

He is young and untrained. I would have killed him, he told himself.

But then he pictured again the ice-blue eyes and the shining axe.

Druss sat under the stars. He was tired, but he could not sleep. A fox moved out into the open, edging towards a corpse. Druss threw a stone at it and the creature slunk away . . . but not far.

By tomorrow the crows would be feasting here, and the other carrion beasts would tear at the dead flesh. Only hours ago this had been a living community, full of people enjoying their own hopes and dreams. Druss stood and walked along the main street of the settlement, past the home of the baker, whose body was stretched out in the doorway with his wife beside him. The smithy was open, the fires still glowing faintly. There were three bodies here. Tetrin the Smith had managed to kill two of the raiders, clubbing them down with his forge hammer. Tetrin himself lay beside the long anvil, his throat cut.

Druss swung away from the scene.

What was it for? Slaves and gold. The raiders cared nothing for the dreams of other men. 'I will make you pay,' said Druss. He glanced at the body of the smith. 'I will avenge you. And your sons. I will avenge you all,' he promised.

And he thought of Rowena and his throat went dry, his heartbeat increasing. Forcing back his fears, he gazed around at the settlement.

In the moonlight the village still seemed strangely alive, its buildings untouched. Druss wondered at this. Why did the raiders not put the settlement to the torch? In all the stories he had heard of such attacks, the plunderers usually fired the buildings. Then he remembered the troop of Drenai cavalry patrolling the wilderness. A column of smoke would alert them, were they close.

Druss knew then what he had to do. Moving to the body of Tetrin he hauled it across the street to the meeting hall, kicking open the door and dragging the corpse inside, laying it at the centre of the hall. Then he returned to the street and began to gather one by one, all the dead of the community. He was tired when he began, and bone-weary by the finish. Forty-four bodies he placed in the long hall, making sure that husbands were beside wives and their children close. He did not know why he did this, but it seemed right.

Lastly he carried the body of Bress into the building, and laid it beside Patica. Then he knelt by the woman and, taking the dead hand in his own, he bowed his head. 'I thank you,' he said quietly, 'for your years of care, and for the love you gave my father. You deserved better than this, Patica.' With all the bodies accounted for, he began to fetch wood from the winter store, piling it against the walls and across the bodies. At last he carried a large barrel of lantern oil from the main storehouse and poured it over the wood, splashing it to the dry walls.

As dawn streaked the eastern sky, he struck a flame to the pyre and blew it into life. The morning breeze licked at the flames in the doorway, caught at the tinder beyond, then hungrily roared up the first wall.

Druss stepped back into the street. At first the blaze made little smoke, but as the fire grew into an inferno a black column of oily smoke billowed into the morning sky, hanging in the light wind, flattening and spreading like an earth-born storm cloud. 'You have been working hard,' said Shadak, moving silently alongside the young axeman.

Druss nodded. 'There was no time to bury them,' he said. 'Now maybe the smoke will be seen.'

'Perhaps,' agreed the hunter, 'but you should have rested. Tonight you will need your strength.' As Shadak moved away, Druss watched him; the man's movements were sure and smooth, confident and strong.

Druss admired that – as he admired the way that Shadak had comforted Tailia in the doorway. Like a father or a brother might. Druss had known that she needed such consolation, but had been unable to provide it. He had never possessed the easy touch of a Pilan or a Yorath, and had always been uncomfortable in the company of women or girls.

But not Rowena. He remembered the day when she and her father had come to the village, a spring day three seasons ago. They had arrived with several other families, and he had seen Rowena standing beside a wagon helping to unload furniture. She seemed so frail. Druss had approached the wagon.

'I'll help if you want,' offered the fifteen-year-old Druss, more gruffly than he had intended. She turned and smiled. Such a smile, radiant and friendly. Reaching up, he took hold of the chair her father was lowering and carried it into the half-built dwelling. He helped them unload and arrange the furniture, then made to leave. But Rowena brought him a goblet of water.

'It was kind of you to help us,' she said. 'You are very strong.'

He had mumbled some inanity, listened as she told him her name, and left without telling her his own. That evening she had seen him sitting by the southern stream and had sat beside him. So close that he had felt remarkably uncomfortable.

'The land is beautiful, isn't it?' she said.

It was. The mountains were huge, like snow-haired giants, the sky the colour of molten copper, the setting sun a dish of gold, the hills bedecked with flowers. But Druss had not seen the beauty until the moment she observed it. He felt a sense of peace, a calm that settled over his turbulent spirit in a blanket of warmth.

'I am Druss.'

'I know. I asked your mother where you were.'

'Why?'

'You are my first friend here.'

'How can we be friends? You do not know me.'

'Of course I do. You are Druss, the son of Bress.'

'That is not knowing. I . . . I am not popular here,' he said, though he did not know why he should admit it so readily. 'I am disliked.'

'Why do they dislike you?' The question was innocently asked, and he turned to look at her. Her face was so close that he blushed. Twisting, he put space between them.

'My ways are rough, I suppose. I don't . . . talk easily. And I . . . sometimes . . . become angry. I don't understand their jests and their humour. I like to be . . . alone.'

501

'Would you like me to go?'

'No! I just . . . I don't know what I am saying.' He shrugged, and blushed a deeper crimson.

'Shall we be friends then?' she asked him, holding out her hand.

'I have never had a friend,' he admitted.

'Then take my hand, and we will start now.' Reaching out, he felt the warmth of her fingers against his calloused palm. 'Friends?' she asked with a smile.

'Friends,' he agreed. She made as if to withdraw her hand, but he held it for a moment longer. 'Thank you,' he said softly, as he released his hold.

She laughed then. 'Why would you thank me?'

He shrugged. 'I don't know. It is just that . . . you have given me a gift that no one else ever offered. And I do not take it lightly. I will be your friend, Rowena. Until the stars burn out and die.'

'Be careful with such promises, Druss. You do not know where they might lead you.'

One of the roof timbers cracked and crashed into the blaze. Shadak called out to him. 'Better choose yourself a mount, axeman. It's time to go.'

Gathering his axe, Druss turned his gaze towards the south. Somewhere out there was Rowena.

'I'm on my way,' he whispered.

And she heard him.

3

The wagons rolled on through the first afternoon, and on into the night. At first the captured women were silent, stunned, disbelieving. Then grief replaced shock, and there were tears. These were harshly dealt with by the men riding alongside the wagons, who ordered silence and, when it was not forthcoming, dismounted and leapt aboard the wagons dealing blows and brutal slaps, and issuing threats of whip and lash.

Rowena, her hands tied before her, sat beside the equally bound Mari. Her friend had swollen eyes, both from weeping and from a blow that had caught her on the bridge of the nose. 'How are you feeling now?' Rowena whispered.

'All dead,' came the response. 'They're all dead.' Mari's eyes gazed unseeing across the wagon, where other young women were sitting.

'We are alive,' continued Rowena, her voice low and gentle. 'Do not give up hope, Mari. Druss is alive also. And there is a man with him – a great hunter. They are following us.'

'All dead,' said Mari. 'They're all dead.'

'Oh, Mari!' Rowena reached out with her bound hands but Mari screamed and pulled away.

'Don't touch me!' She swung round to face Rowena, her eyes fierce and gleaming. 'This was a punishment. For you. You are a witch! It is all your fault!'

'No, I did nothing!'

'She's a witch,' shouted Mari. The other women stared. 'She has powers of Second Sight. She knew the raid was coming, but she didn't warn us.'

'Why did you not tell us?' shouted another woman. Rowena swung and saw the daughter of Jarin the Baker. 'My father is dead. My brothers are dead. Why did you not warn us?'

'I didn't know. Not until the last moment!'

'Witch!' screamed Mari. 'Stinking witch!' She lashed out with her tied hands, catching Rowena on the side of the head. Rowena fell to her left, into another woman. Fists struck as all around her in the wagon women surged upright, lashing out with hands and feet. Riders galloped alongside the wagon and Rowena felt herself lifted clear and flung to the ground. She hit hard, the breath knocked out of her.

'What is going on here?' she heard someone yell.

'Witch! Witch! Witch!' chanted the women.

Rowena was hauled to her feet, then a filthy hand caught her by the hair. She opened her eyes and looked up into a gaunt, scarred face. 'Witch, are you?' grunted the man. 'We'll see about that!' He drew a knife and held it before her, the point resting against the woollen shirt she wore. 'Witches have three nipples, so it's said,' he told her.

'Leave her be!' came another voice, and a horseman rode close alongside. The man sheathed his knife.

'I wasn't going to cut her, Harib. Witch or no, she'll still bring a pretty price.'

'More if she is a witch,' said the horseman. 'Let her ride behind you.'

Rowena gazed up at the rider. His face was swarthy, his eyes dark, his mouth part hidden by the bronze ear-flaps of his battle helm. Touching spurs to his mount the rider galloped on. The man holding her stepped into the saddle, pulling her up behind him. He smelt of stale sweat and old dirt, but Rowena scarcely noticed it. Glancing at the wagon where her former friends now sat silently, she felt afresh the terrible sense of loss.

Yesterday the world was full of hope. Their home was almost complete, her husband coming to terms with his restless spirit, her

503

father relaxed and free from care, Mari preparing for a night of passion with Pilan.

In the space of a few hours it had all changed. Reaching up, she touched the brooch at her breast . . .

And saw the Axeman her husband was becoming. *Deathwalker!*

Tears flowed then, silently coursing down her cheeks.

Shadak rode ahead, following the trail, while Druss and Tailia travelled side by side, the girl on a bay mare, the young man on a chestnut gelding. Tailia said little for the first hour, which suited Druss, but as they topped a rise before a long valley she leaned in close and touched his arm.

'What are you planning?' she asked. 'Why are we following them?'

'What do you mean?' responded Druss, nonplussed.

'Well, you obviously can't fight them all; you'll be killed. Why don't we just ride for the garrison at Padia? Send troops?' He swung to look at her. Her blue eyes were red-rimmed from crying.

'That's a four-day walk. I don't know how long it would take to ride – two days at the least, I would think. Then, if the troop was there – and they may not be – it would take them at least three days to find the raiders. By then they will be in Vagrian territory, and close to the borders of Mashrapur. Drenai soldiers have no jurisdiction there.'

'But you can't do anything. There is no point to this pursuit.'

Druss took a deep breath. 'They have Rowena,' he said. 'And Shadak has a plan.'

'Ah, a plan,' she said derisively, her full-lipped mouth twisting in a sneer. 'Two men with a plan. Then I suppose I am safe?'

'You are alive – and free,' Druss told her. 'If you want to ride to Padia, then do so.'

Her expression softened and she reached out, laying her hand on Druss's forearm. 'I know you are brave, Druss; I saw you kill those raiders and you were magnificent. I don't want to see you die in some meaningless battle. Rowena wouldn't want it either. There are many of them, and they're all killers.'

'So am I,' he said. 'And there are fewer than there were.'

'Well, what happens to me when they cut you down?' she snapped. 'What chance will I have?'

He looked at her for a moment, his eyes cold. 'None,' he told her.

Tailia's eyes widened. 'You never liked me, did you?' she whispered. 'You never liked any of us.'

'I have no time for this nonsense,' he said, touching heels to the gelding and moving ahead. He did not look back, and was not surprised when he heard the sound of her horse galloping off towards the north.

A few minutes later Shadak rode up from the south. 'Where is she?'

504

asked the hunter, letting go of the reins of the two horses he was leading and allowing them to wander close by, cropping the long grass.

'Riding for Padia,' answered Druss. The hunter said nothing for a moment, but he gazed towards the north where Tailia could be seen as a tiny figure in the distance. 'You'll not talk her out of it,' Druss said.

'Did you send her away?'

'No. She thinks we are both dead men, and she doesn't want to risk being taken by the slavers.'

'That's a hard point to argue with,' agreed Shadak. Then he shrugged. 'Ah well, she chose her own road. Let us hope it was a wise one.'

'What of the raiders?' asked Druss, all thoughts of Tailia gone from his mind.

'They rode through the night, and are heading due south. I think they will make camp by the Tigren, some thirty miles from here. There is a narrow valley opening on to a bowl-shaped canyon. It's been used by slavers for years – and horse thieves, cattle stealers and renegades. It is easily defendable.'

'How long until we reach them?'

'Some time after midnight. We'll move on for two more hours, then we'll rest and eat before switching horses.'

'I don't need a rest.'

'The horses do,' said Shadak, 'and so do I. Be patient. It will be a long night, and fraught with peril. And I have to tell you that our chances are not good. Tailia was right to be concerned for her safety; we will need more luck than any two men have a right to ask for.'

'Why are you doing this?' asked Druss. 'The women are nothing to you.' Shadak did not reply and they rode in silence until the sun was almost at noon. The hunter spotted a small grove of trees to the east and turned his horse; the two men dismounted in the shade of several spreading elms beside a rock pool.

'How many did you kill back there?' he asked Druss as they sat in the shade.

'Six,' answered the axeman, taking a strip of dried beef from the pouch at his side and tearing off a chunk.

'You ever kill men before?'

'No.'

'Six is . . . impressive. What did you use?'

Druss chewed for a moment, then swallowed. 'Felling-axe and a hatchet. Oh . . . and one of their daggers,' he said at last. 'And my hands.'

'And you have had no training in combat?'

'No.'

Shadak shook his head. 'Talk me through the fights – everything you can remember.' Druss did so, Shadak listened in silence, and when the axeman had finished his tale the hunter smiled. 'You are a rare young man. You positioned yourself well, in front of the fallen tree. That was a good move – the first of many, it seems. But the most impressive is the last. How did you know the swordsman would jump to your left?'

'He saw I had an axe and that I was right-handed. In normal circumstances the axe would have been raised over my left shoulder and pulled down towards the right. Therefore he moved to his right – my left.'

'That is cool thinking for a man in combat. I think there is a great deal of your grandfather in you.'

'Don't say that!' growled Druss. 'He was insane.'

'He was also a brilliant fighting man. Yes, he was evil. But that does not lessen his courage and his skills.'

'I am my own man,' said Druss. 'What I have is mine.'

'I do not doubt it. But you have great strength, good timing and a warrior's mind. These are gifts that pass from father to son, and on through the line. But know this, laddie, there are responsibilities that you must accept.'

'Like what?'

'Burdens that separate the hero from the rogue.'

'I don't know what you mean.'

'It comes back to the question you asked me, about the women. The true warrior lives by a code. He has to. For each man there are different perspectives, but at the core they are the same: *Never violate a woman, nor harm a child. Do not lie, cheat or steal. These things are for lesser men. Protect the weak against the evil strong. And never allow thoughts of gain to lead you into the pursuit of evil.*'

'This is your code?' asked Druss.

'It is. And there is more, but I shall not bore you with it.'

'I am not bored. Why do you need such a code to live by?'

Shadak laughed. 'You will understand, Druss, as the years go by.'

'I want to understand now,' said the younger man.

'Of course you do. That is the curse of the young, they want it all now. No. Rest a while. Even your prodigious strength will fail after a time. Sleep a little. And wake refreshed. It will be a long – and bloody – night.'

The moon was high, and a quarter full in a cloudless sky. Silver light bathed the mountains, rippling on the river below, making it seem of molten metal. Three camp-fires burned and Druss could just make out the movement of men in the flickering light. The women were huddled between two wagons; there was no fire near them, but guards patrolled close by. To the north of the wagons, around thirty paces from the women, was a large tent. It gleamed yellow-gold, like a great lantern, shimmering shadows being cast on the inside walls; there was obviously a brazier within, and several lamps.

Shadak moved silently alongside the axeman, beckoning him back. Druss edged from the slope, returning to the glade where the horses were tethered.

'How many did you count?' asked Shadak, keeping his voice low.

'Thirty-four, not including those inside the tent.'

'There are two men there, Harib Ka and Collan. But I make it thirty-six outside. They have placed two men by the river-bank to prevent any of the women trying to swim to safety.'

'When do we go in?' asked Druss.

'You are very anxious to fight, laddie. But I need you to have a cool head down there. No baresark warfare.'

'Do not concern yourself about me, hunter. I merely want my wife back.'

Shadak nodded. 'I understand that, but now I want you to consider something. What if she has been raped?'

Druss's eyes gleamed, his fingers tightening on the axe haft. 'Why do you ask this now?'

'It is certain that some of the women will have been violated. It is the way of men such as these to take their pleasures where they want them. How cool do you feel now?'

Druss swallowed back his rising anger. 'Cool enough. I am not a baresark, Shadak. I know this. And I will follow your plan to the last detail, live or die, win or lose.'

'Good. We will move two hours before dawn. Most of them will be deeply asleep by then. Do you believe in the gods?'

'I never saw one – so no.'

Shadak grinned. 'Neither do I. It puts praying for divine help out of the question, I suppose.'

Druss was silent for a moment. 'Tell me now,' he said at last, 'why you need a code to live by.'

Shadak's face was ghostly in the moonlight, the expression suddenly stern and forbidding. Then he relaxed and turned to gaze down at the camp of the raiders. 'Those men down there have only one code. It is simple: *Do what you will is the whole of the law*. Do you understand?'

'No,' admitted Druss.

'It means that whatever their strength can obtain is rightfully theirs. If another man holds something they desire they kill the other man. This is right in their minds; this is the law the world offers – the law of the wolf. But you and I are no different from them, Druss. We have the same desires, the same perceived needs. If we are attracted to a woman, why should we not have her, regardless of her opinions? If another man has wealth, why should we not take it, if we are stronger, deadlier than he? It is an easy trap to fall into. Collan was once an officer in the Drenai lancers. He comes from a good family; he took the Oath as we all did, and when he said the words he probably believed them. But in Drenan he met a woman he wanted desperately, and she wanted him. But she was married. Collan murdered her husband. That was his first step on the road to Perdition; after that the other steps were easy. Short of money, he became a mercenary – fighting for gold in any cause, right or wrong, good or evil. He began to see only what was good for Collan. Villages were there merely for him to raid. Harib Ka is a Ventrian nobleman, distantly related to the Royal House. His story is similar. Both lacked the Iron Code. I am not a good man, Druss, but the Code holds me to the Way of the Warrior.'

'I can understand,' said Druss, 'that a man will seek to protect what is his, and not steal or kill for gain. But it does not explain why you risk your life tonight for women you do not know.'

'Never back away from an enemy, Druss. Either fight or surrender. It is not enough to say I will not *be* evil. It must be fought wherever it is found. I am hunting Collan, not just for killing my son but for being what he is. But if necessary I will put off that hunt tonight in order for the girls to be freed; they are more important.'

'Perhaps,' Druss said, unconvinced. 'For me, all I want is Rowena and a home in the mountains. I care nothing about fighting evil.'

'I hope you learn to care,' said Shadak.

Harib Ka could not sleep. The ground was hard beneath the tent floor and despite the heat from the brazier he felt cold through to his bones. The girl's face haunted him. He sat up and reached for the wine-jug. You are drinking too much, he told himself. Stretching, he poured a full goblet of red wine, draining it in two swallows. Then he pushed back his blankets and rose. His head ached. He sat down on a canvas stool and refilled his goblet.

What have you become? whispered a voice in his mind. He rubbed at his eyes, his thoughts returning to the academy and his days with Bodasen and the young Prince.

'We will change the world,' said the Prince. 'We will feed the poor and ensure employment for all. And we will drive the raiders from Ventria, and establish a kingdom of peace and prosperity.'

Harib Ka gave a dry laugh and sipped his wine. Heady days, a time of youth and optimism with its talk of knights and brave deeds, great victories and the triumph of the Light over the Dark.

'There is no Light and Dark,' he said aloud. 'There is only Power.'

He thought then of the first girl – what was her name, Mari? Yes. Compliant, obedient to his desires, warm, soft. She had cried out with pleasure at his touch. No. She had pretended to enjoy his coarse love-making. 'I'll do anything for you – but don't hurt me.'

Don't hurt me.

The chill winds of autumn rippled the tent walls. Within two hours of enjoying Mari he had felt in need of a second woman, and had chosen the hazel-eyed witch. That was a mistake. She had entered his tent, rubbing at her chafed wrists, her eyes large and sorrowful.

'You intend to rape me?' she had asked him quietly.

He had smiled. 'Not necessarily. That is your choice. What is your name?'

'Rowena,' she told him. 'And how can it be my choice?'

'You can give yourself to me, or you can fight me. Either way the result will be the same. So why not enjoy the love-making?'

'Why do you speak of love?'

'What?'

'There is no love in this. You have murdered those I have loved. And now you seek to pleasure yourself at the expense of what dignity I have left.'

He strode towards her, gripping her upper arms. 'You are not here to debate with me, whore! You are here to do as you are told.'

'Why do you call me a whore? Does it make your actions more simple for you? Oh, Harib Ka, how would Rajica view your actions?'

He reeled back as if struck. 'What do you know of Rajica?'

'Only that you loved her – and that she died in your arms.'

'You are a witch!'

'And you are a lost man, Harib Ka. Everything you once held dear has been sold – your pride, your honour, your love of life.'

'I will not be judged by you,' he said, but he made no move to silence her.

'I do not judge you,' she told him. 'I pity you. And I tell you this: unless you release me and the other women, you will die.'

'You are a seer also?' he said, trying to mock. 'Are the Drenai cavalry close, witch? Is there an army waiting to fall upon me and my men? No. Do not seek to threaten me, girl. Whatever else I may have lost I am still a warrior and, with the possible exception of Collan, the finest swordsman you will ever see. I do not fear death. No. Sometimes I long for it.' He felt his passion ebbing away. 'So tell me, witch, what is this peril I face?'

'His name is Druss. He is my husband.'

'We killed all the men in the village.'

'No. He was in the woods, felling timbers for the palisade.'

'I sent six men there.'

'But they have not returned,' Rowena pointed out.

'You are saying he killed them all?'

'He did,' she told him softly, 'and now he is coming for you.'

'You make him sound like a warrior of legend,' said Harib uneasily. 'I could send men back to kill him.'

509

'I hope you do not.'

'You fear for his life?'

'No, I would mourn for theirs.' She sighed.

'Tell me of him. Is he a swordsman? A soldier?'

'No, he is the son of a carpenter. But once I dreamt I saw him on a mountainside. He was black-bearded and his axe was smeared with blood. And before him were hundreds of souls. They stood mourning their lives. More flowed from his axe, and they wailed. Men of many nations, billowing like smoke until broken by the breeze. All slain by Druss. Mighty Druss. The Captain of the Axe. The *Deathwalker*.'

'And this is your husband?'

'No, not yet. This is the man he will become if you do not free me. This is the man you created when you slew his father and took me prisoner. You will not stop him, Harib Ka.'

He sent her away then, and ordered the guards to let her remain unmolested.

Collan had come to him and had laughed at his misery. 'By Missael, Harib, she is just a village wench and now a slave. She is property. *Our* property. And her gift makes her worth ten times the price we will receive for any of the others. She is attractive and young – I'd say around a thousand gold pieces' worth. There is that Ventrian merchant, Kabuchek; he's always looking for seers and fortune-tellers. I'll wager he'd pay a thousand.'

Harib sighed. 'Aye, you are right, my friend. Take her. We'll need coin upon our arrival. But don't touch her, Collan,' he warned the handsome swordsman. 'She really does have the Gift, and she will see into your soul.'

'There is nothing to see,' answered Collan, with a harsh, forced smile.

Druss edged his way along the river-bank, keeping close to the undergrowth and pausing to listen. There were no sounds save the rustling of autumn leaves in the branches above, no movement apart from the occasional swooping flight of bat or owl. His mouth was dry, but he felt no fear.

Across the narrow river he saw a white jutting boulder, cracked down the centre. According to Shadak, the first of the sentries was positioned almost opposite. Moving carefully Druss crept back into the woods, then angled towards the river-bank, timing his approach by the wind which stirred the leaves above him, the rustling in the trees masking the sound of his movements.

The sentry was sitting on a rock no more than ten feet to Druss's right, and he had stretched out his right leg. Taking Snaga in his left hand, Druss wiped his sweating palm on his trews, his eyes scanning the undergrowth for the second sentry. He could see no one.

510

Druss waited, his back against a broad tree. From a little distance to the left came a harsh, gurgling sound. The sentry heard it too, and rose.

'Bushin! What are you doing there, you fool?'

Druss stepped out behind the man. 'He is dying,' he said.

The man spun, hand snaking down for the sword at his hip. Snaga flashed up and across, the silver blade entering the neck just below the ear and shearing through sinew and bone. The head toppled to the right, the body to the left.

Shadak stepped from the undergrowth. 'Well done,' he whispered. 'Now, when I send the women down to you, get them to wade across by the boulder, then head north up into the canyon to the cave.'

'We've been over this many times,' Druss pointed out.

Ignoring the comment, Shadak laid a hand on the younger man's shoulder. 'Now, whatever happens, do not come back into the camp. Stay with the women. There is only one path up to the cave, but several leading from it to the north. Get the women moving on the north-west route. You hold the path.'

Shadak faded back into the undergrowth and Druss settled down to wait.

Shadak moved carefully to the edge of the camp. Most of the women were asleep, and a guard was sitting by them; his head was resting against a wagon wheel, and Shadak guessed he was dozing. Unbuckling his sword-belt, he moved forward on his belly, drawing himself on his elbows until he reached the wagon. Slipping his hunting-knife from the sheath at his hip, Shadak came up behind the man – his left hand reached through the wheel, fingers closing on the sentry's throat. The knife rammed home into the man's back; his leg jerked once, then he was still.

Moving back from beneath the wagon, Shadak came to the first girl. She was sleeping close to several other women, huddled together for warmth. He clamped a hand over her mouth and shook her. She awoke in a panic and started to struggle.

'I am here to rescue you!' hissed Shadak. 'One of your villagers is by the river-bank and he will lead you to safety. You understand? When I release you, slowly wake the others. Head south to the river. Druss, the son of Bress, is waiting there. Nod if you understand me.'

He felt her head move against his hand. 'Good. Make sure none of the others make a noise. You must move slowly. Which one is Rowena?'

'She is not with us,' whispered the girl. 'They took her away.'

'Where?'

'One of the leaders, a man with a scarred cheek, he rode out with her just after dusk.'

Shadak swore softly. There was no time for a second plan. 'What is your name?'

'Mari.'

'Well, Mari, get the others moving – and tell Druss to follow the original plan.'

Shadak moved away from the girl, gathered his swords and belted them to his waist. Then he stepped out into the open and strolled casually towards the tent. Only a few men were awake, and they paid little heed to the figure moving through the shadows so confidently.

Lifting the tent-flap he swiftly entered, drawing his right-hand sword as he did so. Harib Ka was sitting on a canvas chair with a goblet of wine in his left hand, a sabre in his right. 'Welcome to my hearth, Wolf-man,' he said, with a smile. He drained the goblet and stood. Wine had run into his dark, forked beard, making it shine in the lantern light as if oiled. 'May I offer you a drink?'

'Why not?' answered Shadak, aware that if they began to fight too soon the noise of clashing steel would wake the other raiders and they would see the women fleeing.

'You are far from home,' remarked Harib Ka.

'These days I have no home,' Shadak told him.

Harib Ka filled a second goblet and passed it to the hunter. 'You are here to kill me?'

'I came for Collan. I understand he has gone?'

'Why Collan?' asked Harib Ka, his dark eyes glittering in the golden light.

'He killed my son in Corialis.'

'Ah, the blond boy. Fine swordsman, but too reckless.'

'A vice of the young.' Shadak sipped his wine, his anger controlled like an armourer's fire, hot but contained.

'That vice killed him,' observed Shadak. 'Collan is very skilled. Where did you leave the young villager, the one with the axe?'

'You are well informed.'

'Only a few hours ago his wife stood where you now stand; she told me he was coming. She's a witch – did you know that?'

'No. Where is she?'

'On her way to Mashrapur with Collan. When do you want the fight to begin?'

'As soon as . . .' began Shadak, but even as he was speaking Harib attacked, his sabre slashing for Shadak's throat. The hunter ducked, leaned to the left and kicked out at Harib's knee. The Ventrian crashed to the floor and Shadak's sword touched the skin of Harib's throat. 'Never fight drunk,' he said softly.

'I'll remember that. What now?'

'Now tell me where Collan stays in Mashrapur.'

'The White Bear Inn. It's in the western quarter.'

512

'I know that. Now, what is your life worth, Harib Ka?'

'To the Drenai authorities? Around a thousand gold pieces. To me? I have nothing to offer – until I sell my slaves.'

'You have no slaves.'

'I can find them again. Thirty women on foot in the mountains will pose me no problem.'

'Hunting is not easy with a slit throat,' pointed out Shadak, adding an extra ounce of pressure to the sword-blade, which pricked the skin of Harib's neck.

'True,' agreed the Ventrian, glancing up. 'What do you suggest?' Just as Shadak was about to answer he caught the gleam of triumph in Harib's eyes and he swung round. But too late.

Something cold, hard and metallic crashed against his skull.

And the world spun into darkness.

Pain brought Shadak back to consciousness, harsh slaps to his face that jarred his teeth. His eyes opened. His arms were being held by two men who had hauled him to his knees, and Harib Ka was squatting before him.

'Did you think me so stupid that I would allow an assassin to enter my tent unobserved? I knew someone was following us. And when the four men I left in the pass did not return I guessed it had to be you. Now I have questions for you, Shadak. Firstly, where is the young farmer with the axe; and secondly, where are my women?'

Shadak said nothing. One of the men holding him crashed a fist against the hunter's ear; lights blazed before Shadak's eyes and he sagged to his right. He watched Harib Ka rise and move to the brazier where the coals had burned low. 'Get him outside to a fire,' ordered the leader. Shadak was hauled to his feet and half carried out into the camp. Most of the men were still asleep. His captors pushed him to his knees beside a camp-fire and Harib Ka drew his dagger, pushing the blade into the flames. 'You will tell me what I wish to know,' he said, 'or I will burn out your eyes and then set you free in the mountains.'

Shadak tasted blood on his tongue, and fear in his belly. But still he said nothing.

An unearthly scream tore through the silence of the night, followed by the thunder of hooves. Harib swung to see forty terrified horses galloping towards the camp. One of the men holding the hunter turned also, his grip slackening. Shadak surged upright, head butting the raider who staggered back. The second man, seeing the stampeding horses closing fast, released his hold and ran for the safety of the wagons. Harib Ka drew his sabre and leapt at Shadak, but the first of the horses cannoned into him, spinning him from his feet. Shadak spun on his heel to face the terrified beasts and began to wave his arms. The maddened horses swerved around him and galloped on through the camp. Some men, still wrapped in their blankets, were trampled underfoot. Others tried to halt the charging beasts. Shadak ran back to Harib's tent and found his swords. Then he stepped out into the night. All was chaos.

The fires had been scattered by pounding hooves and several corpses were lying on the open ground. Some twenty of the horses had been halted and calmed; the others were running on through the woods, pursued by many of the warriors.

A second scream sounded and despite his years of experience in warfare and battle, Shadak was astonished by what followed.

Alone, the young woodsman had attacked the camp. The awesome axe shone silver in the moonlight, slashing and cleaving into the surprised warriors. Several took up swords and ran at him; they died in moments.

But he could not survive. Shadak saw the raiders group together, a dozen men spread out in a semi-circle around the black-garbed giant, Harib Ka among them. The hunter, his two short swords drawn, ran towards them yelling the battle-cry of the Lancers. 'Ayiaa! Ayiaa!' At that moment arrows flashed from the woods. One took a raider in the throat, a second glanced from a helm to plunge home into an unprotected shoulder. Combined with the sudden battle-cry, the attack made the raiders pause, many of them backing away and scanning the tree line. At that moment Druss charged the enemy centre, cutting to left and right. The raiders fell back before him, several tumbling to the ground, tripping over their fellows. The mighty blood-smeared axe clove into them, rising and falling with a merciless rhythm.

Just as Shadak reached them, the raiders broke and fled. More arrows sailed after them.

Harib Ka ran for one of the horses, grabbing its mane and vaulting to its bare back. The animal reared, but he held on. Shadak hurled his right-hand sword, which lanced into Harib's shoulder. The Ventrian sagged, then fell to the ground as the horse galloped away

'Druss!' shouted Shadak. 'Druss!' The axeman was pursuing the fleeing raiders, but he stopped at the edge of the trees and swung back. Harib Ka was on his knees, trying to pull the brass-hilted sword from his body.

The axeman stalked back to where Shadak was waiting. He was blood-drenched and his eyes glittered. 'Where is she?' he asked the hunter.

'Collan took her to Mashrapur; they left at dusk.'

Two women emerged from the trees, carrying bows and quivers of arrows. 'Who are they?' asked Shadak.

'The Tanner's daughters. They did a lot of hunting for the village. I gave them the bows the sentries had with them.'

The tallest of the women approached Druss. 'They are fleeing into the night. I don't think they'll come back now. You want us to follow them?'

'No, bring the others down and gather the horses.' The axeman turned towards the kneeling figure of Harib Ka. 'Who is this?' Druss asked Shadak.

'One of the leaders.'

Without a word Druss clove the axe through Harib's neck. 'Not any more,' he observed.

'Indeed not,' agreed Shadak, stepping to the still quivering corpse and pulling free his sword. He gazed around the clearing and counted the bodies. 'Nineteen. By all the gods, Druss, I can't believe you did that!'

'Some were trampled by the horses I stampeded, others were killed by the girls.' Druss turned and stared out over the campsite. Somewhere to his left a man groaned and the tallest of the girls ran to him, plunging a dagger into his throat. Druss turned back to Shadak. 'Will you see the women get safely to Padia?'

'You're going on to Mashrapur?'

'I'm going to find her.'

Shadak laid his hand on the young man's shoulder. 'I hope that you do, Druss. Seek out the White Bear Inn – that's where Collan will stay. But be warned, my friend. In Mashrapur, Rowena is his property. That is their law.'

'This is mine,' answered Druss, raising the double-headed axe.

Shadak took the young man's arm and led him back to Harib's tent where he poured himself a goblet of wine and drained it. One of Harib's linen tunics was draped over a small chest and Shadak threw it to Druss. 'Wipe off the blood. You look like a demon.'

Druss smiled grimly and wiped his face and arms, then cleaned the double blades.

'What do you know of Mashrapur?' asked Shadak.

The axeman shrugged. 'It is an independent state, ruled by an exiled Ventrian Prince. That's all.'

'It is a haven for thieves and slavers,' said Shadak. 'The laws are simple: those with gold to offer bribes are considered fine citizens. It matters not where the gold comes from. Collan is respected there; he owns property and dines with the Emir.'

'So?'

'So if you march in and kill him, you will be taken and executed. It is that simple.'

'What do you suggest?'

'There is a small town around twenty miles from here, due south. There is a man there, a friend of mine. Go to him, tell him I sent you. He is young and talented. You won't like him, Druss; he is a fop and a

515

pleasure-seeker. He has no morals. But it will make him invaluable in Mashrapur.'

'Who is this man?'

'His name is Sieben. He's a poet, a saga-teller, and he performs at palaces; he's very good as a matter of fact. He could have been rich. But he spends most of his time trying to bed every pretty young woman who comes into his line of vision. He never concerns himself whether they are married or single – that has brought him many enemies.'

'Already I don't like the sound of him.'

Shadak chuckled. 'He has good qualities. He is a loyal friend, and he is ridiculously fearless. A good man with a knife. And he knows Mashrapur. Trust him.'

'Why should he help me?'

'He owes me a favour.' Shadak poured a second goblet of wine and passed it to the young man.

Druss sipped it, then drained the goblet. 'This is good. What is it?'

'Lentrian Red. Around five years old, I'd say. Not the best, but good enough on a night like this.'

'I can see that a man could get a taste for it,' Druss agreed.

4

Sieben was enjoying himself. A small crowd had gathered around the barrel, and three men had already lost heavily. The green crystal was small and fitted easily under one of the three walnut shells. 'I'll move a little more slowly,' the young poet told the tall, bearded warrior who had just lost four silver pieces. His slender hands slid the shells around the smooth barrel top, halting them in a line across the centre. 'Which one? And take your time, my friend, for that emerald is worth twenty golden raq.'

The man sniffed loudly and scratched at his beard with a dirty finger. 'That one,' he said at last, pointing to the centre shell. Sieben flipped the shell. There was nothing beneath it. Moving his hand to the right he covered a second shell, expertly palmed the stone under it and showed it to the audience.

'So close,' he said, with a bright smile. The warrior swore, then turned and thrust his way through the crowd. A short swarthy man was next; he had body odour that could have felled an ox. Sieben was tempted to let him win. The fake emerald was only worth a tenth of what he had already cheated from the crowd. But he was enjoying himself too much. The swarthy man lost three silver pieces.

The crowd parted and a young warrior eased his way to the front as Sieben glanced up. The newcomer was dressed in black, with shoulder guards of shining silver steel. He wore a helm on which was blazoned a motif of two skulls on either side of a silver axe. And he was carrying a double-headed axe. 'Try your luck?' asked Sieben, gazing up into the eyes of winter blue.

'Why not?' answered the warrior, his voice deep and cold. He placed a silver piece on the barrel head. The poet's hands moved with bewildering speed, gliding the shells in elaborate figure eights. At last he stopped.

'I hope you have a keen eye, my friend,' said Sieben.

'Keen enough,' said the axeman, and leaning forward he placed a huge finger on the central shell. 'It is here,' he said.

'Let us see,' said the poet, reaching out, but the axeman pushed his hand away.

'Indeed we shall,' he said. Slowly he flipped the shells to the left and right of the centre. Both were empty. 'I must be right,' he said, his pale eyes locked to Sieben's face. 'You may show us.' Lifting his finger, he gestured to the poet.

Sieben forced a smile and palmed the crystal under the shell as he flipped it. 'Well done, my friend. You are indeed hawk-eyed.' The crowd applauded and drifted away.

'Thank you for not exposing me,' said Sieben, rising and gathering his silver.

'Fools and money are like ice and heat,' quoted the young man. 'They cannot live together. You are Sieben?'

'I might be,' answered the other cautiously. 'Who is asking?'

'Shadak sent me.'

'For what purpose?'

'A favour you owe him.'

'That is between the two of us. What has it to do with you?'

The warrior's face darkened. 'Nothing at all,' he said, then turned away and strode towards the tavern on the other side of the street. As Sieben watched him go, a young woman approached from the shadows.

'Did you earn enough to buy me a fine necklace?' she asked. He swung and smiled. The woman was tall and shapely, raven-haired and full-lipped; her eyes were tawny brown, her smile an enchantment. She stepped into his embrace and winced. 'Why do you have to wear so many knives?' she asked, moving back from him and tapping the brown leather baldric from which hung four diamond-shaped throwing-blades.

'Affectation, my love. I'll not wear them tonight. And as for your necklace – I'll have it with me.' Taking her hand he kissed it. 'However, at the moment, duty calls.'

'Duty, my poet? What would you know of duty?'

He chuckled. 'Very little – but I always pay my debts; it is my last finger-hold on the cliff of respectability. I will see you later.' He bowed, then walked across the street.

The tavern was an old, three-storeyed building with a high gallery on the second floor overlooking a long room with open fires at both ends. There was a score of bench tables and seats and a sixty-foot brass-inlaid bar behind which six tavern maids were serving ale, mead and mulled wine. The tavern was crowded, unusually so, but this was market day and farmers and cattle-breeders from all over the region had gathered for the auctions. Sieben stepped to the long bar, where a young tavern maid with honey-blonde hair smiled and approached him. 'At last you visit me,' she said.

'Who could stay away from you for long, dear heart?' he said with a smile, straining to remember her name.

'I will be finished here by second watch,' she told him.

'Where's my ale?' shouted a burly farmer, some way to the left.

'I was before you, goat-face!' came another voice. The girl gave a shy smile to Sieben, then moved down the bar to quell the threatened row.

'Here I am now, sirs, and I've only one pair of hands. Give me a moment, won't you?'

Sieben strolled through the crowds, seeking out the axeman, and found him sitting alone by a narrow, open window. Sieben eased on to the bench alongside him. 'Might be a good idea to start again,' said the poet. 'Let me buy you a jug of ale.'

'I buy my own ale,' grunted the axeman. 'And don't sit so close.'

Sieben stood and moved to the far side of the table, seating himself opposite the young man. 'Is that more to your liking?' he asked, with heavy sarcasm.

'Aye, it is. Are you wearing perfume?'

'Scented oil on the hair. You like it?'

The axeman shook his head, but refrained from comment. He cleared his throat. 'My wife has been taken by slavers. She is in Mashrapur.'

Sieben sat back and gazed at the young man. 'I take it you weren't home at the time,' he said.

'No. They took all the women. I freed them. But Rowena wasn't with them; she was with someone called Collan. He left before I got to the other raiders.'

'Before you got to the other raiders?' repeated Sieben. 'Isn't there a little more to it?'

'To what?'

518

'How did you free the other women?'

'What in Hell's name does that matter? I killed a few of them and the rest ran away. But that's not the point. Rowena wasn't there – she's in Mashrapur.'

Sieben raised a slender hand. 'Slow down, there's a good fellow. Firstly, how does Shadak come into this? And secondly, are you saying that you single-handedly attacked Harib Ka and his killers?'

'Not single-handedly. Shadak was there; they were going to torture him. Also I had two girls with me; good archers. Anyway, all that is past. Shadak said you could help me to find Rowena and come up with a plan to rescue her.'

'From Collan?'

'Yes, from Collan,' stormed the axeman. 'Are you deaf or stupid?'

Sieben's dark eyes narrowed and he leaned forward. 'You have an appealing way of asking for help, my large and ugly friend. Good luck with your quest!' He rose and moved back through the throng, emerging into the late afternoon sunlight. Two men were lounging close to the entrance, a third was whittling a length of wood with a razor-sharp hunting-knife.

The first of the men moved in front of the poet; it was the warrior who had first lost money at the barrel head. 'Get your emerald back, did you?'

'No,' answered Sieben, still angry. 'What a bumptious, ill-bred boor!'

'Not a friend, then?'

'Hardly. I don't even know his name. More to the point, I don't want to.'

'It's said you're crafty with those knives,' said the warrior, pointing to the throwing-blades. 'Is it true?'

'Why do you ask?'

'Could be you'll get the emerald back if you are.'

'You plan to attack him? Why? As far as I could see he carries no wealth.'

'It's not his wealth!' snapped the second warrior. Sieben stepped back as the man's body odour reached him. 'He's a madman. He attacked our camp two days ago, stampeded our horses. Never did find my grey. And he killed Harib. Asta's tits! He must have downed a dozen men with that cursed axe.'

'If he killed a dozen, what makes you think that three of you can deal with him?'

The noxious warrior tapped his nose. 'Surprise. When he steps out, Rafin will ask him a question. As he turns, Zhak and I will move in and gut him. But you could help. A knife through the eye would slow him up some, eh?'

'Probably,' agreed Sieben, and he moved away several paces to seat himself on a hitching rail. He drew a knife from its sheath and began to clean his nails.

'You with us?' hissed the first man.

'We'll see,' said Sieben.

Druss sat at the table and gazed down at the shining blades of the axe. He could see his reflection there, cold-eyed and grim. The features were flat and sullen, the mouth a tight, angry line. He removed the black helm and laid it on the blades, covering the face in the axe.

'*Whenever you speak someone gets angry.*' The words of his father drifted up from the halls of memory. And it was true. Some men had a knack for friendship, for easy chatter and simple jests. Druss envied them. Until Rowena had walked into his life he had believed such qualities were entirely lacking in him. But with her he felt at ease, he could laugh and joke – and see himself for a moment as others saw him, huge and bear-like, short-tempered and frightening. 'It was your childhood, Druss,' Rowena told him one morning, as they sat on the hillside overlooking the village. 'Your father moved from place to place, always frightened he would be recognised, never allowing himself to become close to people. It was easier for him, for he was a man. But it must have been hard for a boy who never learned how to make friends.'

'I don't need friends,' he said.

'I need you.'

The memory of those three softly spoken words made his heart lurch. A tavern maid passed the table and Druss reached out and caught her arm. 'Do you have Lentrian Red?' he asked.

'I'll bring you a goblet, sir.'

'Make it a jug.'

He drank until his senses swam and his thoughts became jumbled and confused. He remembered Alarin, and the punch which broke the man's jaw, and then, after the raid, hauling Alarin's body into the meeting hall. He had been stabbed through the back by a lance which had snapped in half in his body. The dead man's eyes had been open. So many of the dead had open eyes . . . all accusing.

'Why are you alive and we dead?' they asked him. 'We had families, lives, dreams, hopes. Why should you outlive us?'

'More wine!' he bellowed and a young girl with honey-blonde hair leaned over the table.

'I think you've had enough, sir. You've drunk a quart already.'

'All the eyes were open,' he said. 'Old women, children. The children were the worst. What kind of a man kills a child?'

'I think you should go home, sir. Have a little sleep.'

'Home?' He laughed, the sound harsh and bitter. 'Home to the dead? And what would I tell them? The forge is cold. There is no smell

520

of fresh-baked bread; no laughter among the children. Just eyes. No, not even eyes. Just ashes.'

'We heard there was a raid to the north,' she said. 'Was that your home?'

'Bring me more wine, girl. It helps me.'

'It is a false friend, sir,' she whispered.

'It is the only one I have.'

A burly, bearded man in a leather apron moved in close. 'What does he want?' he asked the girl.

'More wine, sir.'

'Then fetch it for him – if he can pay.'

Druss reached into the pouch at his side, drawing out one of the six silver pieces Shadak had given him. He flipped it to the innkeeper. 'Well, serve him!' the man ordered the maid.

The second jug went the way of the first and, when it was finished, Druss pushed himself ponderously to his feet. He tried to don the helm, but it slipped from his fingers and rolled to the floor. As he bent down, he rammed his brow against the edge of the table. The serving maid appeared alongside him. 'Let me help you, sir,' she said, scooping up the helm and gently placing it on his head.

'Thank you,' he said, slowly. He fumbled in his pouch and gave her a silver piece. 'For . . . your . . . kindness,' he told her, enunciating the words with care.

'I have a small room at the back, sir. Two doors down from the stable. It is unlocked; you may sleep there if you wish.'

He picked up the axe, but it too fell to the floor, the prongs of the blades embedding in a wooden plank. 'Go back and sleep, sir. I'll bring your . . . weapon with me later.'

He nodded and weaved his way towards the door.

Pulling open the door, he stepped out into the fading sunlight, his stomach lurching. Someone spoke from his left, asking him a question. Druss tried to turn, but stumbled into the man and they both fell against the wall. He tried to right himself, grabbing the man's shoulder and heaving himself upright. Through the fog in his mind he heard other men running in. One of them screamed. Druss lurched back and saw a long-bladed dagger clatter to the ground. The former wielder was standing alongside him, his right arm raised unnaturally. Druss blinked. The man's wrist was pinned to the inn door by a throwing knife.

He heard the rasp of swords being drawn. 'Defend yourself, you fool!' came a voice.

A swordsman ran at him and Druss stepped in to meet him, parrying the lunging blade with his forearm and slamming a right cross to the warrior's chin. The swordsman went down as if poleaxed.

521

Swinging to meet the second attacker, Druss lost his balance and fell heavily. But in mid-swing the swordsman also stumbled and Druss lashed out with his foot, catching his assailant on the heel and catapulting him to the ground. Rolling to his knees, Druss grabbed the fallen man by the hair and hauled him close, delivering a bone-crunching head butt to the warrior's nose. The man slumped forward, unconscious. Druss released him.

Another man moved alongside him and Druss recognised the handsome young poet. 'Gods, you reek of cheap wine,' said Sieben.

'Who . . . are you?' mumbled Druss, trying to focus on the man with his arm pinned to the door.

'Miscreants,' Sieben told him, moving alongside the stricken warrior and levering his knife clear. The man screamed in pain but Sieben ignored him and returned to the street. 'I think you'd better come with me, old horse.'

Druss remembered little of the walk through the town, only that he stopped twice to vomit, and his head began to ache abominably.

He awoke at midnight and found himself lying on a porch under the stars. Beside him was a bucket. He sat up . . . and groaned as the terrible pounding began in his head. It felt as if an iron band had been riveted to his brow. Hearing sounds from within the house, he stood and moved to the door. Then he halted. The sounds were unmistakable.

'Oh, Sieben . . . Oh . . . Oh . . . !'

Druss swore and returned to the edge of the porch. A breath of wind touched his face, bringing with it an unpleasant smell, and he gazed down at himself. His jerkin was soiled with vomit, and he stank of stale sweat and travel. To his left was a well. Forcing himself upright, he walked to it, and slowly raised the bucket. Somewhere deep within his head a demon began to strike at his skull with a red-hot hammer. Ignoring the pain, Druss stripped to the waist and washed himself with the cold water.

He heard the door open and turned to see a dark-haired young woman emerge from the house. She looked at him, smiled, then ran off through the narrow streets. Lifting the bucket, Druss tipped the last of the contents over his head.

'At the risk of being offensive,' said Sieben from the doorway, 'I think you need a little soap. Come inside. There's a fire burning in the hearth and I've heated some water. Gods, it's freezing out here.'

Gathering his clothes, Druss followed the poet inside. The house was small, only three rooms, all on the ground floor – a cook-room with an iron stove, a bedroom and a square dining-room with a stone-built hearth in which a fire was blazing. There was a table with four wooden chairs and on either side of the hearth were comfort seats of padded leather stuffed with horse-hair.

522

Sieben led him to the cloakroom where he filled a bowl with hot water. Handing Druss a slab of white soap and a towel, he opened a cupboard door and removed a plate of sliced beef and a loaf of bread. 'Come in and eat when you're ready,' said the poet, as he walked back to the dining-room.

Druss scrubbed himself with the soap, which smelled of lavender, then cleaned his jerkin and dressed. He found the poet sitting by the fire with his long legs stretched out, a goblet of wine in one hand. The other slender hand swept through the shoulder-length blond hair, sweeping it back over his head. Holding it in place, he settled a black leather headband over his brow; at the centre of the band was a glittering opal. The poet lifted a small oval mirror and studied himself. 'Ah, what a curse it is to be so good-looking,' he said, laying aside the mirror. 'Care for a drink?' Druss felt his stomach heave and shook his head. 'Eat, my large friend. You may feel as if your stomach will revolt, but it is the best thing for you. Trust me.'

Druss tore off a hunk of bread and sat down, slowly chewing it. It tasted of ashes and bile, but he finished it manfully. The poet was right. His stomach settled. The salted beef was harder to take but, washed down with cool water, he soon began to feel his strength returning. 'I drank too much,' he said.

'No, really? Two quarts, I understand.'

'I don't remember how much. Was there a fight?'

'Not much of one, by your standards.'

'Who were they?'

'Some of the raiders you attacked.'

'I should have killed them.'

'Perhaps – but in the state you were in you should consider yourself lucky to be alive.'

Druss filled a clay cup with water and drained it. 'You helped me, I remember that. Why?'

'A passing whim. Don't let it concern you. Now, tell me again about your wife and the raid.'

'To what purpose? It's done. All I care about is finding Rowena.'

'But you will need my help – otherwise Shadak wouldn't have sent you to me. And I like to know the kind of man I'm expected to travel with. You understand? So tell me.'

'There isn't a great deal to tell. The raiders . . .'

'How many?'

'Forty or so, They attacked our village, killed all the men, the old women, the children. They took the younger women prisoner. I was in the woods, felling timber. Some killers came to the woods and I dealt with them. Then I met Shadak, who was also following them; they raided a town and killed his son. We freed the women. Shadak was captured. I stampeded their horses and attacked the camp. That's it.'

Sieben shook his head and smiled. 'I think you could tell the entire history of the Drenai in less time than it takes to boil an egg. A story-teller you are not, my friend – which is just as well, since that is my main source of income and I loathe competition.'

Druss rubbed his eyes and leaned back in the chair, resting his head on the high padded leather cushion. The heat from the fire was soothing and his body was weary beyond anything he had known before. The days of the chase had taken their toll. He felt himself drifting on a warm sea. The poet was speaking to him, but his words failed to penetrate.

He awoke with the dawn to find the fire was burned down to a few glowing coals and the house empty. Druss yawned and stretched, then walked to the kitchen, helping himself to stale bread and a hunk of cheese. He drank some more water, then heard the main door creak open. Wandering out, he saw Sieben and a young, blonde woman. The poet was carrying his axe and his gauntlets.

'Someone to see you, old horse,' said Sieben, laying the axe in the doorway and tossing the gauntlets to a chair. The poet smiled and walked back out into the sunlight.

The blonde woman approached Druss, smiling shyly. 'I didn't know where you were. I kept your axe for you.'

'Thank you. You are from the inn.' She was dressed now in a woollen dress of poor quality, that once had been blue but was now a pale grey. Her figure was shapely, her face gentle and pretty, her eyes warm and brown.

'Yes. We spoke yesterday,' she said, moving to a chair and sitting down with her hands on her knees. 'You seemed . . . very sad.'

'I am . . . myself now,' he told her gently.

'Sieben told me your wife was taken by slavers.'

'I will find her.'

'When I was sixteen raiders attacked our village. They killed my father and wounded my husband. I was taken, with seven other girls, and we were sold in Mashrapur. I was there two years. I escaped one night, with another girl, and we fled into the wilderness. She died there, killed by a bear, but I was found by a company of pilgrims on their way to Lentria. I was almost dead from starvation. They helped me, and I made my way home.'

'Why are you telling me all this?' asked Druss softly, seeing the sadness in her eyes.

'My husband had married someone else. And my brother, Loric, who had lost an arm in the raid, told me I was no longer welcome. He said I was a *fallen* woman, and if I had any pride I would have taken my own life. So I left.'

Druss reached out and took her hand. 'Your husband was a worthless piece of dung, and your brother likewise. But I ask again, why are you telling me this?'

'When Sieben told me you were hunting for your wife . . . it made me remember. I used to dream Karsk was coming for me. But a slave has no rights, you know, in Mashrapur. Anything the Lord wishes, he can have. You cannot refuse. When you find your . . . lady . . . she may well have been roughly used.' She fell silent and sat staring at her hands. 'I don't know how to say what I mean . . . When I was a slave I was beaten, I was humiliated. I was raped and abused. But nothing was as bad as the look on my husband's face when he saw me, or the disgust in my brother's voice when he cast me out.'

Still holding to her hand, Druss leaned in towards her. 'What is your name?'

'Sashan.'

'If I had been your husband, Sashan, I would have followed you. I would have found you. And when I did I would have taken you in my arms and brought you home. As I will bring Rowena home.'

'You will not judge her?'

He smiled. 'No more than I judge you, save to say that you are a brave woman and any man – any true man – would be proud to have you walk beside him.'

She reddened and rose. 'If wishes were horses, then beggars would ride,' she said, then turned away and walked to the doorway. She looked back once, but said nothing; then she stepped from the house.

Sieben entered. 'That was well said, old horse. Very well said. You know, despite your awful manners and your lack of conversation, I think I like you. Let's go to Mashrapur and find your lady.'

Druss looked hard at the slim young man. He was perhaps an inch taller than the axeman and his clothes were of fine cloth, his long hair barber-trimmed, not hacked by a knife nor cut with shears using a basin for a guide. Druss glanced down at the man's hands; the skin was soft, like that of a child. Only the baldric and the knives gave any evidence Sieben was a fighter.

'Well? Do I pass inspection, old horse?'

'My father once said that fortune makes for strange bedfellows,' said Druss.

'You should see the problem from where I'm standing,' answered Sieben. 'You will travel with a man versed in literature and poetry, a story-teller without equal. While I, on the other hand, get to ride beside a peasant in a vomit-flecked jerkin.'

Amazingly Druss found no rising anger, no surging desire to strike out. Instead he laughed, tension flowing from him.

'I like you, little man,' he said.

Within the first day they had left the mountains behind them, and rode now through valleys and vales, and sweeping grassland dotted with hills and ribbon streams. There were many hamlets and villages beside the road, the buildings of whitewashed stone with roofs of timber or slate.

Sieben rode gracefully, straight of back and easy in the saddle, sunlight gleaming from his riding tunic of pale blue silk and the silver edging on his knee-length riding boots. His long blond hair was tied back in a pony-tail, and he also sported a silver headband. 'How many headbands do you have?' asked Druss as they set off.

'Pitifully few. Pretty though, isn't it? I picked it up in Drenan last year. I've always liked silver.'

'You look like a fop.'

'Just what I needed this morning,' said Sieben, smiling, 'hints on sartorial elegance from a man whose hair has apparently been cut with a rusty saw, and whose only shirt carries wine stains, and . . . no, don't tell me what the other marks are.'

Druss glanced down. 'Dried blood. But it's not mine.'

'Well, what a relief. I shall sleep more soundly tonight for knowing that.'

For the first hour of the journey the poet tried to give helpful advice to the young axeman. 'Don't grip the horse with your calves, just your thighs. And straighten your back.' Finally he gave up. 'You know, Druss, my dear, some men are born to ride. You on the other hand have no feel for it. I've seen sacks of carrots with more grace than you.'

The axeman's reply was short and brutally obscene. Sieben chuckled and gazed up at the sky which was cloudless and gloriously blue. 'What a day to set off in search of a kidnapped princess,' he said.

'She's not a princess.'

'All kidnapped women are princesses,' Sieben told him. 'Have you never listened to the stories? Heroes are tall, golden-haired and wondrously handsome. Princesses are demure and beautiful, spending their lives waiting for the handsome prince who will free them. By the gods, Druss, no one would want to hear tales of the truth. Can you imagine? The young hero unable to ride in search of his sweetheart because the large boil on his buttocks prevents him from sitting on a horse?' Sieben's laughter rippled out.

Even normally grim Druss smiled and Sieben continued. 'It's the romance, you see. A woman in stories is either a goddess or a whore. The princess, being a beautiful virgin, falls into the former category. The hero must also be pure, waiting for the moment of his destiny in the arms of the virginal princess. It's wonderfully quaint – and quite ridiculous of course. Love-making, like playing the lyre, requires enormous practice. Thankfully the stories always end before we see the young couple fumbling their way through their first coupling.'

'You talk like a man who has never been in love,' said Druss.

'Nonsense. I have been in love scores of times,' snapped the poet.

Druss shook his head. 'If that were true, then you would know just

526

how . . . how fine the *fumbling* can be. How far is it to Mashrapur?'

'Two days. But the slave markets are always held on Missael or Manien, so we've time. Tell me about her.'

'No.'

'No? You don't like talking about your wife?'

'Not to strangers. Have you ever been wed?'

'No – nor ever desired to be. Look around you, Druss. See all those flowers on the hillsides? Why would a man want to restrict himself to just one bloom? Just one scent? I had a horse once, Shadira, a beautiful beast, faster than the north wind. She could clear a four-bar fence with room to spare. I was ten when my father gave her to me, and Shadira was fifteen. But by the time I was twenty Shadira could no longer run as fast, and she jumped not at all. So I got a new horse. You understand what I am saying?'

'Not a word of it,' grunted Druss. 'Women aren't horses.'

'That's true,' agreed Sieben. 'Most horses you want to ride more than once.'

Druss shook his head. 'I don't know what it is that you call love. And I don't want to know.'

The trail wound to the south, the hills growing more gentle as the mountain range receded behind them. Ahead on the road they saw an old man shuffling towards them. He wore robes of faded blue and he leaned heavily on a long staff. As they neared, Sieben saw that the man was blind.

The old man halted as they rode closer. 'Can we help you, old one?' asked Sieben.

'I need no help,' answered the man, his voice surprisingly strong and resonant. 'I am on my way to Drenan.'

'It is a long walk,' said Sieben.

'I am in no hurry. But if you have food, and are willing to entertain a guest at your midday meal, I would be glad to join you.'

'Why not?' said Sieben. 'There is a stream some little way to your right; we will see you there.' Swinging his mount Sieben cantered the beast across the grass, leaping lightly from the saddle and looping the reins over the horse's head as Druss rode up and dismounted.

'Why did you invite him to join us?'

Sieben glanced back. The old man was out of earshot and moving slowly towards them. 'He is a seeker, Druss. A mystic. Have you not heard of them?'

'No.'

'Source Priests who blind themselves in order to increase their powers of prophecy. Some of them are quite extraordinary. It's worth a few oats.'

Swiftly the poet prepared a fire over which he placed a copper pot half filled with water. He added oats and a little salt. The old man sat cross-legged nearby. Druss removed his helm and jerkin and stretched out in the sunshine. After the porridge had cooked, Sieben filled a bowl and passed it to the priest.

'Do you have sugar?' asked the Seeker.

'No. We have a little honey. I will fetch it.'

After the meal was concluded the old man shuffled to the stream and cleaned his bowl, returning it to Sieben. 'And now you wish to know the future?' asked the priest, with a crooked smile.

'That would be pleasant,' said Sieben.

'Not necessarily. Would you like to know the day of your death?'

'I take your point, old man. Tell me of the next beautiful woman who will share my bed.'

The old man chuckled. 'A talent so large, yet men only require such infinitesimal examples of it. I could tell you of your sons, and of moments of peril. But no, you wish to hear of matters inconsequential. Very well. Give me your hand.'

Sieben sat opposite him and extended his right hand. The old man took it, and sat silently for several minutes. Finally he sighed. 'I have walked the paths of your future, Sieben the Poet, Sieben the Saga-master. The road is long. The next woman? A whore in Mashrapur, who will ask for seven silver pennies. You will pay it.'

He released Sieben's hand and turned his blind eyes towards Druss. 'Do you wish your future told?'

'I will make my own future,' answered Druss.

'Ah, a man of strength and independent will. Come. Let me at least see, for my own interest, what tomorrow holds for you.'

'Come on, lad,' pleaded Sieben. 'Give him your hand.'

Druss rose and walked to where the old man sat. He squatted down before him and thrust out his hand. The priest's fingers closed around his own. 'A large hand,' he said. 'Strong . . . very strong.' Suddenly he winced, his body stiffening. 'Are you yet young, Druss the Legend? Have you stood at the pass?'

'What pass?'

'How old are you?'

'Seventeen.'

'Of course. Seventeen. And searching for Rowena. Yes . . . Mash-rapur. I see it now. Not yet the *Deathwalker*, the Silver Slayer, the Captain of the Axe. But still mighty.' He released his hold and sighed. 'You are quite right, Druss, you will make your own future; you will need no words from me.' The old man rose and took up his staff. 'I thank you for your hospitality.'

Sieben stood also. 'At least tell us what awaits in Mashrapur,' he said.

'A whore and seven silver pennies,' answered the priest with a dry smile. He turned his blind eyes towards Druss. 'Be strong, axeman.

The road is long and there are legends to be made. But Death awaits, and he is patient. You will see him as you stand beneath the gates in the fourth Year of the Leopard.'

He walked slowly away. 'Incredible,' whispered Sieben.

'Why?' responded Druss. 'I could have foretold that the next woman you meet would be a whore.'

'He knew our names, Druss; he knew everything. Now, when is the fourth Year of the Leopard?'

'He told us nothing. Let's move on.'

'How can you say that it was nothing? He called you Druss the Legend. What legend? How will you build it?'

Ignoring him, Druss walked to his horse and climbed into the saddle. 'I don't like horses,' he said. 'Once we reach Mashrapur I'll sell it. Rowena and I will walk back.'

Sieben looked up at the pale-eyed young man. 'It meant nothing to you, did it? His prophecy, I mean.'

'They were just words, poet. Noises on the air. Let's ride.'

After a while Sieben spoke. 'The Year of the Leopard is forty-three years away. Gods, Druss, you'll live to be an old man. I wonder where the gates are.'

Druss ignored him and rode on.

5

Bodasen threaded his way through the crowds milling on the dock, past the gaudily dressed women with their painted faces and insincere smiles, past the stallholders bellowing their bargains, past the beggars with their deformed limbs and their pleading eyes. Bodasen hated Mashrapur, loathed the smell of the teeming multitudes who gathered here seeking instant wealth. The streets were narrow and choked with the detritus of humanity, the houses built high – three-, four- and five-storey – all linked by alleyways and tunnels and shadowed pathways where robbers could plunge their blades into unsuspecting victims and flee through the labyrinthine back streets before the undermanned city guards could apprehend them.

What a city, thought Bodasen. A place of filth and painted women, a haven for thieves, smugglers, slavers and renegades.

A woman approached him. 'You look lonely, my love,' she said, flashing a gold-toothed smile. He gazed down at her and her smile faded. She backed away swiftly and Bodasen rode on.

He came to a narrow alleyway and paused to push his black cloak above his left shoulder. The hilt of his sabre shone in the fading sunlight. As Bodasen walked on, three men stood in the shadows. He felt their eyes upon him and turned his face towards them, his stare challenging; they looked away, and he continued along the alley until it broadened out to a small square with a fountain at the centre, constructed around a bronze statue of a boy riding a dolphin. Several whores were sitting beside the fountain, chatting to one another. They saw him, and instantly their postures changed. Leaning back to thrust out their breasts, they assumed their customary smiles. As he passed he heard their chatter begin again.

The inn was almost empty. An old man sat at the bar, nursing a jug of ale, and two maids were cleaning tables, while a third prepared the night's fire in the stone hearth. Bodasen moved to a window table and sat, facing the door. A maid approached him.

'Good evening, my lord. Are you ready for your usual supper?'

'No. Bring me a goblet of good red wine and a flagon of fresh water.'

'Yes, my lord.' She curtsied prettily and walked away. Her greeting eased his irritation. Some, even in this disgusting city, could recognise nobility. The wine was of an average quality, no more than four years old and harsh on the tongue, and Bodasen drank sparingly.

The inn door opened and two men entered. Bodasen leaned back in his chair and watched them approach. The first was a handsome man, tall and wide-shouldered; he wore a crimson cloak over a red tunic, and a sabre was scabbarded at his hip. The second was a huge, bald warrior, heavily muscled and grim of feature.

The first man sat opposite Bodasen, the second standing alongside the table. 'Where is Harib Ka?' Bodasen asked.

'Your countryman will not be joining us,' replied Collan.

'He said he would be here; that is the reason I agreed to this meeting.'

Collan shrugged. 'He had an urgent appointment elsewhere.'

'He said nothing of it to me.'

'I think it was unexpected. You wish to do business, or not?'

'I do not *do business*, Collan. I seek to negotiate a treaty with the . . . free traders of the Ventrian Sea. My understanding is that you have . . . shall we say, contacts, among them?'

Collan chuckled. 'Interesting. You can't bring yourself to say *pirates*, can you? No, that would be too much for a Ventrian nobleman. Well, let us think the situation through. The Ventrian fleet has been scattered or sunk. On land your armies are crushed, and the Emperor slain. Now you pin your hopes on the pirate fleet; only they can ensure that the armies of Naashan do not march all the way to the capital. Am I in error on any of these points?'

Bodasen cleared his throat. 'The Empire is seeking friends. The Free Traders are in a position to aid us in our struggle against the forces of evil. We always treat our friends with great generosity.'

'I see,' said Collan, his eyes mocking. 'We are fighting the forces of *evil* now? And there I was believing that Naashan and Ventria were merely two warring empires. How naïve of me. However, you speak of generosity. How generous is the Prince?'

'The *Emperor* is noted for his largess.'

Collan smiled. 'Emperor at nineteen – a rapid rise to power. But he has lost eleven cities to the invader, and his treasury is severely depleted. Can he find two hundred thousand gold raq?'

'Two . . . surely you are not serious?'

'The Free Traders have fifty warships. With them we could protect the coastline and prevent invasion from the sea; we could also shepherd the convoys that carry Ventrian silk to the Drenai and the Lentrians and countless others. Without us you are doomed, Bodasen. Two hundred thousand is a small price to pay.'

'I am authorised to offer fifty. No more.'

'The Naashanites have offered one hundred.'

Bodasen fell silent, his mouth dry. 'Perhaps we could pay the difference in silks and trade goods?' he offered at last.

'Gold,' said Collan. 'That is all that interests us. We are not merchants.'

No, thought Bodasen bitterly, you are thieves and killers, and it burns my soul to sit in the same room with such as you. 'I will need to seek counsel of the ambassador,' he said. 'He can communicate your request to the Emperor. I will need five days.'

'That is agreeable,' said Collan, rising. 'You know where to find me?'

Under a flat rock, thought Bodasen, with the other slugs and lice. 'Yes,' he said, softly, 'I know where to find you. Tell me, when will Harib be back in Mashrapur?'

'He won't.'

'Where is this appointment then?'

'In Hell,' answered Collan.

'You must have patience,' said Sieben, as Druss stalked around the small room on the upper floor of the Tree of Bone Inn. The poet had stretched out his long, lean frame on the first of the two narrow beds, while Druss strode to the window and stood staring out over the dock and the sea beyond the harbour.

'Patience?' stormed the axeman. 'She's here somewhere, maybe close.'

'And we'll find her,' promised Sieben, 'but it will take a little time. First there are the established slave traders. This evening I will ask around, and find out where Collan has placed her. Then we can plan her rescue.'

Druss swung round. 'Why not go to the White Bear Inn and find Collan? He knows.'

'I expect he does, old horse.' Sieben swung his legs from the bed and stood. 'And he'll have any number of rascals ready to plunge knives in our backs. Foremost among them will be Borcha. I want you to picture a man who looks as if he was carved from granite, with muscles that dwarf even yours. Borcha is a killer. He has beaten men to death in fist fights, snapped necks in wrestling bouts; he doesn't need a weapon. I have seen him crush a pewter goblet in one hand, and watched him lift a barrel of ale above his head. And he is just one of Collan's men.'

'Frightened, are you, poet?'

'Of course I'm frightened, you young fool! Fear is sensible. Never make the mistake of equating it with cowardice. But it is senseless to go after Collan; he is known here and has friends in very high places. Attack him and you will be arrested, tried and sentenced. Then there will be no one to rescue Rowena.'

Druss slumped down, his elbows resting on the warped table. 'I hate sitting here doing nothing,' he said.

'Then let's walk around the city for a while,' offered Sieben. 'We can gather some information. How much did you get for your horse?'

'Twenty in silver.'

'Almost fair. You did well. Come on, I'll show you the sights.' Druss stood and gathered his axe. 'I don't think you'll need that,' Sieben told him. 'It's one thing to wear a sword or carry a knife, but the City Watch will not take kindly to that monstrosity. In a crowded street you're likely to cut off someone's arm by mistake. Here, I'll loan you one of my knives.'

'I won't need it,' said Druss, leaving the axe on the table and striding out of the room.

Together they walked down into the main room of the inn, then out into the narrow street beyond.

Druss sniffed loudly. 'This city stinks,' he said.

'Most cities do – at least in the poorest areas. No sewers. Refuse is thrown from windows. So walk warily.'

They moved towards the docks where several ships were being unloaded, bales of silk from Ventria and Naashan and other eastern nations, herbs and spices, dried fruit and barrels of wine. The dock was alive with activity.

'I've never seen so many people in one place,' said Druss.

'It's not even busy yet,' Sieben pointed out. They strolled around the harbour wall, past temples and large municipal buildings, through a small park with a statue-lined walkway and a central fountain.

Young couples were walking hand in hand and to the left an orator was addressing a small crowd. He was speaking of the essential selfishness of the pursuit of altruism. Sieben stopped to listen for a few minutes, then walked on.

'Interesting, don't you think?' he asked his companion. 'He was suggesting that good works are ultimately selfish because they make the man who undertakes them feel good. Therefore he has not been unselfish at all, but has merely acted for his own pleasure.'

Druss shook his head and glowered at the poet. 'His mother should have told him the mouth is not for breaking wind with.'

'I take it this is your subtle way of saying you disagree with his comments?' snapped Sieben.

'The man's a fool.'

'How would you set about proving that?'

'I don't need to prove it. If a man serves up a plate of cow dung, I don't need to taste it to know it's not steak.'

'Explain it,' Sieben urged him. 'Share some of that vaunted frontier philosophy.'

'No,' said Druss, walking on.

'Why not?' asked Sieben, moving alongside him.

'I am a woodsman. I know about trees. Once I worked in an orchard. Did you know you can take cuttings from any variety and graft them to another apple tree? One tree can have twenty varieties. It's the same with pears. My father always said men were like that with knowledge. So much can be grafted on, but it must match what the heart feels. You can't graft apple to pear. It's a waste of time – and I don't like wasting my time.'

'You think I could not understand your arguments?' asked Sieben with a sneering smile.

'Some things you either know or you don't. And I can't graft that knowledge on to you. Back in the mountains I watched farmers plant tree lines across the fields; they did it because the winds can blow away the top-soil. But the trees would take a hundred years to form a real windbreak, so those farmers were building for the future, for others they will never know. They did it because it was right to do it – and not one of them would be able to debate with that pompous windbag back there. Or with you. Nor is it necessary that they should.'

'That *pompous windbag* is the first minister of Mashrapur, a brilliant politician and a poet of some repute. I'm sure he would be mortally humiliated to know that a young uneducated peasant from the frontier disagrees with his philosophy.'

'Then we won't tell him,' said Druss. 'We'll just leave him here serving up his cow-pats to people who *will* believe they're steaks. Now I'm thirsty, poet. Do you know of a decent tavern?'

'It depends what you're looking for. The taverns on the docks are

533

rough, and usually filled with thieves and whores. If we walk on for another half-mile we'll come to a more civilised area. There we can have a quiet drink.'

'What about those places over there?' asked Druss, pointing to a row of buildings alongside the wharf.

'Your judgement is unerring, Druss. That is East Wharf, better known to the residents here as Thieves Row. Every night there are a score of fights – and murders. Almost no one of quality would go there – which makes it perfect for you. You go on. I'll visit some old friends who might have news of recent slave movements.'

'I'll come with you,' said Druss.

'No, you won't. You'd be out of place. Most of my friends, you see, are pompous windbags. I'll meet you back at the Tree of Bone by midnight.' Druss chuckled, which only increased Sieben's annoyance as the poet swung away and strode through the park.

The room was furnished with a large bed with satin sheets, two comfort chairs padded with horsehair and covered with velvet, and a table upon which sat a jug of wine and two silver goblets. There were rugs upon the floor, woven with great skill and soft beneath her bare feet. Rowena sat upon the edge of the bed, her right hand clasping the brooch Druss had fashioned for her. She could see him walking beside Sieben. Sadness overwhelmed her and her hand dropped to her lap. Harib Ka was dead – as she had known he would be – and Druss was now closer to his dread destiny.

She felt powerless and alone in Collan's house. There were no locks upon the door, but there were guards in the corridor beyond. Yet there was no escape.

On the first night, when Collan had taken her from the camp, he had raped her twice. On the second occasion she had tried to empty her mind, losing herself in dreams of the past. In doing so she had unlocked the doors to her Talent. Rowena had floated free of her abused body and hurtled through darkness and Time. She saw great cities, huge armies, mountains that breached the clouds. Lost, she sought for Druss and could not find him.

Then a voice came to her, a gentle voice, warm and reassuring. 'Be calm, sister. I will help you.'

She paused in her flight, floating above a night-dark ocean. A man appeared alongside her; he was slim of build and young, perhaps twenty. His eyes were dark, his smile friendly. 'Who are you?' she asked him.

'I am Vintar of the Thirty.'

'I am lost,' she said.

'Give me your hand.'

Reaching out she felt his spirit fingers, then his thoughts washed over hers. On the verge of panic Rowena felt herself swamped by his memories, seeing a temple of grey stone, a dwelling-place of white-clad monks. He withdrew from her as swiftly as he had entered her thoughts. 'Your ordeal is over,' he said. 'He has left you and now sleeps beside you. I shall take you home.'

'I cannot bear it. He is a vile man.'

'You will survive, Rowena.'

'Why should I wish to?' she asked him. 'My husband is changing, becoming day by day as vicious as the men who took me. What kind of life will I face?'

'I will not answer that, though probably I could,' he told her. 'You are very young, and you have experienced great pain. But you are alive, and while living can achieve great good. You have the Talent, not only to Soar but also to Heal, to Know. Few are blessed with this gift. Do not concern yourself with Collan; he raped you only because Harib Ka said that he should not and he will not touch you again.'

'He has defiled me.'

'No,' said Vintar sternly, 'he has defiled himself. It is important to understand that.'

'Druss would be ashamed of me, for I did not fight.'

'You fought, Rowena, in your own way. You gave him no pleasure. To have tried to resist would have increased his lust, and his satisfaction. As it was – and you know this to be true – he felt deflated and full of melancholy. And you know his fate.'

'I don't want any more deaths!'

'We all die. You . . . me . . . Druss. The measure of us all is established by how we live.'

He had returned her to her body, taking care to instruct her in the ways of Spirit travel, and the routes by which she could return by herself in the future. 'Will I see you again?' she asked him.

'It is possible,' he answered.

Now, as she sat on the satin-covered bed, she wished she could speak with him again.

The door opened and a huge warrior entered. He was bald and heavily muscled. There were scars around his eyes and his nose was flattened against his face. He moved towards the bed but there was no threat, she knew. Silently he laid a gown of white silk upon the bed. 'Collan has asked that you wear this for Kabuchek.'

'Who is Kabuchek?' she enquired.

'A Ventrian merchant. If you do well he will buy you. It won't be a bad life, girl. He has many palaces and treats his slaves with care.'

'Why do you serve Collan?' she asked.

His eyes narrowed. 'I serve no one. Collan is a friend. I help him sometimes.'

'You are a better man than he.'

'That is as may be. But several years ago, when I was first champion, I was waylaid in an alley by supporters of the vanquished champion. They had swords and knives. Collan ran to my aid. We survived. I always pay my debts. Now put on the gown, and prepare your skill. You need to impress the Ventrian.'

'And if I refuse?'

'Collan will not be pleased and I don't think you would like that. Trust me on this, lady. Do your best and you will be clear of this house.'

'My husband is coming for me,' she said softly. 'When he does, he will kill any who have harmed me.'

'Why tell me?'

'Do not be here when he comes, Borcha.'

The giant shrugged. 'The Fates will decide,' he said.

Druss strolled across to the wharf buildings. They were old, a series of taverns created from derelict warehouses and there were recesses and alley entrances everywhere. Garishly dressed women lounged against the walls and ragged men sat close by, playing knucklebones or talking in small groups.

A woman approached him. 'All the delights your mind can conjure for just a silver penny,' she said wearily.

'Thank you, but no,' he told her.

'I can get you opiates, if you desire them?'

'No,' he said, more sternly, and moved on. Three bearded men pushed themselves to their feet and walked in front of him. 'A gift for the poor, my lord?' asked the first.

Druss was about to reply when he glimpsed the man to his left edge his hand into the folds of a filthy shirt. He chuckled. 'If that hand comes out with a knife in it – I'll make you eat it, little man.' The beggar froze.

'You shouldn't be coming here with threats,' said the first man. 'Not unarmed as you are. It's not wise, *my lord*.' Reaching behind his back, he drew a long-bladed dagger.

As the blade appeared Druss stepped forward and casually back-handed the man across the mouth. The robber cartwheeled to the left, scattering a group of watching whores and colliding with a wall of brick. He moaned once, then lay still. Ignoring the other two beggars, Druss strode to the nearest tavern and stepped inside.

The interior was windowless and high-ceilinged, lit by lanterns which hung from the beams. The tavern smelt of burning oil and stale sweat. It was crowded, and Druss eased his way to a long trestle table on which several barrels of ale were set. An old man in a greasy apron approached him. 'You don't want to be drinking before the bouts begin; it'll fill you with wind,' he warned.

'What bouts?'

The man looked at him appraisingly, and his glittering eyes held no hint of warmth. 'You wouldn't be trying to fool Old Thom, would you?'

'I'm a stranger here,' said Druss. 'Now, what bouts?'

'Follow me, lad,' said Thom, and he pushed his way through the crowd towards the back of the tavern and on through a narrow doorway. Druss followed him and found himself standing in a rectangular warehouse where a wide circle of sand had been roped off at the centre. By the far walls were a group of athletes, moving through a series of exercises to loosen the muscles of shoulders and back.

'You ever fought?'

'Not for money.'

Thom nodded, then reached out and lifted Druss's hand. 'A good size, and flat knuckles. But are you fast, boy?'

'What is the prize?' countered the young man.

'It won't work that way – not for you. This is a standard contest and all the entrants are nominated well in advance so that sporting gentlemen can have opportunities to judge the quality of the fighter. But just before the start of the competition there'll be offers to men in the crowd to earn a few pennies by taking on various champions. A golden raq, for example, to the man who can stay on his feet for one turn of the sandglass. They do it to allow the fighters to warm up against low-quality opposition.'

'How long is one turn?' asked Druss.

'About as long as it's been since you first walked into the Blind Corsair.'

'And what if a man won?'

'It doesn't happen, lad. But if it did, then he'd take the loser's place in the main event. No, the main money is made on wagers among the crowd. How much coin are you carrying?'

'You ask a lot of questions, old man.'

'Pah! I'm not a robber, lad. Used to be, but then I got old and slow. Now I live on my wits. You look like a man who could stand up for himself. At first I mistook you for Grassin the Lentrian – that's him over there, by the far door.' Druss followed the old man's pointing finger and saw a powerfully built young man with short-cropped black hair. He was talking to another heavily-muscled man, a blond warrior with a dangling moustache. 'The other one is Skatha, he is a Naashanite sailor. And the big fellow at the back is Borcha. He'll win tonight. No question. Deadly, he is. Most likely someone will be crippled by him before the evening is out.'

Druss gazed at the man and felt the hackles on his neck rise. Borcha was enormous, standing some seven inches above six feet tall. He was bald, his head vaguely pointed as if his skin was stretched over a Vagrian helm. His shoulders were massively muscled, his neck huge with muscles swollen and bulging.

'No good looking at him like that, boy. He's too good for you. Trust me on that. He's skilled and very fast. He won't even step up for the warming bouts. No one would face him – not even for twenty golden raq. But that Grassin now, I think you could stand against him for a turn of the glass. And if you've some coin to wager, I'll find takers.'

'What do you get, old man?'

'Half of what we make.'

'What odds could you bargain for?'

'Two to one. Maybe three.'

'And if I went against Borcha?'

'Put it from your mind, boy. We want to make money – not coffin fuel.'

'How much?' persisted Druss.

'Ten to one – twenty to one. The gods alone know!'

Druss opened the pouch at his side, removing ten silver pieces. Casually he dropped them into the old man's outstretched hand. 'Let it be known that I wish to stand against Borcha for a turn of the glass.'

'Asta's tits, he'll kill you.'

'If he doesn't, you could make a hundred pieces of silver. Maybe more.'

'There is that, of course,' said Old Thom, with a crooked grin.

Crowds slowly began to fill the warehouse arena. Rich nobles clad in silks and fine leathers, their ladies beside them in lace and satin, were seated on high tiers overlooking the sand circle. On the lower levels were the merchants and traders in their conical caps and long capes. Druss felt uncomfortable, hemmed in by the mass. The air was growing foul, the temperature rising as more and more people filed in.

Rowena would hate this place, with its noise and its pressing throng. His mood darkened as he thought of her – a prisoner somewhere, a slave to the whims and desires of Collan. He forced such thoughts from his mind, and concentrated instead on his conversation with the poet. He had enjoyed irritating the man; it had eased his own anger, an anger generated by the unwilling acceptance that much of what the speaker in the park had said was true. He loved Rowena, heart and soul. But he needed her also, and he often wondered which was the stronger, love or need. And was he trying to rescue her because he loved her, or because he was lost without her? The question tormented him.

Rowena calmed his turbulent spirit in a way no other living soul ever could. She helped him to see the world through gentle eyes. It was

538

a rare and beautiful experience. If she had been with him now, he thought, he too would have been filled with distaste at the sweating multitude waiting for blood and pain. Instead the young man stood amidst the crowd and felt his heartbeat quicken, his excitement rise at the prospect of combat.

His pale eyes scanned the crowd, picking out the fat figure of Old Thom talking to a tall man in a red velvet cloak. The man was smiling. He turned from Thom and approached the colossal figure of Borcha. Druss saw the fighter's eyes widen, then the man laughed. Druss could not hear the sound above the chatter and noise about him, but he felt his anger grow. This was Borcha, one of Collan's men – perhaps one of those who had taken Rowena.

Old Thom returned through the crowd and led Druss to a fairly quiet corner. 'I've set events in motion,' he said. 'Now listen to me – don't try for the head. Men have broken their hands on that skull. He has a habit of dipping into punches so that the other man's knuckles strike bone. Go for the lower body. And watch his feet – he's a skilled kicker, lad . . . what's your name, by the way?'

'Druss.'

'Well, Druss, you've grabbed a bear by the balls this time. If he hurts you, don't try to hold on; he'll use that head on you, and cave in the bones of your face. Try backing away and covering up.'

'Let him try backing away,' snarled Druss.

'Ah, you're a cocky lad, for sure. But you've never faced a man like Borcha. He's like a living hammer.'

Druss chuckled. 'You really know how to lift a man's spirits. What odds did you find?'

'Fifteen to one. If you hold to your feet, you'll have seventy-five pieces of silver – plus your original ten.'

'Is that enough to buy a slave?'

'What would you want with a slave?'

'Is it enough?'

'Depends on the slave. Some girls fetch upwards of a hundred. You have someone in mind?'

Druss dipped into his pouch, removing the last four silver pieces. 'Wager these also.'

The old man took the money. 'I take it this is your entire wealth?'

'It is.'

'She must be a very special slave?'

'She's my wife. Collan's men took her.'

'Collan takes lots of women. Your wife's not a witch, is she?'

'What?' snarled Druss.

'No offence, lad. But Collan sold a witch woman to Kabuchek the Ventrian today. Five thousand silver pieces she brought.'

'No, she is not a witch. Just a mountain girl, sweet and gentle.'

'Ah well, a hundred should be enough,' said Thom. 'But first you have to win it. Have you ever been hit?'

'No. But a tree fell on me once.'

'Knock you out?'

'No. I was dazed for a while.'

'Well, Borcha will feel like a mountain fell on you. I hope you've the strength to withstand it.'

'We'll see, old man.'

'If you go down, roll under the ropes. Otherwise he'll stomp you.'

Druss smiled. 'I like you, old man. You don't honey the medicine, do you?'

'Does you no good unless it tastes bad,' replied Thom, with a crooked grin.

Borcha enjoyed the admiring glances from the crowd – fear and respect from the men and healthy lust from the women. He felt he had earned such silent accolades during the past five years. His blue eyes scanned the tiers and he picked out Mapek, the First Minister of Mashrapur, Bodasen the Ventrian envoy, and a dozen more notables from the Emir's government. He kept his face impassive as he gazed around the converted warehouse. It was well known that he never smiled, save in the sand circle when his opponent began to weaken under his iron fists.

He glanced at Grassin, watching the man move through a series of loosening exercises. He had to hold back his smile then. Others might believe Grassin was merely stretching tight muscles, but Borcha could read fear in the man's movements. He focused on the other fighters, staring at them. Few looked his way, and those who did cast fleeting glances, avoiding his eyes.

Losers, all of them, he thought.

He took a deep breath, filling his massive lungs. The air was hot and damp. Signalling to one of his aides, Borcha told the man to open the wide windows at either end of the warehouse. A second aide approached him. 'There is a yokel who wants to try a turn of the glass with you, Borcha.' The fighter was irritated and he surreptitiously studied the crowd. All eyes were on him. So the word was already out! He threw back his head and forced a laugh.

'Who is this man?'

'A stranger from the mountains. Youngster – around twenty, I'd say.'

'That explains his stupidity,' hissed Borcha. No man who had ever seen him fight would relish the prospect of four minutes in the sand circle with the champion of Mashrapur. But still he was annoyed.

Winning involved far more skills than with fists and feet, he knew. It was a complex mix of courage and heart, allied to the planting of the seeds of doubt in the minds of opponents. A man who believed his enemy was invincible had already lost, and Borcha had spent years building such a reputation.

No one in two years had dared to risk a turn of the glass with the champion.

Until now. Which threw up a second problem. Arena fights were without rules: a fighter could legitimately gouge out an opponent's eyes or, after downing him, stamp upon his neck. Deaths were rare, but not unknown, and many fighters were crippled for life. But Borcha would not be able to use his more deadly array of skills against an unknown youngster. It would suggest he feared the boy.

'They're offering fifteen to one against him surviving,' whispered the aide.

'Who is negotiating for him?'

'Old Thom.'

'How much has he wagered?'

'I'll find out.' The man moved away into the crowd.

The tournament organiser, a huge, obese merchant named Bilse, stepped into the sand circle. 'My friends,' he bellowed, his fat chins wobbling, 'welcome to the Blind Corsair. Tonight you will be privileged to witness the finest fist fighters in Mashrapur.'

Borcha closed his mind to the man's droning voice. He had heard it all before. Five years ago his mood had been different. His wife and son sick from dysentery, the young Borcha had finished his work on the docks and had run all the way to the Corsair to win ten silver pieces in a warm-up contest. To his surprise he had beaten his opponent, and had taken his place in the tournament. That night, after hammering six fighters to defeat, he had taken home sixty golden raq. He had arrived at their rooms triumphant, only to find his son dead and his wife comatose. The best doctor in Mashrapur was summoned. He had insisted Caria be removed to a hospital in the rich northern district – but only after Borcha had parted with all his hard-won gold. There Caria rallied for a while, only to be struck down with consumption.

The treatment over the next two years cost three hundred raq.

And still she died, her body ravaged by sickness.

Borcha's bitterness was colossal, and he unleashed it in every fight, focusing his hatred and his fury on the men who faced him.

He heard his name called and raised his right arm. The crowd cheered and clapped.

Now he had a house in the northern quarter, built of marble and the finest timber, with terracotta tiles on the roof. Twenty slaves were on hand to do his bidding, and his investments in slaves and silks brought him an income to rival any of the senior merchants. Yet still he fought, the demons of the past driving him on.

Bilse announced that the warm-up contest would begin and Borcha watched as Grassin stepped into the circle to take on a burly dock-worker. The bout lasted barely a few seconds, Grassin lifting the man from his feet with an uppercut. Borcha's aide approached him. 'They have wagered around nine silver pieces. Is it important?'

Borcha shook his head. Had there been large sums involved it would have indicated trickery of some kind, perhaps a foreign fighter drafted in, a tough man from another city, a bruiser unknown in Mashrapur. But no. This was merely stupidity and arrogance combined.

Bilse called his name and Borcha stepped into the circle. He tested the sand beneath his feet. Too thick and it made for clumsy movement, too thin and a fighter could slide and lose balance. It was well raked. Satisfied, Borcha turned his gaze on the young man who had entered the circle from the other side.

He was young and some inches shorter than Borcha, though his shoulders were enormous. His chest was thick, the pectoral muscles well developed, and his biceps were huge. Watching him move, Borcha saw that he was well balanced and lithe. His waist was thick, but carried little fat, and his neck was large and well protected by the powerful, swollen muscles of the trapezius. Borcha transferred his gaze to his opponent's face. Strong cheekbones and a good chin. The nose was wide and flat, the brows heavy. The champion looked into the challenger's eyes; they were pale, and they showed no fear. Indeed, thought Borcha, he looks as if he hates me.

Bilse introduced the young man as 'Druss from the lands of the Drenai'. The two fighters approached one another. Borcha towered over Druss. The champion held out his hands but Druss merely smiled and walked back to the ropes, turning to wait for the signal to begin.

The casual insult did not concern the champion. Lifting his hands into the orthodox fighting position, left arm extended and right fist held close to the cheek, he advanced on the young man. Druss surged forward, almost taking Borcha by surprise. But the champion was fast and sent a thudding left jab into the young man's face, following it with a stinging right cross that thundered against Druss's jaw. Borcha stepped back, allowing room for Druss to fall, but something exploded against the side of the champion. For a moment he thought a large rock had been hurled from the crowd, then he realised it was the fist of his opponent. Far from falling, the young man had taken the two punches and hit back with one of his own. Borcha reeled from the blow, then counter-attacked with a series of combination strikes that snapped Druss's head back. Yet still he came on. Borcha feinted a jab to the head, then swept an uppercut into the young man's belly, whereupon Druss snarled and threw a wild right. Borcha ducked under it, dipping just in time to meet a rising left uppercut. He managed to roll his head, the blow striking his cheek. Surging upright, he crashed an overhand right into Druss's face, splitting the skin above the man's left eye; then he hit him with a left.

Druss staggered back, thrown off balance, and Borcha moved in for the kill, but a hammer-blow hit him just under the heart and he felt a rib snap. Anger roared through him and he began to smash punches into the youngster's face and body – brutal, powerful blows that forced his opponent back towards the ropes. Another cut appeared, this time over Druss's right eye. The young man ducked and weaved, but more and more blows hammered home. Sensing victory, Borcha increased the ferocity of his attack and the pace of his punches. But Druss refused to go down and, ducking his head, he charged at Borcha. The champion side-stepped and threw a left that glanced from Druss's shoulder. The young man recovered his balance and Borcha stepped in. Druss wiped the blood from his eyes and advanced to meet him. The champion feinted with a left, but Druss ignored it and sent a right that swept under Borcha's guard and smashed into his injured ribs. The champion winced as pain lanced his side. A huge fist crashed against his chin and he felt a tooth snap; he responded with a left uppercut that lifted Druss to his toes and a right hook that almost felled the youngster. Druss hit him with another right to the ribs and Borcha was forced back. The two men began to circle one another, and only now did Borcha hear the baying of the crowd. They were cheering for Druss, just as five years before they had cheered for Borcha.

Druss attacked. Borcha threw a left that missed and a right that didn't. Druss rocked back on his heels, but advanced again. Borcha hit him three times, further opening the cuts that saw blood streaming into the young man's face. Almost blinded, Druss lashed out, one punch catching Borcha on the right bicep, numbing his arm, a second cracking against his brow. Blood seeped from the champion's face now, and a tremendous roar went up from the crowd.

Oblivious to the noise Borcha counter-attacked, driving Druss back across the circle, hitting him time and again with brutal hooks and jabs.

Then the horn sounded. The sandglass had run out. Borcha stepped back, but Druss attacked. Borcha grabbed him around the waist, pinning his arms and hauling him in close. 'It is over, boy,' he hissed. 'You won your wager.'

Druss jerked himself loose and shook his head, spraying blood to the sand. Then he lifted his hand and pointed at Borcha. 'You go to Collan,' he snarled, 'and you tell him that if anyone has harmed my wife I'll tear his head from his neck.'

Then the young man swung away and stalked from the circle.

Borcha turned and saw the other fighters watching him.

They were all willing to meet his eyes now . . . and Grassin was smiling.

Sieben entered the Tree of Bone just after midnight. There were still some hardened drinkers present, and the serving maids moved wearily among them. Sieben mounted the stairs to the gallery above and made his way to the room he shared with Druss. Just as he was about to open the door, he heard voices from within. Drawing his dagger, he threw open the door and leapt inside. Druss was sitting on one of the beds, his face bruised and swollen, the marks of rough stitches over both eyes. A dirt-streaked fat man was sitting on Sieben's bed and a slim, black-cloaked nobleman with a trident beard was standing by the window. As the poet entered the nobleman swung, a shining sabre hissing from its scabbard. The fat man screamed and dived from the bed, landing with a dull thud behind the seated Druss.

'You took your time, poet,' said the axeman.

Sieben gazed down at the point of the sabre which was motionless in the air some two inches from his throat. 'It didn't take you long to make new friends,' he said, with a forced smile. With great care he slipped the knife back into its sheath, and was relieved to see the nobleman return his sabre to its scabbard.

'This is Bodasen; he's a Ventrian,' said Druss. 'And the man on his knees behind me is Thom.'

The fat man rose, grinning sheepishly. 'Good to meet you, my lord,' he said, bowing.

'Who the Devil gave you those black eyes?' asked Sieben, moving forward to examine Druss's wounds.

'Nobody gave them to me. I had to fight for them.'

'He fought Borcha,' said Bodasen, with the faintest trace of an eastern accent. 'And a fine bout it was. Lasted a full turn of the glass.'

'Aye, it was something to see,' added Thom. 'Borcha didn't look none too pleased – especially when Druss cracked his rib! We all heard it. Wonderful, it was.'

'You fought Borcha?' whispered Sieben.

'To a standstill,' said the Ventrian. 'There were no surgeons present, so I assisted with the stitching. You are the poet Sieben, are you not?'

'Yes. Do I know you, my friend?'

'I saw you perform once in Drenan, and in Ventria I read your saga of Waylander. Wonderfully inventive.'

'Thank you. Much needed to be invention since little is known of him. I did not know that the book had travelled so far. Only fifty copies were made.'

'My Emperor acquired one on his travels, bound in leather and embossed with gold leaf. The script is very fine.'

544

'There were five of those,' said Sieben. 'Twenty raq each. Beautiful works.'

Bodasen chuckled. 'My Emperor paid six hundred for it.'

Sieben sighed and sat down on the bed. 'Ah well, better the fame than gold, eh? So tell me, Druss, what made you fight Borcha?'

'I earned a hundred silver pieces. Now I shall buy Rowena. Did you find out where she is held?'

'No, my friend. Collan has sold only one woman recently. A Seer. He must be keeping Rowena for himself.'

'Then I shall kill him and take her – and to Hell with the law of Mashrapur.'

'If I may,' said Bodasen, 'I think I can help. I am acquainted with this Collan. It may be that I can secure the release of your lady – without bloodshed.'

Sieben said nothing, but he noted the concern in the Ventrian's dark eyes.

'I'll not wait much longer,' said Druss. 'Can you see him tomorrow?'

'Of course. You will be here?'

'I'll wait for your word,' promised Druss.

'Very well. I bid you all good night,' said Bodasen, with a short bow.

After he had left Old Thom also made for the door. 'Well, lad, it were quite a night. If you decide to fight again I'd be honoured to make the arrangements.'

'No more for me,' said Druss. 'I'd sooner have trees fall on me than that man again.'

Thom shook his head. 'I wish that I'd had more faith,' he said. 'I only bet one silver piece of my share.' He chuckled and spread his hands. 'Ah well, that is life, I suppose.' His smile faded. 'A word of warning, Druss. Collan has many friends here. And there are those who will slit a man's throat for the price of a jug of ale. Walk with care.' He turned and left the room.

There was a jug of wine on the small table and Sieben filled a clay goblet and sat. 'You are a curious fellow, to be sure,' he said, grinning. 'But at least Borcha has improved your looks. I think your nose is broken.'

'I think you are right,' said Druss. 'So tell me of your day.'

'I visited four well-known slave traders. Collan brought no women with him to the slave markets. The story of your attack on Harib Ka is known everywhere. Some of the men who survived have now joined Collan, and they speak of you as a demon. But it is a mystery, Druss. I don't know where she could be – unless at his home.'

The wound above Druss's right eye began to seep blood. Sieben found a cloth and offered it to the axeman. Druss waved it away. 'It will seal. Forget about it.'

'By the gods, Druss, you must be in agony. Your face is swollen, your eyes black.'

'Pain lets you know you're alive,' said Druss. 'Did you spend your silver pennies on the whore?'

Sieben chuckled. 'Yes. She was very good – told me I was the best love-maker she had ever known.'

'There's a surprise,' said Druss and Sieben laughed.

'Yes – but it's nice to hear.' He sipped his wine, then stood and gathered his belongings.

'Where are you going?' asked Druss.

'Not I . . . we. We'll move rooms.'

'I like it here.'

'Yes, it is quaint. But we need to sleep and – convivial as they both were – I see no reason to trust men I do not know. Collan will send killers after you, Druss. Bodasen may be in his employ, and as for the walking lice-sack who just left I think he'd sell his mother for a copper farthing. So trust me, and let's move.'

'I liked them both – but you are right. I do need sleep.'

Sieben stepped outside and called to a tavern maid, slipping her a silver piece and asking for their move to be kept secret – even from the landlord. She slipped the coin into the pocket of her leather apron and took the two men to the far end of the gallery. The new room was larger than the first, boasting three beds and two lanterns. A fire had been laid in the hearth, but it was unlit and the room was cold.

When the maid had departed Sieben lit the fire and sat beside it, watching the flames lick at the tinder. Druss pulled off his boots and jerkin and stretched out on the widest of the beds. Within moments he was asleep, his axe on the floor beside the bed.

Sieben lifted the baldric of knives from his shoulder and hooked it over the back of the chair. The fire blazed more brightly and he added several thick chunks of wood from the log basket beside the hearth. As the hours passed, all sounds from the inn below faded, and only the crackling of burning wood disturbed the silence. Sieben was tired, but he did not sleep.

Then he heard the sounds of men upon the stairs, stealthy footfalls. Drawing one of his knives he moved to the door, opening it a fraction and peering out. At the other end of the gallery some seven men were crowding around the door of their previous quarters; the landlord was with them. The door was wrenched open and the men surged inside, but moments later they returned. One of the newcomers took hold of the landlord by his shirt and pushed him against the wall. The frightened man's voice rose, and Sieben could just make out some of his words: 'They were . . . honestly . . . lives of my children . . . they

. . . without paying . . .' Sieben watched as the man was hurled to the floor. The would-be assassins then trooped down the gallery stairs and out into the night.

Pushing shut the door, Sieben returned to the fire.

And slept.

6

Borcha sat quietly while Collan berated the men he had sent in search of Druss. They stood shamefaced before him, heads down. 'How long have you been with me, Kotis?' he asked one of them, his voice low and thick with menace.

'Six years,' answered the man at the centre of the group, a tall, wide-shouldered bearded fist-fighter. Borcha remembered his destruction of this man; it had taken no more than a minute.

'Six years,' echoed Collan. 'And in that time have you seen other men fall foul of me?'

'Aye, I have. But we got the information from Old Thom. He swore they were staying in the Tree of Bone – and so they were. But they went into hiding after the fight with Borcha. We've men still looking; they won't be hard to find tomorrow.'

'You're right,' said Collan. 'They won't be hard to find; they'll be coming here!'

'You could give his wife back,' offered Bodasen, who was lounging on a couch on the far side of the room.

'I don't *give women back*. I take them! Anyway, I don't know which farm wench he's talking about. Most of those we took were freed when the madman attacked the camp. I expect his wife took a welcome opportunity to escape from his clutches.'

'He's not a man I'd want hunting me,' said Borcha. 'I've never hit anyone so hard – and seen them stay on their feet.'

'Get back out on the streets, all of you. Scour the inns and taverns near the docks. They won't be far. And understand this, Kotis, if he does walk into my home tomorrow I'll kill you!'

The men shuffled out and Borcha leaned back on the couch, suppressing a groan as his injured rib lanced pain into his side. He had been forced to withdraw from the tournament, and that hurt his pride. Yet he felt a grudging admiration for the young fighter; he, too, would have taken on an army for Caria. 'You know what I think?' he offered.

547

'What?' snapped Collan.

'I think she's the witch you sold to Kabuchek. What was her name?'

'Rowena.'

'Did you rape her?'

'I didn't touch her,' lied Collan. 'And anyway, I've sold her to Kabuchek. He gave me five thousand in silver – just like that. I should have asked for ten.'

'I think you should see the Old Woman,' advised Borcha.

'I don't need a prophet to tell me how to deal with one country bumpkin and an axe. Now to business.' He turned to Bodasen. 'It is too early to have received word on our demands, so why are you here tonight?'

The Ventrian smiled, his teeth startlingly white against the black trident beard. 'I came because I told the young fighter that we were acquainted. I said I might be able to secure the release of his wife. But if you have already sold her, then I have wasted my time.'

'What concern is it of yours?'

Bodasen rose and flung his black cloak around his shoulders. 'I am a soldier, Collan – as you once were. And I know men. You should have seen his fight with Borcha. It wasn't pretty, it was brutal and almost terrifying. You are not dealing with a country bumpkin, you are facing a terrible killer. I don't believe you have the men to stop him.'

'Why should you care?'

'Ventria needs the Free Traders and you are my link to them. I don't want to see you dead just yet.'

'I am a fighter too, Bodasen,' said Collan.

'Indeed you are, Drenai. But let us review what we know. Harib Ka, according to those of his men who survived the raid, sent six men into the woods. They did not return. I spoke to Druss tonight and he told me he killed them. I believe him. Then he attacked a camp where forty armed men were based. The men ran away. Now he has fought Borcha, whom most men, including myself, believed to be invincible. The rabble you just sent out will have no chance against him.'

'True,' admitted Collan, 'but as soon as he kills them the City Watch will take him. And I have only four more days to spend here; then I sail for the Free Trading ports. However, I take it you have some advice to offer?'

'Indeed I do. Get the woman back from Kabuchek and deliver her to Druss. Buy her or steal her – but do it, Collan.'

With a short, perfunctory bow the Ventrian officer left the room.

'I'd listen to him if I were you,' advised Borcha.

'Not you as well!' stormed Collan. 'By the gods, did he scramble your brains tonight? You and I both know what keeps us at the top of this filthy pile. Fear. Awe. Sometimes sheer terror. Where would my reputation be if I gave back a stolen woman?'

'You are quite right,' said Borcha, rising, 'but a reputation can be rebuilt. A life is something else. He said he'd tear off your head and he's a man who could do just that.'

'I never thought to see you running scared, my friend. I thought you were impervious to fear.'

Borcha smiled. 'I am strong, Collan. I use my reputation because it makes it easier to win but I don't *live* it. If I were to be in the path of a charging bull, then I would step aside, or turn and run, or climb a tree. A strong man should always know his limitations.'

'Well, he's helped you know yours, my friend,' said Collan, with a sneer.

Borcha smiled and shook his head. He left Collan's house and wandered through the northern streets. They were wider here, and lined with trees. Officers of the Watch marched by him, the captain saluting as he recognised the champion.

Former champion, thought Borcha. Now it was Grassin who would win the accolades.

Until next year. 'I'll be back,' whispered Borcha. 'I have to. It is all I have.'

Sieben floated to consciousness through layers of dreams. He was drifting on a blue lake, yet his body was dry; he was standing on an island of flowers, but could not feel the earth beneath his feet; he was lying on a satin bed, beside a statue of marble. At his touch she became flesh, but remained cold.

He opened his eyes and the dreams whispered away from his memory. Druss was still asleep. Sieben rose from the chair and stretched his back, then he gazed down on the sleeping warrior. The stitches on Druss's brows were tight and puckered, dried blood had stained both eyelids and his nose was swollen and discoloured. Yet despite the wounds his face radiated strength and Sieben felt chilled by the almost inhuman power of the youth.

Druss groaned and opened his eyes.

'How are you feeling this morning?' asked the poet.

'Like a horse galloped over my face,' answered Druss, rolling from the bed and pouring himself a goblet of water. Someone tapped at the door.

Sieben rose from his chair and drew a knife from its sheath. 'Who is it?'

'It is me, sir,' came the voice of the tavern-maid. 'There is a man to see you; he is downstairs.'

Sieben opened the door and the maid curtsied. 'Do you know him?' asked Sieben.

'He is the Ventrian gentleman who was here last night, sir.'

'Is he alone?'

'Yes, sir.'

'Send him up,' ordered Sieben. While they were waiting he told Druss about the men who had come searching for them the night before.

'You should have woken me,' said Druss.

'I thought we could do without a scene of carnage,' Sieben replied.

Bodasen entered and immediately crossed to where Druss stood by the window. He leaned in and examined the stitches on the axeman's eyebrows. 'They've held well,' said Bodasen, with a smile.

'What news?' asked Druss.

The Ventrian removed his black cloak and draped it over a chair. 'Last night Collan had men scouring the city for you. Assassins. But today he has come to his senses. This morning he sent a man to me with a message for you. He has decided to return your wife to you.'

'Good. When and where.'

'There is a quay about a half-mile west of here. He will meet you there tonight, one hour after dusk, and he will have Rowena with him. But he is a worried man, Druss; he doesn't want to die.'

'I'll not kill him,' promised Druss.

'He wants you to come alone – and unarmed.'

'Madness!' stormed Sieben. 'Does he think he is dealing with fools?'

'Whatever else he may be,' said Bodasen, 'he is still a Drenai noble. His word must be accepted.'

'Not by me,' hissed Sieben. 'He is a murdering renegade who has become rich by dealing in the misery of others. Drenai noble indeed!'

'I'll go,' said Druss. 'What other choices are there?'

'It is a trap, Druss. There is no honour in men like Collan. He'll be there, right enough – with a dozen or so killers.'

'They won't stop me,' insisted the axeman, his pale eyes gleaming.

'A knife through the throat can stop anyone.'

Bodasen stepped forward and laid his hand on Druss's shoulder. 'Collan assured me this was an honest trade. I would not have brought this message had I believed it to be false.'

Druss nodded and smiled. 'I believe you,' he said.

'How did you find us?' enquired Sieben.

'This is where you said you would be,' answered Bodasen.

'Exactly where will this meeting take place?' asked Druss. Bodasen gave directions and then bade them farewell.

When he had left Sieben turned on the young axeman. 'You truly believe him?'

'Of course. He is a Ventrian gentleman. My father told me they are the world's worst traders because they have a hatred of lies and deceit. They are reared that way.'

550

'Collan isn't a Ventrian,' Sieben pointed out.

'No,' agreed Druss, his expression grim. 'No, he is not. He is everything you described. And you are quite right, poet. It will be a trap.'

'And yet you will still go?'

'As I have already said, there are no other choices. But you don't have to be there. You owe Shadak – not me.'

Sieben smiled. 'You are quite right, old horse. So how shall we play this little game?'

An hour before dusk Collan sat in an upper room overlooking the quay. The bearded Kotis stood beside him. 'Is everyone in place?' asked the Drenai swordsman.

'Aye. Two crossbowmen, and six knife-fighters. Is Borcha coming?' Collan's handsome face darkened. 'No.'

'He would make a difference,' observed Kotis.

'Why?' snapped Collan. 'He's already taken one beating from the peasant!'

'You really think he will come alone and unarmed?'

'Bodasen believes he will.'

'Gods, what a fool!'

Collan laughed. 'The world is full of fools, Kotis. That is how we grow rich.' He leaned out of the window and gazed down on the quayside. Several whores were lounging in doorways, and two beggars were accosting passers-by. A drunken dock-worker staggered from a tavern, collided with a wall and slid to the ground by a mooring post. He tried to rise, but as he lifted his work-sack he fell back, and then curled up on the stone and went to sleep. What a city, thought Collan! What a wonderful city. A whore moved to the sleeping man and dipped her fingers expertly into his money-pouch.

Collan stepped back from the window and drew his sabre. Taking a whetstone, he sharpened the edge. He had no intention of facing the peasant, but a man could never be too careful.

Kotis poured a goblet of cheap wine. 'Don't drink too much of that,' warned Collan. 'Even unarmed, the man can fight.'

'He won't fight so well with a crossbow bolt through the heart.'

Collan sat down in a padded leather chair and stretched out his long legs. 'In a few days we'll be rich, Kotis. Ventrian gold – enough to fill this squalid room. Then we'll sail to Naashan and buy a palace. Maybe more than one.'

'You think the pirates will aid Ventria?' asked Kotis.

'No, they've already taken Naashanite gold. Ventria is finished.'

'Then we keep Bodasen's money?'

'Of course. As I said, the world is full of fools. You know, I used to be one of them. I had dreams, I wasted half my life on them. Chivalry, gallantry. My father fed me the concepts until my mind was awash with dreams of knighthood and I truly believed it all.' Collan chuckled. 'Incredible! But I learnt the error of my ways. I became wise to the way of the world.'

'You are in good humour today,' observed Kotis. 'You'll have to kill Bodasen too. He won't be pleased when he learns he's been tricked.'

'Him I'll fight,' said Collan. 'Ventrians! A pox on them! They think they're better than everyone else. Bodasen more than most; he thinks he's a swordsman. We'll see. I'll cut him a piece at a time, a nick here and a slash there. He'll suffer well enough. I'll break his pride before I kill him.'

'He may be better than you,' ventured Kotis.

'No one is better than me, with sabre or short blade.'

'They say Shadak is one of the best who ever lived.'

'Shadak is an old man!' stormed Collan, surging to his feet, 'and even at his best he could not have faced me.'

Kotis paled and began to stammer out an apology. 'Be silent!' snapped Collan. 'Get outside and check that the men are in position.'

As Kotis backed from the room, Collan poured himself a goblet of wine and sat down by the window. Shadak! Always Shadak. What was it about the man that inspired men to revere him? What had he ever done? Shema's balls, I've killed twice as many swordsmen as the old man! But do they sing songs about Collan? No.

One day I'll hunt him out, he promised himself. Somewhere in public view, where men can see the great Shadak humbled. He glanced out of the window. The sun was setting, turning the sea to fire.

Soon the peasant would arrive. Soon the enjoyment would begin.

Druss approached the quayside. There was a ship moored at the far end; dock-workers were untying the mooring ropes and hurling them to the decks, while aloft sailors were unfurling the great square of the main-mast. Gulls swooped above the vessel, their wings silver in the moonlight.

The young warrior glanced along the quayside, which was almost deserted save for two whores and a sleeping man. He scanned the buildings, but all the windows were closed. He could taste fear in his mouth, not for his own safety but for Rowena's should Collan kill him. A life of slavery beckoned for her, and Druss could not bear that.

The wounds above his eyes were stinging, and a dull, thudding headache reminded him of the bout with Borcha. He hawked and spat, then made for the quay. From the shadows to his right a man moved.

'Druss!' came a low voice. He stopped and turned his head to see Old Thom standing just inside the mouth of a dark alleyway.

'What do you want?' asked Druss.

'They're waiting for you, lad. There's nine of them. Go back!'

'I cannot. They have my wife.'

'Damn you, boy, you're going to die.'

'We'll see.'

'Listen to me. Two have crossbows. Keep close to the wall on the right. The bowmen are in upper rooms; they'll not be able to sight their weapons if you keep to the wall.'

'I'll do that,' said Druss. 'Thank you, old man.'

Thom faded back into the shadows and was gone. Drawing in a deep breath, Druss moved on to the quay. Above and ahead of him he saw a window open. Altering his line, he moved in towards the walls of the moonlit buildings.

'Where are you, Collan?' he shouted.

Armed men moved out of the shadows and he saw the tall, handsome figure of Collan among them. Druss walked forward. 'Where is my wife?' he called.

'That's the beauty of it,' answered Collan, pointing at the ship. 'She's on board – sold to the merchant Kapuchek, who is even now sailing for his home in Ventria. Maybe she will even see you die!'

'In your dreams!' snarled Druss as he charged the waiting men. Behind them the drunken dock-worker suddenly rose, two knives in his hands. One blade flashed by Collan's head, burying itself to the hilt in Kotis's neck.

A dagger swept towards Druss's belly, but he brushed the attacker's arm aside and delivered a bone-crunching blow to the man's chin, spinning him into the path of the warriors behind him. A knife plunged into Druss's back. Twisting, he grabbed the wielder by the throat and groin and hurled him into the remaining men.

Sieben pulled Snaga from the work-sack and threw it through the air. Druss caught the weapon smoothly. Moonlight glittered from the terrible blades and the attackers scattered and ran.

Druss ran towards the ship, which was gliding slowly away from the quayside.

'Rowena!' he yelled. Something struck him in the back and he staggered, then fell to his knees. He saw Sieben run forward. The poet's arm went back, then swept down. Druss half turned to see a crossbowman outlined against a window-frame; the man dropped his bow, then tumbled from the window with a knife embedded in his eye.

Sieben knelt alongside Druss. 'Lie still,' he said. 'You've a bolt in your back!'

'Get away from me!' shouted Druss, levering himself to his feet. 'Rowena!'

He stumbled forward but the ship was moving away from the quay more swiftly now, the wind catching the sail. Druss could feel blood from his wounds streaming down his back and pooling above his belt. A terrible lethargy swept over him and he fell again.

Sieben came alongside. 'We must get you to a surgeon,' he heard Sieben say. Then the poet's voice receded away from him, and a great roaring filled his ears. Straining his eyes, he saw the ship angle towards the east, the great sail filling.

'Rowena!' he shouted. 'Rowena!' The stone of the quay was cold against his face, and the distant cries of the gulls mocked his anguish. Pain flowed through him as he struggled to rise. . . .

And fell from the edge of the world.

Collan raced along the quay, then glanced back. He saw the giant warrior down, his companion kneeling beside him. Halting his flight, he sat down on a mooring-post to recover his breath. It was unbelievable! Unarmed, the giant had attacked armed men, scattering them. Borcha was right. The charging bull analogy had been very perceptive. Tomorrow Collan would move to a hiding place in the south of the city and then, as Borcha had advised, seek out the old woman. That was the answer. Pay her to cast a spell, or send a demon, or supply poison. Anything.

Collan rose – and saw a dark figure standing in the moon shadows by the wall. The man was watching him. 'What are you staring at?' he said.

The shadowy figure moved towards him, moonlight bathing his face. He wore a tunic shirt of soft black leather, and two short swords were scabbarded at his hips. His hair was black and long, and tied in a pony-tail. 'Do I know you?' asked Collan.

'You will, renegade,' said the man, drawing his right-hand sword.

'You've chosen the wrong man to rob,' Collan told him. His sabre came up and he slashed the air to left and right, loosening his wrist.

'I'm not here to rob you, Collan,' said the man, advancing. 'I'm here to kill you.'

Collan waited until his opponent was within a few paces and then he leapt forward, lunging his sabre towards the man's chest. There was a clash of steel as their blades met. Collan's sabre was parried and a lightning riposte swept at the swordsman's throat. Collan jumped back, the point of the sword missing his eye by less than an inch. 'You are swift, my friend. I underestimated you.'

'It happens,' said the man.

Collan attacked again, this time with a series of sweeps and thrusts aiming for neck and belly. Their blades glittered in the moonlight and all around them windows were opened as the discordant clashing of steel echoed along the quay. Whores leaned out over the window-sills, yelling encouragement; beggars appeared from alleyways; a nearby tavern emptied and a crowd gathered in a large circle around the duelling men. Collan was enjoying himself. His attacks were forcing his opponent back, and he had now taken the measure of the man. The stranger was fast and lithe, cool under pressure; but he was no longer young and Collan could sense he was tiring. At first he had made several counter-attacks, but these were fewer now as he desperately fended off the younger man's blade. Collan feinted a cut, then rolled, his wrist lunging forward on to his right foot. The stranger blocked too late, the point of the sabre piercing the man's left shoulder. Collan leapt back, his blade sliding clear. 'Almost time to die, old man,' said Collan.

'Yes. How does it feel?' countered his opponent.

Collan laughed. 'You have nerve, I'll say that for you. Before I kill you, will you tell me why you are hunting me? A wronged wife, perhaps? A despoiled daughter? Or are you a hired assassin?'

'I am Shadak,' said the man.

Collan grinned. 'So the night is not a total waste.' He glanced at the crowd. 'The great Shadak!' he said, his voice rising. 'This is the famed hunter, the mighty swordsman. See him bleed? Well, my friends, you can tell your children how you saw him die! How Collan slew the man of legend.'

He advanced on the waiting Shadak, then raised his sabre in a mock salute. 'I have enjoyed this duel, old man,' he said, 'but now it is time to end it.' Even as he spoke he leapt, sending a fast reverse cut towards Shadak's right side. As his opponent parried Collan rolled his wrist, the sabre rolling over the blocking blade and sweeping up towards Shadak's unprotected neck. It was the classic killing stroke, and one Collan had employed many times, but Shadak swayed to his left, the sabre cutting into his right shoulder. Collan felt a searing pain in his belly and glanced down. Horrified, he saw Shadak's sword jutting there.

'Burn in Hell!' hissed Shadak, wrenching the blade clear. Collan screamed and fell to his knees, his sabre clattering against the stones of the quay. He could feel his heart hammering and agony, red-hot acid pain, scorched through him. He cried out: 'Help me!'

The crowd was silent now. Collan fell face down on the stones. 'I can't be dying,' he thought. 'Not me. Not Collan.'

The pain receded, replaced by a soothing warmth that stole across his tortured mind. He opened his eyes and could see his sabre glinting on the stones just ahead. He reached out for it, his fingers touching the hilt.

'I can still win!' he told himself. 'I can. . . .'

Shadak sheathed his sword and stared down at the dead man. Already the beggars were around him, pulling at his boots and ripping at his belt. Shadak turned away and pushed through the crowd.

He saw Sieben kneeling beside the still figure of Druss, and his heart sank. Moving more swiftly, he came alongside the body and knelt down.

'He's dead,' said Sieben.

'In your . . . dreams,' hissed Druss. 'Get me to my feet.'

Shadak chuckled. 'Some men take a sight of killing,' he told the poet. The two men hauled Druss upright.

'She's out there,' said Druss, staring at the ship that was slowly shrinking against the distant horizon.

'I know, my friend,' said Shadak softly. 'But we'll find her. Now let's get you to a surgeon.'

Book Two

The Demon in the Axe

Prologue

The ship glided from the harbour, the early evening swell rippling against the hull. Rowena stood on the aft deck, the tiny figure of Pudri beside her. Above them, unnoticed on the raised tiller deck, stood the Ventrian merchant Kabuchek. Tall and cadaverously thin, he stared at the dock. He had seen Collan cut down by an unknown swordsman, and had watched the giant Drenai warrior battle his way through Collan's men. Interesting, he thought, what men will do for love.

His thoughts flew back to his youth in Varsipis and his desire for the young maiden Harenini. Did I love her then, he wondered? Or has time added colours to the otherwise grey days of youth?

The ship lifted on the swell as the vessel approached the harbour mouth and the surging tides beyond. Kabuchek glanced down at the girl; Collan had sold her cheaply. Five thousand pieces of silver for a talent such as hers? Ludicrous. He had been prepared for a charlatan, or a clever trickster. But she had taken his hand, looked into his eyes and said a single word: '*Harenini*'. Kabuchek had kept the shock from his face. He had not heard her name in twenty-five years, and certainly there was no way that the pirate Collan could have known of his juvenile infatuation. Though already convinced of her talents, Kabuchek asked many questions until finally he turned to Collan. 'It appears she has a modicum of talent,' he said. 'What price are you asking?'

'Five thousand.'

Kabuchek swung to his servant, the eunuch Pudri. 'Pay him,' he said, concealing the smile of triumph and contenting himself with the tormented look which appeared on Collan's face. 'I will take her to the ship myself.'

Now, judging by how close the axeman had come, he congratulated himself upon his shrewdness. He heard Pudri's gentle voice speaking to the girl.

'I pray your husband is not dead,' said Pudri. Kabuchek glanced back at the dock and saw two Drenai warriors were kneeling beside the still figure of the axeman.

'He will live,' said Rowena, tears filling her eyes. 'And he will follow me.'

If he does, thought Kabuchek, I will have him slain.

'He has a great love for you, *Pahtai*,' said Pudri soothingly. 'So it should be between husband and wife. It rarely happens that way, however. I myself have had three wives – and none of them loved me. But then a eunuch is not the ideal mate.'

The girl watched the tiny figures on the dock until the ship had slipped out of the harbour and the lights of Mashrapur became distant twinkling candles. She sighed and sank down on the rail seat, her head bowed, tears spilling from her eyes.

Pudri sat beside her, his slender arm on her shoulders. 'Yes,' he whispered, 'tears are good. Very good.' Patting her back as if she were a small child, he sat beside her and whispered meaningless platitudes.

Kabuchek climbed down the deck steps and approached them. 'Bring her to my cabin,' he ordered Pudri.

Rowena glanced up at the harsh face of her new master. His nose was long and hooked, like the beak of an eagle, and his skin was darker than any she had seen, almost black. His eyes, however, were a bright blue beneath thick brows. Beside her Pudri stood, helping her to her feet, and together they followed the Ventrian merchant down the steps to the aft cabin. Lanterns were lit here, hanging on bronze hooks from low oak beams.

Kabuchek sat down behind a desk of polished mahogany. 'Cast the runes for the voyage,' he ordered Rowena.

'I do not cast runes,' she said. 'I would not know how.'

He waved his hand dismissively. 'Do whatever it is you do, woman. The sea is a treacherous mistress and I need to know how the voyage will be.'

Rowena sat opposite him. 'Give me your hand,' she said. Leaning forward, he struck her face with his open palm. It was not a heavy blow, but it stung the skin.

'You will address me always as *master*,' he said, without any display of anger. His bright blue eyes scrutinised her face for any sign of anger or defiance, but found himself gazing into calm hazel eyes which appeared to be appraising him. Curiously he felt like apologising for the blow, which was a ridiculous thought. It was not intended to hurt, being merely a swift method of establishing authority – ownership. He cleared his throat. 'I expect you to learn swiftly the ways of Ventrian households. You will be well cared for and well fed; your quarters will be comfortable and warm in winter, cool in summer. But you are a slave: understand that. I own you. You are property. Do you understand this?'

'I understand . . . *master*,' said the girl. The title was said with just a touch of emphasis, but without insolence.

'Very well. Then let us move on to more important matters.' He extended his hand.

Rowena reached out and touched his open palm. At first she could see only the details of his recent past, his agreement with the traitors who had slain the Ventrian Emperor, one of them a hawk-faced man. Kabuchek was kneeling before him and there was blood on the man's sleeve. A name whispered into her mind – Shabag.

'What's that you say?' hissed Kabuchek.

Rowena blinked, then realised she must have spoken the name. 'I see a tall man with blood on his sleeve. You are kneeling before him . . .'

'The future, girl! Not the past.' From the decks above came a great flapping as if some giant flying beast was descending from the sky. Rowena was startled. 'It is just the mainsail,' said Kabuchek. 'Concentrate, girl!'

Closing her eyes, Rowena allowed her mind to drift. She could see the ship now from above, floating on a clear sea beneath a sky of brilliant blue. Then another ship hove into sight, a trireme, its three banks of oars sending up a white spray as it sheared through the waves towards them. Rowena floated closer . . . closer. Armed men filled the trireme's deck.

Silver-grey forms swam around the trireme – great fish, twenty feet long, with fins like spear points cutting through the water. Rowena watched as the two ships crashed together, saw men falling into the water and the sleek grey fish rising up towards them. Blood billowed into the sea, and she saw the jagged teeth in the mouths of the fish, saw them rend and tear and dismember the helpless sailors thrashing in the water.

The battle on the ship's deck was short and brutal. She saw herself and Pudri, and the tall form of Kabuchek clambering over the aft rail and leaping out into the waves.

The killer fish circled them – then moved in.

Rowena could watch no more and, jerking her mind to the present, she opened her eyes.

'Well, what did you see?' asked Kabuchek.

'A black-sailed trireme, master.'

'Earin Shad,' whispered Pudri, his face pale, his eyes fearful.

'Do we escape him?' asked Kabuchek.

'Yes,' said Rowena, her voice dull, her thoughts full of despair, 'we escape Earin Shad.'

'Good. I am well satisfied,' announced Kabuchek. He glanced at Pudri. 'Take her to her cabin and give her some food. She is looking pale.'

Pudri led Rowena back along the narrow corridor to a small door. Pushing it open, he stepped inside. 'The bed is very small, but you are not large. I think it will suffice, *Pahtai*.' Rowena nodded dumbly and sat.

'You saw more than you told the master,' he said.

'Yes. There were fish, huge fish, dark with terrible teeth.'

'Sharks,' said Pudri, sitting beside her.

'This ship will be sunk,' she told him. 'And you and I, and Kabuchek, will leap into the sea, where the sharks will be waiting.'

1

Sieben sat in an outer room, sunlight slanting through the shuttered window at his back. He could hear low voices from the room beyond – a man's deep, pleading tones, and the harsh responses from the Old Woman. Muffled by the thick walls of stone and the oak door, the words were lost – which was just as well, since Sieben had no wish to hear the conversation. The Old Woman had many clients; most seeking the murder of rivals – at least, according to the whispered gossip he had heard.

He closed his ears to the voices and concentrated instead on the shafts of light and the gleaming dust motes dancing within them. The room was bare of ornament save for the three seats of plain, unfinished wood. They were not even well made and Sieben guessed they had been bought in the southern quarter, where the poor spent what little money they had.

Idly he swept his hand through a shaft of light. The dust scattered and swirled.

The oak door opened and a middle-aged man emerged. Seeing Sieben, he swiftly turned his face away and hurried from the house. The poet rose and moved towards the open door. The room beyond was scarcely better furnished than the waiting area. There was a broad table with ill-fitting joints, two hard wood chairs and a single shutter window. No light shone through the slats and Sieben saw that old cloths had been wedged between them.

'A curtain would have been sufficient to block the light,' he said, forcing a lightness of tone he did not feel.

The Old Woman did not smile, her face impassive in the light of the red-glassed lantern on the table before her.

'Sit,' she said.

He did so, and tried to stop himself from considering her awesome ugliness. Her teeth were multi-coloured – green, grey and the brown of rotting vegetation. Her eyes were rheumy, and a cataract had formed in the left. She was wearing a loose-fitting gown of faded red, and a gold talisman was partially hidden in the wrinkled folds of her neck.

'Put the gold upon the table,' she said. He lifted a single gold raq from the pouch at his side and slid it towards her. Making no move to pick up the coin, she looked into his face. 'What do you require of me?' she asked him.

'I have a friend who is dying.'

'The young axeman.'

'Yes. The surgeons have done all they can, but there is poison within his lungs, and the knife wound in his lower back will not heal.'

'You have something of his with you?'

Sieben nodded and pulled the silver-knuckled gauntlet from his belt. She took it from his hand and sat in silence, running the calloused skin of her thumb across the leather and metal. 'The surgeon is Calvar Syn,' she said. 'What does he say?'

'Only that Druss should already be dead. The poison in his system is spreading; they are forcing liquids into him, but his weight is falling away and he has not opened his eyes in four days.'

'What would you have me do?'

Sieben shrugged. 'It is said you are very skilled in herbs. I thought you might save him.'

She laughed suddenly, the sound dry and harsh. 'My herbs do not usually prolong life, Sieben.' Laying the gauntlet upon the table, she leaned back in her chair. 'He suffers,' she said. 'He has lost his lady, and his will to live is fading. Without the will, there is no hope.'

'There is nothing you can do?'

'About his will? No. But his lady is on board a ship bound for Ventria and she is safe – for the moment. But the war sweeps on and who can say what will become of a slave-girl if she reaches that battle-torn continent? Go back to the hospital. Take your friend to the house Shadak is preparing for you.'

'He will die, then?'

She smiled, and Sieben tore his eyes from the sudden show of rotting teeth. 'Perhaps . . . Place him in a room where the sunlight enters in the morning, and lay his axe upon his bed, his fingers upon the hilt.' Her hand snaked across the table, and the gold raq vanished into her palm.

'That is all you can tell me for an ounce of gold?'

'It is all you need to know. Place his hand upon the hilt.'

Sieben rose. 'I had expected more.'

'Life is full of disappointments, Sieben.'

He moved to the door, but her voice stopped him. 'Do not touch the blades,' she warned.

'What?'

'Carry the weapon with care.'

Shaking his head, he left the house. The sun was hidden now behind dark clouds, and rain began to fall.

Druss was sitting alone and exhausted upon a grim mountainside, the sky above him grey and forlorn, the earth around him arid and dry. He gazed up at the towering peaks so far above him and levered himself to his feet.

His legs were unsteady, and he had been climbing for so long that all sense of time had vanished. All he knew was that Rowena waited on the topmost peak, and he must find her. Some twenty paces ahead was a jutting finger of rock and Druss set off towards it, forcing his aching limbs to push his weary body on and up. Blood was gushing from the wounds in his back, making the ground treacherous around his feet. He fell. Then he crawled.

It seemed that hours had passed.

He looked up. The jutting finger of rock was now forty paces from him.

Despair came fleetingly, but was washed away on a tidal wave of rage. He crawled on. Ever on.

'I won't give up,' he hissed. 'Ever.'

Something cold touched his hand, his fingers closing around an object of steel. And he heard a voice. 'I am back, my brother.'

Something in the words chilled him. He gazed down at the silver axe – and felt his wounds heal, his strength flooding back into his frame.

Rising smoothly, he looked up at the mountain.

It was merely a hill.

Swiftly he strode to the top. And woke.

Calvar Syn patted Druss's back. 'Put on your shirt, young man,' he said. 'The wounds have finally healed. There is a little pus, but the blood is fresh and the scab contains no corruption. I congratulate you on your strength.'

Druss nodded, but did not reply. Slowly and with care he pulled on his shirt of grey wool, then leaned back exhausted on the bed. Calvar Syn reached out, gently pressing his index finger to the pulse point on the young man's throat. The beat was erratic and fast, but this was to be expected after such a long infection. 'Take a deep breath,' ordered the surgeon and Druss obeyed. 'The right lung is still not operating at full efficiency; but it will. I want you to move out into the garden. Enjoy the sunshine and the sea air.'

The surgeon rose and left the room, walking down the long hall-ways and out into the gardens beyond. He saw the poet, Sieben, sitting beneath a spreading elm and tossing pebbles into a man-made pond. Calvar Syn wandered to the poolside.

'Your friend is improving, but not as swiftly as I had hoped,' he said.

'Did you bleed him?'

'No. There is no longer a fever. He is very silent . . . withdrawn.'

Sieben nodded. 'His wife was taken from him.'

'Very sad, I'm sure. But there are other women in the world,' observed the surgeon.

'Not for him. He loves her, he's going after her.'

565

'He'll waste his life,' said Calvar. 'Has he any idea of the size of the Ventrian continent? There are thousands upon thousands of small towns and villages, and more than three hundred major cities. Then there is the war. All shipping has ceased. How will he get there?'

'Of course he understands. But he's Druss – he's not like you or me, surgeon.' The poet chuckled and threw another pebble. 'He's an old-fashioned hero. You don't see many these days. He'll find a way.'

Calvar cleared his throat. 'Hmmm. Well, your old-fashioned hero is currently as strong as a three-day lamb. He is deep in a melancholic state, and until he recovers from it I cannot see him improving. Feed him red meat and dark green vegetables. He needs food for the blood.' He cleared his throat again, and stood silently.

'Was there something else?' asked the poet.

Calvar cursed inwardly. People were always the same. As soon as they were sick, they sent at speed for the doctor. But when it came to the time for settling accounts . . . No one expected a baker to part with bread without coin. Not so a surgeon. 'There is the question of my fee,' he said coldly.

'Ah, yes. How much is it?'

'Thirty raq.'

'Shema's balls! No wonder you surgeons live in palaces.'

Calvar sighed, but kept his temper. 'I do not live in a palace; I have a small house to the north. And the reason why surgeons must charge such fees is that a great number of patients renege. Your friend has been ill now for two months. During this time I have made more than thirty visits to this house, and I have had to purchase many expensive herbs. Three times now you have promised to settle the account. On each occasion you ask me how much is it. So you have the money?'

'No,' admitted Sieben.

'How much do you have?'

'Five raq.'

Calvar held out his hand and Sieben handed him the coins. 'You have until this time next week to find the rest of the money. After that I shall inform the Watch. In Mashrapur the law is simple: if you do not honour your debts your property will be sequestered. Since this house does not belong to you and, as far as I know, you have no source of income, you are likely to be imprisoned until sold as a slave. Until next week then.'

Calvar turned away and strode through the garden, his anger mounting.

Another bad debt.

One day I really will go to the Watch, he promised himself. He strolled on through the narrow streets, his medicine bag swinging from his narrow shoulders.

'Doctor! Doctor!' came a woman's voice and he swung to see a

566

young woman running towards him. Sighing he waited. 'Could you come with me? It's my son, he has a fever.' Calvar looked down at the woman. Her dress was of poor quality, and old. She wore no shoes.

'And how will you pay me?' he asked, the question springing from the residue of his anger.

She stood silent for a moment. 'You can take everything I have,' she said simply.

He shook his head, his anger finally disappearing. 'That will not be necessary,' he told her, with a professional smile.

He arrived home a little after midnight. His servant had left him a cold meal of meat and cheese. Calvar stretched out on a leather-covered couch and sipped a goblet of wine.

Untying his money-pouch, he tipped the contents to the table. Three raq tumbled to the wooden surface. 'You will never be rich, Calvar,' he said, with a wry smile.

He had sat with the boy while the mother was out buying food. She had returned with eggs, and meat, and milk, and bread, her face glowing. It was worth two raq just to see her expression, he thought.

Druss made his way slowly out into the garden. The moon was high, the stars bright. He remembered a poem of Sieben's: *Glitter dust in the lair of night.* Yes, that's how the stars looked. He was breathing heavily by the time he reached the circular seat constructed around the bole of the elm. Take a deep breath, the surgeon had ordered. Deep? It felt as if a huge lump of stone had been wedged into his lungs, blocking all air.

The crossbow bolt had pierced cleanly, but it had also driven a tiny portion of his shirt into the wound, and this had caused the poison that drained his strength.

The wind was cool, and bats circled above the trees. *Strength.* Druss realised now just how much he had undervalued the awesome power of his body. One small bolt and a hastily thrust knife had reduced him to this shambling, weak shell. How, in this state, could he rescue Rowena?

Despair struck him like a fist under the heart. Rescue her? He did not even know where she was, save that thousands of miles now separated them. No Ventrian ships sailed, and even if they did he had no gold with which to purchase passage.

He gazed back at the house where golden light gleamed from Sieben's window. It was a fine house, better than any Druss had ever visited. Shadak had arranged for them to rent the property, the owner being trapped in Ventria. But the rent was due.

The surgeon had told him it would be two months before his strength began to return.

We'll starve before then, thought Druss. Levering himself to his feet, he walked on to the high wall at the rear of the garden. By the time he reached it his legs felt boneless, his breath was coming in ragged gasps. The house seemed an infinite distance away. Druss struck out for it, but had to stop by the pond and sit at the water's edge. Splashing his face, he waited until his feeble strength returned, then rose and stumbled to the rear doors. The iron gate at the far end of the garden was lost in shadow now. He wanted to walk there once more, but his will was gone.

As he was about to enter the building he saw movement from the corner of his eye. He swung, ponderously, and a man moved from the shadows.

'Good to see you alive, lad,' said Old Thom.

Druss smiled. 'There is an ornate door-knocker at the front of the house,' he said.

'Didn't know as I'd be welcome,' the old man replied.

Druss led the way into the house, turning left into the large meeting room with its four couches and six padded chairs. Thom moved to the hearth, lighting a taper from the dying flames of the fire, then touching it to the wick of a lantern set on the wall. 'Help yourself to a drink,' offered Druss. Old Thom poured a goblet of red wine, then a second which he passed to the young man.

'You've lost a lot of weight, lad, and you look like an old man,' said Thom cheerfully.

'I've felt better.'

'I see Shadak spoke up for you with the magistrates. No action to be taken over the fight at the quay. Good to have friends, eh? And don't worry about Calvar Syn.'

'Why should I worry about him?'

'Unpaid debt. He could have you sold into slavery – but he won't. Soft, he is.'

'I thought Sieben had paid him. I'll not be beholden to any man.'

'Good words, lad. For good words and a copper farthing you can buy a loaf of bread.'

'I'll get the money to pay him,' promised Druss.

'Of course you will, lad. The best way – in the sand circle. But we've got to get your strength up first. You need to work – though my tongue should turn black for saying it.'

'I need time,' said Druss.

'You've little time, lad. Borcha is looking for you. You took away his reputation and he says he'll beat you to death when he finds you.'

'Does he indeed?' hissed Druss, his pale eyes gleaming.

'That's more like it, my bonny lad! Anger, that's what you need! Right, well I'll leave you now. By the way, they're felling trees to the west of the city, clearing the ground for some new buildings. They're looking for workers. Two silver pennies a day. It ain't much, but it's work.'

'I'll think on it.'

'I'll leave you to your rest, lad. You look like you need it.'

Druss watched the old man leave, then walked out into the garden once more. His muscles ached, and his heart was beating to a ragged drum. But Borcha's face was fixed before his mind's eye and he forced himself to walk to the gate and back.

Three times. . . .

Vintar rose from his bed, moving quietly so as not to wake the four priests who shared the small room in the southern wing. Dressing himself in a long white habit of rough wool, he padded barefoot along the cold stone of the corridor and up the winding steps to the ancient battlements.

From here he could see the mountain range that separated Lentria from the lands of the Drenai. The moon was high, half full, the sky cloudless. Beyond the temple the trees of the forest shimmered in the spectral light.

'The night is a good time for meditation, my son,' said the Abbot, stepping from the shadows. 'But you will need your strength for the day. You are falling behind in your sword work.' The Abbot was a broad-shouldered, powerful man who had once been a mercenary. His face bore a jagged scar from his right cheekbone down to his rugged jaw.

'I am not meditating, Father. I cannot stop thinking about the woman.'

'The one taken by slavers?'

'Yes. She haunts me.'

'You are here because your parents gave you into my custody, but you remain of your own free will. Should you desire to leave and find this girl you may do so. The Thirty will survive, Vintar.'

The young man sighed. 'I do not wish to leave, Father. And it is not that I desire her.' He smiled wistfully. 'I have never desired a woman. But there was something about her that I cannot shake from my thoughts.'

'Come with me, my boy. It is cold here, and I have a fire. We will talk.'

Vintar followed the burly Abbot into the western wing and the two men sat in the Abbot's study as the sky paled towards dawn. 'Sometimes,' said the Abbot, as he hung a copper kettle over the flames, 'it is hard to define the will of the Source. I have known men who wished to travel to far lands. They prayed for guidance. Amazingly they found that the Source was guiding them to do just what they wished for. I say *amazingly* because, in my experience, the

569

Source rarely sends a man where he wants to go. That is part of the sacrifice we make when we serve Him. I do not say it never happens, you understand, for that would be arrogance. No, but when one prays for guidance it should be with an open mind, all thoughts of one's own desires put aside.'

The kettle began to hiss, clouds of vapour puffing from the curved spout. Shielding his hands with a cloth, the Abbot poured the water into a second pot, in which he had spooned dried herbs. Placing the kettle in the hearth, he sat back in an old leather chair.

'Now the Source very rarely speaks to us directly, and the question is: How do we know what is required? These matters are very complex. You chose to absent yourself from study, and soar across the Heavens. In doing so you rescued the spirit of a young girl and led her home to her abused body. Coincidence? I distrust coincidence. Therefore it is my belief, though I may be wrong, that the Source led you to her. And that is why she now haunts your mind. Your dealings with her are not yet concluded.'

'You think I should seek her out?'

'I do. Take yourself to the south wing library. There is a small cell beyond it. I will excuse you from all studies tomorrow.'

'But how shall I find her again, Lord Abbot? She was a slave. She could be anywhere.'

'Start with the man who was abusing her. You know his name – Collan. You know where he was planning to take her – Mashrapur. Let your spirit search begin there.'

The Abbot poured tea into two clay cups. The aroma was sweet and heady. 'I am the least talented of all the priests,' said Vintar sorrowfully. 'Surely it would be better to pray for the Source to send someone stronger?'

The Abbot chuckled. 'It is so strange, my boy. Many people say they wish to serve the Lord of All Peace. But in an advisory capacity: "Ah, my God, you are most wondrous, having created all the planets and the stars. However, you are quite wrong to choose me. I know this, for I am Vintar, and I am weak." '

'You mock me, Father.'

'Of course I mock you. But I do so with at least a modicum of love in my heart. I was a soldier, a killer, a drunkard, a womaniser. How do you think I felt when He chose me to become a member of the Thirty? And when my brother priests stood facing death, can you imagine my despair at being told I was the one who must survive? I was to be the new Abbot. I was to gather the new Thirty. Oh Vintar, you have much to learn. Find this girl. I rather believe that in doing so you will find something for yourself.'

The young priest finished his tea and stood. 'Thank you, Father, for your kindness.'

'You told me she has a husband who was searching for her,' said the Abbot.

'Yes. A man named Druss.'

'Perhaps he will still be in Mashrapur.'

An hour later, in the bright sky above the city, the spirit of the young priest hovered. From here, despite the distance that made the buildings and palaces seem tiny, like the building bricks of an infant, he could feel the pulsing heart of Mashrapur, like a beast upon wakening; ravenous, filled with greed and lust. Dark emotions radiated from the city, filling his thoughts and swamping the purity he fought so hard to maintain. He dropped closer, closer still.

Now he could see the dock-workers strolling to work, and the whores plying the early-morning trade and the merchants opening their shops and stalls.

Where to begin? He had no idea.

For hours he flew aimlessly, touching a mind here, a thought there, seeking knowledge of Collan, Rowena or Druss. He found nothing save greed, or want, hunger or dissipation, lust or, so rarely, love.

Tired and defeated, he was ready to return to the Temple when he felt a sudden pull on his spirit, as if a rope had attached itself to him. In panic he tried to pull away, but though he used all his strength he was drawn inexorably down into a room where all the windows had been barred. An elderly woman was sitting before a red lantern. She gazed up at him as he floated just below the ceiling.

'Ah, but you are a treat to these old eyes, my pretty,' she said. Suddenly shocked, Vintar realised that his form was naked and he clothed himself in an instant in robes of white. She gave a dry laugh. 'And modest too.' The smile faded, and with it her good humour. 'What are you doing here? Hmmm? This is my city, child.'

'I am a priest, lady,' he said. 'I am seeking knowledge of a woman called Rowena, the wife of Druss, the slave of Collan.'

'Why?'

'My Abbot instructed me to find her. He believes the Source may want her protected.'

'By you?' Her good humour returned. 'Boy, you can't even protect yourself from an old witch. Were I to desire it, I could send your soul flaming into Hell.'

'Why would you desire such a terrible thing?'

She paused for a moment. 'It might be a whim, or a fancy. What will you give me for your life?'

'I don't have anything to give.'

'Of course you do,' she said. Her old eyes closed and he watched her spirit rise from her body. She took the form of a beautiful woman, young and shapely, with golden hair and large blue eyes. 'Does this form please you?'

'Of course. It is flawless. Is that how you looked when younger?'

'No, I was always ugly. But this is how I choose for you to see me.' She glided in close to him and stroked his face. Her touch was warm, and he felt a ripple of arousal.

'Please do not continue,' he said.

'Why? Is it not pleasurable?' Her hand touched his robes and they disappeared.

'Yes, it is. Very. But my vows . . . do not allow for the pleasures of the flesh.'

'Silly boy,' she whispered into his ear. 'We are not flesh. We are spirit.'

'No,' he said sternly. Instantly he transformed himself into the image of the old woman sitting at the table.

'Clever boy,' said the beautiful vision. 'Yes, very clever. And virtuous too. I don't know if I like that, but it does have the charm of being novel. Very well. I will help you.'

He felt the invisible chains holding him disappear, as did the vision. The old woman opened her eyes.

'She was at sea, heading for Ventria when the ship came under attack. She leapt into the water, and the sharks took her.'

Vintar reeled back and cried out, 'It's my fault! I should have sought her sooner.'

'Go back to your Temple, boy. My time is precious, and I have clients waiting.'

Her laughter rang out and she waved her hand dismissively. Once more he felt the pull on his spirit. It dragged him out, hurling him high into the sky over Mashrapur.

Vintar returned to the tiny cell at the Temple, merging once more with his body. As always he felt nauseous and dizzy and lay still for a few moments, experiencing the weight of his flesh, feeling the rough blanket beneath his skin. A great sadness fell upon him. His talents were far beyond those of normal men, yet they had brought him no pleasure. His parents had treated him with cold reverence, frightened by his uncanny skills. They had been both delighted and relieved when the Abbot came to them one autumn evening, offering to take the boy into his custody. It mattered nothing to them that the Abbot represented a Temple of the Thirty, where men with awesome talents trained and studied with one purpose only – to die in some battle, some distant war, and thus become one with the Source. The prospect of his death could not grieve his parents, for they had never treated him as a human being, flesh of their flesh, blood of their blood. They saw him as a changeling, a demonic presence.

He had no friends. Who wants to be around a boy who can read minds, who can peek into the darkest corners of your soul and know all your secrets? Even in the Temple he was alone, unable to share in the simple camaraderie of others with talents the equal of his.

And now he had missed an opportunity to help a young woman, indeed to save her life.

He sat up and sighed. The old woman had been a witch, and he had felt the malevolence of her personality. Even so the vision she created had aroused him. He could not even withstand such a petty evil.

And then the thought struck him, like a blow between the eyes. Evil! Malice and deceit walked hand in hand beneath the darkness of evil. Perhaps she lied!

He lay back and forced his mind to relax, loosening the spirit once more. Soaring from the Temple, he sped across the ocean, seeking the ship and praying that he was not too late.

Clouds were gathering in the east, promising a storm. Vintar swooped low over the water, spirit eyes scanning the horizon. Forty miles from the coast of Ventria he saw the ships, a trireme with a huge black sail and a slender merchant vessel seeking to avoid capture.

The merchant ship swung away, but the trireme ploughed on, its bronze-covered ram striking the prey amidships, smashing the timbers and ripping into the heart of the vessel. Armed men swarmed over the trireme's prow. On the rear deck Vintar saw a young woman dressed in white, with two men – one tall and dark-skinned, the other small and slightly built. The trio leapt into the waves. Sharks glided through the water towards them.

Vintar flew to Rowena, his spirit hand touching her shoulder as she bobbed in the water, clinging to a length of timber, the two men on either side of her. 'Stay calm, Rowena,' he pulsed.

A shark lunged up at the struggling trio and Vintar entered its mind, tasting the bleakness of its non-thoughts, the coldness of its emotions, the hunger that consumed it. He felt himself becoming the shark, seeing the world through black, unblinking eyes, tasting the environment through a sense of smell a hundred, perhaps a thousand times more powerful than Man's. Another shark glided below the three people, its jaws opening as it swept up towards them.

With a flick of his tail Vintar rammed the beast, which turned and snapped at his side, barely missing his dorsal fin.

Then came a scent in the water, sweet and beguiling, promising infinite pleasure and a cessation of hunger. Almost without thinking Vintar swam for it, sensing and seeing the other sharks racing towards it.

And then he knew, and his soaring lust was quelled as swiftly as it had risen.

Blood. The victims of the pirates were being thrown to the sharks.

Releasing control of the sea beast, he flew back to where Rowena and the others were clinging to the beam. 'Get your friends to kick out.

You must swim away from here,' he told her. He heard her tell the others, and slowly the three of them began to move away from the carnage.

Vintar soared high into the sky and scanned the horizon. Another ship was just in sight, a merchant vessel, and the young priest sped towards it. Dropping to where the captain stood by the tiller Vintar entered the man's mind, screening out his thoughts of wife, family, pirates and bad winds. The ship was manned by two hundred rowers and thirty seamen; it was carrying wine from Lentria to the Naashanite port of Virinis.

Vintar flowed through the captain's body, seeking control. In the lungs he found a small, malignant cancer. Swiftly Vintar neutralised it, accelerating the body's healing mechanism to carry away the corrupt cell. Moving up once more into the brain, he made the captain swing the ship towards the north-west.

The captain was a kindly man, his thoughts mellow. He had seven children, and one of them – the youngest daughter – had been sick with yellow fever when he set sail. He was praying for her recovery.

Vintar imprinted the new course on the man's unsuspecting mind and flew back to Rowena, telling her of the ship that would soon arrive. Then he moved to the pirate trireme. Already they had sacked the merchant vessel and were backing oars, pulling clear the ram and allowing the looted ship to sink.

Vintar entered the captain's mind – and reeled with the horror of his thoughts. Swiftly he made the man see the distant merchant ship and filled his mind with nameless fears. The approaching ship, he made the captain believe, was filled with soldiers. It was an ill omen, it would be the death of him. Then Vintar left him, and listened with satisfaction as Earin Shad bellowed orders to his men to turn about and make for the north-west.

Vintar floated above Rowena and the two men until the merchant ship arrived and hauled them aboard. Then he departed for the Lentrian port of Chupianin, where he healed the captain's daughter.

Only then did he return to the Temple, where he found the Abbot sitting beside his bed.

'How are you feeling, my boy?' he asked.

'Better than I have in years, Father. The girl is safe now. And I have enhanced two lives.'

'Three,' said the Abbot. 'You have enhanced your own.'

'That is true,' admitted Vintar, 'and it is good to be home.'

Druss could hardly believe the chaos at the clearing site. Hundreds of men scurried here and there without apparent direction, felling trees, digging out roots, hacking at the dense, overgrown vegetation. There was no order to the destruction. Trees were hacked down, falling across paths used by men with wheelbarrows who were trying to clear the debris. Even while he waited to see the Overseer he watched a tall pine topple on to a group of men digging out tree roots. No one was killed, but one worker suffered a broken arm and several others showed bloody gashes to face or arm.

The Overseer, a slender yet pot-bellied man, called him over. 'Well, what are your skills?' he asked.

'Woodsman,' answered Druss.

'Everyone here claims to be a woodsman,' said the man wearily. 'I'm looking for men with skill.'

'You certainly need them,' observed Druss.

'I have twenty days to clear this area, then another twenty to prepare footings for the new buildings. The pay is two silver pennies a day.' The man pointed to a burly, bearded man sitting on a tree-stump. 'That's Togrin, the charge-hand. He organises the work-force and hires the men.'

'He's a fool,' said Druss, 'and he'll get someone killed.'

'Fool he may be,' admitted the Overseer, 'but he's also a very tough man. No one shirks when he's around.'

Druss gazed at the site. 'That may be true; but you'll never finish on time. And I'll not work for any man who doesn't know what he's doing.'

'You're a little young to be making such sweeping comments,' observed the Overseer. 'So tell me, how would you re-organise the work?'

'I'd move the axemen further west and allow the rest of the men to clear behind them. If it carries on like this, all movement will cease. Look there,' said Druss, pointing to the right. Trees had been felled in a rough circle, at the centre of which were men digging out huge roots. 'Where will they take the roots?' asked the axeman. 'There is no longer a path. They will have to wait while the trees are hauled away. Yet how will you move horses and trace chains through to them?'

The Overseer smiled. 'You have a point, young man. Very well. The charge-hand earns four pennies a day. Take his place and show me what you can do.'

Druss took a deep breath. His muscles were already tired from the long walk to the site, and the wounds in his back were aching. He was in no condition to fight, and had been hoping to ease himself in to the work. 'How do you signal a break in the work?' he asked.

'We ring the bell for the noon break. But that's three hours away.'

'Have it rung now,' said Druss.

The Overseer chuckled. 'This should break the monotony,' he said. 'Do you want me to tell Togrin he has lost his job?'

Druss looked into the man's brown eyes. 'No. I'll tell him myself,' he said.

'Good. Then I'll see to the bell.'

The Overseer strolled away and Druss picked his way through the chaos until he was standing close to the seated Togrin. The man glanced up. He was large and round-shouldered, heavy of arm and sturdy of chin. His eyes were dark, almost black under heavy brows. 'Looking for work?' he asked.

'No.'

'Then get off my site. I don't like idlers.'

The clanging of a bell sounded through the wood. Togrin swore and rose as everywhere men stopped working. 'What the . . . ?' He swung around. 'Who rang that bell?' he bellowed.

Men began to gather around the charge-hand and Druss approached the man. 'I ordered the bell rung,' he said.

Togrin's eyes narrowed. 'And who might you be?' he asked.

'The new charge-hand,' replied Druss.

'Well, well,' said Togrin, with a wide grin. 'Now there are two charge-hands. I think that's one too many.'

'I agree,' Druss told him. Stepping in swiftly, he delivered a thundering blow to the man's belly. The air left Togrin's lungs with a great whoosh and he doubled up, his head dropping. Druss's left fist chopped down the man's jaw and Togrin hit the ground face first. The charge-hand twitched, then lay still.

Druss sucked in a great gulp of air. He felt unsteady and white lights danced before his eyes as he looked around at the waiting men. 'Now we are going to make some changes,' he said.

Day by day Druss's strength grew, the muscles of his arms and shoulders swelling with each sweeping blow of the axe, each shovelful of hard clay, each wrenching lift that tore a stubborn tree root clear of the earth. For the first five days Druss slept at the site in a small canvas tent supplied by the Overseer. He had not the energy to walk the three miles back to the rented house. And each lonely night two faces hovered in his mind as he drifted to sleep: Rowena, whom he loved more than life, and Borcha, the fist-fighter he knew he had to face.

In the quiet of the tent his thoughts were many. He saw his father differently now and wished he had known him better. It took courage to live down a father like Bardan the Slayer, and to raise a child and build a life on the frontier. He remembered the day when the wandering mercenary had stopped at the village. Druss had been impressed by the man's weapons, knife, short sword and hand-axe, and by his battered breastplate and helm. 'He lives a life of real courage,' he had observed to his father, putting emphasis on the word *real*. Bress had merely nodded. Several days later, as they were walking across the high meadow, Bress had pointed towards the house of Egan the farmer. 'You want to see courage, boy,' he said. 'Look at him working in that field. Ten years ago he had a farm on the Sentran Plain, but Sathuli raiders came in the night, burning him out. Then he moved to the Ventrian border, where locusts destroyed his crops for three years. He had borrowed money to finance his farm and he lost everything. Now he is back on the land, working from first light to last. That's *real* courage. It doesn't take much for a man to abandon a life of toil for a sword. The real heroes are those who battle on.'

The boy had known better. You couldn't be a hero and a farmer.

'If he was so brave, why didn't he fight off the Sathuli?'

'He had a wife and three children to protect.'

'So he ran away?'

'He ran away,' agreed Bress.

'I'll never run from a fight,' said Druss.

'Then you'll die young,' Bress told him.

Druss sat up and thought back to the raid. What would he have done if the choice had been to fight the slavers – or run with Rowena?

His sleep that night was troubled.

On the sixth night as he walked from the site a tall, burly figure stepped into his path. It was Togrin, the former charge-hand. Druss had not seen him since the fight. The young axeman scanned the darkness, seeking other assailants, but there were none.

'Can we talk?' asked Togrin.

'Why not?' countered Druss.

The man took a deep breath. 'I need work,' he said. 'My wife's sick. The children have not eaten in two days.'

Druss looked hard into the man's face, seeing the hurt pride and instantly sensing what it had cost him to ask for help. 'Be on site at dawn,' he said, and strolled on. He felt uncomfortable as he made his way home, telling himself he would never have allowed his own dignity to be lost in such a way. But even as he thought the words, a seed of doubt came to him. Mashrapur was a harsh, unforgiving city. A man was valued only so long as he contributed to the general well-being of the community. And how dreadful it must be, he thought, to watch your children starve.

It was dusk when he arrived at the house. He was tired, but the bone-weariness he had experienced for so long had faded. Sieben was not home. Druss lit a lantern and opened the rear door to the garden allowing the cool sea breeze to penetrate the house.

Removing his money-pouch, he counted out the twenty-four silver pennies he had earned thus far. Twenty was the equivalent of a single raq, and that was one month's rent on the property. At this rate he would never earn enough to settle his debts. Old Thom was right: he could make far more in the sand circle.

He recalled the bout with Borcha, the terrible pounding he had received. The memory of the punches he had taken was strong within him – but so too was the memory of those he had thundered into his opponent.

He heard the iron gate creak at the far end of the garden and saw a shadowy figure making his way towards the house. Moonlight glinted from the man's bald pate, and he seemed colossal as he strode through the shadowed trees. Druss rose from his seat, his pale eyes narrowing.

Borcha halted just before the door. 'Well,' he asked, 'are you going to invite me in?'

Druss stepped into the garden. 'You can take your beating out here,' he hissed. 'I've not the money to pay for broken furniture.'

'You're a cocky lad,' said Borcha amiably, stepping into the house and draping his green cloak across the back of a couch. Nonplussed, Druss followed him inside. The big man stretched out in a padded chair, crossing his legs and leaning his head back against the high back. 'A good chair,' he said. 'Now how about a drink?'

'What do you want here?' demanded Druss, fighting to control his rising temper.

'A little hospitality, farm boy. I don't know about you, but where I come from we normally offer a guest a goblet of wine when he takes the trouble to call.'

'Where I'm from,' responded Druss, 'uninvited guests are rarely welcome.'

'Why such hostility? You won your wager and you fought well. Collan did not take my advice – which was to return your wife – and now he is dead. I had no part in the raid.'

'And I suppose you haven't been looking for me, seeking your revenge?'

Borcha laughed. 'Revenge? For what? You stole nothing from me. You certainly did not beat me – nor could you. You have the strength but not the skill. If that had been a genuine bout I would have broken you, boy – eventually. However, you are quite right – I have been looking for you.'

Druss sat opposite the giant. 'So Old Thom told me. He said you were seeking to destroy me.'

Borcha shook his head and grinned. 'The drunken fool misunderstood, boy. Now tell me, how old do you think I am?'

'What? How in the name of Hell should I know?' stormed Druss.

'I'm thirty-eight, thirty-nine in two months. And yes, I could still beat Grassin, and probably all the others. But you showed me the mirror of time, Druss. No one lasts for ever – not in the sand circle. My day is over; my few minutes with you taught me that. Your day is beginning. But it won't last long unless you learn how to fight.'

'I need no instruction in that,' said Druss.

578

'You think not? Every time you throw a right-hand blow, you drop your left shoulder. All of your punches travel in a curve. And your strongest defence is your chin which, though it may appear to be made of granite, is in fact merely bone. Your footwork is adequate, though it could be improved, but your weaknesses are many. Grassin will exploit them; he will wear you down.'

'That's one opinion,' argued Druss.

'Don't misunderstand me, lad. You are good. You have heart and great strength. But you also know how you felt after four minutes with me. Most bouts last ten times that long.'

'Mine won't.'

Borcha chuckled. 'It will with Grassin. Do not let arrogance blind you to the obvious, Druss. They say you were a woodsman. When you first picked up an axe, did it strike with every blow?'

'No,' admitted the younger man.

'It is the same with combat. I can teach you many styles of punch, and even more defences. I can show you how to feint, and lure an opponent in to your blows.'

'Perhaps you can – but why would you?'

'Pride,' said Borcha.

'I don't understand.'

'I'll explain it – after you beat Grassin.'

'I won't be here long enough,' said Druss. 'As soon as a ship bound for Ventria docks in Mashrapur, I shall sail on her.'

'Before the war such a journey would cost ten raq. Now . . . ? Who knows? But in one month there is a small tournament at Visha, with a first prize of one hundred raq. The rich have palaces in Visha, and a great deal of money can be made on side wagers. Grassin will be taking part, and several of the other notable figures. Agree to let me train you and I will enter your name in my place.'

Druss stood and poured a goblet of wine, which he passed to the bald fighter. 'I have taken employment, and I promised the Overseer I would see the work done. It will take a full month.'

'Then I will train you in the evenings.'

'On one condition,' said Druss.

'Name it!'

'The same one I gave the Overseer. If a ship bound for Ventria docks and I can get passage, then I will up and go.'

'Agreed.' Borcha thrust out his hand. Druss clasped it and Borcha stood. 'I'll leave you to your rest. By the way, warn your poet friend that he is taking fruit from the wrong tree.'

'He is his own man,' said Druss.

Borcha shrugged. 'Warn him anyway. I'll see you tomorrow.'

2

Sieben lay awake, staring at the ornate ceiling. Beside him the woman slept, and he could feel the warmth of her skin against his side and legs. There was a painting on the ceiling, a hunting scene showing men armed with spears and bows pursuing a red-maned lion. What kind of man would have such a composition above the marital bed, he thought? Sieben smiled. The First Minister of Mashrapur must have an enormous ego since, whenever he and his wife made love, she would be gazing up at a group of men more handsome than her husband.

Rolling to his side, he looked down at the sleeping woman. Her back was turned towards him, her arm thrust under the pillow, her legs drawn up. Her hair was dark, almost black against the creamy-white of the pillow. He could not see her face, but he pictured again the full lips and the long, beautiful neck. When first he had seen her she was standing beside Mapek in the market-place. The minister was surrounded by underlings and sycophants, Evejorda looking bored and out of place.

Sieben had stood very still, waiting for her eyes to glance in his direction. When they did, he sent her a smile. One of his best – a swift, flashing grin that said, 'I am bored too. I understand you. I am a linked soul.' She raised an eyebrow at him, signifying her distaste for his impertinence, and then turned away. He waited, knowing she would look again. She moved to a nearby stall and began to examine a set of ceramic bowls. He angled himself through the crowd and she looked up, startled to see him so close.

'Good morning, my lady,' he said. She ignored him. 'You are very beautiful.'

'And you are presumptuous, sir.' Her voice had a northern burr, which he normally found irritating. Not so now.

'Beauty demands presumption. Just as it demands adoration.'

'You are very sure of yourself,' she said, moving in close to disconcert him.

She was wearing a simple gown of radiant blue and a Lentrian shawl of white silk. But it was her perfume that filled his senses – a rich, scented musk he recognised as *Moserche*, a Ventrian import costing five gold raq an ounce.

'Are you happy?' he asked her.

'What a ridiculous question! Who could answer it?'

'Someone who is happy,' he told her.

She smiled. 'And you, sir, are you happy?'

'I am now.'

'I think you are an accomplished womaniser, and there is no truth to your words.'

'Then judge me by my deeds, my lady. My name is Sieben.' He whispered the address of the house he shared with Druss and then, taking her hand, he kissed it.

Her messenger arrived at the house two days later.

She moved in her sleep. Sieben's hand slid under the satin sheet, cupping her breast. At first she did not stir, but he gently continued to caress her skin, squeezing her nipple until it swelled erect. She moaned and stretched. 'Do you never sleep?' she asked him.

He did not reply.

Later, as Evejorda slept again, he lay silently beside her, his passion gone, his thoughts sorrowful. She was without doubt the most beautiful woman he had ever enjoyed. She was bright, intelligent, dynamic and full of passion.

And he was bored . . .

As a poet he had sung of love, but never known it, and he envied the lovers of legend who looked into each other's eyes and saw eternity beckoning. He sighed and slipped from the bed, dressing swiftly and leaving the room, padding softly down the back stairs to the garden before pulling on his boots. The servants were not yet awake, and dawn was only just breaking in the eastern sky. A cockerel crowed in the distance.

Sieben walked through the garden and out on to the avenue beyond. As he walked he could smell the fresh bread baking, and he stopped at a bakery to buy some cheese bread which he ate as he strolled home.

Druss was not there, and he remembered the labouring work the young man had undertaken. God, how could a man spend his days digging in the dirt, he wondered? Moving through to the kitchen, he stoked up the iron stove and set a copper pan filled with water atop it.

Making a tisane of mint and herbs, he stirred the brew and carried it to the main sitting room where he found Shadak asleep on a couch. The hunter's black jerkin and trews were travel-stained, his boots encrusted with mud. He awoke as Sieben entered, and swung his long legs from the couch.

'I was wondering where you were,' said Shadak, yawning. 'I arrived last night.'

'I stayed with a friend,' said Sieben, sitting opposite the hunter and sipping his tisane.

Shadak nodded. 'Mapek is due in Mashrapur later today. He cut short his visit to Vagria.'

581

'Why would that concern me?'

'I'm sure that it does not. But now you know it anyway.'

'Did you come to give me a sermon, Shadak?'

'Do I look like a priest? I came to see Druss. But when I got here he was in the garden, sparring with a bald giant. From the way he moved I concluded his wounds are healed.'

'Only the physical wounds,' said Sieben.

'I know,' responded the hunter. 'I spoke to him. He still intends to sail for Ventria. Will you go with him?'

Sieben laughed. 'Why should I? I don't know his wife. Gods, I hardly know him.'

'It might be good for you, poet.'

'The sea air, you mean?'

'You know what I mean,' said Shadak gravely. 'You have chosen to make an enemy of one of the most powerful men in Mashrapur. His enemies die, Sieben. Poison, or the blade, or a knotted rope around your throat as you sleep.'

'Is my business known all over the city?'

'Of course. There are thirty servants in that house. You think to keep secrets from them when her ecstatic cries reverberate around the building in the middle of the afternoon, or the morning, or in the dead of night?'

'Or indeed all three,' said Sieben, smiling.

'I see no humour in this,' snapped Shadak. 'You are no more than a rutting dog and you will undoubtedly ruin her life as you have ruined others. Yet I would sooner you lived than died – only the gods know why!'

'I gave her a little pleasure, that's all. Which is more than that dry stick of a husband could do. But I will think on your advice.'

'Do not think too long. When Mapek returns he will soon find out about his wife's . . . *little pleasure*. Do not be surprised if he has her killed also.'

Sieben paled. 'He wouldn't . . .'

'He is a proud man, poet. And you have made a profound error.'

'If he touches her I'll kill him.'

'Ah, how noble. The dog bares its fangs. You should never have wooed her. You do not even have the defence of being in love; you merely wanted to rut.'

'Is that not what love is?' countered Sieben.

'For you, yes.' Shadak shook his head. 'I don't believe you'll ever understand it, Sieben. To love means giving, not receiving. Sharing your soul. But this argument is wasted on you, like teaching algebra to a chicken.'

'Oh, please, don't try to spare my feelings with pretty words. Just come right out with it!'

Shadak rose. 'Bodasen is hiring warriors, mercenaries to fight in the Ventrian war. He has chartered a ship which will sail in twelve days. Lie low until then, and do not seek to see Evejorda again – not if you want *her* to live.'

The hunter moved towards the door, but Sieben called out, 'You don't think very highly of me, do you?'

Shadak half turned. 'I think more of you than you think of yourself.'

'I am too tired for riddles.'

'You can't forget Gulgothir.'

Sieben jerked as if struck, then lunged to his feet. 'That is all past. It means nothing to me. You understand? Nothing!'

'If you say so. I'll see you in twelve days. The ship is called *The Thunderchild*. She will sail from Quay 12.'

'I may be on it. I may not.'

'A man always has two choices, my friend.'

'No! No! No!' roared Borcha. 'You are still thrusting out that chin, and leading with your head.' Stepping back from his opponent, Borcha swept up a towel and wiped the sweat from his face and head. 'Try to understand, Druss, that if Grassin gets the opportunity he will take out one – or both – of your eyes. He will step in close, and as you charge he will strike with a sudden thrust, his thumb like a dagger.'

'Let's go again,' said Druss.

'No. You are too angry and it swamps your thoughts. Come and sit for a while.'

'The light is fading,' Druss pointed out.

'Then let it fade. You are four days from the competition. *Four days*, Druss. In that time you must learn to control your temper. Winning is everything. It means nothing if an opponent sneers at you, or mocks you, or claims your mother sold herself to sailors. You understand? These insults are merely weapons in a fighter's armoury. You will be goaded – because every fighter knows that his enemy's rage is his greatest weakness.'

'I can control it,' snapped Druss.

'A few moments ago you were fighting well – your balance was good, the punches crisp. Then I slapped you with a straight left . . . then another. The blows were too fast for your defences and they began to irritate you. Then the curve came back to your punches and you exposed your chin, your face.'

Druss sat beside the fighter and nodded. 'You are right. But I do not like this sparring, this holding back. It does not feel real.'

'It isn't real, my friend, but it prepares the body for genuine combat.' He slapped the younger man on the shoulder. 'Do not despair; you are almost ready. I think your digging in the dirt has brought back your strength. How goes it at the clearing site?'

'We finished today,' said Druss. 'Tomorrow the stonemasons and builders move in.'

'On time. The Overseer must have been pleased – I know I am.'

'Why should it please you?'

'I own a third of the land. The value will rise sharply when the houses are completed.' The bald fighter chuckled. 'Were you happy with your bonus?'

'Was that your doing?' asked Druss suspiciously.

'It is standard practice, Druss. The Overseer received fifty raq for completing within the time allocated. The charge-hand is usually offered one tenth of this sum.'

'He gave me ten raq – in gold.'

'Well, well, you must have impressed him.'

'He asked me to stay on and supervise the digging of the footings.'

'But you declined?'

'Yes. There is a ship bound for Ventria. I told him my assistant, Togrin, could take my place. He agreed.'

Borcha was silent for a moment. He knew of Druss's fight with Togrin on the first day, and how he had welcomed the defeated charge-hand back on the site, training him and giving him responsibility. And the Overseer had told him at their progress meetings how well the men responded to Druss.

'He is a natural leader who inspires by example. No work is too menial, nor too hard. He's a real find, Borcha; I intend to promote him. There is a new site planned to the north, with difficult terrain. I shall make him Overseer.'

'He won't take it.'

'Of course he will. He could become rich.'

Borcha pulled his thoughts back to the present. 'You know you may never find her,' he said softly.

Druss shook his head. 'I'll find her, Borcha – if I have to walk across Ventria and search every house.'

'You are a woodman, Druss, so answer me this: If I marked a single fallen leaf in a forest, how would you begin to search for it?'

'I hear you – but it is not that difficult. I know who bought her: Kabuchek. He is a rich man, an important man; I will find him.' Reaching behind the bench seat, Druss drew forth Snaga. 'This was my grandfather's axe,' he said. 'He was an evil man, they say. But when he was young a great army came out of the north, led by a Gothir King named Pasia. Everywhere there was panic. How could the Drenai stand against such an army? Towns emptied, people piled their possessions on to carts, wagons, coaches, the backs of horses, ponies. Bardan – my grandfather – led a small raiding party deep into the mountains, to where the enemy was camped. He and twenty men walked into the camp, found the King's tent and slew him in the night. In the morning they found Pasia's head stuck atop a lance. The army went home.'

'An interesting story, and one I have heard before,' said Borcha. 'What do you think we learn from it?'

'There is nothing a man cannot achieve if he has the will, the strength and the courage to attempt it,' answered Druss.

Borcha rose and stretched the massive muscles of his shoulders and back. 'Then let's see if it is true,' he said, with a smile. 'Let's see if you have the will, the strength and the courage to keep your chin tucked in.'

Druss chuckled and placed the axe beside the seat as he stood. 'I like you, Borcha. How in the name of Chaos did you ever come to serve a man like Collan?'

'He had a good side, Druss.'

'He *did?*'

'Aye, he paid well.' As he spoke his hand snaked out, the open palm lashing across Druss's cheek. The younger man snarled and leapt at him but Borcha swayed left, his fist glancing from Druss's cheek. 'The chin, you ox! Keep it in!' he bellowed.

'I was hoping for men with more quality,' said Bodasen, as he scanned the crowds milling in the Celebration Field.

Borcha chuckled. 'Do not be misled by appearances. Some of these men *are* quality. It really depends on what you are seeking.'

Bodasen stared moodily at the rabble – some in rags, most filthy. More than two hundred had assembled so far, and a quick glance to the gate showed others moving along the access road. 'I think we have different views on what constitutes quality,' he said gloomily.

'Look over there,' said Borcha, pointing to a man sitting on a fence rail. 'That is Eskodas the Bowman. He can hit a mark no larger than your thumbnail from fifty paces. A man to walk the mountains with, as they say in my home country. And there, the swordsman Kelva – fearless and highly skilled. A natural killer.'

'But do they understand the concept of honour?'

Borcha's laughter rang out. 'You have listened to too many tales of glory and wonder, my friend. These men are fighters; they fight for pay.'

Bodasen sighed. 'I am trapped in this . . . this blemish of a city. My emperor is beset on all sides by a terrible enemy, and I cannot join him. No ship will sail unless it is manned by seasoned troops, and I must choose them from among the gutter scum of Mashrapur. I had hoped for more.'

'Choose wisely, and they may yet surprise you,' advised Borcha.

585

'Let us see the archers first,' Bodasen ordered.

For more than an hour Bodasen watched the bowmen sending their shafts at targets stuffed with straw. When they had finished he selected five men, the youthful Eskodas among them. Each man was given a single gold raq, and told to report to *The Thunderchild* at dawn on the day of departure.

The swordsmen were more difficult to judge. At first he ordered them to fence with one another, but the warriors set about their task with mindless ferocity and soon several men were down with cuts, gashes, and one with a smashed collar-bone. Bodasen called a halt to the proceedings and, with Borcha's help, chose ten. The injured men were each given five silver pieces.

The day wore on, and by noon Bodasen had chosen thirty of the fifty men he required to man *The Thunderchild*. Dismissing the remainder of the would-be mercenaries, he strode from the field with Borcha beside him.

'Will you leave a place for Druss?' asked the fighter.

'No. I will have room only for men who will fight for Ventria. His quest is a personal one.'

'According to Shadak he is the best fighting man in the city.'

'I am not best disposed towards Shadak. Were it not for him the pirates would not be fighting Ventria's cause.'

'Sweet Heaven!' snorted Borcha. 'How can you believe that? Collan would merely have taken your money and given nothing in return.'

'He gave me his word,' said Bodasen.

'How on earth did you Ventrians ever build an empire?' enquired Borcha. 'Collan was a liar, a thief, a raider. Why would you believe him? Did he not tell you he was going to give back Druss's wife? Did he not lie to you in order for you to lure Druss into a trap? What kind of man did you believe you were dealing with?'

'A nobleman,' snapped Bodasen. 'Obviously I was wrong.'

'Indeed you were. You have just paid a gold raq to Eskodas, the son of a goat-breeder and a Lentrian whore. His father was hanged for stealing two horses and his mother abandoned him. He was raised in an orphanage run by two Source priests.'

'Is there some point to this sordid tale?' asked the Ventrian.

'Aye, there is. Eskodas will fight to the death for you; he'll not run. Ask him his opinion, and he'll give an honest answer. Hand him a bag of diamonds and tell him to deliver it to a man a thousand leagues distant, and he will do so – and never once will he consider stealing a single gem.'

'So I should hope,' observed Bodasen. 'I would expect no less from any Ventrian servant I employed. Why do you make honesty sound like a grand virtue?'

586

'I have known rocks with more common sense than you,' said Borcha, struggling to hold his temper.

Bodasen chuckled. 'Ah, the ways of you barbarians are mystifying. But you are quite right about Druss – I was instrumental in causing him grievous wounds. Therefore I shall leave a place for him on *The Thunderchild*. Now let us find somewhere that serves good food and passable wine.'

Shadak, Sieben and Borcha stood with Druss on the quayside as dock-workers moved by them, climbing the gangplank, carrying the last of the ship's stores to the single deck. *The Thunderchild* was riding low in the water, her deck crammed with mercenaries who leaned on the rail, waving goodbyes to the women who thronged the quay. Most were whores, but there were a few wives with small children, and many were the tears.

Shadak gripped Druss's hand. 'I wish you fair sailing, laddie,' the hunter told him. 'And I hope the Source leads you to Rowena.'

'He will,' said Druss. The axeman's eyes were swollen, the lids dis-coloured – a mixture of dull yellow and faded purple – and there was a lump under his left eye, where the skin was split and badly stitched.

Shadak grinned at him. 'It was a good fight. Grassin will long remember it.'

'And me,' grunted Druss.

Shadak nodded, and his smile faded. 'You are a rare man, Druss. Try not to change. Remember the code.'

'I will,' promised Druss. The two men shook hands again, and Shadak strolled away.

'What code?' Sieben asked.

Druss watched as the black-garbed hunter vanished into the crowd. 'He once told me that all true warriors live by a code: *Never violate a woman, nor harm a child. Do not lie, cheat or steal. These things are for lesser men. Protect the weak against the evil strong. And never allow thoughts of gain to lead you into the pursuit of evil.*'

'Very true, I'm sure,' said Sieben, with a dry, mocking laugh. 'Ah well, Druss, I can hear the call of the fleshpots and the taverns. And with the money I won on you, I can live like a lord for several months.' He thrust out his slender hand and Druss clasped it.

'Spend your money wisely,' he advised.

'I shall . . . on women and wine and gambling.' Laughing, he swung away.

Druss turned to Borcha. 'I thank you for your training, and your kindness.'

'The time was well spent, and it was gratifying to see Grassin humbled. But he still almost took out your eye. I don't think you'll ever learn to keep that chin protected.'

'Hey, Druss! Are you coming aboard?' yelled Bodasen from the deck and Druss waved.

'I'm on my way,' he shouted. The two men clasped hands in the warrior's grip, wrist to wrist. 'I hope we meet again,' said Druss.

'Who can say what the fates will decree?'

Druss hefted his axe and turned for the gangplank. 'Tell me now why you helped me?' he asked suddenly.

Borcha shrugged. 'You frightened me, Druss. I wanted to see just how good you could be. Now I know. You could be the best. It makes what you did to me more palatable. Tell me, how does it feel to leave as champion?'

Druss chuckled. 'It hurts,' he said, rubbing his swollen jaw.

'Move yourself, dog-face!' yelled a warrior, leaning over the rail.

The axeman glanced up at the speaker, then turned back to Borcha. 'Be lucky, my friend,' he said, then strode up the gangplank.

With the ropes loosed, *The Thunderchild* eased away from the quayside.

Warriors were lounging on the deck, or leaning over the rail waving goodbye to friends and loved ones. Druss found a space by the port rail and sat, laying his axe on the deck beside him. Bodasen was standing beside the mate at the tiller; he waved and smiled at the axeman.

Druss leaned back, feeling curiously at peace. The months trapped in Mashrapur had been hard on the young man. He pictured Rowena.

'I'm coming for you,' he whispered.

Sieben strolled away from the quay, and off into the maze of alleys leading to the park. Ignoring the whores who pressed close around him, his thoughts were many. There was sadness at the departure of Druss. He had come to like the young axeman; there were no hidden sides to him, no cunning, no guile. And much as he laughed at the axeman's rigid morality, he secretly admired the strength that gave birth to it. Druss had even sought out the surgeon Calvar Syn, and settled his debt. Sieben had gone with him and would long remember the surprise that registered on the young doctor's face.

But Ventria? Sieben had no wish to visit a land torn by war.

He thought of Evejorda and regret washed over him. He'd like to have seen her just one more time, to have felt those slim thighs sliding up over his hips. But Shadak was right; it was too dangerous for both of them.

Sieben turned left and started to climb the Hundred Steps to the park gateway. Shadak was wrong about Gulgothir. He remembered the filth-strewn streets, the limbless beggars and the cries of the dispossessed. But he remembered them without bitterness. And was it his fault that his father had made such a fool of himself with the

Duchess? Anger flared briefly. Stupid fool, he thought. Stupid, stupid man! She had stripped him first of his wealth, then his dignity, and finally his manhood. They called her the Vampire Queen and it was a good description, save that she didn't drink blood. No, she drank the very life force from a man, sucked him dry and left him thanking her for doing it, begging her to do it again.

Sieben's father had been thrown aside – a useless husk, an empty, discarded shell of a man. While Sieben and his mother had almost starved, his father was sitting like a beggar outside the home of the Duchess. He sat there for a month, and finally cut his own throat with a rusty blade.

Stupid, stupid man!

But I am not stupid, thought Sieben as he climbed the steps. I am not like my father.

He glanced up to see two men walking down the steps towards him. They wore long cloaks that were drawn tightly across their bodies. Sieben paused in his climb. It was a hot morning, so why would they be dressed in such a manner? Hearing a sound, he turned to see another man climbing behind him. He also wore a long cloak.

Fear flared suddenly in the poet's heart and, spinning on his heel, he descended towards the single man. As he neared the climber the cloak flashed back, a long knife appearing in the man's hand. Sieben leapt feet first, his right boot cracking into the man's chin and sending him tumbling down the steps. Sieben landed heavily but rose swiftly and began to run, taking the steps three at a time. He could hear the men behind him also running.

Reaching the bottom, he set off through the alleyways. A hunting horn sounded and a tall warrior leapt into his path with a sword in hand. Sieben, at full run, turned his shoulder into the man, barging him aside. He swerved right, then left. A knife sliced past his head to clatter against a wall.

Increasing his speed, he raced across a small square and into a side street. He could see the docks ahead. It was more crowded here and he pushed his way through. Several men shouted abuse, and a young woman fell behind him. He glanced back – there were at least half a dozen pursuers.

Close to panic now, he emerged on to the quay. To his left he saw a group of men emerge from a side street; they were all carrying weapons and Sieben swore.

The Thunderchild was slipping away from the quayside as Sieben ran across the cobbles and launched himself through the air, reaching out to grab at a trailing rope. His fingers curled around it, and his body cracked against the ship's timbers. Almost losing his grip, he clung to the rope as a knife thudded into the wood beside his head. Fear gave him strength and he began to climb.

A familiar face loomed above him and Druss leaned over, grabbing him by the shirt and hauling him on to the deck.

'Changed your mind, I see,' said the axeman. Sieben gave a weak smile and glanced back at the quay. There were at least a dozen armed men there now.

'I thought the sea air would be good for me,' said Sieben.

The captain, a bearded man in his fifties, pushed his way through to them. 'What's going on?' he said. 'I can only carry fifty men. That's the limit.'

'He doesn't weigh much,' said Druss goodnaturedly.

Another man stepped forward. He was tall and broad-shouldered, and wore a dented breastplate, two short swords and a baldric boasting four knives. 'First you keep us waiting, dog-face, and now you bring your boyfriend aboard. Well, Kelva the Swordsman won't sail with the likes of you.'

'Then don't!' Druss's left hand snaked out, his fingers locking to the man's throat, his right slamming home into the warrior's groin. With one surging heave Druss lifted the struggling man into the air and tossed him over the side. He hit with a great splash and came up struggling under the weight of his armour.

The Thunderchild pulled away and Druss turned to the captain. 'Now we are fifty again,' he said, with a smile.

'Can't argue with that,' the captain agreed. He swung to the sailors standing by the mast. 'Let loose the mainsail!' he bellowed.

Sieben walked to the rail and saw that people on the quayside had thrown a rope to the struggling warrior in the water. 'He might have friends aboard the ship,' observed the poet.

'They're welcome to join him,' answered Druss.

3

Each morning Eskodas paced the deck, moving along the port rail all the way to the prow and then back along the starboard rail, rising the six steps to the tiller deck at the stern, where either the captain or the first mate would be standing alongside the curved oak tiller.

The bowman feared the sea, gazing with undisguised dread at the rolling waves and feeling the awesome power that lifted the ship like a piece of driftwood. On the first morning of the voyage Eskodas had climbed to the tiller deck and approached the captain, Milus Bar.

'No passengers up here,' said the captain sternly.

'I have questions, sir,' Eskodas told him politely.

Milus Bar looped a hemp rope over the tiller arm, securing it. 'About what?' he asked.

'The boat.'

'Ship,' snapped Milus.

'Yes, the ship. Forgive me, I am not versed in nautical terms.'

'She's seaworthy,' said Milus. 'Three hundred and fifty feet of seasoned timber. She leaks no more than a man can sweat, and she'll ride any storm the gods can throw our way. She's sleek. She's fast. What else do you need to know?'

'You talk of the . . . ship . . . as a woman.'

'Better than any woman I ever knew,' said Milus, grinning. 'She's never let me down.'

'She seems so small against the immensity of the ocean,' observed Eskodas.

'We are all small against the ocean, lad. But there are few storms at this time of year. Our danger is pirates, and that's why you are here.' He stared at the young bowman, his grey eyes narrowing under heavy brows. 'If you don't mind me saying so, lad, you seem a little out of place among these killers and villains.'

'I don't object to you saying it, sir,' Eskodas told him. 'They might object to hearing it, however. Thank you for your time and your courtesy.'

The bowman climbed down to the main deck. Men were lounging everywhere, some dicing, others talking. By the port rail several others were engaged in an arm-wrestling tourney. Eskodas moved through them towards the prow.

The sun was bright in a blue sky, and there was a good following breeze. Gulls circled high above the ship, and to the north he could just make out the coast of Lentria. At this distance the land seemed misty and unreal, a place of ghosts and legends.

There were two men sitting by the prow. One was the slim young man who had boarded the ship so spectacularly. Blond and handsome, long hair held in place by a silver headband, his clothes were expensive – a pale blue shirt of fine silk, dark blue leggings of lambswool seamed with soft leather. The other man was huge; he had lifted Kelva as if the warrior weighed no more than a few ounces, and hurled him into the sea like a spear. Eskodas approached them. The giant was younger than he had first thought, but the beginnings of a dark beard gave him the look of someone older. Eskodas met his gaze. Cold blue eyes, flint-hard and unwelcoming. The bowman smiled. 'Good morning,' he said. The giant grunted something, but the blond dandy rose and extended his hand.

'Hello, there. My name is Sieben. This is Druss.'

591

'Ay, yes. He defeated Grassin at the tournament – broke his jaw, I believe.'

'In several places,' said Sieben.

'I am Eskodas.' The bowman sat down on a coiled rope and leaned his back against a cloth-bound bale. Closing his eyes, he felt the sun warm on his face. The silence lasted for several moments, then the two men resumed their conversation.

Eskodas didn't listen too intently . . . something about a woman and assassins.

He thought of the journey ahead. He had never seen Ventria, which according to the story books was a land of fabled wealth, dragons, centaurs and many wild beasts. He tended to disbelieve the part about the dragons; he was widely travelled, and in every country there were stories of them, but never had Eskodas seen one. In Chiatze there was a museum where the bones of a dragon had been re-assembled. The skeleton was colossal, but it had no wings, and a neck that was at least eight feet long. No fire could have issued from such a throat, he thought.

But dragons or not, Eskodas looked forward with real pleasure to seeing Ventria.

'You don't say much, do you?' observed Sieben.

Eskodas opened his eyes and smiled. 'When I have something to say, I will speak,' he said.

'You'll never get the chance,' grunted Druss. 'Sieben talks enough for ten men.'

Eskodas smiled politely. 'You are the saga-master,' he said.

'Yes. How gratifying to be recognised.'

'I saw you in Corteswain. You gave a performance of *The Song of Karnak*. It was very good; I particularly enjoyed the tale of Dros Purdol and the siege, though I was less impressed by the arrival of the gods of war, and the mysterious princess with the power to hurl lightning.'

'Dramatic licence,' said Sieben, with a tight smile.

'The courage of men needs no such licence,' said Eskodas. 'It lessens the heroism of the defenders to suggest that they had divine help.'

'It was not a history lesson,' Sieben pointed out, his smile fading. 'It was a poem – a song. The arrival of the gods was merely an artistic device to highlight that courage will sometimes bring about good fortune.'

'Hmmm,' said Eskodas, leaning back and closing his eyes.

'What does that mean?' demanded Sieben. 'Are you disagreeing?'

Eskodas sighed. 'It is not my wish to provoke an argument, sir poet, but I think the device was a poor one. You maintain it was inserted to supply dramatic effect. There is no point in further discussion; I have no desire to increase your anger.'

592

'I am not angry, damn you!' stormed Sieben.

'He doesn't take well to criticism,' said Druss.

'That's very droll,' snapped Sieben, 'coming as it does from the man who tosses shipmates over the side at the first angry word. Now why was it a poor device?'

Eskodas leaned forward. 'I have been in many sieges. The point of greatest courage comes at the end, when all seems lost; that is when weak men break and run, or beg for their lives. You had the gods arrive just before that moment, and offer divine assistance to thwart the Vagrians. Therefore the truly climactic moment was lost, for as soon as the gods appeared we knew victory was assured.'

'I would have lost some of my best lines. Especially the end, where the warriors wonder if they will ever see the gods again.'

'Yes, I remember . . . *the eldritch rhymes, the wizard spells, the ringing of sweet Elven bells*. That one.'

'Precisely.'

'I prefer the grit and the reality of your earlier pieces:

> *But came the day, when youth was worn away,*
> *and locks once thought of steel and fire,*
> *proved both ephemeral and unreal*
> *against the onslaught of the years.*
> *How wrong are the young to believe in secrets*
> *or enchanted woods.'*

He lapsed into silence.

'Do you know all my work?' asked Sieben, clearly astonished.

Eskodas smiled. 'After you performed at Corteswain I sought out your books of poetry. There were five, I think. I have two still – the earliest works.'

'I am at a loss for words.'

'That'll be the day,' grunted Druss.

'Oh, be quiet. At last we meet a man of discernment on a ship full of rascals. Perhaps this voyage will not be so dreadful. So, tell me, Eskodas, what made you sign on for Ventria?'

'I like killing people,' answered Eskodas.

Druss's laughter bellowed out.

For the first few days the novelty of being at sea kept most of the mercenaries amused. They sat up on the deck during daylight hours, playing dice or telling stories. At night they slept under a tarpaulin that was looped and tied to the port and starboard rails.

Druss was fascinated by the sea and the seemingly endless horizons. Berthed at Mashrapur *The Thunderchild* had looked colossal, unsinkable. But here on the open sea she seemed fragile as a flower stem in a river torrent. Sieben had grown bored with the voyage very swiftly. Not so Druss. The sighing of the wind, the plunging and the rising of the ship, the call of the gulls high above – all these fired the young axeman's blood.

One morning he climbed the rigging to the giant cross-beam that held the mainsail. Sitting astride it he could see no sign of land, only the endless blue of the sea. A sailor walked along the beam towards him, barefooted, and using no hand-holds. He stood in delicate balance with hands on hips and looked down at Druss.

'No passengers should be up here,' he said.

Druss grinned at the young man. 'How can you just stand there, as if you were on a wide road? A puff of breeze could blow you away.'

'Like this?' asked the sailor, stepping from the beam. He twisted in mid-air, his hands fastening to a sail rope. For a moment he hung there, then lithely pulled himself up alongside the axeman.

'Very good,' said Druss. His eye was caught by a silver-blue flash in the water below and the sailor chuckled.

'The gods of the sea,' he told the passenger. 'Dolphins. If they are in the mood, you should see some wonderful sights.' A gleaming shape rose out of the water, spinning into the air before entering the sea again with scarcely a splash. Druss clambered down the rigging, determined to get a closer look at the sleek and beautiful animals performing in the water. High-pitched cries echoed around the ship as the creatures bobbed their heads above the surface.

Suddenly an arrow sped from the ship, plunging into one of the dolphins as it soared out of the water.

Within an instant the creatures had disappeared.

Druss glared at the archer while other men shouted at him, their anger sudden, their mood ugly.

'It was just a fish!' said the archer.

Milus Bar pushed his way through the crowd. 'You fool!' he said, his face almost grey beneath his tan. 'They are the gods of the sea; they come for us to pay homage. Sometimes they will even lead us through treacherous waters. Why did you have to shoot?'

'It was a good target,' said the man. 'And why not? It was my choice.'

'Aye, it was, lad,' Milus told him, 'but if our luck turns bad now it will be my choice to cut out your innards and feed them to the sharks.' The burly skipper stalked back to the tiller deck. The earlier good mood had evaporated now and the men drifted back to their pursuits with little pleasure.

Sieben approached Druss. 'By the gods, they were wondrous,' said the poet. 'According to legend, Asta's chariot is drawn by six white dolphins.'

Druss sighed. 'Who would have thought that anyone would consider killing one of them? Do they make good food, do you know?'

'No,' said Sieben. 'In the north they sometimes become entangled in the nets and drown. I have known men who cooked the meat; they say it tastes foul, and is impossible to digest.'

'Even worse then,' Druss grunted.

'It is no different from any other kind of hunting for sport, Druss. Is not a doe as beautiful as a dolphin?'

'You can eat a doe. Venison is fine meat.'

'But most of them don't hunt for food, do they? Not the nobles. They hunt for *pleasure*. They enjoy the chase, the terror of the prey, the final moment of the kill. Do not blame this man alone for his stupidity. He comes, as do we all, from a cruel world.'

Eskodas joined them. 'Not very inspiring, was he?' said the bowman.

'Who?'

'The man who shot the fish.'

'We were just talking about it.'

'I didn't know you understood the skills of archery,' said Eskodas, surprised.

'Archery? What are you talking about?'

'The bowman. He drew and loosed in a single movement. No hesitation. It is vital to pause and sight your target; he was over-anxious for the kill.'

'Be that as it may,' said Sieben, his irritation rising, 'we were talking about the morality of hunting.'

'Man is a killer by nature,' said Eskodas amiably. 'A natural hunter. Like him there!' Sieben and Druss both turned to see a silver-white fin cutting through the water. 'That's a shark. He scented the blood from the wounded dolphin. Now he'll hunt him down, following the trail as well as a Sathuli scout.'

Druss leaned over the side and watched the shimmering form slide by. 'Big fellow,' he said.

'They come bigger than that,' said Eskodas. 'I was on a ship once that sank in a storm off the Lentrian coast. Forty of us survived the wreck, and struck out for shore. Then the sharks arrived. Only three of us made it – and one of those had his right leg ripped away. He died three days later.'

'A storm, you say?' ventured Druss.

'Aye.'

'Like that one?' asked Druss, pointing to the east, where massive dark clouds were bunching. A flash of lightning speared across the sky, followed by a tremendous roll of thunder.

'Yes, like that. Let's hope it is not blowing our way.'

Within minutes the sky darkened, the sea surging and rising. *The Thunderchild* rolled and rose on the crests of giant waves, sliding into ever larger valleys of water. Then the rain began, faster and faster, icy needles that came from the sky like arrows.

Crouching by the port rail Sieben glanced to where the unfortunate archer was huddled. The man who had shot the dophin was alone, and holding fast to a rope. Lightning flashed above the ship.

'I would say our luck has changed,' observed Sieben.

But neither Druss nor Eskodas could hear him above the screaming of the wind.

Eskodas hooked his arms around the port rail and clung on as the storm raged. A huge wave crashed over the side of the ship, dislodging several men from their precarious holds on ropes and bales, sweeping them across the deck to crash into the dipping starboard rail. A post cracked, but no one heard it above the ominous roll of thunder booming from the night-dark sky. *The Thunderchild* rode high on the crest of an enormous wave, then slid down into a valley of raging water. A sailor carrying a coiled rope ran along the deck trying to reach the warriors at the starboard rail. A second wave crashed over him, hurling him into the struggling men. The port rail gave way, and within the space of a heartbeat some twenty men were swept from the deck. The ship reared like a frightened horse. Eskodas felt his grip on the rail post weaken. He tried to readjust his hold, but the ship lurched again. Torn from his position of relative safety, he slid headlong towards the yawning gap in the starboard rail.

A huge hand clamped down around his ankle, then he was hauled back. The axeman grinned at him, then handed him a length of rope. Swiftly Eskodas slipped it around his waist, fastening the other end to the mast. He glanced at Druss. The big man was *enjoying* the storm. Secure now, Eskodas scanned the deck. The poet was clinging to a section of the starboard rail that seemed none too secure, and high on the tiller deck the bowman could see Milus Bar wrestling with the tiller, trying to keep *The Thunderchild* ahead of the storm.

Another massive wave swept over the deck. The starboard rail cracked and Sieben slid over the edge of the deck. Druss untied his rope and rose. Eskodas shouted at him, but the axeman either did not hear, or ignored him. Druss ran across the heaving deck, fell once, then righted himself until he came alongside the shattered rail. Dropping to his knees Druss leaned over, dragging Sieben back to the deck.

Just behind them the man who had shot the dolphin was reaching for a rope with which to tie himself to a hauling ring set in the deck. The ship reared once more. The man tumbled to the deck, then slid on his back, cannoning into Druss who fell heavily. Still holding Seiben with one hand, the axeman tried to reach the doomed archer, but the man vanished into the raging sea.

Almost at that instant the sun appeared through broken clouds and the rain lessened, the sea settling. Druss rose and gazed into the water. Eskodas untied the rope that held him to the mast and stood, his legs unsteady. He walked to where Druss stood with Sieben.

The poet's face was white with shock. 'I'll never sail again,' he said. 'Never!'

Eskodas thrust out his hand. 'Thank you, Druss. You saved my life.'

The axeman chuckled. 'Had to, laddie. You're the only one on this boat who can leave our saga-master speechless.'

Bodasen appeared from the tiller deck. 'That was a reckless move, my friend,' he told Druss, 'but it was well done. I like to see bravery in the men who fight alongside me.'

As the Ventrian moved on, counting the men who were left, Eskodas shivered. 'I think we lost nearly thirty men,' he said.

'Twenty-seven,' said Druss.

Sieben crawled back to the edge of the deck and vomited into the sea. 'Make that twenty-seven and a half,' Eskodas added.

4

The young Emperor climbed down from the battlement walls and strode along the quayside, his staff officers following; his aide, Nebuchad, beside him. 'We can hold for months, Lord,' said Nebuchad, squinting his eyes against the glare from the Emperor's gilded breastplate. 'The walls are thick and high, and the catapults will prevent any attempt to storm the harbour mouth from the sea.'

Gorben shook his head. 'The walls will not protect us,' he told the young man. 'We have fewer than three thousand men here. The Naashanites have twenty times that number. Have you ever seen tiger ants attack a scorpion?'

'Yes, Lord.'

'They swarm all over it – that is how the enemy will storm. Capalis.'

'We will fight to the death,' promised an officer.

Gorben halted and turned. 'I know that,' he said, his dark eyes angry now. 'But dying will not bring us victory, will it, Jasua?'

'No, Lord.'

Gorben strode on, along near-empty streets, past boarded, deserted shops and empty taverns. At last he reached the entrance to the Magisters' Hall. The City Elders had long since departed and the ancient building had become the headquarters of the Capalis militia.

Gorben entered the hallway and stalked to his chambers, waving away his officers and the two servants who ran towards him – one bearing wine in a golden goblet, the second carrying a towel soaked with warm, scented water.

Once inside, the young Emperor kicked off his boots and hurled his white cloak across a nearby chair. There was one large window facing east, and before it was a desk of oak upon which were laid many maps, and reports from scouts and spies. Gorben sat down and stared at the largest map; it was of the Ventrian Empire and had been commissioned by his father six years ago.

He smoothed out the hide and gazed with undisguised fury at the map. Two-thirds of the Empire had been overrun. Leaning back in his chair, he remembered the palace at Nusa where he had been born and raised. Built on a hill overlooking a verdant valley, and a glistening city of white marble, the palace had taken twelve years to construct, and at one time more than eight thousand workers had laboured on the task, bringing in blocks of granite and marble and towering trunks of cedar, oak and elm to be fashioned by the Royal masons and carpenters.

Nusa – the first of the cities to fall. 'By all the gods of Hell, Father, I curse thee!' hissed Gorben. His father had reduced the size of the national army, relying on the wealth and power of his Satraps to protect the borders. But four of the nine Satraps had betrayed him, opening a path for the Naashanites to invade. His father had gathered an army to confront them, but his military skills were non-existent. He had fought bravely, so Gorben had been informed – but then they would say that to the new Emperor.

The new Emperor! Gorben rose now and walked to the silvered mirror on the far wall. What he saw was a young, handsome man, with black hair that gleamed with scented oils, and deep-set dark eyes. It was a strong face – but was it the face of an Emperor? Can you overcome the enemy, he asked himself silently, aware that any spoken word could be heard by servants and repeated. The gilded breastplate had been worn by warrior Emperors for two hundred years, and the cloak of purple was the mark of ultimate royalty. But these were merely adornments. What mattered was the man who wore them. Are you man enough? He gazed hard at his reflection, taking in the broad shoulders and the narrow waist, the muscular legs and powerful arms. But these too were merely adornments, he knew. The cloak of the soul.

Are you man enough?

The thought haunted him and he returned to his studies. Leaning forward with his elbows on the table, Gorben stared down at the map once more. Scrawled across it in charcoal was the new line of defence: Capalis to the west, Larian and Ectanis to the east. Gorben hurled the map aside. Beneath it lay a second map of the port city of Capalis.

Four gates, sixteen towers and a single wall which stretched from the sea in the south in a curving half-circle to the cliffs of the north. Two miles of wall, forty feet high, guarded by three thousand men, many of them raw recruits with no shields nor breastplates.

Rising, Gorben moved to the window and the balcony beyond. The harbour and the open sea met his gaze. 'Ah, Bodasen, my brother, where are you?' he whispered. The sea seemed so peaceful under the clear blue sky and the young Emperor sank into a padded seat and lifted his feet to rest on the balcony rail.

On this warm, tranquil day it seemed inconceivable that so much death and destruction had been visited upon the Empire in so short a time. He closed his eyes and recalled the Summer Banquet at Nusa last year. His father had been celebrating his forty-fourth birthday, and the seventeenth anniversary of his accession to the throne. The banquet had lasted eight days and there had been circuses, plays, knightly combat, displays of archery, running, wrestling and riding. The nine Satraps were all present, smiling and offering toasts to the Emperor. Shabag, tall and slim, hawk-eyed, and cruel of mouth. Gorben pictured him. He always wore black gloves, even in the hottest weather, and tunics of silk buttoned to the neck. Berish, fat and greedy, but a wonderful raconteur with his tales of orgies and humorous calamities. Darishan, the Fox of the North, the cavalryman, the Lancer, with his long silver hair braided like a woman. And Ashac, the Peacock, the lizard-eyed lover of boys. They had been given pride of place on either side of the Emperor, while his eldest son was forced to sit on the lower table, gazing up at these men of power!

Shabag, Berish, Darishan, and Ashac! Names and faces that burned Gorben's heart and soul. Traitors! Men who swore allegiance to his father, then saw him done to death, his lands overrun and his people slaughtered.

Gorben opened his eyes and took a deep breath. 'I will seek you out – each one of you,' he promised, 'and I will pay you back for your treachery.'

The threat was as empty as the treasury coffers, and Gorben knew it.

A soft tapping came at the outer door. 'Enter!' he called.

Nebuchad stepped inside and bowed low. 'The scouts are in, Lord. The enemy is less than two days' march from the walls.'

'What news from the east?'

'None, Lord. Perhaps our riders did not get through.'

'What of the supplies?'

Nebuchad reached inside his tunic and produced a parchment scroll which he unrolled. 'We have sixteen thousand loaves of unleavened bread, a thousand barrels of flour, eight hundred beef cattle, one hundred and forty goats. The sheep have not been counted yet. There is little cheese left, but a great quantity of oats and dried fruit.'

'What about salt?'

'Salt, Lord?'

'When we kill the cattle, how will we keep the meat fresh?'

'We could kill them only when we need them,' offered Nebuchad, reddening.

'To keep the cattle we must feed them, but there is no food to spare. Therefore they must be slaughtered, and the meat salted. Scour the city. And, Nebuchad?'

'Lord?'

'You did not mention water?'

'But, Lord, the river flows through the city.'

'Indeed it does. But what will we drink when the enemy dam it, or fill it with poisons?'

'There are artesian wells, I believe.'

'Locate them.'

The young man's head dropped. 'I fear, Lord, that I am not serving you well. I should have anticipated these requirements.'

Gorben smiled. 'You have much to think of and I am well pleased with you. But you do need help. Take Jasua.'

'As you wish, Lord,' said Nebuchad doubtfully.

'You do not like him?'

Nebuchad swallowed hard. 'It is not a question of "like", Lord. But he treats me with . . . contempt.'

Gorben's eyes narrowed, but he held the anger from his voice. 'Tell him it is my wish that he assist you. Now go.'

As the door closed, Gorben slumped down on to a satin-covered couch. 'Sweet Lords of Heaven,' he whispered, 'does my future depend on men of such little substance?' He sighed, then gazed once more out to sea. 'I need you, Bodasen,' he said. 'By all that is sacred, I need you!'

Bodasen stood on the tiller deck, his right hand shading his eyes, his vision focusing on the far horizon. On the main deck sailors were busy repairing the rail, while others were aloft in the rigging, or refastening bales that had slipped during the storm.

'You'll see pirates soon enough if they are near,' said Milus Bar.

Bodasen nodded and swung back to the skipper. 'With a mere twenty-four warriors, I am hoping not to see them at all,' he said softly.

The captain chuckled. 'In life we do not always get what we want, my Ventrian friend. I did not want a storm. I did not want my first wife to leave me – nor my second wife to stay.' He shrugged. 'Such is life, eh?'

'You do not seem unduly concerned.'

'I am a fatalist, Bodasen. What will be will be.'

'Could we outrun them?'

Milus Bar shrugged once more. 'It depends on which direction they are coming from.' He waved his hand in the air. 'The wind. Behind us? Yes. There is not a swifter ship on the ocean than my *Thunderchild*. Ahead and to the west – probably. Ahead and to the east – no. They would ram us. They have a great advantage, for many of their vessels are triremes with three banks of oars. You would be amazed, my friend, at the speed with which they can turn and ram.'

'How long now to Capalis?'

'Two days – maybe three if the wind drops.'

Bodasen moved across the tiller deck, climbing down the six steps to the main deck. He saw Druss, Sieben and Eskodas by the prow and walked towards them. Druss saw him and glanced up.

'Just the man we need,' said the axeman. 'We are talking about Ventria. Sieben maintains there are mountains there which brush the moon. Is it so?'

'I have not seen all of the Empire,' Bodasen told him, 'but according to our astronomers the moon is more than a quarter of a million miles from the surface of the earth. Therefore I would doubt it.'

'Such eastern nonsense,' mocked Sieben. 'There was a Drenai archer once, who fired a shaft into the moon. He had a great bow called Akansin, twelve feet long and woven with spells. He fired a black arrow, which he named Paka. Attached to the arrow was a thread of silver, which he used to climb to the moon. He sat upon it as it sailed around the great plate of the earth.'

'Mere fable,' insisted Bodasen.

'It is recorded in the library at Drenan – in the *Historic* section.'

'All that tells me is how limited is your understanding of the universe,' said Bodasen. 'Do you still believe the sun is a golden chariot drawn by six white, winged horses?' He sat down upon a coiled rope. 'Or perhaps that the earth sits upon the shoulders of an elephant, or some such beast?'

Sieben smiled. 'No, we do not. But would it not be better if we did? Is there not a certain beauty in the tale? One day I shall craft a bow and shoot at the moon.'

'Never mind the moon,' said Druss. 'I want to know about Ventria.'

'According to the census ordered by the Emperor fifteen years ago, and concluded only last year, the Greater Ventrian empire is 214,969 square miles. It has an estimated population of fifteen and a half million people. On a succession of fast horses, a rider galloping along the borders would return to where he started in just under four years.'

Druss looked crestfallen. He swallowed hard. 'So large?'

'So large,' agreed Bodasen.

Druss's eyes narrowed. 'I will find her,' he said at last.

'Of course you will,' said Bodasen. 'She left with Kabuchek and he will have headed for his home in Ectanis, which means he will have docked at Capalis. Kabuchek is a famous man, senior advisor to the Satrap, Shabag. He will not be hard to find. Unless . . .'

'Unless what?' queried Druss.

'Unless Ectanis has already fallen.'

'Sail! Sail!' came a cry from the rigging. Bodasen leapt up, eyes scanning the glittering water. Then he saw the ship in the east with sails furled, three banks of oars glistening like wings. Swinging back towards the main deck, he drew his sabre.

'Gather your weapons,' he shouted.

Druss donned his jerkin and helm and stood at the prow, watching the trireme glide towards them. Even at this distance he could see the fighting men thronging the decks.

'A magnificent ship,' he said.

Beside him Sieben nodded. 'The very best. Two hundred and forty oars. See there! At the prow!'

Druss focused on the oncoming ship, and saw a glint of gold at the waterline. 'I see it.'

'That is the ram. It is an extension of the keel, and it is covered with reinforced bronze. With three banks of oars at full stretch, that ram could punch through the hull of the strongest vessel!'

'Will that be their plan?' Druss asked.

Sieben shook his head. 'I doubt it. This is a merchant vessel, ripe for plunder. They will come in close, the oars will be withdrawn, and they'll try to drag us in with grappling-hooks.'

Druss hefted Snaga and glanced back along the deck. The remaining Drenai warriors were armoured now, their faces grim. Bowmen, Eskodas among them, were climbing the rigging to hook themselves into place high above the deck, ready to shoot down into the enemy. Bodasen was standing on the tiller deck with a black breastplate buckled to his torso.

The Thunderchild swung away towards the west, then veered back. In the distance two more sails could be seen and Sieben swore. 'We can't fight them all,' he said. Druss glanced at the billowing sail, and then back at the newly sighted vessel.

'They don't look the same,' he observed. 'They're bulkier. No oars. And they're tacking against the wind. If we can deal with the trireme, they'll not catch us.'

Sieben chuckled. 'Aye, aye, captain. I bow to your superior knowledge of the sea.'

'I'm a swift learner. That's because I listen.'

'You never listen to me. I've lost count of the number of times you've fallen asleep during our conversations on this voyage.'

The Thunderchild swung again, veering away from the trireme.

Druss swore and ran back along the deck, climbing swiftly to where Bodasen stood with Milus Bar at the tiller.

'What are you doing?' he yelled at the skipper.

'Get off my deck!' roared Milus.

'If you keep this course, we'll have three ships to fight,' Druss snarled.

'What other choices are there?' queried Bodasen. 'We cannot defeat a trireme.'

'Why?' asked Druss. 'They are only men.'

'They have close to one hundred fighting men – plus the oarsmen. We have twenty-four, and a few sailors. The odds speak for themselves.'

Druss glanced back at the sailing-ships to the west. 'How many men do they have?'

Bodasen spread his hands and looked to Milus Bar. The captain thought for a moment. 'More than two hundred on each ship,' he admitted.

'Can we outrun them?'

'If we get a mist, or if we can keep them off until dusk.'

'What chance of either?' enquired the axeman.

'Precious little,' said Milus.

'Then let's at least take the fight to them.'

'How do you suggest we do that, young man?' the captain asked.

Druss smiled. 'I'm no sailor, but it seems to me their biggest advantage lies in the oars. Can we not try to smash them?'

'We could,' admitted Milus, 'but that would bring us in close enough for their grappling-hooks. We'd be finished then; they'd board us.'

'Or we board them!' snapped Druss.

'Milus laughed aloud. 'You are insane!'

'Insane and quite correct,' said Bodasen. 'They are hunting us down like wolves around a stag. Let's do it, Milus!'

For a moment the captain stood and stared at the two warriors, then he swore and leaned in to the tiller. *The Thunderchild* swung towards the oncoming trireme.

His name was Earin Shad, though none of his crew used it. They addressed him to his face as Sea Lord, or Great One, while behind his back they used the Naashanite slang – *Bojeeba*, The Shark.

Earin Shad was a tall man, slim and round-shouldered, long of neck, with protruding eyes that glimmered pearl-grey and a lipless mouth that never smiled. No one aboard the *Darkwind* knew from whence he came, only that he had been a pirate leader for more than two decades. One of the Lords of the Corsairs, mighty men who ruled the seas, he was said to own palaces on several of the Thousand

Islands, and to be as rich as one of the eastern kings. This did not show in his appearance. He wore a simple breastplate of shaped bronze, and a winged helm looted from a merchant ship twelve years before. At his hip hung a sabre with a simple hilt of polished wood and a fist-guard of plain brass. Earin Shad was not a man who liked extravagance.

He stood at the stern as the steady, rhythmic pound of the drums urged the rowers to greater efforts, and the occasional crack of the whip sounded against the bare skin of a slacker's back. His pale eyes narrowed as the merchant vessel swung towards the *Darkwind*.

'What is he doing?' asked the giant Patek.

Earin Shad glanced up at the man. 'He has seen Reda's ship and he is trying to cut by us. He won't succeed.' Swinging to the steersman, a short toothless old man named Luba, Earin Shad saw that the man was already altering course. 'Steady now,' he said. 'We don't want her rammed.'

'Aye, Sea Lord!'

'Make ready with the hooks!' bellowed Patek. The giant watched as the men gathered coiled ropes, attaching them to the three-clawed grappling-hooks. Then he transferred his gaze to the oncoming ship. 'Look at that, Sea Lord!' he said, pointing at *The Thunderchild's* prow. There was a man there, dressed in black; he had raised a double-headed axe above his head in a gesture of defiance.

'They'll never cut all the ropes,' said Patek. Earin Shad did not reply – he was scanning the decks of the enemy ship, seeking any sign of female passengers. He saw none, and his mood darkened. To compensate for his disappointment he found himself remembering the last ship they had taken three weeks ago, and the Satrap's daughter she had carried. He licked his lips at the memory. Proud, defiant, and comely – the whip alone had not tamed her, nor the stinging slaps. And even after he had raped her repeatedly, still her eyes shone with murderous intent. Ah, she was lively, no doubt about that. But he had found her weakness; he always did. And when he had he experienced, as always, both triumph and disappointment. The moment of conquest, when she had begged him to take her – had promised to serve him always, in any way that he chose – had been exquisite. But then sadness had flowed within him, followed by anger. He had killed her quickly, which disappointed the men. But then she had earned that, he thought. She had held her nerve for five days in the darkness of the hold, in the company of the black rats.

Earin Shad sniffed, then cleared his throat. This was no time to be considering pleasures.

A cabin door opened behind him and he heard the soft footfalls of the young sorcerer.

'Good day, Sea Lord,' said Gamara. Patek moved away, avoiding the sorcerer's gaze.

604

Earin Shad nodded to the slender Chiatze. 'The omens are good, I take it?' he asked.

Gamara spread his hands in an elegant gesture. 'It would be a waste of power to cast the stones, Sea Lord. During the storm they lost half their men.'

'And you are sure they are carrying gold?'

The Chiatze grinned, showing a perfect line of small, white teeth. Like a child's, thought Earin Shad. He looked into the man's dark, slanted eyes. 'How much are they carrying?'

'Two hundred and sixty thousand gold pieces. Bodasen gathered it from Ventrian merchants in Mashrapur.'

'You should have cast the stones,' said Earin Shad.

'We will see much blood,' answered Gamara. 'Aha! See, my good Lord, the sharks, as ever, follow in your wake. They are like pets, are they not?'

Earin Shad did not glance at the grey forms slipping effortlessly through the water, fins like raised sword-blades. 'They are the vultures of the sea,' he said, 'and I like them not at all.'

The wind shifted and *The Thunderchild* swung like a dancer on the white-flecked waves. On the decks of the *Darkwind* scores of warriors crouched by the starboard rail as the two ships moved ever closer. It will be close, thought Earin Shad; they will veer again and try to pull away. Anticipating the move he bellowed an order to Patek, who now stood on the main deck among the men. The giant leaned over the side and repeated the instruction to the oars chief. Immediately the starboard oars lifted from the water, the 120 rowers on the port side continuing to row. *Darkwind* spun to starboard.

The Thunderchild sped on, then veered towards the oncoming vessel. On the prow the dark-bearded warrior was still waving the gleaming axe – and in that instant Earin Shad knew he had miscalculated. 'Bring in the oars!' he shouted.

Patek glanced up, astonished. 'What, Lord?'

'The oars, man! They're attacking *us*!'

It was too late. Even as Patek leaned over the side to shout the order *The Thunderchild* leapt to the attack, swinging violently towards *Darkwind*, the prow striking the first ranks of oars. Wood snapped violently with explosive cracks, mingled with the screams of the slave rowers as the heavy oars smashed into arms and skulls, shoulders and ribs.

Grappling-lines were hurled out, iron claws biting into wood or hooking into *The Thunderchild*'s rigging. An arrow slashed into the chest of a corsair; the man pitched back, struggled to rise, then fell again. The corsairs hauled on the grappling-lines and the two ships edged together.

Earin Shad was furious. Half the oars on the starboard side had

605

been smashed, and the gods alone knew how many slaves were crippled. Now he would be forced to limp to port. 'Ready to board!' he yelled.

The two ships crashed together. The corsairs rose and clambered to the rails.

In that moment the black-bearded warrior on the enemy ship stepped up to the prow and leaped into the massed ranks of waiting corsairs. Earin Shad could hardly believe what he was seeing. The black-garbed axeman sent several men spinning to the deck, almost fell himself, then swung his axe. A man screamed as blood sprayed from a terrible wound in his chest. The axe rose and fell – and the corsairs scattered back from the apparently deranged warrior.

He charged them, the axe cleaving into their ranks. Further along the deck other corsairs were still trying to board the merchant ship and meeting ferocious resistance from the Drenai warriors, but at the centre of the main deck all was chaos. A man ran in behind the axeman, a curved knife raised to stab him in the back. But an arrow slashed into the assailant's throat and he stumbled and fell.

Several Drenai warriors leapt to join the axeman. Earin Shad swore and drew his sabre, vaulting the rail and landing smoothly on the deck below. When a swordsman ran at him he parried the lunge and sent a riposte that missed the neck but opened the man's face from cheek-bone to chin. As the warrior fell back Earin Shad plunged his blade into the man's mouth and up into the brain.

A lithe warrior in black breastplate and helm despatched a corsair and moved in on Earin Shad. The Corsair captain blocked a fierce thrust and attempted a riposte, only to leap back as his opponent's blade slashed by his face. The man was dark-skinned and dark-eyed, and a master swordsman.

Earin Shad stepped back and drew a dagger. 'Ventrian?' he enquired.

The man smiled. 'Indeed I am.' A corsair leapt from behind the swordsman. He spun and disembowelled the man, then swung back in time to block a thrust from Earin Shad. 'I am Bodasen.'

The corsairs were tough, hardy men, long used to battles and the risk of death. But they had never had to face a phenomenon like the man with the axe. Watching from the tiller deck of *The Thunderchild*, Sieben saw them fall back, again and again, from Druss's frenzied, tireless assaults. Though the day was warm Sieben felt a chill in his blood as he watched the axe cleaving into the hapless pirates. Druss was unstoppable – and Sieben knew why. When swordsmen fought the outcome rested on skill, but armed with the terrible double-headed axe there was no skill needed, just power and an eagerness for combat – a battle lust that seemed unquenchable. No one could stand against him, for the only way to win was to run within the reach of those deadly blades. Death was not a risk; it was a certainty. And Druss himself seemed to possess a sixth sense. Corsairs circled behind him, but even as they rushed in he swung to face them, the axe-blades slashing through skin, flesh and bone. Several of the corsairs threw down their weapons, backing away from the huge, blood-smeared warrior. These Druss ignored.

Sieben flicked his gaze to where Bodasen fought with the enemy captain. Their swords, shimmering in the sunlight, seemed fragile and insubstantial against the raw power of Druss and his axe.

A giant figure bearing an iron war hammer leapt at Druss – just as Snaga became embedded in the ribs of a charging corsair. Druss ducked under the swinging weapon and sent a left hook that exploded against the man's jaw. Even as the giant fell, Druss snatched up his axe and near beheaded a daring attacker. Other Drenai warriors ran to join him and the corsairs backed away, dismayed and demoralised.

'Throw your weapons down!' bellowed Druss, 'And live!'

There was little hesitation and swords, sabres, cutlasses and knives clattered to the deck. Druss turned to see Bodasen block a thrust and send a lightning counter that ripped across the enemy captain's throat. Blood sprayed from the wound. The captain half fell, and tried for one last stab. But his strength fled from him and he pitched face first to the deck.

A man in flowing green robes appeared at the tiller deck rail. Slender and tall, his hair waxed to his skull, he lifted his hands. Sieben blinked. He seemed to be holding two spheres of glowing brass – no, the poet realised, not brass – but fire!

'Look out, Druss!' he shouted.

The sorcerer threw out his hands and a sheet of flame seared towards the axeman. Snaga flashed up; the flames struck the silver heads.

Time stopped for the poet. In a fraction of a heartbeat he saw a scene he would never forget. At the moment when the flames struck the axe, a demonic figure appeared above Druss, its skin iron-grey and scaled, its long, powerful arms ending in taloned fingers. The flames rebounded from the creature and slashed back into the sorcerer. His robes blazed and his chest imploded – a gaping hole appearing in his torso, through which Sieben could see the sky. The sorcerer toppled from the deck and the demon disappeared.

'Sweet mother of Cires!' whispered Sieben. He turned to Milus Bar. 'Did you see it?'

'Aye! The axe saved him right enough.'

'Axe? Did you not see the creature?'

'What are you talking about, man?'

Sieben felt his heart hammering. He saw Eskodas climbing down from the rigging and ran to him. 'What did you see when the flames came at Druss?' he asked, grabbing the bowman's arm.

'I saw him deflect them with his axe. What is wrong with you?'

'Nothing. Nothing at all.'

'We'd better cut free these ropes,' said Eskodas. 'The other ships are closing in.'

The Drenai warriors on the *Darkwind* also saw the two battle vessels approaching. With the defeated corsair standing by, they hacked at the ropes and then leapt back to *The Thunderchild*. Druss and Bodasen came last. None tried to stop them.

The giant Druss had felled rose unsteadily, then ran to the rail and leapt after the axeman, landing amidst a group of Drenai warriors and scattering them.

'It's not over!' he yelled. 'Face me!'

The Thunderchild eased away from the corsair ship, the wind gathering once more in her sails as Druss dropped Snaga to the deck and advanced on the giant. The corsair – almost a foot taller than the blood-drenched Drenai – landed the first blow, a juddering right that split the skin above Druss's left eye. Druss pushed through the blow and sent an uppercut that thundered against the man's rib-cage. The corsair grunted and smashed a left hook into Druss's jaw, making him stumble, then hit him again with lefts and rights. Druss rode them and hammered an overhand right that spun his opponent in a half-circle. Following up he hit him again, clubbing the man to his knees. Stepping back, Druss sent a vicious kick that almost lifted the giant from the deck. He slumped down, tried to rise, then lay still.

'Druss! Druss! Druss!' yelled the surviving Drenai warriors as *The Thunderchild* slipped away from the pursuing vessels.

Sieben sat down and stared at his friend.

No wonder you are so deadly, he thought. Sweet Heaven, Druss, you are possessed!

Druss moved wearily to the starboard rail, not even looking at the pursuing ships which were even now falling further behind *The Thunderchild*. Blood was clotting on his face, and he rubbed his left eye where the lashes were matted and sticky. Dropping Snaga to the deck Druss peeled off his jerkin, allowing the breeze to cool his skin.

Eskodas appeared alongside him, carrying a bucket of water. 'Is any of that blood yours?' the bowman asked.

Druss shrugged, uncaring. Removing his gauntlets, he dipped his hands into the bucket, splashing water to his face and beard. Then he lifted the bucket and tipped the contents over his head.

Eskodas scanned his body. 'You have minor wounds,' he said, probing at a narrow cut on Druss's shoulder and a gash in the side. 'Neither are deep. I'll get needle and thread.'

Druss said nothing. He felt a great weariness settle on him, a dullness of the spirit that left him leached of energy. He thought of Rowena, her gentleness and tranquillity, and of the peace he had known when beside her. Lifting his head, he leaned his huge hands on the rail. Behind him he heard laughter, and turned to see some of the warriors baiting the giant corsair. They had tied his hands behind his back and were jabbing at him with knives, forcing him to leap and dance.

Bodasen climbed down from the tiller deck. 'Enough of that!' he shouted.

'It's just a little sport before we throw him to the sharks,' replied a wiry warrior with a black and silver beard.

'No one will be thrown to the sharks,' snapped Bodasen. 'Now untie him.'

The men grumbled, but obeyed the order, and the giant stood rubbing his chafed wrists. His eyes met Druss's gaze, but the corsair's expression was unreadable. Bodasen led the man to the small cabin door below the tiller deck and they disappeared from view.

Eskodas returned and stitched the wounds in the axeman's shoulder and side. He worked swiftly and expertly. 'You must have had the gods with you,' he said. 'They granted you good luck.'

'A man makes his own luck,' said Druss.

Eskodas chuckled. 'Aye. Trust in the Source – but keep a spare bowstring handy. That's what my old teacher used to tell me.'

Druss thought back to the action on the trireme. 'You helped me,' he said, remembering the arrow that had killed the man coming in behind him.

'It was a good shot,' agreed Eskodas. 'How are you feeling?'

Druss shrugged. 'Like I could sleep for a week.'

'It is very natural, my friend. Battle lust roars through the blood, but the aftermath is unbearably depressing. Not many poets sing songs about that.' Eskodas took up a cloth and sponged the blood from Druss's jerkin, handing it back to the axeman. 'You are a great fighter, Druss – perhaps the best I've seen.'

Druss slipped on his jerkin, gathered Snaga and walked to the prow where he stretched out between two bales. He slept for just under an hour, but was woken by Bodasen; he opened his eyes and saw the Ventrian bending over him as the sun was setting.

'We need to talk, my friend,' said Bodasen and Druss sat up. The stitches in his side pulled tight as he stretched. He swore softly. 'I'm tired,' said the axeman. 'So let's make this brief.'

'I have spoken with the corsair. His name is Patek . . .'

'I don't care what his name is.'

Bodasen sighed. 'In return for information about the numbers of corsair vessels, I have promised him his liberty when we reach Capalis. I have given him my word.'

'What has this to do with me?'

'I would like your word also that you will not kill him.'

'I don't want to kill him. He means nothing to me.'

'Then say the words, my friend.'

Druss looked into the Ventrian's dark eyes. 'There is something else,' he said, 'something you are not telling me.'

'Indeed there is,' agreed Bodasen. 'Tell me that you will allow my promise to Patek to be honoured, and I shall explain all.'

'Very well. I will not kill him. Now say what you have to say – and then let me get some sleep.'

Bodasen drew in a long, deep breath. 'The trireme was the *Dark-wind*. The captain was Earin Shad, one of the leading Corsair . . . kings, if you like. They have been patrolling these waters for some months. One of the ships they . . . plundered . . .' Bodasen fell silent. He licked his lips. 'Druss, I'm sorry. Kabuchek's ship was taken and sunk, the passengers and crew thrown to the sharks. No one survived.'

Druss sat very still. All anger vanished from him.

'I wish there was something I could say or do to lessen your pain,' said Bodasen. 'I know that you loved her.'

'Leave me be,' whispered Druss. 'Just leave me be.'

5

Word soon spread among the warriors and crew of the tragedy that had befallen the huge axeman. Many of the men could not understand the depth of his grief, knowing nothing of love, but all could see the change in him. He sat at the prow, staring out over the sea, the massive axe in his hands. Sieben alone could approach him, but even the poet did not remain with him for long.

There was little laughter for the remaining three days of the voyage, for Druss's brooding presence seemed to fill the deck. The corsair giant, Patek, remained as far from the axeman as space would allow, spending his time on the tiller deck.

On the morning of the fourth day the distant towers of Capalis could be seen, white marble glinting in the sun.

Sieben approached Druss. 'Milus Bar intends to pick up a cargo of spices and attempt the return journey. Shall we stay on board?'

'I'm not going back,' said Druss.

'There is nothing here for us now,' pointed out the poet.

'There is the enemy,' the axeman grunted.

'What enemy?'

'The Naashanites.'

Sieben shook his head. 'I don't understand you. We don't even know a Naashanite!'

'They killed my Rowena. I'll make them pay.'

Sieben was about to debate the point, but he stopped himself. The Naashanites had bought the services of the corsairs and in Druss's mind this made them guilty. Sieben wanted to argue, to hammer home to Druss that the real villain was Earin Shad, and that he was now dead. But what was the use? In the midst of his grief Druss would not listen. His eyes were cold, almost lifeless, and he clung to the axe as if it were his only friend.

'She must have been a very special woman,' observed Eskodas when he and Sieben stood by the port rail as *The Thunderchild* eased her way into the harbour.

'I never met her. But he speaks of her with reverence.'

Eskodas nodded, then pointed to the quayside. 'There are no dock-workers,' he said, 'only soldiers. The city must be under siege.'

Sieben saw movement at the far end of the quay, a column of soldiers wearing black breastplates adorned with silver marching behind a tall, wide-shouldered nobleman. 'That must be Gorben,' he said. 'He walks as if he owns the world.'

Eskodas chuckled. 'Not any more – but I'll agree he is a remarkably handsome fellow.'

The Emperor wore a simple black cloak above an unadorned breastplate, yet he still – like a hero of legend – commanded attention. Men ceased in their work as he approached, and Bodasen leapt from the ship even before the mooring ropes were fastened, landing lightly and stepping into the other man's embrace. The Emperor clapped him on the back, and kissed Bodasen on both cheeks.

'I'd say they were friends,' observed Eskodas dryly.

'Strange customs they have in foreign lands,' said Sieben, with a grin.

The gangplank was lowered and a squad of soldiers moved on board, vanishing below decks and reappearing bearing heavy chests of brass-bound oak.

'Gold, I'd say,' whispered Eskodas and Sieben nodded. Twenty chests in all were removed before the Drenai warriors were allowed to disembark. Sieben clambered down the gangplank just behind the bowman. As he stepped ashore he felt the ground move beneath him and he almost stumbled, then righted himself.

'Is it an earthquake?' he asked Eskodas.

'No, my friend, it is merely that you are so used to the pitching and rolling of the ship that your legs are unaccustomed to solid stone. It will pass very swiftly.'

Druss strode down to join them as Bodasen stepped forward, the Emperor beside him.

'And this, my Lord, is the warrior I spoke of – Druss the Axeman. Almost single-handedly he destroyed the corsairs.'

'I would like to have seen it,' said Gorben. 'But there is time yet to admire your prowess. The enemy are camped around our city and the attacks have begun.'

Druss said nothing, but the Emperor seemed unconcerned. 'May I see your axe?' he asked. Druss nodded and passed the weapon to the monarch. Gorben accepted it and lifted the blades to his face. 'Remarkable workmanship. Not a nick or a rust mark – the surface is entirely unblemished. A rare kind of steel.' He examined the black haft and the silver runes. 'This is an ancient weapon, and has seen much death.'

'It will see more,' said Druss, his voice low and rumbling. At the sound Sieben shivered.

Gorben smiled and handed back the axe, then turned to Bodasen. 'When you have settled your men into their quarters you will find me at the Magisters' Hall.' He strode away without another word.

Bodasen's face was white with anger. 'When you are in the presence of the Emperor you should bow deeply. He is a man to respect.'

'We Drenai are not well versed in subservient behaviour,' Sieben pointed out.

'In Ventria such disrespect is punishable by disembowelling,' said Bodasen.

'But I think we can learn,' Sieben told him cheerfully.

Bodasen smiled. 'See that you do, my friends. These are not Drenai lands, and there are other customs here. The Emperor is a good man, a fine man. Even so he must maintain discipline, and he will not tolerate such bad manners again.'

The Drenai warriors were billeted in the town centre, all save Druss and Sieben who had not signed on to fight for the Ventrians. Bodasen took the two of them to a deserted inn and told them to choose their own rooms. Food, he said, could be found at either of the two main barracks, although there were still some shops and stalls in the town centre.

'Do you want to look at the city?' asked Sieben, after the Ventrian general had left. Druss sat on a narrow bed staring at his hands; he did not seem to hear the question. The poet sat alongside him. 'How are you feeling?' he asked softly.

'Empty.'

'Everyone dies, Druss. Even you and I. It is not your fault.'

'I don't care about *fault*. I just keep thinking about our time in the mountains together. I can still feel . . . the touch of her hand. I can still

612

hear . . .' He stumbled to silence, his face reddened and his jaw set in a tight line. 'What was that about the city?' he growled.

'I thought we could take a look around.'

'Good. Let's go.' Druss rose, gathered his axe and strode through the door. The inn was situated on Vine Street. Bodasen had given them directions through the city and these were easy to follow, the roads being wide, the signs in several languages including the western tongue. The buildings were of white and grey stone, some more than four levels high. There were gleaming towers, domed palaces, gardens and tree-lined avenues. The scent of flowers, jasmine and rose, was everywhere.

'It is very beautiful,' observed Sieben. They passed a near-deserted barracks and headed on towards the eastern wall. From the distance they could hear the clash of blades and the thin cries of wounded men. 'I think I've seen enough,' announced Sieben, halting.

Druss gave a cold smile. 'As you wish,' he said.

'There's a temple back there I'd like to see more of. You know, the one with the white horses?'

'I saw it,' said Druss. The two men retraced their steps until they came to a large square. The temple was domed, and around it were twelve exquisitely sculpted statues of rearing horses, three times larger than life. A huge arched gateway, with open gates of polished brass and silver between beckoned the two men into the temple. The domed roof had seven windows, all of coloured glass, and beams of light criss-crossed the high altar. There were benches that could seat almost a thousand people, Sieben calculated, and upon the altar was a table on which was set a hunting horn of gold encrusted with gems. The poet walked down the aisle and climbed to the altar. 'It's worth a fortune,' he said.

'On the contrary,' came a low voice, 'it is priceless.' Sieben turned to see a priest in robes of grey wool, embroidered with silver thread. The man was tall, his shaven head and long nose giving him a birdlike appearance. 'Welcome to the shrine of Pashtar Sen.'

'The citizens here must be worthy of great trust,' said Sieben. 'Such a prize as this would gain a man enormous wealth.'

The priest gave a thin smile. 'Not really. Lift it!'

Sieben reached out his hand, but his fingers closed on air. The golden horn, so substantial to the eye, was merely an image. 'In-credible!' whispered the poet. 'How is it done?'

The priest shrugged and spread his thin arms. 'Pashtar Sen worked the miracle a thousand years ago. He was a poet and a scholar, but also a man of war. According to myth he met the goddess, Ciris, and she gave him the hunting horn as a reward for his valour. He placed it here. And the moment it left his grasp it became as you see it.'

'What is its purpose?' Sieben asked.

'It has healing properties. Barren women are said to become fertile if they lie upon the altar and cover the horn. There is some evidence that this is true. And once every ten years the horn is said to become solid once more and then, so we are told, it can bring a man back from the halls of death, or carry his spirit to the stars.'

'Have you ever seen it become solid?'

'No. And I have been a servant here for thirty-seven years.'

'Fascinating. What happened to Pashtar Sen?'

'He refused to fight for the Emperor and was impaled on a spike of iron.'

'Not a good ending.'

'Indeed not, but he was a man of principle and believed the Emperor to be in the wrong. Are you here to fight for Ventria?'

'No. We are visitors.'

The priest nodded and turned to Druss. 'Your mind is far away, my son,' he said. 'Are you troubled?'

'He has suffered a great loss,' said Sieben swiftly.

'A loved one? Ah, I see. Would you wish to commune with her, my son?'

'What do you mean?' growled Druss.

'I could summon her spirit. It might bring you peace.'

Druss stepped forward. 'You could do that?'

'I could try. Follow me.' The priest led them into the shadowed recesses at the rear of the temple, then along a narrow corridor to a small, windowless room. 'You must leave your weapons outside,' said the priest. Druss leaned Snaga against the wall, and Sieben hung his baldric of knives to the haft. Inside the room there were two chairs facing one another; the priest sat in the first, beckoning Druss to take the second. 'This room,' said the priest, 'is a place of harmony. No profane language has ever been heard here. It is a room of prayer and kind thoughts. It has been so for a thousand years. Whatever happens, please remember that. Now give me your hand.'

Druss stretched out his arm and the priest took hold of his hand, asking who it was that he wished to call. Druss told him. 'And your name, my son?'

'Druss.'

The man licked his lips and sat, eyes closed, for several minutes. Then he spoke. 'I call to thee, Rowena, child of the mountains. I call to thee on behalf of Druss. I call to thee across the plains of Heaven, I speak to thee across the vales of Earth. I reach out to thee, even unto the dark places below the oceans of the world, and the arid deserts of Hell.' For a moment nothing happened. Then the priest stiffened and cried out. He slumped down in the chair, head dropping to his chest.

His mouth opened and a single word issued forth: 'Druss!' It was a woman's voice. Sieben was startled. He glanced at the axeman; all colour faded from Druss's face.

'Rowena!'

'I love you, Druss. Where are you?'

'In Ventria. I came for you.'

'I am here waiting. Druss! Oh no, everything is fading. Druss, can you hear . . . ?'

'Rowena!' shouted Druss, storming to his feet. The priest jerked and awoke. 'I am sorry,' he said. 'I did not find her.'

'I spoke to her,' said Druss, hauling the man to his feet. 'Get her again!'

'I cannot. There was no one. Nothing happened!'

'Druss! Let him go!' shouted Sieben, grabbing Druss's arm. The axeman released his hold on the priest's robes and walked from the room.

'I don't understand,' whispered the man. 'There was nothing!'

'You spoke with the voice of a woman,' Sieben told him. 'Druss recognised it.'

'It is most peculiar, my son. Whenever I commune with the dead I know their words. But it was as if I slept.'

'Do not concern yourself,' said Sieben, fishing in his money-pouch for a silver coin.

'I take no money,' said the man, with a shy smile. 'But I am perplexed and I will think on what just happened.'

'I'm sure he will too,' said Sieben.

He found Druss standing by the altar, reaching out to the shimmering golden horn, his huge fingers trying to close around it. The axeman's face was set in concentration, the muscles of his jaw showing through the dark beard.

'What are you doing?' asked Sieben, his voice gentle.

'He said it could bring back the dead.'

'No, my friend. He said that was the *legend*. There is a difference. Come away. We'll find a tavern somewhere in this city, and we'll drink.'

Druss slammed his hand down on to the altar, the golden horn apparently growing through the skin of his fist. 'I don't need to drink! Gods, I need to fight!' Snatching up the axe, the big man strode from the temple.

The priest appeared alongside Sieben. 'I fear that, despite my good intentions, the result of my labour was not as I had hoped,' he said.

'He'll survive, Father.' Sieben turned to the priest. 'Tell me, what do you know of demon possession?'

'Too much – and too little. You think you are possessed?'

'No, not I. Druss.'

615

The priest shook his head. 'Had he been so . . . afflicted . . . I would have sensed it when I touched his hand. No, your friend is his own man.'

Sieben sat down on a bench seat and told the priest what he had seen on the deck of the corsair trireme. The priest listened in silence. 'How did he come by the axe?' he asked.

'Family heirloom, I understand.'

'If there is a demonic presence, my son, I believe you will find it hidden within the weapon. Many of the ancient blades were crafted with spells, in order to give the wielder greater strength or cunning. Some even had the power to heal wounds, so it is said. Look to the axe.'

'What if it is just the axe? Surely that will only help him in times of combat?'

'Would that were true,' said the priest, shaking his head. 'But evil does not exist in order to serve, but to rule. If the axe is possessed it will have a history – a dark history. Ask him of its past. And when you hear it, and of the men who wielded it, you will understand my words.'

Sieben thanked the man and left the temple. There was no sign of Druss, and the poet had no wish to venture near the walls. He strolled through the near deserted city until he heard the sound of music coming from a courtyard nearby. He approached a wrought-iron gate and saw three women sitting in a garden. One of them was playing a lyre, the others were singing a gentle love song as Sieben stepped into the gateway.

'Good afternoon, ladies,' he said, offering them his most dazzling smile. The music ceased and the three all gazed at him. They were young and pretty – the oldest, he calculated, around seventeen. She was dark-haired and dark-eyed, full-lipped and slender. The other two were smaller, their hair blonde, their eyes blue. They were dressed in shimmering gowns of satin, the dark-haired beauty in blue and the others in white.

'Have you come to see our brother, sir?' asked the dark-haired girl, rising from her seat and placing the lyre upon it.

'No, I was drawn here by the beauty of your playing and the sweet voices which accompanied it. I am a stranger here, and a lover of all things beautiful, and I can only thank the fates for the vision I find here.' The younger girls laughed, but the older sister merely smiled.

'Pretty words, sir, well phrased, and I don't doubt well rehearsed. They have the smooth edges of weapons that have seen great use.'

Sieben bowed. 'Indeed, my lady, it has been my pleasure and my privilege to observe beauty wherever I can find it; to pay homage to it; to bend the knee before it. But it makes my words no less sincere.'

She gave a full smile, then laughed aloud. 'I think you are a rascal, sir, and a libertine, and in more interesting times I would summon a servant to see you from the premises. However, since we are at war and that makes for the dullest entertainment, I shall welcome you – but only for so long as you are entertaining.'

'Sweet lady, I think I can promise you entertainment enough, both in word and deed.' He was delighted that she did not blush at his words, though the younger sisters reddened.

'Such fine promises, sir. But then perhaps you would feel less secure in your boasting were you aware of the quality of entertainment I have enjoyed in the past.'

Now it was Sieben's turn to laugh. 'Should you tell me that Azhral, the Prince of Heaven, came to your chambers and transported you to the Palace of Infinite Variety, then truly I might be mildly concerned.'

'Such a book should not be mentioned in polite company,' she chided.

He stepped closer and took her hand, raising it to his lips and turning it to kiss her palm. 'Not so,' he said softly, 'the book has great merit, for it shines like a lantern in the hidden places. It parts the veils and leads us to the paths of pleasure. I recommend the sixteenth chapter for all new lovers.'

'My name is Asha,' she said, 'and your deeds will need to be as fine as your words, for I react badly to disappointment.'

'You were dreaming, *Pahtai*,' said Pudri as Rowena opened her eyes and found herself sitting in the sunshine beside the lake.

'I don't know what happened,' she told the little eunuch. 'It was as if my soul was dragged from my body. There was a room, and Druss was sitting opposite me.'

'Sadness gives birth to many visions of hope,' quoted Pudri.

'No, it was real, but the hold loosened and I came back before I could tell him where I was.'

He patted her hand. 'Perhaps it will happen again,' he said reassuringly, 'but for now you must compose yourself. The master is entertaining the great Satrap, Shabag. He is being sent to command the forces around Capalis and it is very important that you give him good omens.'

'I can offer only the truth.'

'There are many truths, *Pahtai*. A man may have only days to live, yet in that time will find great love. The seeress who tells him he is about to die will cause him great sorrow – but it will be the truth. The prophet who says that love is only a few hours away will also be telling the truth, but will create great joy in the doomed man.'

Rowena smiled. 'You are very wise, Pudri.'

He shrugged and smiled. 'I am old, Rowena.'

'That is the first time you have used my name.'

He chuckled. 'It is a good name, but so is *Pahtai*; it means *gentle dove*. Now we must go to the shrine. Shall I tell you something of Shabag? Would it help your talent?'

She sighed. 'No. Tell me nothing. I will see what there is to see – and I will remember your advice.'

Arm in arm they strolled into the palace, along the richly carpeted corridors, past the beautifully carved staircase that led to the upper apartments. Statues and busts of marble were set into recesses every ten feet on both sides of the corridor, and the ceiling above them was embellished with scenes from Ventrian literature, the architraves covered with gold leaf.

As they approached the shrine room a tall warrior stepped out from a side door. Rowena gasped, for at first she took the man to be Druss. He had the same breadth of shoulder and jutting jaw, and his eyes beneath thick brows were startlingly blue. Seeing her, he smiled and bowed.

'This is Michanek, *Pahtai*. He is the champion of the Naashanite Emperor – a great swordsman and a respected officer.' Pudri bowed to the warrior. 'This is the Lady Rowena, a guest of the Lord Kabuchek.'

'I have heard of you, lady,' said Michanek, taking her hand and drawing it to his lips. His voice was low and vibrant. 'You saved the merchant from the sharks, no mean feat. But now I have seen you I can understand how even a shark would wish to do nothing to mar your beauty.' Keeping hold of her hand he smiled and moved in close. 'Can you tell me my fortune, lady?'

Her throat was dry, but she met his gaze. 'You will . . . you will achieve your greatest ambition, and realise your greatest hope.'

His eyes showed his cynicism. 'Is that it, lady? Surely any street charlatan could say the same. How will I die?'

'Not fifty feet from where we stand,' she said. 'Out in the courtyard. I see soldiers with black cloaks and helms, storming the walls. You will gather your men for a last stand outside these walls. Beside you will be . . . your strongest brother and a second cousin.'

'And when will this be?'

'One year after you are wed. To the day.'

'And what is the name of the lady I shall marry?'

'I will not say,' she told him.

'We must go, Lord,' said Pudri swiftly. 'The Lords Kabuchek and Shabag await.'

'Of course. It was a pleasure meeting you, Rowena. I hope we will meet again.'

Rowena did not reply, but followed Pudri into the shrine room.

At dusk the enemy drew back, and Druss was surprised to see the Ventrian warriors leaving the walls and strolling back through the city streets. 'Where is everyone going?' he asked the warrior beside him.

618

The man had removed his helm and was wiping his sweat-streaked face with a cloth.

'To eat and rest,' the warrior answered.

Druss scanned the walls. Only a handful of men remained, and these were sitting with their backs to the ramparts. 'What if there is another attack?' asked the axeman.

'There won't be. That was the fourth.'

'Fourth?' queried Druss, surprised.

The warrior, a middle-aged man with a round face and keen blue eyes, grinned at the Drenai. 'I take it that you are no student of strategy. Your first siege, is it?' Druss nodded. 'Well, the rules of engagement are precise. There will be a maximum of four attacks during any twenty-four-hour period.'

'Why only four?'

The man shrugged. 'It's a long time since I studied the manual, but, as I recall, it is a question of morale. When Zhan Tsu wrote *The Art of War* he explained that after four attacks the spirit of the attackers can give way to despair.'

'There won't be very much despair among them if they attack now – or after night falls,' Druss pointed out.

'They won't attack,' said his comrade slowly, as if speaking to a child. 'If a night attack was planned there would have only been three assaults during the day.'

Druss was nonplussed. 'And these rules were written in a book?'

'Yes, a fine work by a Chiatze general.'

'And you will leave these walls virtually unmanned during the night because of a book?'

The man laughed. 'Not the *book*, the rules of engagement. Come with me to the barracks and I'll explain a little more.'

As they strolled the warrior, Oliquar, told Druss that he had served in the Ventrian army for more than twenty years. 'I was even an officer once, during the Opal Campaign. Damn near wiped out we were, so I got to command a troop of forty men. It didn't last. The General offered me a commission, but I couldn't afford the armour, so that was it. Back to the rankers. But it's not a bad life. Comradeship, two good meals a day.'

'Why couldn't you afford the armour? Don't they pay officers?'

'Of course, but only a *disha* a day. That's half of what I earn now.'

'The officers receive less than the rankers? That's stupid.'

Oliquar shook his head. 'Of course it isn't. That way only the rich can afford to be officers, which means that only noblemen – or the sons of merchants, who desire to be noblemen – can command. In this way the noble families retain power. Where are you from, young man?'

'I am Drenai.'

'Ah, yes. I have never been there of course, but I understand the mountains of Skeln are exceptionally beautiful. Green and lush, like the Saurab. I miss the mountains.'

Druss sat with Oliquar in the Western Barracks and ate a meal of beef and wild onions before setting off back to the empty tavern. It was a calm night, with no clouds, and the moon turned the white, ghostly buildings to a muted silver.

Sieben was not in their room and Druss sat by the window, staring out over the harbour, watching the moonlit waves and the water which looked like molten iron. He had fought in three of the four attacks – the enemy, red-cloaked, with helms boasting white horsehair plumes, running forward carrying ladders which they leaned against the walls. Rocks had been hurled down upon them, arrows peppered them. Yet on they came. The first to reach the walls were speared, or struck with swords, but a few doughty fighters made their way to the battlements, where they were cut down by the defenders. Half-way through the second attack a dull, booming sound, like controlled thunder, was heard on the walls.

'Battering-ram,' said the soldier beside him. 'They won't have much luck, those gates are reinforced with iron and brass.'

Druss leaned back in his chair and stared down at Snaga. In the main, he had used the axe to push back ladders, sliding them along the wall, sending attackers tumbling to the rocky ground below. Only twice had the weapon drawn blood. Reaching out Druss stroked the black haft, remembering the victims – a tall, beardless warrior and a swarthy, pot-bellied man in an iron helm. The first had died when Snaga crunched through his wooden breastplate, the second when the silver blades had sheared his iron helm in two. Druss ran his thumb along the blades. Not a mark, or a nick.

Sieben arrived at the room just before midnight. His eyes were red-rimmed and he yawned constantly. 'What happened to you?' asked Druss.

The poet smiled. 'I made new friends.' Pulling off his boots he settled back on one of the narrow beds.

Druss sniffed the air. 'Smells like you were rolling in a flower-bed.'

'A bed of flowers,' said Sieben, with a smile. 'Yes, almost exactly how I would describe it.'

Druss frowned. 'Well, never mind that, do you know anything about rules of engagement?'

'I know everything about *my* rules of engagement, but I take it you are talking about Ventrian warfare?' Swinging his legs from the bed, he sat up. 'I'm tired, Druss, so let's make this conversation brief. I have a meeting in the morning and I need to build up my strength.'

Druss ignored the exaggerated yawn with which Sieben accompanied his words. 'I saw hundreds of men wounded today, and scores

620

killed. Yet now, with only a few men on the walls, the enemy sits back and waits for sunrise. Why? Does no one want to win?'

'Someone will win,' answered Sieben. 'But this is a *civilised* land. They have practised warfare for thousands of years. The siege will go on for a few weeks, or a few months, and every day the combatants will count their losses. At some point, if there is no breakthrough, either one or the other will offer terms to the enemy.'

'What do you mean, terms?'

'If the besiegers decide they cannot win, they will withdraw. If the men here decide all is lost, they will desert to the enemy.'

'What about Gorben?'

Sieben shrugged. 'His own troops might kill him, or hand him over to the Naashanites.'

'Gods, is there no honour among these Ventrians?'

'Of course there is, but most of the men here are mercenaries from many eastern tribes. They are loyal to whoever pays them the most.'

'If the rules of war here are so civilised,' said Druss, 'why have the inhabitants of the city fled? Why not just wait until the fighting is over, and serve whoever wins?'

'They would, at best, be enslaved; at worst, slaughtered. It may be a civilised land, Druss, but it is also a harsh one.'

'Can Gorben win?'

'Not as matters stand, but he may be lucky. Often Ventrian sieges are settled by single combat between champions, though such an event would take place only if both factions were of equal strength, and both had champions they believed were invincible. That won't happen here, because Gorben is heavily outnumbered. However, now that he has the gold Bodasen brought he will send spies in to the enemy camp to bribe the soldiers to desert to his cause. It's unlikely to work, but it might. Who knows?'

'Where did you learn all this?' asked Druss.

'I have just spent an informative afternoon with the Princess Asha – Gorben's sister.'

'What?' stormed Druss. 'What is it with you? Did you learn nothing from what happened in Mashrapur? One day! And already you are rutting!'

'I do not *rut*,' snapped Sieben. 'I make love. And what I do is none of your concern.'

'That's true,' admitted Druss, 'and when they take you for disembowelling, or impaling, I shall remind you of that.'

'Ah, Druss!' said Sieben, settling back on the bed. 'There are some things worth dying for. And she is very beautiful. By the gods, a man could do worse than marry her.'

Druss stood and turned away to the window. Sieben was instantly contrite. 'I am sorry, my friend. I wasn't thinking.' He approached

Druss and laid his hand on his shoulder. 'I am sorry about what happened with the priest.'

'It was her voice,' said Druss, swallowing hard and fighting to keep his emotions in check. 'She said she was waiting for me. I thought that if I went to the wall I might be killed, and then I'd be with her again. But no one came with the skill or the heart. No one ever will . . . and I don't have the courage to do the deed myself.'

'That would not be courage, Druss. And Rowena would not want it. She'd want you to be happy, to marry again.'

'Never!'

'You are not yet twenty, my friend. There are other women.'

'None like her. But she's gone, and I'll speak no more of her. I'll carry her here,' he said, touching his chest, 'and I'll not forget her. Now go back to what you were saying about Eastern warfare.'

Sieben lifted a clay goblet from a shelf by the window, blew the dust from it, and filled it with water which he drained at a single swallow. 'Gods, that tastes foul! All right . . . Eastern warfare. What is it you wish to know now?'

'Well,' said Druss, slowly, 'I know that the enemy can attack four times in a day. But why did they only attack one wall? They have the numbers to surround the city and attack in many places at once.'

'They will, Druss, but not in the first month. This is the testing time. Untried new soldiers are judged on their courage during the first few weeks; then they will bring up the siege-engines. That should be the second month. After that perhaps ballistae, hurling huge rocks over the walls. If at the end of the month there has been no success, they will call in the engineers and they will burrow under the walls, seeking to bring them down.'

'And what rules over the besieged?' asked the axeman.

'I don't understand you?'

'Well, suppose we were to attack them. Could we only do it four times? Can we attack at night? What are the rules?'

'It is not a question of rules, Druss, it's more a matter for common sense. Gorben is outnumbered by around twenty to one; if he attacked, he'd be wiped out.'

Druss nodded, and lapsed into silence. Finally he spoke. 'I'll ask Oliquar for his book. You can read it to me, then I'll understand.'

'Can we sleep now?' asked Sieben.

Druss nodded and took up his axe. He did not remove his boots or jerkin and stretched out on the second bed with Snaga beside him.

'You don't need an axe in bed in order to sleep.'

'It comforts me,' answered Druss, closing his eyes.

'Where did you get it?'

'It belonged to my grandfather.'

'Was he a great hero?' asked Sieben, hopefully.

'No, he was a madman, and a terrible killer.'

'That's nice,' said Sieben, settling down on his own bed. 'It's good to know you have a family trade to fall back on if times get hard.'

6

Gorben leaned back in his chair as his servant, Mushran, carefully shaved the stubble from his chin. He glanced up at the old man. 'Why do you stare so?' he asked.

'You are tired, my boy. Your eyes are red-rimmed and there are purple patches beneath them.'

Gorben smiled. 'One day you will call me, "great Lord" or "my Emperor". I live for that day, Mushran.'

The old man chuckled. 'Other men can bestow upon you these titles. They can fall to the ground before you and bounce their brows from the stone. But when I look upon you, *my boy*, I see the child that was before the man, and the babe who was before the child. I prepared your food and I wiped your arse. And I am too old to crash my poor head to the stones every time you walk into a room. Besides, you are changing the subject. You need more rest.'

'Has it escaped your notice that we have been under siege for a month? I must show myself to the men; they must see me fight, or they will lose heart. And there are supplies to be organised, rations set – a hundred different duties. Find me some more hours in a day and I will rest, I promise you.'

'You don't need more hours,' snapped the old man, lifting the razor and wiping oil and stubble from the blade. 'You need better men. Nebuchad is a good boy – but he's slow-witted. And Jasua . . .' Mushran raised his eyes to the ceiling. 'A wonderful killer, but his brain is lodged just above his . . .'

'Enough of that!' said Gorben amiably. 'If my officers knew how you spoke of them, they'd have you waylaid in an alley and beaten to death. Anyway, what about Bodasen?'

'The best of them – but let's be fair, that isn't saying much.'

Gorben's reply was cut off as the razor descended to his throat and he felt the keen blade gliding up over his jawline and across to the edge of his mouth. 'There!' said Mushran proudly. 'At least you look like an Emperor now.'

Gorben stood and wandered to the window. The fourth attack was under way; it would be repulsed, he knew, but even from here he could see the huge siege-towers being dragged into place for tomorrow. He pictured the hundreds of men pulling them into position, saw in his mind's eye the massive attack ramps crashing down on to the battlements, and heard the war-cries of the Naashanite warriors as they clambered up the steps, along the ramp, and hurled themselves on to the defenders. Naashanites? He laughed bitterly. Two-thirds of the *enemy* soldiers were Ventrians, followers of Shabag, one of the renegade Satraps. Ventrians killing Ventrians! It was obscene. And for what? How much richer could Shabag become? How many palaces could a man occupy at one time? Gorben's father had been a weak man, and a poor judge of character, but for all that he had been an Emperor who cared for his people. Every city boasted a university, built from funds supplied by the Royal treasury. There were colleges where the brightest students could learn the arts of medicine, listen to lectures from Ventria's finest herbalists. There were schools, hospitals, and a road system second to none on the continent. But his greatest achievement had been the forming of the Royal Riders, who could carry a message from one end of the Empire to another in less than twelve weeks. Such swift communication meant that if any satrapy suffered a natural disaster – plague, famine, flood – then help could be sent almost immediately.

Now the cities were either conquered or besieged, the death toll was climbing towards a mountainous total, the universities were closed, and the chaos of war was destroying everything his father had built. With great effort he forced down the heat of anger, and concentrated coolly on the problem facing him at Capalis.

Tomorrow would be a pivotal day in the siege. If his warriors held, then dismay would spread among the enemy. If not . . . He smiled grimly. If not we are finished, he thought. Shabag would have him dragged before the Naashanite Emperor. Gorben sighed.

'Never let despair enter your mind,' said Mushran. 'There is no profit in it.'

'You read minds better than any seer.'

'Not minds, faces. So wipe that expression clear and I'll fetch Bodasen.'

'When did he arrive?'

'An hour ago. I told him to wait. You needed the shave – and the rest.'

'In a past life you must have been a wonderful mother,' said Gorben. Mushran laughed, and left the room. Returning, he ushered Bodasen inside and bowed. 'The general Bodasen, great Lord, my Emperor,' he said, then backed out, pulling shut the door behind him.

'I don't know why you tolerate that man, Lord!' snapped Bodasen. 'He is always insolent.'

'You wished to see me, general?'

Bodasen snapped to attention. 'Yes, sir. Druss the Axeman came to see me last night, he has a plan concerning the siegetowers.'

'Go on.'

Bodasen cleared his throat. 'He wants to attack them.'

Gorben stared hard at the general, observing the deep blush that was appearing on the warrior's cheeks. 'Attack them?'

'Yes, Lord. Tonight, under cover of darkness – attack the enemy camp and set fire to the towers.'

'You feel this is feasible?'

'No, Lord . . . well . . . perhaps. I watched this man attack a corsair trireme and force fifty men to throw down their weapons. I don't know whether he can succeed this time, but . . .'

'I'm still listening.'

'We have no choice. They have thirty siege-towers, Lord. They'll take the wall and we'll not hold them.'

Gorben moved to a couch and sat. 'How does he intend to set these fires? And what does he think the enemy will be doing while he does so? The timbers are huge, old, weathered. It will take a great flame to bring one of them down.'

'I appreciate that, Lord. But Druss says the Naashanites will be too busy to think of towers.' He cleared his throat. 'He intends to attack the centre of the camp, kill Shabag and the other generals, and generally cause enough mayhem to allow a group of men to sneak out from Capalis and set fires beneath the towers.'

'How many men has he asked for?'

'Two hundred. He says he's already chosen them.'

'*He* has chosen them?'

Bodasen glanced down at the floor. 'He is a very . . . popular man, Lord. He has fought every day and he knows many of the men well. They respect him.'

'Has he chosen any officers?'

'Only one . . . Lord.'

'Let me guess. You?'

'Yes, Lord.'

'And you are willing to lead this . . . insane venture?'

'I am, Lord.'

'I forbid it. But you can tell Druss that I agree, and that I will choose an officer to accompany him.'

Bodasen seemed about to protest, but he held his tongue, and bowed deeply. He backed to the door.

'General,' called Gorben.

'Yes, Lord?'

'I am well pleased with you,' said Gorben, not looking at the man. He walked out to the balcony and breathed the evening air. It was cool and flowing from the sea.

Shabag watched the setting sun turn the mountains to fire, the sky burning like the vaults of Hades, deep crimson, flaring orange. He shuddered. He had never liked sunsets. They spoke of endings, inconstancy – the death of a day.

The siege-towers stood in a grim line facing Capalis, monstrous giants promising victory. He gazed up at the first. Tomorrow they would be dragged to the walls, then the mouths of the giants would open, the attack ramps would drop to the ramparts like stiff tongues. He paused. How would one continue the analogy? He pictured the warriors climbing from the belly of the beast and hurling themselves on to the enemy. Then he chuckled. Like the breath of death, like a dragon's fire? No, more like a demon disgorging acid. Yes, I like that, he thought.

The towers had been assembled from sections brought on huge wagons from Resha in the north. They had cost twenty thousand gold pieces, and Shabag was still angry that he alone had been expected to finance them. The Naashanite Emperor was a parsimonious man.

'We will have him tomorrow, sir?' said one of his aides. Shabag jerked his mind to the present and turned to his staff officers. The *him* was Gorben. Shabag licked his thin lips.

'I want him alive,' he said, keeping the hatred from his voice. How he loathed Gorben! How he despised both the man and his appalling conceit. A trick of fate had left him with a throne that was rightly Shabag's. They shared the same ancestors, the kings of glory who had built an empire unrivalled in history. And Shabag's grandfather had sat upon the throne. But he died in battle leaving only daughters surviving him. Thus had Gorben's father ascended the golden steps and raised the ruby crown to his head.

And what happened then to the Empire? Stagnation. Instead of armies, conquest and glory, there were schools, fine roads and hospitals. And to what purpose? The weak were kept alive in order to breed more weaklings, peasants learned their letters and became obsessed with thoughts of betterment. Questions that should never have been voiced were debated openly in city squares: *By what right do the noble families rule our lives? Are we not free men?* By what right? By the right of blood, thought Shabag. By the right of steel and fire!

He thought back with relish to the day when he had surrounded the university at Resha with armed troops, after the students there had voiced their protests at the war. He had called out their leader, who came armed not with a sword, but with a scroll. It was an ancient work, written by Pashtar Sen, and the boy had read it aloud. What a fine voice he had. It was a well-written piece, full of thoughts of honour, and patriotism, and brotherhood. But then when Pashtar Sen had written it the serfs knew their places, the peasants lived in awe of their betters. The sentiments were outworn now.

He had allowed the boy to finish the work, for anything less would have been ill-mannered, and ill befitting a nobleman. Then he had gutted him like a fish. Oh, how the brave students ran then! Save that there was nowhere to run, and they had died in their hundreds, like maggots washed from a pus-filled sore. The Ventrian Empire was decaying under the old emperor, and the only chance to resurrect her greatness was by war. Yes, thought Shabag, the Naashanites will think they have won, and I will indeed be a vassal king. But not for long.

Not for long . . .

'Excuse me, sir,' said an officer and Shabag turned to the man.

'Yes?'

'A ship has left Capalis. It is heading north along the coast. There are quite a number of men aboard.'

Shabag swore. 'Gorben has fled,' he announced. 'He saw our *giants* and realised he could not win.' He felt a sick sense of disappointment, for he had been anticipating tomorrow with great expectation. He turned his eyes towards the distant walls, half expecting to see the Herald of Surrender. 'I shall be in my tent. When they send for terms wake me.'

'Yes, sir.'

He strode through the camp, his anger mounting. Now some whore-born corsair would capture Gorben, maybe even kill him. Shabag glanced up at the darkening sky. 'I'd give my soul to have Gorben before me!' he said.

But sleep would not come and Shabag wished he had brought the Datian slave girl with him. Young innocent, and exquisitely compliant, she would have brought him sleep and sweet dreams.

He rose from his bed and lit two lanterns. Gorben's escape – if he managed to avoid the corsairs – would prolong the war. But only by a few months, reasoned Shabag. Capalis would be his by tomorrow, and after that Ectanis would fall. Gorben would be forced to fall back into the mountains, throwing himself upon the mercy of the wild tribes who inhabited them. It would take time to hunt him down, but not too much. And the hunt might afford amusement during the bleak winter months.

He thought of his palace in Resha, deciding that after organising the surrender of Capalis he would return home for a rest. Shabag pictured the comforts of Resha, the theatres, the arena and the gardens. By now the flowering cherry trees would be in bloom by the lake, dropping their petals to the crystal waters, the sweet scent filling the air.

627

Was it only a month since he had sat by the lake with Darishan beside him, sunlight gleaming upon his braided silver hair?

'Why do you wear those gloves, cousin?' Darishan had asked, tossing a pebble into the water. A large golden fish flicked its tail at the sudden disturbance, then vanished into the depths.

'I like the feel of them,' answered Shabag irritated. 'But I did not come here to discuss matters sartorial.'

Darishan chuckled. 'Always so serious? We are on the verge of victory.'

'You said that half a year ago,' Shabag pointed out.

'And I was correct then. It is like a lion hunt, cousin. While he is in the dense undergrowth he has a chance, but once you have him on open ground, heading into the mountains, it is only a matter of time before he runs out of strength. Gorben is running out of strength *and* gold.'

'He still has three armies.'

'He began with seven. Two of them are now under my command. One is under yours, and one has been destroyed. Come, cousin, why the gloom?'

Shabag shrugged. 'I want to see an end to the war, so I can begin to rebuild.'

'I? Surely you mean *we*?'

'A slip of the tongue, cousin,' said Shabag swiftly, forcing a smile. Darishan leaned back on the marble seat and idly twisted one of his braids. Though not yet forty his hair was startlingly pale, silver and white, and braided with wires of gold and copper.

'Do not betray me, Shabag,' he warned. 'You will not be able to defeat the Naashanites alone.'

'A ridiculous thought, Darishan. We are of the same blood – and we are friends.'

Darishan's cold eyes held to Shabag's gaze, then he too smiled. 'Yes,' he whispered, 'friends and cousins. I wonder where our cousin – and former friend – Gorben is hiding today.'

Shabag reddened. 'He was never my friend. I do not betray my friends. Such thoughts are unworthy of you.'

'Indeed, you are right,' agreed Darishan, rising. 'I must leave for Ectanis. Shall we have a small wager as to which of us conquers first?'

'Why not? A thousand in gold that Capalis falls before Ectanis.'

'A thousand – plus the Datian slave girl?'

'Agreed,' said Shabag, masking his irritation. 'Take care, cousin.' The men shook hands.

'I shall.' The silver-haired Darishan swung away, then glanced back over his shoulder. 'By the way, did you see the wench?'

'Yes, but she told me little of use. I think Kabuchek was swindled.'

628

'That may be true, but she saved him from the sharks and predicted a ship would come. She also told me where to find the opal brooch I lost three years ago. What did she tell you?'

Shabag shrugged. 'She talked of my past, which was interesting, but then she could easily have been schooled by Kabuchek. When I asked her about the coming campaign she closed her eyes and took hold of my hand. She held it for maybe three heartbeats, then pulled away and said she could tell me nothing.'

'Nothing at all?'

'Nothing that made any sense. She said . . . "*He is coming!*" She seemed both elated and yet, moments later, terrified. Then she told me not to go to Capalis. That was it.'

Darishan nodded and seemed about to speak. Instead he merely smiled and walked away.

Putting thoughts of Darishan from his mind, Shabag moved to the tent entrance. The camp was quiet. Slowly he removed the glove from his left hand. The skin itched, red open sores covering the surface as they had done since adolescence. There were herbal ointments and emollients that could ease them, but nothing had ever healed the diseased skin, nor fully removed the other sores that stretched across his back and chest, thighs and calves.

Slowly he peeled back the right-hand glove. The skin here was clean and smooth. This was the hand she had held.

He had offered Kabuchek sixty thousand gold pieces for her, but the merchant had politely refused. When the battle is over, thought Shabag, I shall have her taken from him.

Just as he was about to turn into the tent Shabag saw a line of soldiers marching slowly down towards the camp, their armour gleaming in the moonlight. They were moving in columns of twos, with an officer at the head; the man looked familiar, but he was wearing a plumed helm with a thick nasal guard that bisected his face. Shabag rubbed at his tired eyes to focus more clearly on the man; it was not the face but the walk that aroused his interest. One of Darishan's officers, he wondered? Where have I seen him before?

Pah, what difference does it make, he thought suddenly, pulling shut the tent-flap. He had just blown out the first of the two lanterns when a scream rent the air. Then another. Shabag ran to the entrance, tearing aside the flap.

Warriors were running through his camp, cutting and killing. Someone had picked up a burning brand and had thrown it against a line of tents. Flames rippled across the bone-dry cloth, the wind carrying the fire to other tents.

At the centre of the fighting Shabag saw a huge warrior dressed in black, brandishing a double-headed axe. Three men ran at him, and he

629

killed them in moments. Then Shabag saw the officer – and remembrance rose like a lightning blast from the halls of his memory.

Gorben's soldiers surrounded Shabag's tent. It had been set at the centre of the camp, with thirty paces of clear ground around it to allow the Satrap a degree of privacy. Now it was ringed by armed men.

Shabag was bewildered by the speed at which the enemy had struck, but surely, he reasoned, it would avail them nothing. Twenty-five thousand men were camped around the besieged harbour city. How many of the enemy were here? Two hundred? Three hundred? What could they possibly hope to achieve, save to slay Shabag himself? And how would that serve them, for they would die in the act?

Nonplussed, he stood – a still, silent spectator as the battle raged and the fires spread. He could not tear his eyes from the grim, blood-smeared axeman, who killed with such deadly efficiency, such a minimum of effort. When a horn sounded, a high shrill series of notes that flowed above the sounds of combat, Shabag was startled. The trumpeter was sounding the truce signal and the soldiers fell back, momentarily bewildered. Shabag wanted to shout at his men: 'Fight on! Fight on!' But he could not speak. Fear paralysed him. The silent circle of soldiers around him stood ready, their blades shining in the moonlight. He felt that were he to even move they would fall upon him like hounds upon a stag. His mouth was dry, his hands trembling.

Two men rolled a barrel into view, up-ending it and testing the top. Then the enemy officer stepped forward and climbed on to the barrel, facing out towards the massed ranks of Shabag's men. The Satrap felt bile rise in his throat.

The officer threw back his cloak. Armour of gold shone upon his breast and he removed his helm.

'You know me,' he bellowed, his voice rich and resonant, compelling. 'I am Gorben, the son of the God King, the heir of the God King. In my veins runs the blood of Pashtar Sen, and Cyrios the Lord of Battles, and Meshan Sen, who walked the Bridge of Death. I am Gorben!' The name boomed out, and the men stood silently, spellbound. Even Shabag felt the goose-flesh rising on his diseased skin.

Druss eased back into the circle and stared out at the massed ranks of the enemy. There was a kind of divine madness about the scene which he found himself enjoying immensely. He had been angry when Gorben himself had appeared at the harbour to take command of the troops, and doubly so when the Emperor casually informed him there would be a change of plan.

'What's wrong with the plan we have?' asked Druss.

Gorben chuckled, and, taking Druss's arm, led him out of earshot of the waiting men. 'Nothing is wrong with it, axeman – save for the objective. You seek to destroy the towers. Admirable. But it is not the towers that will determine success or failure in this siege; it is the men. So tonight we do not seek to hamper them, we seek to defeat them.'

Druss chuckled. 'Two hundred against twenty-five thousand?'

'No. One against one.' He had outlined his strategy and Druss had listened in awed silence. The plan was audacious and fraught with peril. Druss loved it.

The first phase had been completed. Shabag was surrounded and the enemy were listening to Gorben speak. But now came the testing time. Success and glory or failure and death? Druss did not know, but he sensed that the strategy was now teetering on a razor's edge. One wrong word from Gorben and the horde would descend upon them.

'I am Gorben!' roared the Emperor again. 'And every man of you has been led into treachery by this . . . this miserable wretch here behind me.' He waved his hand contemptuously in the direction of Shabag. 'Look at him! Standing like a frightened rabbit. Is this the man you would set upon the throne? It will not be easy for him, you know. He will have to ascend the Royal steps. How will he accomplish this with his lips fastened to a Naashanite arse?'

Nervous laughter rose from the massed ranks. 'Aye, it is an amusing thought,' agreed Gorben, 'or it would be were it not so tragic. Look at him! How can warriors follow such a creature? He was lifted to high position by my father; he was trusted; and he betrayed the man who had helped him, who loved him like a son. Not content with causing the death of my father, he has also done everything within his power to wreak havoc upon Ventria. Our cities burn. Our people are enslaved. And for why? So that this quivering rodent can pretend to be a king. So that he can creep on all fours to lie at the feet of a Naashanite goat-breeder.'

Gorben gazed out over the ranks. 'Where are the Naashanites?' he called. A roar went up from the rear. 'Ah yes,' he said, 'ever at the back!' The Naashanties began to shout, but their calls were submerged beneath the laughter of Shabag's Ventrians. Gorben raised his hands for silence. 'No!' he bellowed. 'Let them have their say. It is rude to laugh, to mock others because they do not have your skills, your understanding of honour, your sense of history. I had a Naashanite slave once – ran off with one of my father's goats. I'll say this for him, though – he picked a pretty one!' Laughter rose in a wall of sound and Gorben waited until it subsided. 'Ah, my lads,' he said at last. 'What are we doing with this land we love? How did we allow the Naashanites to rape our sisters and daughters?' An eerie silence settled over the camp. 'I'll tell you how. Men like Shabag opened the doors to them. "Come in," he shouted, "and do as you will. I will be your dog. But please, please, let me have the crumbs that fall from your table. Let me lick the scrapings from your plates!" ' Gorben drew his sword and raised it high as his voice thundered out. 'Well, I'll have none of it!

631

I am the Emperor, anointed by the gods. And I'll fight to the death to save my people!'

'And we'll stand by you!' came a voice from the right. Druss recognised the caller. It was Bodasen; and with him were the five thousand defenders of Capalis. They had marched silently past the siege-towers while the skirmish raged and had crept up to the enemy lines while the soldiers listened to the voice of Gorben.

As Shabag's Ventrians began to shift nervously, Gorben spoke again. 'Every man here – save the Naashanites – is forgiven for following Shabag. More than this, I will allow you to serve me, to purge your crimes by freeing Ventria. And more than this, I shall give you each the pay that is owed you – and ten gold pieces for every man who pledges to fight for his land, his people and his Emperor.' At the rear the nervous Naashanites eased away from the packed ranks, forming a fighting square a little way distant.

'See them cower!' shouted Gorben. 'Now is the time to earn your gold! Bring me the heads of the enemy!'

Bodasen forced his way through the throng. 'Follow me!' he shouted. 'Death to the Naashanites!' The cry was taken up, and almost thirty thousand men hurled themselves upon the few hundred Naashanite troops.

Gorben leapt down from the barrel and strode to where Shabag waited. 'Well, cousin,' he said, his voice soft yet tinged with acid, 'how did you enjoy my speech?'

'You always could talk well,' replied Shabag, with a bitter laugh.

'Aye, and I can sing and play the harp, and read the works of our finest scholars. These things are dear to me – as I am sure they are to you, cousin. Ah, what an awful fate it must be to be born blind, or to lose the use of speech, the sense of touch.'

'I am noble born,' said Shabag, sweat gleaming on his face. 'You cannot maim me.'

'I am the Emperor,' hissed Gorben. 'My will is the law!'

Shabag fell to his knees. 'Kill me cleanly, I beg of you . . . cousin!'

Gorben drew a dagger from the jewel-encrusted scabbard at his hip, tossing the weapon to the ground before Shabag. The Satrap swallowed hard as he lifted the dagger and stared with grim malevolence at his tormentor. 'You may choose the manner of your passing,' said Gorben.

Shabag licked his lips, then held the point of the blade to his chest. 'I curse you, Gorben,' he screamed. Then taking the hilt with both hands, he rammed the blade home. He groaned and fell back. His body twitched, and his bowels opened.

'Remove . . . it,' Gorben ordered the soldiers close by. 'Find a ditch and bury it.' He swung to Druss and laughed merrily. 'Well, axeman, the deed is done.'

'Indeed it is, my Lord,' answered Druss.

'*My Lord?* Truly this is a night of wonders!'

At the edge of the camp the last of the Naashanites died begging for mercy, and a grim quiet descended. Bodasen approached the Emperor and bowed deeply. 'Your orders have been obeyed, Majesty.'

Gorben nodded. 'Aye, you have done well, Bodasen. Now take Jasua and Nebuchad and gather Shabag's officers. Promise them anything, but take them into the city, away from their men. Interrogate them. Kill those who do not inspire your confidence.'

'As you order it, so shall it be,' said Bodasen.

Michanek lifted Rowena from the carriage. Her head lolled against his shoulder, and he smelt the sweetness of her breath. Tying the reins to the brake bar, Pudri scrambled down and gazed apprehensively at the sleeping woman.

'She is all right,' said Michanek. 'I will take her to her room. You fetch the servants to unload the chests.' The tall warrior carried Rowena towards the house. A slave girl held open the door and he moved inside, climbing the stairs to a sunlit room in the eastern wing. Gently he laid her down, covering her frail body with a satin sheet and a thin blanket of lamb's wool. Sitting beside her, he lifted her hand. The skin was hot and feverish; she moaned, but did not stir.

Another slave girl appeared and curtsied to the warrior. He rose. 'Stay by her,' he ordered.

He found Pudri standing in the main doorway of the house. The little man looked disconsolate and lost, his dark eyes fearful. Michanek summoned him to the huge oval library, and bade him sit on a couch. Pudri slumped down, wringing his hands.

'Now, from the beginning,' said Michanek. 'Everything.'

The eunuch looked up at the powerful soldier. 'I don't know, Lord. At first she seemed merely withdrawn, but the more the Lord Kabuchek made her tell fortunes the more strange she became. I sat with her and she told me the Talent was growing within her. At first she needed to concentrate her mind upon the subject, and then visions would follow – short, disjointed images. Though after a while no concentration was needed. But the visions did not stop when she released the hands of Lord Kabuchek's . . . guests. Then the dreams began. She would talk as if she was old, and then in different voices. She stopped eating, and moved as if in a trance. Then, three days ago, she collapsed. Surgeons were called and she was bled, but to no avail.' His lip trembled and tears flowed to his thin cheeks. 'Is she dying, Lord?'

Michanek sighed. 'I don't know, Pudri. There is a doctor here whose opinions I value. He is said to be a mystic healer; he will be here within the hour.' He sat down opposite the little man. He thought he

633

could read the fear in the eunuch's eyes. 'No matter what happens, Pudri, you will have a place here in my household. I did not purchase you from Kabuchek merely because you are close to Rowena. If she . . . does not recover I will not discard you.'

Pudri nodded, but his expression did not change. Michanek was surprised. 'Ah,' he said softly, 'you love her, even as I do.'

'Not as you, Lord. She is like a daughter to me. She is sweet, without a feather's weight of malice in her whole body. But such Talent as she has should not have been used so carelessly. She was not ready, not prepared.' He stood. 'May I sit with her, Lord?'

'Of course.'

The eunuch hurried from the room and Michanek rose and opened the doors to the gardens, stepping through into the sunlight. Flowering trees lined the paths and the air was full of the scent of jasmine, lavender and rose. Three gardeners were working, watering the earth and clearing the flower-beds of weeds. As he appeared they stopped their work and fell to their knees, their foreheads pressed into the earth. 'Carry on,' he said, walking past them and entering the maze, moving swiftly through it to the marble bench at the centre where the statue of the Goddess was set in the circular pool. Of white marble, it showed a beautiful young woman, naked, her arms held aloft, her head tilted back to stare at the sky. In her hands was an eagle with wings spread, about to fly.

Michanek sat and stretched out his long legs. Soon the story would spread all over the city. The Emperor's champion had paid two thousand silver pieces for a dying seeress. Such folly! Yet, since the day he had first seen her, he had not been able to push her from his mind. Even on the campaign, while fighting against Gorben's troops, she had been with him. He had known more beautiful women, but at twenty-five had found none with whom he wished to share his life.

Until now. At the thought that she might be dying, he found himself trembling. Recalling the first meeting, he remembered her prophecy that he would die in this city, in a last stand against black-cloaked troops.

Gorben's Immortals. The Ventrian Emperor had re-formed the famous regiment, manning it with the finest of his fighters. Seven cities had been retaken by them, two of them after single combat between Gorben's new champion, a Drenai axeman they called *Deathwalker*, and two Naashanite warriors, both known to Michanek. Good men, strong and brave, skilful beyond the dreams of most soldiers. Yet they had died.

Michanek had asked for the right to join the army and challenge this axeman. But his Emperor had refused. 'I value you too highly,' said the Emperor.

'But, Lord, is this not my role? Am I not your champion?'

'My seers tell me that the man cannot be slain by you, Michanek. They say his axe is demon-blessed. There will be no more single-combat settlements; we will crush Gorben by the might of our armies.'

But the man was not being crushed. The last battle had been no more than a bloody draw, with thousands slain on both sides. Michanek had led the charge which almost turned the tide, but Gorben had withdrawn into the mountains, two of his general officers having been slain by Michanek.

Nebuchad and Jasua. The first had little skill; he had charged his white horse at the Naashanite champion, and had died with Michanek's lance in his throat. The second was a canny fighter, fast and fearless – but not fast enough, and too fearless to accept that he had met a better swordsman. He had died with a curse on his lips.

'The war is not being won,' Michanek told the marble goddess. 'It is being lost – slowly, day by day.' Three of the renegade Ventrian Satraps had been slain by Gorben: Shabag at Capalis; Berish, the fat and greedy sycophant, hanged at Ectanis; and Ashac, Satrap of the south-west, impaled after the defeat at Gurunur. Only Darishan, the silver-haired fox of the north, survived. Michanek liked the man. The others he had treated with barely concealed contempt, but Darishan was a warrior born. Unprincipled, amoral, but gifted with courage.

His thoughts were interrupted by the sound of a man moving through the maze. 'Where in Hades are you, lad?' came a deep voice.

'I thought you were a mystic, Shalatar,' he called.

The response was both an obscenity and an instruction. 'If I could do that,' replied Michanek, chuckling, 'I could make a fortune with public performances.'

A bald, portly man in a long white tunic appeared and sat beside Michanek. His face was round and red and his ears protruded like those of a bat. 'I hate mazes,' he said. 'What on earth is the point of them? A man walks three times as far to reach a destination, and when he arrives there's nothing there. Futile!'

'Have you seen her?' asked Michanek.

Shalatar's expression changed, and he turned his eyes from the warrior's gaze. 'Yes. Interesting. Why ever did you buy her?'

'That is beside the point. What is your prognosis?'

'She is the most talented seer I have ever known – but that Talent overwhelmed her. Can you imagine what it must be like to *know* everything about everyone you meet? Their pasts and their futures. Every hand you touch flashes an entire life and death into your mind. The influx of such knowledge – at such speed – has had a catastrophic effect on her. She doesn't just see the lives, she experiences them, lives them. She became not Rowena but a hundred different people – including you, I might add.'

'Me?'

'Yes. I only touched her mind fleetingly, but your image was there.'

'Will she live?'

Shalatar shook his head. 'I am a mystic, my friend, but not a prophet. I would say she has only one chance: we must close the doors of her talent.'

'Can you do this?'

'Not alone, but I will gather those of my colleagues with experience of such matters. It is not unlike the casting-out of demons. We must close off the corridors of her mind that lead to the source of her power. It will be expensive, Michanek.'

'I am a rich man.'

'You will need to be. One of the men I need is a former Source priest and he will ask for at least ten thousand in silver for his services.'

'He will have it.'

Shalatar laid his hand on his friend's shoulder. 'You love her so dearly?'

'More than life.'

'Did she share your feelings?'

'No.'

'Then you will have a chance to start anew. For after we have finished she will have no memory. What will you tell her?'

'I don't know. But I will give her love.'

'You intend to marry her?'

Michanek thought back to her prophecy. 'No, my friend. I have decided never to marry.'

Druss wandered along the dark streets of the newly captured city, his head aching, his mood restless. The battle had been bloody and all too brief, and he was filled with a curious sense of anti-climax. He sensed a change in himself, unwelcome and yet demanding; a need for combat, to feel the axe crushing bone and flesh, to watch the light of life disappear from an enemy's eyes.

The mountains of his homeland seemed an eternity from him, lost in some other time.

How many men had he slain since setting off in search of Rowena? He no longer knew, nor cared. The axe felt light in his hand, warm and companionable. His mouth was dry and he longed for a cool drink of water. Glancing up, he saw a sign proclaiming 'Spice Street'. Here in more peaceful times traders had delivered their herbs and spices to be packed into bales for export to the west. Even now there was a scent of pepper in the air. At the far end of the street, where it intersected with the market square, was a fountain and beside it a brass pump with a long curved handle and a copper cup attached by a slender chain to an iron ring. Druss filled the cup, then resting the axe against the side of the fountain wall he sat quietly drinking. Every so often, though, his hand would drop to touch Snaga's black haft.

When Gorben had ordered the last attack on the doomed Naashanites, Druss had longed to hurl himself into the fray, had felt the call of blood and the need to kill. It had taken all of his strength to resist the demands of his turbulent spirit. For the enemy in the keep had begged to surrender and Druss had known with certainty that such a slaughter was wrong. The words of Shadak came back to him:

'The true warrior lives by a code. He has to. For each man there are different perspectives, but at the core they are the same. Never violate a woman, nor harm a child. Do not lie, cheat or steal. These things are for lesser men. Protect the weak against the evil strong. And never allow thoughts of gain to lead you into pursuit of evil.'

Numbering only a few hundred, the Naashanites had had no chance. But Druss still felt somehow cheated, especially when, as now, he recalled the warm, satisfying, triumphant surging of spirit during the fight in the camp of Harib Ka, or the blood-letting following his leap to the deck of the corsair trireme. Pulling clear his helm, he dipped his head into the water of the fountain pool and then stood, removed his jerkin and washed his upper body. Movement from his left caught his eye as a tall, bald man in robes of grey wool came into sight.

'Good evening, my son,' said the priest from the temple back in Capalis. Druss nodded curtly, then donned his jerkin and sat down. The priest made no move to walk on but stood gazing down at the axeman. 'I have been looking for you these past months.'

'You have found me,' said Druss, his voice even.

'May I join you for a few moments?'

'Why not?' responded Druss, making room on the seat where the priest sat alongside the black-garbed warrior.

'Our last meeting troubled me, my son. I have spent many an evening in prayer and meditation since then; finally I walked the Paths of Mist to seek out the soul of your loved one, Rowena. This proved fruitless. I journeyed through the Void on roads too dark to speak of. But she was not there, nor did I find any souls who knew of her death. Then I met a spirit, a grossly evil creature, who in this life bore the name Earin Shad. A corsair captain also called *Bojeeba*, the Shark, he knew of your wife, for this was the ship that plundered the vessel on which she was sailing. He told me that when his corsairs boarded the ship a merchant named Kabuchek, another man and a young woman leapt over the side. There were sharks everywhere, and much blood in the water once the slaughter started on the deck.'

'I don't need to know how she died!' snapped Druss.

'Ah, but that is my point,' said the priest. 'Earin Shad believes that she and Kabuchek were slain. But they were not.'

'What?'

'Kabuchek is in Resha, building more fortunes. He has a seeress with him whom they call *Pahtai*, the little dove. I have seen her, in spirit. I read her thoughts; she is Rowena, your Rowena.'

'She is alive?'

'Yes,' said the priest softly.

'Sweet Heaven!' Druss laughed and threw his arms around the priest's scrawny shoulders. 'By the gods, you have done me a great service. I'll not forget it. If ever there is anything you need from me, you have only to ask.'

'Thank you, my son. I wish you well in your quest. But there is one more matter to discuss: the axe.'

'What about it?' asked Druss, suddenly wary, his hands reaching down to curl around the haft.

'It is an ancient weapon, and I believe that spells were cast upon the blades. Someone of great power, in the distant past, used sorcery to enhance the weapon.'

'So?'

'There were many methods. Sometimes the spell would merely involve the armourer's blood being splashed upon the blades. At other times a binding spell would be used. This served to keep the edge keen, giving it greater cutting power. Small spells, Druss. Occasionally a master of the arcane arts would bring his skills to bear on a weapon, usually one borne by a king or lord. Some blades could heal wounds, others could cut through the finest armour.'

'As indeed can Snaga,' said Druss, hefting the axe. The blades glittered in the moonlight and the priest drew back. 'Do not be frightened,' said Druss. 'I'll not harm you, man.'

'I do not fear you, my son,' the priest told him. 'I fear what lives within those blades.'

Druss laughed. 'So someone cast a spell a thousand years ago? It is still an axe.'

'Yes, an axe. But the greatest of spells was woven around these blades, Druss. An enchantment of colossal skill was used. Your friend Sieben told me that when you were attacking the corsairs a sorcerer cast a spell at you, a spell of fire. When you lifted your axe Sieben saw a demon appear, scaled and horned; he it was who turned back the fire.'

'Nonsense,' said Druss, 'it bounced from the blades. You know, Father, you shouldn't take a great deal of notice when Sieben speaks. The man is a poet. He builds his tales well, but he embroiders them, adds little touches. A demon indeed!'

'He needed to add no touches, Druss. I know of Snaga the Sender. For in finding your wife I also learned something of you, and the weapon you bear: Bardan's weapon. Bardan the Slayer, the butcher of babes, the rapist, the slaughterer. Once he was a hero, yes? But he was corrupted. Evil wormed into his soul, and the evil came from that!' he said, pointing to the axe.

'I don't believe it. I am not evil, and I have carried this axe for almost a year now.'

'And you have noticed no change in yourself? No lusting after blood and death? You do not feel a need to hold the axe, even when battle is not near? Do you sleep with it beside you?'

'It is not possessed!' roared Druss. 'It is a fine weapon. It is my. . . .' he stumbled to silence.

'My *friend*? Is that what you were going to say?'

'What if I was? I am a warrior, and in war only this axe will keep me alive. Better than any friend, eh?' As he spoke he lifted the axe . . . and it slipped from his grip. The priest threw up his hands as Snaga plunged down towards his throat, but in that instant Druss's left hand slammed into the haft, just as the priest pushed at the shining blades. The axe crashed to the stones, sending up a shower of sparks from the flints embedded in the paving slabs.

'God, I'm sorry. It just slipped!' said Druss. 'Are you hurt?'

The priest rose. 'No, it did not cut me. And you are wrong, young man. It did not slip; it wanted me dead, and had it not been for your swift response, so would I have been.'

'It was an accident, Father, I assure you.'

The priest gave a sad smile. 'You saw me push away the blades with my hand?'

'Aye?' responded Druss, mystified.

'Then look,' said the priest, lifting his hand with the palm outward. The flesh was seared and blackened, the skin burned black, blood and water streaming from the wound. 'Beware, Druss, the beast within will seek to kill any who threaten it.'

Druss gathered the axe and backed from the priest. 'Look after that wound,' he said. Then he turned and strode away.

He was shocked by what he had seen. He knew little of demons and spells, save what the storytellers sang of when they had visited the village. But he did know the value of a weapon like Snaga – especially in an alien, war-torn land. Druss came to a halt and, lifting the axe, he gazed into his own reflection in the blades.

'I need you,' he said softly. 'If I am to find Rowena and get her home.' The haft was warm, the weapon light in his hand. He sighed. 'I'll not give you up. I can't. And anyway, damn it all, you are mine!'

You are mine! came an echo deep inside his mind. *You are mine!*

639

Book Three

The Chaos Warrior

1

Varsava was enjoying the first sip of his second goblet of wine when the body hit the table. It arrived head-first, splintering the central board of the trestle table, striking a platter of meat and sliding towards Varsava. With great presence of mind the bladesman lifted his goblet high and leaned back as the body hurtled past to slam head-first into the wall. Such was the impact that a jagged crack appeared in the white plaster, but there was no sound from the man who caused it as he toppled from the table and hit the floor with a dull thud.

Glancing to his right, Varsava saw that the inn was crowded, but the revellers had moved back to form a circle around a small group struggling to overcome a black-bearded giant. One fighter – a petty thief and pickpocket Varsava recognised – hung from the giant's shoulders, his arms encircling the man's throat. Another was slamming punches into the giant's midriff, while a third pulled a dagger and ran in. Varsava sipped his wine. It was a good vintage – at least ten years old, dry and yet full-bodied.

The giant hooked one hand over his shoulder, grabbing the jerkin of the fighter hanging there. Spinning, he threw the man into the path of the oncoming knifeman, who stumbled and fell into the giant's rising boot. There followed a sickening crack and the knifeman slumped to the floor, either his neck or his jaw broken.

The giant's last opponent threw a despairing punch at the black-bearded chin and the fist landed – to no effect. The giant reached forward and pulled the fighter into a head butt. The sound made even Varsava wince. The fighter took two faltering steps backwards, then keeled over in perfect imitation of a felled tree.

'Anyone else?' asked the giant, his voice deep and cold. The crowd melted away and the warrior strode through the inn, coming to Varsava's table. 'Is this seat taken?' he asked, slumping down to sit opposite the bladesman.

'It is now,' said Varsava. Lifting his hand he waved to a tavern maid and, once he had her attention, pointed to his goblet. She smiled and brought a fresh flagon of wine. The bench table was split down the centre, and the flagon sat drunkenly between the two men. 'May I offer you some wine?' Varsava asked.

'Why not?' countered the giant, filling a clay goblet. A low moan came from behind the table.

'He must have a hard head,' said Varsava. 'I thought he was dead.'

'If he comes near me again, he will be,' promised the man. 'What is this place?'

'It's called the All but One,' Varsava told him.

'An odd name for an inn?'

Varsava looked into the man's pale eyes. 'Not really. It comes from a Ventrian toast: *may all your dreams – save one – come true.*'

'What does it mean?'

'Quite simply that a man must always have a dream unfulfilled. What could be worse than to achieve everything one has ever dreamed of? What would one do then?'

'Find another dream,' said the giant.

'Spoken like a man who understands nothing about dreams.'

The giant's eyes narrowed. 'Is that an insult?'

'No, it is an observation. What brings you to Lania?'

'I am passing through,' said the man. Behind him two of the injured men had regained their feet; both drew daggers and advanced towards them, but Varsava's hand came up from beneath the table with a huge hunting-knife glittering in his fist. He rammed the point into the table and left the weapon quivering there.

'Enough,' he told the would-be attackers, the words softly spoken, a smile upon his face. 'Pick up your friend here and find another place to drink.'

'We can't let him get away with this!' said one of the men, whose eye was blackened and swollen almost shut.

'He did get away with it, my friends. And if you persist in this foolishness, I think he will kill you. Now go away, I am trying to hold a conversation.' Grumbling, the men sheathed their blades and moved back into the crowd. 'Passing through to where?' he asked the giant. The fellow seemed amused.

'You handled that well. Friends of yours?'

'They know me,' answered the bladesman, offering his hand across the table. 'I am Varsava.'

'Druss.'

'I've heard that name. There was an axeman at the siege of Capalis. There's a song about him, I believe.'

'Song!' snorted Druss. 'Aye, there is, but I had no part in the making of it. Damn fool of a poet I was travelling with – he made it up. Nonsense, all of it.'

Varsava smiled. '*They speak in hushed whispers of Druss and his axe, even demons will scatter when this man attacks.*'

Druss reddened. 'Asta's tits! You know there's a hundred more lines of it?' He shook his head. 'Unbelievable!'

'There are worse fates in life than to be immortalised in song. Isn't there some part of it about a lost wife? Is that also an invention?'

'No, that's true enough,' admitted Druss, his expression changing as he drained his wine and poured a second goblet. In the silence that followed, Varsava leaned back and studied his drinking companion. The man's shoulders were truly immense and he had a neck like a bull. But it was not the size that gave him the appearance of a giant, Varsava realised, it was more a power that emanated from him. During the fight he had seemed seven feet tall, the other warriors puny by comparison. Yet here, sitting quietly drinking, Druss seemed no more than a large, heavily muscled young man. Intriguing, thought Varsava.

'If I remember aright, you were also at the relief of Ectanis, and four other southern cities?' he probed. The man nodded, but said nothing. Varsava called for a third flagon of wine and tried to recall all he had heard of the young axeman. At Ectanis, it was said, he had fought the Naashanite champion, Cuerl, and been one of the first to scale the walls. And two years later he had held, with fifty other men, the pass of Kishtay, denying the road to a full legion of Naashanite troops until Gorben could arrive with reinforcements.

'What happened to the poet?' asked Varsava, searching for a safe route to satisfy his curiosity.

Druss chuckled. 'He met a woman . . . several women, in fact. Last I heard he was living in Pusha with the widow of a young officer.' He laughed again and shook his head. 'I miss him; he was merry company.' The smile faded from Druss's face. 'You ask a lot of questions?'

Varsava shrugged. 'You are an interesting man, and there is not much of interest these days in Lania. The war has made it dull. Did you ever find your wife?'

'No. But I will. What of you? Why are you here?'

'I am paid to be here,' said Varsava. 'Another flagon?'

'Aye, and I'll pay for it,' promised Druss. Reaching out, he took hold of the huge knife embedded in the table and pulled it clear. 'Nice weapon, heavy but well balanced. Good steel.'

'Lentrian. I had it made ten years ago. Best money I ever spent. You have an axe, do you not?'

Druss shook his head. 'I had one once. It was lost.'

'How does one lose an axe?'

Druss smiled. '*One* falls from a cliff into a raging torrent.'

'Yes, I would imagine that would do it,' responded Varsava. 'What do you carry now?'

'Nothing.'

'Nothing at all? How did you cross the mountains to Lania without a weapon?'

'I walked.'

'And suffered no attacks from robbers? Did you travel with a large group?'

645

'I have answered enough questions. Now it is your turn. Who pays you to sit and drink in Lania?'

'A nobleman from Resha who has estates near here. While he was away fighting alongside Gorben, raiders came down from the mountains and plundered his palace. His wife and son were taken, his servants murdered – or fled. He has hired me to locate the whereabouts – if still alive – of his son.'

'Just the son?'

'Well, he wouldn't want the wife back, would he?'

Druss's face darkened. 'He would – if he loved her.'

Varsava nodded. 'Of course, you are a Drenai,' he said. 'The rich here do not marry for love, Druss; they wed for alliances or wealth, or to continue family lines. It is not rare for a man to find that he does love the woman he has been told to marry, but neither is it common. And a Ventrian nobleman would find himself a laughing-stock if he took back a wife who had been – shall we say – abused. No, he has already divorced her; it is the son who matters to him. If I can locate him, I receive one hundred gold pieces. If I can rescue him, the price goes up to one thousand.'

Another flagon of wine arrived. Druss filled his goblet and offered the wine to Varsava, who declined. 'My head is already beginning to spin, my friend. You must have hollow legs.'

'How many men do you have?' asked Druss.

'None. I work alone.'

'And you know where the boy is?'

'Yes. Deep in the mountains there is a fortress called Valia, a place for thieves, murderers, outlaws and renegades. It is ruled by Cajivak – you have heard of him?' Druss shook his head. 'The man is a monster in every respect. Bigger than you, and terrifying in battle. He is also an axeman. And he is insane.'

Druss drank the wine, belched and leaned forward. 'Many fine warriors are considered mad.'

'I know that – but Cajivak is different. During the last year he has led raids which have seen mindless slaughter that you would not believe. He has his victims impaled on spikes, or skinned alive. I met a man who served him for almost five years; that's how I found out where the boy was. He said Cajivak sometimes speaks with a different voice, low and chilling, and that when he does so his eyes gleam with a strange light. And always – when such madness is upon him – he kills. It could be a servant or a tavern wench, or a man who looks up just as Cajivak's eyes meet his. No, Druss, we are dealing with madness . . . or possession.'

'How do you intend to rescue the boy?'

Varsava spread his hands. 'I was contemplating that when you arrived. As yet, I have no answers.'

'I will help you,' said Druss.

Varsava's eyes narrowed. 'For how much?'

'You can keep the money.'

'Then why?' asked the bladesman, mystified.

But Druss merely smiled and refilled his goblet.

Druss found Varsava an agreeable companion. The tall bladesman said little as they journeyed through the mountains and up into the high valleys far above the plain on which Lania sat. Both men carried packs, and Varsava wore a wide-brimmed brown leather hat with an eagle feather tucked into the brim. The hat was old and battered, the feather ragged and without sheen. Druss had laughed when first he saw it, for Varsava was a handsome man – his clothes immaculately styled from fine green wool, his boots of soft lambskin. 'Did you lose a wager?' asked Druss.

'A wager?' queried Varsava.

'Aye. Why else would a man wear such a hat?'

'Ah!' said the bladesman. 'I imagine that is what passes as humour among you barbarians. I'll have you know that this hat belonged to my father.' He grinned. 'It is a magic hat and it has saved my life more than once.'

'I thought Ventrians never lied,' said Druss.

'Only noblemen,' Varsava pointed out. 'However, on this occasion I am telling the truth. The hat helped me escape from a dungeon.' He removed it and tossed it to Druss. 'Take a look under the inside band.'

Druss did so and saw that a thin-saw blade nestled on the right side, while on the left was a curved steel pin. At the front he felt three coins and slipped one clear; it was gold. 'I take it all back,' said Druss. 'It is a fine hat!'

The air was fresh and cool here and Druss felt free. It had been almost four years since he had left Sieben in Ectanis and journeyed alone to the occupied city of Resha, searching for the merchant Kabuchek and, through him, Rowena. He had found the house, only to discover that Kabuchek had left a month before to visit friends in the lands of Naashan. He had followed to the Naashanite city of Pieropolis, and there lost all traces of the merchant.

Back once more in Resha, he discovered that Kabuchek had sold his palace and his whereabouts were unknown. Out of money and supplies, Druss took employment with a builder in the capital who had been commissioned to rebuild the shattered walls of the city. For four months he laboured every day until he had enough gold to head back to the south.

In the five years since the victories at Capalis and Ectanis the Ventrian Emperor, Gorben, had fought eight major battles against the Naashanites and their Ventrian allies. The first two had been won

647

decisively, the last also. But the others had been fought to stalemate, with both sides suffering huge losses. Five years of bloody warfare and neither side, as yet, could claim they were close to victory.

'Come this way,' said Varsava. 'There is something I want you to see.'

The bladesman left the path and climbed a short slope to where a rusted iron cage had been set into the earth. Within the domed cage was a pile of mouldering bones, and a skull that still had vestiges of skin and hair clinging to it.

Varsava knelt down by the cage. 'This was Vashad – the peace-maker,' he said. 'He was blinded and his tongue cut out. Then he was chained here to starve to death.'

'What was his crime?' asked Druss.

'I have already told you: he was a peacemaker. This world of war and savagery has no place for men like Vashad.' Varsava sat down and removed his wide-brimmed leather hat.

Druss eased his pack from his shoulders and sat beside the blades-man. 'But why would they kill him in such a fashion?' he asked.

Varsava smiled, but there was no humour in his eyes. 'Do you see so much and know so little, Druss? The warrior lives for glory and battle, testing himself against his fellows, dealing death. He likes to see himself as noble, and we allow him such vanities because we admire him. We make songs about him; we tell stories of his greatness. Think of all the Drenai legends. How many concern peacemakers or poets? They are stories of *heroes* – men of blood and carnage. Vashad was a philosopher, a believer in something he called the *nobility of man*. He was a mirror, and when warmakers looked into his eyes they saw themselves – their true selves – reflected there. They saw the darkness, the savagery, the lust and the enormous stupidity of their lives. They could not resist killing him, they had to smash the mirror: so, they put out his eyes and they ripped out his tongue. Then they left him here . . . and here he lies.'

'You want to bury him? I'll help with the grave.'

'No,' said Varsava sadly, 'I don't want to bury him. Let others see him, and know the folly of trying to change the world.'

'Did the Naashanites kill him?' asked Druss.

'No, he was killed long before the war.'

'Was he your father?'

Varsava shook his head, his expression hardening. 'I only knew him long enough to put out his eyes.' He stared hard at Druss's face, trying to read his reaction, then he spoke again. 'I was a soldier then. Such eyes, Druss – large and shining, blue as a summer sky. And the last sight they had was of my face, and the burning iron that melted them.'

'And now he haunts you?'

Varsava stood. 'Aye, he haunts me. It was an evil deed, Druss. But those were my orders and I carried them out as a Ventrian should. Immediately afterwards, I resigned my commission and left the army.' He glanced at Druss. 'What would you have done in my place?'

'I would not be in your place,' said Druss, hoisting his pack to his shoulder.

'Imagine that you were. Tell me!'

'I would have refused.'

'I wish I had,' Varsava admitted, and the two men returned to the trail. They walked on in silence for a mile, then Varsava sat down beside the path. The mountains loomed around them, huge and towering, and a shrill wind was whistling through the peaks. High overhead two eagles were circling. 'Do you despise me, Druss?' asked Varsava.

'Yes,' admitted Druss, 'but I also like you.'

Varsava shrugged. 'I do so admire a plain speaker. I despise myself sometimes. Have you ever done anything which shamed you?'

'Not yet, but I came close in Ectanis.'

'What happened?' asked Varsava.

'The city had fallen several weeks before, and when the army arrived the walls were already breached. I went in with the first assault and I killed many. And then, with the bloodlust on me, I forced my way into the main barracks. A child ran at me. He was carrying a spear and before I could think about what I was doing I cut at him with my axe. He slipped, and only the flat of the blade caught him; he was knocked out. But I had tried to kill him. Had I succeeded it would not have sat well with me.'

'And that is all?'

'It is enough,' said Druss.

'You have never raped a woman? Or killed an unarmed man? Or stolen?'

'No. And I never shall.'

Varsava rose. 'You are an unusual man, Druss. I think this world will either come to hate you or revere you.'

'I don't much care which,' said Druss. 'How far to this mountain city?'

'Another two days. We'll camp in the high pines, where it will be cold but the air is wonderfully fresh. By the way, you haven't told me yet why you offered to help me.'

'That's true,' said Druss, with a grin. 'Now let us find a camp-site.'

They walked on, through a long pass which opened out on to a stand of pine trees and a wide pear-shaped valley beyond. Houses dotted the valley, clustered in the main along both banks of a narrow river. Druss scanned the valley. 'There must be fifty homes here,' he said.

'Yes,' agreed Varsava. 'Farmers mostly. Cajivak leaves them alone, for they supply him with meat and grain during the winter months. But it will be best if we make a cold camp in the trees, for Cajivak will have spies in the village, and I don't want our presence announced.'

The two men moved out from the pass and into the shelter of the trees. The wind was less powerful here and they walked on, seeking a camp-site. The landscape was similar to the mountains of home and Druss found himself once more thinking of days of happiness with Rowena. When he had set out with Shadak to find her, he had been convinced that only a matter of days separated them. Even on board ship he had believed his quest was almost over. But the months, and years, of pursuit had gnawed at his confidence. He knew he would never give up the hunt, but to what purpose? What if she were wed, or had children? What if she had found happiness without him? What then, as he walked back into her life?

His thoughts were broken by the sounds of laughter echoing through the trees. Varsava stopped and moved silently from the trail and Druss followed him. Ahead and to the left was a hollow through which ran a ribbon stream, and at the centre of the hollow a group of men were throwing knives at a tree-trunk. An old man was tied to the trunk, his arms spread. A blade had nicked the skin of his face, there were wounds to both arms and a knife jutted from his thigh. It was obvious to Druss that the men were playing a game with the old man, seeing how close they could come with their knives. To the left of the scene three other men were struggling with a young girl, who screamed as they tore her dress and pushed her to the earth. As Druss loosed his pack and started down the slope, Varsava grabbed him. 'What are you doing? There are ten of them!'

But Druss shrugged him off and strode through the trees to come up behind the seven knife-throwers. Intent as they were on their victim, they did not notice his approach. Reaching out, he grabbed the heads of the two nearest knifemen and rammed them together; there followed a sickening crack and both men dropped without a murmur. A third man swung at the sound, but had no time to register surprise as a silver-skinned gauntlet slammed into his mouth, splintering teeth. Unconscious, the knifeman flew backwards to cannon into a comrade. A warrior leapt at Druss, thrusting his blade towards his belly, but Druss slapped the blade aside and hammered a straight left into the man's chin. The remaining warriors ran at him, and a knife-blade slashed through his jerkin, ripping a narrow gash across his hip. Druss grabbed the nearest warrior, dragging him into a ferocious head butt, then swung and backhanded another attacker. The man cartwheeled across the hollow, struggled to rise, then sat back against a tree having lost all interest in the fight.

Grappling with two men, Druss heard a bloodcurdling scream. His attackers froze. Druss dragged an arm free and struck the first of the

650

men a terrible blow to the neck. The second released his hold on the axeman and sprinted from the hollow. Druss's pale eyes scanned the area, seeking new opponents. But only Varsava was standing there, his huge hunting-knife dripping blood. Two corpses lay beside him. Three other men Druss had struck lay where they had fallen, and the warrior he had backhanded was still sitting by the tree. Druss walked to where he sat, then hauled him to his feet. 'Time to go, laddie!' said Druss.

'Don't kill me!' pleaded the man.

'Who said anything about killing? Be off with you!'

The man tottered away on boneless legs as Druss moved to the old man tied to the tree. Only one of his wounds was deep. Druss untied him and eased him to the ground. Swiftly he dragged the knife clear of the man's thigh as Varsava came alongside. 'That will need stitching,' he said. 'I'll get my pack.'

The old man forced a smile. 'I thank you, my friends. I fear they would have killed me. Where is Dulina?'

Druss glanced round, but the girl was nowhere in sight. 'She was not harmed,' he said. 'I think she ran when the fight started.' Druss applied a tourniquet to the thigh wound, then stood and moved back to check the bodies. The two men who had attacked Varsava were dead, as was one other, his neck broken. The remaining two were unconscious. Rolling them to their backs, Druss shook them awake and then pulled them upright. One of the men immediately sagged back to the ground.

'Who are you?' asked the warrior still standing.

'I am Druss.'

'Cajivak will kill you for this. Were I you, I would leave the mountains.'

'You are not me, laddie. I go where I please. Now pick up your comrade and take him home.'

Druss dragged the fallen warrior to his feet and watched as the two men left the hollow. When Varsava returned with his pack, a young girl was walking beside him. She was holding her ruined dress in place. 'Look what I found,' said Varsava. 'She was hiding under a bush.' Ignoring the girl, Druss grunted and moved to the stream where he knelt and drank.

Had Snaga been with him, the hollow would now be awash in blood and bodies. He sat back and stared at the rippling water.

When the axe was lost Druss had felt as if a burden had been lifted from his heart. The priest back in Capalis had been right: it was a demon blade. He had felt its power growing as the battles raged, had enjoyed the soaring, surging blood-lust that swept over him like a tidal wave. But after the battles came the sense of emptiness and disenchantment. Even the spiciest food was tasteless; summer days seemed grey and colourless.

Then came the day in the mountains when the Naashanites had come upon him alone. He had killed five, but more than fifty men had pursued him through the trees. He had tried to traverse the cliff, but holding to the axe made his movements slow and clumsy. Then the ledge had given way and he had fallen, twisting and turning through the air. Even as he fell he hurled the axe from him, and tried to turn the fall into a dive; but his timing was faulty and he had landed on his back, sending up a huge splash, the air exploding from his lungs. The river was in flood and the currents swept him on for more than two miles before he managed to grab a root jutting from the river-bank. Hauling himself clear he had sat, as now, staring at the water.

Snaga was gone.

And Druss felt free. 'Thank you for helping my grandfather,' said a sweet voice and he turned and smiled.

'Did they hurt you?'

'Only a little,' said Dulina. 'They hit me in the face.'

'How old are you?'

'Twelve – almost thirteen.' She was a pretty child with large hazel eyes and light brown hair.

'Well, they've gone now. Are you from the village?'

'No. Grandfather is a tinker. We go from town to town; he sharpens knives and mends things. He's very clever.'

'Where are your parents?'

The girl shrugged. 'I never had any; only grandfather. You are very strong – but you are bleeding!'

Druss chuckled. 'I heal fast, little one.' Removing his jerkin, he examined the wound on his hip. The surface skin had been sliced, but the cut was not deep.

Varsava joined them. 'That should also be stitched, *great hero*,' he said, irritation in his voice.

Blood was still flowing freely from the wound. Druss stretched out and lay still while Varsava, with little gentleness, drew the flaps of skin together and pierced them with a curved needle. When he had finished the bladesman stood. 'I suggest we leave this place and head back for Lania. I think our friends will return before too long.'

Druss donned his jerkin. 'What about the city and your thousand gold pieces?'

Varsava shook his head in disbelief. 'This . . . escapade . . . of yours has put paid to any plan of mine. I shall return to Lania and claim my hundred gold pieces for locating the boy. As to you, well, you can go where you like.'

'You give up very easily, bladesman. So we cracked a few heads! What difference does that make? Cajivak has hundreds of men; he won't interest himself in every brawl.'

'It is not Cajivak who concerns me, Druss. It is you. I am not here to rescue maidens or kill dragons, or whatever else it is that makes heroes of myth. What happens when we walk into the city and you see some . . . some hapless victim? Can you walk by? Can you hold fast to a plan of action that will see us succeed in our mission?'

Druss thought for a moment. 'No,' he said at last. 'No, I will never walk by.'

'I thought not, damn you! What are you trying to prove, Druss? You want more songs about you? Or do you just want to die young?'

'No, I have nothing to prove, Varsava. And I may die young, but I'll never look in a mirror and be ashamed because I let an old man suffer or a child be raped. Nor will I ever be haunted by a peacemaker who died unjustly. Go where you will, Varsava. Take these people back to Lania. I shall go to the city.'

'They'll kill you there.'

Druss shrugged. 'All men die. I am not immortal.'

'No, just stupid,' snapped Varsava and spinning on his heel, the bladesman strode away.

Michanek laid his bloody sword on the battlements and untied the chin-straps of his bronze helm, lifting it clear and enjoying the sudden rush of cool air to his sweat-drenched head. The Ventrian army was falling back in some disarray, having discarded the huge battering-ram which lay outside the gate, surrounded by corpses. Michanek walked to the rear of the ramparts and yelled orders to a squad of men below.

'Open the gate and drag that damned ram inside,' he shouted. Pulling a rag from his belt, he wiped his sword clean of blood and sheathed it.

The fourth attack of the day had been repulsed; there would be no further fighting today. However, few of the men seemed anxious to leave the wall. Back in the city the plague was decimating the civilian population. No, he thought, it is worse than decimation. Far more than one in ten were now suffering the effects.

Gorben had not dammed the river. Instead he had filled it with every kind of corruption – dead animals, bloated and maggot-ridden, rotting food, and the human waste from an army of eleven thousand men. Small wonder that sickness had ripped into the population.

Water was now being supplied by artesian wells, but no one knew how deep they were or how long the fresh water would last. Michanek gazed up at the clear blue sky: not a cloud in sight, and rain had not fallen for almost a month.

A young officer approached him. 'Two hundred with superficial wounds, sixty dead, and another thirty-three who will not fight again,' he said.

Michanek nodded, his mind elsewhere. 'What news from the inner city, brother?' he asked.

'The plague is abating. Only seventy dead yesterday, most of them either children or old people.'

Michanek stood and smiled at the young man. 'Your section fought well today,' he said, clapping his hand on his brother's shoulder. 'I shall see that a report is placed before the Emperor when we return to Naashan.' The man said nothing and their eyes met, the unspoken thought passing between them: *If* we return to Naashan. 'Get some rest, Narin. You look exhausted.'

'So do you, Michi. And I was only here for the last two attacks – you've been here since before dawn.'

'Yes, I am tired. *Pahtai* will revive me; she always does.'

Narin chuckled. 'I never expected love to last so long for you. Why don't you marry the girl? You'll never find a better wife. She's revered in the city. Yesterday she toured the poorest quarter, healing the sick. It's amazing; she has more skill than any of the doctors. It seems that all she needs to do is lay her hands upon the dying and their sores disappear.'

'You sound as if you're in love with her yourself,' said Michanek.

'I think I am – a little,' admitted Narin, reddening. 'Is she still having those dreams?'

'No,' lied Michanek. 'I'll see you this evening.' He moved down the battlement steps and strode through the streets towards his home. Every other house, it seemed, boasted the white chalked cross denoting plague. The market was deserted, the stalls standing empty. Everything was rationed now, the food – four ounces of flour, and a pound of dried fruit – doled out daily from storehouses in the west and east.

Why don't you marry her?

For two reasons he could never share. One: she was already wed to another, though she did not know it. And secondly, it would be like signing his death warrant. Rowena had predicted that he would die here, with Narin beside him, one year to the day after he was wed.

She no longer remembered this prediction either, for the sorcerers had done their work well. Her Talent was lost to her, and all the memories of her youth in the lands of the Drenai. Michanek felt no guilt over this. Her Talent had been tearing her apart and now, at least, she smiled and was happy. Only Pudri knew the whole truth, and he was wise enough to stay silent.

Michanek turned up the Avenue of Laurels and pushed open the gates of his house. There were no gardeners now, and the flower-beds were choked with weeds. The fountain was no longer in operation, the fish-pool dry and cracked. As he strode to the house, Pudri came running out to him.

654

'Master, come quickly, it is the *Pahtai*!'

'What has happened?' cried Michanek, grabbing the little man by his tunic.

'The plague, master,' he whispered, tears in his dark eyes. 'It is the plague.'

Varsava found a cave nestling against the rock-face to the north; it was deep and narrow, and curled like a figure six. He built a small fire near the back wall, below a split in the rock that created a natural chimney. The old man, whom Druss had carried to the cave, had fallen into a deep, healing sleep with the child, Dulina, alongside him. Having walked from the cave to check whether the glare of the fire could be seen from outside, Varsava was now sitting in the cave-mouth staring out over the night-dark woods.

Druss joined him. 'Why so angry, bladesman?' he asked. 'Do you not feel some satisfaction at having rescued them?'

'None at all,' replied Varsava. 'But then no one ever made a song about me. I look after myself.'

'That does not explain your anger.'

'Nor could I explain it in any way that would be understood by your simple mind. Borza's Blood!' He rounded on Druss. 'The world is such a mind-numbingly uncomplicated place for you, Druss. There is good, and there is evil. Does it ever occur to you that there may be a vast area in between that is neither pure nor malevolent? Of course it doesn't! Take today as an example. The old man could have been a vicious sorcerer who drank the blood of innocent babes; the men punishing him could have been the fathers of those babes. You didn't know, you just roared in and downed them.' Varsava shook his head and took a deep breath.

'You are wrong,' said Druss softly. 'I have heard the arguments before, from Sieben and Bodasen – and others. I will agree that I am a simple man. I can scarcely read more than my name, and I do not understand complicated arguments. But I am not blind. The man tied to the tree wore homespun clothes, old clothes; the child was dressed in like manner. These were not rich, as a sorcerer would be. And did you listen to the laughter of the knife-throwers? It was harsh, cruel. These were not farmers; their clothes were bought, their boots and shoes of good leather. They were scoundrels.'

'Maybe they were,' agreed Varsava, 'but what business was it of yours? Will you criss-cross the world seeking to right wrongs and protect the innocent? Is this your ambition in life?'

'No,' said Druss, 'though it would not be a bad ambition.' He fell silent for several minutes, lost in thought. Shadak had given him a code, and impressed upon him that without such an iron discipline he would soon become as evil as any other reaver. Added to this there was Bress, his father, who had lived his whole life bearing the terrible burden of being the son of Bardan. And lastly there was Bardan himself, driven by a demon to become one of the most hated and vilified villains in history. The lives, the words and deeds of these three men had created the warrior who now sat beside Varsava. But Druss had no words to explain, and it surprised him that he desired them; he had never felt the need to explain to Sieben or Bodasen. 'I had no choice,' he said at last.

'No choice?' echoed Varsava. 'Why?'

'Because I was there. There wasn't anyone else.'

Feeling Varsava's eyes upon him, and seeing the look of blank incomprehension, Druss turned away and stared at the night sky. It made no sense, he knew that, but he also knew that he felt good for having rescued the girl and the old man. It might make no sense, but it was *right*.

Varsava rose and moved back to the rear of the cave, leaving Druss alone. A cold wind whispered across the mountainside, and Druss could smell the coming of rain. He remembered another cold night, many years before, when he and Bress had been camped in the mountains of Lentria. Druss was very young, seven or eight, and he was unhappy. Some men had shouted at his father, and gathered outside the workshop that Bress had set up in a small village. He had expected his father to rush out and thrash them but instead, as night fell, he had gathered a few belongings and led the boy out into the mountains.

'Why are we running away?' he had asked Bress.

'Because they will talk a lot, and then come back to burn us out.'

'You should have killed them,' said the boy.

'That would have been no answer,' snapped Bress. 'Mostly they are good men, but they are frightened. We will find somewhere where no one knows of Bardan.'

'I won't run away, not ever,' declared the boy and Bress had sighed. Just then a man approached the camp-fire. He was old and bald, his clothes ragged, but his eyes were bright and shrewd.

'May I share your fire?' he asked and Bress had welcomed him, offering some dried meat and a herb tisane which the man accepted gratefully. Druss had fallen asleep as the two men talked, but had woken several hours later. Bress was asleep, but the old man was sitting by the fire feeding the flames with twigs. Druss rose from his blankets and walked to sit alongside him.

'Frightened of the dark, boy?'

'I am frightened of nothing,' Druss told him.

'That's good,' said the old man, 'but I am. Frightened of the dark, frightened of starvation, frightened of dying. All my life I've been frightened of something or other.'

'Why?' asked the boy, intrigued.

The old man laughed. 'Now there's a question! Wish I could answer it.' As he picked up a handful of twigs and reached out, dropping them to the dying flames, Druss saw his right arm was criss-crossed with scars.

'How did you get them?' asked the boy.

'Been a soldier most of my life, son. Fought against the Nadir, the Vagrians, the Sathuli, corsairs, brigands. You name the enemy, and I've crossed swords with them.'

'But you said you were a coward.'

'I said no such thing, lad. I said I was *frightened*. There's a difference. A coward is a man who knows what's right, but is afraid to do it; there're plenty of them around. But the worst of them are easy to spot: they talk loud, they brag big, and given a chance they're as cruel as sin.'

'My father is a coward,' said the boy sadly.

The old man shrugged. 'If he is, boy, then he's the first in a long, long while to fool me. And if you are talking about him running away from the village, there's times when to run away is the bravest thing a man can do. I knew a soldier once. He drank like a fish, rutted like an alley-cat and would fight anything that walked, crawled or swam. But he got religion; he became a Source priest. When a man he once knew, and had beaten in a fist-fight, saw him walking down the street in Drenan, he walked up and punched the priest full in the face, knocking him flat. I was there. The priest surged to his feet and stopped. He wanted to fight – everything in him wanted to fight. But then he remembered what he was, and he held back. Such was the turmoil within him that he burst into tears. And he walked away. By the gods, boy, that took some courage.'

'I don't think that was courage,' said Druss.

'Neither did anyone else who was watching. But then that's something you'll learn, I hope. If a million people believe a foolish thing, it is still a foolish thing.'

Druss's mind jerked back to the present. He didn't know why he had remembered that meeting, but the recollection left him feeling sad and low in spirit.

2

A storm broke over the mountains, great rolls of thunder that made the walls of the cave vibrate, and Druss moved back as the rain lashed into the cave-mouth. The land below was lit by jagged spears of lightning which seemed to change the very nature of the valley – the gentle woods of pine and elm becoming shadow-haunted lairs, the friendly homes looking like tombstones across the vault of Hell.

Fierce winds buffeted the trees and Druss saw a herd of deer running from the woods, their movements seeming disjointed and ungainly against the flaring lightning bolts. A tree was struck and seemed to explode from within, splitting into two halves. Fire blazed briefly from the ruined trunk, but died within seconds in the sheeting rain.

Dulina crept alongside him, pushing herself against him. He felt the stitches in his side pull as she snuggled in, but he lifted his arm around her shoulders. 'Is is only a storm, child,' he said. 'It cannot harm us.' She said nothing and he drew her to his lap, holding her close. She was warm, almost feverish, he thought.

Sighing, Druss felt again the weight of loss, and wondered where Rowena was on this dark and ferocious night. Was there a storm where she lay? Or was the night calm? Did she feel the loss, or was Druss just a dim memory of another life in the mountains? He glanced down to see that the child was asleep, her head in the crook of his arm.

Holding her firmly but gently, Druss rose and carried her back to the fireside, laying her down on her blanket and adding the last of the fuel to the fire.

'You are a good man,' came a soft voice. Druss looked up and saw that the old tinker was awake.

'How is the leg?'

'It hurts, but it will heal. You are sad, my friend.'

Druss shrugged. 'These are sad times.'

'I heard your talk with your friend. I am sorry that in helping me you have lost the chance to help others.' He smiled. 'Not that I would change anything, you understand?'

Druss chuckled. 'Nor I.'

'I am Ruwaq the Tinker,' said the old man, extending a bony hand.

Druss shook it and sat beside him. 'Where are you from?'

'Originally? The lands of Matapesh, far to the east of Naashan and north of the Opal Jungles. But I have always been a man who needed to see new mountains. People think they are all the same, but it is not so. Some are lush and green, others crowned with shining ice and snow. Some are sharp, like sword-blades, others old and rounded, comfortable within eternity. I love mountains.'

'What happened to your children?'

'Children? Oh, I never had children. Never married.'

'I thought the child was your grand-daughter?'

'No, I found her outside Resha. She had been abandoned and was starving to death. She is a good girl. I love her dearly. I can never repay the debt to you for saving her.'

658

'There is no debt,' said Druss.

The old man lifted his hand and wagged his finger. 'I don't accept that, my friend. You gave her – and me – the gift of life. I do not like storms, but I was viewing this one with the greatest pleasure. Because until you entered the hollow I was a dead man, and Dulina would have been raped and probably murdered. Now the storm is a vision of beauty. No one ever gave me a greater gift.' The old man had tears in his eyes and Druss's discomfort grew. Instead of feeling elated by his gratitude he experienced a sense of shame. A true hero, he believed, would have gone to the man's aid from a sense of justice, of compassion. Druss knew that was not why he had helped them.

Not even close. The right deed . . . for the wrong reason. He patted the old man's shoulder and returned to the cave-mouth where he saw that the storm was moving on towards the east, the rain lessening. Druss's spirits sank. He wished Sieben were with him. Irritating as the poet could be, he still had a talent for lifting the axeman's mood.

But Sieben had refused to accompany him, preferring the pleasures of city life to an arduous journey across the mountains to Resha. No, thought Druss, not the journey; that was just an excuse.

'I'll make a bargain with you though, old horse,' said Sieben on that last day. 'Leave the axe and I'll change my mind. Bury it. Throw it in the sea. I don't care which.'

'Don't tell me you believe that nonsense?'

'I saw it, Druss. Truly. It will be the death of you – or at least the death of the man I know.'

Now he had no axe, no friend, and no Rowena. Unused to despair Druss felt lost, his strength useless.

Dawn brightened the sky, the land glistening and fresh from the rain as Dulina came alongside him. 'I had a wonderful dream,' she said brightly. 'There was a great knight on a white horse. And he rode up to where grandfather and I were waiting, and he leaned from his saddle and lifted me to sit beside him. Then he took off his golden helmet and he said, "I am your father." And he took me to live in a castle. I never had a dream like it. Do you think it will come true?'

Druss did not answer. He was staring down at the woods at the armed men making their way towards the cave.

The world had shrunk now to a place of agony and darkness. All Druss could feel was pain as he lay in the windowless dungeon, listening to the skittering of unseen rats which clambered over him. There was no light, save when at the end of the day the jailer strode down the dungeon corridor and a tiny, flickering beam momentarily lit the narrow grille of the door-stone. Only in those seconds could Druss see his surroundings. The ceiling was a mere four feet from the floor, the airless room six feet square. Water dripped from the walls, and it was cold.

Druss brushed a rat from his leg, the movement causing him a fresh wave of pain from his wounds. He could hardly move his neck, and his right shoulder was swollen and hot to the touch. Wondering if the bones were broken, he began to shiver.

How many days? He had counted to sixty-three, but then lost track for a while. Guessing at seventy, he had begun to count again. But his mind wandered. Sometimes he dreamt of the mountains of home, under a blue sky, with a fresh northerly wind cooling his brow. At other times he tried to remember events in his life.

'I will break you, and then I will watch you beg for death,' said Cajivak on the day they had hauled Druss into the castle Hall.

'In your dreams, you ugly whoreson.'

Cajivak had beaten him then, pounding his face and body with brutal blows. His hands tied behind him, a tight rope around his neck, Druss could do nothing but accept the hammering.

For the first two weeks he was kept in a larger cell. Every time he slept men would appear alongside his narrow bed to beat him with clubs and sticks. At first he had fought them, grabbing one man by the throat and cracking his skull against the cell wall. But deprived of food and water for days on end, his strength had given out and he could only curl himself into a tight ball against the merciless beatings.

Then they had thrown him into this tiny dungeon, and he had watched with horror as they slid the door-stone into place. Once every two days a guard would push stale bread and a cup of water through the narrow grille. Twice he caught rats and ate them raw, cutting his lips on the tiny bones.

Now he lived for those few seconds of light as the guard walked back to the outside world.

'We caught the others,' the jailer said one day, as he pushed the bread through the grille. But Druss did not believe him. Such was Cajivak's cruelty that he would have dragged Druss out to see them slain.

He pictured Varsava pushing the child up into the chimney crack in the cave, urging her to climb, and remembered lifting Ruwaq up to where Varsava could haul the old man out of sight. Druss himself was about to climb when he heard the warriors approaching the cave. He had turned.

And charged them . . .

But there were too many, and most bore clubs which finally smashed him from his feet. Boots and fists thundered into him and he awoke to find a rope around his neck, his hands bound. Forced to walk behind a horseman, he was many times dragged from his feet, the rope tearing the flesh of his neck.

Varsava had described Cajivak as a monster, which could not be more true. The man was close to seven feet tall, with an enormous breadth of shoulder and biceps as thick as most men's thighs. His eyes were dark, almost black, and no hair grew on the right side of his head where the skin was white and scaly, covered in scar tissue that only a severe burn could create. Madness shone in his eyes, and Druss had glanced to the man's left and the weapon that was placed there, resting against the high-backed throne.

Snaga!

Druss shook himself free of the memory now and stretched. His joints creaked and his hands trembled in the cold that seeped from the wet walls. Don't think of it, he urged himself. Concentrate on something else. He tried to picture Rowena, but instead found himself remembering the day when the priest of Pashtar Sen had found him in a small village, four days east of Lania. Druss had been sitting in the garden of an inn, enjoying a meal of roast meat and onions and a jug of ale. The priest bowed and sat opposite the axeman. His bald head was pink and peeling, burned by the sun.

'I am glad to find you in good health, Druss. I have searched for you for the last six months.'

'You found me,' said Druss.

'It is about the axe.'

'Do not concern yourself, Father. It is gone. You were right, it was an evil weapon. I am glad to be rid of it.'

The priest shook his head. 'It is back,' he said. 'It is now in the possession of a robber named Cajivak. Always a killer, he succumbed far more swiftly than a strong man like yourself and now he is terrorising the lands around Lania, torturing, killing and maiming. With the war keeping our troops from the area, there is little that can be done to stop him.'

'Why tell me?'

The priest said nothing for a moment, averting his eyes from Druss's direct gaze. 'I have watched you,' he said at last. 'Not just in the present, but through the past, from your birth through your childhood, to your marriage to Rowena and your quest to find her. You are a rare man, Druss. You have iron control over those areas of your soul which have a capacity for evil. And you have a dread of becoming like Bardan. Well, Cajivak is Bardan reborn. Who else can stop him?'

'I don't have time to waste, priest. My wife is somewhere in these lands.'

The priest reddened and hung his head. His voice was a whisper, and there was shame in the words. 'Recover the axe and I will tell you where she is,' he said.

Druss leaned back and stared long and hard at the slender man before him. 'This is unworthy of you,' he observed.

661

The priest looked up. 'I know.' He spread his hands. 'I have no other . . . payment . . . to offer.'

'I could take hold of your scrawny neck and wring the truth from you,' Druss pointed out.

'But you will not. I know you, Druss.'

The warrior stood. 'I'll find the axe,' he promised. 'Where shall we meet?'

'You find the axe – and I'll find you,' the priest told him.

Alone in the dark, Druss remembered with bitterness the confidence he had felt. Find Cajivak, recover the axe, then find Rowena. So simple!

What a fool you are, he thought. His face itched and he scratched at the skin of his cheek, his grimy finger breaking a scab upon his cheek. A rat ran across his leg and Druss lunged for it, but missed. Struggling to his knees, he felt his head touch the cold stone of the ceiling.

Torchlight flickered as the guard moved down the corridor. Druss scrambled to the grille, the light burning his eyes. The jailer, whose face Druss could not see, bent and thrust a clay cup into the door-stone cavity. There was no bread. Druss lifted the cup and drained the water. 'Still alive, I see,' said the jailer, his voice deep and cold. 'I think the Lord Cajivak has forgotten about you. By the gods, that makes you a lucky man – you'll be able to live down here with the rats for the rest of your life.' Druss said nothing and the voice went on, 'The last man who lived in that cell was there for five years. When we dragged him out his hair was white and all his teeth were rotten. He was blind, and bent like a crippled old man. You'll be the same.'

Druss focused on the light, watching the shadows on the dark wall. The jailer stood, and the light receded. Druss sank back.

No bread . . .

You'll be able to live down here with the rats for the rest of your life.

Despair struck him like a hammer blow.

Pahtai felt the pain recede as she floated clear of her plague-racked body. I am dying, she thought, but there was no fear, no surging panic, merely a peaceful sense of harmony as she rose into the air.

It was night, and the lanterns were lit. Hovering just below the ceiling, she gazed down on Michanek as he sat beside the frail woman in the bed, holding to her hand, stroking the fever-dry skin and whispering words of love. That is me, thought *Pahtai*, staring down at the woman.

'I love you, I love you,' whispered Michanek. 'Please don't die!'

He looked so tired, and *Pahtai* wanted to reach out to him. He was all the security and love she had ever known, and she recalled the first morning when she had woken in his home in Resha. She remembered the bright sunshine and the smell of jasmine from the gardens, and she

662

knew that the bearded man sitting beside her should have been known to her. But when she reached into her mind she could find no trace of him. It was so embarrassing. 'How are you feeling?' he had asked, the voice familiar but doing nothing to unlock her memory. She tried to think of where she might have met him. That was when the second shock struck, with infinitely more power than the first.

She had no memory! Nothing! Her face must have reacted to the shock, for he leaned in close and took her hand. 'Do not concern yourself, *Pahtai*. You have been ill, very ill. But you are getting better now. I know that you do not remember me, but as time passes you will.' He turned his head and called to another man, tiny, slender and dark-skinned. 'Look, here is Pudri,' said Michanek. 'He has been worried about you.'

She had sat up then, and seen the tears in the little man's eyes. 'Are you my father?' she asked.

He shook his head. 'I am your servant and your friend, *Pahtai*.'

'And you, sir,' she said, turning her gaze on Michanek. 'Are you my . . . brother?'

He had smiled. 'If that is what you wish, that is what I will be. But no, I am not your brother. Nor am I your master. You are a free woman, *Pahtai*.' Taking her hand, he kissed the palm, his beard soft as fur against her skin.

'You are my husband, then?'

'No, I am merely a man who loves you. Take my hand and tell me what you feel.'

She did so. 'It is a good hand, strong. And it is warm.'

'You see nothing? No . . . visions?'

'No. Should I?'

He shook his head. 'Of course not. It is only . . . that you were hallucinating when the fever was high. It just shows how much better you are.' He kissed her hand again.

Just as he was doing now. 'I love you,' she thought, suddenly sad that she was about to die. She rose through the ceiling and out into the night, gazing up at the stars. Through spirit eyes they no longer twinkled, but sat perfect and round in the vast bowl of the night. The city was peaceful, and even the camp-fires of the enemy seemed merely a glowing necklace around Resha.

She had never fully discovered the secrets of her past. It seemed she was a prophet of some kind, and had belonged to a merchant named Kabuchek, but he had fled the city long before the siege began. *Pahtai* remembered walking to his house, hoping that the sight of it would stir her lost memories. Instead she had seen a powerful man, dressed in black and carrying a double-headed axe. He was talking to a servant. Instinctively she had ducked back into an alley, her heart hammering. He looked like Michanek but harder,

663

more deadly. Unable to take her eyes from him, she found the oddest sensations stirring within her.

Swiftly she turned and ran back the way she had come.

And had never since sought to find out her background.

But sometimes as she and Michanek were making love, usually in the garden beneath the flowering trees, she would find herself suddenly thinking of the man with the axe, and then fear would come and with it a sense of betrayal. Michanek loved her, and it seemed disloyal that another man – a man she didn't even know – could intrude into her thoughts at such a time.

Pahtai soared higher, her spirit drawn across the war-torn land, above gutted houses, ruined villages and ghostly, deserted towns. She wondered if this was the route to Paradise? Coming to a range of mountains, she saw an ugly fortress of grey stone. She was thinking of the man with the axe, and found herself drawn into the citadel. There was a hall and within it sat a huge man, his face scarred, his eyes malevolent. Beside him was the axe she had seen carried by the man in black.

Down she journeyed, to a dungeon deep and dark, cold and filthy, the haunt of rats and lice. The axeman lay there, his skin covered in sores. He was asleep and his spirit was gone from the body. Reaching out she tried to touch his face, but her spectral hand flowed beneath the skin. In that moment she saw a slender line of pulsing light radiating around the body. Her hand stroked the light and instantly she found him.

He was alone and in terrible despair. She spoke with him, trying to give him strength, but he reached for her and his words were shocking and filled her with fear. He disappeared then, and she guessed that he had been woken from sleep.

Back in the citadel she floated through the corridors and rooms, the antechambers and halls. An old man was sitting in a deserted kitchen. He too was dreaming, and it was the dream that drew her to him. He was in the same dungeon; he had lived there for years. *Pahtai* entered his mind and spoke with his dream spirit. Then she returned to the night sky. 'I am not dying,' she thought. 'I am merely free.'

In an instant she returned to Resha and her body. Pain flooded through her, and the weight of flesh sank down like a prison around her spirit. She felt the touch of Michanek's hand, and all thoughts of the axeman dispersed like mist under the sun. She was suddenly happy, despite the pain. He had been so good to her, and yet . . .

'Are you awake?' he asked, his voice low. She opened her eyes.

'Yes. I love you.'

'And I you. More than life.'

'Why did we never wed?' she said, her throat dry, the words rasping clear. She saw him pale.

'Is that what you wish for? Would it make you well?'

'It would . . . make me . . . happy,' she told him.

'I will send for a priest,' he promised.

She found him on a grim mountainside where winter winds were howling through the peaks. He was frozen and weak, his limbs trembling, his eyes dull. 'What are you doing?' she asked.

'Waiting to die,' he told her.

'That is no way for you to behave. You are a warrior, and a warrior never gives up.'

'I have no strength left.'

Rowena sat beside him and he felt the warmth of her arms around his shoulders, smelt the sweetness of her breath. 'Be strong,' she said, stroking his hair. 'In despair there is only defeat.'

'I cannot overcome cold stone. I cannot shine a light through the darkness. My limbs are rotting, my teeth shake in their sockets.'

'Is there nothing you would live for?'

'Yes,' he said, reaching for her. 'I live for you! I always have. But I can't find you.'

He awoke in the darkness amidst the stench of the dungeon and crawled to the door-stone grille, finding it by touch. Cool air drifted down the corridor and he breathed deeply. Torchlight flickered, burning his eyes. He squinted against it and watched as the jailer tramped down the corridor. Then the darkness returned. Druss's stomach cramped and he groaned. Dizziness swamped him, and nausea rose in his throat.

A faint light showed and, rolling painfully to his knees, he pushed his face against the narrow opening. An old man with a wispy white beard knelt outside the dungeon stone. The light from the tiny clay oil lamp was torturously bright, and Druss's eyes stung.

'Ah, you are alive! Good,' whispered the old man. 'I have brought you this lamp and an old tinder-box. Use it carefully. It will help accustom your eyes to light. Also I have some food.' He thrust a linen package through the door-stone and Druss took it, his mouth too dry for speech. 'I'll come back when I can,' said the old man. 'Remember, only use the light once the jailer has gone.'

Druss listened to the man slowly make his way down the corridor. He thought he heard a door shut, but could not be sure. With unsteady hands he drew the lamp into the dungeon, placing it on the floor beside him. Then he hauled in the package and the small iron tinder-box.

Eyes streaming from the light, he opened the package to find there were two apples, a hunk of cheese and some dried meat. When he bit into one of the apples it was unbearably delicious, the juices stinging his bleeding gums. Swallowing was almost painful, but the minor irritation was swamped by the coolness. He almost vomited, but held it down, and slowly finished the fruit. His shrunken stomach rebelled after the second apple, and he sat holding the cheese and the meat as if they were treasures of gems and gold.

While waiting for his stomach to settle he stared around at his tiny cell, seeing the filth and decay for the first time. Looking at his hands, he saw the skin was split and ugly sores showed on his wrists and arms. His leather jerkin had been taken from him and the woollen shirt was alive with lice. He saw the small hole in the corner of the wall from which the rats emerged.

And despair was replaced by anger.

Unaccustomed to the light, his eyes continued to stream. Removing his shirt, he gazed down at his wasted body. The arms were no longer huge, the wrists and elbows jutting. But I am alive, he told himself. And I will survive.

He finished the cheese and half of the meat. Desperate as he was to consume it all, he did not know if the old man would come back, and he rewrapped the meat and pushed it into his belt.

Examining the working of the tinder-box he saw that it was an old design, a sharp piece of flint that could be struck against the serrated interior, igniting the powdered tinder in the well of the box. Satisfied he could use it in the dark, he reluctantly blew out the lamp.

The old man did return – but not for two days. This time he brought some dried peaches, a hunk of ham and a small sack of tinder. 'It is important that you keep supple,' he told Druss. 'Stretch out on the floor and exercise.'

'Why are you doing this for me?'

'I sat in that cell for years, I know what it is like. You must build your strength. There are two ways to do this, or so I found. Lie on your stomach with your hands beneath your shoulders and then, keeping the legs straight, push yourself up using only your arms. Repeat this as many times as you can manage. Keep count. Each day try for one more. Also you can lie on your back and raise your legs, keeping them straight. This will strengthen the belly.'

'How long have I been here?' asked Druss.

'It is best not to think of that,' the old man advised. 'Concentrate on building your body. I will bring some ointments next time for those sores, and some lice powder.'

'What is your name?'

'Best you don't know – in case they find the lamp.'

'I owe you a debt, my friend. And I always pay my debts.'

'You'll have no chance of that – unless you become strong again.'

'I shall,' promised Druss.

When the old man had gone Druss lit the lamp and lay down on his belly. With his hands beneath his shoulders he forced his body up. He managed eight before collapsing to the filthy floor.

A week later it was thirty. And by the end of a month he could manage one hundred.

3

The guard at the main gate narrowed his eyes and stared at the three riders. None was known to him, but they rode with casual confidence, chatting to one another and laughing. The guard stepped out to meet them. 'Who are you?' he asked.

The first of the men, a slim blond-haired warrior wearing a baldric from which hung four knives, dismounted from his bay mare. 'We are travellers seeking lodging for the night,' he said. 'Is there a problem? Is there plague in the city?'

'Plague? Of course there's no plague,' answered the guard, hastily making the sign of the Protective Horn. 'Where are you from?'

'We've ridden from Lania, and we're heading for Capalis and the coast. All we seek is an inn.'

'There are no inns here. This is the fortress of Lord Cajivak.'

The other two horsemen remained mounted. The guard looked up at them. One was slim and dark-haired, a bow slung across his shoulder and a quiver hanging from the pommel of his saddle. The third man wore a wide leather hat and sported no weapons save an enormous hunting-knife almost as long as a short sword.

'We can pay for our lodgings,' said the blond man with an easy smile. The guard licked his lips. The man dipped his hand into the pouch by his side and produced a thick silver coin which he dropped into the guard's hand.

'Well . . . it would be churlish to turn you away,' said the guard, pocketing the coin. 'All right. Ride through the main square, bearing left. You'll see a domed building, with a narrow lane running down its eastern side. There is a tavern there. It's a rough place, mind, with much fighting. But the keeper – Ackae – keeps rooms at the back. Tell him that Ratsin sent you.'

'You are most kind,' said the blond man, stepping back into the saddle.

As they rode in to the city the guard shook his head. Be unlikely to see them again, he thought, not with that much silver on them and not a sword between them.

The old man came almost every day, and Druss grew to treasure the moments. He never stayed long, but his conversation was brief, wise and to the point. 'The biggest danger when you get out is to the eyes, boy. They get too used to the dark, and the sun can blind them – permanently. I lost my sight for almost a month after they dragged me out. Stare into the lamp flame, close as you can, force the pupils to contract.'

Druss was now as strong as he would ever be in such a place, and last night he had told the man, 'Do not come tomorrow, or the next day.'

'Why?'

'I'm thinking of leaving,' answered the Drenai. The old man had laughed. 'I'm serious, my friend. Don't come for two days.'

'There's no way out. The door-stone alone requires two men to move it, and there are two bolts holding it in place.'

'If you are correct,' Druss told him, 'then I will see you here in three days.'

Now he sat quietly in the dark. The ointments his friend had supplied had healed most of his sores, and the lice powder – while itching like the devil's touch – had convinced all but the most hardy of the parasites to seek alternative accommodation. The food over the last months had rebuilt Druss's strength, and his teeth no longer rattled in their sockets. Now was the time, he thought. There'll never be a better.

Silently he waited through the long day.

At last he heard the jailer outside. A clay cup was pushed into the opening, with a hunk of stale bread by it. Druss sat in the dark, unmoving.

'Here is it, my black-bearded rat,' the jailer called.

Silence. 'Ah well, suit yourself. You'll change your mind before long.'

The hours drifted by. Torchlight flickered in the corridor and he heard the jailer halt. Then the man walked on. Druss waited for an hour, then he lit his lamp and chewed on the last of the meat the old man had left the night before. Lifting the lamp to his face he stared hard into the tiny flame, passing it back and forth before his eyes. The light didn't sting as once it had. Blowing out the light he turned over on to his stomach, pushing himself through one hundred and fifty press raises.

He slept . . .

And awoke to the arrival of the jailer. The man knelt down at the

668

narrow opening, but Druss knew he could not see more than a few inches into the dark. The food and water was untouched. The only question now was whether the jailer cared if his prisoner lived or died. Cajivak had threatened to have Druss dragged before him in order to plead for death. Would the Lord be pleased that his jailer had robbed him of such delights?

He heard the jailer curse, then move off back the way he had come. Druss's mouth was dry, and his heart pounded. Minutes passed – long, anxious minutes. Then the jailer returned; he was speaking to someone.

'It's not my fault,' he was saying. 'His rations were set by the Lord himself.'

'So it's *his* fault? Is that what you're saying?'

'No! No! It's nobody's *fault*. Maybe he had a weak heart or something. Maybe he's just sick. That's it, he's probably sick. We'll move him to a bigger cell for a while.'

'I hope you're right,' said a soft voice, 'otherwise you'll be wearing your own entrails for a necklace.'

A grating sound followed, then another, and Druss guessed the bolts were being drawn back. 'All right, together now,' came a voice. 'Heave!' The stone groaned as the men hauled it clear.

'Gods, but it stinks in there!' complained one of the guards as a torch was thrust inside. Druss grabbed the wielder by the throat, hauling him in, then he dived through the opening and rolled. He rose, but dizziness caused him to stagger and a guard laughed.

'There's your dead man,' he said, and Druss heard the rasp of a sword being drawn. It was so hard to see – there were at least three torches, and the light was blinding. A shape moved towards him. 'Back in your hole, rat!' said the guard. Druss leapt forward to smash a punch to the man's face. The guard's iron helm flew from his head as his body shot backwards, his head cannoning into the dungeon wall. A second guard ran in. Druss's vision was clearing now and he saw the man aim a blow at his head. He ducked and stepped inside the blow, thundering his fist in the man's belly. Instantly the guard folded, a great whoosh of air rushing from his lungs. Druss brought his clenched fist down on the man's neck, there was a sickening crack and the guard fell to his face.

The jailer was trying to wriggle clear of the dungeon opening as Druss turned on him. The man squealed in fright and elbowed his way back into the dungeon. Druss hauled the first guard to the entrance, thrusting the unconscious body through into the cell. The second guard was dead; his body followed the first. Breathing heavily Druss looked at the door-stone. Anger rose in him like a sudden fire. Squatting down, he took the stone in both hands and heaved it into place. Then he sat before it and pushed it home with his legs. For several minutes he sat exhausted, then he crawled to the door-stone and pushed the bolts home.

Lights danced before Druss's eyes, and his heart was hammering so fast he could not count the beats. Yet he forced himself upright and moved carefully to the door, which was partly open, and glanced into the corridor beyond. Sunlight was shining through a window, the beam highlighting dust motes in the air. It was indescribably beautiful.

The corridor was deserted. He could see two chairs and a table with two cups upon it. Moving into the corridor, he halted at the table and, seeing the cups contained watered wine, he drained them both. More dungeons lined the walls, but these all had doors of iron bars. He moved on to a second wooden door, beyond which was a stairwell, dark and unlit.

His strength was fading as he slowly climbed the stairs, but anger drove him on.

Sieben gazed down with undisguised horror at the small black insect upon the back of his hand. 'This,' he said, 'is insufferable.'

'What?' asked Varsava from his position at the narrow window.

'The room has fleas,' answered Sieben, taking the insect between thumb and forefinger and crushing it.

'They seem to prefer you, poet,' put in Eskodas with a boyish grin.

'The risk of death is one thing,' said Sieben icily. 'Fleas are quite another. I have not even inspected the bed, but I would imagine it is teeming with wild-life. I think we should make the rescue attempt at once.'

Varsava chuckled. 'After dark would probably be best,' he said. 'I was here three months ago when I took a child back out to his father. That's how I learned that Druss was here. The dungeons are – as you would expect – on the lowest level. Above them are the kitchens, and above them the main Hall. There is no exit from the dungeons save through the Hall, which means we must be inside the Keep by dusk. There is no night jailer; therefore, if we can hide within the Keep until around midnight, we should be able to find Druss and get him out. As to leaving the fortress, that is another matter. As you saw, the two gates are guarded by day and locked by night. There are sentries on the walls, and lookouts in the towers.'

'How many?' asked Eskodas.

'When I was here before, there were five near the main gate.'

'How did you get out with the child?'

'He was a small boy. I hid him in a sack and carried him out just after dawn, draped behind my saddle.'

'I can't see Druss fitting in a sack,' said Sieben.

Varsava moved to sit alongside the poet. 'Do not think of him as you knew him, poet. He has been over a year in a tiny, windowless cell.

670

The food would be barely enough to keep him alive. He will not be the giant we all knew. And he's likely to be blind – or insane. Or both.'

Silence fell upon the room as each man remembered the axeman they had fought alongside. 'I wish I'd known sooner,' muttered Sieben.

'I did not know myself,' said Varsava. 'I thought they'd killed him.'

'It's strange,' put in Eskodas, 'I could never imagine Druss being beaten – even by an army. He was always so – so indomitable.'

Varsava chuckled. 'I know. I watched him walk unarmed into a hollow where a dozen or so warriors were torturing an old man. He went through them like a scythe through wheat. Impressive.'

'So, how shall we proceed?' Sieben asked.

'We will go to the main Hall to pay our respects to the Lord Cajivak. Perhaps he won't kill us outright!'

'Oh, that's a good plan,' said Sieben, his voice dripping with sarcasm.

'You have a better?'

'I believe that I have. One would imagine that a sordid place like this would be short of entertainment. I shall go alone and announce myself by name; I will offer to perform for my supper.'

'At the risk of being considered rude,' said Eskodas, 'I don't think your epic poems will be as well received as you think.'

'My dear boy, I am an entertainer. I can fashion a performance to suit any audience.'

'Well, this audience,' said Varsava, 'will be made up of the dregs of Ventria and Naashan and all points east and west. There will be Drenai renegades, Vagrian mercenaries and Ventrian criminals of all kinds.'

'I shall dazzle them,' promised Sieben. 'Give me half an hour to make my introductions, then make your way into the Hall. I promise you no one will notice your entrance.'

'Where did you acquire such humility?' asked Eskodas.

'It's a gift,' replied Sieben, 'and I'm very proud of it.'

Druss reached the second level and paused at the top of the stairwell. He could hear the sounds of many people moving around, the scrape of pans being cleaned and of cutlery being prepared. He could smell fresh bread cooking, mixed with the savoury aroma of roasting beef. Leaning against the wall, he tried to think. There was no way through without being seen. His legs were tired, and he sank down to his haunches.

What to do?

He heard footsteps approaching and pushed himself upright. An old man appeared, his back hideously bent, his legs bowed. He was carrying a bucket of water. His head came up as he approached Druss, his nostrils quivering. The eyes, Druss saw, were rheumy and covered with an opal film. The old man put down the bucket and reached out. 'Is it you?' he whispered.

'You are blind?'

'Almost. I told you I spent five years in that cell. Come, follow me.' Leaving the bucket, the old man retraced his steps, round a winding corridor and down a narrow stair. Pushing open a door, he led Druss inside. The room was small, but there was a slit window that allowed a shaft of sunshine. 'Wait here,' he said. 'I will bring you some food and drink.'

He returned within minutes with a half-loaf of fresh baked bread, a slab of cheese and a jug of water. Druss devoured the food and drank deeply, then leaned back on the cot-bed.

'I thank you for your kindness,' he said. 'Without it I would be worse than dead; I would have been lost.'

'I owed a debt,' said the cripple. 'Another man fed me, just as I fed you. They killed him for it – Cajivak had him impaled. But I would never have found the courage had the goddess not appeared to me in a dream. Was it she who brought you from the dungeon?'

'Goddess?'

'She told me of you, and your suffering, and she filled me with shame at my cowardice. I swore to her that I would do all in my power to help you. And she touched my hand, and when I awoke all pain had gone from my back. Did she make the stone disappear?'

'No, I tricked the jailer.' He told the man of the ruse, and his fight with the guards.

'They will not be discovered until later tonight,' said the cripple. Ah, but I would love to hear their screams as the rats come at them in the dark.'

'Why do you say the woman in your dream was a goddess?' asked Druss.

'She told me her name, *Pahtai*, and that is the daughter of the earth mother. And in my dream she walked with me upon the green hillsides of my youth. I shall never forget her.'

'*Pahtai*,' said Druss softly. 'She came to me also in that cell, and gave me strength.' He stood and laid his hand on the old man's back. 'You risked much to help me, and I've no time left in this world in which to repay you.'

'No time?' echoed the old man. 'You can hide here and escape after dark. I can get a rope; you can lower yourself from the wall.'

'No. I must find Cajivak – and kill him.'

'Good,' said the old man. 'The goddess will give you powers, yes? She will pour strength into your body?'

'I fear not,' said Druss. 'In this I shall be alone.'

'You will die! Do not attempt this,' pleaded the old man, tears

672

streaming from the opal eyes. 'I beg you. He will destroy you; he is a monster with the strength of ten men. Look at yourself. I cannot see you clearly, but I know how weak you must be. You have a chance at life, freedom, sunshine on your face. You are young – what will you achieve if you attempt this foolishness? He will crush you, and either kill you or throw you back into that hole in the ground.'

'I was not born to run,' said Druss. 'And, trust me, I am not as weak as you think. You saw to that. Now tell me of the Keep, and where the stairwells lead.'

Eskodas had no fear of death, for he had no love of life – a fact he had known for many years. Ever since his father was dragged from their home and hanged, he had known no depth of joy. He felt the loss, but accepted it in a calm and tranquil manner. On board ship he had told Sieben that he enjoyed killing people, but this was not true. He experienced no sensation whatever when his arrow struck home, save for a momentary satisfaction when his aim was particularly good.

Now, as he strolled with Varsava towards the grey, forbidding Hall, he wondered if he would die. He thought of Druss imprisoned beneath the Keep in a dark, dank dungeon, and found himself wondering what such incarceration would do to his own personality. He took no especial pleasure from the sights of the world, the mountains and lakes, the oceans and valleys. Would he miss them? He doubted it.

Glancing at Varsava, he saw that the bladesman was tense, expectant. Eskodas smiled. No need for fear, he thought.

It is only death.

The two men climbed the stone steps to the Keep gates, which were open and unguarded. Moving inside, Eskodas heard a roar of laughter from the Hall. They walked to the main doors and looked inside. There were some two hundred men seated around three great tables and, at the far end, on a dais raised some six feet from the floor, sat Cajivak. He was seated in a huge, ornately carved chair of ebony, and he was smiling. Before him, standing on the end table, was Sieben.

The poet's voice sang out. He was telling them a tale of such mind-bending raunchiness that Eskodas's jaw dropped. He had heard Sieben tell epic stories, recite ancient poems and discuss philosophy, but never had he heard the poet talk of whores and donkeys. Varsava laughed aloud as Sieben finished the story with an obscene *double entendre*.

Eskodas gazed around the hall. Above them was a gallery, and he located the recessed stairway that led to it. This might be a good place to hide. He nudged Varsava. 'I'll take a look upstairs,' he whispered. The bladesman nodded and Eskodas strolled unnoticed through the throng and climbed the stairs. The gallery was narrow and flowed round the Hall. There were no doors leading from it, and a man seated here would be invisible to those below.

Sieben was now telling the story of a hero captured by a vicious enemy. Eskodas paused to listen:

'He was taken before the leader, and told that he had one opportunity for life: he must survive four trials by ordeal. The first was to walk barefoot across a trench filled with hot coals. The second to drink a full quart of the most powerful spirit. Thirdly he had to enter a cave and, with a small set of tongs, remove a bad tooth from a mankilling lioness. Lastly, he was told, he had to make love to the ugliest crone in the village.

'Well, he pulled off his boots and told them to bring on the hot coals. Manfully he strode through them to the other side of the trench, where he lifted the quart of spirit and drained it, hurling the pot aside. Then he stumbled into the cave. There followed the most terrible sounds of spitting, growling, and banging and shrieking. The listening men found their blood growing cold. At last the warrior staggered out into the sunlight. "Right," he said. "Now where's the woman with the toothache?" '

Laughter echoed around the rafters and Eskodas shook his head in amazement. He had watched Sieben back in Capalis listening to warriors swapping jests and jokes. Not once had the poet laughed, or appeared to find the stories amusing. Yet here he was, performing the same tales with apparent relish.

Transferring his gaze to Cajivak, the archer saw that the leader was no longer smiling, but was sitting back in his chair, his fingers drumming on the arm-rest. Eskodas had known many evil men, and knew well that some could look as fine as angels – handsome, clear-eyed, golden-haired. But Cajivak looked what he was, dark and malevolent. He was wearing Druss's jerkin of black leather, with the silver shoulder guards, and Eskodas saw him reach down and stroke the black haft of an axe that was resting against the chair. It was Snaga.

Suddenly the colossal warrior rose from his chair. 'Enough!' he bellowed and Sieben stood silently before him. 'I don't like your performance, bard, so I'm going to have you impaled on an iron spike.' The Hall was utterly silent now. Eskodas drew a shaft from his quiver and notched it to his bow. 'Well? Any more jests before you die?' Cajivak asked.

'Just the one,' answered Sieben, holding to the madman's gaze. 'Last night I had dream, a terrible dream. I dreamt I was beyond the gates of Hell; it was a place of fire and torture, exquisitely ghastly. I was very frightened and I said to one of the demon guards, "Is there any way out of here?" And he said there was only one, and no one had ever achieved the task set. He led me to a dungeon, and through a narrow grille I saw the most loathsome woman. She was leprous, with weeping sores, toothless and old beyond time. Maggots crawled in what was left of her hair. The guard said, "If you can make love to her all night, you will be allowed to leave." And, you know, I was prepared to have a try. But as I stepped forward I saw a second door, and I glanced through. And you know what I saw, Lord? I saw you. You were making love to one of the most beautiful women I have ever seen. So I said to the guard, "Why is it that I have to bed a crone, when Cajivak gets a beauty?" "Well," he said, " 'tis only fair that the women also have a chance to get out." ' '

Even from the gallery Eskodas could see Cajivak's face lose its colour. When he spoke, his voice was harsh and trembling. 'I will make your death last an eternity,' he promised.

Eskodas drew back on his bowstring . . . and paused. A man had appeared at the back of the dais, his hair and beard matted and filthy, his face blackened with ingrained dirt. He ran forward, throwing his shoulder into the high back of Cajivak's chair, which hurtled forward to catapult the warlord from the dais. He fell head-first on to the table upon which Sieben stood.

The filth-covered warrior swept up the shining axe, and his voice boomed out through the Hall: 'Now do you want me to beg, you miserable whoreson?'

Eskodas chuckled. There were moments in life worth cherishing, he realised.

As he swept up the axe, feeling the cool, black haft in his hand, power surged through him. It felt like fire roaring through his veins to every muscle and sinew. In that moment Druss felt renewed, reborn. Nothing in his life had ever been so exquisite. He felt light-headed and full of life, like a paralysed man who regains the use of his limbs.

His laughter boomed out over the Hall, and he gazed down on Cajivak who was scrambling to his feet amongst the dishes and goblets. The warlord's face was bloody, his mouth contorted.

'It is mine!' shouted Cajivak. 'Give it back!'

The men around him looked surprised at his reaction. Where they had expected fury and violence, they saw instead their dread Lord reaching out, almost begging.

'Come and get it,' invited Druss.

Cajivak hesitated and licked his thin lips. 'Kill him!' he screamed suddenly. The warriors surged to their feet, the nearest man drawing his sword and running towards the dais. An arrow slashed into his throat, pitching him from his feet. All movement ceased then as scores of armed men scanned the Hall, seeking the hidden bowman.

'What a man you chose to follow!' said Druss, his voice booming in the sudden silence. 'He stands with his feet in your stew, too frightened to face a man who has been locked in his dungeon and fed on scraps. You want the axe?' he asked Cajivak. 'I say again, Come and get it.' Twisting the weapon, he slammed it down into the boards of the dais where it stood quivering, the points of the butterfly blades punching deep into the wood. Druss stepped away from the axe and the warriors waited.

Suddenly Cajivak moved, taking two running steps and leaping towards the dais. He was a huge man, with immense shoulders and powerful arms; but he leapt into a straight left from the former champion of Mashrapur which smashed his lips into his teeth, and a right cross that hit his jaw like a thunderbolt. Cajivak fell to the dais and rolled back to the floor, landing on his back. He was up fast, and this time he slowly mounted the steps to the dais.

'I'll break you, little man! I'll rip out your entrails and feed them to you!'

'In your dreams!' mocked Druss. As Cajivak charged, Druss stepped in to meet him, slamming a second straight left into Cajivak's heart. The larger man grunted, but then sent an overhand right that cannoned against Druss's brow, forcing him back. Cajivak's left hand snapped forward with fingers extended to rip out Druss's eyes. Druss dropped his head so that the fingers stabbed into his brow, the long nails gashing the skin. Cajivak grabbed for him, but as his hands closed around Druss's shirt the rotted material gave way. As Cajivak staggered back, Druss stepped in to thunder two blows to his belly. It felt as if he were beating his hands against a wall. The giant warlord laughed and struck out with an uppercut that almost lifted Druss from his feet. His nose was broken and streaming blood, but as Cajivak leapt in for the kill Druss side-stepped, tripping the larger man. Cajivak hit the floor hard, then rolled and came up swiftly.

Druss was tiring now, the sudden surge of power from the axe fading away from his muscles. Cajivak lunged forward, but Druss feinted with a left and Cajivak swayed back from it – straight into the path of a right hook that hammered into his mouth, impaling his lower lip on his teeth. Druss followed this with a left, then another right. A cut opened above Cajivak's right eye, blood spilling to the cheek, and he fell back. Then he pulled the punctured lip from his teeth – and gave a bloody grin. For a moment Druss was nonplussed, then Cajivak leaned over and dragged Snaga from the boards.

The axe shone red in the lantern light. 'Now you die, little man!' Cajivak snarled.

He raised the axe as Druss took one running step and leapt, his right foot coming down hard on Cajivak's knee. The joint gave way with an explosive crack and the giant fell screaming to the ground, losing his hold on the axe. The weapon twisted in the air – then plunged down,

676

the twin points striking the warlord just below the shoulder-blades, lancing through the leather jerkin and the skin beyond. Cajivak twisted and the axe ripped clear of his body. Druss knelt and retrieved the weapon.

Cajivak, his face twisted in pain, pushed himself into a sitting position and stared at the axeman with undisguised hatred. 'Let the blow be a clean one,' he said softly.

Still kneeling Druss nodded, then swept Snaga in a horizontal arc. The blades bit into Cajivak's bull neck, slicing through the muscle, sinew and bone. The body toppled to the right, the head falling left where it bounced once on the dais before rolling to the hall floor below. Druss stood and turned to face the stunned warriors. Suddenly weary, he sat down on Cajivak's throne. 'Someone bring me a goblet of wine!' he ordered.

Sieben grabbed a pitcher and a goblet and moved slowly to where the axeman sat.

'You took your damned time getting here,' said Druss.

4

From the back of the Hall Varsava watched the scene with fascination. Cajivak's body lay on the dais, blood staining the floor around it. In the Hall itself the warriors stood with their eyes locked to the man sitting slumped on Cajivak's throne. Varsava glanced up at the gallery where Eskodas waited, an arrow still strung to his bow.

What now, thought Varsava, scanning the Hall. There must be over a hundred killers here. His mouth was dry. At any moment the unnatural calm would vanish. What then? Would they rush the dais? And what of Druss? Would he take up his axe and attack them all?

I don't want to die here, he thought, wondering what he would do if they did attack Druss. He was close to the rear door – no one would notice if he just slipped away into the night. After all, he owed the man nothing. Varsava had done more than his share, locating Sieben and setting up the rescue attempt. To die now, in a meaningless skirmish, would be nonsense.

Yet he did not move but stood silently, waiting, with all the other men, and watched Druss drain a third goblet of wine. Then the axeman rose and wandered down into the hall, leaving his axe on the dais. Druss moved to the first table and tore a chunk of bread from a fresh-baked loaf. 'None of you hungry?' he asked the men.

A tall, slim warrior wearing a crimson shirt stepped forward. 'What are your plans?' he asked.

'I'm going to eat,' Druss told him. 'Then I'm going to bathe. After that I think I'll sleep for a week.'

'And then?' The Hall was silent, the warriors milling closer to hear the axeman's answer.

'One thing at a time, laddie. When you sit in a dungeon, in the dark, with only rats for company, you learn never to make too many plans.'

'Are you seeking to take his place?' persisted the warrior, pointing to the severed head.

Druss laughed. 'By the gods, look at him! Would *you* want to take his place?' Chewing on the bread, Druss returned to the dais and sat. Then he leaned forward and addressed the men. 'I am Druss,' he said. 'Some of you may remember me from the day I was brought here. Others may know of my service with the Emperor. I have no ill-will towards any of you . . . but if any man here wishes to die, then let him take up his weapons and approach me. I'll oblige him.' He stood and hefted the axe. 'Anyone?' he challenged. No one moved and Druss nodded. 'You are all fighting men,' he said, 'but you fight for pay. That is sensible. Your leader is dead – best you finish your meal, and then choose another.'

'Are you putting yourself forward?' asked the man in the crimson shirt.

'Laddie, I've had enough of this fortress. And I have other plans.'

Druss turned back to Sieben, and Varsava could not hear their conversation. The warriors gathered together in small groups, discussing the various merits and vices of Cajivak's under-leaders, and Varsava strolled out of the Hall, confused by what he had seen. Beyond the Hall was a wide antechamber where the bladesman sat on a long couch – his feelings mixed, his heart heavy. Eskodas joined him.

'How did he do it?' asked Varsava. 'A hundred killers, and they just accepted his murder of their leader. Incredible!'

Eskodas shrugged and smiled. 'That's Druss.'

Varsava swore softly. 'You call that an answer?'

'It depends what you are looking for,' responded the bowman. 'Perhaps you should be asking yourself why you are angry. You came here to rescue a friend, and now he is free. What more did you want?'

Varsava laughed, but the sound was dry and harsh. 'You want the truth? I half desired to see Druss broken. I wanted confirmation of his stupidity! The great *hero*! He rescued an old man and child – that's why he's spent a year or more in this cesspit. You understand? It was meaningless. Meaningless!'

'Not for Druss.'

'What is so special about him?' stormed Varsava. 'He's not blessed with a fine mind, he has no intellect to speak of. Any other man who has just done what he did would be ripped to pieces by that mangy crew. But no, not Druss! Why? He could have become their leader – just like that! They would have accepted it.'

'I can give you no definitive answers,' said Eskodas. 'I watched him storm a ship filled with blood-hungry corsairs – they threw down their weapons. It is the nature of the man, I suppose. I had a teacher once, a great bowman, who told me that when we see another man we instinctively judge him as either threat or prey. Because we are hunting, killing animals. Carnivores. We are a deadly breed, Varsava. When we look at Druss we see the ultimate threat – a man who does not understand compromise. He breaks the rules. No, more than that, I think. For him there *are* no rules. Take what happened back there. An ordinary man might well have killed Cajivak – though I doubt it. But he would not have hurled aside the axe and fought the monster hand to hand. And when he'd slain the leader he would have looked out at all those killers and, in his heart, he would have expected death. They would have sensed it . . . and they would have killed him. But Druss didn't sense it; he didn't care. One at a time, or all at once. He'd have fought them all.'

'And died,' put in Varsava.

'Probably. But that's not the point. After he killed Cajivak he sat down and called for a drink. A man doesn't do that if he expects further battles. That left them confused, uncertain – no rules, you see. And when he walked down among them he left the axe behind. *He* knew he wouldn't need it – and they knew too. He played them like a harp. But he didn't do it consciously, it is just the nature of the man.'

'I can't be like him,' said Varsava sadly, remembering the peace-maker and the terrible death he suffered.

'Few can,' agreed Eskodas. 'That's why he is becoming a legend.'

Laughter echoed from the Hall. 'Sieben is entertaining them again,' said Eskodas. 'Come on, let's go and listen. We can get drunk.'

'I don't want to get drunk. I want to be young again. I want to change the past, wipe a wet rag over the filthy slate.'

'It's a fresh day tomorrow,' said Eskodas softly.

'What does that mean?'

'The past is dead, bladesman, the future largely unwritten. I was on a ship once with a rich man when we hit a storm, and the ship went down. The rich man gathered as much gold as he could carry. He drowned. I left behind everything I owned. I survived.'

'You think my guilt weighs more than his gold?'

'I think you should leave it behind,' said Eskodas, rising. 'Now, come and see Druss – and let's get drunk.'

'No,' said Varsava sadly. 'I don't want to see him.' He stood and placed his wide leather hat upon his head. 'Give him my best wishes, and tell him . . . tell him . . .' His voice faded away.

'Tell him what?'

Varsava shook his head, and smiled ruefully. 'Tell him goodbye,' he said.

Michanek followed the young officer to the base of the wall, then both men knelt with their ears to the stone. At first Michanek could hear nothing, but then came the sound of scraping, like giant rats beneath the earth, and he swore softly.

'You have done well, Cicarin. They are digging beneath the walls. The question is, from where? Follow me.' The young officer followed the powerfully built champion as Michanek scaled the rampart steps and leaned out over the parapet. Ahead was the main camp of the Ventrian army, their tents pitched on the plain before the city. To the left was a line of low hills with the river beyond them. To the right was a higher section of hills, heavily wooded. 'My guess,' said Michanek, 'would be that they began their work on the far side of that hill, about half-way up. They would have taken a bearing and know that if they hold to a level course they would come under the walls by around two feet.'

'How serious is it, sir?' asked Cicarin nervously.

Michanek smiled at the young man. 'Serious enough. Have you ever been down a mine?'

'No, sir.'

Michanek chuckled. Of course he hadn't. The boy was the youngest son of a Naashanite Satrap who until this siege had been surrounded by servants, barbers, valets and huntsmen. His clothes would have been laid out each morning, his breakfast brought to him on a silver tray as he lay in bed with satin sheets. 'There are many aspects to soldiering,' he said. 'They are mining beneath our walls, removing the foundations. As they dig, they are shoring up the walls and ceiling with very dry timber. They will dig along the line of the wall, then burrow on to the hills by the river, emerging somewhere around . . . there.' He pointed to the tallest of the low hills.

'I don't understand,' said Cicarin. 'If they are shoring up the tunnel, what harm can it do?'

'That's an easy question to answer. Once they have two openings there will be a through draught of air; then they will soak the timbers with oil and, when the wind is right, set fire to the tunnel. The wind will drive the flames through, the ceiling will collapse and, if they have done their job well, the walls will come crashing down.'

'Can we do nothing to stop them?'

'Nothing of worth. We could send an armed force to attack the workings, maybe kill a few miners, but they would just bring in more. No. We cannot act, therefore we must react. I want you to assume that this section of wall will fall.' He turned from the parapet and scanned

680

the line of houses behind the wall. There were several alleyways and two major roads leading into the city. 'Take fifty men and block the alleys and roads. Also fill in the ground-floor windows of the houses. We must have a secondary line of defence.'

'Yes, sir,' said the young man, his eyes downcast.

'Keep your spirits up, boy,' advised Michanek. 'We're not dead yet.'

'No, sir. But people are starting to talk openly about the relief army; they say it's not coming – that we've been left behind.'

'Whatever the Emperor's decision, we will abide by it,' said Michanek sternly. The young man reddened, then saluted and strode away. Michanek watched him, then returned to the battlements.

There was no relief force. The Naashanite army had been crushed in two devastating battles and was fleeing now towards the border. Resha was the last of the occupied cities. The intended conquest of Ventria was now a disaster of the first rank.

But Michanek had his orders. He, and the renegade Ventrian Darishan, were to hold Resha as long as possible, tying down Ventrian troops while the Emperor fled back to the safety of the mountains of Naashan.

Michanek dug into the pouch at his side and pulled clear the small piece of parchment on which the message had been sent. He gazed down at the hasty script.

Hold at all costs, until otherwise ordered. No surrender.

The warrior slowly shredded the message. There were no farewells, no tributes, no words of regret. Such is the gratitude of princes, he thought. He had scribbled his own reply, folding it carefully and inserting it into the tiny metal tube which he then tied to the leg of the pigeon. The bird soared into the air and flew east, bearing Michanek's last message to the Emperor he had served since a boy:

As you order, so shall it be.

The stitched wound on his side was itching now, a sure sign of healing. Idly he scratched it. You were lucky, he thought. Bodasen almost had you. By the western gate he saw the first of the food convoys wending its way through the Ventrian ranks, and he strode down to meet the wagons.

The first driver waved as he saw him; it was his cousin Shurpac. The man leapt down from the plank seat, throwing the reins to the fat man beside him.

'Well met, cousin,' said Shurpac, throwing his arms around Michanek and kissing both bearded cheeks. Michanek felt cold, the thrill of fear coursing through him as he remembered Rowena's warning: '*I see soldiers with black cloaks and helms, storming the walls. You will gather your men for a last stand outside these walls. Beside you will be . . . your youngest brother and a second cousin.*'

'What's wrong, Michi? You look as if a ghost has drifted across your grave.'

Michanek forced a smile. 'I did not expect to see you here. I heard you were with the Emperor.'

'I was. But these are sad times, cousin; he is a broken man. I heard you were here and was trying to find a way through. Then I heard about the duel. Wonderful. The stuff of legends! Why did you not kill him?'

Michanek shrugged. 'He fought well, and bravely. But I pierced his lung and he fell. He was no threat after that, there was no need to make the killing thrust.'

'I'd love to have seen Gorben's face. He is said to have believed Bodasen unbeatable with the blade.'

'No one is unbeatable, cousin. No one.'

'Nonsense,' announced Shurpac. 'You are unbeatable. That's why I wanted to be here, to fight beside you. I think we'll show these Ventrians a thing or three. Where is Narin?'

'At the barracks, waiting for the food. We will test it on Ventrian prisoners.'

'You think Gorben may have poisoned it?'

Michanek shrugged. 'I don't know . . . perhaps. Go on, take them through.'

Shurpac clambered back to his seat, lifted a whip and lightly cracked it over the heads of the four mules. They lurched forward into the traces and the wagon rolled on. Michanek strolled out through the gates and counted the wagons. There were fifty, all filled with flour and dried fruit, oats, cereal, flour and maize. Gorben had promised two hundred. Will you keep your word? wondered Michanek.

As if in answer a lone horseman rode from the enemy camp. The horse was a white stallion of some seventeen hands, a handsome beast built for power and speed. It charged towards Michanek, who held his ground with arms crossed against his chest. At the last moment the rider dragged on the reins. The horse reared, and the rider leapt down. Michanek bowed as he recognised the Ventrian Emperor.

'How is Bodasen?' asked Michanek.

'Alive. I thank you for sparing the last thrust. He means much to me.'

'He's a good man.'

'So are you,' said Gorben. 'Too good to die here for a monarch who has deserted you.'

Michanek laughed. 'When I made my oath of allegiance, I do not

682

recall it having a clause that would allow me to break it. You have such clauses in your own oath of fealty?'

Gorben smiled. 'No. My people pledge to support me to the death.'

Michanek spread his arms. 'Well then, my Lord, what else would you expect this poor Naashanite to do?'

Gorben's smile faded and he stepped in close. 'I had hoped you would surrender, Michanek. I do not seek your death – I owe you a life. You must see now that even with these supplies, you cannot hold out much longer. Why must I send in my Immortals to see you all cut to pieces? Why not merely march out in good order and return home? You may pass unmolested; you have my word.'

'That would be contrary to my orders, my Lord.'

'Might I ask what they are?'

'To hold until ordered otherwise.'

'Your Lord is in full flight. I have captured his baggage train, including his three wives and his daughters. Even now one of his messengers is in my tent, negotiating for their safe return. But he asks nothing for you, his most loyal soldier. Do you not find that galling?'

'Of course,' agreed Michanek, 'but it alters nothing.'

Gorben shook his head and turned to his stallion. Taking hold of rein and pommel, he vaulted to the horse's back. 'You are a fine man, Michanek. I wish you could have served me.'

'And you, sir, are a gifted general. It has been a pleasure to thwart you for so long. Give my regards to Bodasen – and if you wish to stake it all on another duel, I will meet whoever you send.'

'If my champion was here I would hold you to that,' said Gorben, with a wide grin. 'I would like to see how you would fare against Druss and his axe. Farewell, Michanek. May the gods grant you a splendid afterlife.'

The Ventrian Emperor heeled the stallion into a run and galloped back to the camp.

Pahtai was sitting in the garden when the first vision came to her. She was watching a bee negotiate an entry into a purple bloom when suddenly she saw an image of the man with the axe – only he had no axe, and no beard. He was sitting upon a mountainside overlooking a small village with a half-built stockade wall. As quickly as it had come, it disappeared. She was troubled, but with the constant battles upon the walls of Resha, and her fears for Michanek's safety, she brushed her worries away.

But the second vision was more powerful than the first. She saw a ship, and upon it a tall, thin man. A name filtered through the veils of her mind:

Kabuchek.

He had owned her once, long ago in the days when Pudri said she had a rare Talent, a gift for seeing the future and reading the past. The gift was gone now, and she did not regret it. Amid a terrible civil war it was, perhaps, a blessing not to know what perils the future had to offer.

She told Michanek of her visions and watched as the look of sorrow touched his handsome face. He had taken her into his arms, holding her tight, just as he had throughout her sickness. Michanek had risked catching the plague, yet in her fever dreams she drew great strength from his presence and his devotion. And she had survived, though all the surgeons predicted her death. True her heart was now weak, so they said, and any exertion tired her. But her strength was returning month by month.

The sun was bright above the garden, and *Pahtai* moved out to gather flowers with which to decorate the main rooms. In her arms she held a flat wicker basket in which was placed a sharp cutting knife. As the sun touched her face she tilted her head, enjoying the warmth upon her skin. In the distance a high-pitched scream suddenly sounded and her eyes turned towards the direction of the noise. Faintly she could hear the clash of steel on steel, the shouts and cries of warriors in desperate combat.

Will it never end? she thought.

A shadow fell across her and she turned and saw that two men had entered the garden. They were thin, their clothes ragged and filthy.

'Give us food,' demanded one, moving in towards her.

'You must go to the ration centre,' she said, fighting down her fear.

'You don't live on rations, do you, you Naashanite whore!' said the second man, stepping in close. He stank of stale sweat and cheap ale, and she saw his pale eyes glance towards her breasts. She was wearing a thin tunic of blue silk, and her legs were bare. The first man grabbed her arm, dragging her towards him. She thought of grabbing for the cutting knife, but in that instant found herself staring down at a narrow bed in a small room. Upon it lay a woman and a sickly child; their names flashed into her mind.

'What of Katina?' she said suddenly. The man groaned and fell back, releasing his hold, his eyes wide and stricken with guilt. 'Your baby son is dying,' she said softly. 'Dying while you drink and attack women. Go to the kitchen, both of you. Ask for Pudri, and tell him that . . .' she hesitated . . . 'that *Pahtai* said you could have food. There are some eggs and unleavened bread. Go now, both of you.'

The men backed away from her, then turned and ran for the house. *Pahtai*, trembling from the shock, sat down on a marble seat.

Pahtai? Rowena . . . The name rose up from the deepest levels of her memory, and she greeted it like a song of morning after a night of storms.

Rowena. I am Rowena.

A man came walking along the garden path, bowing as he saw her. His hair was silver, and braided, yet his face was young and almost unlined. He bowed again. 'Greetings, *Pahtai*, are you well?'

'I am well, Darishan. But you look tired.'

'Tired of sieges, that's for sure. May I sit beside you?'

'Of course. Michanek is not here, but you are welcome to wait for him.'

He leaned back and sniffed the air. 'I do love roses. Exquisite smell; they remind me of my childhood. You know I used to play with Gorben? We were friends. We used to hide in bushes such as these, and pretend we were being hunted by assassins. Now I am hiding again, but there is not a rose bush large enough to conceal me.'

Rowena said nothing, but she gazed into his handsome face and saw the fear lurking below the surface.

'I saddled the wrong horse, my dear,' he said, with a show of brightness. 'I thought the Naashanites would be preferable to watching Gorben's father destroy the Empire. But all I have done is to train a younger lion in the ways of war and conquest. Do you think I could convince Gorben that I have, in fact, done him a service?' He looked into her face. 'No, I suppose I couldn't. I shall just have to face my death like a Ventrian.'

'Don't talk of death,' she scolded. 'The walls still hold and now we have food.'

Darishan smiled. 'Yes. It was a fine duel, but I don't mind admitting that my heart was in my mouth throughout. Michanek might have slipped, and then where would I have been, with the gates open to Gorben?'

'There is no man alive who could defeat Michanek,' she said.

'So far. But Gorben had another champion once . . . Druss, I think his name was. Axeman. He was rather deadly, as I recall.'

Rowena shivered. 'Are you cold?' he asked, suddenly solicitous. 'You're not getting a fever, are you?' Lifting his hand, he laid his palm on her brow. As he touched her she saw him die, fighting upon the battlements, black-cloaked warriors all around him, swords and knives piercing his flesh.

Closing her eyes, she forced the images back. 'You are unwell,' she heard him say, as if from a great distance.

Rowena took a deep breath. 'I am a little weak,' she admitted.

'Well, you must be strong for your celebration. Michanek has found three singers and a lyre player – it should be quite an entertainment. And I have a full barrel of the finest Lentrian Red, which I shall have sent over.'

At the thought of the anniversary Rowena brightened. It was almost a year since she had recovered from the plague . . . A year since Michanek had made her happiness complete. She smiled at

Darishan. 'You will join us tomorrow? That is good. I know Micha-nek values your friendship.'

'And I his.' Darishan rose. 'He's a good man, you know, far better than the rest of us. I'm proud to have known him.'

'I'll see you tomorrow,' she said.

'Tomorrow,' he agreed.

'I have to admit, old horse, that life without you was dull,' said Sieben. Druss said nothing, but sat staring into the flames of the small fire, watching them dance and flicker. Snaga was laid beside him, the blades upwards resting against the trunk of a young oak, the haft wedged against a jutting root. On the other side of the fire Eskodas was preparing two rabbits for the spit. 'When we have dined,' continued Sieben, 'I shall regale you with the further adventures of Druss the Legend.'

'No, you damned well won't,' grunted Druss.

Eskodas laughed. 'You really should hear it, Druss. He has you descending into Hell to rescue the soul of a princess.'

Druss shook his head, but a brief smile showed through the black beard and Sieben was heartened. In the month since Druss had killed Cajivak the axeman had said little. For the first two weeks they had rested at Lania, then they had journeyed across the mountains, heading east. Now, two days from Resha, they were camped on a wooded hillside above a small village. Druss had regained much of his lost weight, and his shoulders almost filled the silver-embossed jerkin he had removed from Cajivak's body.

Eskodas placed the spitted rabbits across the fire and sat back, wiping grease and blood from his fingers. 'A man can starve to death eating rabbit,' he observed. 'Not a lot of goodness there. We should have gone down to the village.'

'I like being outside,' said Druss.

'Had I known, I would have come sooner,' said Sieben softly and Druss nodded.

'I know that, poet. But it is in the past now. All that matters is that I find Rowena. She came to me in a dream while I was in that dungeon; she gave me strength. I'll find her.' He sighed. 'Some day.'

'The war is almost over,' said Eskodas. 'Once it is won, I think you'll find her. Gorben will be able to send riders to every city, village and town. Whoever owns her will know that the Emperor wants her returned.'

'That's true,' said Druss, brightening, 'and he did promise to help. I feel better already. The stars are bright, the night is cool. Ah, but it's good to be alive! All right, poet, tell me how I rescued the princess from Hell. And put in a dragon or two!'

'No,' said Sieben, with a laugh, 'You are now in altogether too good

686

a mood. It is only amusing when your face is dark as thunder and your knuckles are clenched white.'

'There is truth in that,' muttered Druss. 'I think you only invent these tales to annoy me.'

Eskodas lifted the spit and turned the roasting meat. 'I rather liked the tale, Druss. And it had the ring of truth. If the Chaos Spirit did drag your soul into Hell, I'm sure you'd twist his tail for him.'

Conversation ceased as they heard movement from the woods. Sieben drew one of his knives; Eskodas took up his bow and notched a shaft to the string; Druss merely sat silently, waiting. A man appeared. He was wearing long flowing robes of dusty grey, though they shone like silver in the bright moonlight.

'I was waiting for you in the village,' said the priest of Pashtar Sen, sitting down alongside the axeman.

'I prefer it here,' said Druss, his voice cold and unwelcoming.

'I am sorry, my son, for your suffering, and I feel a weight of shame for asking you to take up the burden of the axe. But Cajivak was laying waste to the countryside, and his power would have grown. What you did . . .'

'I did what I did,' snarled Druss. 'Now live up to your side of the bargain.'

'Rowena is in Resha. She . . . lives . . . with a soldier named Michanek. He is a Naashanite general, and the Emperor's champion.'

'*Lives* with?'

The priest hesitated. 'She is married to him,' he said swiftly.

Druss's eyes narrowed. 'That is a lie. They might force her to do many things, but she would never marry another man.'

'Let me tell this in my own way,' pleaded the priest. 'As you know I searched long and hard for her, but there was nothing. It was as if she had ceased to exist. When I did find her it was by chance – I saw her in Resha just before the siege and I touched her mind. She had no memory of the lands of the Drenai, none whatever. I followed her home and saw Michanek greet her. Then I entered his mind. He had a friend, a mystic, and he employed him to take away Rowena's Talent as a seeress. In doing this they also robbed her of her memories. Michanek is now all she has ever known.'

'They tricked her with sorcery. By the gods, I'll make them pay for that! Resha, eh?' Reaching out Druss curled his hand around the haft of the axe, drawing the weapon to him.

'No, you still don't understand,' said the priest. 'Michanek is a fine man. What he . . .'

'Enough!' thundered Druss. 'Because of you I have spent more than a year in a hole in the ground, with only rats for company. Now get out of my sight – and never, *ever* cross my path again.'

The priest slowly rose and backed away from the axeman. He seemed about to speak, but Druss turned his pale eyes upon the man and the priest stumbled away into the darkness.

Sieben and Eskodas said nothing.

High in the cliffs, far to the east, the Naashanite Emperor sat, his woollen cloak wrapped tightly around him. He was fifty-four years of age and looked seventy, his hair white and wispy, his eyes sunken. Beside him sat his staff officer, Anindais; he was unshaven, and the pain of defeat was etched into his face.

Behind them, down the long pass, the rearguard had halted the advancing Ventrians. They were safe . . . for the moment.

Nazhreen Connitopa, Lord of the Eyries, Prince of the Highlands, Emperor of Naashan, tasted bile in his mouth and his heart was sick with frustration. He had planned the invasion of Ventria for almost eleven years, and the Empire had been his for the taking. Gorben was beaten – everyone knew it, from the lowliest peasant to the highest Satraps in the land. Everyone, that is, except Gorben.

Nazhreen silently cursed the gods for snatching away his prize. The only reason he was still alive was because Michanek was holding Resha and tying down two Ventrian armies. Nazhreen rubbed at his face and saw, in the firelight, that his hands were grubby, the paint on his nails cracked and peeling.

'We must kill Gorben,' said Anindais suddenly, his voice harsh and cold as the winds that hissed through the peaks.

Nazhreen gazed sullenly at his cousin. 'And how do we do that?' he countered. 'His armies have vanquished ours. His Immortals are even now harrying our rearguard.'

'We should do now what I urged two years ago, cousin. Use the Darklight. Send for the Old Woman.'

'No! I will not use sorcery.'

'Ah, you have so many other choices then, cousin?' The tone was derisive, contempt dripping from every word. Nazhreen swallowed hard. Anindais was a dangerous man, and Nazhreen's position as a losing Emperor left him exposed.

'Sorcery has a way of rebounding on those who use it,' he said softly. 'When you summon demons they require payment in blood.'

Anindais leaned forward, his pale eyes glittering in the firelight. 'Once Resha falls, you can expect Gorben to march into Naashan. Then there'll be blood aplenty. Who will defend you, Nazhreen? Our troops have been cut to pieces, and the best of our men are trapped in Resha and will be butchered. Our only hope is for Gorben to die; then the Ventrians can fight amongst themselves to choose a successor and that will give us time to rebuild, to negotiate. Who else can guarantee his death? The Old Woman has never failed, they say.'

'*They say*,' mocked the Emperor. 'Have you used her yourself then? Is that why your brother died in so timely a fashion?' As soon as the words were spoken he regretted them, for Anindais was not a man to offend, not even in the best of times. And these were certainly not the best of times.

Nazhreen was relieved to see his cousin smile broadly, as Anindais leaned in and placed his arm around the Emperor's shoulder. 'Ah, cousin, you came so close to victory. It was a brave gamble and I honour you for it. But times change, needs change.'

Nazhreen was about to answer when he saw the firelight glint from the dagger blade. There was no time to struggle or to scream, and the blade plunged in between his ribs, cutting through his heart.

There was no pain, only release as he slumped sideways, his head resting on Anindais' shoulder. The last feeling he experienced was of Anindais stroking his hair.

It was soothing . . .

Anindais pushed the body from him and stood. A figure shuffled from the shadows, an old woman in a wolfskin cloak. Kneeling by the body, she dipped her skeletal fingers into the blood and licked them. 'Ah, the blood of kings,' she said. 'Sweeter than wine.'

'Is that enough of a sacrifice?' Anindais asked.

'No – but it will suffice as a beginning,' she said. She shivered. 'It is cold here. Not like Mashrapur. I think I shall return there when this is over. I miss my house.'

'How will you kill him?' asked Anindais.

She glanced up at the general. 'We shall make it poetic. He is a Ventrian nobleman, and the sign of his house is the Bear. I shall send Kalith.'

Anindais licked his dry lips. 'Kalith is just a dark legend, surely?'

'If you want to see him for yourself I can arrange it,' hissed the Old Woman.

Anindais fell back. 'No, I believe you.'

'I like you, Anindais,' she said softly. 'You do not have a single redeeming virtue – that is rare. So I will give you a gift, and charge nothing for it. Stay by me and you will see the Kalith kill the Ventrian.' She stood and walked to the cliff-face. 'Come,' she called and Anindais followed. The Old Woman gestured at the grey rock and the wall became smoke. Taking the general's hand, she led him through.

A long dark tunnel beckoned and Anindais shrank back. 'Not a single redeeming feature,' she repeated, 'not even courage. Stay by me, general, and no harm will befall you.'

The walk was not long, but to Anindais it stretched on for an eternity. He knew they were passing through a world that was not his own, and in the distance he could hear screams and cries that were not human. Great bats flew in a sky of dark ash, and not a living plant could be seen. The Old Woman followed a slender path, and took him across a narrow bridge that spanned an awesome chasm. At last she came to a fork in the path, and moved to the left towards a small cave. A three-headed dog guarded the entrance, but it backed away from her and they passed through. Within was a circular room stacked with tomes and scrolls. Two skeletons were hanging from hooks in the ceiling, their joints bound with golden wire. A cadaver lay across a long table, its chest and belly cut open, the heart lying beside the body like a grey stone about the size of a human fist.

The Old Woman lifted the heart and showed it to Anindais. 'Here it is,' she said, 'the secret of life. Four chambers and a number of valves, arteries and veins. Just a pump. No emotions, no secret storehouse for the soul.' She seemed disappointed. Anindais said nothing. 'Blood,' she went on, 'is pumped into the lungs to pick up oxygen, then distributed through the atria and the ventricles. Just a pump. Now, where were we? Ah yes, the Kalith.' She sniffed loudly and threw the heart back towards the table; it hit the cadaver, then fell to the dusty floor. Swiftly she rummaged through the books on a high shelf, pulling one clear and flicking through the yellowed pages. Then she sat at a second desk and laid the book on the table. The left-hand page bore a neat script, the letters tiny. Anindais could not read, but he could see the picture painted on the right-hand page. It showed a huge bear, with claws of steel, its eyes of fire, its fangs dripping venom.

'It is a creature of earth and fire,' said the Old Woman, 'and it will take great energy to summon it. That is why I need your assistance.'

'I know no sorcery,' said Anindais.

'You need to know none,' she snapped. 'I will say the words, you will repeat them. Follow me.'

She led him further back into the cave, to an altar stone surrounded by gold wire fastened to a series of stalagmites. The stone sat at the centre of a circle of gold, and she bade Anindais step over the wires and approach the altar, upon which was a silver bowl full of water.

'Look into the water,' she said, 'and repeat the words I speak.'

'Why do you stay outside the wire?' he asked.

'There is a seat here and my old legs are tired,' she told him. 'Now let us begin.'

5

Oliquar was the first of the Immortals to see Druss striding down the hill. The soldier was sitting on an upturned barrel darning the heel of a sock when the axeman appeared. Laying the worn garment aside, Oliquar stood and called out Druss's name. Several of the soldiers sitting nearby looked up as Oliquar ran to meet him, throwing his brawny arms around Druss's neck.

Hundreds of other warriors gathered round, craning to see the Emperor's champion, the famed axeman who fought like ten tigers. Druss grinned at his old comrade. 'There are more grey hairs in that beard than I remember,' he said.

Oliquar laughed. 'I earned every one. By the Holy Hands, it is good to see you, friend!'

'Life has been dull without me?'

'Not exactly,' answered Oliquar, gesturing towards the walls of Resha. 'They fight well, these Naashanites. And they have a champion too: Michanek, a great warrior.'

The smile left Druss's face. 'We'll see how great he is,' he promised.

Oliquar turned to Sieben and Eskodas. 'We hear that you did not need to rescue our friend. It is said he slew the great killer Cajivak, and half the men of his fortress. Is it true?'

'Wait until you hear the song,' Sieben advised.

'Aye, there are dragons in it,' put in Eskodas.

Oliquar led the trio through the silent ranks of warriors to a tent set up near the river's edge. Producing a jug of wine and several clay goblets, he sat down and looked at his friend. 'You are a little thinner,' he said, 'and your eyes are tired.'

'Pour me a drink and you'll see them shine again. Why the black cloaks and helms?'

'We are the new Immortals, Druss.'

'You don't look immortal, judging by that,' said Druss, pointing to the bloodstained bandage on Oliquar's right bicep.

'It is a title – a great title. For two centuries the Immortals were the Emperor's hand-picked honour guard. The finest soldiers, Druss: the elite. But twenty or so years ago the Immortal general, Vuspash, led a revolt, and the regiment was disbanded. Now the Emperor has re-formed them – us! It is a wondrous honour to be an Immortal.' He leaned forward and winked. 'And the pay is better – double, in fact!'

Filling the goblets, he passed one to each of the newcomers. Druss drained his in a single swallow and Oliquar refilled it. 'And how goes the siege?' asked the axeman.

Oliquar shrugged. 'This Michanek holds them together. He is a lion, Druss, tireless and deadly. He fought Bodasen in single combat. We thought the war would be over. The Emperor offered two hundred wagons of food, for there is starvation in the city. The wager was that if Bodasen lost, the food would be delivered, but if he won then the city gates would be opened and the Naashanites allowed to march free.'

'He killed Bodasen?' put in Eskodas. 'He was a great swordsman.'

'He didn't kill him; he put him down with a chest wound, then stepped back. The first fifty wagons were delivered an hour ago and the rest go in tonight. It will leave us on short rations for a while.'

'Why didn't he strike the killing blow?' asked Sieben. 'Gorben could have refused to send the food. Duels are supposed to be to the death, aren't they?'

'Aye, they are. But this Michanek, as I said, is special.'

'You sound as if you like the man,' snapped Druss, finishing the second goblet.

'Gods, Druss, it's hard not to like him. I keep hoping they'll surrender; I don't relish the thought of slaughtering such bonny fighters. I mean, the war's over – this is just the last skirmish. What point is there in more killing and dying?'

'Michanek has my wife,' said Druss, his voice low and cold. 'He tricked her into marrying him, stole her memory. She does not know me at all.'

'I find that hard to believe,' said Oliquar.

'Are you calling me a liar?' hissed Druss, his hand snaking round the haft of his axe.

'And I find *this* hard to believe,' said Oliquar. 'What is the matter with you, my friend?'

Druss's hand trembled on the haft, and he snatched it clear and rubbed at his eyes. Taking a deep breath, he forced a smile. 'Ah, Oliquar! I am tired, and the wine has made me stupid. But what I said was true; it was told to me by a priest of Pashtar Sen. And tomorrow I will scale those walls, and I will find Michanek. Then we will see how special he is.'

Druss levered himself to his feet and entered the tent. For a while the three men sat in silence, then Oliquar spoke, keeping his voice low. 'Michanek's wife is called *Pahtai*. Some of the refugees from the city spoke of her. She is a gentle soul, and when plague struck the city she went to the homes of the sick and dying, comforting them, bringing them medicines. Michanek adores her, and she him. This is well known. And I say again, he is not the man to take a woman by trickery.'

692

'It doesn't matter,' said Eskodas. 'It is like fate carved into stone. Two men and one woman; there must be blood. Isn't that right, poet?'

'Sadly you are correct,' agreed Sieben. 'But I can't help wondering how she will feel when Druss marches in to her, drenched in the blood of the man she loves. What then?'

Lying on a blanket within the tent, Druss heard every word. They cut his soul with knives of fire.

Michanek shielded his eyes against the setting sun and watched the distant figure of the axeman walk down towards the Ventrian camp, saw the soldiers gather round him, heard them cheer.

'Who is it, do you think?' asked his cousin, Shurpac.

Michanek took a deep breath. 'I'd say it was the Emperor's champion, Druss.'

'Will you fight him?'

'I don't think Gorben will offer us the chance,' answered Michanek. 'There's no need – we can't hold for long now.'

'Long enough for Narin to return with reinforcements,' put in Shurpac, but Michanek did not reply. He had sent his brother out of the city with a written request for aid, though he knew there would be no help from Naashan; his one purpose had been to save his brother.

And yourself. The thought leapt unbidden from deep within him. Tomorrow was the first anniversary of his marriage, the day Rowena had predicted he would die with Narin on one side of him, Shurpac on the other. With Narin gone, perhaps the prophecy could be thwarted. Michanek squeezed shut his tired eyes. It felt as if sand was lodged under the lids.

The mining under the walls had stopped now and soon, when the winds permitted, the Ventrians would fire the timbers in the tunnel. He gazed out over the Ventrian camp. At least eleven thousand warriors were now gathered before Resha, and the defenders numbered only eight hundred. Glancing to left and right, Michanek saw the Naashanite soldiers sitting slumped by the battlements. There was little conversation, and much of the food that had just been carried up from the city was left untouched.

Michanek moved to the nearest soldier, a young man who was sitting with his head resting on his knees. His helm was beside him; it was split across the crown, dislodging the white horsehair plume.

'Not hungry, lad?' asked Michanek.

The boy looked up. His eyes were dark brown, his face beardless and feminine. 'Too tired to eat, general,' he said.

'The food will give you strength. Trust me.'

The boy lifted a hunk of salted beef and stared down at it. 'I'm going to die,' he said, and Michanek saw a tear spill to his duststained cheek.

The general laid his hand on the boy's shoulder. 'Death is merely another journey, lad. But you won't be walking that road alone – I'll be with you. And who knows what adventures wait?'

'I used to believe that,' said the soldier sadly, 'but I've seen so much death. I saw my brother die yesterday, his guts spilling out. His screams were terrible. Are you frightened of dying, sir?'

'Of course. But we are soldiers of the Emperor. We knew the risks when we first strapped on the breastplate and greaves. And what is better, lad, to live until we are toothless and mewling, our muscles like rotted string, or to face down our enemies in the fullness of our strength? We are all destined to die one day.'

'I don't want to die; I want to get out of here. I want to marry and father children. I want to watch them grow.' The boy was openly weeping now and Michanek sat beside him, taking him in his arms and stroking his hair.

'So do I,' he said, his voice barely above a whisper.

After a while the sobbing ceased and the boy drew himself up. 'I'm sorry, general. I won't let you down, you know.'

'I knew that anyway. I've watched you, and you're a brave lad: one of the best. Now eat your ration and get some sleep.'

Michanek rose and walked back to Shurpac. 'Let's go home,' he said. 'I'd like to sit in the garden with *Pahtai* and watch the stars.'

Druss lay still, his eyes closed, allowing the buzz of conversation to drift over him. He could not remember feeling so low – not even when Rowena was taken. On that dreadful day his anger had been all-consuming, and since then his desire to find her had fuelled his spirit, giving him a strength of purpose that bound his emotions in chains of steel. Even in the dungeon he had found a way to fend off despair. But now his stomach was knotted, his emotions unravelling.

She was in love with another man. He formed the words in his mind, and they ground into his heart like broken glass in a wound.

He tried to hate Michanek, but even that was denied him. Rowena would never love a worthless or an evil man. Druss sat up and stared down at his hands. He had crossed the ocean to find his love, and these hands had killed, and killed, and killed in order that Rowena could be his once more.

He closed his eyes. Where should I be? he asked himself. In the front rank as they storm the walls? On the walls defending Rowena's city? Or should I just walk away?

Walk away.

The tent entrance flapped as Sieben ducked under it. 'How are you faring, old horse?' asked the poet.

'She loves him,' said Druss, his voice thick, the words choking him.

Sieben sat alongside the axeman. He took a deep breath. 'If her memories were taken, then what she has done is no betrayal. She does not know you.'

'I understand that. I bear her no ill-will – how could I? She is the most . . . beautiful . . . I can't explain it, poet. She doesn't understand hatred, or greed, or envy. Soft but not weak, caring but not stupid.' He swore and shook his head. 'As I said, I can't explain it.'

'You're doing fine,' said Sieben softly.

'When I'm with her there is no . . . no fire in my mind. No anger. When I was a child I hated to be laughed at. I was big and clumsy – I'd knock over pots, trip over my own big feet. But when people laughed at my clumsiness I wanted to . . . I don't know . . . crush them. But I was with Rowena one day on the mountainside, and it had been raining. I lost my footing and fell headlong into a muddy pool. Her laughter was bright and fresh; I sat up, and I just laughed with her. And it was so good, poet, it was so good.'

'She's still there, Druss. Just across the wall.'

The axeman nodded. 'I know. What do I do – scale the wall, kill the man she loves and then march up to her and say, "Remember me?" I cannot win here.'

'One step at a time, my friend. Resha will fall. From what I gathered from Oliquar, Michanek will fight to the end, to the death. You don't have to kill him, his fate is already sealed. And then Rowena will need someone. I can't advise you, Druss, I have never truly been in love and I envy you that. But let us see what tomorrow brings, eh?'

Druss nodded and took a deep breath. 'Tomorrow,' he whispered.

'Gorben has asked to see you, Druss. Why not come with me? Bodasen is with him – and there'll be wine and good food.'

Druss stood and gathered Snaga to him. The blades glittered in the light from the brazier burning at the centre of the tent. 'A man's best friend is said to be a dog,' said Sieben, stepping back as Druss lifted the axe.

The axeman ignored him and stepped out into the night.

Rowena stood by with a long robe as Michanek stepped from the bath. Smiling, she brushed two rose petals from his shoulder, then held the robe open. Michanek slid his arms into the sleeves, then tied the satin belt and turned towards her. Taking her hand he led her into the garden. Rowena leaned in towards him and he stopped and took her into his arms, kissing the top of her head. His body was rich with the smell of rose oil and she put her arms around him, snuggling in to the soft robe. Tilting back her head, she looked up into his dark brown eyes. 'I love you,' she said.

Cupping her chin he kissed her, lingeringly. His mouth tasted of the peaches he had eaten while lazing in the bath. But there was no passion in the kiss and he drew away from her.

695

'What is wrong?' she asked. He shrugged and forced a smile.
'Nothing.'

'Why do you say that?' she chided. 'I hate it when you lie to me.'

'The siege is almost over,' he said, leading her to a small circular bench beneath a flowering tree.

'When will you surrender?' she asked.

He shrugged. 'When I receive orders to do so.'

'But the battle is unnecessary. The war is over. If you negotiate with Gorben he will allow us to leave. You can show me your home in Naashan. You always promised to take me to your estates near the Lakes; you said the gardens there would dazzle me with their beauty.'

'So they would,' he told her. Slipping his hands around her waist he stood and lifted her swiftly, lightly kissing her lips.

'Put me down. You'll tear the stitches – you know what the surgeon said.'

He chuckled. 'Aye, I listened to him. But the wound is almost healed.' Kissing her twice more, he lowered her to the ground and they walked on. 'There are matters we must discuss,' he said, but when she waited for him to continue he merely glanced up at the stars and the silence grew.

'What matters?'

'You,' he said at last. 'Your life.' Rowena looked at him, saw the lines of tension on his moonlit face, the tightening of the muscle in his jaw.

'My life is with you,' she said. 'That's all I want.'

'Sometimes we want more than we can have.'

'Don't say that!'

'You used to be a seer – a good one. Kabuchek charged two hundred silver pieces for a single reading from you. You were never wrong.'

'I know all this, you have told me before. What difference does it make now?'

'All the difference in the world. You were born in the lands of the Drenai, you were taken by slavers. But there was a man . . .'

'I don't want to hear this,' she said, pulling away from him and walking to the edge of the tiny lake. He did not follow, but his words did.

'The man was your husband.' Rowena sat down by the water's edge, trailing her fingers across the surface, sending ripples through the moon's reflection.

'The man with the axe,' she said dully.

'You remember?' he asked, walking forward and sitting beside her.

'No. But I saw him once – at the house of Kabuchek. And also in a dream, when he lay in a dungeon.'

'Well, he is not in a dungeon now, *Pahtai*. He is outside the city. He is Druss the Axeman, Gorben's champion.'

'Why are you telling me this?' she asked him, turning to face him in the bright moonlight.

His white robe shimmered, and he looked ghostly, almost ethereal. 'Do you think I want to?' he countered. 'I'd sooner fight a lion with my hands than have this conversation. But I love you, *Pahtai*. I have loved you since our first meeting. You were standing with Pudri in the main corridor of Kabuchek's home, and you told my future.'

'What did I tell you?'

He smiled. 'You told me I would wed the woman I loved. But that is not important now. I think soon you will meet your . . . first . . . husband.'

'I don't want to.' Her heart was beating fast and she felt faint. Michanek put his arms around her.

'I don't know much about him, but I do know you,' he said. 'You are Drenai; your customs are different from ours. You were not high-born, therefore it is likely you married for love. And think on this: Druss has followed you across the world for seven years. He must love you deeply.'

'I don't want to talk about this!' she said, her voice rising as panic flooded her. She tried to rise, but he held her close.

'Neither do I,' he whispered, his voice hoarse. 'I wanted to sit here with you and watch the stars. I wanted to kiss you, and to make love.' His head dropped, and she saw tears in his eyes.

Her panic disappeared and the cold touch of fear settled on her soul. She looked up into his face. 'You talk as if you are going to die.'

'Oh, I will some day,' he said, with a smile. 'Now I must go. I am meeting Darishan and the other officers to discuss tomorrow's strategy. They should be in the house now.'

'Don't go!' she pleaded. 'Stay with me a little while . . . just a little while?'

'I'll always be with you,' he said softly.

'Darishan will die tomorrow. On the walls. I saw it; it was a vision. He was here today and I saw him die. My Talent is coming back. Give me your hand! Let me see our future.'

'No!' he said, rising and moving back from her. 'A man's fate is his own. You read my future once. Once was enough, *Pahtai*.'

'I predicted your death, didn't I?' she said, but it was not a question for she knew the answer even before he spoke.

'You told me about my dreams, and you mentioned my brother, Narin. I don't remember much of it now. We'll talk later.'

'Why did you mention Druss? You think that if you die I will just go to him, and take up a life I know nothing of? If you die, I will have

697

nothing to live for.' Her eyes locked to his. 'And I will not live,' she said.

A figure moved out of the shadows. 'Michi, why are you keeping us all waiting?' Rowena saw her husband flinch and glanced up to see Narin striding towards them.

'I sent you away,' said Michanek. 'What are you doing here?'

'I made it as far as the hills, but the Ventrians are everywhere. I came in through the sewers; the guards there recognised me, thank the gods. What is the matter with you? Are you not pleased to see me?'

Michanek did not answer. Turning to Rowena he smiled, but she saw the fear in his eyes. 'I'll not be long, my love. We'll talk again later.'

She remained on the seat as the two men walked away. Closing her eyes she thought of the axeman, picturing the pale grey eyes and the broad, flat face. But even as she pictured him, another image came to her:

The face of a terrible beast, with talons of steel and eyes of fire.

Gorben leaned back on his couch and watched with appreciation the sword jugglers before the huge fire, the five razor-sharp blades spinning in the air between the two men. It was a display of rare skill as the jugglers deftly caught the swords, before sending them soaring back across the open ground. The men were clad in loincloths, their skin shone red-gold in the firelight. Around them sat more than five hundred Immortals, enjoying the martial display.

Beyond the dancing flames of the camp-fire Gorben could see the walls of Resha, and the few defenders there. It was all but over. Against all the odds he had won.

Yet there was no sense of joy in his heart. The years of battle, the stresses and the fears had taken their toll on the young Emperor. For every victory he had seen childhood friends cut down: Nebuchad at Ectanis, Jasua in the mountains above Porchia, Bodasen before the gates of Resha. He glanced to his right where Bodasen was lying on a raised bed, his face pale. The surgeons said he would live, and they had managed to re-inflate his collapsed lung. You are like my Empire, thought Gorben, wounded almost unto death. How long would it take to rebuild Ventria? Years? Decades?

A great roar went up from the watching men as the sword jugglers completed their performance. The men bowed to the Emperor. Gorben rose and tossed them a pouch full of gold pieces. There was great laughter when the first of the jugglers reached out and failed to catch the pouch.

'You are better with blades than coins,' said Gorben.

'Money has always slipped through his fingers, Lord,' said the second man.

Gorben returned to his seat and smiled down at Bodasen. 'How are you feeling, my friend?'

'My strength is returning, Lord.' The voice was weak, his breathing ragged as Gorben reached out and patted his shoulder. The heat of the skin and the sharpness of the bone beneath his hand almost made him recoil. Bodasen's eyes met his. 'Do not concern yourself about me, Lord. I'll not die on you.' The swordsman's eyes flickered to the left, and he smiled broadly. 'By the gods, there's a sight to gladden the eyes!'

Gorben turned to see Druss and Sieben walking towards them. The poet dropped to one knee, bowing his head. Druss gave a perfunctory bow.

'Well met, axeman,' said Gorben, stepping forward and embracing Druss. Turning, he took Sieben's arm and raised him to his feet. 'And I have missed your talents, saga-master. Come, join us.'

Servants brought two couches for the Emperor's guests, and golden goblets filled with fine wine. Druss moved to Bodasen. 'You look as weak as a three-day kitten,' he said. 'Are you going to live?'

'I'll do my best, axeman.'

'He cost me two hundred wagons of food,' said Gorben. 'I blame myself for believing him to be unbeatable.'

'How good is this Michanek?' asked Druss.

'Good enough to leave me lying here scarce able to breathe,' answered Bodasen. 'He's fast, and he's fearless. The best I ever met. I tell you truly, I wouldn't want to face him again.'

Druss turned to Gorben. 'You want me to take him?'

'No,' said Gorben. 'The city will fall in the next day or two – there is no need for single combat to decide the issue. The walls are undermined. Tomorrow, if the wind is good, we will fire them. Then the city will be ours and this ghastly war will be over. Now, tell me about your adventures. I hear you were held captive?'

'I escaped,' Druss told him, then drained his goblet. A servant ran forward to refill it.

Sieben laughed. 'I will tell you, Lord,' he said, and launched into a richly embroidered account of Druss's time in the dungeons of Cajivak.

The huge camp-fire was burning low and several men moved forward to throw logs upon it. Suddenly the ground heaved beneath one of them, pitching him to the earth. Gorben looked up, and watched the man struggle to rise. All around the fire the seated men were scrambling back. 'What is happening?' asked Gorben, rising and striding forward. The ground lurched beneath him.

'Is it an earthquake?' he heard Sieben ask Druss.

Gorben stood still and gazed down. The earth was writhing. The camp-fire suddenly flared, sending bright sparks into the night sky.

The heat was intense and Gorben moved back from it, staring into the flames. Logs exploded out from the blaze and a huge shape appeared within the fire, a beast with outspread arms. The flames died and Gorben found himself staring at a colossal bear, more than twelve feet tall.

Several soldiers carrying spears ran at the creature, plunging their weapons into the great belly. The first of the spears snapped on impact. The beast roared, a deafening sound like captured thunder. One of the mighty arms swept down, steel talons ripping through the first soldier, cutting him in half at the waist.

Surging from the fading fire, the beast leapt towards Gorben.

As the creature of fire appeared Sieben, who was sitting alongside Bodasen, found all sensation of time and reality slipping away from him. His eyes fastened on the beast, and an image flew from the halls of his memory, linking what he could see in terrifying life to a still, small moment three years ago in the main Library at Drenan. Researching for an epic poem, he had been scanning the ancient leather-bound books in the archives. The pages were dry and yellow, and much of the ink and paint had faded from them, but on one page the colours were still vibrant, fierce hues – glowing gold, savage crimsons, sun-bright yellows. The figure painted there was colossal, and flames sprouted like blooms from its eyes. Sieben could still picture the carefully painted letters above the painting . . .

The Kalith of Numar

Beneath the heading were the words:

The Chaos Beast, the Stalker, the Hound of the Invincible, whose skin no blade of man shall pierce. Where he walks, death follows.

As Sieben recalled the night of the monster in later days, he would wonder anew at the lack of fear he experienced. He watched men die horribly, saw a beast from the depths of Hell tear human limbs asunder, disembowelling warriors, ripping their lives from them. He heard the ghastly howling and smelt the stench of death on the night breeze. Yet there was no fear.

A dark legend had come to life and he, the saga-master, was on hand to witness it.

Gorben was standing stock-still, rooted to the spot. A soldier Sieben recognised as Oliquar threw himself at the beast, slashing at it with a sabre; but the blade clanged against the creature's side, and the sound that followed was like the dim tolling of a distant bell. A taloned paw swept down, and Oliquar's face and head disappeared in a bloody spray of shattered bone. Several archers shot arrows, but these either shattered on impact or ricocheted away. The creature advanced on Gorben.

Sieben saw the Emperor flinch, then hurl himself to his right, rolling to his feet smoothly. The enormous beast turned ponderously, the glowing coals of its eyes seeking out Gorben.

Loyal soldiers, showing incredible bravery, threw themselves into the path of the beast, stabbing at it ineffectually. Each time the talons slashed down, and blood sprayed across the camp-site. Within a few heartbeats there were at least twenty dead or maimed soldiers. The Chaos Beast's talons ripped into a soldier's chest, lifting him from his feet and hurling him across the dying fire. Sieben heard the man's ribs snap, and saw his entrails spill out like a tattered banner as the corpse sailed through the air.

Druss, axe in his hand, strode out towards the creature. Soldiers were falling back before it, but still they formed a wall between the beast and the Emperor. Looking tiny and insubstantial against the colossal frame of the Kalith, Druss stepped into its path. The moon was bright in the night sky, shining from his shoulder-guards and glinting on Snaga's terrible blades.

The Chaos Beast paused and seemed to stare down at the tiny man before it. Sieben's mouth was dry, and he could feel the hammering of his own heart.

And the Kalith spoke, voice deep and rumbling, words slurred by its foot-long tongue.

'Step aside, brother,' it said. 'I have not come for you.'

The axe began to glow as red as blood. Druss stood his ground, with Snaga held in both hands.

'Step aside,' repeated the Kalith, 'or I must kill you!'

'In your dreams,' said Druss.

The creature lunged forward, one great paw sweeping in towards the axeman. Druss dropped to one knee and swung the blood-red axe, the blade striking the beast's wrist and cleaving through. As the taloned paw fell to the ground beside the axeman, the Kalith reeled back. No blood issued from the wound, but an oily smoke pumped out into the air, billowing and growing. Fire blazed from the creature's mouth and it lunged again at the mortal before it. But instead of jumping back Druss leapt in to meet it, swinging Snaga high over his head and bringing the weapon down in a lethal arc that clove into the Kalith's chest, smashing the sternum and ripping a wound from throat to groin.

Flames exploded from the beast, engulfing the axeman. Druss staggered – and the Kalith fell back, and as the huge form struck the ground even Sieben, some thirty feet away, felt the tremor of the earth. A breeze blew up, the smoke disappearing.

701

And there was no sign of the Kalith . . .

Sieben ran to where Druss stood. The axeman's eyebrows and beard were singed, but he bore no marks of burns. 'By the gods, Druss,' Sieben shouted, slapping his friend's back. 'Now that'll make a song to bring us both fame and riches!'

'It killed Oliquar,' said Druss, shrugging off Sieben's embrace and letting fall the axe.

Gorben moved alongside him. 'That was nobly done, my friend. I'll not forget – I owe you my life.' Bending his body, he lifted the axe. It was now black and silver once more. 'This is an enchanted weapon,' whispered the Emperor. 'I will give you twenty thousand in gold for it.'

'It is not for selling, my Lord,' said Druss.

'Ah, Druss, and I thought you liked me.'

'I do, laddie. That's why I'll not sell it to you.'

A cold wind swirled around the cave. Anindais felt the chill and swung from the altar, looking back to see the Old Woman rise from her seat outside the golden circle. 'What is happening?' he asked. 'The axeman has killed the beast. Can we send another?'

'No,' she told him. 'But he did not kill it, he merely sent it back to the Pit.'

'Well, what now?'

'Now we pay for the services of the Kalith.'

'You said the payment would be the blood of Gorben.'

'Gorben did not die.'

'Then I do not understand you. And why is it so cold?'

A shadow fell across the Naashanite, who swung round to see a huge shape rearing above him. Talons flashed down, slicing into his chest.

'Not even intelligence,' repeated the Old Woman, turning her back on his screams. Returning to her apartments, she sat back in an old wicker chair. 'Ah, Druss,' she whispered, 'perhaps I should have let you die back in Mashrapur.'

6

Rowena opened her eyes and saw Michanek sitting at her bedside. He was wearing his ceremonial armour of bronze and gold, the helm with the red crest, and the enamelled cheek-guards, the moulded breastplate covered in sigils and motifs.

'You look very handsome,' she said sleepily.

'And you are very beautiful.'

Rubbing her eyes, she sat up. 'Why are you wearing that today? It is not as strong as your old breastplate of iron.'

'It will lift morale among the men.' Taking her hand he kissed her palm, then rose and moved towards the door. At the doorway he paused and spoke without looking back. 'I have left something for you – in my study. It is wrapped in velvet.'

And then he was gone.

Within minutes Pudri appeared, bearing a tray which he laid down beside her. There were three honey-cakes and a goblet of apple-juice. 'The Lord looks very magnificent today,' said the little man, and Rowena saw that his expression was sorrowful.

'What is wrong, Pudri?'

'I don't like battles,' he told her. 'So much blood and pain. But it is even worse when the reasons for battle have long been overtaken by events. Men will die today for no reason. Their lives will be snuffed out like midnight candles. And for why? And will it end here? No. When Gorben is strong enough he will lead a vengeance invasion against the people of Naashan. Futile and stupid!' He shrugged. 'Maybe it is because I am a eunuch that I do not understand such matters.'

'You understand them very well,' she said. 'Tell me, was I a good seeress?'

'Ah, you must not ask me this, my lady. That was yesterday, and it has flown away into the past.'

'Did the Lord Michanek ask you to withhold my past from me?'

He nodded glumly. 'It was for love that he asked this of me. Your Talent almost killed you and he did not wish for you to suffer again. Anyway, your bath is prepared. It is hot and steaming, and I managed to find some rose oil for the water.'

An hour later Rowena was walking through the garden when she saw that the window to Michanek's study was open. This was unusual, for there were many papers here and the summer breezes would often scatter them around the room. Moving inside, she opened the door and pulled shut the small window. Then she saw the package on the oak desk. It was small and, as Michanek had said, was wrapped in purple velvet.

Slowly she unwrapped the velvet to find a small, unadorned wooden box with a hinged lid, which she opened. Within lay a brooch which was simply, even crudely, made of soft copper strands surrounding a moonstone. Her mouth was suddenly dry. A part of her mind told her the brooch was new to her, but a tiny warning bell was ringing in the deep recesses of her soul.

This is mine!

Her right hand dropped slowly towards the brooch, then stopped, the fingers hovering just above the moonstone. Rowena drew back, then sat down. She heard Pudri enter the room.

703

'You were wearing that when I first saw you,' he said gently. She nodded, but did not answer. The little Ventrian approached and handed her a letter, sealed with red wax. 'The Lord asked me to give you this when you had seen his . . . gift.'

Rowena broke the seal and opened the letter. It was written in Michanek's bold, clear script.

Greetings, Beloved.

I am skilled with the sword, and yet, at this moment, I would sell my soul to be as skilful with words. A long time ago, as you lay dying, I paid three sorcerers to seal your Talents deep within you. In doing so they closed also the doorways of memory.

The brooch was, they told me, made for you as a gift of love. It is the key to your past, and a gift for your future. Of all the pain I have known, there is no suffering greater than the knowledge that your future will be without me. Yet I have loved you, and would not change a single day. And if, by some miracle, I was allowed to return to the past and court you once more, I would do so in the same way, in full knowledge of the same outcome.

You are the light in my life and the love of my heart.

Farewell, Pahtai. May your paths be made easy, and your soul know many joys.

The letter fell from her hands, floating to the floor. Pudri stepped forward swiftly and placed his slender arm around her shoulders. 'Take the brooch, my lady!'

She shook her head. 'He's going to die.'

'Yes,' admitted the Ventrian. 'But he bade me urge you to take the brooch. It was his great wish. Do not deny him!'

'I'll take the brooch,' she said solemnly, 'but when he dies, I shall die with him.'

Druss sat in the near deserted camp and watched the attack on the walls. From this distance it seemed that the attackers were insects, swarming up tiny ladders. He watched bodies topple and fall, heard the sound of battle horns and the occasional high-pitched scream that drifted on the shifting breeze. Sieben was beside him.

'The first time I've ever seen you miss a fight, Druss. Are you mellowing in your old age?'

Druss did not answer. His pale eyes watched the fighting and saw the smoke seeping out from under the wall. The timber and brushwood in the tunnels were burning now, and soon the foundations of the wall would disappear. As the smoke grew thicker the attackers fell back and waited.

Time passed slowly now in the great silence that descended over the plain. The smoke thickened, then faded. Nothing happened.

704

Druss gathered his axe and stood. Sieben rose with him. 'It didn't work,' said the poet.

'Give it time,' grunted Druss and he marched forward, Sieben followed until they were within thirty yards of the wall. Gorben was waiting here with his officers around him. No one spoke.

A jagged line, black as a spider's leg, appeared on the wall, followed by a high screeching sound. The crack widened and a huge block of masonry dislodged itself from a nearby tower, thundering down to crash on the rocks before the wall. Druss could see defenders scrambling back. A second crack appeared . . . then a third. A huge section of wall crumbled and a high tower pitched to the right, smashing down on the ruined wall and sending up an immense cloud of dust. Gorben covered his mouth with his cloak, and waited until the dust settled.

Where moments before there had been a wall of stone, there were now only jagged ruins like the broken teeth of a giant.

The battle horns sounded. The black line of the Immortals surged forward.

Gorben turned to Druss. 'Will you join them in the slaughter?'

Druss shook his head. 'I have no stomach for slaughter,' he said.

The courtyard was littered with corpses and pools of blood. Michanek glanced to his right where his brother Narin was lying on his back with a lance jutting from his chest, his sightless eyes staring up at the crimson-stained sky.

Almost sunset, thought Michanek. Blood ran from a wound in his temple and he could feel it trickling down his neck. His back hurt, and when he moved he could feel the arrow that was lodged above his left shoulder-blade gouging into muscle and flesh. It made holding the heavy shield impossible, and Michanek had long since abandoned it. The hilt of his sword was slippery with blood. A man groaned to his left. It was his cousin Shurpac; he had a terrible wound in his belly, and was attempting to stop his entrails from gushing forth.

Michanek transferred his gaze to the enemy soldiers surrounding him. They had fallen back now, and were standing in a grim circle. Michanek turned slowly. He was the last of the Naashanites still standing. Glaring at the Immortals, he challenged them. 'What's the matter with you? Frightened of Naashanite steel?' They did not move. Michanek staggered and almost fell, but then righted himself.

All pain was fading now.

It had been quite a day. The undermined wall had collapsed, killing a score of his men, but the rest had regrouped well and Michanek was proud of them. Not one had suggested surrender. They had fallen back to the second line of defence and met the Ventrians with arrows, spears and even stones. But there were too many, and it had been impossible to hold a line.

705

Michanek had led the last fifty warriors towards the inner Keep, but they were cut off and forced down a side road that led to the courtyard of Kabuchek's old house.

What were they waiting for?

The answer came to him instantly: *They are waiting for you to die.*

He saw a movement at the edge of the circle, the men moving aside as Gorben appeared – dressed now in a robe of gold, a seven-spiked crown upon his head. He looked every inch the Emperor. Beside him was the axeman, the husband of *Pahtai*.

'Ready for another duel . . . my Lord?' called Michanek. A racking cough burst from his lungs, spraying blood into the air.

'Put up your sword, man. It is over!' said Gorben.

'Do I take it you are surrendering?' Michanek asked. 'If not, then let me fight your champion!'

Gorben turned to the axeman, who nodded and moved forward. Michanek steadied himself, but his mind was wandering. He remembered a day with *Pahtai*, by a waterfall. She had made a crown of white water-lilies which she placed on his brow. The flowers were wet and cool; he could feel them now . . .

No. Fight! Win!

He looked up. The axeman seemed colossal now, towering above him, and Michanek realised he had fallen to his knees. 'No,' he said, the words slurring, 'I'll not die on my knees.' Leaning forward he tried to push himself upright, but fell again. Two strong hands took hold of his shoulders, drawing him upright, and he looked into the pale eyes of Druss the Axeman.

'Knew . . . you would . . . come,' he said. Druss half carried the dying warrior to a marble bench at the wall of the courtyard, laying him gently to the cool stone. An Immortal removed his own cloak and rolled it into a pillow for the Naashanite general.

Michanek gazed up at the darkening sky, then turned his head. Druss was kneeling alongside him, and beyond the axeman the Immortals waited. At an order from Gorben they drew their swords and held them high, saluting their enemy.

'Druss! Druss!'

'I am here.'

'Treat . . . her . . . gently.'

Michanek did not hear his answer.

He was sitting on the grass by a waterfall, the cool petals of a water-lily crown against his skin.

There was no looting in Resha, nor any organised slaughter amongst the population. The Immortals patrolled the city, having first marched through to the centre past cheering crowds who were waving banners and hurling flower petals beneath the feet of the soldiers. In the first

706

hours there were isolated outbursts of violence, as angry citizens gathered in mobs to hunt down Ventrians accused of collaborating with the Naashanite conquerors.

Gorben ordered the mobs dispersed, promising judicial inquiries at a later date to identify those who could be accused of treason. The bodies of the slain were buried in two mass graves beyond the city walls, and the Emperor ordered a monument built above the Ventrian fallen, a huge stone lion with the names of the dead carved into the base. Above the Naashanite grave there was to be no stone. Michanek, however, was laid to rest in the Hall of the Fallen, below the Great Palace on the Hill that stood like a crown at the centre of Resha.

Food was brought in to feed the populace, and builders began work, removing the dams that had starved the city of water, rebuilding the walls and repairing those houses and shops damaged by the huge stones of the ballistae that had hurtled over the walls during the past three months.

Druss had no interest in the affairs of the city. Day by day he sat at Rowena's bedside, holding to her cold, pale hand.

After Michanek had died Druss had sought out his house, the directions supplied by a Naashanite soldier who had survived the last assault. With Sieben and Eskodas he had run through the city streets until at last he had come to the house on the hill, entering it through a beautiful garden. There he saw a small man, sitting weeping by an ornamental lake. Druss seized him by his woollen tunic, hauling him to his feet. 'Where is she?' he demanded.

'She is dead,' wailed the man, his tears flowing freely. 'She took poison. There is a priest with the body.' He pointed to the house, then fell to weeping again. Releasing him, Druss ran in to the house and up the curved stairs. The first three rooms were empty, but in the fourth he found the priest of Pashtar Sen sitting by the bedside.

'Gods, no!' said Druss as he saw the still form of his Rowena, her face grey, her eyes closed. The priest looked up, his eyes tired.

'Say nothing,' urged the priest, his voice weak and seemingly far away. 'I have sent for a . . . a friend. And it is taking all my power to hold her to life.' He closed his eyes. At a loss, Druss walked to the far side of the bed and gazed down on the woman he had loved for so long. It was seven years since last he had laid eyes on her, and her beauty tore at his heart with talons of steel. Swallowing hard, he sat at the bedside. The priest was holding to her hand; sweat was flowing down his face, making grey streaks on his cheeks, and he seemed mortally weary. When Sieben and Eskodas entered the room Druss waved them to silence, and they sat and waited.

It was almost an hour before another man entered: a bald, portly man with a round red face and comically protruding ears. He was dressed in a long white tunic, and carried a large leather bag slung

707

from his shoulder by a long gold-embroidered strap. Without a word to the three men he moved to the bedside, placing his fingers against Rowena's neck.

The priest of Pashtar Sen opened his eyes. 'She has taken *yasroot*, Shalitar,' he said.

The bald man nodded. 'How long ago?'

'Three hours, though I have prevented most of it from spreading through the blood. But a minute part has reached the lymphatic system.'

Shalitar clicked his teeth, then delved into the leather bag. 'One of you fetch water,' he ordered. Eskodas stood and left the room, returning moments later with a silver jug. Shalitar told him to stand close to the head of the bed, then from the bag he produced a small packet of powder which he tipped into the jug. It foamed briefly, then settled. Delving into the bag again, he pulled clear a long grey tube and a funnel. Reaching down, he opened Rowena's mouth.

'What are you doing?' stormed Druss, grabbing the man's hand.

The surgeon was unperturbed. 'We must get the potion into her stomach. As you can see, she is in no condition to drink, therefore I intend to insert this tube in her throat and pour the potion in through the funnel. It is a delicate business, for I would not want to flood her lungs. It would be hard for me to do it correctly with a broken hand.'

Druss released him, and watched in silent anguish as the tube was eased into her throat. Shalitar held the funnel in place and ordered Eskodas to pour. When half of the contents of the jug had vanished, Shalitar nipped the tube between thumb and forefinger and withdrew it. Kneeling by the bed, he pressed his ear to Rowena's breast.

'The heartbeat is very slow,' he said, 'and weak. A year ago I treated her for plague; she almost died then, but the illness left its mark. The heart is not strong.' He turned to the men. 'Leave me now, for I must keep her circulation strong, and that will involve rubbing oil into her legs, arms and back.'

'I'll not leave,' said Druss.

'Sir, this *lady* is the widow of the Lord Michanek. She is well loved here – despite being wed to a Naashanite. It is not fitting for men to observe her naked – and any man who causes her shame will not survive the day.'

'I am her husband,' hissed Druss. 'The others can go. *I stay.*'

Shalitar rubbed his chin, but looked ready to argue no further. The priest of Pashtar Sen touched the surgeon's arm. 'It is a long story, my friend, but he speaks truly. Now do your best.'

'My best may not be good enough,' muttered Shalitar.

Three days passed. Druss ate little and slept by the bedside. There was no change in Rowena's condition, and Shalitar grew ever more

708

despondent. The priest of Pashtar Sen returned on the morning of the fourth day.

'The poison is gone from her body,' said Shalitar, 'yet she does not wake.'

The priest nodded sagely. 'When first I came, as she was sinking into the coma, I touched her spirit. It was fleeing from life; she had no will to live.'

'Why?' asked Druss. 'Why would she want to die?'

The man shrugged. 'She is a gentle soul. She first loved you, back in your own lands, and carried that love within as something pure in a tarnished world. Knowing you were coming for her, she was ready to wait. Her Talents grew astonishingly swiftly and they overwhelmed her. Shalitar, and some others, saved her life by closing the pathways of that Talent, but in doing so they also took her memory. So here she woke, in the house of Michanek. He was a good man, Druss, and he loved her – as much as you love her. He nursed her to health, and he won her heart. But he did not tell her his greatest secret – that she had, as a seeress, predicted his death . . . one year to the day after he was wed. For several years they lived together, and she succumbed to the plague. During her illness and, as I have said, with no knowledge of her life as a seeress, she asked Michanek why he had never married her. In his fear at her condition, he believed that a marriage would save her. Perhaps he was right. Now we come to the taking of Resha. Michanek left her a gift – this gift,' he said, passing the brooch to Druss.

Druss took the delicate brooch in his huge hand and closed his fingers around it. 'I made this,' he said. 'It seems like a lifetime ago.'

'This was the key which Michanek knew would unlock her memory. He thought, as I fear men will, that a return of memory would help her assuage her grief at his passing. He believed that if she remembered you, and that if you still loved her, she would have a safe future. His reasoning was flawed, for when she touched the brooch what struck her most was a terrible guilt. *She* had asked Michanek to marry her, thus assuring – as she saw it – his death. *She* had seen you, Druss, at the house of Kabuchek, and had run away, frightened to find out her past, terrified it would destroy her new-found happiness. In that one moment she saw herself as a betrayer, and as a harlot and, I fear, as a killer.'

'None of it was her fault,' said Druss. 'How could she think it was?'

The priest smiled, but it was Shalitar who spoke. 'Any death produces guilt, Druss. A son dies of plague, and the mother will berate herself for not taking the child away to somewhere safe before the disease struck. A man falls to his death, and his wife will think, "If only I had asked him to stay home today." It is the nature of good people to draw burdens to themselves. All tragedy could be avoided, if only we knew it; therefore when it strikes we blame ourselves. But for Rowena, the weight of guilt was overpowering.'

'What can I do?' the axeman asked.

'Nothing. We must just hope she returns.'

The priest of Pashtar Sen seemed about to speak, but instead stood and walked to the window. Druss saw the change in the man. 'Speak,' he said. 'What were you about to say?'

'It doesn't matter,' he said softly.

'Let me be the judge of that, if it concerns Rowena.'

The priest sat down and rubbed his tired eyes. 'She hovers,' he said at last, 'between death and life, her spirit wandering in the Valley of the Dead. Perhaps, if we could find a sorcerer, we could send his spirit after her to bring her home.' He spread his hands. 'But I do not know where to find such a man – or woman. And I don't think we have the time to search.'

'What about your Talent?' asked Druss. 'You seem to know of this place.'

The man's eyes swung away from Druss's gaze. 'I . . . I do have the Talent, but not the courage. It is a terrible place.' He forced a smile. 'I am a coward, Druss. I would die there. It is no place for men of little spirit.'

'Then send me. I'll find her.'

'You would have no chance. We are talking of a . . . a realm of dark magic and demons. You would be defenceless against them, Druss; they would overwhelm you.'

'But you could send me there?'

'There is no point. It would be madness.'

Druss turned to Shalitar. 'What will happen to her if we do nothing?'

'She has maybe a day . . . perhaps two. Already she is fading.'

'Then there are no choices, priest,' said Druss, rising and moving to stand before the man. 'Tell me how I reach this Valley.'

'You must die,' the priest whispered.

A grey mist swirled, though there was no discernible breeze, and strange sounds echoed eerily from all around him.

The priest was gone now, and Druss was alone.

Alone?

Around him shapes moved in the mist, some huge, some low and slithering. 'Keep to the path,' the priest had said. 'Follow the road through the mist. Under no circumstances allow yourself to be led from the road.'

Druss glanced down. The road was seamless and grey, as if it had been created from molten stone. It was smooth and flat and the mist held to it, floating and swaying in cold tendrils that swirled around his legs and lower body.

A woman's voice called to him from the side of the road. He paused and glanced to his right. A dark-haired woman, scarce more than a girl, was sitting on a rock with legs apart, her right hand stroking her thigh. She licked her lips and tossed her head. 'Come here,' she called. 'Come here!'

Druss shook his head. 'I have other business.'

She laughed at him. 'Here? You have other business here?' Her laughter rang out and she moved closer to him, but he saw that she did not set foot upon the road. Her eyes were large and golden but there were no pupils, merely black slits in the gold. When her mouth opened a forked tongue darted between her lips, which Druss now saw were grey-blue. Her teeth were small and sharp.

Ignoring her he walked on. An old man was sitting in the centre of the road with shoulders hunched. Druss paused. 'Which way, brother?' asked the old man. 'Which way do I go? There are so many paths.'

'There is only one,' said Druss.

'So many paths,' repeated the other man. Again Druss moved on, and behind him he heard the woman's voice speaking to the old man. 'Come here! Come here!' Druss didn't look back, but only moments later he heard a terrible scream.

The road moved ever on through the mist, level and straight as a spear. There were others on the road, some walking tall, others shuffling. No one spoke. Druss moved through them silently, scanning their faces, seeking Rowena.

A young woman stumbled from the path, falling to her knees. Instantly a scaled hand caught at her cloak, dragging her back. Druss was too far back to help, and he cursed and moved on.

Many pathways merged with the road and Druss found himself travelling with a multitude of silent people, young and old. Their faces were blank, their expressions preoccupied. Many left the path and wandered through the mist.

It seemed to the axeman that he had walked for many days. There was no sense of time here, nor any fatigue, nor hunger. Gazing ahead, he could see vast numbers of souls wending their way through the mist-enveloped road.

Despair touched him. How would he find her among so many? Ruthlessly he pushed the fear from his mind, concentrating only on scanning the faces as he moved ever on. Nothing would ever have been achieved, he thought, if men had allowed themselves to be diverted by the scale of the problems faced.

After a while Druss noted that the road was rising. He could see further ahead, and the mist was thinning. There were no more merging pathways now; the road itself was more than a hundred feet wide.

On and on he moved, forcing his way through the silent throng. Then he saw that the road was beginning to diverge once more, into scores of pathways leading to arched tunnels, dark and forbidding.

711

A small man in a robe of coarse brown wool was moving back through the river of souls. He saw Druss and smiled. 'Keep moving, my son,' he said, patting Druss's shoulder.

'Wait!' called the axeman as the man moved past him. Brown Robe swung back, surprised. Stepping to Druss, he gestured him to the side of the road.

'Let me see your hand, brother,' he said.

'What?'

'Your hand, your right hand. Show me the palm!' The little man was insistent. Druss held out his hand and Brown Robe grasped it, peering intently at the calloused palm. 'But you are not ready to pass over, brother. Why are you here?'

'I am looking for someone.'

'Ah,' said the man, apparently relieved. 'You are the despairing heart. Many of you try to pass through. Did your loved one die? Has the world treated you savagely? Whatever the answer, brother, you must return whence you came. There is nothing for you here – unless you stray from the path. And then there is only an eternity of suffering. Go back!'

'I cannot. My wife is here. And she is alive – just like me.'

'If she is alive, brother, then she will not have passed the portals before you. No living soul can enter. You do not have the coin.' He held out his own hand. Nestling there was a black shadow, circular and insubstantial. 'For the Ferryman,' he said, 'and the road to Paradise.'

'If she could not pass the tunnels, then where could she be?' asked Druss.

'I don't know, brother. I have never left the path and I know not what lies beyond, save that it is inhabited by the souls of the damned. Go to the Fourth Gateway. Ask for Brother Domitori. He is the Keeper.'

Brown Robe smiled, then moved away to be swallowed up by the multitude. Druss joined the flow and eased his way through to the Fourth Gateway where another man in a brown, hooded robe stood silently by the entrance. He was tall and round-shouldered, with sad, solemn eyes. 'Are you Brother Domitori?' asked Druss.

The man nodded, but did not speak.

'I am looking for my wife.'

'Pass on, brother. If her soul lives you will find her.'

'She had no coin,' said Druss. The man nodded and pointed to a narrow, winding path that led up and around a low hill.

'There are many such,' said Domitori, 'beyond the hill. There they flicker and fade, and rejoin the road when they are ready, when their bodies give up the fight, when the heart ceases.'

Druss turned away, but Domitori called out to him. 'Beyond the hill the road is no more. You will be in the Valley of the Dead. Best you arm yourself.'

'I have no weapons here.'

712

Domitori raised his hand and the flow of souls ceased to move through the Gateway. He stepped alongside Druss. 'Bronze and steel have no place here, though you will see what appear to be swords and lances. This is a place of Spirit, and a man's spirit can be steel or water, wood or fire. To cross the hill – and return – will require courage, and so much more. Do you have faith?'

'In what?'

The man sighed. 'In the Source? In yourself? What do you hold most dear?'

'Rowena – my wife.'

'Then hold fast to your love, my friend. No matter what assails you. What do you fear most?'

'Losing her.'

'What else?'

'I fear nothing.'

'All men fear something. And that is your weakness. This place of the Damned and the Dead has an uncanny talent for bringing a man face to face with what he fears. I pray that the Source will guide you. Go in peace, brother.'

Returning to the Gateway he lifted his hand once more, and the entrance opened, the grim, silent flow of souls continuing without pause.

'You gutless whoreson!' stormed Sieben. 'I should kill you!'

The surgeon Shalitar stepped between Sieben and the priest of Pashtar Sen. 'Be calm,' he urged. 'The man has admitted to lacking courage and has no need to apologise for it. Some men are tall, some short, some brave, others not so brave.'

'That may be true,' conceded Sieben, 'but what chance does Druss have in a world of enchantment and sorcery? Tell me that!'

'I don't know,' Shalitar admitted.

'No, but he does,' said Sieben. 'I have read of the Void; a great many of my tales are centred there. I have spoken to Seekers and mystics who have journeyed through the Mist. All agree on one point – without access to the powers of sorcery a man is finished there. Is that not true, priest?'

The man nodded, but did not look up. He was sitting beside the wide bed upon which lay the still figures of Druss and Rowena. The axeman's face was pale, and he did not seem to be breathing.

'What will he face there?' insisted Sieben. 'Come on, man!'

'The horrors of his past,' answered the priest, his voice barely audible.

'By the gods, priest, I tell you this: If he dies, you will follow him.'

Druss had reached the brow of the hill and gazed down into a parched valley. There were trees, black and dead, silhouetted against the slate-grey

713

earth, as if sketched there with charcoal. There was no wind, no movement save for the few souls who wandered aimlessly across the face of the valley. A little way down the hill he saw an old woman sitting on the ground with head bowed and shoulders hunched. Druss approached her.

'I am looking for my wife,' he said.

'You are looking for more than that,' she told him.

He squatted down opposite her. 'No, just my wife. Can you help me?'

Her head came up and he found himself staring into deep-set eyes that glittered with malice. 'What can you give me, Druss?'

'How is it you know me?' he countered.

'The Axeman, the Silver Slayer, the man who fought the Chaos Beast. Why should I not know you? Now, what can you give me?'

'What do you want?'

'Make me a promise.'

'What promise?'

'You will give me your axe.'

'I do not have it here.'

'I know that, boy,' she snapped. 'But in the world above you will give me your axe.'

'Why do you need it?'

'That is no part of the bargain. But look around you, Druss. How will you begin to find her in the time that is left?'

'You can have it,' he said. 'Now, where is she?'

'You must cross a bridge. You will find her there. But the bridge is guarded, Druss, by an awesome warrior.'

'Just tell me where it is.'

A staff lay beside the old woman and she used it to lever herself to her feet. 'Come,' she said, and began to walk towards a low line of hills. As they walked, Druss saw many new souls wandering down into the valley.

'Why do they come here?' he asked.

'They are weak,' she told him. 'Victims of despair, of guilt, of longing. Suicides, mostly. As they wander here their bodies are dying – like Rowena.'

'She is not weak.'

'Of course she is. She is a victim of love – just as you are. And love is the ultimate downfall of Man. There is no abiding strength in love, Druss. It erodes the natural strength of man, it taints the heart of the hunter.'

'I do not believe that.'

She laughed, a dry sound like the rattling of bones. 'Yes, you do,' she said. 'You are not a man of love, Druss. Or was it love that led you to leap upon the decks of the corsair ship, cutting and killing? Was it love that sent you over the battlements at Ectanis? Was it love that carried you through the battles in the sand circles of Mashrapur?' She halted in her stride and turned to face him. 'Was it?'

714

'Yes. Everything was for Rowena – to help me find her. I love her.'

'It is not love, Druss; it is perceived need. You cannot bear what you are without her – a savage, a killer, a brute. But with her it is a different story. You can leach from her purity, suck it in like fine wine. And then you can see the beauty in a flower, smell the essence of life upon the summer breeze. Without her you see yourself as a creature without worth. And answer me this, axeman: If it was truly love, would you not wish for her happiness above all else?'

'Aye, I would. And I do!'

'Really? Then when you found that she was happy, living with a man who loved her, her life rich and secure, what did you do? Did you try to persuade Gorben to spare Michanek?'

'Where is this bridge?' he asked.

'It is not easy to face, is it?' she persisted.

'I am no debater, woman. I only know that I would die for her.'

'Yes, yes. Typical of the male – always look for the easy solutions, the simple answers.' She walked on, cresting the hill, and paused, resting on her staff. Druss gazed down into the chasm beyond. Far, far below a river of fire, at this distance a slender ribbon of flame, flowed through a black gorge. Across the gorge stretched a narrow bridge of black rope and grey timber. At the centre stood a warrior in black and silver with a huge axe in his hands.

'She is on the far side,' said the old woman. 'But to reach her you must pass the guardian. Do you recognise him?'

'No.'

'You will.'

The bridge was secured by thick black ropes tied to two blocks of stone. The wooden slats that made up the main body of the structure were, Druss judged, around three feet long and an inch thick. He stepped out on to the bridge, which immediately began to sway. There were no guiding ropes attached by which a man could steady himself and, looking down, Druss felt a sick sense of vertigo.

Slowly he walked out over the chasm, his eyes fixed to the boards. He was half-way to the man in black and silver before he looked up. Then shock struck him like a blow.

The man smiled, bright teeth shining white against the black and silver beard. 'I am not you, boy,' he said. 'I am everything you could have been.'

Druss stared hard at the man. He was the very image of Druss himself, except that he was older and his eyes, cold and pale, seemed to hold many secrets.

'You are Bardan,' said Druss.

'And proud of it. I used my strength, Druss. I made men shake with fear. I took my pleasures where I wanted them. I am not like you, strong in body but weak in heart. You take after Bress.'

715

'I take that as a compliment,' said Druss. 'For I would never have wanted to be like you – a slayer of babes, an abuser of women. There is no strength in that.'

'I fought men. No man could accuse Bardan of cowardice. Shemak's balls, boy, I fought armies!'

'I say you were a coward,' said Druss. 'The worst kind. What strength you had came from that,' he said, pointing to the axe. 'Without it you were nothing. Without it you are nothing.'

Bardan's face reddened, then grew pale. 'I don't need this to deal with you, you weak-kneed whoreson. I could take you with my hands.'

'In your dreams,' mocked Druss.

Bardan made as if to lay down the axe, but then hesitated. 'You can't do it, can you?' taunted Druss. 'The mighty Bardan! Gods, I spit on you!'

Bardan straightened, the axe still in his right hand. 'Why should I lay aside my only friend? No one else stood by me all those lonely years. And here – even here he has been my constant aid.'

'Aid?' countered Druss. 'He destroyed you, just as he destroyed Cajivak and all others who took him to their hearts. But I don't need to convince you, Grandfather. You know it, but you are too weak to acknowledge it.'

'I'll show you weakness!' roared Bardan, leaping forward with axe raised. The bridge swayed perilously, but Druss leapt in under the swinging axe, hammering a ferocious punch to Bardan's chin. As the other man staggered, Druss took one running step and leapt feet first, his boots thudding into Bardan's chest to hurl him back. Bardan lost his grip on the axe and teetered on the edge.

Druss rolled to his feet and dived at the man. Bardan, recovering his footing, snarled and met him head-on. Druss smashed a blow to the other man's chin, but Bardan rolled with the punch, sending an uppercut which snapped the axeman's head back. The power in the blow was immense and Druss reeled. A second blow caught him above the ear, smashing him to the boards. Rolling as a booted foot slashed past his ear, he grabbed Bardan's leg and heaved. The warrior fell heavily. As Druss pushed himself upright, Bardan launched himself from the boards, his hands circling Druss's throat. The bridge was swaying wildly now and both men fell and rolled towards the edge. Druss hooked his foot into the space between two boards, but he and Bardan were hanging now over the awesome drop.

Druss tore himself free of Bardan's grip and thundered a punch to the warrior's chin. Bardan grunted and toppled from the bridge. His hand snaked out to grab Druss's arm – the wrenching grasp almost pulled Druss over the edge.

Bardan hung above the river of fire, his pale eyes looking up into Druss's face.

'Ah, but you're a bonnie fighter, laddie,' said Bardan softly. Druss got a grip on the other man's jerkin and tried to pull him up on to the bridge.

'Time to die at last,' said Bardan. 'You were right. It was the axe, always the axe.' Releasing his hold, he smiled. 'Let me go, boy. It's over.'

'No! Damn you, take my hand!'

'May the gods smile on you, Druss!' Bardan twisted up and hit out at Druss's arm, dislodging his grip. The bridge swayed again and the black and silver warrior fell. Druss watched him fall, spinning down, down, until he was just a dark speck swallowed up by the river of fire.

Pushing himself to his knees he glanced at the axe. Red smoke swirled from it to form a crimson figure – the skin scaled, the head horned at the temples. There was no nose, merely two slits in the flesh above a shark-like mouth.

'You were correct, Druss,' said the demon affably. 'He was weak. As was Cajivak, and all the others. Only you have the strength to use me.'

'I want no part of you.'

The demon's head lifted and his laughter sounded. 'Easy to say, mortal. But look yonder.' At the far end of the bridge stood the Chaos Beast, huge and towering, its taloned paws glinting, its eyes glowing like coals of fire.

Druss felt a swelling of despair and his heart sank as the axe-demon stepped closer, his voice low and friendly. 'Why do you hesitate, Man? When have I failed you? On the ship of Earin Shad, did I not turn away the fire? Did I not slip in Cajivak's grasp? I am your friend, Mortal. I have always been your friend. And in these long and lonely centuries I have waited for a man with your strength and determination. With me you can conquer the world. Without me you will never leave this place, never feel the sun upon your face. Trust me, Druss! Slay the beast – and then we can go home.'

The demon shimmered into smoke, flowing back into the black half of the axe.

Druss glanced up to see the Chaos Beast waiting at the far end of the bridge. It was even more monstrous now: massive shoulders beneath the black fur, saliva dripping from its huge maw. Stepping forward, Druss gripped the haft of Snaga, swinging the blades into the air.

Instantly his strength returned, and with it a soaring sense of hatred and a lust to cleave and kill. His mouth was dry with the need for battle, and he moved towards the flame-eyed bear. The beast waited with arms at its sides.

It seemed to Druss then that all the evil of the world rested in the creature's colossal frame, all the frustrations of life, the angers, the jealousies, the vileness – everything that he had ever suffered could be laid upon the black soul of the Chaos Beast. Fury and madness made his limbs tremble and he felt his lips draw back in a snarl as he lifted high the axe and ran at the creature.

The beast did not move. It stood still, arms down and head drooping. Druss slowed in his charge. Kill it! Kill it! Kill it! He reeled with the

717

intensity of his need to destroy, then looked down at the axe in his hand.

'No!' he shouted, and with one tremendous heave hurled the axe high in the air and out over the chasm. It spun glistening towards the ribbon of flame, and Druss saw the demon spew from it, black against the silver of the blades. Then the axe struck the river of fire. Exhausted, Druss turned back to face the beast.

Rowena stood alone and naked, her gentle eyes watching him.

He groaned and walked towards her. 'Where is the beast?' he said.

'There is no beast, Druss. Only me. Why did you change your mind about killing me?'

'You? I would never hurt you! Sweet heaven, how could you think it?'

'You looked at me with hate and then you ran at me with your axe.'

'Oh, Rowena! I saw only a demon. I was bewitched! Forgive me!' Stepping in close he tried to put his arms around her, but she moved back from him.

'I loved Michanek,' she said.

He sighed and nodded. 'I know. He was a good man – perhaps a great one. I was with him at the end. He asked me . . . urged me to look after you. He didn't need to ask that of me. You are everything to me, you always were. Without you there was no light in my life. And I've waited so long for this moment. Come back with me, Rowena. Live!'

'I was looking for him,' she said, tears in her eyes, 'but I couldn't find him.'

'He's gone where you cannot follow,' said Druss. 'Come home.'

'I am both a wife and widow. Where is my home, Druss? Where?'

Her head drooped and bright tears fell to her cheeks. Druss took her in his arms, drawing her in to him. 'Wherever you choose to make your home,' he whispered, 'I will build it for you. But it should be where the sun shines, and where you can hear the birdsong, smell the flowers. This place is not for you – nor would Michanek want you here. I love you, Rowena. But if you want to live without me I will bear it. Just so long as you live. Come back with me. We'll talk again in the light.'

'I don't want to stay here,' she said, clinging to him. 'But I miss him so.'

The words tore at Druss, but he held her close and kissed her hair. 'Let's go home,' he said. 'Take my hand.'

Druss opened his eyes and drew in a great gulp of air. Beside him Rowena slept. He felt a moment of panic, but then a voice spoke. 'She is alive.' Druss sat up, and saw the Old Woman sitting in a chair by the bedside.

'You want the axe? Take it!'

She chuckled, the sound dry and cold. 'Your gratitude is over-whelming, axeman. But no, I do not need Snaga. You exorcised the demon from the weapon and he is gone. But I shall find him. You did

718

well, boy. All that hatred and lust for death – yet you overcame it. What a complex creature is Man.'

'Where are the others?' asked Druss.

Taking up her staff, she eased herself to her feet. 'Your friends are sleeping. They were exhausted and it took little effort to send them deep into dreams. Good luck to you, Druss. I wish you and your lady well. Take her back to the Drenai mountains, enjoy her company while you can. Her heart is weak, and she will never see the white hair of a human winter. But you will, Druss.'

She sniffed and stretched, her bones creaking. 'What did you want with the demon?' asked Druss as she made her way to the door.

She turned in the doorway. 'Gorben is having a sword made – a great sword. He will pay me to make it an enchanted weapon. And I shall, Druss. I shall.'

And then she was gone.

Rowena stirred and woke.

Sunlight broke through the clouds and bathed the room.

Book Four

Druss the Legend

Druss took Rowena back to the lands of the Drenai, and, with the gold presented to him by a grateful Gorben, bought a farm in the high mountains. For two years he lived quietly, struggling to be a loving husband and a man of peace. Sieban travelled the land, performing his songs and tales before princes and courtiers, and the legend of Druss spread across the continent.

At the invitation of the King of Gothir Druss travelled north, and fought in the Second Campaign against the Nadir, earning the title *Deathwalker*[*]. Sieban joined him and together they travelled through many lands.

And the legend grew.

Between campaigns Druss would return to his farm, but always he would listen for the siren call to battle and Rowena would bid him farewell as he set off, time and again, to fight, what he assured her, would be his last battle.

Faithful Pudri remained at Rowena's side. Sieban continued to scandalise Drenai society and his travels with Druss were usually undertaken to escape the vengeance of outraged husbands.

In the east the Ventrian Emperor, Gorben, having conquered all his enemies, turned his attention to the fiercely independent Drenai.

Druss was forty five, and once more had promised Rowena there would be no more journeying to distant wars.

What he could not know was, this time, the war was coming to him.

[*]From the **second** chronicles of Druss the Legend.

Druss sat in the sunshine, watching the clouds glide slowly across the mountains, and thought of his life. Love and friendship had been with him always, the first with Rowena, the latter with Sieben, Eskodas and Bodasen. But the greater part of his forty-five years had been filled with blood and death, the screams of the wounded and dying.

He sighed. A man ought to leave more behind him than corpses, he decided. The clouds thickened, the land falling into shadow, the grass of the hillside no longer gleaming with life, the flowers ceasing to blaze with colour. He shivered. It was going to rain. The soft, dull, arthritic ache had begun in his shoulder. 'Getting old,' he said.

'Who are you talking to, my love?' He turned and grinned. Rowena seated herself beside him on the wooden bench, slipping her arm around his waist, resting her head on his shoulder. His huge hand stroked her hair, noting the grey at the temples.

'I was talking to myself. It's something that happens when you get old.'

She stared up into his grizzled face and smiled. 'You'll never get old. You're the strongest man in the world.'

'Once, princess. Once.'

'Nonsense. You hefted that barrel of sand at the village fair right over your head. No one else could do that.'

'That only makes me the strongest man in the village.'

Pulling away from him, Rowena shook her head, but her expression, as always, was gentle. 'You miss the wars and the battles?'

'No. I . . . I am happy here. With you. You give my soul peace.'

'Then what is troubling you?'

'The clouds. They move in front of the sun. They cast shadows. Then they are gone. Am I like that, Rowena? Will I leave nothing behind me?'

'What would you wish to leave?'

'I don't know,' he answered, looking away.

'You would have liked a son,' she said, softly. 'As would I. But it was not to be. Do you blame me for it?'

'No! No! Never.' His arms swept around her, drawing her to him. 'I love you. I always have. I always will. You are my wife!'

'I would have liked to have given you a son,' she whispered.

'It does not matter.'

725

They sat in silence until the clouds darkened and the first drops of rain began to fall.

Druss stood, lifting Rowena into his arms, and began the long walk to the stone house. 'Put me down,' she commanded. 'You'll hurt your back.'

'Nonsense. You are as light as a sparrow wing. And am I not the strongest man in the world?'

A fire was blazing in the hearth, and their Ventrian servant, Pudri, was preparing mulled wine for them. Druss lowered Rowena into a broad-backed leather armchair.

'Your face is red with the effort,' she chided him.

He smiled and did not argue. His shoulder was hurting, his lower back aching like the devil. The slender Pudri grinned at them both.

'Such children you are,' he said, and shuffled away into the kitchen.

'He's right,' said Druss. 'With you I am still the boy from the farm, standing below the Great Oak with the most beautiful woman in the Drenai lands.'

'I was never beautiful,' Rowena told him, 'but it pleased me to hear you say it.'

'You were – and are,' he assured her.

The firelight sent dancing shadows on to the walls of the room as the light outside began to fail. Rowena fell asleep and Druss sat silently watching her. Four times in the last three years she had collapsed, the surgeons warning Druss of a weakness in her heart. The old warrior had listened to them without comment, his ice-blue eyes showing no expression. But within him a terrible fear had begun to grow. He had forsaken his battles and settled down to life in the mountains, believing that his presence nearby would hold Rowena to life.

But he watched her always, never allowing her to become too tired, fussing over her meals, waking in the night to feel her pulse, then being unable to sleep.

'Without her I am nothing,' he confided to his friend Sieben the Poet, whose house had been built less than a mile from the stone house. 'If she dies, part of me will die with her.'

'I know, old horse,' said Sieben. 'But I am sure the princess will be fine.'

Druss smiled. 'Why did you make her a princess? Are you poets incapable of the truth?'

Sieben spread his hands and chuckled. 'One must cater to one's audience. The saga of Druss the Legend had need of a princess. Who would want to listen to the tale of a man who fought his way across continents to rescue a farm girl?'

'Druss the Legend? Pah! There are no real heroes any more. The likes of Egel, Karnak and Waylander are long gone. Now they were heroes, mighty men with eyes of fire.'

Sieben laughed aloud. 'You say that only because you have heard the songs. In years to come men will talk of you in the same way. You and that cursed axe.'

The cursed axe.

Druss glanced up to where the weapon hung on the wall, its twin silver steel blades glinting in the firelight. Snaga the Sender, the blades of no return. He stood and moved silently across the room, lifting the axe from the brackets supporting it. The black haft was warm to the touch, and he felt, as always, the thrill of battle ripple through him as he hefted the weapon. Reluctantly he returned the axe to its resting place.

'They are calling you,' said Rowena. He swung and saw that she was awake and watching him.

'Who is calling me?'

'The hounds of war. I can hear them baying.' Druss shivered and forced a smile.

'No one is calling me,' he told her, but there was no conviction in his voice. Rowena had always been a mystic.

'Gorben is coming, Druss. His ships are already at sea.'

'It is not my war. My loyalties would be divided.'

For a moment she said nothing. Then: 'You liked him, didn't you?'

'He is a good Emperor – or he was. Young, proud, and terribly brave.'

'You set too much store by bravery. There was a madness in him you could never see. I hope you never do.'

'I told you, it is not my war. I'm forty-five years old, my beard is going grey and my joints are stiff. The young men of the Drenai will have to tackle him without me.'

'But the Immortals will be with him,' she persisted. 'You said once there were no finer warriors in the world.'

'Do you remember all my words?'

'Yes,' she answered, simply.

The sound of hoofbeats came from the yard beyond, and Druss strode to the door, stepping out on to the porch.

The rider wore the armour of a Drenai officer, white plumed helm and silver breastplate, with a long scarlet cloak. He dismounted, tied the reins of his horse to a hitching rail and walked towards the house.

'Good evening. I am looking for Druss the Axeman,' said the man, removing his helm and running his fingers through his sweat-drenched fair hair.

'You found him.'

'I thought so. I am Dun Certak. I have a message from Lord Abalayn. He wonders if you would agree to ride east to our camp at Skeln.'

'Why?'

727

'Morale, sir. You are a legend. The Legend. It would boost the men during the interminable waiting.'

'No,' said Druss. 'I am retired.'

'Where are your manners, Druss?' called Rowena. 'Ask the young man to come in.'

Druss stepped aside and the officer entered, bowing deeply to Rowena.

'It is a pleasure to meet you, my lady. I have heard so much about you.'

'How disappointing for you,' she replied, her smile friendly. 'You hear of a princess and meet a plump matron.'

'He wants me to travel to Skeln,' said Druss.

'I heard. I think you should go.'

'I am no speechmaker,' growled Druss.

'Then take Sieben with you. It will do you good. You have no idea how irritating it is to have you fussing around me all day. Be honest, you will enjoy yourself enormously.'

'Are you married?' Druss asked Certak, his voice almost a growl.

'No, sir.'

'Very wise. Will you stay the night?'

'No, sir. Thank you. I have other despatches to deliver. But I will see you at Skeln . . . and look forward to it.' The officer bowed once more and backed away towards the door.

'You will stay for supper,' ordered Rowena. 'Your despatches can wait for at least one hour.'

'I'm sorry, my lady, but . . .'

'Give up, Certak,' advised Druss. 'You cannot win.'

The officer smiled and spread his hands. 'An hour then,' he agreed.

The following morning, on borrowed horses, Druss and Sieben waved farewell and headed east. Rowena waved and smiled until they were out of sight, then returned to the house, where Pudri was waiting.

'You should not have sent him away, lady,' said the Ventrian sadly. Rowena swallowed hard, and the tears began to flow. Pudri moved alongside her, his slender arms encircling her.

'I had to. He must not be here when the time comes.'

'He would want to be here.'

'In so many ways he is the strongest man I have ever known. But in this I am right. He must not see me die.'

'I will be with you, lady. I will hold your hand.'

'You will tell him that it was sudden, and there was no pain – even if it is a lie?'

'I will.'

Six days later, after a dozen changes of mount, Certak galloped into the camp. There were four hundred white tents set in unit squares in

728

the shadow of the Skeln range, each housing twelve men. Four thousand horses were picketed in the surrounding fields, and sixty cookfires were blazing under iron pots. The odour of stew assailed him as he reined in outside the large red-striped tent used by the general and his staff.

The young officer handed over his despatches, saluted and left to rejoin his company at the northern edge of the camp. Leaving his lathered mount with a groom, he removed his helm and pushed aside the tent flap of his quarters. Inside his companions were dicing and drinking. The game broke up as he entered.

'Certak!' said Orases, grinning and rising to meet him. 'Well, what was he like?'

'Who?' asked Certak innocently.

'Druss, you moron.'

'Big,' said Certak, moving past the burly blond officer and throwing his helm to the narrow pallet bed. He unbuckled his breastplate, letting it drop to the floor. Freed of its weight, he took a deep breath and scratched his chest.

'Now don't be annoying, there's a good fellow,' said Orases, his smile fading. 'Tell us about him.'

'Do tell him,' urged the dark-eyed Diagoras. 'He's been talking about the axeman non-stop since you left.'

'That's not true,' muttered Orases, blushing. 'We've all been talking about him.' Certak slapped Orases on the shoulder, then ruffled his hair.

'You get me a drink, Orases, and then I'll tell you all.'

As Orases fetched a flagon of wine and four goblets, Diagoras moved smoothly to his feet and pulled up a chair, reversing it before sitting opposite Certak, who had streched out on the bed. The fourth man, Archytas, joined them, accepting a goblet of light honey mead wine from Orases and draining it swiftly.

'As I said, he is big,' said Certak. 'Not as tall as the stories claim, but built like a small castle. The size of his arms? Well, his biceps are as long as your thighs, Diagoras. He is bearded and dark, though there is some grey in his hair. His eyes are blue, and they seem to look right through you.'

'And Rowena?' asked Orases eagerly. 'Is she as fabulously beautiful as the poem says?'

'No. She is nice enough, in a matronly sort of way. I suppose she would have been lovely once. It's hard to tell with some of these older women. Her eyes are gorgeous, though, and she has a pretty smile.'

'Did you see the axe?' asked Archytas, a wand-slender nobleman from the Lentrian border.

'No.'

'Did you ask Druss about his battles?' asked Diagoras.

'Of course not, you fool. He may be only a farmer now, but he's still Druss. You don't just march up and ask how many dragons he's downed.'

'There are no dragons,' said Archytas loftily.

Certak shook his head, staring at the man through narrowed eyes.

'It was a figure of speech,' he said. 'Anyway, they invited me to join them for supper and we chatted about horses and the running of the farm. He asked my opinion about the war, and I told him I thought Gorben would sail for Penrac Bay.'

'It's a safe bet,' said Diagoras.

'Not necessarily. If it's that safe, how come we're stuck here with five regiments?'

'Abalayn is over-cautious,' answered Diagoras, grinning.

'That's the trouble with you westerners,' said Certak. 'You live so long with your horses that you start to think like them. Skeln Pass is a gateway to the Sentran Plain. If Gorben took that we would starve during the winter. So would half of Vagria, for that matter.'

'Gorben is no fool,' offered Archytas. 'He knows Skeln can be defended forever with two thousand men. The pass is too narrow for the numbers of his army to be of any real use. And there's no other way through. Penrac makes more sense. It's only three hundred miles from Drenan and the countryside around is as flat as a lake. There his army could spread and cause real problems.'

'I don't particularly care where he lands,' said Orases, 'as long as I'm close by to see it.'

Certak and Diagoras exchanged glances. Both had fought the Sathuli and had seen the true, bloody face of battle, and watched the crows peck out the eyes of dead friends. Orases was a newcomer who had urged his father to buy him a commission in Abalayn's lancers when news of the invasion fleet reached Drenan.

'What about the Cuckold King?' asked Archytas. 'Was he there?'

'Sieben? Yes, he arrived for supper. He looks ancient. I can't see the ladies swooning over him any longer. Bald as a rock and thin as a stick.'

'You think Druss will want to fight alongside us?' asked Diagoras. 'That would be something to tell the children.'

'No. He's past it. Tired. You can see it in him. But I liked him. He's no braggart, that's for sure. Down to earth. You'd never believe he was the subject of so many songs and ballads. They say Gorben has never forgotten him.'

'Maybe he sailed the fleet just for a reunion with his friend Druss,' said Archytas, with a sneer. 'Perhaps you should put that idea to the general. We could all go home.'

'It's an idea,' admitted Certak, biting back his anger. 'But if the regiments separate, we'd be deprived of your delightful company, Archytas. And nothing is worth that.'

'I could live with it,' said Diagoras.

'And I could do without being forced to share a tent with a pack of ill-bred hounds,' said Archytas. 'But needs must.'

'Well, woof woof,' said Diagoras. 'Do you think we've been insulted, Certak?'

'Not by anyone worth worrying about,' he replied.

'Now that is an insult,' said Archytas, rising. A sudden commotion from outside the tent cut through the gathering drama. The flap was pulled aside. A young soldier pushed his head inside.

'The beacons are lit,' he said. 'The Ventrians have landed at Penrac.'

The four warriors leapt to their feet, rushing to gather their armour.

Archytas turned as he buckled his breastplate.

'This changes nothing,' he said. 'It is a question of honour.'

'No,' said Certak. 'It is a question of dying. And you'll do that nicely, you pompous pig.'

Archytas grinned mirthlessly back at him.

'We'll see,' he said.

Diagoras pulled down the earflaps of his bronze helmet and tied them under his chin. He leaned conspiratorially close to Archytas.

'A thought to remember, goat-face. If you kill him – which is extremely doubtful – I shall cut your throat while you're sleeping.' He smiled pleasantly and patted Archytas' shoulder. 'You see, I'm no gentleman.'

The camp was in uproar. Along the coast the warning beacons were blazing from the Skeln peaks. Gorben, as expected, had landed in the south. Abalayn was there with twenty thousand men. But he would be outnumbered at least two to one. It was a hard five days' ride to Penrac and the orders were being issued at speed, the horses saddled, and the tents packed away. Cooking fires were doused and wagons loaded as men scurried about the camp in seeming chaos.

By morning only six hundred warriors remained in the mouth of Skeln Pass, the bulk of the army thundering south to bolster Abalayn.

Earl Delnar, Warden of the North, gathered the men together just after dawn. Beside him stood Archytas.

'As you know, the Ventrians have landed,' said the Earl. 'We are to stay here in case they send a small force to harry the north. I know many of you would have preferred to head south, but, to state the obvious, someone has to stay behind to protect the Sentran Plain. And we've been chosen. The camp here is no longer suitable for our needs and we will be moving up into the pass itself. Are there any questions?'

There were none and Delnar dismissed the men, turning to Archytas.

'Why you have been left here I do not know,' he said. 'But I don't

731

like you at all, lad. You are a troublemaker. I would have thought your skills would have been welcome at Penrac. However, be that as it may. You cause any trouble here and you will regret it.'

'I understand, Lord Delnar,' replied Archytas.

'Understand this also: As my aide I will require you to work, passing on my instructions exactly as I give them to you. I am told you are a man of surpassing arrogance.'

'That is hardly fair.'

'Perhaps. I cannot see that it should be true, since your grandfather was a tradesman and your nobility is scarce two generations old. You will find as you grow older that it is what a man does that counts, and not what his father did.'

'Thank you for your advice, my lord. I shall bear it in mind,' said Archytas stiffly.

'I doubt that you will. I do not know what drives you, but then I don't care overmuch. We should be here about three weeks and then I'll be rid of you.'

'As you say, my lord.'

Delnar waved him away, then glanced beyond him to the edge of the trees bordering the field to the west. Two men were walking steadily towards them. Delnar's jaw tightened as he recognised the poet. He called Archytas back.

'Sir?'

'The two men approaching yonder. Go out to meet them and have them brought to my tent.'

'Yes, sir. Who are they, do you know?'

'The large one is Druss the Legend. The other is the saga poet Sieben.'

'I understand you know him very well,' said Archytas, barely disguising his malice.

'It doesn't look much of an army,' said Druss, shading his eyes against the sun rising over the Skeln peaks. 'Can't be more than a few hundred of them.'

Sieben didn't answer. He was exhausted. Early the previous day Druss had finally tired of riding the tall gelding borrowed in Skoda. He had left it with a stock breeder in a small town thirty miles west, determined to walk to Skeln. In a moment – in which Sieben could only consider he had been struck by transient and massive stupidity – he had agreed to walk with him. He seemed to remember thinking that it would be good for him. Now, even with Druss carrying both packs, the poet stumbled wearily alongside, his legs boneless and numb, his ankles and wrists swollen, his breathing ragged.

'You know what I think?' said Druss. Sieben shook his head, concentrating on the tents. 'I think we're too late. Gorben has landed

732

at Penrac and the army's gone. Still, it's been a pleasant journey. Are you all right, poet?'

Sieben nodded, his face grey.

'You don't look it. If you weren't standing here beside me I'd think you were dead. I've seen corpses that looked in better health.' Sieben glared at him. It was the only response his fading strength would allow. Druss chuckled. 'Lost for words, eh? This was worth coming for.'

A tall young officer was making his way towards them, fastidiously avoiding small patches of mud and the more obvious reminders of the horses picketed in the field the night before.

Halting before them, he bowed elaborately.

'Welcome to Skeln,' he said. 'Is your friend ill?'

'No, he always looks like this,' said Druss, running his eyes over the warrior. He moved well, and handled himself confidently, but there was something about the narrow green eyes and the set of his features that nettled the axeman.

'Earl Delnar asked me to conduct you to his tent. I am Archytas. And you?'

'Druss. This is Sieben. Lead on.'

The officer set a fast pace which Druss made no effort to match on the last few hundred paces uphill. He walked slowly beside Sieben. The truth of it was that Druss himself was tired. They had walked most of the night, both trying to prove they still had a claim to youth.

Delnar dismissed Archytas and remained seated behind the small folding table on which were strewn papers and despatches. Sieben, oblivious of the tension, slumped to Delnar's narrow bed. Druss lifted a flagon of wine to his lips, taking three great swallows.

'He is not welcome here – and, therefore, neither are you,' said Delnar, as Druss replaced the flagon.

The axeman wiped his mouth with the back of his hand. 'Had I been sure you were here, I would not have brought him,' he said. 'I take it the army has moved on.'

'Yes. They travelled south. Gorben has landed. You may borrow two horses, but I want you gone by sundown.'

'I came to give the men something to think about besides waiting,' said Druss. 'They won't need me now. So I'll just rest here for a couple of days then head back to Skoda.'

'I said you're not welcome here,' said Delnar.

The axeman's eyes grew cold as he stared at the Earl. 'Listen to me,' said Druss, as softly as he could. 'I know why you feel as you do. In your place I would feel the same. But I am not in your place. I am Druss. And I walk where I will. If I say I will stay here then I shall. Now I like you, laddie. But cross me and I'll kill you.'

Delnar nodded and rubbed his chin. The situation had gone as far

733

as he could allow it. He had hoped Druss would leave, but he could not force him. What could be more ludicrous than the Earl of the North ordering Drenai warriors to attack Druss the Legend? Especially since the man had been invited to the camp by the Lord of Hosts. Delnar did not fear Druss, because he did not fear death. His life had been ended for him six years before. Since then his wife, Vashti, had shamed him with many more affairs. Three years ago she had delivered to him a daughter, a delightful child he adored, even if he doubted his part in her conception. Vashti had run away to the capital soon after, leaving the child at Delnoch. The Earl had heard his wife was now living with a Ventrian merchant in the rich western quarter. Taking a deep, calming breath, he met Druss' eyes.

'Stay then,' he said. 'But keep him from my sight.'

Druss nodded. He glanced down at Sieben. The poet was asleep.

'This should never have come between us,' said Delnar.

'These things happen,' said Druss. 'Sieben always had a weakness for beautiful women.'

'I shouldn't hate him. But he was the first I knew about. He was the man who destroyed my dreams. You understand?'

'We will leave tomorrow,' said Druss wearily. 'But for now let's walk in the pass. I need some air in my lungs.'

The Earl rose and donned his helm and red cape, and together the two warriors walked through the camp and on up the steep rocky slope to the mouth of the pass. It ran for almost a mile, narrowing at the centre to less than fifty paces, where the ground dropped away gently in a rolling slope down to a stream that flowed across the valley floor, angling towards the sea some three miles distant. From the mouth of the pass, through the jagged peaks, the sea glittered in the fragmented sunlight, glowing gold and blue. A fresh easterly wind cooled Druss's face.

'Good place for a defensive battle,' said the axeman, scanning the pass. 'At the centre any attacking force would be funnelled in and numbers would be useless.'

'And they would have to charge uphill,' said Delnar. 'I think Abalayn was hoping Gorben would land here. We could have sealed him in the bay. Left his army to starve, and brought the fleet round to harry his ships.'

'He's too canny for that,' said Druss. 'A more wily warrior you will not find.'

'You liked him?'

'He was always fair with me,' said Druss, keeping his tone neutral.

Delnar nodded. 'They say he's become a tyrant.'

Druss shrugged. 'He once told me it was the curse of kings.'

'He was right,' said Delnar. 'You know your friend Bodasen is still one of his top generals?'

'I wouldn't doubt it. He's a loyal man, with a good eye for strategy.'

'I should think you are relieved to miss this battle, my friend,' commented the Earl.

Druss nodded. 'The years I served with the Immortals were happy ones, I'll grant that. And I have other friends among them. But you are right, I would hate to come up against Bodasen. We were brothers in battle, and I love the man dearly.'

'Let's go back. I'll arrange some food for you.'

The Earl saluted the sentry at the mouth of the pass and the two men made their way up the slope to the camp. Delnar took him to a square white tent, lifting the flap for Druss to enter first. Within were four men. They leapt to their feet as the Earl followed Druss inside.

'Stand easy,' said Delnar. 'This is Druss, an old friend of mine. He'll be staying with us for a while. I'd like you to make him welcome.' He turned to Druss. 'I believe you know Certak and Archytas. Well, this black-bearded reprobate is Diagoras.' Druss liked the look of the man; his smile was quick and friendly, and the gleam in his dark eyes bespoke humour. But more than this he had what soldiers call 'the look of eagles' and Druss knew instantly he was a warrior born.

'Nice to meet you, sir. We've heard a lot about you.'

'And this is Orases,' said Certak. 'He's new with us. From Drenan.'

Druss shook hands with the young man, noting the fat around his middle and the softness of his grip. He seemed pleasant enough, but beside Diagoras and Certak he seemed boyish and clumsy.

'Would you like some food?' asked Diagoras, after the Earl had departed.

'I certainly would,' muttered Druss. 'My stomach thinks my throat's been sliced.'

'I'll get it,' said Orases swiftly.

'I think he's a little in awe of you, Druss,' said Diagoras as Orases raced from the tent.

'It happens,' said Druss. 'Why don't you ask me to sit down?'

Diagoras chuckled and pulled up a chair. Druss reversed it and sat. The others followed suit and the atmosphere eased. The world is getting younger, thought Druss, wishing he had never come.

'May I see your axe, sir?' asked Certak.

'Certainly,' said Druss, pulling Snaga smoothly from the oiled sheath. In the older man's hands the weapon seemed almost weightless, but as it passed to Certak the officer grunted.

'The blade that smote the Chaos Hound,' whispered Certak, turning it over in his hands, then returning it to Druss.

'Do you believe everything you hear?' said Archytas, sneering.

'Did it happen, Druss?' said Diagoras, before Certak could answer.

'Yes. A long time ago. But it scarce pierced its hide.'

'Was it true they were sacrificing a princess?' asked Certak.

735

'No. Two small children. But tell me about yourselves,' said Druss. 'Wherever I go people ask me the same questions and I get very bored.'

'If you're that bored,' said Archytas, 'why do you take the poet with you on all your adventures?'

'What does that mean?'

'Quite simply that it seems strange for a man as modest as you seem to be to take a saga master with him. Although it proved very convenient.'

'Convenient?'

'Well, he created you, didn't he? Druss the Legend. Fame and fortune. Surely any wandering warrior with such a companion could have been boosted into legend?'

'I suppose that's true,' said Druss. 'I've known a lot of men in my time whose deeds are forgotten, but who were worthy of remembrance in song or tale. I never really thought of it before.'

'How much of Sieben's great saga is exaggerated?' asked Archytas.

'Oh do shut up,' snapped Diagoras.

'No,' said Druss, lifting his hand. 'You've no idea how good this is. Always people ask me about the stories, and whenever I tell them they are – shall we say – rounded, they disbelieve me. But it's true. The stories are not about me. They are based on the truth, but they have grown. I was the seed; they have become the tree. I never met a princess in my life. But to answer your first question. I never took Sieben on my quest. He just came. I think he was bored and wanted to see the world.'

'But did you slay the werebeast in the mountains of Pelucid?' said Certak.

'No. I just killed a lot of men in a lot of battles.'

'Then why do you allow the poems to be sung?' asked Archytas.

'If I could have stopped them I would,' Druss told him. 'The first few years of my return were a nightmare. But I've got used to it since. People believe what they want to believe. The truth rarely makes a difference. People need heroes, and if they don't have any, they invent them.'

Orases returned with a bowl of stew and a loaf of black bread. 'Have I missed anything?' he asked.

'Not really,' said Druss. 'We were just chatting.'

'Druss has been telling us that his legend is all lies,' said Archytas. 'It's been most revealing.'

Druss chuckled with genuine humour and shook his head. 'You see,' he told Diagoras and Certak, 'people believe what they want to believe, and hear only what they wish to hear.' He glanced across at the tight-lipped Archytas. 'Boy, there was a time when your blood would now be staining the walls of this tent. But I was younger then,

736

and headstrong. Now I get no delight from killing puppies. But I am still Druss, so I tell you this, walk softly around me from now on.'

Archytas forced a laugh. 'You cause me no concern, old man,' he said. 'I don't think . . .'

Druss rose swiftly and backhanded him across the face. Archytas hurtled backwards over his chair to lie groaning on the tent floor, his nose smashed and leaking blood.

'No, you don't think,' said Druss. 'Now give me that stew, Orases. It must be getting cold.'

'Welcome to Skeln, Druss,' said Diagoras, grinning.

For three days Druss remained at the camp. Sieben had woken in Delnar's trent, complaining of chest pains. The regimental surgeon examined him and ordered him to rest, explaining to Druss and Delnar that the poet had suffered a serious spasm of the heart.

'How bad is it?' asked Druss.

The surgeon's eyes were bleak. 'If he rests for a week or two he could be fine. The danger is that the heart might cramp suddenly – and fail. He's not a young man, and the journey here was hard for him.'

'I see,' said Druss. 'Thank you.' He turned to Delnar. 'I am sorry, but we must stay.'

'Do not concern yourself, my friend,' responded the Earl, waving his hand. 'Despite what I said when you arrived, you are welcome. But, tell me, what happened between you and Archytas? It looks like a mountain fell on his face.'

'His nose tapped my hand,' grunted Druss.

Delnar smiled. 'He's a somewhat loathsome character. But you had better watch out for him. He's stupid enough to challenge you.'

'No, he won't,' said Druss. 'He may be foolish, but he's not in love with death. Even a puppy knows to hide from a wolf.'

On the morning of the fourth day, as Druss sat with Sieben, one of the lookout sentries came running headlong into the camp. Within minutes chaos reigned as men raced for their armour. Hearing the commotion, Druss walked from the tent. A young soldier ran by. Druss's arm snaked out, catching the man's cloak and wrenching him to a stop.

'What's going on?' asked Druss.

'The Ventrians are here!' shouted the soldier, tearing himself loose and running towards the pass. Druss swore and strode after him. At the mouth of the pass he halted, staring out over the stream.

Standing in armoured line upon line, their lances gleaming, were the warriors of Gorben, filling the valley from mountainside to mountainside. At the centre of the mass was the tent of the Emperor, and around it were massed the black and silver ranks of the Immortals.

Drenai warriors scurried past him as Druss made his slow way to Delnar's side.

'I told you he was cunning,' said Druss. 'He must have sent a token force to Penrac, knowing it would draw our army south.'

'Yes. But what now?'

'You're not left with many choices,' said Druss.

'True.'

The Drenai warriors spread out across the narrow centre of the pass in three ranks, their round shields glinting in the morning sun, their white horsehair-crested helms flowing in the breeze.

'How many here are veterans?' asked Druss.

'About half. I've placed them at the front.'

'How long will it take a rider to reach Penrac?'

'I've sent a man. The army should be back in about ten days.'

'You think we've got ten days?' asked Druss.

'No. But, as you say, there aren't too many choices. What do you think Gorben will do?'

'First he'll talk. He'll ask you to surrender. You'd better request a few hours to make up your mind. Then he'll send the Panthians in. They're an undisciplined bunch but they fight like devils. We should see them off. Their wicker shields and stabbing spears are no match for Drenai armour. After that he'll test all his troops on us . . .'

'The Immortals?'

'Not until the end, when we're weary and finished.'

'It's a gloomy picture,' said Delnar.

'It's a bitch,' agreed Druss.

'Will you stand with us, axeman?'

'Did you expect me to leave?'

Delnar chuckled suddenly. 'Why shouldn't you? I wish I could.'

In the first Drenai line Diagoras sheathed his sword, wiping his sweating palm on his red cloak.

'There are enough of them,' he said.

Beside him Certak nodded. 'Masterly understatement. They look like they could run right over us.'

'We'll have to surrender, won't we?' whispered Orases from behind them, blinking sweat from his eyes.

'Somehow I don't think that's likely,' said Certak. 'Though I admit it's a welcome thought.'

A rider on a black stallion forded the stream and galloped towards the Drenai line. Delnar walked through the ranks, Druss beside him, and waited.

The rider wore the black and silver armour of a general of the Immortals. Reining in before the two men, he leaned forward on the pommel of his saddle.

'Druss?' he said. 'Is that you?'

Druss studied the gaunt features, the silver-streaked dark hair hanging in two braids.

'Welcome to Skeln, Bodasen,' answered the axeman.

'I'm sorry to find you here. I was meaning to ride for Skoda as soon as we took Drenan. Is Rowena well?'

'Yes. And you?'

'As you see me. Fit and well. Yourself?'

'I'm not complaining.'

'And Sieben?'

'He's asleep in a tent.'

'He always knew when to avoid battles,' said Bodasen, forcing a smile. 'And that's what this is looking like unless commonsense prevails. Are you the leader?' he asked Delnar.

'I am. What message do you bring?'

'Merely this. Tomorrow morning my Emperor will ride through this pass. He would consider it a courtesy if you could remove your men from his path.'

'We will think on it,' said Delnar.

'I would advise you to think well,' said Bodasen, turning his mount. 'I'll be seeing you, Druss. Take care!'

'You too.'

Bodasen spurred the stallion back towards the stream and on through the Panthian ranks.

Druss beckoned Delnar aside, away from the men. 'It's pointless standing here all day staring at them,' he said. 'Why don't you order them to stand down and we'll send half of them back to bring up some blankets and fuel?'

'You don't think they'll attack today?'

'No. Why should they? They know we'll not be reinforced tonight. Tomorrow will come soon enough.' Druss tramped back to the camp, stopping in to see the poet. Sieben was asleep. Druss pulled up a chair and stared down at the poet's lined face. Uncharacteristically he stroked the balding head. Sieben opened his eyes.

'Oh it's you,' he said. 'What's all the fuss about?'

'The Ventrians tricked us. They're on the other side of the mountain.'

Sieben swore softly. Druss chuckled. 'You just lie here, poet, and I'll tell you all about it once we've sent them running.'

'The Immortals are here too?' asked Sieben.

'Of course.'

'Wonderful. A nice little outing you promised me. A few speeches. And what do we get? Another war.'

'I saw Bodasen. He's looking well.'

'Marvellous. Maybe after he's killed us we can have a drink together and chat about old times.'

'You take things too seriously, poet. Rest now, and later I'll have some men carry you up to the pass. You'd hate to miss the action, now, wouldn't you?'

'Couldn't you get them to carry me all the way back to Skoda?'

'Later,' grinned Druss. 'Anyway, I must be getting back.'

The axeman walked swiftly up the mountain slopes and sat on a boulder at the mouth of the pass, gazing intently at the enemy camp.

'What are you thinking about?' asked Delnar, moving up to join him.

'I was remembering something I told an old friend a long time ago.'

'What was that?'

'If you want to win: Attack.'

Bodasen dismounted before the Emperor and knelt, pressing his forehead to the earth. Then he rose. From a distance the Ventrian looked as he always had, powerful, black-bearded and keen of eye. But he could no longer stand close inspection. His hair and beard showed the unhealthy sheen of heavy, dark dye, his painted face glowed with unnatural colour and his eyes saw treachery in every shadow. His followers, even those like Bodasen who had served him for decades, knew never to stare into his face, addressing all their remarks to the gilded griffin on his breastplate. No one was allowed to approach him bearing a weapon, and he had not granted a private audience to anyone in years. Always he wore armour – even, it was said, when he slept. His food was tasted by slaves, and he had taken to wearing gloves of soft leather, in the belief that poison might be spread on the outside of his golden goblets.

Bodasen waited for permission to speak, glancing up swiftly to read the expression on the Emperor's face. Gorben was staring moodily.

'Was that Druss?' he asked.

'Aye, my lord.'

'So even he has turned against me.'

'He is a Drenai, my lord.'

'Do you dispute with me, Bodasen?'

'No, sire. Of course not.'

'Good. I want Druss brought before me for judgement. Such treachery must be answered with swift justice. You understand?'

'Yes, sire.'

'Will the Drenai give us the way?'

'I think not, sire. But it will not take long to clear the path. Even with Druss there. Shall I order the men to stand down and prepare camp?'

'No. Let them stay in ranks for a while. Let the Drenai see their power and their strength.'

'Yes, sire.'

Bodasen backed away.

'Are you still loyal?' asked the Emperor, suddenly.

Bodasen's mouth was dry. 'As I have always been, lord.'

'Yet Druss was your friend.'

'Even though that is true, sire, I will see him dragged before you in chains. Or his head presented to you, should he be slain in the defence.'

The Emperor nodded, then turned his painted face to stare up at the pass.

'I want them dead. All dead,' he whispered.

In the cool of the pre-dawn haze the Drenai formed their lines, each warrior bearing a rounded shield and a short stabbing sword. Their sabres had been put aside, for in close formation a swinging long-sword could be as deadly to a comrade standing close as to an enemy bearing down. The men were nervous, constantly rechecking breastplate straps, or discovering the bronze greaves protecting their lower legs were too tight, too loose, too anything. Cloaks were removed and left in tight red rolls by the mountain wall behind the ranks. Both Druss and Delnar knew this was the time a man's courage was under the greatest strain. Gorben could do many things. The dice were in his hands. All the Drenai could do was wait.

'Do you think he'll attack immediately the sun comes up?' asked Delnar.

Druss shook his head. 'I don't think so. He'll let the fear work for about an hour. But then again – you can never tell with him.'

The two hundred men in the front rank shared the same emotions now, with varying intensity. Pride, for they had been singled out as the best; fear, for they would be the first to die. Some had regrets. Many had not written home for weeks, others had left friends and relatives with bitter words. Many were the thoughts.

Druss made his way to the centre of the first line, calling for Diagoras and Certak to stand on either side of him.

'Move away from me a little,' he said. 'Give me swinging room.' The line shuffled apart. Druss loosened his shoulders, stretching the muscles of his arms and back. The sky lightened. Druss cursed. The disadvantage for the defenders – apart from the numbers of the enemy – was that the sun rose in their eyes.

Across the stream the black-skinned Panthians sharpened their spears. There was little fear among them. The ivory-skins facing them were few in number. They would be swept away like antelope before a veldt blaze. Gorben waited until the sun cleared the peaks, then gave the order to attack.

The Panthians surged to their feet, a swelling roar of hatred rising from their throats, a wall of sound that hurtled up into the pass, washing over the defenders.

'Listen to that!' bellowed Druss. 'That's not strength you hear. That's the sound of terror!'

Five thousand warriors raced towards the pass, their feet drumming a savage beat on the rocky slopes, echoing high into the peaks.

Druss hawked and spat. Then he began to laugh, a rich, full sound that brought a few chuckles from the men around him.

'Gods, I've missed this,' he shouted. 'Come on, you cowsons!' he yelled at the Panthians. 'Move yourselves!'

Delnar, at the centre of the second line, smiled and drew his sword.

With the enemy a bare hundred paces distant, the men of the third line looked to Archytas. He raised his arm. The men dropped their shields and stooped, rising with barbed javelins. Each man had five of them at his feet.

The Panthians were almost upon them.

'Now!' yelled Archytas.

Arms flew forward and two hundred shafts of death hurtled into the black mass.

'Again!' bellowed Archytas.

The front ranks of the advancing horde disappeared screaming, to be trampled by the men behind them. The charge faltered as the tribesmen tripped and fell over fallen comrades. The mountain walls, narrowing like an hour-glass, slowed the attack still further.

Then the lines clashed.

A spear lunged for Druss. Blocking it with his axe blades, he dragged a back-hand cut that sheared through the wicker shield and the flesh beyond. The man grunted as Snaga clove through his ribcage. Druss tore the weapon clear, parried another thrust and hammered his axe into his opponent's face. Beside him Certak blocked a spear with his shield, expertly sliding his gladius into a gleaming black chest. A spear sliced his upper thigh, but there was no pain. He counter-thrust, and his attacker fell across the growing pile of corpses in front of the line.

The Panthians now found themselves leaping upon the bodies of their comrades in their desperation to breach the line. The floor of the pass became slippery with blood, but the Drenai held.

A tall warrior threw aside his wicker shield and hurdled the wall of dead, spear raised. He hurtled towards Druss. Snaga buried itself in his chest, but the weight of the man bore Druss back, tearing his axe from his hands. A second man leapt at him. Druss turned aside the thrusting spear with his mail-covered gauntlets, and smashed a cruel punch to the man's jaw. As the warrior crumpled Druss grabbed him by the throat and groin and hoisted the body above his head, hurling him back over the corpse wall into the faces of the advancing warriors. Twisting, he wrenched his axe clear of the first man's body.

'Come on, my lads,' he bellowed. 'Time to send them home!'

Leaping up on the corpses, he cut left and right, opening up a space in the Panthian ranks. Diagoras couldn't believe his eyes. He swore. Then leapt to join him.

The Drenai advanced, clambering over the Panthian dead, their swords red, their eyes grim.

At the centre the tribesmen struggled first to overcome the madman with the axe, then to get back from him, as other Drenai warriors joined him.

Fear flashed through their ranks like a plague.

Within minutes they were streaming back across the valley floor.

Druss led the warriors back into position. His jerkin was stained with blood, and his beard spotted with crimson. Opening his shirt, he removed a towel and wiped his sweating face. Doffing his helm of black and silver, he scratched his head.

'Well, lads,' he called out, his deep voice echoing in the crags, 'how does it feel to have earned your pay?'

'They're coming again!' someone shouted.

Druss' voice cut through the rising fear. 'Of course they are,' he bellowed. 'They don't know when they're beaten. Front rank fall back, second rank stand to. Let's spread the glory!'

Druss remained with the front line, Diagoras and Certak alongside him.

By dusk they had beaten off four charges for the loss of only forty men – thirty dead, ten wounded.

The Panthians had lost over eight hundred men.

It was a macabre scene that night as the Drenai sat around small campfires, the dancing flames throwing weird shadows across the wall of corpses in the pass making it seem as if the bodies writhed in the darkness. Delnar ordered the men to gather all the wicker shields they could find and recover as many javelins and spears as were still usable.

Towards midnight many of the veterans were asleep, but others found the excitement of the day too fresh, and they sat in small groups, talking in low tones.

Delnar walked from group to group, sitting with them, joking and lifting their spirits. Druss slept in the tent of Sieben, high in the mouth of the pass. The poet had watched part of the day's action from his bed, and fallen asleep during the long afternoon.

Diagoras, Orases and Certak sat with half a dozen other men as Delnar approached and joined them.

'How are you feeling?' asked the Earl.

The men smiled. What answer could they give?

'Can I ask a question, sir?' asked Orases.

'Certainly.'

'How is it that Druss has stayed alive so long? I mean, he has no defence to speak of.'

'It's a good point,' said the Earl, doffing his helm and running his fingers through his hair, enjoying the cool of the night. 'The reason is contained in your question. It is because he has no defence. That terrible axe rarely leaves a man with a non-mortal wound. To kill Druss you have to be prepared to die. No, not just prepared. You would have to attack Druss in the sure knowledge that he will kill you. Now, most men want to live. You understand?'

'Not really, sir,' admitted Orases.

'Do you know the one kind of warrior no one wants to face?' asked Delnar.

'No, sir.'

'The baresark, sometimes called the berserker, a man whose killing frenzy makes him oblivious to pain and uncaring about life. He throws his armour away and attacks the enemy, cutting and killing until he himself is cut to pieces. I saw a baresark once who had lost an arm. As the blood spewed from the stump he aimed it in the faces of his attackers and carried on fighting until he dropped.

'No one wants to fight such a man. Now, Druss is even more formidable than the berserker. He has all the virtues, but his killing frenzy is controlled. He can think clearly. And when you add the man's awesome strength he becomes a veritable machine of destruction.'

'But surely a chance thrust amid the melee,' said Diagoras. 'A sudden slip on a pool of blood. He could die as well as any other man.'

'Yes,' admitted Delnar. 'I do not say that he won't die in such a way; only that the odds are all with Druss. Most of you saw him today. Those who fought alongside him had no time to study his technique, but others of you caught a glimpse of the Legend. He's always balanced, always moving. His eyes are never still. His peripheral vision is incredible. He can sense danger even amid chaos. Today a very brave Panthian warrior hurled himself on the axe, dragging it from Druss's hand. A second warrior followed. Did anyone see it?'

'I did,' said Orases.

'But you didn't really learn from it. The first Panthian died to remove Druss's weapon. The second was to engage him while the others breached the line. Had they come through then, our force might have been split and pushed back into the walls of the mountain. Druss saw that instantly. That's why, although he could have just knocked his attacker senseless and retrieved his axe, he hurled the man back into the breach. Now think on this: in that instant Druss had seen the danger, formulated a plan of action, and carried it out. More even than this. He retrieved the axe and took the battle to the enemy. That's what broke them. Druss had judged exactly the right moment to attack. It's the instinct of the born warrior.'

'But how did he know we would follow him?' asked Diagoras. 'He could have been cut to pieces.'

'Even in this he was confident. That's why he asked you and Certak to stand alongside him. Now that's a compliment. He knew you would respond, and that others who might not follow him would follow you.'

'He has told you this?' asked Certak.

The Earl chuckled. 'No. In a way Druss would be as surprised to hear it as you are. His actions are not reasoned. As I said, they are instinctive. If we live through this you will learn much.'

'Do you think we will?' asked Orases.

'If we are strong,' lied Delnar smoothly, surprised at himself.

The Panthians came again at dawn, creeping up through the pass as the Drenai waited, swords drawn. But they did not attack. Under the bewildered eyes of the defenders, they hauled away the bodies of their comrades.

It was a bizarre scene. Delnar ordered the Drenai back twenty paces to make room for the work, and the warriors waited. Delnar sheathed his sword and moved alongside Druss in the front line.

'What do you think?'

'I think they're preparing the ground for chariots,' said Druss.

'Horses will never attack a solid line. They'll pull up short,' the Earl pointed out.

'Take a look yonder,' muttered the axeman.

On the far side of the stream, the Ventrian army had parted, making way for the gleaming bronze chariots of the Tantrians. With their huge wheels bearing sickle blades, serrated and deadly, each chariot was drawn by two horses and manned by a driver and a spear carrier.

For an hour the clearing of bodies continued, while the chariots formed a line in the valley below. As the Panthians withdrew, Delnar ordered forward thirty men carrying the wicker shields retrieved from the battle the day before. The shields were spread in a line across the pass and doused with lantern oil.

Delnar placed his hand on Druss's shoulder. 'Take the line fifty paces forward, beyond the shields. When they attack, break formation left and right and make for the cover of the rocks. Once they are through we will fire the shields. Hopefully that will stop them. The second rank will engage the chariots while your line holds the following infantry.'

'Sounds good,' said Druss.

'If it doesn't work we won't try it again,' said Delnar.

745

Druss grinned.

Along the line of chariots the drivers were pulling silken hoods over the eyes of the horses. Druss led his two hundred men forward, hurdling the wall of wicker shields, Diagoras, Certak and Archytas beside him.

The thunder of hooves on the valley floor echoed through the crags as two hundred charioteers whipped their horses into the gallop.

With the chariots almost upon them Druss bellowed the order to break ranks. As men raced to the safety of the mountain walls on either side, the enemy thundered on towards the second line. Flaming torches were flung upon the wall of oil-soaked wicker shields. Black smoke billowed instantly, followed by dancing flames. The breeze carried the smoke towards the east, burning the flaring nostrils of the hooded horses. Whinnying their terror, they tried to turn, ignoring the biting whips of the charioteers.

Instantly all was confusion. The second line of chariots tore into the first, horses falling, vehicles overturning, hurling screaming men to the jagged rocks.

And into the milling chaos leapt the Drenai, hurdling the dying flames to fall upon the Ventrian spearmen, whose lances were useless at such close quarters.

Gorben, from his vantage point a half-mile away, ordered a legion of infantry into the fray.

Druss and the two hundred Drenai swordsmen re-formed across the pass, locking shields against the new attack, presenting a glittering wall of blades to the silver-armoured infantry.

Crushing the skull of one man and gutting a second, Druss stepped back, casting a lightning glance to left and right.

The line held.

More Drenai fell in this attack than on the previous day, but their numbers were few compared with the losses suffered by the Ventrians.

Only a handful of chariots burst back through the Drenai front line, there to crash and cut a path through their own infantry in their desire to be free of the pass.

Hour upon bloody hour the battle continued, savagely fought by both sides, with no thought of quarter.

The silver-clad Ventrian infantry continued to press their attack, but by dusk their efforts lacked conviction and weight.

Furious, Gorben ordered their general forward into the pass.

'Lead them hard, or you'll beg to be allowed to die,' he promised.

The general's body fell within the hour, and the infantry slunk back across the stream in the gathering gloom of twilight.

Ignoring the dancing troupe performing before him, Gorben lay back on the silk-covered couch, conversing in low tones with Bodasen. The

Emperor wore full battle-dress, and behind him stood the massively muscled Panthian bodyguard who for the last five years had been Gorben's executioner. He killed with his hands, sometimes by strangling his victims slowly, at other times gouging his thumbs through the eye sockets of the hapless prisoners. All executions were performed before the Emperor, and scarcely a week passed without such a grisly scene.

The Panthian had once killed a man by crushing his skull between his hands, to the applause of Gorben and his courtiers.

Bodasen was sickened by it all, but he was caught within a web of his own making. Through the years, naked ambition had driven him to the heights of power. He now commanded the Immortals and was, under Gorben, the most powerful man in Ventria. But the position was perilous. Gorben's paranoia was such that few of his generals survived for long, and Bodasen had begun to feel the Emperor's eyes upon him.

Tonight he had invited Gorben to his tent, promising him an evening of entertainment, but the king was in a surly, argumentative mood, and Bodasen trod warily.

'You thought the Panthians and the chariots would fail, did you not?' asked Gorben. The question was loaded with menace. If the answer was yes, the Emperor would ask why Bodasen had not stated his view. Was he not the Emperor's military advisor? What was the use of an advisor who gave no advice? If the answer was no, then his military judgement would prove to be lacking.

'We have fought many wars over the years, my lord,' he said. 'In most of them we have suffered reverses. You have always said "Unless we try we will never know how to succeed".'

'You think we should send in my Immortals?' asked Gorben. Always before the Emperor had called them *your* Immortals. Bodasen licked his lips and smiled.

'There is no doubt they could clear the pass swiftly. The Drenai are fighting well. They are disciplined. But they know they cannot withstand the Immortals. But that decision is yours alone, my lord. Only you have the divine mastery of tactics. Men like myself are mere reflections of your greatness.'

'Then where are the men who can think for themselves?' snapped the Emperor.

'I must be honest with you, sire,' said Bodasen quickly. 'You will not find such a man.'

'Why?'

'You seek men who can think as rapidly as you yourself, with your own penetrating insight. Such men do not exist. You are supremely gifted, sire. The gods would visit such wisdom on only one man in ten generations.'

747

'You speak truly,' said Gorben. 'But there is little joy in being a man apart, separated from his fellows by his god-given gifts. I am hated, you know,' he whispered, eyes darting to the sentries beyond the tent entrance.

'There will always be those that are jealous, sire,' said Bodasen.

'Are you jealous of me, Bodasen?'

'Yes, sire.'

Gorben rolled to his side, eyes gleaming. 'Speak on.'

'In all the years I have served and loved you, lord, I have always wished I could be more like you. For then I could have served you better. A man would be a fool not to be jealous of you. But he is insane if he hates you because you are what he never can be.'

'Well said. You are an honest man. One of the few I can trust. Not like Druss, who promised to serve me, and now thwarts my destiny. I want him dead, my general. I want his head brought to me.'

'It shall be done, sire,' said Bodasen.

Gorben leaned back, gazing around him at the tent and its contents. 'Your quarters are almost as lavish as my own,' he said.

'Only because they are filled with gifts from you, sire,' answered Bodasen swiftly.

Faces and armour blackened by dirt mixed with oil, Druss and fifty swordsmen silently waded the narrow stream under a moonless sky.

Praying the clouds would not part, Druss led the men single-file towards the eastern bank, axe in hand, blackened shield held before him. Once ashore Druss squatted at the centre of the small group, pointing towards two dozing sentries by a dying fire. Diagoras and two others ghosted from the group, approaching the sentries silently, daggers in hand. The men died without a sound. Removing torches hastily constructed from the wicker shields of Panthian warriors, Druss and the soldiers approached the sentries' fire.

Stepping over the bodies, Druss lit his torch and ran towards the nearest tent. His men followed suit, racing from tent to tent, until flames leapt thirty feet into the night sky.

Suddenly all was chaos, as screaming men burst from blazing canopies to fall before the swords of the Drenai. Druss raced ahead, cutting a crimson path through the confused Ventrians, his eyes fixed on the tent ahead, its glowing griffin outlined in the towering flames. Close behind came Certak and a score of warriors bearing torches. Wrenching open the flaps, Druss leapt inside.

'Damn,' he grunted, 'Gorben's not here! Curse it!'

Setting torch to silk, Druss shouted for his men to regroup, then led them back towards the stream. No concerted effort was made to stop them, as Ventrians milled in confusion, many of them half-clothed, others filling helmets with water, forming human chains to battle the fierce inferno racing on the wings of the wind throughout the Ventrian camp.

A small group of Immortals, swords in hand, collided with Druss as he raced towards the stream. Snaga leapt forward, braining the first. The second died as Diagoras back-handed a slash across his throat. The battle was brief and bloody, but the element of surprise was with the Drenai. Bursting through the front line of swordsmen, Druss crashed his axe through one man's side before reversing a slashing swipe across another's shoulder.

Bodasen ran from his tent, sword in hand. Swiftly gathering a small group of Immortals, he raced past the flames towards the battle. A Drenai warrior loomed before him. The man aimed a thrust at Bodasen's unprotected body. The Ventrian parried and launched a devastating riposte that tore open the man's throat. Bodasen stepped over the body and led his men forward.

Druss killed two men, then bellowed for the Drenai to fall back.

The pounding of feet from behind caused him to swivel and face the new force. With the fire behind them Druss could not make out faces.

Nearby Archytas despatched a warrior, then saw Druss standing alone.

Without thinking, he raced towards the Immortals. In that instant Druss charged. His axe rose and fell, shearing through armour and bone. Diagoras and Certak joined him, with four other Drenai warriors. The battle was brief. Only one Ventrian broke clear, hurling himself to the right and rolling to his feet behind Archytas. The tall Drenai turned on his heel and engaged the man. Archytas grinned as their swords met. The man was old, though skilful, and no match for the young Drenai. Their swords glittered in the firelight: parry, riposte, counter, thrust and block. Suddenly the Ventrian seemed to trip. Archytas leapt forward. His opponent ducked and rolled to his feet in one flowing movement, his sword ramming into Archytas' groin.

'You live and learn, boy,' hissed Bodasen, dragging his blade clear. Bodasen turned as more Immortals ran forward. Gorben wanted Druss's head. Tonight he would give it to him.

Druss wrenched his axe from a man's body and sprinted for the stream and the relative sanctuary of the pass.

A warrior leapt into his path. Snaga sang through the air, smashing the man's sword to shards. A back-hand cut shattered his ribs. As Druss passed him, the man reached out, grabbing his shoulder. In the gleam of the flames, the axeman saw it was Bodasen. The dying Immortal general gripped Druss's jerkin, trying to slow him. Druss kicked him aside and ran on.

Bodasen fell heavily and rolled, watching the burly figure of the axeman and his companions fording the stream.

The Ventrian's vision swam. He closed his eyes. Weariness settled on him like a cloak. Memories danced in his mind. He heard a great noise like the crashing of the sea, and saw again the corsair ship bearing down upon them, gliding out of the past. Once more he raced with Druss to board her, carrying the fight to the aft deck.

Damn! He should have realised Druss would never change.

Attack. Always attack.

He opened his eyes, blinking to clear his vision. Druss was safely on the other side of the stream now, leading the warriors back to the Drenai line.

Bodasen tried to move, but agony lanced him. Carefully he probed the wound in his side, his sticky fingers feeling the broken ribs and the rush of arterial blood from the gaping gash.

It was over.

No more fear. No more insanity. No more bowing and scraping to the painted madman.

In a way he was relieved.

His whole life had been an anticlimax after that battle with Druss against the corsairs. In that one towering moment he had been alive, standing with Druss against . . .

They brought his body to the Emperor in the pink light of dawn.

And Gorben wept.

Around them the camp was a shambles. Gorben's generals stood beside the throne, uneasy and silent. Gorben covered the body with his own cloak and dried his eyes on a white linen towel. Then he turned his attention to the man kneeling before him, flanked by Immortal guards.

'Bodasen dead. My tent destroyed. My camp in flames. And you, you pathetic wretch, were the officer of the guard. A score of men invade my camp, killing my beloved general, and you still live. Explain yourself!'

'My lord, I sat with you in Bodasen's tent – by your order.'

'So now it is my fault the camp was attacked!'

'No, sire . . .'

'No, sire,' mimicked Gorben. 'I should think not. Your sentries were sleeping. Now they are dead. Do you not think it fitting for you to join them?'

'Sire?'

'Join them, I say. Take your blade and slice your veins.'

The officer drew his ornamental dagger, reversed it, then plunged the blade into his belly. For a moment there was no movement. Then the man began to scream and writhe. Gorben drew his sword, slashing the blade through the man's neck.

'He couldn't even do that right,' said Gorben.

Druss entered Sieben's tent and hurled his axe to the floor. The poet was awake, but lying silently watching the stars when Druss arrived.

The axeman sat down on the floor, his great head slumped to his chest, staring at his hands, clenching and unclenching his fists. The poet sensed his despair. He struggled to sit up, the ache in his chest becoming a stabbing pain. He grunted. Druss's head came up, his back straightened.

'How are you feeling?' asked Druss.

'Fine. I take it the raid failed?'

'Gorben was not in his tent.'

'What is wrong, Druss?'

The axeman's head slumped forward and he didn't answer. Sieben climbed from the bed and made his way to Druss, sitting beside him.

'Come along, old horse, tell me.'

'I killed Bodasen. He came at me out of shadows and I cut him down.'

Sieben put his arm on Druss's shoulder. 'What can I say?'

'You could tell me why – why it had to be me.'

'I can't tell you that. I wish I could. But you did not travel across the ocean, seeking to kill him, Druss. He came here. With an army.'

'I only ever had a few friends in my life,' said Druss. 'Eskodas died in my home. I've killed Bodasen. And I've brought you here to die for a pile of rock in a forgotten pass. I'm so tired, poet. I should never have come here.'

Druss rose and left the tent. Dipping his hands in the water-barrel outside, he washed his face. His back was painful, especially under the shoulder-blade where the spear had cut him so many years before. A swollen vein in his right leg nagged at him.

'I don't know if you can hear me, Bodasen,' he whispered, staring up at the stars, 'but I am sorry it had to be me. You were a good friend in happier days, and a man to walk the mountains with.'

Returning to the tent, he found Sieben had fallen asleep in the chair. Druss lifted him gently and carried him to his bed, covering him with a thick blanket. 'You're worn out, poet,' he said. He felt for Sieben's pulse. It was ragged but strong. 'Stay with me, Sieben,' he told him. 'I'll get you home.'

As the dawn's rays bathed the peaks Druss walked slowly down the rocky slope to stand again with the Drenai line.

For eight terrible days Skeln became a charnel house, littered with swelling corpses and the foul stench of putrefaction. Gorben threw legion after legion up into the pass, only to see them stumble back defeated and dejected. The dwindling band of defenders was held together by the indomitable courage of the black-garbed axeman, whose terrifying skill dismayed the Ventrians. Some said he was a demon, others a god of war. Old tales were recalled.

The Chaos Warrior walked again in the stories told around Ventrian camp-fires.

751

Only the Immortals stayed aloof from the fears. They knew it would fall to them to clear the pass, and they knew it would not be easy.

On the eighth night Gorben at last gave in to the insistent demands of his generals. Time was running out. The way had to be taken tomorrow lest the Drenai army trap them in this cursed bay.

The order was given and the Immortals honed their swords.

At dawn they rose silently, forming their black and silver line across the stream, staring stonily ahead at the three hundred men who stood between them and the Sentran Plain.

Tired were the Drenai, bone-weary and hollow-eyed.

Abadai, the new general of the Immortals, walked forward and lifted his sword in silent salute to the Drenai, as was the Immortal custom. The blade swept down and the line moved forward. To the rear three drummers began the doleful marching beat, and the Immortals' swords flashed into the air.

Grim were the faces as the cream of Ventria's army slowly marched towards the Drenai.

Druss, bearing a shield now, watched the advance, his cold blue eyes showing no expression, his jaw set, his mouth a tight line. He stretched the muscles of his shoulders, and took a deep breath.

This was the test. This was the day of days.

The spear-point of Gorben's destiny against the resolution of the Drenai.

He knew the Immortals were damned fine warriors, but they fought now for glory alone.

The Drenai, on the other hand, were proud men, and sons of proud men, descended from a race of warriors. They were fighting for their homes, their wives, their sons, and sons yet unborn. For a free land and the right to make their own way, run their own lives, fulfil the destiny of a free race. Egel and Karnak had fought for this dream, and countless more like them down through the centuries.

Behind the axeman, Earl Delnar watched the nearing enemy line. He was impressed by their discipline and, in a strangely detached way, found himself admiring them. He transferred his gaze to the axeman. Without him they could never have held this long. He was like the anchor of a ship in a storm, holding the prow into the wind, allowing it to ride clear and face the might of the elements without being broken upon the rocks or overturned by the power of the sea. Strong men drew courage from his presence. For he was a constant in a world of shifting change – a colossal force that could be trusted to endure.

As the Immortals loomed ever nearer, Delnar could feel the fear spreading among the men. The line shifted as shields were gripped more firmly. The Earl smiled. Time for you to speak, Druss, he thought.

With the instinct of a lifetime of war, Druss obliged. Raising his axe he bellowed at the advancing Immortals.

'Come in and die, you whoresons! I am Druss and this is death!'

Rowena was picking flowers in the small garden behind the house when the pain struck her, cutting beneath her ribs through to her back. Her legs collapsed beneath her and she toppled into the blooms. Pudri saw her from the meadow gate and ran to her side, shouting for help. Sieben's wife, Niobe, came running from the meadow and between them they lifted the unconscious woman and carried her into the house. Pudri forced a little foxglove powder into her mouth, then poured water into a clay goblet. Holding it to her lips, he pinched her nostrils, forcing her to swallow.

But this time the pain did not pass, and Rowena was carried upstairs to her bed while Niobe rode to the village for the physician.

Pudri sat by Rowena's bedside, his lined leathery face sunken and filled with concern, his large dark eyes moist with tears.

'Please do not die, lady,' he whispered. 'Please.'

Rowena floated from her body and opened her spirit eyes, gazing down with pity at the matronly form in her bed. She saw the wrinkled face and greying hair, the dark rings below the eyes. Was this her? Was this tired, worn-out shell the Rowena that had been taken to Ventria years before?

And poor Pudri, so shrunken and old. Poor devoted Pudri.

Rowena felt the pull of the Source. She closed her eyes and thought of Druss.

On the wings of the wind, the Rowena of yesterday's dreams soared above the farm, tasting the sweetness of the air, enjoying the freedom of those born to the sky. Lands swept below her, green and fertile, dappled with the gold of cornfields. Rivers became satin ribbons, seas rippling lakes, cities peopled with insects scurrying without purpose.

The world shrank until it became a plate studded with gems of blue and white, and then a stone, rounded as if by the sea, and finally a tiny jewel. She thought of Druss once more.

'Oh, not yet!' she begged. 'Let me see him once. Just once.'

Colours swam before her eyes, and she fell, twisting and spinning through the clouds. The land below her was gold and green, the cornfields and meadows of the Sentran Plain, rich and verdant. To the east it seemed as if a giant's cloak had been carelessly thrown on to the land, grey and lifeless, the mountains of Skeln merely folds in the cloth. Closer she flew until she hovered over the pass, gazing down on the embattled armies.

Druss was not hard to find.

He stood, as always, at the centre of the carnage, his murderous axe cutting and killing.

Sadness touched her then, a sorrow so deep it was like a pain in her soul.

'Goodbye, my love,' she said.

And turned her face to the heavens.

The Immortals hurled themselves on the Drenai line, and the clash of steel on steel sounded above the insistent drums. Druss hammered Snaga into a bearded face, then sidestepped a murderous thrust, disembowelling his assailant. A spear cut his face, a sword-blade ripped a shallow wound in his shoulder. Forced back a pace, Druss dug his heel into the ground, his bloody axe slashing into the black and silver ranks before him.

Slowly the weight of the Immortals forced back the Drenai line.

A mighty blow to Druss's shield split it down the middle. Hurling it from him, the axeman gripped Snaga with both hands, slashing a red swathe through the enemy. Anger turned to fury within him.

Druss's eyes blazed, power flooding his tired, aching muscles.

The Drenai had been pushed back nearly twenty paces. Ten more and the pass widened. They would not be able to hold.

Druss's mouth stretched in a death's-head grin. The line was bending like a bow on either side of him, but the axeman himself was immovable. The Immortals pushed towards him, but were cut down with consummate ease. Strength flowed through him.

He began to laugh.

It was a terrible sound, and it filled the veins of the enemy with ice. Druss lashed Snaga into the face of a bearded Immortal. The man was catapulted into his fellows. The axeman leapt forward, cleaving Snaga into the chest of the next warrior. Then he hammered left and right. Men fell back from his path, opening a space in the ranks. Bellowing his rage to the sky, Druss charged into the mass. Certak and Diagoras followed.

It was suicidal, yet the Drenai formed a wedge, Druss at the head, and sheared into the Ventrians.

The giant axeman was unstoppable. Warriors threw themselves at him from every side, but his axe flashed like quicksilver. A young soldier called Eericetes, only accepted into the Immortals a month before, saw Druss bearing down on him. Fear rose like bile in his throat. Dropping his sword he turned, pushing at the man behind him.

'Back,' he shouted. 'Get back!'

The men made way for him, and the cry was taken up by others, thinking it was an order from the officers.

'Back! Back to the stream!' The cry swept through the ranks and the Immortals turned, streaming towards the Ventrian camp.

From his throne Gorben watched in horror as his men waded the shallow stream, disorganised and bewildered.

754

His eyes flicked up to the pass, where the axeman stood waving Snaga in the air.

Druss's voice floated down to him, echoing from the crags.

'Where is your legend now, you eastern sons of bitches?'

Abadai, blood streaming from a shallow cut in his forehead, approached the Emperor, dropping to his knees, head bowed.

'How did it happen?' demanded Gorben.

'I don't know, sire. One moment we were pushing them back, and then the axeman went mad, charging our line. We had them. We really had them. But somehow the cry went up to fall back, and then all was chaos.'

In the pass Druss swiftly honed the dulled blades of his axe.

'We beat the Immortals,' said Diagoras, slapping Druss on the shoulder. 'By all the gods in Missael, we beat the damned Immortals.'

'They'll be back, lad. And very soon. You'd better pray the army is moving at speed.'

With Snaga razor-edged once more, Druss looked to his wounds. The cut on his face stung like the devil, but the flow of blood had ceased. His shoulder was more of a problem, but he strapped it as best he could. If they survived the day, he would stitch it that night. There were several smaller cuts to his legs and arms but these had congealed and sealed themselves.

A shadow fell across him. He looked up. Sieben stood there, wearing breastplate and helm.

'How do I look?' asked the poet.

'Ridiculous. What do you think you're doing?'

'I'm getting into the thick of it, Druss old horse. And don't think you can stop me.'

'I wouldn't dream of it.'

'You're not going to tell me I'm stupid?'

Druss stood and grabbed his friend's shoulders. 'These have been good years, poet. The best I could have wished for. There are few treasures in a man's life. One of them comes with the knowledge that a man has a friend to stand beside him when the hour grows dark. And let's be honest, Sieben . . . It couldn't get much darker, could it?'

'Now you come to mention it, Druss my dear, it does seem a tiny bit hopeless.'

'Well, everybody has to die sometime,' said Druss. 'When death comes for you, spit in his eye, poet.'

'I'll do my best.'

'You always did.'

The drums sounded again and the Immortals massed. Fury was in their eyes now, and they glared balefully at the defenders. They would not be turned back. Not by Druss. Not by the pitiful two hundred facing them.

From the first clash the Drenai line was forced back. Even Druss, needing room to swing his axe, could find space only by retreating a pace. Then another. Then another. He battled on, a tireless machine, bloody and bloodied, Snaga rising in a crimson spray and falling with pitiless efficiency.

Time and again he rallied the Drenai. But ever on came the Immortals, striding across the bodies of their dead, their eyes grim, their mood resolute.

Suddenly the Drenai line broke, and the battle degenerated in moments to a series of skirmishes, small circles of warriors forming shield rings amid the black and silver sea filling the pass.

The Sentran Plain lay open to the conqueror.

The battle was lost.

But the Immortals were desperate to erase the memory of defeat. They blocked the pathway to the west, determined to kill the last of the defenders.

From his vantage point on the eastern hill Gorben threw down his sceptre in fury, turning on Abadai.

'They have won. Why are they not pushing on? Their bloodlust leaves them blocking the pass!'

Abadai could not believe his eyes. With time a desperate enemy waiting to betray them, the Immortals were unknowingly continuing the work of the defenders. The narrow pass was now gorged with warriors as the rest of Gorben's army jostled behind them, waiting to sweep through to the plain beyond.

Druss, Delnar, Diagoras and a score of others had formed a ring of steel by a cluster of jutting boulders. Fifty paces to the right Sieben, Certak and thirty men were surrounded and fighting furiously. The poet's face was grey and terrible pain grew in his chest. Dropping his sword he scrambled atop a grey boulder, pulling his throwing knife from its wrist sheath.

Certak parried one thrust, but a spear punched through his breastplate, ripping into his lungs. Blood welled in his throat and he fell. A tall Ventrian leapt to the boulder. Sieben hurled his blade. It took the man through the right eye.

A spear flashed through the air, lancing Sieben's chest. Strangely, far from causing him pain, it released the agony from his cramped heart. He toppled from the rock, to be swallowed by the black and silver horde.

Druss saw him fall – and went berserk.

Breaking from the shield ring, he launched his giant frame into the massed ranks of the warriors before him, cutting them aside like wheat before a scythe. Delnar closed the ring behind him, disembowelling a Ventrian lancer and locking shields with Diagoras.

Surrounded now by Immortals, Druss hammered his way forward. A spear took him high in the back. He swung round, braining the lancer. A sword bounced from his helm, gashing his cheek. A second spear pierced his side, and a clubbing blow from the flat of a sword thundered into his temple. Grabbing one assailant, he hauled him forward, butting him viciously. The man sagged in his grip. More enemies closed in around the axeman. Using the unconscious Ventrian as a shield, Druss dropped to the ground. Swords and spears slashed at him.

Then came the sound of bugles.

Druss struggled to rise, but a booted foot lashed into his temple and he fell into darkness.

He awoke and cried out. His face was swathed in bandages, his body racked with pain. He tried to sit, but a hand pushed gently on his shoulder.

'Rest, axeman. You've lost a lot of blood.'

'Delnar?'

'Yes. We won, Druss. The army arrived just in time. Now rest.'

The last moments of battle surged back into Druss's mind. 'Sieben!'

'He is alive. Barely.'

'Take me to him.'

'Don't be a fool. By rights you should be dead. Your body was pierced a score of times. If you move, the stitches will open and you'll bleed to death.'

'Take me to him, damn you!'

Delnar cursed and helped the axeman to his feet. Calling an orderly who took the weight on the left side, he half-carried the wounded giant to the back of the tent and the still, sleeping form of Sieben the Sagamaster.

Lowering Druss into a seat by the bedside, Delnar and the orderly withdrew. Druss leaned forward, gazing at the bandages around Sieben's chest, and the slowly spreading red stain at the centre.

'Poet!' he called softly.

Sieben opened his eyes.

'Can nothing kill you, axeman?' he whispered.

'It doesn't look like it.'

'We won,' said Sieben. 'And I want you to note that I didn't hide.'

'I didn't expect you to.'

'I'm awfully tired, Druss old horse.'

'Don't die. Please don't die,' said the axeman, tears causing him to blink furiously.

'There are some things even you cannot have, old horse. My heart is almost useless. I don't know why I've lived this long. But you were right. They have been good years. I wouldn't change anything. Not even this. Look after Niobe and the children. And make sure some sagamaster does me justice. You'll do that?'

'Of course I will.'

'I wish I could be around to add to this saga. What a fitting climax.'

'Yes. Fitting. Listen, poet. I'm not good with words. But I want to tell you . . . I want you to know you've been like a brother to me. The best friend I ever had. The very best. Poet? Sieben?'

Sieben's eyes stared unseeing at the tent ceiling. His face was peaceful and looked almost young again. The lines seemed to vanish before Druss's eyes. The axeman began to shake. Delnar approached and closed Sieben's eyes, covering his face with a sheet. Then he helped Druss back to his bed.

'Gorben is dead, Druss. His own men slew him as they ran. Our fleet has the Ventrians bottled up in the bay. At the moment one of their generals is meeting with Abalayn to discuss surrender. We did it. We held the pass. Diagoras wants to see you. He made it through the battle. Can you believe it, even fat Orases is still with us! Now, I'd have laid ten to one odds he wouldn't survive.'

'Give me a drink, will you,' whispered Druss.

Delnar came back to his side, bearing a goblet of cool water. Druss sipped it slowly. Diagoras entered the tent, carrying Snaga. The axe had been cleaned of blood and polished to shine like silver.

Druss gazed at it, but did not reach out. The dark-eyed young warrior smiled.

'You did it,' he said. 'I have never seen the like. I would not have believed it possible.'

'All things are possible,' said Druss. 'Never forget that, laddie.'

Tears welled in the axeman's eyes, and he turned his head away from them. After a moment he heard them back away. Only then did he allow the tears to fall.